PENGUIN BOOKS

MARCH OF THE ARYANS

Bhagwan S. Gidwani was India's additional director general of tourism and director general of civil aviation till 1978. He served as India's counsel at the International Court of Justice at the Hague and as representative of India on the council of International Civil Aviation Organization (ICAO), United Nations from 1978 to 1981. Thereafter, he joined ICAO as director, serving as adviser to foreign governments till 1985.

Gidwani is the author of the bestselling novel *The Sword of Tipu Sultan* which was translated into many languages and also made into a major TV series for which Gidwani wrote the script and screenplay. His previous novel *Return of the Aryans*, published by Penguin Books India, was also highly successful. *March of the Aryans* is adapted from that novel.

Bhagwan S. Gidwani is based in Montreal and divides his time between international efforts to promote the safety and security of air transport and tourism, and historical writing, research and teaching.

MARCH
OF THE
ARYANS

BHAGWAN S. GIDWANI

PENGUIN BOOKS

PENGUIN BOOKS
Published by the Penguin Group
Penguin Books India Pvt. Ltd, 7th Floor, Infinity Tower C, DLF Cyber City,
Gurgaon 122 002, Haryana, India
Penguin Group (USA) Inc., 375 Hudson Street, New York, New York 10014, USA
Penguin Group (Canada), 90 Eglinton Avenue East, Suite 700, Toronto, Ontario,
M4P 2Y3, Canada
Penguin Books Ltd, 80 Strand, London WC2R 0RL, England
Penguin Ireland, 25 St Stephen's Green, Dublin 2, Ireland (a division of Penguin
Books Ltd)
Penguin Group (Australia), 707 Collins Street, Melbourne, Victoria 3008, Australia
Penguin Group (NZ), 67 Apollo Drive, Rosedale, Auckland 0632, New Zealand
Penguin Books (South Africa) (Pty) Ltd, Block D, Rosebank Office Park, 181 Jan
Smuts Avenue, Parktown North, Johannesburg 2193, South Africa

Penguin Books Ltd, Registered Offices: 80 Strand, London WC2R 0RL, England

First published by Penguin Books India 2012

Copyright © Bhagwan S. Gidwani 2012

ISBN 9780143418986

Typeset in Sabon by Suman Srinivasan
Printed at Repro India Ltd, Navi Mumbai

A PENGUIN RANDOM HOUSE COMPANY

INTRODUCTION

This book is adapted from my earlier novel, *Return of the Aryans*. It tells the story of the Aryans—of how and why they moved out of their homeland in Bharat Varsha (India) in 5000 BCE, their adventures and exploits, the battles and bloodshed forced on them, their trials and triumphs overseas, and finally their return to their home and heritage of India.

I have presented this as a work of fiction. Unfortunately, I had no records, written or otherwise, to rely on while writing this book. Strange as it may seem, the fact is that while thousands upon thousands of books have been written on or about India, by foreign and Indian authors, they all relate to the post-Vedic period. Not a single writer has taken the trouble to research or write about the pre-Vedic period from 8000 BCE to 4000 BCE—the period at the dawn of civilization during which Sanatana Dharma was established in India with ideals of human dignity, respect for all creeds, equality, justice and the protection of the environment; or even about the period—5000 BCE—when the Aryans began their movement to distant parts of the world—as far as Germany in the west, and China in the east.

Thus, in order to write this book, I have had to rely on oral history tradition—the songs of the ancients from prehistory which still remain somewhat in the traditional memory of the people of Sindh, Angkor, Bali, Java, Burma, China, Bhutan, Tibet, Nepal, Iran, Iraq, Turkey, Egypt, Norway, Sweden, Denmark, Finland, Italy, Russia, Lithuania, Greece, Germany and India. The message in these songs is clear—the Aryans originated from India and from nowhere else. The language is archaic, the idiom strange and the images unfamiliar. Yet, they carry the imperishable remembrance of the Aryan movement and migration from India. It is the substance of these songs that dominates my story.

∽

While I wish to focus on the story of the Aryans, the hero of my novel is the pre-ancient Hindu. History is rooted in continuity and advance, and it would be strange to believe that Aryans arrived on the world stage without precedents and ancestors. The Aryans of 5000 BCE were born, grew up and died as Hindus. They were anchored in the timeless foundation of the Hindu tradition, and it is inappropriate to consider them 'strays', without their cultural precedents, traditional links and spiritual ancestry of the Hindu.

∽

I cannot say that I found this subject. Rather, the subject found me, and gradually it came to obsess me. The impulse to study the history of the Hindu first came to me as I witnessed the anguish of my uncle Dr Choithram P. Gidwani, president of the Indian National Congress in Sindh under the inspiration of Mahatma Gandhi, and my father, Shamdas P. Gidwani, president of the Sindh Hindu Maha Sabha, when the partition of India was announced in 1947. They both had different political faiths, though they lived under the same roof in Karachi. Both spoke of the cultural continuity of Bharat Varsha (India) and its age-old political and spiritual frontiers. They felt that by a succession of acts of surrender, the leaders of India had agreed to divide the country as they saw no other immediate possibility of securing power in their own lifetime, thus exiling the Indian from his own land. Both also feared the threat to partitioned India from *outside*, and a far

To the land where poets are no more, and the historian
never was;
To Leila, my wife, who helped so much with research for
this book;
To Manu, my son; Lori, my daughter-in-law; and their
children, Leah, Katy and Jay;
To Sachal, my son; Anju, my daughter-in-law; and their
children, Neil, Chris and Kyle;
To Papu, my niece; and her husband Gulu Chablani for
their cheerful assistance;
and
To all those who will try to keep alive the memory of their
roots for generations
Waiting to be born

CONTENTS

greater menace from *within* that the spiritual tradition of the race would not be able to keep at bay.

When Dr Choithram died, he willed everything to me. The 'everything' contained books, an old watch and eighty rupees. (In those days, politicians and their families did not acquire many assets and wealth and they were judged by the 'magnitude of their non-possession'. It is only in the era after Mahatma Gandhi's assassination that politics became the most lucrative of all professions in India.) He also left me a package containing many hastily scribbled songs about the Aryans. Ever since, I felt a perpetual restlessness to study the subject. Initially, my wife, Leila and I contented ourselves with trying to collect material from various sources. It was in 1978, after I completed research for my novel, *The Sword of Tipu Sultan*, that I started on the Aryans in true earnest.

One version of the Aryans' history is that they originated *not* in India but elsewhere. However, historians have not been able to isolate any single region as the home of the Aryans. At last count, the list of locations in the west and the north from where the Aryans could have originated numbered twenty-two.

The difficulty historians face in choosing one location from the twenty-two is understandable. None of the twenty-two regions showed even the slightest link with the high civilization and classical art and literature of India. Especially, as all these clearly flowered in India, independently and unrelated to any other region, with no parallels or precedents elsewhere.

The main argument supporting the theory that the Aryans originated outside India is that Sanskrit is so similar to Greek and Latin and all the languages now known as Indo-Iranian and Indo-European (including Italic, Germanic, Gothic, Armenian, Tocharian, Celtic, Albanian, Lithuanian and Balto-Slavic). But, is it not possible that these western languages were enriched by the Aryans relocating from India to other regions? And could it not have been Sanskrit that travelled to those countless lands instead of the opposite?

The second hypothesis of the mainstream historical view is weaker still. It relies on the divergence of skin colour and the physique of the races in India and, in particular, between the north and the south.

The link between the pre-ancient Hindu and the Aryans should be clear by now, given the plethora of clues that exist. I have read every word of the Vedas, the Upanishads, ancient epics and other Aryan literature. If the Aryans came from the far north or west, it would be amazing that they, who wrote so much on so many subjects, simply forgot to mention their original homeland.

೧

It is a perilous undertaking to criticize the mainstream historical view, but it cannot be denied that new discoveries and versions of our shared past deserve to exist. I am not arguing here for a revisionist view of history; I have no political axe to grind. Having said that, let me continue my argument. Initially, it was believed that the entire culture of India had to be refracted through the prism of Aryan life and that only decadence and darkness existed until the Aryans invaded the land.

Then, in one of history's more subtle ironies, came the excavations at Mohenjodaro and Harappa, clearly pointing to a flourishing civilization that existed thousands of years in the past, distinct from all others, independent and deeply rooted in the Indian soil and environment. After these discoveries, no further attempts were made to explain the origins of Hindu civilization in terms of immigration from outside.

Faced with this evidence, the histories of the civilization had to admit that the pre-Aryan Indus Valley civilization, with no known beginnings, was highly developed, thoroughly individual, and specifically Indian. Even so, strangely, it was maintained that the Aryans did not spring from the indigenous culture of India, but were from a different culture and arrived from somewhere else at a later stage.

What led to this confusion was evidence of Aryan influence in many foreign lands. But, I submit that this was probably because the Aryans travelled from India to those foreign lands and returned, having left behind, in various regions, the imprint of their language and cultural, social and spiritual affinities.

The British, in presenting the Aryan Invasion Theory, had offered no proof. They did not need to. Hundreds of Indian historians, encouraged by the British, rushed to earn their doctorates, promotions, patronage and government-aided jobs and positions for supporting the British theory. Their proof? Largely quoting those very hundreds of articles and books, written by British-aided historians—and asking, how could so many learned books and serious articles by countless British and Indian historians be wrong! Some did murmur that the British theory was aimed at proving to the Indians that they were incapable of governing themselves, had always been ruled by foreigners, and that it was always the foreign invader, like the Aryans (and eventually the British), who brought progress and enlightenment.

Hopefully, my presentation updates much of the research from scholarly and historical sources, archaeological records, oral traditions and memory songs to present facts and evidence to show that the Aryan Invasion Theory was not only flawed, but frivolous, brought forth by the British for political propaganda.

Hopefully, also, this novel will give a mosaic of a long-forgotten past to show that the Aryans did not belong to a different species, culture or race. Their cradle-grounds were the Sindhu, Ganga, Madhya, Bangla and Dravidian civilizations, and there is an unbroken continuity—spiritual, social and secular—between the pre-ancient civilization of

Bharat Varsha and the Aryans of 5000 BCE.

༄

Even those who initially suspected that the Aryans might have originated in India, failed to follow up on their hunch. This inability was probably because they could not believe the Aryans would leave their homes, but not to loot, plunder and conquer, or to persecute in the name of dogma and propagate their faith while destroying the gods and idols of others. But like all Hindus, they believed in the ideal of Sanatan Dharma—of respect for all creeds and recognition of spiritual nature of man *wherever* he is from and acceptance of *every* culture as an expression of eternal values. To them, as Hindus, it was clear that God wills a rich harmony, not a colourless uniformity based on dogma.

The Aryans who left Bharat Varsha were not adventurers or conquerors or even religious crusaders. They were travellers guided by the dream of finding a land that was pure and free from evil. Unfortunately for them, it was a road that led everywhere and finally nowhere, and at last they came to realize that there was no land of the pure, except what a man might make by his own efforts.

There is some truth in the assumption that some Aryans came to India from foreign lands. Many Aryans from India married there, and returned with their wives and children. But more so, many locals came with them—and kept coming —inspired by the faith and values of the Aryans of Bharat Varsha. These locals came in large numbers from Iran, Assyria, Sumeria, Egypt, Finland, Sweden, Lithuania, Estonia, Latvia, Russia and Scythia, Turkey, Italy, Spain, Greece, Germany and even from Bali, Java, Angkor, Malaysia and Singapore.

Intellectually and emotionally, these men and women from foreign lands came to bind themselves together with the

Aryans of India in a web of common ideas and reciprocal knowledge, with fellowship of spirit, a communion of minds and a union of hearts. It did not take too long for these visitors to be assimilated into India.

～

If the reader is looking for a golden age of peace and plenty in the past, this novel will disappoint him.

Our ancients were not all heroes or hermits—they did not walk hand-in-hand with gods and angels. As we closely examine prehistory, we find in it a cast of characters as varied as any around today. There was cowardice and courage; hermits and harlots; loyalty and treachery; yogis and tricksters; greatness and stupidity—all existing simultaneously. Nor were the majority of people immersed in matters of the spirit. Some sang, others danced or told stories; some tried out new herbs and medicines, while still others sought to discover the physical laws of nature and find unity in diversity. Some occupied themselves with chiselling stone, drawing pictures, burnishing gold and weaving rich fabrics; many dug wells or built reservoirs; some constructed granaries, dock-yards, huts, cottages; others made water-clocks, cloth-looms, boats, carts, chariots and toys; many more toiled in fields and farms, while a few assisted in making ships to cross the ocean. Even some of the rulers then were no less corrupt than those who are in power today. The only difference is that the means available to present-day rulers to manipulate the masses and spread evil are vast, if not unlimited.

As a generalization, however, it can be said that the pre-ancient Hindu had more faith, less superstition, and therefore enjoyed greater laughter and joy in life. The affectionate bonds of the large family nourished him; he did not grow up inwardly torn, largely deprived of love, with his sights shattered and values confused. He did not allow many vague cults to exploit his credulity, nor did he idolize leaders who depended on disunity in the land for their existence or enriched themselves, and their near ones, through corruption and unlawful means.

There was also greater respect for, even fear of, the idea of karma and immense preoccupation with achieving moksha. Judged by today's standards, the corrupt rulers themselves displayed less greed and greater self-restraint. But then as a wag uncharitably, and even crudely, put it, 'Mistake him not; his goodness arises not from his heart; he is simply afraid lest he go down the evolutionary ladder and be reborn as a cockroach or diseased and limbless.'

The distortion of the caste system had not then entered Hindu society, but even then there was the system of slavery, howsoever benign. Fortunately, the system of slavery lasted only a few short centuries and was abolished both in law and fact in 5000 BCE.

I have tried to present our past as it was, with all its triumphs, trials, tragedies and terror, and not in a rosy light. In fact, the Aryans considered themselves exiled and moved out of their homeland only because they were disenchanted with the condition there. That they found greater degradation, corruption, discord, superstition, anarchy, folly and frustration in every other country is quite a different matter.

Compared to other regions, there is no doubt that the Aryans sprang from a society of stability behind which lay ages of civilized existence and thought. No wonder then that the Aryans, soon after leaving their homeland, had the burning desire to return to the healing power of their roots, hometown and heritage. Yet it would be totally fictional to describe India, then, as a society of purity and perfection.

I firmly believe that everyone must know where he comes from, where his ancestors resided and what his roots were. A civilization is kept alive only when its past values and traditions are recreated in men's minds, faithfully and thoroughly, without the element of fancy and distortion. A generation that remains unaware of its roots is truly orphaned. The present silence, blankness, oblivion about our ancient past represents a theft from the future generations as well, and the tragedy we face is that the soul of our culture could well wither away. Already, we are moving towards a cultural holocaust in which our children may acquire much intelligence, power and intellect, but neither wisdom nor virtue, and not even the faith to serve as the consolation of their dreams.

We have inherited an ancient culture. It has faced many waves of invasions, among others, from the Greeks, Persians, Pathans, Mongols, French, Dutch and the English. They all attempted to suppress our culture, often with savagery, yet the flame of hope burnt brightly against the dark background of foreign rule. Our culture endured, though our land has shrunk to less than half its size compared to the past. But then freedom in 1947 did not bring a fulfilment of our dreams. Day by day, the menace grows from within. In the final analysis, the greatest danger lies not *outside* our borders, but *inside,* and in our soul and spirit.

What saved us in the past was the awareness of our age-old culture and the need to hold on to it, while weaving and refining it for the future. What might doom us in the future is our ignorance about our culture. Culture is tradition and tradition is memory. The ancients knew that and that is why Bharat, who led the Sindhu clan, reintroduced memory songs in 5095 BCE, to keep alive the knowledge of the past, lest we run the risk of building our future without the foundation or roots of growth.

In this era of vanishing worth and fading memory,

historians have a role to play, to rekindle the dying embers of life and light in our society. But where history falters for lack of fact or interpretation, the field is open to the novelist.

Bhagwan S. Gidwani
April 2012

ONE

THE BIRTH OF SINDHU PUTRA

5068 BCE

Bharat, the nineteenth karkarta—supreme elected chief of the Sindhu clan—retired at the age of sixty to become a hermit, as ordained by custom; he was now known as Bharatjogi. Mataji, his wife, chose an island on the Sindhu river as his retreat. This was his third year in isolation except for three dogs—two male and one female—who adopted him after he had arrived on the island.

One morning, while meditating, Bharat heard the dogs barking. He saw a small boat drifting aimlessly in the river. Perhaps the boatman was inattentive, sleeping or drunk, while the river kept tossing the boat around. The absence of the family flag on the small, floundering vessel was a sign that it was not their family boat that came once a month, bringing news, food, delicacies, herbs and casks of wine. Even so, the dogs continued to bark furiously.

'You have no desire to pray with me and I have no desire to play with you,' Bharat admonished them before returning to his hut.

Meanwhile, the rain came, pouring from the heavy, velvet sky, amidst thunder and lightning. Sheena, one of the dogs, entered the hut, wet and dripping, looking miserable, and started urgently tugging at his feet. He followed her out, and she led him to the river.

Bharat's pace quickened when he saw the battered boat wedged between the heavy poles supporting the pier; there was someone in the boat. Carefully, he stepped inside.

A young woman lay crumpled on the floor, naked, with an infant nestled against her right breast. Bharat felt her pulse and put his ear to her heart. She was dead. He gently separated the infant from her breast. The child—a boy, barely a few hours old—also appeared to be dead. As he held the limp body of the infant, Bharat wondered why he had been given life if it was to be snatched away immediately.

Sheena began to lick the child's face. Bharat did not stop her. In each life, there should be at least one moment of love and it pleased him that Sheena was giving her love to the babe who, perhaps, had died loveless. Or was Sheena licking the last remains of mother's milk that had dried on his face? But as Sheena's tongue reached the baby's lips, Bharat noticed his lips move imperceptibly; it was as if the infant felt the nearness of his mother's breast. Suddenly, new hope sprang in Bharat's heart. He looked at the mother, her frail body, and marvelled at her strength with which, with her final breath, she had fed her son so that he might survive.

I shall be back for you, he silently told the mother.

He left the boat, the child in his arms, and rushed to his hut with speed he had not known he was capable of. He set the baby on a rug and rubbed his body dry. Then he moistened his fingertips with water and placed them on the child's tongue—no movement.

Gratefully, he looked at the huge drum in the corner intended to summon help from the nearby village. His wife had hired the best artisans in the land to make the drum, the sound of which, they had boasted, could wake the dead. And although Bharat had said then that he would never use the drum, choosing instead to live in silence and privacy, he began to beat the drum with all his strength, hoping that someone in the village would come to his aid.

While he waited, he decided to rescue the mother from the boat. She was entitled to the last prayers and a funeral pyre. But, when he reached the pier, the boat was no longer there. Had it sunk? Bharat looked around and plunged into the river, but there was no sign of the wreckage. He suspected that stormy gusts of wind had pried the boat loose from the poles of the pier and set it adrift.

Disheartened, he was returning to his hut when he remembered that he had seen petals of wet, wilted, white flowers—the kind women wore in their hair—in the boat. Such flowers grew on the island, too. He went to a nearby plant, plucked some flowers and reverently placed them in the river. As he saw them float away, he hoped they would carry his prayer for the soul of the departed mother.

Suddenly, he heard the distant sound of hooves. Someone from the village must have heard the drum and was coming to help! He ran back to the hut where he saw a horseman dismounting. He was Gatha, who had once belonged to Bharat's household as a slave. Mataji had granted him freedom when their son was born. Gatha had chosen to remain with Bharat's family, no longer as a slave but a wage-earner. A year before Bharat retired, Gatha had left to seek his fortune elsewhere.

Gatha bowed low as Bharat approached and asked, 'Is everything all right, master?'

Bharat exclaimed, 'You! Gatha!'

Gatha replied, 'Yes, master, I am the village headman.'

Bharat smiled. He saw his wife's hand at work. Obviously, she had contrived to keep the old family retainer in the village near him.

Gatha asked again, 'Are you well, master?'

Gatha had not yet seen the infant, hidden from view by the dogs. His eyes were anxiously fixed on his old master who could hardly speak, panting from exertion. Bharat pointed to the baby. Gatha went nearer and was startled by what he saw—was it a child or a doll? He touched it and stared at Bharat questioningly.

Bharat nodded and said softly, 'I think this infant may possibly be alive. Can anyone in your village nurse him?'

Gatha picked up the infant gently and went outside where his men were dismounting and spoke to his men. They took the infant and left. Gatha remained and assured Bharat that the child would receive all possible care and added, 'Our village has women with newborn babes. They will nurse him and, if not, there are other villages. I have friends there and their headmen respect me.'

Relieved, Bharat put his hand on Gatha's shoulder. Touched by this affectionate gesture, Gatha continued, 'The vaid is on his way here. My men will intercept him and he will attend to the child.'

'Gatha, please spare no expense,' Bharat said. 'God, in his wisdom, has separated the infant from his mother and placed him in our charge. Do ensure that anyone who cares for the infant is rewarded. When our boat arrives, I shall send a message to my family and they will respond generously.'

Gatha was surprised. 'But, master, surely you know that Mataji has given me ample funds to provide anything you may desire.'

No, Bharat had not known that, just as he had not known that she had arranged for Gatha to be nearby. His wife had broken yet another commandment by earmarking funds for a hermit. Yet, Bharat knew that to his wife every commandment was sacred but if it stood in the way of the safety or happiness of her loved ones, she rejected it. 'This is not what a hermit must do!' he had protested when she was making arrangements to ensure his retirement would be comfortable. 'But this is what a wife must do,' she had retorted. 'Let them come with their laws and customs and commands to bind me, but I shall evade them forever. I am bound only to you, not their sightless laws.' And despite his protests, he had learned to relish the luxuries and comforts she had provided on his lonely retreat. Well, as Karkarta, he had always been kind to hermits, so why not be kind to himself now!

Gatha asked the question which had mystified him. 'Master, where did the infant come from?'

Too tired to speak, Bharat wearily looked at the river, and pointed at it.

Gatha followed his master's gaze and turned back to face him. A tremor passed through him as he recalled Bharatjogi's recent words: *God, in his divine wisdom, has separated the infant from his mother and placed it in our charge.* Overwhelmed by the thoughts rushing in his mind, Gatha asked, 'The infant . . . he comes from the Sindhu river?'

Bharat nodded. Gatha was astonished. 'That little child . . . master, you mean the little one is . . . is Sindhu Putra? Son of the Sindhu river?'

Bharat's eyes met Gatha's and he simply nodded again, the exertions and tensions of the day having taken their toll on him. Gatha was not a man of immense curiosity, but he certainly was a man of great faith. Dimly, deep in his consciousness, he began to realize that he was witnessing the fulfilment of an age-old prophecy that said the son of Mother Goddess Sindhu would come to walk the earth one day. Still, he wanted to be sure. Since it would be disrespectful to ask the same question again, he thought for a moment till inspiration struck. 'Master, by what name should the infant be known?'

'You gave him the name yourself, Gatha,' Bharat responded.

'What name?' Gatha wondered aloud and then added in hushed tones, 'Sindhu Putra?'

When Bharat nodded, Gatha followed with another question. 'To which family should I say the infant belongs?'

Bharat recognized the practical aspect of the question. It was important for a nursing mother to know whose child she was suckling, and if the child were to die, it would be necessary to know his family name to perform the funeral rites.

'Say that he is of my family.'

'Rajavansi?' Gatha asked, referring to Bharat's ancestral family.

Bharat thought for a moment—no, he could not confer on anyone the name of the family from which he had retired as a hermit. 'No, Gatha. Not Rajavansi. My family.'

'Your family?'

'Yes, my family. My own—Bharatvansi.'

There was no such family, Gatha knew, for old slaves and servants are more knowledgeable than their lords about such matters. Gatha knew that if his old master hesitated to adopt the infant into his ancestral family, he also lacked the right, as a hermit, to start his own family. But Bharat was his master. Who was he to question him? Gatha voiced no more questions though his mind was in a whirl. Respectfully, he looked at the pale, tired face in front of him and said, 'I shall do all I can, master. Rely on me.'

Bharat was sure he would. 'God will bless you for looking after this infant whom He has given to our care,' he said, clasping his hand on the old retainer's shoulder.

The next morning Bharat was at his prayers when Gatha arrived, beaming with pleasure. 'Sindhu Putra is crying, master! He is crying!' And lest he be misunderstood, he added, 'They say that an infant that cries so lustily will have a long life.'

Happily, Bharat asked, 'Crying all the time, is he?'

'No, no, mostly he is glued to Sonama's breast. She lost her twins in childbirth and is grateful to have Sindhu Putra.' Gatha saw his old master smiling with pleasure and continued, 'She says he is hungry all the time, as a healthy infant should be, and he is greedy enough for two babes, which is as it should be, because she lost her twins.'

'Poor Sonama,' Bharat lamented.

'Poor Sonama!' Gatha snorted. 'Sonama is radiant with joy. She finds total solace in Sindhu Putra. She is the happiest mother today.' Bharat believed him; he knew that only those who endure real sorrow can truly experience happiness. But Gatha had not finished, 'The vaid is confident that Sindhu Putra shall live.'

Twice more during the day, Gatha came to Bharat to tell him that the infant was doing well and saw his obvious delight. The villagers, too, were excited over the astounding news that Mother Sindhu had sent her son—Sindhu Putra—to be brought up in their village and Gatha, their own headman, had been given the high honour of serving as Sindhu Putra's guardian! Their joy was boundless. For his part, Gatha was untroubled and his faith firm. After all, how could an infant, barely an hour old, arrive at Bharatjogi's hut on his own? Surely, Goddess Sindhu had brought him there. He was thoroughly enjoying his status in the village, not only as the headman, but also as custodian of the infant Sindhu Putra. The new tone of authority in his voice, and the expression of grave concern were only fitting in a man whom the gods had chosen for such high responsibility.

The vaid and the mahant announced that if Sindhu Putra lived through the next twenty-four hours, it would be a sign that he had decided to reside in their village, otherwise he would leave his body here and take birth elsewhere.

None in the village slept. With bated breath, they waited for the twenty-fourth hour to begin and end. At the end of the hour, a loud cheer went up throughout the village. Sindhu Putra was brought out in Sonama's arms with Gatha by her side. The child was crying lustily and Sonama put him to her naked breast in view of everyone. The onlookers were struck silent by this wondrous sight and all bowed in respect. And although the hour was late, none went to bed. Now that Sindhu Putra had decided to make their village his home, the celebrations would begin.

Thus passed Sindhu Putra his first day on Earth.

ᕳ

After a day of rejoicing, most of the villagers dropped off to sleep under a silvery moon, their beings flooded with a sense of serenity. Even in their dreams, they felt that with Sindhu Putra's arrival, their lives had been touched by something that was gentle, noble, beautiful and pure.

Later, when some wondered how the Mother Goddess had deposited her child, unseen by all, with the hermit, the mahant reminded them of the oft-repeated, age-old prophecy that said Sindhu Putra would arrive amongst them on a dark, stormy night, adding, 'This, then, was the gracious will of the Mother Goddess, yet such was her sadness at parting with her child that the sky was overcast and the Sindhu was covered as though by a blanket of furious rain, interrupted by threatening wind and thunder which shook the trees from limb to limb! But all the Mother Goddess had to do was stretch her arms over water and earth, till they reached the hermit's hut and leave her child in his arms, choosing him to serve as the earthly father of her infant.' When asked why the Mother Goddess chose their small, unimportant village which did not even have a temple, the mahant was delighted and repeated from the text of the long prophecy:

He shall come, where you light up his way
With worship and devotion, night and day;
And with reverence and love, you shall wait;
Where no false preacher's foot shall be set;
Where no false temple shall you erect;
Where no false idols shall you install,
Forgetful of Him who is to come for us all.

He went on to add, 'You are right. Our village has no

temple, nor have we installed any idols. Maybe that is why we have been honoured by His arrival. Now is the time to build a great temple to He who has come,' hoping to advance his life-long ambition to set up a temple in the village.

Then someone asked, 'Why did the Mother Goddess choose an unknown hermit of no consequence as the earthly father of her son?'

Seeing this as an insult against Bharatjogi, Gatha lost his temper and shouted, 'An unknown hermit of no consequence? Know this, you ignorant, foolish woman! He is the greatest in our land and shall always be so. He is Bharat, our most honoured karkarta.'

If any doubts still lingered, they were set to rest. But in his anger, Gatha had forgotten Mataji's orders never to reveal the hermit's identity. Many now expressed awe at the fact that such a great personage as Karkarta Bharat was living among them; surely, the Mother Goddess could never have found a worthier choice as the earthly father for her son.

Despite his outburst, Gatha knew that if there was heaven on earth, he was in it—right at its centre. He had performed the simple errand of bringing the infant to the village, and he was now called the Sentinel of the River and Sky. The villagers knew their headman used to go out at all hours of the night to see if the lookouts were awake and vigilant. When the wind broke into a riot and storms followed, he would run to repair fences to prevent wild beasts from straying into the village where they had seen nothing to protect. Surely, then, he had been waiting for the auspicious moment when someone, suddenly, silently, would arrive. And now He had come! It mattered little that Gatha could not tell stories or sing songs. They knew now that his heart was resonant with the melody of a faraway song, floating from unknown shores to sing of the coming of Sindhu Putra. They now looked at their headman in awe, with pride and joy as the Sentinel. Gatha saw their new wave of respect for him and happiness surged through him. In the past, the villagers had tolerated him only because of his gifts to them and for his hard work. Many had suspected that he had acquired the position of headman immediately upon his arrival in the village through bribes and the influence of unknown friends. Indeed, it was Bharat's wife who had managed to steer him to that position, but the village now clearly saw the hand of the Mother Goddess to prepare for the coming of Her Son—Sindhu Putra.

TWO

BHARATJOGI AND HIS MEMORIES

5068 BCE

Bharatjogi was resting in his hut, tired from the events of the previous day, but happy that the infant had survived. Silently, he thanked his wife for the drum and for placing Gatha nearby.

His wife, he knew, longed to visit him, and while he would have enjoyed it too, hermits could not have visitors. He realized that he could no longer meet his wife to make love, but then they were more than lovers, they were companions in spirit. He appreciated that women were not obligated to become hermits and face isolation. Although he had found this a discriminatory practice, he soon realized that a woman could never be asked to retire because her work never ceased. From being a wife, she moved smoothly and selflessly into the roles of mother and grandmother, giving unselfishly of herself, body and soul, to serve the generations that followed, until her dying day.

Bharat himself could easily have avoided the life of a hermit. After all, he was the karkarta of the clan, the one who held the rod of authority and established the law. The first karkarta was chosen eighteen generations ago when people realized that the clan's lands were expanding rapidly and, with it, its problems. As the council of chiefs could never act promptly and was often divided, an elected chief was necessary to act promptly. As karkartas, each one of his eighteen predecessors had died in office before reaching the age of sixty. There had never been a karkarta who had retired, and it was assumed that he too was free from such bondage.

Bharat suspected that at least some karkartas had violated this law. True, a man's age could not easily be hidden, given the custom of planting a tree for each year of a man's life, from birth till retirement, and planting new trees to replace those that died. But so what! Some people just wouldn't count what they didn't wish to count.

Yet, Bharat had declined to consider the option and insisted that the council meet to establish a date for elections to choose his successor. After a long debate, the council decided that the karkarta need not retire; after all, a karkarta who interprets god's laws to man was holy enough, and did not need to become a hermit. Bharat had thanked the council, but spoke of his conviction that the higher the office of the man, the fewer his rights and more numerous his obligations.

'You spoke of my rights,' he had said, 'but as karkarta and leader of our clan, I have no rights, only duties. I am subject to the same laws and subordinate to the same duties and have the same obligations to fulfil as the rest of us in this land, and it is unacceptable that I, as leader of our people, should sacrifice the law which I have sworn to uphold. The unalterable, inevitable course of my destiny therefore leads me to retire and my anguish is no less than yours.'

Thus, sadly, Bharat banished himself. The irony was that he never believed that a man who was obliged to be a hermit forged stronger bonds with the gods. He honoured those who retired as hermits by choice well before the age of sixty. Some even went in their early youth, seeking isolation and immersion in meditation, prompted by devotion and faith. Those were the men, he thought, who would achieve a lasting relationship with the divine.

However, deep in his heart, Bharat was happy, for during

his stewardship as karkarta, his clan had prospered and progressed magnificently in housing, architecture, agriculture, arts, crafts, music, dance, sports, yoga and other fields. The early days of fear and flight were over. No longer would his clan have to run from raiders to the safety of the forests. He had led his people to decisive victories against hostile tribes; those who had raided from the north and the east were enemies no more. As he had gone into each battle, there had been fear in his heart. His friend Suryata, who knew of his fear, had told him, 'Only the dead are without fear.'

Bharat never willingly started a war. He wanted no conquest of land that belonged to others. He hated war; anguish and death were its bitter fruits, he had concluded early on upon seeing all those lost on battlefields and the countless widows and orphans left behind. Yet, he also knew that battles were inevitable and to remain unprepared against a sudden, brutal offensive was the surest way to invite more such attacks.

He had always tried to be gracious and chivalrous after winning in battle, extending to the lands of his conquests the rights, dignity and freedoms of Sanatan Dharma. The last major battle had taken place many years ago and the enemy had fallen—burned, blinded, with fractured faces and limbless bodies—and since that victory, an era of unbroken peace had prevailed during which tribes themselves sought to be a part of the larger fabric of the Hindu clan. For more than two decades now, there had not been a single armed attack.

～

Bharat's mind now dwelt on his wife. Long before his retirement, his wife had come to the island with artisans to construct and equip his large hut. She had herself chosen this site—close to a village and yet almost invisible from it—and had fruit trees and flowering bushes planted, streams widened and fences erected to keep out wild animals.

'Am I, as a hermit, to live so lavishly?' Bharat had protested.

'You must live safely and serenely as a hermit. And am I not entitled to live with peace of mind, assured of your safety? Or do I live with anguish, sleepless, worrying over what may happen to you?'

Haltingly, he said, 'But other hermits . . . '

'Other hermits! I am not married to other hermits,' she had interrupted fiercely and proceeded with the arrangements, many of which he had known nothing about until yesterday.

∽

Bharat's mind now shifted to the mighty Sindhu river. As a child, he had believed that it flowed far beyond the villages of his clan, into some far-away terrain where no man had set foot. Songs about the Sindhu fascinated him; he remembered a song he had heard, when he was eight years old, sung by a wandering hermit about the haunting beauty and endless bounty of the Sindhu river. The song had ended thus:

Sindhu flows majestically; along the way, many rivers and streams come rushing from different directions to pay homage to her;
She accepts them all lovingly, and thus overflowing, she goes on to meet her lover at a magical place where there is the River of all Rivers, with winds of crushing force and enormous waves;
And together, then, in the ecstasy of a tumultuous embrace, with pounding hearts and heaving chests and the cry of joy and pain that is heard when two lovers surrender to each other, she goes on in the lap of the mighty River of all Rivers, onto distant shores that none have seen.

Bharat, fascinated by the hermit's description, had asked,

'But have you seen those unknown distant shores?'

'I have dreamt of them,' was the hermit's reply.

'Oh, a dream!' Bharat said, disillusioned.

'Everything, my son, has at least two faces—its face in a dream and its face in reality.'

'But if it is merely a dream,' Bharat blurted out, 'what reality can it have?'

'My son, only that which cannot be dreamed of is devoid of reality. Everything that is great and blessed begins as a dream.'

Perhaps, Bharat had thought, the old man was always dreaming. The hermit sensed he had disappointed the child and said, 'But there are those who have seen the great waters and their distant shores.'

'Where are they?'

The hermit had turned to face the river, his hand half raised; Bharat was not sure if the hand was directed to the sky to indicate the answer lay above, or simply to admit his ignorance.

Bharat persisted. 'Tell me, is this your song or did you hear it from others?'

'My grandfather used to sing this song; it was sung by many during his time.'

Bharat had wondered why such songs faded away from the memories of the generations that followed. He hoped, some day, someone would reveal the secret of the Sindhu's source and destination. A hope that was realized after he became karkarta.

Bharat had been holding Bindu's hand while listening to the wandering hermit's song. Bindu and he were to get married when they grew up; their parents had already exchanged marriage vows. It was only when the hermit left and Bharat released Bindu's hand that he noticed the white marks his grip had caused and realized how excited he had been during the conversation. He looked at her hand with concern and smiled a special smile in apology. She smiled back at him and pressed her hand lightly to her lips. That was the last time they had exchanged smiles for she had died, along with her two brothers, during the unexpected enemy raid the following day.

Bharat had shed no tears at her funeral or even that of his own father the year before. Some said that Bharat had achieved manhood before becoming a man, and others said that when the hurt is very deep, the heart cries tears that do not reach the eyes. After Bindu's funeral, he had quietly gone to the river. He called out to the sky and then to the river to bear witness to his terrible, eternal oath of vengeance against the tribes of the north and the east. But the sky remained impassive and in the flowing waters of the Sindhu, he saw visions that melted his resolve—the serene face of his father, his eyes full of love, and Bindu, a heart-warming smile in her shining eyes as she waved to him. He understood that she was not waving goodbye, but telling him that she would come back to him, to be with him always. As tears welled up in his eyes and coursed down his cheeks, he wondered if they would reach the River of Rivers and unknown shores that the hermit had described.

∽

Bharat's mother was looking for eligible girls for Bharat to marry, but he begged her to stop, saying Bindu would reappear in her own house.

'Those who left, have left for ever,' she told him. 'They will not return and we must not wish for it either.'

He had been rebellious. 'Why?' he had demanded, leaving his mother in an untenable situation. How could she explain to him the mysteries of life and death when she herself did not understand them all! Still, she tried.

'Son, we are all part of God. He sends us out on this earth and expects us to do good deeds during our life. But there are those who perform acts of evil, commit sins and live with unholy desires. They do not return to God when they die.

They are reborn, again and again, until they learn to live a moral, decent life, a life of goodness. Only then are their sins wiped out and they are allowed to go back to God and be one with Him.'

She was wondering if he had understood her, when he nodded and asked, 'And what about those who do good deeds on this earth and live sinless lives?'

'Son, those people attain moksha, the liberation of the soul from the cycle of birth and death. So, when a person lives an innocent life—one of love, goodness and purity like Bindu— they go into God's loving arms and become one. Then that person is no longer a person but a part of the One Supreme, who is God of us all.'

He looked at her intently, 'You mean Bindu is a god!'

His mother nodded warily; it was not her intention to confer godhood on anyone.

'Then she is a god!' Bharat said triumphantly. His mother did not understand his jubilation until he added, 'Then she can come back if she wants; gods can do anything.'

Lamely, she had replied, 'Gods have no desire for this earth.'

'But gods don't lie,' he retorted. 'Bindu told me herself in the river and in my dreams, that she will come back and always be with me.'

Listening to Bharat, his mother could only hope that time would heal the wound in her child's heart.

After some months, it became known that Bindu's mother was expecting a child. This surprised all, as she was long past the child-bearing age. Many feared a miscarriage. When Bharat heard the news, he quietly told his mother that he would marry the girl who would be born.

His mother smiled and asked, 'How do you know it will be a daughter? Bindu's mother visits the river each day to pray for a son. Her husband has promised the gods that he will erect a temple in their honour if he has a son. Even their family astrologer predicts a son.'

'Are astrologers always right when they predict a son?'
She had smiled, 'They are right, half the time.'

He shared her smile, but then asked, 'Why do they want a son? Were they not happy with Bindu?'

'Of course, they were. Bindu was the sweetest girl who ever lived, but with her, her two elder brothers also passed away. Can you blame them for wanting a son?'

Ignoring this, Bharat had simply said, 'I shall marry her.'

∞

In time, a daughter was born to Bindu's mother. She, too, was named Bindu. Years later, when Bharat was twenty-four and Bindu was fifteen, they were married.

Actually, Bindu was younger than her fifteen years, but that was because the clan used the lunar calendar, in which each month began with the appearance of the new moon, to determine a girl's age. A man's age, on the other hand, was determined using the solar calendar. The cycles of the moon corresponded well with women's menstrual cycles so it was natural to rely on the moon as a measure of their age. Also, the moon was considered auspicious and attractive, even mystical, romantic and enchanting, certainly cool and calm, and therefore, appropriate for women. Whereas man—the farmer, cattle breeder, hunter, builder, trader and traveller—was more concerned with the change of seasons, the months of heat and cold and rain, and the rhythm of the Sindhu river with its ebb and flow. The warmth of the sun and the heavenly gift of rain decided the fate of crops and determined the time to sow and reap. Over the centuries, the clan had perceived that the sun, not the moon, was the surest guide to the change and return of the seasons. Thus it was that the solar year, divided into three hundred sixty-five and a quarter days, was considered the appropriate calendar for official business, and determining a man's age.

Even so, for festivals and other auspicious events, it was

the moon and its cycles that guided the clan, for they had always had a primeval fascination and affection for the moon. An old, half-remembered song spoke of the moon as a worshipper of Mother Goddess Sindhu and Mother Earth:

Even though we sometimes do not see it, the Moon always revolves around Mother Earth, sometimes shining near our view, but half the time away and hidden, shining over distant, unknown shores where Mother Sindhu goes on her enchanted journey into the passionate bosom of the mighty River of Rivers.
So, Sisters, let men order their lives around seasons of the Sun while we have the endless seasons of love with the Moon—that handsome, pale wanderer in the sky.

Since the lunar year had fewer days (and it took a pregnant woman longer—ten months—under that calendar to give birth), it sometimes happened that when a woman was only one year younger than a man on their marriage, it took around thirty-three years for her to reach the same age as her husband.

Bharat thought of their wedding night, of his wife decked in flowers and pearls, her face flushed with pride. He remembered hearing the murmur of admiration from the crowds as she had walked in, dressed in gold and brocade, to hold his hand and take her marriage vows. As the sacred fire burnt, Bindu's father had formally offered her to Bharat after he made the five ritual promises of *piety, permanence, pleasure, property* and *progeny*. Then, while the priest recited the sacred mantras and made offerings of grain and flowers to the gods, their garments were knotted together and Bharat led her around the sacred fire seven times, as they both repeated their vows.

The welcoming bark of the dogs interrupted Bharat's wandering thoughts. He looked up and saw Gatha approaching, no doubt to tell him of the infant's progress.

THREE

PATH OF GLORY: BHARAT'S ELECTION AS KARKARTA

5068 BCE with flashbacks

After Gatha left, Bharatjogi returned to his reflections of the past. He thought of his father who had gathered groups to strike enemy raiders but when he had fallen in battle, fatally stabbed, his men had tried to flee and many had lost their lives. His father's actions had been against the advice of the then karkarta who feared that such an attempt, apart from being futile, would further infuriate their enemies into taking swift, deadly vengeance. Undeterred, Bharat's father had spoken of the shame of passively submitting to the enemy, and having to live with the fear of continued attacks if they failed to resist.

Bharat was only seven years old when he lost his father. He had regarded his father as a permanent fixture in his world—a part of the great universe—never imagining that he could die. Before the year was out, he lost Bindu, too.

Fuelled by grief and rage, he had accosted his friend Suryata, 'When you become karkarta, you must lead our people against them.'

Suryata had understood his anguish and said, 'I am the karkarta's son and cannot become karkarta myself.' Bharat was unaware of the convention prohibiting a family member from succeeding as the karkarta. 'But,' Suryata continued, 'God willing, when you are karkarta, I swear by the light of the sun, I shall be by your side against the enemy.' Suryata belonged to a family of sun-worshippers and would never swear by the sun in vain.

Later, as they went for a swim, eight-year-old Bharat had smiled at Suryata's words—*when you are karkarta*—but as he plunged into the river, he wondered, 'Why not!' As he floated on the river he felt the sun's warm glow and the presence of his father, of Bindu, and those who had died in the raids. He focused his thoughts on the living then, on his people, on the panorama of the land along the life-giving waters of the Sindhu, the valleys and plains, the forests and broad fields, on the men, women and children who lived, loved, laughed, worked and prayed there.

'God! Help me to bring peace to them,' he had pled. 'Help me give them hope, restore their dignity and renew their faith. Use me as You will, but help me protect our clan.'

When he came out of the water, he was determined to devote his life to his resolve.

At the age of fourteen, when he could bear arms, Bharat had begun going into battle against the raiders. Soon, he became a leader among the men, hoping the gods would grant him the opportunity to bring safety and peace to his land. Victory in battle, Bharat realized, did not necessarily go to those who fought with courage, but to those who also had foresight to prepare for it.

He told Suryata, 'We do poorly whenever the enemy ventures into our land. So either we must go and confront them on their land or prevent them from setting foot on ours.'

'How?' Suryata had asked. 'By praying to the sun to dissolve the enemy as my father, the karkarta, does?'

Bharat knew his friend's wrath was directed at his father. The karkarta had led their men to a distant hilltop for prayers during the sun's eclipse when raiders had attacked the unguarded village. Suryata's brothers and sisters had been speared to death and his mother had been dragged away by the raiders and was undoubtedly experiencing unspeakable horrors. Yet his father, the karkarta, did no more than renew his prayers to the sun for the souls of those slain. Suryata himself no longer worshipped the sun. Nevertheless, he spent his time watching the fiery ball in the sky, making drawings of its movements, size and direction. At night, when the sun went into hiding, he watched the stars while many thought he waited for the sun to reappear.

Some, who considered themselves wise, thought that the sun splintered into innumerable stars at night so that people may sleep under their cool cover, and then at dawn, the sun gathered them all in its fiery fold once again, and made a majestic entrance to revive the universe. Others, with playful minds and bold imaginations, saw the constantly flowing waters of the Sindhu, and wondered: Does the sun move out of our lives every day, or do we move out of its realm every evening, only to re-enter it at dawn? But then they were asked that if the earth was indeed moving, how was it that people neither saw nor felt it? But their response was designed to infuriate, rather than explain:

'How is it that you see with your eyes and yet you cannot see your own eyes? What arrogance that you must see and hear something before you can accept its existence! You grow old, moment by moment, but do you see or feel the growth of each moment? Is any heavenly body or element ever stationary or unmoving? So why are you surprised that the earth moves! Or that we move! If you do not see the earth moving, so what? How can you see what the gods designed to remain invisible? How can you even imagine that the sun, a deity of the gods, loses its vigour and might at dusk, and sinks in the west? Instead, is it not possible that the earth itself moves us out of the sun's brightness each night to bring us under the restful glow of the moon?'

Many regarded the sun as the 'local star linked to earth'. They believed there were other countless worlds beyond our outer space and galaxy. Some proudly exclaimed, 'Our own star—the sun—is so much bigger than all other stars!' But the retort was, 'Yes, just as a sparrow in your garden appears larger than an eagle flying high in the sky.'

There were other wise men who held that the rising and setting of the sun over land showed that there were other lands far away, and the sun set over us only to rise in those lands. Then there were those, considered the wisest, who neither supported nor rejected these diverse theories. They welcomed every idea, hoping it would be tested and help mankind understand the mystery of the universe in time.

Bharat, then, knew only a little of such philosophical speculation and theories, though the Sage Ekantra had taught him much. He and Suryata focused their attention on keeping the raiders away from their lands, distinguishing themselves in many skirmishes. Still, they realized that much more needed to be done and racked their brains to devise ways of foiling the enemy—volunteers had to be trained in the use of bows, arrows, daggers, spears, swords and other weaponry; the quality of their weapons needed improving; weapons had to be forged in advance and stored in their huts and concealed in the forests and nearby areas; strategic locations had to be chosen to serve as lookout points to watch for the enemy's approach . . .

The list of things that had to be done was long, but what was really most pressing, paramount in fact, was discovering the secret of the enemy's poisoned arrows. The clan's arrows were well made and could be used over a long range but they were not deadly, whereas the enemy applied a substance to the tips of their arrows which numbed and often killed after piercing the body. Yet, no one seemed to know what that poison was. Finally, their friend, Yadodhra, surprised them by admitting, 'My father knows the secret, but will not tell.' However, Bharat and Suryata did not believe him for Yadodhra often boasted that his father Ekantra knew everything under the sun. True, Ekantra knew a lot, but he had always shared his knowledge with the clan, and if he knew, would he not have said so!

⌒

Although he was well below the age of sixty, and under no obligation to do so, Ekantra had chosen to become a hermit and retired to the forests. However, he refused to believe that as a hermit, he must lead an austere life. It was common knowledge that this part of life's road had to be walked in a single file, in prayer and meditation. But Ekantra had different views; he travelled in style, often mounted on his elephant, carrying home-made food, fruits, candles and herbs for himself and as gifts for the hermits, sadhus, sages and ascetics he met.

When Karkarta Suryakarma criticized Ekantra's lifestyle, the hermit replied, 'If the way of one devotee is different from the other, so be it. When God himself does not dictate, how can you? Man has many God-given rights, and amongst them is the freedom to decide if and how he shall do God's work. That freedom is mine.'

Suryakarma cautioned him, 'But then you will never know God or even recognize Him.'

'It is enough,' responded Ekantra, 'if God knows me and recognizes me.'

Wherever Ekantra went, he took his six elephants, and when he returned to his large cave, the elephants roamed free till he commanded them to go to his family home. There, the elephants moved to the river to frolic in the water. Ekantra's wife would give them a brisk rub-down with pine-needle brushes and herbal soap. Finally, five of the elephants were loaded with provisions for Ekantra, and the last carried Ekantra's wife to the cave where she remained with Ekantra for weeks, sometimes taking her son Yadodhra and his friends to Ekantra's cave.

Bharat had learnt much from Ekantra about the beginnings of Sanatan Dharma some three thousand years earlier, and the ideals that became the foundation of the ageless faith of the Hindus—recognizing the spiritual nature of man irrespective of his origins; accepting every culture as the expression of eternal values; and man's obligation to respect and protect the environment, and all creatures, tame and wild. Sanatan Dharma held that God's grace is withdrawn from none and His gracious purpose includes all human beings and all creation. The idols one worshipped or the images one bowed to did not matter, as long as one's conduct remained pure and virtuous. Even an atheist would not be denied grace if his conduct was pure, for after all he was simply exercising his God-given right to assess for himself the eternal rhythm of the spirit; and the hope was that some day, precious echoes of God's voice would reach his soul.

Ekantra had also talked about some principles of Sanatan Dharma, including karma—the natural law of cause and effect. 'Do good, reap good—that is good karma,' he explained simply. 'Man makes his own destiny. He has liberty of thought and action; he is neither a pawn of fate nor a slave of necessity nor bound by any pre-arranged or pre-determined plan. He is an active agent, a doer, a creator, and the spirit in him can triumph to rise above and beyond his obstacles; clearly, he makes choices for good or evil. Good karma leads him to moksha, releasing him from the cycle of birth and death, and re-identifies him as part of God himself, whereby God and that person become One entity.

'Among other things, Sanatan Dharma,' Ekantra had said, 'holds that the individual is not all matter. Far greater is the unseen and unperceived spiritual portion. On death, the body burns on a pyre, while the spirit—where identity resides—is alive, invisible, undying, immeasurable, indestructible and changeless. In reincarnation, the self comes back to Earth again and again in different bodies unless moksha is achieved.'

∽

Ekantra was silent when Bharat asked if he knew the secret of the enemy's poisoned arrows. Later, as Bharat and Suryata persisted, the sage said that the arrows were not essential as their clan was stronger than the tribals. The clan had recently built walls to halt and harass the enemy; its arrows, though not poisoned, were superior; the swords and spears sharper; and the horses better trained and faster. Surely, the clan could do without poisoned arrows. Besides, Ekantra confessed, he was under oath to divulge the secret only in a dire emergency, which, he hoped, would never arise.

It was after many murderous raids that Ekantra had finally succumbed and agreed to share the secret. He took Bharat, Suryata and Yadodhra, no longer boys but young men, on a journey through many forests, to a rocky region where he led them to a cluster of rocks concealing a broken-down hut. Beyond the hut was what they were looking for—a clump of small trees. These were not joy-giving, life-sustaining trees, but ones that yielded poison. Even at a distance, they had a persistent, inviting aroma. There was a deep, man-made pit that prevented them from reaching the trees. Obviously, someone had seen to it that no animal or man, attracted by their fragrance, strayed near the copse of death. They found logs in the hut that served as a bridge across the pit. Bharat and his friends were afraid to touch the trees, but Ekantra assured them that the trees, as such, were harmless. The poison was in the sticky sap which oozed when a deep cut was made in the trunk. When the sap was dried in the sun till its perfume disappeared, it turned into a deadly poison.

Before he divulged the secret of the poisoned arrows, Ekantra had made them vow that they would not be the first to strike with the arrows, using them only to retaliate to the raiders' attack, and that a tribal prisoner would be sent back with a poisoned arrow to warn his people that such weapons would be used against them, if ever they used their own poisoned arrows. Even after all these years, Bharat remembered Ekantra asking them to swear that only those with proven skill for marksmanship would use the arrows, aiming them at the enemy, not the innocent animal he was riding, and avoid the danger of their falling into the river, lest the fish and other creatures in the waters were poisoned. The sage had even demanded that after the battle, search parties must retrieve the stray arrows lying around or stuck in trees, in case they harm the birds and animals of the forest.

Ekantra insisted that the route to Trees of Death be known only to Bharat, Suryata and Yadodhra, and they reveal it to no one.

'Let it be known that only one of you knows the secret location, lest all of you face questions.' He selected Bharat. 'Not only because he is proving to be a natural leader but also because he is the least talkative among the three of you.'

Thus, the credit for discovering the poisoned arrows belonged to Bharat alone, and he was applauded not only as a protector of the land, but also as a great discoverer.

～

When the karkarta, Suryakarma, fell ill and expressed his reluctance to continue as the supreme chief, Ekantra had told Bharat that he should be the next karkarta of the land.

Bharat laughed and Ekantra said, 'You laugh as if you have not heard of such a possibility, earlier.'

Bharat confessed that, when they were eight, Suryata had once spoken of his becoming karkarta, and he had seen a vision of the panorama of the land and its people, and of his resolve to serve them.

Ekantra nodded and said, 'He who leads people must be

guided by a vision. And he who holds a weapon of destruction, must be guided by responsibility.'

Bharat had thought no more of Ekantra's suggestion that he become karkarta, but he had misjudged Ekantra's persistence. Soon, it became public knowledge that Suryakarma would not be standing for re-election when his seven-year term ended. A karkarta was, of course, elected by the people, but the outgoing karkarta and council members had enormous influence with the people.

Every adult in the clan could, and was obliged to, vote. The failure to do so, except in case of an illness or emergency, resulted in a fine and disqualification from holding public office. Adults cast their own votes and on behalf of their minor children, as it was recognized that a person must vote not only for the present, but also for future of his children. The fact that Suryata had twin children delighted Yadodhra for it meant four votes for Bharat.

It was to Suryakarma that Ekantra went to prepare the ground for Bharat's election. The karkarta was surprised. What were Bharat's credentials? True, he had discovered the secret of the poisoned arrows and was a fine soldier, but were these the only virtues required in a karkarta! Suryakarma, like many pious persons, was contemptuous of soldiers, whom he regarded a necessary evil. For him, it was unthinkable to support Bharat for this high office. Even if he made a list of one thousand eligible candidates, Suryakarma told Ekantra, Bharat's name would not appear on that list.

But Ekantra was not the only person canvassing for Bharat. Yadodhra had organized large groups of friends to seek support for Bharat's candidature. Many spoke of Bharat's ceaseless search for the secret of the poisoned arrow and the arduous journeys he undertook, in the face of grave danger, to protect his land. Every soldier knew of his bravery on the battlefield and old soldiers remembered how Bharat's father had sacrificed his life fighting the raiders. When it was time for Bharat to marry, many recalled how he had exchanged marriage vows with a girl even before she was born; the story was not exactly true, but it appealed to the romantic sentiment. There were those who wondered if his youth was against him, but often forgot this when they saw his handsome face and figure.

The council chiefs, too, were impressed with Bharat. Initially, the only council member promoting Bharat's candidature was Ekantra's wife, who was responsible for the welfare of hermits. Though most hermits were unconcerned, some listened and believed the kind, gentle lady whose mission in life was to see to their well-being! Thus, a few hermits did spread the word in Bharat's favour to anyone who listened to them.

Yadodhra had taken over Ekantra's task of distributing supplies to them and respectfully conveyed to them his father's view in Bharat's favour. While many remained silent, there were those who endorsed it. Yadodhra saw to it that messages of those who endorsed Bharat or even politely wished him well, reached Suryakarma and the council chiefs. With so many messages pouring in from the ascetics in the nearby forests, Suryakarma began to entertain doubts. He sent Suryata to investigate; Suryata returned, not only to confirm the messages already received, but with many more. It was clear that all those men of God, who had never taken the slightest interest in the elections before, had suddenly become deeply enamoured of Bharat's success.

Suryakarma began to waver—had he misjudged young Bharat? It was Suryata again who provided the clinching argument. Almost casually, he spoke of Bharat's worship and veneration for Surya.

Surprised, the karkarta had asked, 'Does your friendship for Bharat misguide you into that belief?'

But Suryata responded, 'Bharat's reverence for the Sun is as great as mine—if not greater.' Since Suryakarma would not believe it, Suryata swore it was so. And as he himself no longer had any reverence for the Sun, it was the truth!

This decided the issue for Suryakarma. He had no personal ambitions any more, but the hope that a sun-worshipper becomes the next karkarta filled his heart. The fact that he had not known about Bharat's devotion to the Sun puzzled him, but he realized he knew so very little about the young man anyway. Suryakarma ignored his misgivings and convinced himself that Bharat was the ideal candidate.

The election was still some time away, but Suryakarma's health began failing. He sent for the council chiefs and sought their influence to elect Bharat. They, too, had received messages from all quarters in favour of the youngster. Some of the council chiefs saw merit in having an immature youth as the karkarta for he would undoubtedly listen to their advice with respect. For the rest, Bharat's youthful looks, his military bearing, his exploits on the battlefield, his discovery of the poison, his ancestry, and even his romantic marriage, were enough to endear him to young and old.

Yadodhra had insisted that, as a candidate, Bharat ought to address people with a flourish and eloquence. But people saw in Bharat's silence a sense of humility and modesty that they liked. Suryata suggested that the least Bharat could do was to close his eyes and tell people—'Let us all pray together,' that the warm glow of joint prayer would heighten people's belief in his godly ways. Bharat said that would be dishonest. Yadodhra retorted that honest men never stood in elections, but looking at Suryata, who possibly considered this as a dig against his father, he changed the subject.

Later, as he recalled the vision he had seen of the land and the people of his clan, he found his eloquence; his words flowed easily as he spoke of Sanatan Dharma, of the spiritual nature of man, and the hopes of the first Hindus who had settled by the banks of the life-giving waters of the Sindhu. He often ended his speech with the prayer—'God bring peace to our people; give them hope, restore their dignity and renew their faith.'

One by one, other candidates dropped out and, on election-day Bharat stood unopposed. Even so, everyone in the clan had to cast their votes, for the winning candidate had to secure three-fourths of the vote, even if he was the sole candidate.

Bharat had greeted his success with an emotion that he could not describe. Pride, humility, happiness, fear, hope, inadequacy, responsibility assailed him at once.

'God, guide my way,' he prayed.

FOUR

DEFENCE OF THE CLAN AND MEMORY SONGS

5068 BCE with flashbacks

Caught up in his memories, Bharatjogi recalled his happiness on being elected the next karkarta. Many had thronged around him with congratulations. When he reached home, he had touched his mother's feet to seek her blessings.

Later, when he was alone with his young wife, she had asked, 'How does it feel to be elected karkarta?'

Bharat responded, 'I feel profoundly in love with all my people who have elected me. This love I must reciprocate with all my heart, soul and being. And you here, now, represent the entire clan and I feel obliged to shower that love on to you right away!'

∽

After Bharat assumed office, his first decision was to grant volunteers selected for the clan's active defence, free, two-storey cottages. The number of applicants grew enormously. Cottages were to be built on the outer fringe of settlements, nearest to lines of attack from the north-east. They were designed so that the first and second floors were connected by a removable ladder which could be pulled up from the second floor where the families could be sheltered behind heavy wooden doors. The second floor and roof had a similar structure; the ladder could be moved up to the roof where the fighters would gather to shoot arrows and fling jagged stones stored there in abundance along with food and water.

The volunteer army was responsible for building the cottages and had to learn brick-making, stone-cutting, masonry, carpentry and other skills along with architectural and building concepts. Several artists, artisans and builders came to supervise and teach. Some of them were nearing retirement, but Bharat declared that their continued service would postpone their retreat as hermits.

'Are prayers more important than God's work to defend our land and our people and to protect our hermits while they pray and meditate?' Bharat's question was answered with silent acquiescence for in recent attacks, raiders had been merciless with groups of hermits in the forest.

Huts, built earlier with mud, wood and straw, were improved and reinforced. Still, they remained easy prey and were vulnerable to being burnt down by raiders. It was necessary for the huts to be located in the inner circle, protected by an outer ring of well-defended cottages. As a result of this extensive cottage-building activity, huts began to disappear except as forest retreats or second homes, with the clansfolk vying with each other to build cottages using newer building techniques and architectural innovations. Bharat welcomed this trend and saw in it rising economic and defensive activity for the clan. He even assured newcomers to the clan that men from the volunteer army would assist them in building their homes, *after* the defensive structures and cottages had been built in the outer circle.

However, the cottages were not the first line of defence. Their aim was to prevent the enemy from entering the clan's territory. Most volunteers, initially, were used for defensive works on walls, pits, mounds, and trenches from which to resist an attack. Scouts were sent into enemy lands in case it became necessary to mount an attack and foil an offensive or create a diversion or simply punish them for earlier raids.

Large bushes with prickly thorns were planted on the approach to the clan's territory in haphazard patterns to slow down the raiders' horses and gain time before an impending attack. Drums were positioned at various points with selected persons assigned the responsibility to warn about attacks and call on volunteers to reach their positions, with different patterns of drum-beats to announce 'all clear' if raiders retreated or to summon help in particular sectors.

Although defending the clan against raiders was his foremost priority, Bharat realized that his people ought to know more about the continuity of their civilization and culture. Such knowledge would give greater incentives to his people to preserve their way of life and protect it from outsiders. One way, he thought, of achieving that was to revive the past for future generations. He knew that stories of past legends, of people who had lived before his time, of rivers, mountains and valleys, of the struggles, longings and aspirations of generations gone by, were all woven into songs and poems— some of which had survived, while others were half-remembered or had been forgotten altogether.

And so, along with introducing defensive and retaliatory measures against raiders, Bharat pioneered a system of 'Memory Songs'—eternal songs that would always be remembered, never forgotten, handed down from one generation to the next to keep alive the knowledge of the past, a gift for the future of humanity.

'Much of our past is covered with the dust of time. Shall it always be thus? No! Our Memory Songs,' he explained, 'shall be the treasury, trustee and guardian of the knowledge of our generation, and through these songs the tales of our times shall be passed to mankind forever. And, thus, our own age shall be endless, not a mere fleeting, unnoticed moment in history.'

Bharat sought to convince his people that some knowledge had to remain permanent, that culture had to be preserved, so that even when they were gone, their culture could continue. It was unfortunate, he said, that only a few stray fragments of past knowledge remained.

'How will future generations discover how we lived, loved, worked, prayed and thought, and know of our hopes, fears, and aspirations? By a dream? By a vision? No, there must be an unbroken bridge of knowledge; otherwise, man will be forever groping in the dark to discover what previous generations had already found and possibly even discarded.' Bharat continued, 'Who amongst us will deny the legacy of wisdom to our children and to the children of our children of the far future!'

No one objected to Bharat's idea, realizing that while their karkarta was trying to pass on the knowledge of the past and the present to future generations, he was also adding immensely to the storehouse of their entertainment; more singers, poets and song-composers meant that at the end of the day's work people could hope to listen to new melodies and fascinating lyrics. So readily, they applauded the measure.

Most information on pre-Vedic times comes from those Memory Songs. One of the earliest songs of Hindus (*Sanatan Dharma*) sung possibly in 8000 BCE or earlier, but remembered only by a few in Bharat's time, was the very first song to be designated as a Memory Song. It was the 'Hymn of Creation', rendered as under:

Then nothingness was not, nor existence then,
Nor air nor depths nor heavens beyond their ken,
What covered it? Where was it? In whose keeping?
In unfathomed folds, was it cosmic water seeping?
Then there was no life, no birth, no death,
Neither night nor day nor wind nor breath,
At last One sighed—a self-sustained Mother,

There was that One then—and none, none other.
Then there was darkness wrapped in darkness;
Was this unlit water, unseen, dry, wetless?
That One which came to be, enclosed in naught,
Arose, who knows, how, from the power of what!
But after all, who knows and who can say
Who, how, why, whence began creation's day?
Gods came after creation, did they not?
So who knows truly, whence it was wrought! . . .
Does that First Mother herself know, now?
Did She create, or was She created somehow;
She, who surveys from heavens, above us all,
She knows—or maybe She knows not at all.
Did She Herself create the One God!
And gladly gave Him the Creator's Rod!
But so re-fashioned Time and Space,
That He was more, and She was less?
Did She then turn future into past?
So He came first and She was last!
But surely, She told Him all, all!
Then how could He not know at all?
Or perhaps He knows it not, and cannot tell
Oh! He knows, He knows, but will not tell . . .

This pre-ancient song also appears in the *Rig Veda*—
'Hymn of Creation'—X:l 29.

There are however notable differences between this song
and the *Rig Veda* hymn. In particular, the *Rig Veda* does not
refer to:

- Creation of the First Mother
- The First Mother as the Creator of the One God
- The future turning into the past
- Time and space being re-fashioned by the First Mother,
  so that She becomes *less* and *last,* while God becomes
  more and *first.*

BHAGWAN S. GIDWANI

It is not possible to discover how these elements of this pre-ancient song, which was sung at least up to 5122 BCE, came to be omitted in the *Rig Veda*, composed around 4000 BCE.

Many songs, then, of early Hindus (*Sanatan Dharma*) sung possibly from 8000 BCE but remembered by only a few in Bharat's era, on various subjects—spiritual and temporal—came to be regarded as Memory Songs. Some of those sang of the impossibility of describing the One-Supreme though they presented a glimmer of promise that The Absolute is attainable in silence—the silence of within, and that the heart has an inner ear and can hear all that the soul silently whispers. Other songs related to making pots and pans or even wine-making—and then there were songs on love-making—to be recited only to adult audience.

The system of Memory Songs was slowly taking root but it really began to flourish after success in the wars with the Tribals.

FIVE

HINDU! HINDU!

5068 BCE with flashbacks

As he sat down to pray, Bharatjogi's thoughts strayed and he recalled the last battle with the tribes of the north-east, when he, as karkarta, had led his army deep into their territory.

'Hindu! Hindu!' The legendary cry echoed in his mind, and he saw himself at the head of his men, charging at the enemy.

'Hindu! Hindu!' The cry repeated itself and he felt tall, powerful and alive, certain that nothing could stop the onslaught of his people against the enemy.

'Hindu! Hindu!' he heard, as his spear pierced the enemy breast; and he felt the spirits of the gods with him.

'Hindu! Hindu!' the enemy wailed as he charged across the battlefield littered with the dead, the wounded, and the dying.

'Hindu! Hindu!' the shrill, piercing scream of the enemy rent the air as they fled in terror. Yet, there had been a time when the tribals had uttered those words with ridicule.

'Hindu! Hindu!' Bharat heard the low moan of the enemy's chief, who lay wounded on the battlefield. Bharat understood the voiceless cry. The chief was crying, not for mercy, but for a swift death. He was in pain from terrible wounds, his men were either dead or fleeing, and his own son had abandoned him. What he feared was a slow, lingering death, and, worse still, a life of slavery to the victorious Hindu. His hands rendered powerless, his eyes kept darting to a spear nearby.

Bharat looked at the chief; their eyes held each other in

silent understanding. He glanced at the spear and shook his head, denying the chief's appeal, and motioned to a soldier to remove him respectfully from the battlefield. But the soldier misunderstood his command and swiftly pierced the chief's chest with a sharp spear. Enraged, Bharat glared at the soldier, but the deed was done.

'Remove the chief's body and give it to his people with utmost respect,' he ordered, and thought he saw a flicker of gratitude flash in the dying man's eyes before they closed forever. The soul of one man, Bharat recalled, when liberated from the body, is the soul of all men and, eventually, we all become one soul, indivisible and merged with the One-Supreme.

Before the soldier could carry out Bharat's orders, a voice behind him thundered, 'Yes, give his body to his people, but not his head.'

It was Dhru—also known as Dhrupatta—Bharat's deputy commander. With his sword Dhru separated the chief's head from his body, and holding it aloft as trophy, he galloped to the hill where the enemy had retreated.

The enemy watched, as Dhru approached, their eyes were focused on the head of their fallen leader. A mournful chant rose from the hill as the tribals dwelled on the enormity of the situation. Their chief held the spirit of their god that he would have surrendered to his son before dying. But the young man had fled when the chief fell in battle, and could never be anointed chief. The spirit of their god would fly away, always wandering, eternally unfulfilled. The tribals knew that the departing spirit of their god demanded sacrifice, and in the silence that followed, they brought forth the chief's son; he was the one who would be sacrificed.

Meanwhile, Dhru stood up on his horse, the fallen warrior's head on his spear, and kept whirling it high in the air. Far away, Bharat shouted, 'What are you doing?' and though Dhru could not hear him, he understood the karkarta's question and said, 'I think fresh air will do him good.'

The tribals stood still; they knew the spirit of their god would escape from the body of the dead chief if clouds concealed the sun, or at the latest, at sunset. The sacrifice had to be completed quickly; already, the sky was threatened with clouds. A priest brought out his axe while others held the trembling youngster. They chanted prayers for the sacrifice, their eyes focused on the whirling head of their chief, waiting for it to stop before striking the boy with the axe.

Dhru's arm was tiring and with one last furious whirl, he flung the head towards his own troops. The chief's son saw his chance as the astonished priests watched the disembodied head fly through air and fled.

Dhru's sword was ready to strike, but he saw it was only an unarmed boy, obviously intent on surrendering. He gently prodded the boy with the back of his sword, making him run even faster towards the clan's troops. Gasping for breath, the boy knelt at Bharat's feet, moaning at the sight of his father's dismembered body. Bharat gently raised the boy and held him in a comforting embrace.

Bharat did not know the enemy's language. A slave—a tribal captured long ago by his troops—was brought forth. He understood the situation clearly. He said the boy was doomed to die, but worse still, the entire tribe was doomed as their chief could not bequeath their god's power to his son who had fled the battlefield when his father fell. The tribe, consequently, had to leave their land and move elsewhere.

'Move where?' Bharat asked.

'Anywhere, everywhere, but they cannot remain in their present habitation, which is forever doomed.'

Bharat was concerned: where would they move? Perhaps they would infiltrate into his own clan's lands! At other times they had come to raid the land, always going back. But now they would stay and die in the attempt, rather than return to their accursed land! He asked, 'What happens if the boy does not go back?'

'They will hunt for him all their lives. He is the one who must be sacrificed to the spirit of our departing god.'

So, feared Bharat, our land will always be their target.

What will hold them back in their lands, Bharat asked. Nothing, he was told. Their land was doomed, for the spirit of their god would wander forever, without repose.

Bharat reached a decision. 'Go, tell them, their chief gave me the spirit of their god. It reposes in my breast, happy, fulfilled.'

The interpreter objected, 'The chief could bequeath the god's spirit only to his eldest son, as the system of dynastic rule must be maintained.'

Could the chief adopt a son, Bharat asked. Yes, the slave explained, but only under special circumstances—if his natural son agreed to such an adoption or if he chose to become a priest or if he fled from battle, deserting his father, as in the present case.

'Can your people adopt a son from our clan?' Bharat asked.

'Why not! Our people have adopted many children captured from your clan.'

'I thought you people killed or enslaved all those you captured!'

'Only a barbarian kills a child, away from the heat of battle. And only a barbarian would enslave a child or keep him captive,' came the reply.

Everything from Bharat's mind was erased except the thought of his clan's captured children. He had thought the tribals massacred or enslaved captured children and he asked, 'How is it, then, that we never hear about our captured children?'

'They are no longer children of your clan. They are children of our tribe.'

'And when they grow?' Bharat asked.

'When they grow, they are our people. Some become

hata—hunters, some itta—magistrates, and some even atta—priests, and all become ita—warriors. It is only in your clan that those captured are slaves for ever.'

The enemy is always a barbarian, Bharat thought, but if you look with the eyes of the enemy, the barbarian is nowhere but within ourselves!

Quietly, he said, 'Very well then, tell them, their chief adopted me as his son, as his own son wishes to be a priest.'

The interpreter explained that the breast of he who is to be adopted must be pierced in order to take in blood from the breast of he who is to adopt. Bharat asked Dhru to draw blood from his breast with his dagger.

'With great pleasure,' said Dhru. But for all his flamboyance, Dhru stopped when the first hesitant drop of blood appeared. Bharat prodded him to dig deeper. As more blood flowed, Dhru threw away the dagger and said, 'Enough, we killed their chief today; we don't have to kill ours. I can wait.' His words—'I can wait'—brought smiles all round, as he was expected to be karkarta, after Bharat.

'Go now,' Bharat told the slave-interpreter. 'Tell them, I am their chief now, for their old chief adopted me as his son and surrendered to me their god's spirit.'

'Only a priest can make such an announcement.'

'Who can appoint a priest?' Bharat asked.

'Only the chief of the tribe can.'

'Very well then, I am chief now. I appoint you as a priest.'

'No,' the interpreter objected. 'You cannot. I am unclean.'

'Unclean! How?' Bharat asked.

'My tribe knows that I have been a slave. A slave is not clean.'

Bharat understood the slave's sadness and responded with the traditional words: 'I, Bharat, karkarta of the land, here and now, set you free. From this moment, you are no longer a slave but a free man of the Rya of the land.'

The slave shook his head. A slave, he explained, cannot

instantly become clean. Purification ceremonies for a moon-month must cleanse his spirit. 'My freedom cannot serve your purpose. You can take it back,' he said, contemptuously.

Bharat shook his head too. Words granting him freedom had been spoken. The slave was a slave no more. A free man of the Rya—the people—could not be enslaved unless convicted of a grievous offence.

Inwardly, Bharat smiled, happy he had freed him. He did not have the absolute right to free him since the slave belonged to a land-owner, but during hostilities, the karkarta could dispose of private property in the clan's interest. In any case, Bharat had decided to pay the owner from his own funds.

The problem of sending a priest to the tribe remained. The freed slave suggested that the old chief's son could go as a priest if the karkarta, as the new chief, appointed him as priest.

'But how!' asked Bharat. 'You said they will hunt him down and kill him!'

'Not if he is a priest. No one can dare to kill a priest. In fact, your right to be adopted by our chief is stronger if his natural son surrenders his succession to be a priest.'

Bharat understood. Since he'd been adopted by the old chief as his eldest son and had received the god's spirit from him, he was now the tribe's chief and as such he could appoint anyone as a priest and that person could not be held accountable for any faults—including fleeing the battlefield—committed prior to attaining priesthood.

The interpreter also explained that a witness must accompany the priest when he announces the transfer of the god's power from one chief to another. And the priest must wear a red head-dress. Dhru solved the problem by dipping a piece of white cloth in the blood of the tribals who had died on the battlefield. The boy's head was draped with red cloth, narrow rivers of blood flowing down his face. Earlier, the boy had trembled in terror at the prospect of facing his people.

But the head-dress transformed him. He stood erect, unafraid and full of confidence in his priestly dignity.

How outward symbols change the spirit inside us! Bharat marvelled.

The interpreter also explained that anyone could be a witness.

Bharat ordered, 'Then you must go as witness.' Something in the man's eyes held Bharat's attention.

He seemed lost in thought, and then, finally, he nodded blankly and said, 'Of course, I must. You shall be obeyed, karkarta.' Yet his anguish was evident.

On the hill, the eyes of the tribesmen were raised towards the sky, fearful of the impending sunset when the spirit of their god would leave the dead chief's body and wander away.

The interpreter asked for a cask of wine.

'Is this the time to drink!' Bharat asked.

'No,' he explained, 'the new chief invariably sends a gift to the priests.'

'Would they be happy if I sent many casks of wine?'

'The more, the better. The more you send, the more the priests shall believe; and hope for more in future; and they will wonder what reason can he have to lie, who has so much to give, now and later!'

Bharat smiled, 'They do not suspect that he who comes bearing many gifts has his eyes on something in return?'

'Perhaps they do. But they think that what you give is theirs to keep, and what you seek, you will grab from people.'

'The priests and the people—are they not one?'

The interpreter shook his head. 'The priests? They are a class apart—the privileged class. How can they know how another class feels!'

Silently, Bharat asked himself: is it not true of my land too? Why is it that those who are known as men of god are the least godly!

'What happens if the priests do not believe you?' asked Bharat.

'They shall believe me,' the interpreter replied, 'because they shall *want* to believe. Or else they shall wander homeless, without their priestly dignity and comfort. Soon, they shall come to bow to you as their chief.'

Bharat ordered four mules to be loaded with wine casks brought for the campaign. 'These are my gifts to the priests. They can expect more in future.'

The interpreter nodded and then astonished everyone by taking off his clothes. He explained, 'A witness must appear as God made him—naked.'

He turned to the dead chief's son, who went ahead, and followed with the mules bearing the wine.

Bharat's troops watched. Only Dhru laughed, 'If our old slave goes naked, as God made him, would the tribals also think that God made him with four mules loaded with wine?'

From the hill, the tribals watched two men and four mules moving towards them. The chief's son stopped at the base of the hill while the interpreter climbed up after securing the mules.

Not a sound was heard as everyone waited for the naked messenger to reach them.

The interpreter stood before the head priest. His face and his arms were raised towards the sky as if he was speaking to the gods. When he finished speaking, the head priest left the hill and walked towards the old chief's son. The two men spoke for a while and then the head priest returned to the hilltop, raised his hands and remained gazing at the sky. The other priests and the tribals followed his example and did likewise. A few moments later, everyone lowered their arms, except the naked interpreter.

The head priest draped a white cloth around the naked man and knelt before him, as did the other priests.

Bharat and his men had been watching the spectacle intently, and Dhru said, 'They have believed him. They are kneeling to our former slave!'

'But why are they kneeling to him?' the troops asked.

'Why not?' Dhru rejoined. 'He announced the movement of the god's spirit from one chief to another. Is he not then the god's messenger? Surely, they must kneel to him!'

The head priest escorted the chief's son to the hilltop, from where the boy pointed in Bharat's direction.

Led by the head priest, the tribals began chanting, 'Hindu! Hindu!' It was a soulful cry. They had not lost their god's spirit! It had not disappeared into nothingness! The void they dreaded was no more! The spirit of their god was alive in the heart of the chief of Hindus. He was their chief now. They were not doomed. They were saved!

'Hindu! Hindu!' It was a joyous cry, of relief, gratitude, and thanksgiving.

'What happens now?' Bharat wondered.

'They will come and kneel before you as their new chief,' Dhru said. 'But as our good former slave said, you have to wait till sunset.'

When the sun went into hiding, a mighty roar went up from the tribals. 'Hindu! Hindu!' they chanted as they rushed forward in an almost never-ending stream. The head priest paused only to inspect the dagger wound on Bharat's breast before kneeling in front of him. The tribals knelt as one, their cries of 'Hindu! Hindu!' echoing across the battlefield.

At a signal from the head priest, they all rose and quickly improvised a platform of boulders and wooden frames. Bharat stood on it, raised his hand in benediction and the chant was heard once more.

'Hindu! Hindu!'

That evening, Bharat asked for the former slave. I must thank him, he thought, he earned for us a victory that will last!

Moments later, the head priest brought the dead body of the former slave, cut up in several pieces and wrapped in a rug.

Bharat was horrified. 'Why!' he asked, at last.

The head priest misunderstood, for he did not know the language of his new chief and explained that the body was cut into the correct number of pieces—one for the sun, one for the moon, seven for the planets, one for the mother earth, one for . . .

Bharat realized that he who had witnessed their god's spirit being surrendered by one chief to the other must die. 'Why?' he asked.

'He who is a false witness goes straight to hell, so none shall bear false witness,' the head priest explained. 'And he who is a true witness shall go straight to heaven. What more can one want! But that none shall come forth lightly to bear witness, except that he be inspired by a cause greater than his life . . . for his life shall be forfeit as soon he bears witness.'

Where would I go? Bharat wondered. I, who encouraged him to bear false witness. Why did he not tell me what would happen to him! Did he not know?

'Perhaps more than his life, he loved his people,' Dhru said.

'His people!'

'Yes, his people—we were his people, for he became one of us when you granted him freedom. But he died also for those amongst whom he was born; he realized that they, too, must be saved from the catastrophe that would inevitably result if the spirit of their god was lost and they became homeless, rootless.'

'But perhaps he did not know that he must die!' .Bharat cried, as though to escape the guilt of sending the man to his death.

'He knew. He was a priest amongst his people before we captured him. I have checked.' Dhru added, 'He also left a message for us with the old chief's son, saying, "If all goes well, tell the karkarta that I go where I must for bearing false witness, but I go without tears, for what is false should have been true so that the children of my ancestors remain unharmed, and the people of the karkarta's land remain in peace, and the battle cry is heard no more."'

Bharat listened in anguish. He did not believe in heaven or hell, but he was convinced that the man who had died with such infinite love for people—his own and the clan's—was not of this earth. For him, should be moksha, total liberation, and complete identity with the One-Supreme.

Dhru interrupted Bharat's reverie. 'He left another message of a personal kind. He said that all his clothes should be given to Dhanumati, a slave-girl who was his only friend; and if he was entitled to a day's wages as a soldier—since he was a free man at least for one day—those, too, should be given to her.'

'Dhanumati shall receive his wages for all her life. Who is she? Where is she?' Bharat asked feverishly.

'They were slaves together in Sutukat's plantation.'

'Send a courier. Now, this instant. Send an order in my name that Dhanumati is no longer a slave.'

'I have already taken the liberty of doing that.'

'Thank you, Dhru, you always know what is in my heart.'

'Of course. How else can I become karkarta?' Dhru replied, hoping for a smile. Seeing Bharat's obvious distress, Dhru added: 'What is done is done. All we can do now is to pray for his soul.'

'Pray *for* his soul! No, Dhru, no! We do not pray *for* such souls. We pray *to* such souls.'

SIX

PARLIAMENT OF HINDU & 'SONG OF HINDU'

5068 BCE with flashbacks

As Bharatjogi sat in his hut, his thoughts went back to Dhanumati, the wife of the former slave.

Together, they had run away from their tribe. The former slave, as priest, could not take a wife or live with the same woman for more than six days in any moon-month or more than twelve days in nine months. Were he to break the rules, though nothing would happen to him, Dhanumati would be killed for corrupting a priest, and her body fed to hyenas. Unfortunately, the lovers found no sanctuary. They were caught by Bharat's clan, treated as enemy spies, and promptly enslaved. The former slave tried to comfort Dhanumati through her tears; his own tears were for her, never for himself, when he said, 'He who runs from the gods has to be caught by the devil. He has no other destiny!'

Indeed, he was right to call us the devil, thought Bharat. Is it not devilish to hold two innocent lovers in slavery? To hold *anyone* in slavery?

Bharat wondered if it was the former slave's sacrifice that eventually hardened his own heart against slavery all the more intensely. Who knew how God revealed his heart to man! A sudden flash, an inward illumination—and all life is seen afresh, anew.

∽

Bells had rung throughout the Hindu clan when they heard of Bharat's victory. There had been victories before against scattered tribal outposts and villages, but this was against the combined armies of the tribes, right in the heart of enemy territory; most of the tribal chieftains had been killed, and the hated tribal chief decapitated.

Some from the clan arrived even before the battle ended, hoping to buy captured prisoners as slaves at a cheap price given their abundance. From a distance, they saw the ghastly spectacle of flight and pursuit, slaughter and capture, fallen men and beasts. The enemy was defeated everywhere, and the battlefield was strewn with corpses, only small patches of bloodstained earth showing here and there. All that remained was to completely occupy the enemy's territory and exact swift vengeance for all their past outrages.

More and more people began arriving at Bharat's tent, the battle headquarters. Some were slave traders, others came to buy land in the tribal areas for farming and cattle, some needed mining rights for metals, others for precious stones, and some sought recruits for whore-houses. But there were many who wanted nothing.

'You do not conquer men by war, but with love,' they said. 'Evil is greed for gold and lust for power,' they urged, 'and avarice will destroy our honour and virtue and tempt us to hold nothing too sacred to buy and sell.'

Bharat told the slave traders there would be no slaves to buy, for none would be enslaved. They smiled, thinking the karkarta was trying to bargain for higher prices. Surely the clan, with its increasing territory, needed slaves, and the karkarta's dwindling treasury needed money.

But the karkarta was adamant. The council chiefs were also baffled. 'Why?' asked Nandan, their spokesman.

'Because they, too, are Hindus,' Bharat replied. 'And a Hindu shall not be a slave.'

'When did they become Hindus?' Nandan asked.

'When they called themselves Hindus, accepted our protection, our way of life and our gods.'

'There are those who say that you have accepted their gods!'

'Of course,' replied Bharat.

'Then it is you who have ceased to be a Hindu.'

Bharat did not flinch. 'When has a Hindu failed to accept the gods of others? When have we ever rejected a god in our endless quest for supremacy? Did our ancestors, who first came to live by the side of the river, not accept the gods of those who were there before them? And did we not embrace the gods of those who came in peace after them? Their gods, like ours, serve the One-Supreme, whose gracious purpose is to . . .'

Nandan interrupted, 'Bharatji, we are speaking of slaves, not of gods.'

'No! We are not speaking of slaves. We are speaking of God and His love for His Creation, of man and his humanity, of the tribals and their right to freedom.'

'Yet you think nothing of the horrors those tribals perpetrated on our people!'

'Is it vengeance you seek? Or is it profit from the slave trade?'

'Both. They tore the children of our clan out of their parents' arms, ravished our women and pillaged our temples and homes. They ravaged . . . '

'And they shall do so again, unless *we* show wisdom and restraint. Can you not see that vengeance sows vengeance, hate engenders hate, and bloodshed breeds still more bloodshed! What satisfaction can revenge bring? Does one war end all wars? No. The enemy rises again. How can a victory today guarantee a victory in future? The answer to war is not enslaving the enemy, but ending enmity.'

Nandan and Bharat spoke for a long time, but both remained inflexible. At last Nandan said, 'All right, they are

Hindus. But how does that protect them from slavery? The slaves we already own also call themselves Hindus. They pray as we do and serve the same gods. See how wrong your position is!'

'It is not I who am wrong, but those who own slaves in our land.'

'Yet you yourself own slaves!' Nandan retorted. 'How many slaves does your household have?' he asked when Bharat nodded sadly in response.

'Many,' Bharat answered, as though admitting to a charge.

'And you will, of course, free them instantly?' Nandan asked, with heavy irony.

Bharat looked at him, as if pondering over the question, and then said, 'Yes, half of them, instantly.'

'Half of them!' Nandan was astonished at the unexpected answer.

'Half, I can liberate,' Bharat explained. 'My wife and I own property in common; what right do I have to dispose of her portion, unless she agrees!'

Nandan wondered if Bharat was losing his mind, and asked, 'How did this idea come to you?'

'It came from you. And I am very grateful. I must liberate my slaves.'

'No, I mean the idea that the tribals must not be enslaved.'

Bharat replied, 'Who knows! Maybe a slave spoke to me, or a priest or a witness or someone seeking refuge, or a lover, or his sweetheart. Who knows!' But Bharat thought of the man who had been a priest, a lover, a refugee, a slave, and a witness, and had chosen to die for others.

'You are in error, Bharatji, those barbarians will never be good Hindus,' Nandan said.

'Are we good Hindus ourselves? It may take centuries for men to be fully men but we must prepare for that day.'

To those who wanted to exploit the tribals, Bharat said, 'Go, help them; peace is our primary need. Poverty and riches must not grow side by side. For your own peace and prosperity, share god's bounty with your neighbouring tribes. Their failure to grow is your failure.'

Many thought it was simply the poet in the karkarta's heart taking charge, and ignored him.

But then Bharat did free his slaves. Not just half, but all of them, for Bindu immediately agreed.

∾

In an imposing ceremony, Bharat addressed the tribals: 'Your gods are our gods . . . Your people are our people. Know this then that from this moment, all of you are free, never to be enslaved, except for seven grave offences for which the Law prescribes slavery.'

The clan's chief priest recited:

Let us think of the splendour
Of Her that is the One-Supreme,
She, that is one without second,
That She may inspire our minds,
Our words, thoughts and deeds.
To Her, who is the unending time
To Her, who is without beginning
To Her, who is without end
To Her, who began it all
To Her, who is seed of all
To Her, who is source of all
And to Her, who is the Self
In the innermost heart of all.
To Her, our prayer, our devotion, our love
That She may inspire us, together, all, all.

He sprinkled water and grain over the ceremonial fire and uncovered fruits and flowers.

Bharat spoke: 'Mother Sindhu's holy water is sprinkled in worship of the One-Supreme. The grain is sacrificed to Goddess Agni, to carry it to all the deities on the earth, in the air, water, space, outer space and beyond. These flowers and fruits are our homage to the gods; we hope they shall accept a subtle part of the fruits, leaving the rest for their worshippers. For know this: such are the only sacrifices that gods accept. For gods do not desire the sacrifice of blood and flesh—neither of humans, nor of animals, nor of birds; the surest way of inviting the wrath of the gods is to abominate their presence with the blood and flesh of unwilling sacrificial victims.'

'Unwilling!' a tribal priest protested. He explained that for them it was the finest death to perish under a sacrificial knife. 'Such a fate to honour the gods is known as an honourable death.'

The tribal head priest was unhappy with Bharat's decree ending human and animal sacrifices to the gods, but remained silent. How did one argue with a conqueror who spared the lives and liberty of the conquered! Yet, later he asked the karkarta, 'Everything has life—human, animal and bird. Flowers, fruits and grains, trees and stones, every drop of water that we sprinkle has life. All creation has life. Sacrificing one or the other, is it not the same?'

Bharat was pleased. He knew that those who believed that all creation had life were on the right path; the next step to enlightenment would arise only from such faith. 'Everything has life,' he agreed. 'But then every life has a purpose and its own fulfilment and salvation to seek.'

The tribals received Bharat's decree that none would be enslaved with relief. They assumed there would be sacrifices to the gods; virgins and warriors had already been chosen. Now, instead, each was offered grain, nuts and fruits to place before the idols. They found it strange that this conquering clan should have such tame, undeveloped ideas of sacrifice. How would the gods be satisfied with so little!

BHAGWAN S. GIDWANI

But the tribal head priest, true to his oath of loyalty, said, 'Be silent. Their karkarta is now the chief of our chiefs and speaks with the spirit of Prajapati, the lord of all beings. Obey him in all things.'

Many obeyed, but some wondered: can the chief of chiefs offend against the Way and Will of the gods as revealed by our ancestors?

It was to them that the former chief's son, now a priest, spoke. 'Their karkarta is now our chief and he speaks truly. The gods of the Hindu are not hungry or thirsty, and that is why their clan is well fed and prosperous.'

The rebel leader asked with contempt, 'So we desert our gods, who are thirsty and hungry, and run after gods of wealth and plenty!'

'No!' the young priest pleaded. 'Their gods are our gods and our gods are theirs—and they all serve the same Creator.'

'Foolish youth!' the rebel leader raged. 'Gods are not like these animal skins we wear, to be worn or discarded at will. They are with us, always and forever!' When the young priest did not respond, he continued, 'You were the son of he who was the chief of our chiefs; you were to be our chief after him, but that glory is denied to you, as your own father disowned you to adopt another. Now you are nothing more than a junior priest. To what lower depths you will sink, in time, I know not, but be sure, there is a place in hell for those like you who abandon their gods.'

Many looked at the youth, some sympathetic over his father's death, others remembering the days when they bowed reverently to his father, and to him as the heir-apparent. As the moon came out from behind the clouds in an overcast, starless sky, they saw a glow on the young priest's handsome face, but it did not come from the moonlight alone. There was no distress on his face; all the tension had left him. Maybe he felt the stirring of an emotion that thrilled him. He forgot the pain of his father's death; he forgot the gnawing guilt of deserting his father in battle; he even forgot his sin for lies leading to his appointment as priest. No longer was his spirit overwhelmed. Peace had returned to his anguished soul. Unafraid, he looked at the man who cursed him.

He stood transformed, as though a vision rose before him. Then he spoke in a faraway voice: 'The Creator bleeds when any of His creatures bleed. Do not carry the sin of His blood!'

This is all they heard. Perhaps he said no more, or perhaps he did, but they did not hear any more, for rain came down accompanied by thunder and lightning that played hide and seek on his face, bringing out its glow and shadow. His lips moved in prayer, and though they could not hear him, they felt his words echo in the thunder: 'The Creator bleeds . . . bleeds, when any of His creatures bleed. The Creator bleeds . . .'

A vast majority of the tribals accepted the new wave of leadership. Only a few chose to escape to the mountains beyond and build a shrine to continue human and animal sacrifices.

When Bharat heard what the old chief's son had said, he had his words woven into a Memory Song—*The Creator bleeds . . . bleeds when any of His Creatures bleed. Do not carry the sin of His blood!*

∾

Relieved at being spared the fate of slavery, the tribals were surprised when their chief of chiefs exercised his limitless powers and freed all the slaves that they had owned. It was a heavy price, but they had been prepared for worse. However, while they no longer had any slaves, Bharat's own clan still had slaves, for the karkarta did not have the right to interfere with the clan's pre-existing privileges.

Many at the clan's council meeting complained bitterly about being denied their traditional right to enslave the tribals even after they had been victorious on the battlefield. But Bharat had insisted that their real victory had not been on the battlefield, but later when the tribals made peace and extended their hand of friendship.

'We could have annihilated them,' cried a council member. 'And we should have. Their entire race should have been wiped out.'

Dhru interrupted, 'Then we would not have had a single slave; so why complain!'

There were those who laughed, but Bharat turned to his accuser, 'Who would bear the responsibility for the evil of annihilating another race? He who leads our people or the entire Hindu clan? To whose karma would it be accounted? Who shall suffer the consequences of being denied moksha? I must know if I am ever to lead our people in battle again. The entire clan must know before going into battle again.'

Dhru smiled. Trust the karkarta to divert a political discussion into the spiritual realm of karma and moksha.

Bharat continued, 'But what exactly is your complaint? That you are being denied a few more slaves? That tribal lands are not open to your greed and exploitation? For that, you think that I should have rejected the peace and friendship the tribes offered? The pity is that not many of you know the value of peace. This discussion must be continued in an open assembly of the people of the clan.'

The threat was obvious. The karkarta wanted a public debate so he could appeal to people directly. Most of the clan did not own slaves and had no intention to grab tribal lands. Many had had to enlist as soldiers in campaigns against the tribals and go through mud, filth, blood and the horror of war. They had sufficient common sense to realize that the idea of annihilating the tribals was foolhardy. Surely, in that rough terrain with impassable barriers and hidden caves, the enemy could easily retreat and prepare for future attacks. The clan wanted peace, and would surely shout down the council if it opposed the karkarta's plans for amity.

Nandan, who led the critics, now found himself in a conciliatory mood. He needed time to influence the clan into rejecting the idea of a union with the tribals. He said, 'We respect Bharatji. Undoubtedly, he had the clan's best interest at heart when he made his decisions. Only time will tell what the future holds in store for us. Let the night give us counsel before we meet tomorrow. It would of course be unthinkable that a matter be referred to the people before the council fully debates the issues.'

The discussion would have ended for the day, but Devdatta (Deva) intervened. He belonged to no party and had no affiliations; he admired reason and logic above all. 'Our karkarta,' Deva said, 'leads our people by the power of his intelligence, his reason and his charisma. But even intelligent men can sometimes be wrong. Is he not wrong to say that he has not interfered with traditional rights? True, he has not interfered with the rights of our clan, but has he not interfered with the traditional rights of the tribals by depriving them of their slaves?'

'I made that decision as the chief of chiefs of the tribals, not as the karkarta,' Bharat responded, 'and it cannot be questioned in this council.'

'Very true,' Deva agreed. 'I take it, then, that our clan will not control the tribals and their lands.'

Bharat sensed a trap. Or was it an invitation? He replied, 'There should be no question of control. I foresee a unity of two peoples, not dominion over one by the other. I visualize a joint council and joint assembly, where both our clan and the tribes have equal rights.'

'Splendid. I feared you intended to treat the tribals as subjects under our rule. But I was wrong. You, karkarta, are honourable as always, and I salute you for combining the interests of the tribes and those of our clan to everyone's benefit.'

Nandan seethed over the fact that Bharat had arrogated complete power as the chief of the tribals, as if the victory on the battlefield was his alone. And how could the karkarta dream of bringing those barbarians into the council and assembly with equal rights!

'Karkarta . . . ' he shouted.

But Deva interrupted, 'Nandanji, await your turn. I have not yielded the floor to you yet.' Nandan glared, but sat down as the other man continued, 'I must say now that this meeting is clearly out of order.'

Everyone was surprised; the meeting was being held on the fourth day of the month, as usual. There was a quorum with only two council chiefs out of the seventy-seven missing; even the galleries for headmen and spectators were overcrowded.

'Whenever the council discusses questions affecting the interests of a particular group, that group is invited to participate even if it cannot vote. For instance, when questions affect farmers, their guild is invited. The same is done for hunters, fishermen, artisans, teachers, singers, dancers, painters, sculptors, builders and others. Regrettably, I do not see the representatives . . . '

Nandan was furious. What was Deva suggesting? That the tribals be invited to the council meeting! He could not be allowed to utter that impossible, preposterous demand. No, he had to be silenced before he infected the other council members.

Nandan thundered, 'What utter nonsense is this! Have we lost all sense, all reason? Is this a council of chiefs or a meeting of jokers, buffoons and comics! If the tribals are allowed to participate in the meeting, tomorrow you might ask that slaves be included in the council as well!'

'Nandan,' Deva responded gently but firmly, 'your habit of interrupting grows tiresome. Even if the karkarta does not call you to order, out of the goodness of his heart, you must try to control yourself.' He continued, 'Did I speak of inviting tribals or even slaves to participate? Although, maybe, if they participated, more sense would emerge at our meetings.'

'But you spoke of the tribals,' Nandan shot back. 'Tribals in the council of the clan!'

'Did I?' Deva innocently looked at Bharat, who, as the presiding officer, was expected to clarify doubts about the proceedings. But the karkarta was silent. 'No,' Deva continued, 'I did not ask that the tribals be invited to this meeting. Nandan has a gift of looking into the future, and certainly I shall welcome the tribals' participation in future joint councils. But my present concern is different, and I beg permission to speak without interruption if Nandan will graciously restrain himself.' After a pause, he continued, 'Whenever special problems affecting particular groups come up before the council, persons from that group are invited to the meeting. I confess I am mystified that this meeting should be unattended by those who are primarily concerned. You understand my difficulty, Karkarta?'

Bharat did not. He hesitantly responded, 'The issue here is of war and peace with the tribals, and is of vital importance to all of us . . . but the special interests of a particular group are not involved.'

'No!' Deva challenged. 'How many in this council have lost their sons in countless wars with the tribals? My impression is that when battles take place, not only are councillors far away from the battle, but also their sons. They all are engaged in so-called important clan-building activities, far away from the fields where arrows fly and blood flows. I must ask, for I have carried on my shoulders the coffins of my three sons who died in battle, and I assure you no load is heavier than bearing the body of one's child towards the funeral pyre. And those who have lit the funeral pyre of their sons know that that fire does not lighten your burden or diminish the darkness of despair in your heart; no, the fire mocks at you and even promises to return to consume more of your sons, perhaps in the hope that when all your sons are gone, there will be an end to the madness in your minds that seeks war, instead of peace.'

Deva's voice rose as he continued. 'Would you, Karkarta, ask how many council members have lost sons in battle? If they have not, how are they qualified to speak of war and peace? Have you, Karkarta, lost a son in the war?'

Bharat replied softly, 'No, I have not.' He did not add that his sons were too young for battle. Nor did he add that his own father had died in battle when he himself was a child. But Deva knew that; he was one of those who had carried his father's coffin on that last, mournful journey.

Deva continued, 'I spoke of my tears for my sons, but I speak also for those who have lost their husbands and those who lost their fathers when they were children.' His eyes turned to Bharat momentarily, and then his voice rose, 'But I deny that the council alone can speak for the tears of the clan. Let us recognize that a special interest exists: of women who lost their husbands to those dreadful wars, of children who lost their fathers, and of fathers who lit the funeral pyres of their sons.

'Let that special interest be invited if the question of war is to be debated again. Let them tell you what is in their hearts. Then, let us see if what they say makes an impression on those who have never shed tears for the loss of their loved ones.'

This was the first time that anyone had seen or heard Deva display emotion or speak with passion. He was usually cool and collected, and always spoke precisely, with reason and logic.

∾

At another stormy meeting, some preachers declared that

the tribals could not be considered Hindus. Deva asked, 'How can the horizons of our God be bound by the limits of our clan! Do we or do we not worship a universal God? Or is it that we reject the God of the universe in favour of a local god whose boundaries are limited to a stone's throw?'

When Bharat thanked him for interceding in the council, Deva said, 'Thank me by all means, Bharatji! But in my heart is anguish for insult to our land.'

'What insult?' Bharat asked with concern.

'The tribal land today is the Land of the Free, for you abolished slavery there. But here, slavery still flourishes. Is that not an insult? Tell me, you who always think of the future, what will the coming ages say of us?'

'They will say that in our midst lived a man of honour like Deva who sought to right a wrong and showed the true path.'

'Flatterer! No wonder people love and admire you.'

'And I,' Bharat replied, 'love and admire you.'

'Then I shall die happy.'

'No, you shall live happily,' Bharat said. But both knew that Deva was terminally ill and had only eighteen months to two years of life left.

'Perhaps,' Deva said, 'I shall do you one last favour after I die. You do need someone to intercede for you in the world beyond.'

'I need someone to intercede for me here.'

'You! You who are karkarta of our clan! You who are the chief of chiefs of the tribals! You need someone to intercede for you here?'

Bharat smiled, for he knew that despite his heavy irony, Deva understood his predicament. Even so, he said, 'So much is being said so often by so many against giving equal rights to the tribals. Preachers, slave owners, their hirelings . . . oh, so many . . . they are just out to mislead, misguide and inflame!'

'Surely our people will know what is right and wrong!'

'Will they? Who will silence the thousand voices calling for vengeance! In their fury, those voices rise far above the soft and gentle murmurings of the few who urge mercy, compassion, brotherhood. How will our people ever understand? Through a miracle? By a vision? From a dream? Inspiration? No, my friend, I need people to intercede here. A karkarta is powerless unless his people are behind him.'

They held each other's gaze for a moment, then Deva said, 'I think I shall intercede for you on this earth itself.'

Bharat smiled politely, but did not know what Deva intended to do. When they parted, he saw the other man walk away erect, with the light, precise steps of a soldier.

Deva died two months later, far from his home. He had been on the road night and day, through mud, slush and rain, speaking of the moral and spiritual need to unite with the tribals as Hindus, under the One-Supreme, and to strengthen the karkarta's attempts to achieve a union with the tribal lands based on peace, friendship and goodwill.

Sadly Bharat reminisced over his last conversation with Deva who had offered to help. He realized the lengths to which Deva had gone despite his fragile health! The vaid said, 'He was a law unto himself. I did not even know where he went or when and why. He squandered his life in two months when he could have lived for two years.'

But Bharat felt Deva had died like a soldier on the battlefield, for a cause greater than life. He had not squandered his life; he lived it to the fullest. Yet Bharat's sadness remained.

He was informed of Deva's dying wish that his ashes be immersed in the Sindhu by the villages that he was unable to visit, while repeating his desire for peace and unity with the tribal lands. 'Add my apology that my death prevents me from visiting you but let my dead ashes immersed nearby speak for me, not only to confound those that lie, but also to accuse those who, knowing better, fail to speak,' he had said before he died.

Deva was right, Bharat thought. Mercy and goodness must speak out themselves and only then can they silence the evil tongues that forever try to overwhelm the truth. It is not enough to have truth and honour on our side. One must fight for them. *There is guilt in silence.* Deva was not really dead, for now a hundred living tongues carried his message across the land and his words would be heard throughout the clan.

'Ultimately,' Bharat said, 'the truth will prevail. People will respond to Deva's appeal.'

'Maybe so,' Dhru replied. 'People love to listen to the voice of the dead. Not many listened to Deva while he lived, but now that he is dead they possibly think that he spoke with the combined wisdom of all the sages. I am sure that if I were to end my life now, people would begin to think of me as amongst the wisest on this earth, which of course I am, though not many are aware of it.'

'I certainly know the extent of your wisdom,' Bharat responded. 'But to test your theory of the people's reaction, would it not be worthwhile for you to end your life now?'

'And deprive you of my constant advice! Never! I love you too much to do you that ill turn. It is enough that you and I know of my wisdom.'

'Enough, if only one of us knows of it.'

But Bharat was wrong to believe that people would be willing to agree to a union with the tribals. His adversaries had mounted a widespread campaign against the tribals, reminding them of their past savagery. The rich and mighty slave owners and landowners had much to lose from such a union, and even ordinary people understood that equality for tribals meant that the Hindu clan would initially spend a lot on their welfare. Why—asked the preachers—do we sacrifice our comforts and benefits for those who sought to violate our land and people? Is it not right to compensate the clan for the past depredation by the raiders? Think of your loved ones who died battling against them! Did they die in vain? How can we be one with these savages! No, they are a race apart, and we need only just and honourable reprisals for the havoc they have wreaked on us in the past.

Bharat knew he had sufficient strength in the council and the assembly to win support for a union with the tribals. Yet he said, 'I shall not impose this decision on our people; they must be the ones to decide.' His adversaries were certain that the public was hardening against the tribals.

Bharat recalled stories that Ekantra had told him in his childhood, of the birth of Hinduism and the dreams and hopes of ancient Hindus. He recalled Deva's words and remembered conversations with Muni of the Rocks. What Ekantra, Deva and Muni had said was no different from the earliest ideals of Sanatan Dharma and the songs of Hindus in pre-ancient times. For himself, Bharat had no more doubts. He was no longer overwhelmed by uncertainty. He had understood the essence of the Hindu way of life. There was now no hesitation in his words, no effort, no groping. His words came out in a torrent, and later the once-blind singer composed a song called the 'Song of the Hindu' to commemorate Bharat's words, which echoed what the ancients had always said. The song was heard throughout the clan. To recite it fully, one needed the hours from sunset to midnight.

Our desires have grown immeasurable. But they should be desires to give, not merely to receive; to accept and not to reject; to honour and respect, not to deny or belittle . . .
God's gracious purpose includes all human beings and all creation
For God is the Creator; and God is the Creation . . .
Each man has his own stepping stones to reach the One-Supreme . . .
God's grace is withdrawn from no one; not even from

those who have chosen to withdraw from God's grace . . .
How does it matter what idols they worship, or what images they bow to, so long as their conduct remains pure . . .
It is conduct then—theirs and ours—that needs to be purified . . .
There can be no compulsion; each man must be free to worship his gods as he chooses . . .
Does every Hindu worship all the gods of all the Hindus? No, he has a free will; a free choice . . .
A Hindu may worship Agni and ignore other deities. Do we deny that he is a Hindu . . .
Another may worship God through an idol of his choosing. Do we deny that he is a Hindu . . .
Yet another will find God everywhere and not in any image or idol. Is he not a Hindu . . .
He who was karkarta before me was a sun-worshipper. Did the worshippers of Siva ever say that he was not a good Hindu . . .
Do the worshipers of Vishnu feel that he who worships before the image of Brahma is not a Hindu . . .
How can salvation be limited to a single view of God's nature and worship . . .
Is God, then, not an all-loving Universal God . . .
Know this then, that whatever god you choose, He is that One God, and dharma is His Will . . .
Clearly then, he who seeks to deny protection to another on the basis of his faith, offends against the Hindu way of life, and denies an all-loving God . . .
Those who love their own sects, idols and images more than the Truth, will end up by loving themselves more than their gods . . .
He who seeks to convert another to his own faith, offends against his own soul and the will of God and the law of humanity . . .

In the Kingdom of God, there is no higher or lower. The passion for perfection burns equally in all, for there is only one class even as there is only one God . . .
The Hindu way of life . . . Always it has been and always it shall be . . . God wills a rich harmony, not a colourless uniformity . . .
A Hindu must enlarge the heritage of mankind . . .
For a Hindu is not a mere preserver of custom . . .
For a Hindu is not a mere protector of present knowledge . . .
Hinduism is a movement, not a position; a growing tradition, not a fixed revelation . . .
A Hindu must grow and evolve, with all that was good in the past, with all that is good in the present, and with all goodness that future ages shall bring . . .
Yet he remains a Hindu . . .
Hinduism is the law of life, not a dogma; its aim is not to create a creed but character, and its goal is to achieve perfection through the most varied spiritual knowledge which rejects nothing, and yet refines everything, through continuous testing and experiencing . . .
Yet a Hindu must remain strong and united, for a Hindu must know that no external, outside force can ever crush him, except when he is divided and betrays his own . . .
What then is the final goal of the Hindu? Through strength, unity, discipline, selfless work, to reach the ultimate in being, ultimate in awareness and ultimate in bliss, not for himself alone, but for all . . .
This was the silent pledge that our ancient ancestors had taken, when they called themselves the Hindu . . .
If I cannot abide by that pledge, how can I retain the right to call myself a Hindu?

There was nothing specific in the 'Song of the Hindu' about protecting tribals or forming a union with them. Bharat's adversaries saw nothing ominous in it. To them, it was simply an irrelevancy to restate the basic beliefs of Hinduism.

Yet, overwhelmingly, the clan came to support the idea of a union when the time came to vote. When Bharat's adversaries asked why, they were told that the 'Song of the Hindu' had challenged their inner faith. A union with the tribes was achieved with equal rights, equal protection and representation in the council and the assembly, which came to be known simply as 'The Parliament of the Hindu'.

SEVEN

SINDHU RIVER: ITS SOURCE AND DESTINATION

5068 BCE with flashbacks

Bharatjogi's thoughts now shifted to the expeditions he had organized as karkarta to discover the source and destination of the Sindhu river. Like other ancients, he too was enamoured of the voices that seemed to come from the heavens and the unending parade of God's glory in the sky and on earth. But his greatest affection was for the Sindhu, which had sustained countless generations of his clan from time immemorial. He longed to know the source of the gracious river, and where it rested.

As karkarta, he organized two large groups—one of 140 men headed north to discover the source of the Sindhu, and the other of eighty men to travel south to find the river's destination. Bharat decided to lead the latter group.

Bindu, Bharat's wife, was concerned, 'Why are you taking only eighty men while the other group has 140?'

'Didn't you once say that I am equal to at least sixty men?'

'No, I have always said you are equal to a thousand, so why don't you go alone?' Bindu retorted.

Bharat explained that he was taking Yadodhra, who had examined charts discovered by Sage Ekantra, and had also studied the currents, terrain and much more. Clearly, the southward journey would be swift and easy. Besides, as karkarta, he could not be away for long and if it took more time, he would return, leaving Yadodhra in charge.

∾

Poets have described, often in detail, the northern route which the explorers took to discover the source of the Sindhu river in 5000 BCE, ascribing the trials and tribulations en route to demons and the achievements to divine inspiration.

For nine long years, the 140-strong expedition was not heard from and given up for lost, until, at last, four survivors returned, exhausted, dazed and crazed, unable for days to tell a coherent story of their incredible journey, covering 320 yojnas (1600 miles) each way. In terms of time and distance, they had covered less than a mile per day, but each day was fraught with danger, and sometimes disaster. Only twenty-four had survived to reach the source of the Sindhu as it rose at an altitude of 16,000 feet in southwestern Tibet. Nandan's two brothers were among those twenty-four, though they were not among the four who finally returned.

Initially, the progress of the explorers was brisk. They had mules, horses and great enthusiasm. It did not take them long to reach the confluence of the Sindhu, at an elevation of 2000 feet, with the river from Kubha, the present-day Kabul river. From there, the expedition moved to a spot beyond which lay what poets have described as Taraka Desa—the land of the demon Taraka. Later Vedic legends describe Skanda, born from the marriage of Shiva and Parvati, as a warrior god who destroyed the terrible demon Taraka. However, in pre-ancient, pre-Vedic times, Skanda was regarded as a god of fertility, gentle and kind, concerned with improving the earth's bounty. All that Skanda was reputed to have done was to keep a watch on Taraka who was under a curse that if ever he came to fertile lands, his demonic powers would be taken away. As long as he remained in the region of turbulent storms, named Taraka Desa, he could do as he pleased. It was this terrible land of Taraka Desa that the expedition had to cross.

Rishi Skanda Dasa, and fifteen of his disciples, joined the expedition. The rishi was convinced that when Taraka Desa ended, they would reach Skanda Desa from where, it was alleged, that Skanda himself was watching Taraka—and the hope was that the source of the Sindhu would be found there. Yet, it was the rishi himself who warned them that the route through Taraka Desa would be long, hard and treacherous. From his brief excursions up and down, he knew something of the sudden dangers that might be ahead in that mountainous region.

The members of the expedition knew little about mountains. They were simply going forward, in faith, to discover the source of Mother Goddess Sindhu, and if mountains came in the way—well, they would somehow cross them with God's help. The rishi cautioned them that the gods may not be able to see them all the time through the blinding snow and fog that would envelop them. Certain that this man of god knew the ways of the gods better, the men heeded his advice and equipped themselves with the things the rishi obtained for them—dry foodstuff, skins to wear, stitched skins to serve as sleeping bags, tents, thick ropes, rope ladders, poles with sharp edges on one end, and several balms and herbal remedies. All these were in addition to their own equipment which included axes, spears and hammers.

'How can we carry all this all the way?' the men asked in dismay.

The rishi's ominous response was, 'Maybe you won't have to carry them all the way. The mountains may demand their due.'

Resignedly, the men loaded their mules and together with the rishi and his disciples entered Taraka Desa. Their horses were left behind at the rishi's ashram as it was feared that they would be useless in this rocky terrain.

Initially it seemed that Taraka was in a playful mood and though the journey was slow and painful, they could still manage it. But soon the lofty mountains began to close in towards the Sindhu river. Like a torrent in fury, the deep, relentless, dark grey river hurled itself through ravines of naked rock. Their mules, terrified by the forbidding terrain and the roar of thunder, became a source of danger to them. They had to let the mules go. Perilously, the expedition continued on foot, through terrible storms. They heaved a sigh of relief, thinking that their journey was nearing its end, when they saw the valley widen and a clear, jade green river foaming down to meet the Sindhu. It was the river that came from the mountain range which Sadhu Gandhara had named Hindu Kush to mark the birth of his son, Kush, at the foot of those mountains.

Compared to the torrential, forbidding grey waters of the Sindhu, this tributary appeared so inviting with its clear, transparent waters that despite the icy winds, they went in for a brief swim. Here they had their first casualty. An avalanche of boulders hurtled down suddenly from the mountainside. The leader of the expedition was killed. The waters changed colour from jade green to grey, as boulders and mud kept pouring in. They called this river 'Girgit'— chameleon. Later this river would come to be known as the Gilgit river.

There would be more casualties, thereafter. The Sindhu was narrowly confined within the mountain walls with no outlet and forced to turn south-west. Another river joined the Sindhu from the east, and, reinforced, the Sindhu twisted and swirled down the trough between the Hindu Kush to the west and the huge ramparts of the Nanga Parbat to the east.

Even though a confluence is considered holy, this meeting of rivers actually frightened them. They were in the midst of appalling storms and landslides and fearsome noise, as though the demon Taraka, was challenging them to a demonic duel. They named this tributary 'Asura'. Inch by painful inch, they went on, sometimes protected by clefts, crevices and caves from blizzards, landslides and falling rocks. The entire area was filled with chasms and gorges seemingly made by some superhuman, malignant will. They heard the earth and sky shake and rumble. They did not know then that they were passing through an unstable region subject to severe storms and earthquakes which had left their mark on the terrain. They lost three more men where the Asura river met the Sindhu. Often they gave up skirting along the Sindhu to take other passes to shelter themselves from falling rocks, though they always kept the river in sight, so as to retrace their steps to follow its course.

Eventually, they reached another confluence of rivers, having battled through snow and fog and taken a route both treacherous and circuitous. Skanda Dassa saw a few plants and shrubs ahead, and assured them that Skanda Desa must be near. No one was in the mood to believe him, but the rishi pointed towards the tributary river on which floated the remnant of a glacier. 'Sikhara! Sikhara!' the rishi shouted with joy. The expedition named it the Sikhara river.

From the confluence, the rishi rushed forward, the men following him till they reached a spot which the rishi immediately declared was Skanda Desa. He had good reason for saying so, for legend had it that the demon Taraka could not hold sway where the land became fertile, blessed by the benign hand of Skanda.

The expedition rested in Skanda Desa—presently known as Skandu or Skardu, in Pakistan. The rishi's search was over. He had reached the end of his quest—the land of the god Skanda. With his fifteen disciples, he remained there, while the others prepared to move on. Like his gentle god, whose life was one of toil and labour, the rishi, too, wanted a life of toil, to establish an ashram, to tend the earth and make it fertile. But that had to wait. He collected herbs so that he could treat the sick among the explorers. Thereafter, he devoted his energy to repairing and making tools and equipment for their journey since so much had been lost on the way. To their food-store, the rishi added nuts and berries collected on the mountainside.

It was only after the expedition members left that the rishi set about establishing his ashram in Skanda Desa along with his disciples. He started planting walnuts, apples, melons, nectarines, apricots and several crops of cereals. Later, far away, in small pockets and caves, he came across locals and encouraged them to cluster around his ashram. In the course of time they, too, became devotees of Skanda, the god of fertility.

Being a devotee of Skanda himself, the rishi did not believe in brahmacharya but in the institution of marriage. He felt that the right time for brahmacharya was before the age of seventeen and after the age of seventy-two. Most of his disciples, at his original ashram, had been married couples. It was not uncommon for bachelors, unmarried girls, widows and widowers to join his ashram, although sooner or later they all married. At the new ashram, however, only five of his disciples were bachelors; the rest had left their wives behind. With unmarried local girls joining the ashram, the bachelors were getting anxious to marry but the rishi withheld his blessing until he was satisfied that the local men and women joining his ashram clearly understood that they could have only one spouse, and that marriage was a bond for life, indissoluble.

The rishi, too, had left his wife behind. He made many excursions, near and far, into the fringes of Taraka Desa to study the right season and proper route to travel to his old ashram and bring his wife and the wives of ten others. There are those who say that he prayed not only to Skanda but also to Taraka, and even a poem is attributed to him, questioning the gods for their harsh treatment of the demon, who in his previous life had been a holy man.

I ask not what his sin was
Nor how he broke your laws,
But to banish him for all time!
Does the punishment fit the crime?
He deserves no mercy, you say!
Gods! You too may need mercy, one day!

While the gods may have been indifferent to the rishi's plea, it seems that Taraka was delighted with his sympathy for him. The result was that all the demon's thunderbolts were kept in abeyance while Skanda Dasa travelled back to his old ashram, with his five bachelor disciples and thirty-eight locals, without a single casualty.

After a brief rest there, Skanda Dasa appointed his worthiest disciple as the head of the old ashram, and left with his wife, the wives of ten disciples and 176 others—men, women and children—this time taking care not to separate men from their wives or parents from their children. He guided the entire group to Skanda Desa without mishap. All along the way, the demon Taraka, the poets say, was playful, but never vicious. His demonic laughter howled after them right through the journey. He also hurled boulders, but always just before the group arrived at a particular spot or just after they left it so nobody was ever hurt.

The rishi even performed two marriages on the way and it is said that Taraka's laughter followed the rhythm of the mantras recited at the ceremony.

Another poem has been attributed to the rishi—interceding with the gods on behalf of Taraka, who clearly had listened to his prayers for a safe journey.

Banished he is, banished in pain
Yet he heard and heard again;
Count! For all the mistakes he made,
Has he not fully, finally paid?

The rishi's pleas seeking forgiveness for the demon were, however, not too excessive. Like some others of his era, he realized that Taraka was only a myth which presented an aspect of the innermost self. All gods and demons, all heavens and hells, all worlds and all voids were within us—and the myth was intended simply as a story, in the setting of a dream, to manifest the symbols of images within us. Thus, a myth was not to be confused with actual events; the adventures and exploits of gods and demons were simply markers to the way of the spirit. Even his own god, Skanda, and all the idols were no more than symbols to lead man to the One-Supreme and to focus man's faith on Him and Him alone. The rishi was not one to take a myth literally and dissect it as a reflection or replica of day-to-day events, but then nor was he one to take a myth lightly. All he saw was that the demon Taraka, like other troubled spirits, had a human face.

According to legend, not only Skanda, but also Taraka blessed the land where the rishi established his new ashram, and it is said that poplars, walnuts, lemons, melons, nectarines and apples grew to enormous sizes. Those who did not believe in such myths of course saw that the land grew green and fertile as a result of Skanda Dasa's endless toil, and the labours of the growing number of disciples around his ashram.

～

Meanwhile, the expedition to discover the source of the Sindhu river plodded on. They had thought their troubles were over on reaching Skanda Desa, but greater ordeals awaited them.

Tragedy struck at the confluence of yet another river that they named Shok. Fed by the mighty glaciers on the slopes of the Nanga Parbat Massif, Karakoram and Kohistan ranges, the Shok did not, at first, seem terrifying. Through storms, and fog, they did not see the mighty glacier floating down the river, nor did they see when the ice dam broke with its implacable waters rising cliff-high. They lost six more men in a single catastrophic sweep of the river. Two were wounded, unable to move. It was decided that they would be taken back to Skanda Desa to the rishi's ashram in the morning, but the two men died during the night.

Clearly, the explorers were now in a region far more severe and merciless than Taraka Desa. Instead of risking all their lives, their leader asked for volunteers to return to the rishi in Skanda Desa and wait there, while he went onwards with just twelve men. He cajoled, begged, and ordered—but none of the men agreed to return.

The fearsome journey continued, slowly, painfully. For days on end, they had to find shelter under mountain clefts, unable to advance even a few yards. At another confluence, where the Sindhu joined another river, blocks of solid ice were falling around them. The invisible sky rumbled and it felt as though the earth below their feet was shaking and rattling. They named that river—the present-day Zanskar in Ladakh—'Ghar Ghar'—an imitative sound to describe fearsome conditions of thunder and rumbling. The distance between the Shok and the Ghar Ghar rivers, as they met the Sindhu, was possibly 150 miles and yet it took months to cross.

Between the Shok and Ghar Ghar, the team lost three men. If one life can be considered more valuable than another, then they lost their three most valuable men—their leader, the vaid, and the artist who had been charting the route to keep a record for future explorers. The pieces of bark and leaves on which he had been drawing had lost their shape and form, and the pigments and colours had dried up. All he had was a long pointed needle, but he was forbidden to use it for etching on skins, which were being used for clothing, tents and sleeping bags. But he had an eye for detail and a sharp memory. He hoped that on his return, in the warm sunshine of his home, with a cup of soma wine in one hand and a paint brush in the other, he would draw and paint a thousand pictures of every little twist and turn in the route. Thus he concentrated on naming and remembering the rivers, mountains, gorges on the way, for Karkarta Bharat had told him, 'You will not be the last to go on that route; your charts must speak to those that follow you, so they neither falter nor fail.' To many features, he gave names to help him recall the scenes, and, lest he forgot, he would tap everyone's head playfully and make them repeat the name. The last name he had given to a place was Tribhanga where over high cliffs rose pinnacles of ice in various forms and figures. One such pinnacle, slim and taller than the rest, stood out, distinct from the rest, and they all had to agree with the artist that it was the figure of a lovely woman, decked in all her jewellery and colourful dress, striking a playful dancing pose, with one leg bent and the body slightly turned at the hips. But the artist knew that ice formations can be temperamental, changing from moment to moment, and what appeared to be the figure of a dancing girl today would later possibly look like a ferocious lion or a clowning monkey. But the others charged him with trying to keep to himself the memory of the voluptuous dancer—Tribhanga.

It was at the confluence of the Ghar Ghar and the Sindhu that boulders fell and the earth seemed to give way, instantly killing their leader and the vaid, and burying the artist under a mass of rubble. When the others dug him out, he was unconscious. From the state of his legs, it was evident that the artist would never walk again. Long after, when he opened his eyes through the pain and delirium, he saw his friends had tied him to a stretcher and were carrying him perilously over treacherous, pathless terrain. Weakly, he begged them to leave him behind but they ignored his pleas. Some time later, he asked for his sketching needle. That was not surprising in itself for he often waved it in the air, making imaginary etchings that would remained embedded in his memory. His companions gave him the needle, though for some time his hand was too shaky to hold it. After a while, when they set the stretcher down, they realized that they had been carrying a dead man, for the artist had slashed his wrist with the needle and bled to death; the blood had congealed.

They knew he had died by his own hand to save them from carrying him at the risk of their own lives. But to take one's own life! Was it not a denial of God? No, in their hearts, they knew that in this case, it was a renewal of faith—a sacrifice for a cause that was bigger than all of them. Yet, no one would admit to the other that he had killed himself, and it was as though by common—but unspoken—consent that the fiction arose that he, too, had died along with the vaid and the leader.

The expedition moved along in the domain of falling rocks of ice, where blizzards ran wild and the cold was congealing. What kept them going was not faith alone. In some of the ice-covered caves where they sought shelter, they found evidence that others had been there, long before them. There were no footprints, no skeletons, and yet there were unmistakable traces of travellers having passed through, or even lived there. As they tried to break out of a cave where they were trapped, the men came upon a few beads with holes through them, similar to beads found near the Sindhu river. Later, in another cave, they found a stone idol—merely the face, crudely chiselled, but unmistakably that of the God Rudra. In yet another cave in Taraka Desa they found a two-sided statue with the face of Rudra on one side and Shiva on the other. They also found a stone axe, a round plate engraved with three triangles, a child's rattle, and a flute.

'We will go on,' they resolved. 'If a Hindu has been here before and crossed over, how can we fail!'

Yet, many died around them. Something even died *within* them. Each step was like a mile. In the thin cold air, they had difficulty in breathing. Their minds and bodies fought desperately to conquer fatigue and they feared that they would not be able to go on. They did not then know what later Hindu explorers of the Himalayas would discover—that the higher one goes, the severer is the environment, and the lungs are unable to push in that rarefied atmosphere the required amount of oxygen for the bloodstream.

But what did these men—untrained and inexperienced—know of the mountains! They came from the lowlands of the Sindh and knew little of the conditions that still awaited them. In fact they would not even have known how to clothe and equip themselves for the journey had it not been for the rishi's assistance. They understood nothing of the constant headaches, breathlessness, inability to drag their bodies, and sometimes, even loss of control over their muscles. Often they could not find an even patch on the terrain to rest. Caves were not easy to come by. They often had no strength to make an ice-shelter.

Yes, something had died within them and they felt it deeply. But their new leader cried out, 'We shall not die of this cold, nor of the mountains. No, we shall die of having lived!' His words by themselves made little sense to the others, but they all understood his determination to survive.

From the Ghar Ghar river in Ladakh, with painful steps, they skirted the Sindhu as it crossed the south-eastern boundary of Jammu and Kashmir, while the mighty Himalayas closed in on them. Almost every yojna took its toll of life. They were dazed most of the time and sometimes moved as though in a trance, but often they were not moving even an inch. Then there would be times when their bodies seemed to them like terrible dead loads—standing apart from their mind and spirit. Many lost their equipment, others lost their lives. They could no longer build fires to cremate bodies. They had no idea that the ice would preserve the bodies and that future explorers might find them for cremation.

They had crossed possibly about forty yojnas from the Ghar Ghar when they heard a continuous noise above the wind. They paused to listen. It was the sound of a lion's roar, but a constant, unending roar. For some reason—or perhaps for no reason—the twenty-four who had survived felt that they had reached. And indeed they had.

They had found, at long last, the source of the Sindhu.

Silently, the twenty-four survivors stood at the source of the river and heard its lion-like roar with mixed feelings, their minds dwelling possibly on those that fell on the way, and wondering how many would fall on the return journey. But there was also a quiet glow in their hearts. In awe, they gazed upon the source of the Sindhu, unable to speak. It was their leader—their twelfth leader; eleven before him had died on the way—who realized the inappropriateness of silence on so auspicious an occasion. Surely, a prayer was called for. Maybe the men were even waiting for him to begin. He spoke, 'Tat tvam bhagwant—thou art from God.'

He kept repeating the phrase, not knowing what to add. They joined his chant, repeating after him, 'Tat tvam bhagwant.'

Louder and louder they chanted, so that the Sindhu might hear them above its lion-like roar. Peace entered their hearts. The questions, whirling in their minds, ceased. They felt blessed. At last, the leader spoke loudly, clearly: 'Daughter of God, who art our Mother Goddess! With the roar of the lioness you leap and, at your command, mountains part to give way, to tear for you a route to our land, so that you may nourish us, sustain us, give us your grace and bind us with your everlasting love . . . '

He did not finish, but stood along with the others, eyes

closed in silent meditation. After a long while, he opened his eyes, and repeated the chant again:

'Tat tvam bhagwant.'

There are those who say that this oft-repeated chant—Tat tvam bhagwant—along with the few simple words of the expedition leader came to be regarded as a mantra, though much was added to it later. The mantra itself was called by the shortened, simplified name Tibata Mantra, and that is how possibly the entire region of the Sindhu's source got the name of Tibet. That may be so. But inspired by those Sindhu pioneers, the river would come to be known even to Tibetans of later ages as Seng-ge-Kha-bab—out of the lion's mouth.

Doubts were expressed about how many reached the Sindhu's source. Some poets had said that twenty-four survivors were present at the source of the Sindhu whereas others said that twenty-two saw the spectacle. Both figures are correct, for as another poet explains:

Twenty-four reached that awesome height
But only twenty-two saw that glorious sight,
For two, it was as dark as the darkest night,
Robbed as they were by the Giver of light.
Shining he was, yes, softly, up, high, above
Shooting from ice below, cruel arrows somehow.

The reflection of the sun's rays, as they fell on ice and snow, blinded two of the twenty-four men. At the time they did not understand how men could lose their eyesight because of sunlight leaping back from ice. But later, as more Hindu explorers went into the Himalayas, the realization came that the sun's rays, even those of a softly shining sun, reflected by ice and snow, can be deadly to the eyesight.

The twenty-four survivors remained in Tibet for months. They needed time to heal their wounds and prepare for the journey home. Their first task was to build a hut which would stand the wind and the vagaries of various seasons. They saw many animals nearby—mostly small—and every kind of bird—pheasants, cuckoos, nightingales, robins, mynahs, larks, owls, hawks, eagles, jungle-fowl and even ducks, cranes and gulls. The streams abounded with fish. They also heard the sounds of bigger animals. Once they had heard the growl of a lone tiger. From a distance, they had seen bears, a wild boar and a leopard. These wild animals were not likely to attack them with so many smaller animals around. Even so, they built their hut well above the ground, with strong support from the poles and planks they had cut from trees. Even the stairs, which they made to lead to the entrance of the hut, were light and portable, and when they were out, the stairs were kept away from the hut.

It was a region of wild flowers, edible roots and fruit trees. They built fires and for the first time after such a long deprivation, ate cooked food, and it seemed to them that its aroma was so great that it would reach their own homes far away.

Forests surrounded them—large willow trees, oaks, birches, teak, bamboo, spruce, fir, pines, spreading yews, poplars, thorn trees, babul and several others. They experimented. From these trees, bushes and vines, mixed with the rushes found in streams, they made ropes stronger than they had before. They sharpened their spears and axes and made many more—though wooden, for they did not find any metals there. They found that they could make better baskets with willow than with bamboo. From the durable Khrespa tree, they made not only bowls and food-containers, but also a sort of helmet to protect their heads, if not from falling blocks of ice or boulders, then at least small rocks, splinters and ice stones. Every basket and container was wound with thick ropes so that most of these could be dragged, instead of being carried—and ropes, which had often saved their lives, would in any case be necessary, even if baskets had to be discarded. Skins to wear, skins as sleeping bags and even for tents, they had enough, for many had died and their gear was carried by the living. Even so, the skins were tattered. Pine needles and thread from the river rushes helped to repair them.

This silk-like thread also proved useful as a lining within two folds of skins, to provide better protection against the biting cold. Patiently, they made ropes from thread, which were then flattened with rock hammers and tied at appropriate spots to hold as lining between two layers of skins. The guild of tailors, back home, would not have thought much of their handiwork but it served its purpose.

'Are we going to be here for ever?' one of the men asked.

'Some of us are,' the leader replied.

They knew he had decided that the two blind men in the group had to stay back. One more, whose arm had lost all its feeling and strength, also had to be left behind. Who else! they wondered.

They were certain there would be human habitation in this region, but they were not too keen to discover people as yet. People, they knew, could be temperamental—and the group of twenty-four felt they were far too few and much too weak to take the risk.

To domesticate cattle, the survivors erected two large pens outside the hut, one at ground level, and another connected to it by a movable ramp, on a higher level. It took several trips to the forest and a long time to coax and cajole cattle into the pens and for them to be responsive. The first cup of milk that their cattle yielded was like nectar to them—better than any soma that they had ever tasted. In time the cattle became so mild that even the blind could milk them.

When their strength returned the men prepared to return. The two blind men and the one with the disabled arm had to remain. Three of the bachelors were selected to be with them. The leader organized endurance contests amongst the bachelors for running, climbing and obstacle clearance. They all assumed that those who did the worst would be left behind. Each strained to excel—and those who did, were chosen to remain. The leader justified it by saying, 'We know what dangers we will face, and we have faced them before, but what of the unknown dangers these men we leave behind may encounter!'

Of these six men, only the one with the disabled arm was married. Eventually, the others too got married to local girls from communities in the nearby areas. Years later, Skanda Dasa travelled to this region, and was able to revive strength in the paralysed arm of the disabled man who had been left behind. Nothing, however, is known about him—whether he crossed the mountains to return or remained there.

∾

The return journey was as terrifying as before. The men did not suffer as much from the overpowering headaches, fatigue, depression and breathlessness which had earlier tortured them—they had become better acclimatized to higher altitudes and the rarefied atmosphere. But the danger from falling rocks, cascading ice and sudden landslides lurked everywhere. The threat of ice and snow, trembling mountainsides and rumbling rocks, blizzards and avalanches were with them all the time. Yet they were fortunate, for it seemed their leader had developed a sixth sense which warned them of the hazards ahead. At every change in the wind, at every faraway rumble, he guessed the right direction for his group, the right time to rest, and the right spot to choose for shelter. But their good fortune did not last long. As always, the leader walked ahead of them, scouting the route, when, suddenly, he was lost from view. The snow and ice under him had given way. Two others, though much behind, but tied to him with the same rope, were being pulled forward. The others held on to them, pulling at the rope with every ounce of their strength, hoping that somehow their leader would come back to them at the end of it. Impossible!

Then came blizzards—terrifying, unending and deadly. Whatever was not tied to their bodies was blown away— and they too were in the same danger, throughout. Much of their equipment was lost. In the thick fog, even with just inches between them they could not see each other. All seemed to be lost. One of them at last reached Skanda Desa. The rishi himself, accompanied by many others, led the search for more survivors. Two more were found the next day, half-dead, but they revived back at the ashram. Another was found far away by a half-wolf belonging to one of the local devotees, trapped in a cave surrounded by ice and boulders. He was not in a terrible state, for he had his sleeping bag, tent and enough food to sustain him for a few days. But it would have taken him months to break out from the cave; it took the rishi's men four days to break through the ice at the mouth of the cave. Eventually, five bodies were also located, but no more after that even though the search went on for months.

The four returning survivors continued their journey from Skanda Desa after a rest there. The journey to the rishi's old ashram at the entrance of Taraka Desa posed no real danger. The rishi himself accompanied them with a large group. It was a route which by now had become familiar to him and his disciples and even his mules. Already, the rishi had established sixteen shelters on the way, and hoped to have ninety-two more built. Some of his local devotees were even housed at five of those shelters to plant trees and bushes there. 'Why?' many asked. There was so much land around Skanda Desa itself, with springs, streams and tributaries of the Sindhu. Why, then, go into the inhospitable, rough terrain of Taraka Desa? The rishi's reply was simple: 'This is also God's earth. Who knows—another Hindu like you may wish to cross over to pay his homage to the high mountains beyond. Why should any demons bar his way?'

Even before the four survivors reached the rishi's old ashram, some of the rishi's men had rushed to the lowlands to convey the glad tidings of their safe return, along with the news of the six who had remained behind in Tibet.

There was joy—wild and tumultuous. All 140 explorers had been feared lost. The news that ten of them had survived unleashed a wave of happiness. Yet it also renewed the pain of those whose loved ones would never return. True, in the years gone by, they had given up hope of their ever coming back, but with the return of these four, their grief, allayed for so long, came back to wrench their hearts more cruelly than before. Even so, every house, even those who had lost someone to the expedition, was brilliantly illuminated with myriad twinkling earthen lamps.

Bharat, Dhrupatta, Yadodhra, Nandan and others had sped to the rishi's ashram to welcome the survivors on behalf of the clan and to escort them back home. The four men embraced Nandan first, for two of the men lost on their return journey were his younger brothers.

∼

These four survivors told the story of their travels and how, ultimately, twenty-four of the original 140 had reached the source of the Mother Goddess Sindhu—this greatest of the trans-Himalayan rivers rising at an enormous altitude of 16,000 feet, near Mount Kailas in southwestern Tibet. They did not know then that it was one of the longest rivers in the world, though certainly they knew that it was longer than any that crossed their land, nor did they know that its annual flow of 450,000 square miles, of which about one-third would be in the Himalayan mountains and foothills, while much of the rest found its way into their own land, was twice that of the Nile in Egypt and three times that of the Tigris and

Euphrates combined. No, they did not know all that—for the age of statistics, and even of the written word, had not yet arrived. Nor did they know of the existence of the Nile, the Tigris or the Euphrates. If they had been called upon to estimate the distance they had covered, they would possibly have considered it to be colossal, beyond reckoning, but actually, they had covered only about 1,600 miles each way.

Yet, these men who were not the children of the mountains and were brought up in the warm sunshine of the lowlands of India, were among the first to witness the source of this great river, hidden in the midst of the most formidable mountains of the world.

∽

As the four survivors returned from the source of the Sindhu river, they wondered: What came first? The mountains through which the Sindhu flows or the river itself? For years, Yadodhra, who later came to be regarded as a sage, considered the question and finally gave his verdict on the antiquity of the Sindhu, recorded in a memory song:

> The Sindhu river was always there, long before the mountains came. And then slowly, imperceptibly, the mountains rose, but each day no more than one-millionth measure of one angula, and thus the mountains were uplifted gradually, completing in each cycle of a million days the rise of one angula.
> . . . If the mountains had come in all their might and height in one single sweep, perhaps the rivers would have been blocked and the mountains themselves would have lost the sure foundation that they now have— and who would wish to obstruct the flow of Mother Goddess Sindhu or provide the mountains with a floating foundation, rendering them unsure of their

place on earth! Nature works with patience; mighty mountains will not bang into the waters and the earth, nor will rivers explode suddenly to rise to the height of the mountains and the sky.

. . . Everything evolves gently, slowly, smoothly as a continuous drama in time with the same tranquil calmness of the ONE who fashioned it all.

Yadodhra had worked on this theory for several years. By his reckoning, for a mountain to rise one metre, it would take 140,000 years and 140 million years for it to grow 1000 metres. On the basis of this calculation, the highest peak in the Himalayas should have taken about 1,238 million years to form.

Yadodhra was undoubtedly foremost among those who sought to discover natural and physical laws. His ashram was a beehive of scientific activity (though he chided those who characterized his ashram as a beehive and assured everyone of his own findings that bees were lazy and indolent and certainly could not be compared to his diligent, hard-working students). His students were busy planting crops and flowers in different kinds of soils, treating various metals, studying the effect of still water and dripping water and rushing water on diverse materials including rocks and stones, making and mixing various dyes and paints, charting the growth pattern of various trees . . . Their activities were endless, but to what end? 'Until the mystery is no more,' Sage Yadodhra would reply.

He saw the Hand of God in everything, but this did not limit his investigations, because he believed, as did the other sages of those times, that God Himself followed the physical laws which He had created for observance by His creations.

The journey to discover the destination of the Sindhu posed no real danger. None of the trials and tragedies that assailed their compatriots on the northern route affected the contingent of eighty that was being led by Bharat.

Spellbound, the men watched the foaming bodies of water with enormous, frighteningly powerful waves as the Sindhu merged with the river of rivers, the Sindhu Samundar, now known as the Arabian Sea.

Bharat and his men mingled with the people of the region and were charmed by them. They all seemed to delight in poetry, song and music. They loved conversation not only because each thought they had much to learn from others, but also for sheer pleasure. Their huts and cottages were smaller than those of the clan, but better equipped, their boats superior and their tools far more advanced. These sea people were friendly, forever laughing, joking, and making merry. They loved life. They painted beautifully, but there was no evidence of great architecture. Trees could be cut down only in parks on the fringes of the forests, with the requirement to replant. There was equal respect for men and women and both went in for fishing, farming, weaving and other activities, though generally, it was the man's task to cook food while women served communal meals. It was prohibited to hunt in the forest or to kill birds; they raised poultry and cattle in pens and meat was eaten by a few on special occasions. They generally ate fish and seafood, poultry, eggs and vegetables and they loved their wines. They fished no more than three days in the week saying the fish needed time to grow and multiply. They had no notion of money and relied on barter.

There were no temples as the earth, sky and the sea were themselves regarded as temples, and a person could pray anywhere; most of them however kept idols—made with great art and intricacy—though the guest huts reserved for visitors, and parks and public places were kept free of idols for each visitor may have his own favourite gods. Why impose a god when they possibly believe in another? Why impose a god at all, when they believe only in the One-Supreme?

There were no whores, no slaves, and no priests. They belonged to an ancient order which they called Sanatanah or Sanathana—all pervading, ageless, insoluble, awake, alert, infinite, abiding and eternal—and one that is indestructible and imperishable like the soul itself, and it imposed a requirement to watch that no action should be performed or contemplated to hurt or harm another or offend against nature.

Many including the Shreshtha, the headman of the area, came to see them off. Bharat, Yadodhra and their contingent gazed on the Sindhu Samundar for the last time and then embraced the Shreshtha and others affectionately.

Bharat was silent, but Yadodhra spoke, pointing to the Shreshtha's heart and his own to show that they were the same people from the same race. The Shrestha, despite the language barrier, had no difficulty understanding him. He had always believed that all men were brothers and that God and the human soul were the same.

On the way back, Yadodhra was lost in thought. More than finding the destination of the Sindhu river, more than the sight of the vast ocean, what had enchanted him most was discovering these people with their pre-ancient link with the Sanatan Dharma that his father Ekantra had spoken of with such feeling and emotion. He did not know then that, later, people from the Sindhu-Saraswati region would meet the people from the greater Ganga civilization and discover a common ancestry, culture and link that bound all of them as one people, from one single race. There they would see how their own holy river, the Saraswati, met with the Ganga and the Yamuna, merging some of its waters with these two rivers while charting a majestic path of its own and ultimately flowing into the Sindhu Samundar. Nor did Yadodhra know that people from his region would one day meet people of the magnificent Dravidian civilization in the south and discover the long-forgotten link that had once bound them together in their ways of living, thought, attitude, ideals and culture, though the language they spoke was different.

However, Yadodhra's mind was not on the unseen future. He was thinking of the past, convinced that somehow, hidden in the mists of the centuries gone by, there had been a close and continuous relationship between his people and the people who lived beside the confluence of the Sindhu river and the Sindhu sea.

'These people . . . truly, they are the people of the Sanatan Dharma!' he told Bharat.

But Bharat shook his head, 'No, they are more ancient than that. They are the people of the Sanathana. It is from them that Sanatan Dharma came.'

∽

Somehow, the discoverers had believed that once the source and destination of the Sindhu were revealed, they would have far greater insight into the secrets of the Mother Goddess. And though they experienced the joy of discovery, it was accompanied by the realization that with each discovery, the mystery deepened.

> 'She reveals much to conceal more
> Behind each gate, a closed door,
> Play your games, God, it matters not
> I know what is in my lot
> And if in seeking You, I fail
> You will find me—is it not?'

EIGHT

GO! BUILD YOUR TEMPLE!

5068 BCE with flashbacks

Bharatjogi smiled in the midst of his yogic exercise when he saw his dogs wagging their tails. Gatha was approaching.

'I hope I am not interrupting, master,' said Gatha.

'No,' Bharat replied, 'I am glad you have come.'

'They want to build a huge temple for Sindhu Putra in the village,' Gatha said in a sombre voice.

'A huge temple for that little infant?' Bharat asked, adding, 'Gatha, your people must understand that the infant is not a god,' when Gatha nodded.

The old retainer nodded again. He knew the little one was not yet a god, but he *was* the son of the Mother Goddess Sindhu, brought by her to walk on this earth. Godhood would come to him later, by the grace of his mother, when he was older.

'It is to be a great temple, the biggest in the land.'

Bharat smiled. Dreams cost nothing. Large temples were, however, expensive. He said so. But Gatha assured him, 'Money is not a problem.'

'No?' Bharat was surprised. Anyone ambitious to build a temple always needed money.

Gatha assured him, 'We have money. More than enough.'

'You have hidden treasure in the village?'

'No, someone will pay for it all . . . a . . . a lady . . . a woman . . . a female.'

Bharat ignored the confusion in Gatha's words and said,

'Even if you have the money, the question is: Shouldn't it be put to better use?'

But the question troubling Gatha was different. 'About the woman, some have asked: Is it not inauspicious to build a temple with her money?'

'Why? Who is she?'

Gatha told Bharat that Kanta, the woman donating the fabulous sum of money for the temple, had a troubled past and was a prostitute. Bharat's memory raced back to when he was karkarta and a headman had complained bitterly that a whore had set up a field where helpless, elderly cows could graze, 'bringing everlasting disgrace to the village and she must be stopped'. He had silenced the headman by saying that neither the holiness of the cows nor their morality was adversely affected by a whore paying for it all. Besides, the headman himself was to be complimented for creating an atmosphere in which even sinners conquered their nature and performed saintly acts.

Just moments earlier, Bharat had been determined to persuade Gatha to give up the idea of a temple. He saw no evidence of godhood in the infant. All he knew was that mother and child had somehow reached the riverbank in a boat, the mother dead, the baby still alive, and a gust of wind swept the boat—with the mother in it—away while the baby was left with him. How did that confer godhood? However, now that Bharat heard of thoughtless objections against a former prostitute donating for a temple, he changed his mind. Why should villagers object? Should we not celebrate when sinners wish to perform saintly acts?

Gatha saw Bharatjogi in deep thought, and wondered if his old master was offended by the idea of accepting a prostitute's donation. He asked, 'We should refuse, master?'

'Refuse what?' Bharat asked.

'Her donation for the temple,' Gatha said. 'Many have said we should refuse. Even the vaid.'

'Tell your villagers that God would never refuse an offering made with love; tell them, they lack the right to dictate to God whose offering He shall accept. And tell the vaid that his very profession expects him to be compassionate and if he aspires to be blessed by God, he should develop a little more compassion.'

Gatha looked troubled; how could he speak so harshly to the vaid! But Bharat misunderstood his expression and asked, 'Tell me, are you also against Kanta?'

'Me? No. I like her I . . . I . . . ' He blushed and said no more. He did not want to admit that he had longed to spend nights of pleasure with Kanta, but had abandoned the idea, realizing that a headman must seek such pleasures outside his village.

'I am glad,' Bharat said. 'God's goodness and mercy shall reach her. There are no sins that He cannot forgive. Tell your villagers to object no more, for His grace is denied to none. If they doubt your word, tell them this is the message from him who is to serve as father of Sindhu Putra.'

Gatha beamed. This was the first time that Bharat had referred to himself as Sindhu Putra's earthly father, and shown enthusiasm over the temple intended for the child. Obviously then, contrary to his earlier words, Bharat had no doubt about the godhood of Sindhu Putra.

There was happiness in Bharatjogi's heart, too, as he referred to Sindhu Putra as his son. For years, in this lonely retreat, his mind had dwelled on the past because he had no future to dream of, but now, the gods in their wisdom had willed that he, a hermit, should adopt a son and assist in shaping his future.

'Gatha, do something for me? Tell Kanta that I honour her pious thought to build the temple. Say that in front of everyone. But also tell her privately that I have requested her to never resume her profession. And even if she has compelling reasons, she should persevere and somehow God will show her the way.'

'I will so order her.'

'No, let it be my request. It is for her to decide.'

'As you wish, master.'

'No. As she wishes,' Bharat clarified, leaving no room for doubt.

Bharat need not have worried that Kanta might become a prostitute once again.

Kanta had lived a life of purity until she was forced into prostitution by her husband's misdeeds. Satrash, her husband, had seduced her innocent sister who was a devdasi and a brahmacharini. For this revolting outrage against the laws of God and man, Satrash would have faced terrible punishment, but he escaped from his village, compelling Kanta to go with him. He dared not leave Kanta behind; she was pregnant, and her father would have him hunted down for seducing one daughter and abandoning the other. Kanta was his protection. They reached the far-away retreat where Muni of the Rocks and his wife Roopa lived. Muni and Roopa treated them with kindness

There, Kanta gave birth to a son, but the baby died after two days. She shivered as she remembered the ancient curse from a time well before Sanatan Dharma: *For ever and ever, he and his seed shall burn eternally in the fires of hell for committing the grievous sin of plucking the chaste flower of God in a Brahmacharini.*

Kanta held her dead baby against her breast. She had no tears, no words; her unspoken grief cast a pall over them all. When Satrash came near, she recoiled as if his shadow on her dead son would doom him for eternity. She cried piteously: 'Muniji, out of your mercy, save my child.'

'Your child is already saved,' Muni replied.

She met his eyes. They were soft, tender. She kissed her baby's face and silently placed him at Muni's feet. He picked up the baby and cried out to the river:

'Goddess of Sindhu! Princess of limitless treasures! I behold your beautiful vision, robed in white and blue, and I bow to you.

'For nine months, this infant lay in the womb of his mother, in innocence. For two days he lived among us in innocence.

'For the innocence in which he lived and died, let him go to the realm of the Liberated.

'Count also that I pray for him with my heart.'

Kanta heard Muni's prayers calmly, but as he was lighting the cremation fire, she cried, 'No, no, do not burn him. Spare him, for he will always burn in the fires of hell.'

Her inauspicious utterance upset Muni; he shouted, 'How can you speak of this little one burning in hell; he who was helpless, innocent. He suffered, yes, but he caused no suffering!'

Kanta was in the grip of a nameless terror. Hoarsely, she whispered, 'He is of the accursed seed, eternally to burn.'

'Who told you this?' Muni asked in anger.

'It is the curse of the gods for the sins of his father.'

Muni was aghast; in a towering rage he said, 'A god that would curse an innocent child is the one who deserves to be cursed! How can ancestral sins be on our heads! Are our own sins not enough?'

Kanta believed him. The torment within her ceased as she heard Muni praying to the Sindhu, the sun, fire, the atmosphere, outer space. 'Protect his soul. Keep the winds and waters sweet for him; let his nights and days, dawns and sunsets be sweet; may all the regions he passes through be sweet; may his resting places be sweet.'

The ache in Kanta's heart returned when she was sprinkling her son's ashes in the river. Muni realized there was a heavy burden in her heart and began his invocation again. 'Goddess of Sindhu! This mother has placed in your loving fold the ashes of her son, who is henceforth your son. Be then the loving mother of this child.'

Kanta saw a ripple in the waters; Muni saw nothing, but with inner feeling, said, 'Sindhu accepts. Grieve no more. Your child is now the putra of Sindhu.'

'Putra of Sindhu! Sindhu Putra?' she asked, in a voice hushed with wonder, remembering the age-old prophecy that spoke of the arrival of Sindhu Putra.

Muni nodded, though he had not been thinking about the prophecy. 'Goddess Sindhu accepts your child. If there is a hidden burden of anyone's guilt in your heart, it cannot hurt your child's soul. The sin of a father cannot affect the child, nor can it affect you. The love of Goddess Sindhu for your child will be no less than yours.'

Kanta heard him with relief flooding her heart. But then, there never is an end to human wishing and she asked wistfully: 'Only, I shall never see my child again!'

'Who knows! Goddess Sindhu may bring him back for a sojourn here!'

'He can come back! To me, as my son?'

Muni realized that this was a question every grieving mother might ask. Yet how could he explain to her that the soul seeks liberation from the cycle of rebirth and death only to be reunited with the One-Supreme!

Earlier, when Muni invoked deities, he had felt confident, powerful. But now he found it difficult to answer a simple question from a simple woman. It was easier to speak to gods than humans, for gods, possibly, neither hear nor reply, he thought irreverently and smiled.

Kanta saw that smile; she needed no more assurance.

But Muni's mind was still on what she had asked. He was thinking of the goal to attain moksha—liberation from the cycle of birth and death, in the final, eternal ecstasy of union with the One-Supreme. Attainment of liberation? Muni knew it was not an attainment as such because moksha was a birthright. Man frees himself to reach that highest level of emancipation; a man's life is simply the soul's pilgrimage, back to man's original goal of mystical and spiritual union with the One-Supreme. Even if liberation is not realized in one, two or more lives, an individual is sustained in all stages of transmigration by the message that none is denied his birthright—to be one with the One-Supreme.

Then how is it possible, Muni wondered, that the child would not attain moksha! He thought of karma—the law of action and retribution, which governs mankind and operates in the moral realm as inexorably as in the physical realm. Each creature is fashioned by his past deeds, and not by blind chance, fate, destiny or the configuration of the stars. Yet this child had lived in innocence and God could not possibly will that he be given another life to pay for the sins of earlier lives. The Supreme was just, not capricious and if He wanted the child to expiate for the sins of his past lives, his life could not have ended in two days. The child of two days had committed no sin—neither denied his soul nor betrayed his Self—and if he had not acquired true knowledge, it *was* God who needed forgiveness, not the child, for he had been denied time and opportunity to acquire it.

Muni was now certain that he had the answer. He told Kanta, 'Your child is no longer a creature of God. He is one with God; his self is united with the Creator. He is free, pure, and limitless, without beginning, without end. If he chooses, he may even visit you.'

Kanta looked at Muni, fascinated.

Lest she harbour hopes of seeing her child again, he added, 'Yes, your child and the Creator are united; all you can do is to have a temple in your heart for your son and the Creator, who together are one.'

'A temple in my heart!'

'The heart is where temples of love are. Temples of stone, brick and straw do not last! My parents built such a temple here. It burnt. They died in a fire. Again, it burnt, after I came here.'

Soulfully, Kanta said, 'I shall always have a temple in my heart. But I shall also build a temple, a great temple, for my Sindhu Putra.'

Muni did not hear her. Briskly, he walked away to attend to his prayers. But Roopa heard and, hoping to divert the grieving mother's mind, said, 'Yes, you do that.'

'A temple with gardens, flowers, fountains,' Kanta said.

Later, she was in a deep trance, imagining her son with thousands cheering him, calling him the healer, teacher, pathfinder. And he, to whom everyone was bowing, bowed to her and kissed her cheek, saying, 'Now, mother mine . . . '

The remaining words were lost, for then, her husband Satrash finally shook her out of her trance. She heard him in a daze, desperately trying to recapture her lost dream and wondering what it was that her son had left unsaid. Plaintively, she asked, 'Where is my son?'

Grimly, hoping to shock her into reality, Satrash replied, 'He is in the Sindhu river.'

But Kanta nodded, as though she was glad that he knew. 'Yes, of course. He came to me. I must build a temple for him.'

'Of course,' Satrash quickly agreed, for he was a marksman with many arrows, and if one fell short, he had another. 'That is why we must leave in the morning. We have to hurry. The temple must be built . . . '

Kanta stared at him. The memory of what he had done to her little sister would never leave her, it would haunt her forever, but at that moment his words swayed her, 'The temple shall be my atonement or else the burden of my sins will be heavy . . . for us . . . for our son.'

And as she heard these words, and looked at his downcast face, she recalled Roopa's words, 'There is no sin for which there is no atonement, for God in his limitless mercy . . . '

Kanta was ready to leave.

Muni was meditating, so Kanta stopped some steps away

from him and silently prayed, 'Protect my son, tell Sindhu to give me back my son. He is not Sindhu Putra . . . he is my son, mine! Protect him.'

And though she had not spoken the words out loud, Muni opened his eyes, as if awakening from a dream. His voice was calm as he spoke, 'The body of your son died. The God in him did not die—cannot die. Unborn, undead, he shall live and love, for he is the Creation of God and he is the Creator of God, for God and he are one.'

Kanta asked the question that tore her heart. 'But will he return to me?'

Muni smiled, and thought, she pines for him whose soul is liberated and is with the One-Supreme! But why not! His brow cleared and in the gladness of a song he said: *'He comes, He comes, Ever He comes, Ever, Ever, He . . . .'*

His voice rose above the tumult of the wind that blew across the rocks. His eyes were closed and his face glowed as if the vision he was seeing clasped him to its bosom. Roopa put a comforting arm around Kanta and also watched her husband, enthralled. They saw the rapture on his face—a new glow, a new radiance—luminous, shining! Roopa could hear in her heart the song—*'He comes, He comes, Ever He comes, Ever, Ever, He . . .'*—and she knew that one day she would sing that song in its fullness so that everyone could hear it. Love, she realized, was the liberating force—love, mercy and compassion for God's creation. To Kanta, she said, 'Go with God, and may He guide your steps to build your temple with love.'

Kanta left with Satrash who remained as warped in mind and as corrupt in his actions as ever before. They stopped in a large town where Satrash knew it would be easy to get lost in the crowds and harder for pursuers to catch them. And his misdeeds continued.

Jhadrov, a rich financier, agreed to have a huge temple built with Satrash as manager. Satrash was full of ideas to attract large numbers of devotees and tempt them into making generous donations to the temple. Land for the temple was cleared and his house was littered with statues of idols that would be installed in the temple, including imaginative statues depicting Sindhu Putra, for the prophecy of his arrival was well known. However, in return for financing the temple and providing ample funds, Jhadrov had demanded that Satrash ensure Kanta slept with him. Jhadrov reminded him: 'You promised that you *and* your wife would serve me, body and soul'.

Kanta was given a highly intoxicating substance mixed with the temple Prasad, and she passed out. When she woke up from her sleep and saw what had happened, she was furious. She clutched a nearby metal statue and struck Jhadrov three times on the head. Satrash heard Jhadrov's cry and rushed into the room. In her anger, all Kanta saw was a man who had seduced her sister and allowed a fiend to ruin her. She flung the statue at Satrash. Bleeding, whimpering, he fell to the ground with the statue stuck in his head.

In a daze, Kanta noticed that it was the statue of her son, Sindhu Putra, 'My son, Sindhu Putra, is powerful, is he not!'

Hiran, a prostitute, was Kanta's neighbour and respected her. Passing by, she saw the carnage and feared that many would soon arrive at the scene to investigate. She herself was trying to flee as she was responsible for the death of a man who had long ago killed her mother and molested Hiran when she was young and innocent, unwittingly pushing her towards a life of prostitution. Hiran persuaded Kanta to escape with her and Vassi, her servant.

The next morning, the dead bodies of Jhadrov and Satrash were discovered. Inquiries began, but by then Kanta was far away with Hiran and Vassi. They found sanctuary with one of Hiran's relatives—Ghulat, a gangster—who ran a whorehouse and a gambling den in a frontier town. He insisted that the newcomers must earn their keep. Hiran was sick and old, but Kanta was pretty enough to serve as a decoy for the gambling joint and to sleep with the richer customers. Otherwise, Ghulat said he would surrender them to the authorities in exchange for the generous reward that was being offered for the capture of Jhadrov and Satrash's killers.

The suggestion horrified Kanta, but Hiran said, 'You must live to fulfil your cherished dream to build the temple. Maybe that will atone for some of my many sins, too. Promise me that you shall build the temple, Kanta.'

Hiran trained Kanta for her new role. Later, as the older woman was dying, her last words were, 'Remember, Kanta, Sindhu Putra's temple.'

'I remember,' Kanta replied, tearfully.

Some months later, Ghulat was attacked by rival gangsters. Bleeding from deadly wounds, Ghulat whispered to Kanta to go to a distant village where a vast horde of wealth was hidden in a secure place. He asked her to bring it all to him. She was amazed; such a journey would take a long time and surely he was dying. He understood her silence, but defiantly shouted, 'No, I shall live . . . I shall li . . . ' His voice trailed off, blood spurted from his wounds and he died.

Kanta left the same day with Vassi, taking all they could. Together, they moved from place to place till they reached Gatha's village and settled down there. Later, they went to the hiding place Ghulat had described. There, digging under the solitary statue of a cow, in an isolated valley, they found wealth secreted by Ghulat, his father and grandfathers over five generations of crime. 'We are immeasurably rich,' Vassi said, and Kanta responded, 'The temple shall be immeasurably rich.' Vassi agreed. It took them several weeks to transport all the wealth hidden there.

Then, like an avalanche, came the momentous news of the coming of Sindhu Putra. Kanta rushed out with tears of joy, certain it was her son. Surprisingly, the infant gave up Sonama's breast, and crying, looked in Kanta's direction.

Kanta looked at the headman. When Gatha nodded, she took the babe in her arms and the infant nestled against her bosom and slept. Kanta felt whole. She said with authority, 'There shall be a grand temple for my Sindhu Putra.'

Gatha said, 'That will cost money.'

'Yes, the money is all there,' Kanta said and she spoke to Vassi who returned after a while with a heavy box and spread out gold, jewellery, rubies . . . .

The crowd gasped. 'What? How! So much! Whose?'

'It always belonged to him,' said Kanta, pointing at the infant. 'For his temple; there is more, ten times as much, perhaps even more, for it must be the biggest, the greatest temple for . . . '

She did not have to complete the sentence; the infant woke up from the nap in her arms to face the crowd, and it seemed that he nodded as though in approval. The crowd bowed. Truly, miracles were multiplying! Mother Goddess Sindhu sending her son to them! So much wealth in their village! The infant Sindhu Putra nodding approval!

Only Gatha seemed worried and the vaid looked stern. They knew Kanta had been a prostitute.

∽

The allotment of village land was not a complicated process and whenever land was required for building huts, cottages, schools or the business of buying and selling, or activities involving arts, crafts and sports, only the headman's permission was needed. However, when large tracts of land were needed—such as when building a temple—it was necessary to seek the karkarta's permission. This permission could no longer be given freely, for during Bharat's reign as karkarta, an incident now known as the Sadhu's Curse had taken place in a distant village.

At a large meeting that was being presided over by Asudra,

Bharat's representative, a sadhu, had learnt that a strip of land was being cleared in a half-burnt forest to build a temple.

'Destroy a thousand ancient temples of God for a new temple of man!' the sadhu protested. When told that many trees had already been destroyed by fire, he said, 'Forests grow! They regrow! God's temples renew themselves. But man must not rob them of the part of the earth that is theirs. Thousands of trees have perished, homes of birds destroyed, animals of the woods scattered and slaughtered. But that beautiful landscape is not gone for ever. It will regrow unless man is too stupid, too greedy and too thoughtless.'

He continued: 'Your karkarta is endowed with reason. He cannot create a beautiful, plentiful forest, but he has the power to preserve what he is powerless to create. They say your karkarta encourages memory songs that people will hear thousands of years from now. Should he not help the earth to remain richer, more abundant and beautiful, ten thousand years from now? If you prevent the forests from reappearing, what will you leave behind—an earth that is scarred, poor, ugly and desolate? Is that the legacy he wants to leave the future? Sores and wounds on the face of the earth? Remember, many will then curse him for it.'

Asudra tried to reason with the sadhu, saying, 'Please understand, the forest is nearly dead. While the fires raged, the karkarta prayed that the fires would stop, but they did not. It was God's will . . .'

'Then let God's will prevail,' the sadhu interrupted. 'Do nothing. When the rains come, all nature will sigh and wake up refreshed. The forest will grow once again, its bounty will return, the animals will come back and the birds will fill the air with their songs. I shall tell them to sing songs to bless your karkarta and his memory for ever, and beyond.'

But when the various headmen present at the meeting objected to his suggestions, he lost his temper, 'Protest all you want till you are blue in the face and till the river starts flowing backwards! But you shall never again see me in your villages and in your lands. I renounce you and your lands. I am not your *rya* anymore. I am *Arya*.'*

Asudra sensed the sadhu's agony and pleaded, 'Sadhuji, I beg of you, renounce your last words. Do not leave in anger, please.'

The sadhu responded, 'I do not curse you nor your karkarta for you know not what you do. But tell your karkarta that God's thunderbolt shall strike him and his land if he ever listens to those who rob ancient temples of gods to build false temples of man.'

After that incident, a set of twenty-eight guidelines for sanctioning land for temples was created. Among them were:

* Extent of forest land needed for the temple.
* Names of donors, and to ensure that they receive nothing of the temple's income.
* A committee of seven appointed by the headman to oversee donations and to ensure that they are applied strictly for the temple or for approved the charities to which income from the temple is to flow.
* Remuneration and facilities for those employed to serve the temple.

Gatha sent the mahant to meet Dhru, who had been elected karkarta after Bharat retired. The mahant returned with Sushma, Dhru's representative. She had no difficulty in allocating land as the proposed temple ended at the edge of the forest. A large balcony overlooked the forest and the wildlife. The other side of the temple ended a little away from

---

* This ancient practice of attaching 'a' to a word in order to give it the opposite meaning, continues till today in languages in India. Thus rya means 'people of the land' but the prefix of 'a' changes its meaning to 'exiles'. Later though, the words Arya and Aryan achieved different significance and came to mean 'noble' because of the noble aims and goals of Aryans.

the river so as not to interfere with bathers, visitors or worshippers there, but again with balconies with a clear view of the river, and stairs for easy access for bathers and visitors to reach the temple. The temple revenues would not be used for paying its workers as Kanta had assumed responsibility for those payments. In any case, volunteers from near and far were ready to pour in. Offerings or donations intended for the temple's continuing activities were being made, and any surplus would be credited to the karkarta's list of sixty-six charities, which included the defence of the realm; support of veterans, and the widows and orphans of those killed in battle; protection of hermits; care for the sick, infirm and handicapped; feeding troughs and watering holes for birds and wildlife . . .

Sushma returned to the headquarters, satisfied that the temple project met the guidelines fully. Karkarta Dhru also gave his approval and construction of the temple began in earnest. Volunteers, artisans and builders poured in to work on it not only from Gatha's village but also surrounding and distant villages. The story of Sindhu Putra's arrival began to be known in every town and village of the land along with accounts of the magnificent temple that was being built. People came from all over to bow to Sindhu Putra and to witness the frenzied work in progress at the temple site. The mahant, who never believed in relying on a single donor for the temple's funds, encouraged all the visitors to leave generous offerings, assuring them that their donations would be made known to Sindhu Putra. Of course, since the gods know everything, there was really no need for the mahant to recite their names to Sindhu Putra. Each donor was given a saffron armband with a colourful painting of the Mother Goddess standing in the midst of the waters of the Sindhu, her infant son in her outstretched arms, held aloft for the world to see. It served as a proud badge of honour for the donors and came to be coveted by all.

NINE

SHOULD GODS BE EDUCATED?

5068 to 5065 BCE

Gatha arrived one morning, a few months later, crying out in delight, 'Sindhu Putra speaks, master! He speaks!'

'He speaks, does he? And what does he say?' Bharat asked with a smile.

Thrilled, Gatha repeated the infant's first words, 'Da da da.'

'He is a true Hindu, then!' Bharat rejoined.

Gatha was surprised, 'How so, master?'

Bharat had no intention of being serious. 'Did you not say that the infant's words were "Da da da"? What else could they mean, other than daya (compassion), dana (charity) and dharma!'

Gatha had not seen deep significance in those first sounds of the infant, barely five months old. Nor did it occur to him now to doubt his old master's words. 'I never thought of that, master!' he said, awed.

Immediately, Bharat regretted his thoughtless jest and said, 'No, Gatha, I was joking—a foolish jest. Forget it.'

But how could Gatha ever forget it! Earlier, Bharatjogi was at pains to deny the infant's divinity. Yet now he had invested Sindhu Putra's initial words with divine significance. Soulfully, he looked at his master, as though to thank him for giving him that meaningful clue to the infant's first utterance.

'Thank you, master,' Gatha said, brimming with gratitude.

As Bharat was in the process of offering Gatha a cup of

wine, he was not surprised at the headman's words, and attributed the joy in Gatha's voice to a desire for wine. 'Yes,' said Bharat, 'let us have a drink to celebrate the first words of the infant.'

Gatha spoke only as he was leaving, in a sombre voice, 'Today Sindhu Putra speaks of daya, dana, and dharma; imagine what he will say and do when he walks on this earth with firm footsteps!'

When the mahant visited him, Gatha asked, 'Did you hear Sindhu Putra's words?'

'Of course! Da da da.'

'And do you know what they mean?' Before the startled mahant could reply, Gatha explained, 'They mean daya, dana and dharma!'

The mahant did not bat an eyelid. 'But of course! This is what I came to tell you. But you are great, Gatha! You know everything!'

Gatha nodded. Here was confirmation of what Bharatjogi had said. 'Have you told the others of their significance?'

'No,' the mahant replied. 'I came to suggest that you should.'

This was one of the things Gatha admired most about the mahant; he was always humble, wanting Gatha to be in the forefront.

'Call the people here, then,' Gatha ordered.

'Here! Such announcements are made in the village square.'

'No, call them here.' Gatha knew that the wine had rendered him incapable of walking to the village square.

The mahant left to call the villagers. Let them laugh at Gatha, he thought. He himself would distance himself from the foolishness of giving profound significance to a babe's babble.

When the villagers gathered outside Gatha's hut, he dragged his cot out and stood on it so they could all see him.

'Da da da,' he began. 'Today was Sindhu Putra's first discourse. He said daya, dana, dharma . . . daya, daya, da . . .' He fell down on his cot, overpowered by the wine. The audience followed his obviously prayerful posture and knelt, all the way, on the ground.

The mahant, too, followed their example to avoid inviting public wrath. But the pain in his joints forced him to get up. He pulled the cot with the sleeping Gatha inside the hut, wondering what to tell the villagers who thought that Gatha, their Sentinel of River and Sky, was in a deep trance. What do I tell these dolts? That their headman is drunk and babbling? Who will believe me?

He spoke slowly at first, and then gathered momentum, as he spoke of Sindhu Putra's discourse on daya, dana and dharma. This only confirmed for the villagers what Gatha had said before falling into a trance. Impressed by his own oratory and his speech, the mahant went on till it began to rain, at which point the villagers went back, with souls uplifted.

Later, people spoke not of the simple babble of Sindhu Putra, but of his entire discourse on daya and dana as two of the essential pillars of dharma. When the story reached other villages, it grew to include songs sung and stories told by an infant who could not as yet utter a single word! Devotees came from all over and remained to pray.

౿

Meanwhile Bharatjogi remembered Gatha's joyful words, 'Imagine what Sindhu Putra will say and do when he walks on the earth!' Bharat recalled them not with joy but with dread. The little one is not a god, he thought. What will he be when he grows up? A god that failed?

Bharat did not see the beautiful landscape that glorious morning. In his mind's eye, all he saw was the lone figure of a child passing silently through a desolate graveyard of shattered dreams, lost illusions and crushed hopes.

∼

Time passed. Sindhu Putra was three years old. His every wish was a command. He went through mountains of toys made by loving devotees and it took him only a moment to break them and demand new ones. The child threw tantrums.

'He is not of this earth,' Gatha said. The villagers echoed Gatha's words, 'He is not of this earth!'

Bharat understood. A child without training and instruction is unfit for this earth or any realm of God. Yet none dared to teach him differently, overcome by blind love and unquestioning obedience to a child of three!

Bharat felt responsible. It was I who picked up the child from his dead mother's arms. Did I not then make covenant with her and the gods that I would look after her orphaned babe? But I failed to squash even the image of his divinity! In a moment of utter foolishness I even blessed the temple for the infant, just to oppose the villagers' prejudice against Kanta's donation! Why was I so blind? The gods imposed a duty on me and I failed. A mother left her babe in my arms and I let her down!

When he tried to speak to Gatha, the headman did not seem to understand the need to discipline a god. Actually, Bharat had not reached the point of desperation; he realized that children knew when and where they could misbehave. How sweet-tempered the child was during his weekly visits with him! Maybe, the environment he was being raised in mattered. In the village, everyone was trying to meet every possible or impossible demand of the child. Here, with him, the child played happily on the ground with the dogs. During his visits to Bharatjogi's retreat, the child was playful and smiling; he cried only when Gatha tried to take him back.

But from all accounts, he was a terror in the village. The time, Bharat concluded, was ripe for Sindhu Putra's education. Later, it might be too late.

Bharat wondered if he should send the child to his wife, but he feared that thousands would collect there, too, to worship the child. He then thought of Muni and Roopa, the daughter of the once-blind singer. He had often visited the rocks to meet them, long before he retired. But are they still there? He considered sending Gatha to find out, but decided against it; Gatha would know why and where Sindhu Putra had been sent, and might not be able to keep it a secret from the insistent villagers.

Then inspiration struck. Bharat asked Gatha to go to the singer and beg him to come to the retreat, adding that 'Sometimes, I get an urge to hear old songs again.'

After travelling for two days, Gatha reached the singer late at night. When Gatha suggested they leave the next day, the singer said, 'Why tomorrow? I am ready now.' Before an hour had passed, they were on their way. There was fear in the singer's heart. Gatha had said that Bharatjogi wanted to hear old songs. He recalled his last words with the karkarta, 'Allow me to come to you in your retirement to sing for you.' But Bharat had said, 'No, your songs are for people here, not for a hermit.'

Yet he had been summoned now. Why?

Upon arriving at the retreat, the singer embraced Bharat and asked, 'Are you well?'

Bharat reassured him, 'Would I trouble you if it was merely a question of my health! Is an old man like me afraid to face the gods?'

The singer was delighted. Then he really had been called for his songs!

'That,' Bharat said, 'and much more.'

What could be more important than Bharat's health and his own songs, the singer wondered.

Having secured the boat, Gatha walked up to them, but waited only to extract a promise from the singer to sing for the villagers later.

Bharat opened his heart to the singer. The singer had already heard much about Sindhu Putra. Who had not? Bharat then told him how he had found the child and how a foolish myth about the child's divinity had grown.

'What makes you certain that this is not God's own miracle?' asked the singer.

'I do not deny God's ability to perform any miracle of His choosing. But in my sixty-six years, the only miracles I have seen are those which are contrived by humans to mislead and misguide.'

Bharat continued: 'I believe God had a choice when He created this universe and He had freedom to choose the laws that the universe obeys. That is the real, everlasting miracle which arose from the mind of God. But if I am to believe in an unending string of miracles, which are talked of from day to day, I must also believe that the initial choices of God were so imperfect as to need the aid of constant miracles to support His universe. And this I cannot believe—that God's mind conceived something imperfect!'

The singer smiled, 'Would you really say that everything in this God's universe is clear to you? Everything?'

'No, not even a fraction of a fraction. But that is a failure of our knowledge. As our knowledge grows, so will our understanding, and the realization that what we consider a miracle is fully in accord with God's plans when He began His universe is inevitable.'

The singer did not wish to argue and contented himself with the observation, 'Every time I look at the earth and the sky, I know He, that created us all, is there, and with each day that dawns, He creates a new miracle.'

'Yes, that is His miracle,' Bharat interrupted, 'but must I accept the notion that He sends the son of the Mother

Goddess to us to take on our sins, or lead us on paths of purity, or cure us, all with a wave of his hand!'

'My eyesight with which I see you, Bharatji, is a miracle in itself.'

Bharat knew the story. He recalled his own belief that Bindu would be reincarnated. But those were miracles of man's faith and followed God's laws.

Their conversation continued. Bharat said finally, 'Even if Sindhu Putra is destined to be a god, do you not see that he must learn the ways of the earth if he is to live on it. How can a god be without proper education!'

The singer confirmed that Muni and Roopa were still at the rocks. Muni, he said, no longer had a quarrel with the gods and was even rebuilding the temple destroyed by fire. What had delayed the temple was that during the last six years Roopa had had three children—two daughters and a son.

That night, the singer slept little. His mind was on what Bharatjogi had said about miracles. The singer certainly knew of charlatans who contrived 'miracles' to mislead others for their personal gain. But then he also believed that God lives among us, around us, above us—everywhere—and His miracles are unceasing. He recalled how he, who was totally blind, suddenly regained his eyesight, and Bharat as karkarta had pressed him to put the story into a memory song.

That miracle had started with his five-year-old daughter, who often saw a young ascetic walking towards the forest. One day, she brought him a long staff for his walks, saying that it belonged to her father, but he also had another staff. The ascetic asked her to bring the other one as well: 'Possibly, your father may not need it.' The girl refused, protesting that her father was blind and invariably needed it. When she reached home, she tearfully told her poor blind father of the impossible demand of the ascetic. But her father said that it was improper to refuse a holy man, and he handed over the staff to his daughter. She went tearfully, and reluctantly gave it to the holy man, but in her anger she asked him, 'How can you take this staff? Do you not know my father is blind?'

Gently he said, 'I knew, little one, that your father *was* blind. But is he *still* blind?'

The girl stamped her foot in disgust and ran back to her hut. Her father was asleep. In a surge of sympathy, she placed her hand on her father's forehead and said, 'I shall be your staff, Father, and we shall walk together, always, hand in hand.'

Her tears flowed and some of those tears fell into her father's eyes. The father opened his eyes. And then . . . miraculously, he could see! He was blind no more!

Trembling with joy, the singer went to thank the ascetic, but he replied, 'I had nothing to do with that, old man. Maybe your daughter's tears washed away your blindness.'

And when the singer said he would go to the temple to render thanks, the ascetic said, 'Men go to temples sometimes to lose sight, not to gain it.'

The ascetic became angry when the old man wanted to touch his feet, but calmed down when the little girl quickly sat in his lap.

That ascetic was Muni of the Rocks. The once blind singer recalled how, at the age of eighteen, his daughter went to the rocks and another miracle of love occurred and his daughter Roopa and Muni were married.

∼

Even Bharatjogi did not sleep much that night with his mind on what the singer had said about the miracles of God.

He recalled the conversations he had had as a young boy

with Sage Ekantra, his mentor, about a prehistoric cave that contained carvings dating back to 7000 BCE. Ekantra could explain some carvings but there were some he could not. There was one series of carvings, covering an entire wall from ceiling to floor. A series of figures were arranged in a circle—a lotus flower; a plant with leaves; a plant with flowers; a tree; insects; a butterfly; birds in flight; fish in water; bigger fish, dolphins, whales; a tortoise emerging from water onto land; a peacock on the ground; a snake entering water; a boar in the forest; lions, tigers deer, many animals, both small and large; monkeys in a tree, apes on the ground; and finally a sole human being.

All the figures were evenly spaced, but a large gap remained between the human being and the lotus. What was the intention of the artist? Did this distance warn that all creation must remain at a distance from man, to avoid destruction from the human species? Or did this space indicate that there would be yet another species after human beings— that evolution was not complete?

Even more mysterious were the side-by-side figures of mammoths, and monstrous animals with the faces of crocodiles, their mouths wide open with other animals visible on their tongues as though about to be swallowed; birds with wolf faces; flying fish with large canine fangs and sweeping tongues with tusks; followed by smaller figures of apes with some human features; and finally, a vroun—half man–half ape, standing on hind legs—bleeding as he was being stabbed by three or four human figures.

Was the artist telling the story of the extinction of certain species? Had the race of vroun been wiped out by man? Who caused the extinction of other species? There were many questions in Bharatjogi's mind. Were the miracles of evolution and extinction of certain species a part of God's design when He first created the universe? Or was the singer right in believing that God performed miracles from time to time to support His universe?

He gave up, saying to himself: 'If my little mind cannot discover what the fish in the water or the bird in flight is thinking, what arrogance is this that I should presume to understand God's design!'

~

The following day, the singer and Bharatjogi left for Muni's Rocks. When they returned Bharat announced that Sindhu Putra would soon leave for his education. This announcement almost caused a riot in the village. How could he, who was destined to dispense enlightenment, go elsewhere to receive enlightenment! No, they could not let Sindhu Putra go!

Even the singer found no favour with the villagers when he sang mythological songs to show that those who came to be honoured as gods had received the most rigorous training in childhood. The mahant protested that those people were not gods initially, rather humans who had achieved godhood, whereas here an attempt was being made to reduce a god to an ordinary human. Unfortunately, the singer had no songs to prove that a god who sprang from the river had ever been educated on earth. The mahant's argument was, thus, unquestionable. But could it stand against the resolve of Sindhu Putra's earthly father!

Kanta was devastated. Hers was an important, vital voice. She employed hundreds to work on the construction of the temple. Everyone respected her smallest wish. She put her foot down: Sindhu Putra would not go.

When Bharatjogi and Kanta met, she cried, 'Where and why do you wish to send my Sindhu Putra away from me? Do you not know how long I waited for my son to come back to me!' With tears, she began her incoherent story. He hardly understood her but discerned a deep wound in her heart as she kept asking, 'Where would you send him—why?'

His heart went out to her. He begged, 'Please, do not tell anyone, but I must send him to Muni of the Rocks and Roopa.'

Bharat was astonished to see Kanta's transformation as he uttered those words. It was as though a flash of light split the darkness in every corner of her mind and her entire soul was illuminated. Her tears stopped, and she smiled.

'But of course, of course,' she cried out. 'What a fool I am! Of course, yes, of course.' She fell at Bharatjogi's feet and wept. Bharat lifted her face from his feet, not knowing what to make of her. She kept smiling through her tears, 'Thank you, thank you! Yes, that is where my son must go. He ended his last journey there. That is where he must begin his next. Where else! Send him! Send him there!'

Kanta left, promising that no one would hear from her of Sindhu Putra's destination. Bharatjogi insisted on that, certain of Muni's wrath if crowds gathered around his home to catch a glimpse of Sindhu Putra.

When Kanta returned, the villagers saw her face, serene and happy. Obviously, the battle with the hermit was won. But Kanta cried out, 'No, my son must go where his earthly father takes him.'

Who could oppose Kanta! She was, they knew, the first miracle which Sindhu Putra wrought on earth. Had untold wealth not dropped from the sky into her house when Sindhu Putra arrived? Was she not building a magnificent temple to him? And what was it, if not a miracle, that a lowly prostitute had given up her sinful ways overnight and devoted herself to Sindhu Putra? Truly, she was dwija—twice born or born again. If some doubted the divine inspiration in her, they were quiet; nobody wanted to question a person of such immense wealth who had given gainful employment to so many.

Later, with a smile, Bharat admitted to the singer that he would begin to believe in miracles because the woman, convinced that she was Sindhu Putra's mother, came storming in to quarrel with him, but ended by kissing his feet!

TEN

SINDHU PUTRA AT MUNI'S ROCKS

5068 BCE

Bharatjogi and the singer escorted Sindhu Putra to the boat at night to leave for Muni's Rocks. Bharat heard the mournful wail from his dogs at being left behind. The prospect of parting with the child saddened him.

Moonlight illuminated the night and Bharat had no difficulty in rowing the small boat. He thought of what lay ahead of the child, in years to come.

Like most children his age, Bharat, too, had attended school with a large number of students. School discipline, though firm, was never as demanding as under a guru. Nor did school concentrate on God-realization, as a guru would. Teaching at school was devoted to the rules of good conduct, polite speech, health, yoga, arithmetic, painting, poetry, music, sculpture, swimming, boating, horse riding, sports and activities like farming, cattle-breeding and mining. Compulsory classes were few, and a student could skip many, except those related to conduct, health, yoga, arithmetic and sports.

Bharat had pleasant memories of his school and given a choice, he would have sent the child to a large school. A guru would not accept so young a child; a student went to a guru of his own free will and in order to exercise such a personal choice, a student had to be much older. In fact, the search for a guru often began well after the student had completed school sessions.

He wondered if Muni's Rocks would have the advantages of a large school. But do I have a choice, Bharat asked himself. All I want is an escape for him into anonymity so that he grows up as a normal child should, away from the worshipful glances of those who treat him as a god. Besides, he will have Muni and Roopa to teach him and their three children as playmates. After all, did I really learn that much at my school, he thought. God guided my path to Ekantra and it was he who orchestrated my rise to the position of karkarta. After that campaign for my first election, there never was need for another campaign. People gave me their love in abundance; Ekantra taught me, helped me, and inspired me to keep my pledge to the gods and to my clan of the Hindu. Why then this strange, desolate feeling! Ekantra is no more. But this child will have Muni and Roopa to guide him. How can I ask for more!

He looked at the child sleeping peacefully as the boat moved. Where is the need for sorrow, he asked himself, but he knew his sorrow was not for the child, but for himself. In his loneliness on the retreat, his one ray of happiness had been the weekly visits of this child. He would have little to look forward to in the years ahead. Only memories of his clan and the knowledge that he had left his people self-sufficient, strong and happy.

Yet, he was in danger of being robbed of those memories, too. The singer told him of all that was happening in the land, with division and disunity fast creeping into the clan. Bharat wondered where this new sickness, this deadly disease of disunity in the hearts of his people would lead them?

Gently, the boat moved on. The singer saw Bharat looking sadly at the sleeping child. With a reassuring smile, he said, 'When he returns from Muni's Rocks, he shall walk as a god should.'

'Let him walk as a son should,' was Bharat's reply.

Let him unite our people, he prayed silently. God, give him the vision to walk as my son should, and give him the strength to unite the people of my land.

∼

Bharat had sought no assurances from them, but Muni and Roopa had given them, generously, abundantly. Muni told the singer, 'Tell his father to worry no more about the child.'

'His father!' the singer asked.

'Yes, of course, Bharatjogi,' Muni said. 'He has no other. God brought him to his shore and Bharatjogi accepted him as his own.'

Yes, the child, Bharat felt, was a part of him, like his own son.

Together, he and the singer left, comforted by Muni and Roopa's affectionate words and the obvious delight of their three children at gaining a new playmate.

∼

On the return journey, the singer was busy composing new melodies. Bharatjogi shook off his sadness at parting from the child and thought of Muni and how gracious, kind and considerate he was. It amused him now to recall that years ago when he was karkarta, a deputation of influential headmen and villagers had bitterly complained at a council meeting that this so-called Muni was not a man of god, but a believer in the devil who insulted and cursed the gods and their idols and ought to be banished forthwith from the land. They had even claimed that Muni had possibly set fire to the temple on the Rocks.

That was the very first time that Bharat had met the singer and his daughter Roopa. They had rushed to the council meeting to defend Muni against the villagers' charges. The singer was dying to speak and interrupted to say that the villagers and headmen were talking utter nonsense. But Bharat had silenced him, 'Let the accusers be the first to speak.'

After hearing the accusers and questioning them closely, Bharat told them, 'The testimony given by some of you reveals that Muni was far away from the scene and the fire was probably caused by lightning; some of you even concede that that there are signs of lightning strike on nearby trees. So the charge of setting fire to the temple is hereby dropped.'

On the charge of being insulting to the gods, Bharat said, 'It is a question between the gods and Muni. Do our gods need our protection from Muni? A quarrel between a man and his gods is a private affair. How can we accept that a man cannot ask the gods the questions that torment his spirit! If the gods do not answer, or his understanding is not illuminated, why can he not question the gods further? And even if a crime has been committed against the gods, it is for the gods—not man—to avenge it.'

On the charge of Muni being a believer in the devil, Bharat said, 'Does it matter what gods or devils he believes in? Your own preachers say their gods are true, but the gods of others are devils. Tell me then, who the true gods are and who the devil is? As long as Muni believes in a creature of god, maybe he will come to believe in god. Is the devil a creature of god, or is he created independent of god? If he is created independently, then you admit that there are two creators— god and the devil. Besides, what right do we have to interfere with a person's beliefs, or the path he chooses to reach the truth?'

On the question of banishing Muni, Bharat said, 'You ask that he be banished. Where to? Is it your suggestion that he be sent to other villages, far from you? Then you must concede the principle that undesirables from other villages, scoffers of gods and blasphemers can be banished to your villages. He stays at his own Rocks; he does not come to you, having effectively banished himself. You are the ones who go to disturb his peace, and then come crying that the company of this godless man degrades you! Did it not occur to you to let him be in his isolation and keep yourself away from the temptation of his company so that you might achieve your self-appointed goal of remaining chaste and pure?'

Finally, raising his voice, Bharat said, 'But if you have come seeking his banishment from our clan and our land, then you are guilty of harbouring evil in your hearts, for remember this, he, like all of us, is a rya and no one, and I repeat, no one has the right to exile a rya, and make him arya. As karkarta, I do not have that right; the council of chiefs has no such right. Why, even if all our rya in this entire land are unanimous, they cannot deprive any man of his basic right as a rya and make him arya and be forced to leave this land.'

Courteously then, Bharat dismissed their plea but also promised them that he would personally meet Muni to understand the matter fully. The villagers left disappointed though consoled by the karkarta's promise to meet this so-called Muni. The council chiefs had smiled; this was always the way of the karkarta—let none be sent out empty-handed.

It was then that the singer wanted to speak, but Bharat stopped him again and said, 'The case is decided and judgment given. Do you want to reopen it?'

The singer shook his head, 'No, all I wanted was to sing a song.'

Bharat was delighted and the singer sang soulfully of how Muni restored his eyesight, bringing tears to many eyes.

∼

Bharat was sincere in telling the villagers that he would meet Muni of the Rocks personally. He wanted to see for himself if Muni was such a forbidding personality as the villagers made him out to be or if he was the soul of kindness and compassion that the singer and his daughter had described. To arrange the meeting, he sent his representative to the Rocks.

Bharat's representative bowed respectfully and said, 'Muniji, I bring greetings from our karkarta, Bharatji. He seeks the honour of visiting you.'

Dark clouds of suspicion gathered on Muni's brow. 'Tell me, young man, is your karkarta coming here to charge me with burning the temple? Tell him, I did not burn it. Or does he want to get me out of these rocks? Tell him, I shall not leave. If need be, I shall lift these rocks with my bare hands from their very foundations and hurl them to the centre of the karkarta's town. Do you hear me?'

The representative replied sincerely, 'The karkarta has no such designs. He seeks the honour to visit you with utmost respect.'

Muni felt contrite. 'I am sorry. The karkarta is welcome. Forgive me, I spoke harshly.'

'You had every right; I believe many disturb you foolishly.'

'No. The foolishness has been mine, to disturb the villagers' faith in their idols.' Impressed with the youth's bearing, he added, 'I wish I had your elegance of speech, but I suppose some people are born lucky.'

Muni saw a fleeting shadow of sadness in the youth's eyes and realized that somehow he had, again, said the wrong thing. As a gesture of friendship, he asked: 'What is your name, son?'

'Asudra,' the young man replied. The peculiar name surprised Muni.

Sudra literally meant a slave. By the addition of 'a', Asudra would mean a non-slave or a person who once was a slave but is now free. Later, with the abolition of slavery, the expression 'Sudra' went into disuse. In those pre-ancient times, the caste system did not exist. However, many long centuries after the Aryans returned to India, slowly, the caste system came to be introduced; and the term Sudra came to be revived to mean a person of low caste; and caste oppression grew in India only due to unsavoury effect of foreign domination.

Thus in the larger historical context, the caste system of the Hindu is recent, so much so that even the Sanskrit language—both ancient and modern—has no word which directly or indirectly means 'caste'. By no means, therefore, can caste system be considered a tenet of Sanatan Dharma or Hinduism. It has no sanction in the Vedas. Yet the caste system is believed to have become necessary to avoid disintegration of Hinduism. In those early times, the caste system was flexible, and it was clearly recognized that one could attain the highest state by one's deeds, not by one's family or birth—for instance, Vasistha, a celebrated sage of the Vedic era, was born of a prostitute; Vyasa, another celebrated sage, was the son of a fisherwoman; and similarly, Sage Parasara's mother was a chandala girl, belonging to a family that dealt with the disposal of corpses; Karna, a charioteer's son, was appointed as King of Angadesha and elevated to the position of kshatriya by Duryodhana. Note also: Valmiki, who was an untouchable, became a brahmin, and was recognized as a sage after he changed his wild ways and wrote the most celebrated Hindu epic, the Ramayana. Also, the Maratha armies under seventeenth-century freedom fighter Shivaji, were elevated from sudra to the higher kshatriya status to match their military achievements.' Every Hindu must of course know what Lord Krisna said: 'Birth is not the cause; it is virtues which are the cause of auspiciousness.' A chandala (lower caste) observing the vow is considered a brahmin (highest caste) by the gods. Clearly also, the Bhagvad Gita says: 'All those who take refuge in me, whatever their birth, race, sex, or caste, will attain the supreme goal; this realization can be attained even by those whom society scorns. Kings and sages too seek this goal with devotion.' In the Mahabharata, Yuddhishthir affirms that an individual is defined by qualities of head and heart, not by his birth.

It was later, after the incursion into India of foreigners, that the caste system came to acquire rigidity, making it somewhat difficult for anyone to move to higher castes.

There are of course many reasons for Christian missionaries and foreign commentators to portray the caste system as the ultimate horror.

'Asudra! What family?' Muni asked.

'I am of no family. My mother was a slave. She could not tell who my father was. I hope I have not dishonoured you with my presence.'

'Dishonoured me! No, son, no, I dishonour myself for allowing such a thought to enter your mind.'

Asudra proceeded to tell Muni his story.

In order to keep up the population of slaves, and to ensure that the offspring were healthy, the strongest of male slaves were sent by slave owners, to impregnate female slaves. Asudra was the product of one such loveless union. No one knew who his father was. His mother had died when he was three. He was not strong, having inherited the physical weakness of his mother, so his master was keen to part with him. Mataji Bindu purchased him. She called him Asudra and instantly gave him free status. Later, when he grew up to manhood, the karkarta appointed Asudra to serve as his liaison officer with the headmen. Some people had suggested to him that Asudra was not an appropriate name, but he was proud of it, for it was given to him by Mataji at the moment of his freedom. It was, for him, the only sure link between his unknown past and uncertain future.

Bharat had wanted to adopt him, but by law an adoption could take place only when the natural father of the child agreed to it or if the natural father was dead. As nothing was known about his natural father, these conditions could not be met. However, Bharat had already set up a body of learned men to consider a revision of the law since he felt that a father who abandoned his child or who could not be found for three years should be presumed to have agreed to such adoption.

Meanwhile, Bharat gave Asudra the right to use his family name—Rajavansi. He used that name for official duties as Asudra Rajavansi. But he had felt that he could not appear before Muni in the garb that really was not his.

The life of every man is always a deep, dark forest, Muni thought. He said, 'Karkarta Bharat is wrong to believe that an adoption requires the permission of the natural father, even if no one can locate him. The law cannot be so inflexible.'

'This law, inspired by the ancient sage, Yakantra, is repeated and reinforced by many. Nobody questions it, believe me.'

'I do, but I also believe that there is much that is wrong in treating unrelated songs or stories as sources of true law.'

Muni then explained, 'Yakantra was a poet, a singer and a storyteller, who drew more from his imagination than from reality. His song, in which he referred briefly to the gods adopting a child, was simply a story to amuse children. Yakantra loved children. Rather than be in awe of them, he wanted children to love the gods. Children, he felt, must not regard the gods as infallible. He believed that once children loved the gods as one of their own, there would be time enough, later, for them to understand the ways of God. Let me tell you Yakantra's story, and you be the judge.

'"I, Yakantra, when five years old, was playing with wooden marbles, and I saw Yama charging on a buffalo. Yama, as you know, is a cheerful fellow, always merry and playful and comes to help those who are to die and convey them to the world of the gods. This world, as you know, is only one of the many that God has created and is still creating.

'"But that day no one was to die on the street, otherwise

my parents, who know all, would have told me. I wanted to ask Yama why he had come, but my question remained unasked for his buffalo had displaced my marble just as it was reaching the winning hole. I was so angry that I threw the marble at the buffalo, but it hit Yama instead. Enraged that his master had been hit, the buffalo charged at me.

'"I ran, rushing to the forest, and collided with a lion cub. The lion cub's mother and father, who were nearby, rushed at me, thinking I was attacking their little one, with help from the buffalo and its rider behind me. Yama wanted to protect me from the ferocious lion attack, so he quickly picked me out of the path of lions. But that was his mistake, because Yama cannot touch anyone who is alive. And so I died and went to heaven.

'"Oh! It was great fun to be in heaven! I loved it. But my father called to the gods and asked them to explain Yama's conduct. All the gods met to discuss the situation. They were worried because it was not my time to die—and yet, I was with them. So how could they answer my father's charge!

'"The gods decided to adopt me as their own son. They told my father that I was no longer his son, but theirs. My father protested: 'What right do you gods have to adopt my son, when I, his father, am living and have not given consent?'

'"Now children, the gods could have set Yama on my father also. Then he, too, would have died, and been unable to question them. But the gods are fair and just. They said, 'Two wrongs cannot make a right.'

'"You know children, even if the gods wanted my father to die, I could have prevented that. Because as I had been adopted by the gods, I was a god myself. But the gods are good, fair, just and kind. Their hearts are full of love. So they met again and agreed to send me back to earth, to my parents.

'"But as the gods had already adopted me—and an adoption cannot be broken—I go to heaven whenever I like. I take my dog there too, and Indra shouts when my dog chews his rug.

'"And, as I have already died, I cannot die again, so I shall always be here, and when your children and grandchildren are born, tell them to visit me, for I shall still be here to tell them stories.

'"Ah children, you are laughing. You don't believe my story! Well, I don't believe it myself either."'

∾

Muni continued, 'I have given you merely the gist of a long story that speaks also of the duties of children, parents and the gods. But do you see that Yakantra ends his story by saying that he didn't believe the story himself? Even Yakantra's adopted son, who became a respected sage himself, said that Yakantra laughed at his story of adoption as did the children, who did not believe a word of it though they enjoyed it immensely.'

Asudra stared. 'Surely, this story could not be the basis for the belief that a father must be proved dead or found, to consent to adoption!'

'I know of no other source. Words from his story were taken out of context and woven by later poets into their songs. In particular, the words "What right did you have to adopt my son, when I, his father, have not given consent?" Yet,' Muni paused to smile, 'our people, wise with age and old with white hair—or none at all—choose to consider such stories the true foundation of the Law.'

'Why?' Asudra asked.

'There are those among us who believe that whatever is rooted in antiquity is authentic, worthy, pious. For them, it is as if the ancients never laughed, and all they were concerned with was to leave their ponderous utterances to guide us. There are, of course, others who credit the ancients with nothing but primitiveness, ignorance and indolence—devoid of reason, rationality and intelligence. But the truth . . . '

'The truth?' Asudra prompted.

'The truth? Our ancients had their half-truths and we have ours. I wish I could say that the truth lies somewhere in between. But man's quest for the truth continues and the ultimate truth is still beyond us. Meanwhile, we must simply follow the path of ananda, so long as it is with ahimsa to others and oneself.'

'Ahimsa to oneself?' Asudra wondered aloud.

'Of course,' said Muni. 'Your body is the temple of your soul. Must it not be kept away from impurity? If ahimsa imposes a duty to avoid hurt or harm to another, how can you conceive of hurting your own body! Is it not then necessary to avoid inebriation, over-eating, indiscriminate sex, and even associating with people of violence!' Muni added smilingly, 'Yes, people of violence, like me.'

He continued, 'Yes, you can hurt your body, willingly, for a higher cause, or to protect your soul—and when such rare demands are made, one must respond, even to sacrifice one's life.' Asudra nodded and Muni added, 'But above all, it is your own soul that you must protect with ahimsa, in thought and deed. Man's soul is a part of the Supreme. When liberated, it attains the world of the Lord of Creation and becomes one with the Lord. Your soul is not a creature of God, but God himself. God is pure. Your self—the soul within you—must remain undefiled, untouched by sin. For remember, the soul has to be in union with the ultimate for eternal bliss. Therefore, practice ahimsa also with your self and soul.'

Asudra nodded. 'I had thought ahimsa meant avoiding physical injury to other people.'

'To people? No, my son. Ahimsa is not restricted to humanity alone. There may be forgiveness for transgressions against humanity, for humans can provoke and retaliate. But what forgiveness is there for a man who will wantonly offend against a cow, an elephant, a lamb or a deer! Or for a man who aims an arrow at a parrot or an owl, or destroys trees and offends against nature! What use can the soul of God have for the soul of a man who permits himself to do dark, evil, ugly things to other creatures of God! Do you believe that man was created simply to destroy beauty and the treasures of the earth in which God Himself breathed life with infinite love and endless patience! Do you believe it is man's destiny to become a destroyer of those things that live with nature and be surrounded by creatures hostile to him, fearful of him, fleeing in terror at the scent of his flesh and the sound of his footsteps!'

Asudra felt Muni's rising vehemence as he continued, 'You also spoke of physical injury. But the hurt to the heart can be deeper. It is that which I often forget. Yet neither knowledge, nor wisdom, nor prayer is above the principle of ahimsa.'

'Perhaps I am too old to learn God's ways,' Muni added gently. 'But you, who are young, should never be without the hope of moksha, to unite with the very soul of God, as your mother has done.'

'Moksha!' Asudra was shaken to the core. 'My mother has moksha!'

'What else! She was a slave, you said—chained to man's will, with no pleasures of her own, unable to speak her heart out, living in filth, misery, subject to man's cruelties. You think God does not reserve a special place in the heart of His soul for victims of man?'

Asudra was in a daze. 'My mother! Moksha!' Asudra whispered to himself.

'Yes, your mother,' Muni said slowly, measuring each word, 'because the *soul* of God has the *heart* of God.'

A flash of ecstasy passed over Asudra's face, as Muni continued, 'Yes, we are discussing that one must follow one's own ananda and if it can be achieved with honour, go fearlessly where you want to go. So, if Bharatji still wishes to adopt you, he should.'

'My adoption! Bharatji considered it when I was a child.

Only children younger than twelve can be adopted.'

Muni laughed. 'Let me then summarize for you another song by Sage Yakantra.'

Children of this valley prayed to God, sad that their parents came home weary from work, with no time to tell stories. So they asked God either to abolish work or give them a storyteller,

God stroked his long, white beard, and thought long and hard; then he decided that work could not be abolished, but the children's request for a storyteller was just.

Now God had a young angel, who was only ninety years old, and he was His best storyteller. But God said, 'I cannot send him, for everyone on earth must have a father, so I must ask someone worthy, someone good and honourable on earth to adopt this angel.'

But then a three-year-old child cried out, 'I will adopt him.'

Again, God thought long and hard, and said: 'Who can be more worthy and more honourable than a three-year old child!'

So, children, that is how I, Yakantra, an angel who was ninety years old, came to be adopted by a child of three.

Concluding the story, Muni smiled, 'So if Yakantra's stories for children are being regarded as an authority on adoption, you are eligible for it till the age of ninety!'

Asudra laughed. 'I love, respect and honour Bharatji, but now I would not wish to be adopted. I shall remain the son of my departed mother and my nameless father. If I had hatred in my heart, it was for my father who brought me, loveless, to this world. But now I know that he too was helpless—a victim—as much as my mother was.'

'Of course,' Muni said softly, 'a victim of his own past life, for which he paid in this life, to go to his final goal of moksha.'

Asudra nodded. 'I shall go to Sage Yakantra's ashram and hear his songs to try and separate fact from fantasy.'

'Not an easy task. There is, sometimes, more truth in fantasy than in fact. But let us not misjudge Yakantra. His moments of laughter were few, but when he was with the children his heart was full of cheer and he could laugh easily. For the rest, his was an eternal, unceasing search, but again with faith, certain that God shall reach him. You should hear all his songs.'

Asudra nodded. 'Yes, I must.'

'Go to Lurkan. They will guide you to the ashram of the yogi of a thousand years. That is how Yakantra is known by some. Each successor of Yakantra takes the same name. Thus he keeps his promise to children to remain a thousand years on earth and a thousand years in heaven.' Then Muni asked, 'Bharatji was concerned over the phantom of an adoption law, torn from Yakantra's words of laughter? And yet, is there not a law that persons from slave stock cannot be taken into public service? Then how did he give you this position?'

'The law preventing former slaves from joining public service was adopted only a century ago, in fear that the then karkarta would give a place of honour to a son born from his affair with a slave woman. It was not a law based on immemorial custom and Bharatji could abolish it.'

'And no one objected to his admitting former slaves into public service?'

'Many grumbled, but they were consoled by the belief that former slaves would never reach the level of intelligence needed for public service.'

'Is that the reason Bharatji gave?'

'No, Bharatji said freedom is freedom, and when a slave is freed, he must have all the attributes and opportunities of a free man.'

'Did not people realize that Bharat was changing the law in order to appoint you?'

'No, Muniji. Bharatji abolished that odious law long before he gave me the position. At the time, he had no individual in mind—only the principle.'

'And were you as good as the others when Bharatji selected you?'

'I had to be, because Bharatji said that my past entitled me to receive two times the training, but for the sake of my future, I had to be three times better than the others.'

'But if Bharatji is so enlightened, how is it that he does not abolish slavery altogether, if indeed he wants the gods to be on his side?'

'He also wants the people on his side,' Asudra replied. 'When he first suggested the abolition of slavery, they made such a noise that if he had persisted, they would have removed him from office.'

'And is it good to hold office amongst such people?'

'Should not a man lead his people in the hope that one day he might change them? This karkarta is a man of God, but he is also a man of the people. He will bring the two nearer each other.'

Muni sensed Asudra's love for Bharat and ceased his questions. 'Tell the karkarta, he is welcome here, and if he brings you I shall be doubly pleased.'

~

Karkarta Bharat, impressed by Asudra's detailed report of his conversation with Muni, travelled to the Rocks. He had planned a few hours' visit, but stayed for two days. That was his first visit and so charmed was he with Muni and Roopa that he visited them often until some years before his retirement.

Their discussions, during Bharat's visits to Muni, had

touched on many subjects including slavery which, they both agreed, violated the tenets of Sanatan Dharma and ahimsa. They spoke also of the carvings that Ekantra had discovered in the cave, depicting different figures in a circle and other mysterious etchings. Muni agreed with Bharat that the artists who had carved those figures were trying to tell the story of the extinction of certain species including the possible destruction of the vroun by man. Muni also spoke of the giant birds and animals that had vanished from the face of the earth—the 250-foot-long makar or magar, the predecessor of the crocodile, whose fossils had been seen by some; of the Garuda bird, that was as tall as the combined height of twenty men; of the Ajay bird, larger than a cloud, whose flight caused a shadow to fall from one end of the village to the other, and who was known to lay an egg each spring, but later shrunk in size and laid a single egg throughout its lifespan of 150 years; of the Doli fish which carried camels, elephants and other animals from one shore to another during a flood or a drought or simply for pleasure; of the Humana ape-bird, which flew from one mountain top to another, throwing down herbs and plants for sick animals and fish; and of the biggest of them all, the mighty Candara, that could, with one flick of his abrasive tongue, gather in his mouth weeds, thorns and underbrush for a tenth of a yojna (half a mile) uprooting everything, but leaving the trees untouched, and spitting out insects and birds, unharmed.

Maybe, said Muni, the stories of what these mammoth creatures did were all a myth. But there was no doubt in his mind that these creatures really and truly had existed for there were those who had seen their remains. But no one knew what those creatures actually did for after all, man, howsoever ancient, came to inhabit the earth long after those giant birds and animals were gone.

But why did they disappear? To make place for man? But if they went, would not man also abide his hour or two in this vast scheme of eternity and disappear? Was it then possible that evolution was still in the making and that man might be eventually eliminated by another being!

'Who knows!' Muni said, but he also reminded Bharat of what Sage Bhardwaj had said, 'The earth is eternal, and so is man if he lives in harmony with nature. But man cannot destroy the earth; and if he tries that by folly or design, then only mankind shall perish, not the eternal ground on which man walks.'

Bharat also mentioned Yadodhra's theory to Muni.

'The possibility of life on the planets remains,' Yadodhra had said. 'How can we be arrogant enough to believe that life exists nowhere except on this earth! But if there is no life on some planets now, the chances are that there was life there in the past, which is now extinct because of misuse of the planet and the violation of God's laws; and God waits with His immeasurable patience to renew life there, perhaps in a form and shape altogether different. Here, too, on this earth, were we to abuse God's laws, it is not as if the earth would vanish. No. Only we, mankind, would disappear.

'And then there are planets and stars still in the making, as the miracle of evolution continues endlessly. What is building is forever building, unstopped and unstoppable; and surely there shall be life in those planets and stars in the future.'

Muni fully endorsed the view that the misuse of or violence against nature could bring about the extinction of life, and that God would wait with immeasurable wisdom to create new life. He also pointed out that all the carvings which depicted the emergence of the human figure long after so many species had disappeared, including the vroun, were in a circle. Possibly, he suggested, the circle indicated the earth itself. But was the earth circular? At least all those early artists seemed to think so. But why not! The moon, sun and stars were circular. Was anything in nature in the form of a square or rectangle? The human body, the face, hips, buttocks,

BHAGWAN S. GIDWANI

women's breasts—were they not all in curves and circles?

In those early visits, Bharat had also seen Muni in meditation. He knew that before a worshipper becomes one with the spirit through yoga, certain visions of mist, nebulous smoke, lightning, are experienced within, with an inner glow, and then the yogi's face is transformed and there is a certain radiance on it when passing into samadhi. He saw the same glow and radiance on Muni's face. Clearly, the peace and love of God were within him.

Bharat had also discussed several worldly affairs and asked Muni's advice on how to accelerate the development of 'a language that could be seen'—a written language, on building larger, faster and more dependable boats for longer voyages in rough weather in the Sindhu Samundar. Based on Muni's advice, Bharat had expanded the programme of sending men and materials to the lower Sindhu to assist in the project of boat-building. Also, teachers all over the land were encouraged to familiarize themselves with the alphabet of the written language being evolved.

～

It had been ten years since Bharat had last visited Muni. Yet the affection with which he and Roopa had received him and Sindhu Putra and their obvious delight in taking charge of the child's education convinced Bharat that his decision to entrust Sindhu Putra to their care was right, and no other alternative could even remotely match the wisdom of this choice.

ELEVEN

THE ENEMY WITHIN

5068 BCE

Bharat returned to his retreat along with the singer to a loud, ecstatic welcome from the dogs.

'How I wish humans could learn to demonstrate such love and happiness over reunion!' the singer remarked.

Next day, they resumed their conversation about the affairs of the clan under the new karkarta, Nandan.[*]

The singer told Bharat much of what was happening. The clan was more prosperous; the diversion of the Sindhu and Saraswati rivers into new channels, commenced in Bharat's time, had begun to pay rich dividends; new lands were under cultivation; new villages and towns were springing up; expeditions to faraway lands had met with astonishing success; the clan's territory had expanded. People had more wealth, more amenities, and more leisure. But clearly, also, a new wind was blowing. Nepotism and wealth were obstructing the rule of law, and new kinds of divisions and hatreds were creeping in, bringing the threat of disunity with them. Karkarta Nandan had pitted different guilds against each other and even enlisted preachers to support the causes he championed.

---

[*] After Bharat retired, Dhru was elected as karkarta but was soon assassinated. There were whispered rumours that Council Chief Nandan had masterminded the assassination but there was no evidence at all and the rumours were untrue. Nandan was elected as twenty-first karkarta. For Dhru's achievements and Nandan's election, see *Return of the Aryans*.

'Why does Nandan wish to create divisions? To what end?' Bharat asked.

The singer replied, 'So that each guild may learn to quarrel with the other, and each may look to him, alone, and none other, for protection.'

Bharat was also sad when the singer told him that headmen were no longer to be elected but appointed by the karkarta. 'Nandan could do a lot of damage in these fifteen years as karkarta,' said Bharat.

'Fifteen years! Why only fifteen years?' the singer asked.

'He is, I think, forty-five years old now. Did I not establish a principle that a karkarta, like everyone else, must retire at sixty?'

'Did you really!' the singer asked. 'The council and the assembly ruled that a karkarta can serve till the end of his natural life. You simply chose to walk away and did not offer yourself for re-election. When Nandan became karkarta, his first official act was to approve a number of the decisions made by the council and the assembly and amongst them was the decree that the karkarta does not have to retire.'

'And the precedent I set has no value then?' Bharat asked.

'To a man of honour, yes. To Nandan, no.'

'But what about the people? Surely Nandan faces them for re-election, after each seven-year term!'

'Exactly. That is why he has to create even more divisions among them, so that he alone remains the single, solid symbol of unity.'

The singer told Bharat of the sense of complacency growing in the clan, as more wealth poured in with less effort. With new territories came greater comforts and luxuries. New expeditions were being sent out to claim more land, and those who undertook such enterprises were allowed to deal as they chose with the indigenous people.

True, the singer added, some had begun to worry over the divisions and blocks forming in the land that Bharat had left united. Voices of unity—a few, isolated and scattered—were lost in the wilderness. 'And you know the faith our people generally have in those that lead them! In any case, Nandan has loyal supporters who, with fakery and fraud, propagate his false doctrines and cruel hatreds, and invent perilous lies to splinter the clan's ancient beliefs into fragments.'

Bharat again wondered where the disunity in the hearts of his people would lead them. He thought it strange that these new and vile hatreds should lift their deadly heads when prosperity had begun to smile on his clan after he had defeated the raiders from the north and east, and united them with the land of the Hindu. Is it that when danger does not threaten from *outside,* that people choose to create demons *inside* themselves and rush to self-destruction? Surely, that was not so! He believed what the people of Sanatan Dharma had believed for countless generations—the gods, with their mercy and compassion, sought to *unite*, not *divide* mankind.

The singer then told him that Nandan's adherents criticized Bharat for abolishing slavery in tribal lands and declaring that if any slave of the clan entered tribal land with the permission or connivance of his owner, that slave would be deemed free. In doing so, they said, he had not only interfered with their age-old custom, but prevented them from taking their slaves to tribal lands to take advantage of many real opportunities there.

'Yes, of course, I did that,' Bharat explained, 'I could not abolish slavery in our land. I was helpless and lacked public support. But I certainly did not want the slaves in our land to be sent to exploit tribal lands. It would have sent a wrong message and encouraged the tribals to reintroduce slavery in their land. So the least I could do was to keep our slave owners and their slaves away from tribal lands, hoping that the future would provide the opportunity to abolish slavery in our own land itself.'

'I know and I honour you for it. Yet, Nandan's adherents

think you imposed a burden on your own people and often refer to it as an unpatriotic act on your part. Why, Nandan himself had the temerity to mention this to Sage Yadodhra. I have even composed a memory song about the exchange between Nandan and Yadodhra.'

NANDAN: 'I can never consider Bharat unpatriotic, but there are some who complain that Bharat was unpatriotic in imposing this burden on our own people when the tribals never asked for this protection.'

YADODHRA: 'Fidelity to one's own land and culture is consistent with compassion for humanity. Maybe Bharat heard a voice in his heart saying that all men are children of the Immortal and it is treason to the Majesty of the One who is Real to permit or promote slavery. How can we prevent a · yogi from hearing the voice of his conscience?'

NANDAN: 'Yadodhra! Please understand! Bharat became a yogi recently when he retired to become a hermit. I speak of the time when he was karkarta, when the union with the tribals was established.'

YADODHRA: 'I know Bharat became a yogi recently. But in my view, he was always a yogi at heart.'

NANDAN LAUGHED: 'I suppose, next, you will compare Bharat not to a yogi but even to a god!'

YADODHRA: 'Is there a difference between a yogi and a god?'

NANDAN: 'But slavery, Yadodhraji, is ancient . . . .'

YADODHRA INTERRUPTED: 'Humanity, I think, is more ancient.'

The singer continued, 'Since then, Nandan himself has avoided making the charge that you were unpatriotic, but his supporters have not been so restrained.'

TWELVE

MY LAND, MY PEOPLE! TIMES OF KARKARTA NANDAN

5053 BCE

'Honour the hermit by all means . . . but remember that the interests of humanity cannot lie simply in deep passions of spiritualism. For a civilization to grow, it must first learn to harness the forces of bounteous nature, and with effort, labour and persistence, it must nurture them to grow to eliminate hunger and want and to achieve for its people material joys and rewards . . . Then only can it be possible for humanity to think of a higher life, to be serene with the love of wisdom, to lead a life of meaningful self-denial, and to dream strange dreams and burst forth in joyous songs . . . The first condition, then, for thinking minds to blossom, is a settled society which provides material needs, wealth, security and absence of external and internal enemies . . . Leisure shall then follow and only then is renunciation well earned . . . '

(From Karkarta Nandan's address to the Parliament of the Hindu—5065 BCE)

Nandan, the twenty-first karkarta, sat idly under a great tree in the garden of his house. It was his sixtieth birthday and also the first holiday he had permitted himself during his fifteen-year tenure as karkarta.

As he contemplated the Sindhu river and the silvery vista of the city on either side, he felt that he could look deep into the entire north and south. His mind went far beyond his field of vision to the foaming sea and distant mountains with their immense range and elevation; to mighty rivers with their abundant bounty; to lush forests and broad fields; to well-built towns with their wide avenues, and to the valleys and plains, teeming with life and activity.

The election of karkarta was now a mere formality, and undoubtedly Nandan was karkarta of his people for life. After which, he wanted to see his younger son, Sharat, elected to the office for he could think of no worthier successor.

Sharat shall be one of the council chiefs now, resolved Nandan. In time, he will be senior enough to head the council, and then I can retire and he can succeed me as karkarta.

The only obstacle to overcome was the age-old prohibition that a karkarta's family members could not succeed him to the office. 'Well, one more hurdle to encounter—and to overcome,' Nandan told himself.

Deep down, Nandan loved his clan passionately. He was convinced that the inscrutable wisdom of Providence and the inexorable process of destiny had ordained that his clan would always be in a preeminent position. If he needed any proof of that, all he had to do was to look around at the barbarism of the tribes around them. As a young boy, he had joined Bharat's expeditions against the raiders and in those arduous battles he saw the terrible condition of various tribes. And while his companions were moved to pity, he was thankful for the culture of his own clan. He found Bharat's friendly treatment of tribals distasteful and gave up soldiering, determined to dictate policy rather than be a puppet of policy. With his family's wealth and prestige supporting him and his success in several civic fields, he was soon elected as an assembly member.

Nandan loved his clan as he saw it—free, proud, clothed in honour, steeped in culture, industrious, frugal, just and benevolent. Like Sadhu Gandhara, he, too, did not know how far the earth extended, but he was convinced that his own land and clan were the greatest. He deeply regretted Bharat and Dhru's obsession with uniting the clan with various tribes. Maybe their initial motives were not foolish or evil, as they felt that their clan's rich culture could assimilate new tribes, so why have enemies on their borders! But when the clan had expanded so far, it was time to call a halt. It was extremely expensive to assimilate tribals. They had to be provided with food, clothing and shelter, at least initially, and the clan ran the risk of contaminating its own culture.

Nandan had developed something in the nature of a religious faith in the paramount importance of his own clan and its culture. He would tolerate no challenge to it. When he became karkarta, he resolved, he would be benevolent, even helpful to the new territories, but he would see to it that his clan remained cold, aloof and distant from their culture and way of life. Nothing must stand in the way of the greater glory of the Hindu clan.

'God! Let me be the one to lead the Hindu on to the path of glory.'

❧

Nandan looked up as a messenger approached with a bulky package.

'From Naudhyaksa. The superintendent of ships sends his regards on the auspicious occasion of your birthday,' the messenger said.

'Naudhyaksa!' Nandan asked. 'From my son Vasistha, you mean! Now he is called Naudhyaksa, is he?'

'It was a title conferred on him by the combined decision of sixty-five shreshthas of the sea-people of the lower Sindhu.'

'Sixty-five shreshthas! I thought the lower Sindhu had sixty-six shreshthas.'

'We still do,' the messenger responded, smiling. The sixty-sixth shreshtha was, as they both knew, Vasistha's wife. Naturally, the wife and close relatives abstained from resolutions seeking to honour their own.

Vasistha, Nandan's elder son, had gone to the lower Sindhu several years earlier as a junior member of a large group sent by Karkarta Bharat under Naupati,* an experienced boat-builder, to study the boat-building techniques of the sea-people.

Most members of the group had returned after a while, but Vasistha, along with Naupati and Pilava, remained behind. They were making phenomenal progress in building bigger, faster and more dependable boats for longer voyages in rough weather. Under Naupati's guidance, they had built a huge vessel with upraised bow and stern to overtake the fastest boats and withstand the turbulence of the waves. Naupati was killed during the ship's experimental voyage when a loosely tied anchor-stone struck him. After Naupati's death, Vasistha worked under Pilava, with more than two hundred sea-people, to build sturdy sea-faring vessels. Under Karkarta Bharat's orders, every assistance was sent to them. The land was scoured for suitable wood, leather, baskets, and ropes. Special cutting, trimming and sanding implements were made for them.

Pilava, too, died tragically when he went out to sea alone at night during a storm to study the behaviour of waves. He never returned. That night, the town was celebrating

---

*   It was in Naupati's honour that all ships were called *nau*. His name literally meant husband of Nau. As the poet explains, his original name was Thukra, son of Bhoja, but he changed his name to Naupati at the death of his wife who was named Nau, because she, with her dying breath, called him Naupati.

Vasistha's wedding.

After Pilava's death, Vasistha led the ship-building enterprise, putting his heart and soul into it. Nandan was unable to persuade Vasistha to return home, for Vasistha was unmoved by his father's suggestions that one day he might become the council chief or even the karkarta. It was then that Nandan decided to groom his younger son Sharat for the karkarta's office.

Vasistha's dedication to his work and the continued assistance from the clan helped him make remarkable progress in ship-building. He had also discovered a suitable location for a dockyard, southeast of the mouth of the Sindhu river, near the Sindhu Samundar. It was a sheltered harbour into which the Bhogava and Savarmati rivers flowed. In this ideal setting, both for sea and river navigation, he began construction of a massive dockyard of burnt brick reinforced by mortar, bitumen and other building materials. When completed, it measured 170 dhanus by 35 dhanus (approximately 1000 feet by 200 feet). Through a gap in the eastern embankment, ships were intended to be sluiced into the dockyard at high tide through an inlet 40 feet wide. Where the inlet cut into the side of the dockyard, a low wall retained sufficient water within the docks at low tide to permit the ships to be moved. A loading platform, about 1100 feet long, ran along the western embankment of the dockyard.

Nandan was impressed with Vasistha's achievements, but could not resist adding that had slaves been permitted, it would have finished even sooner.

'But there would have been no pride in our achievement then,' Vasistha replied simply.

Nandan silently regretted that his son had assimilated Bharat's philosophy and the beliefs of the sea-people so completely. He had thought that the time Vasistha spent with Bharat involved discussions related only to ship-building. But later he learnt that Bharat had talked about far more with

Vasistha, including the need to honour the sea-people's repugnance towards the system of slavery and how such a system involved the negation of god-given principles. Still, Nandan loved his son, and the sea-people, for he, like Bharat, believed that 'the links that bound them to our people were far stronger, more ancient and abiding than those that divided them.'

Nandan broke free of his thoughts as his wife and grandson came out to see Vasistha's gift. His wife opened the large package, covered with layers of bark. The child shouted with excitement, 'It is a toy! For me!'

It was not a toy. It was a miniature model of a sea-faring vessel. Apparently, Vasistha's team had nearly completed the vessel. As he examined the model, Nandan began counting the many tiny oars in it, but soon gave up.

'It will have a hundred oars?' he asked the messenger.

'One hundred and eight,' the messenger responded.

'What is this on the sides?' Nandan asked, pointing to two projections on the sides.

'They are devices to serve as the ship's stabilizer,' the messenger replied. 'They will help the ship withstand a heavy battering from a storm-tossed sea.' He referred to them as 'nau-manda'. He further explained that their present ships largely hugged the coast, afraid to go into the deep, except in fine weather, but the new vessels would be different.

'Naudhyaksa, your son,' the messenger added, 'also has a request.'

'Consider it granted,' Nandan promptly responded.

'He seeks your permission to name his ship after you, and fly your flag.'

Nandan felt thrilled that his son should wish to honour him so. But he said, 'Thank my son and tell him that my time to receive such an honour, if it is ever to come, has not arrived yet. But if he wants my suggestion, he should name the ship after Pilava, his senior who first dreamt of such a ship and who died in the effort to discover what angry waves can do to our vessels.'

The grandchild looked sadly at the projections on the ship's model which he had thought were wings. 'Why did he put in nau-manda?'

'Did you not hear? To stabilize the ship,' Nandan replied.

'He should have put wings instead. The ship could fly then.'

'Ships don't fly.'

'They do! Ma tells me stories of flying ships in which gods and goddesses travel. I saw a flying chariot in a drama.'

'Yes, ships and chariots fly in stories and dramas, but in real life flying ships are yet to arrive.'

'When?'

'When little ones like you grow up, when they dare a dream and work to realize it, then ships and chariots shall fly.'

'They will?'

'Certainly they will,' replied Nandan. 'With persistence of effort and labour, I know of no dream that can remain unfulfilled.'

His grandson still had questions—'will flying ships go to the moon?'

'In time, why not!' Nandan smiled. 'Maybe beyond, to the planets, stars, and galaxies unseen and unknown.'

'Are there people living on the stars and planets?'

'Maybe,' Nandan replied wondering, like all grandparents, why children always asked unanswerable questions.

But it seemed that the child knew the answer and was merely testing the limits of his grandfather's knowledge. Jubilantly, he said, 'Ma says that Sage Yadodhra said that people live on other planets.'

'If your mother told you that, why must you ask me?'

'She said you would know better.'

Nandan smiled. Indeed he did know better—not if there was life on the planets, but what Yadodhra had said. The idea of life on other planets was charming, but Nandan was interested in this world, in this life, and the question of life on other planets did not concern him. He was certain of only one thing: life existed all over, on earth itself—beyond the snow-capped peaks of the Himalayas, beyond the rushing rivers and the vast sea surging in the lower Sindhu.

Affectionately, he looked at the model of the ship Vasistha had sent. The sea was vast but, he thought, it must end somewhere—and then their ships would lead them to discover the lands beyond.

Silently, he resolved to halt all other public works that could wait, so as to send unlimited materials and men to assist the ship-building projects.

Let those ships be a reality in my lifetime, Nandan prayed, and let me be the one to guide my people to lands beyond—and to glory.

∼

Two years later, *Pilava*—the first major ship—was ready to sail in the Sindhu Sammundar. Unfortunately, it met with disaster on its maiden voyage and Vasistha and his crew perished with it.

Nandan was devastated. Yet, he redoubled his efforts to continue the ship-building projects. Six years later, his perseverance was rewarded as ships crossed the Sindhu Samundar and reached the deserted coastlines of Persia and the Gulf. The years that followed were even more eventful in the clan's nautical enterprise, with many explorations using bigger, better ships.

Meanwhile, on the mainland, Nandan was succeeding in his project to discover new territories. He had sent out teams in all directions to discover and occupy distant lands. He even encouraged his people to go and settle in those new territories. He was convinced, like Rishi Skanda Dasa—

though their aims and ends were different—that lands left unoccupied would attract demons.

What Nandan really longed for was to blaze new trails and expand 'Hindu Varsha'—the land of the Hindu. The clan made remarkable advances in shipping, exploration and other areas. Naturally, Nandan could take credit for all those developments even though the projects had been initiated by Bharat during his time as karkarta.

೬

The efforts of Muni Manu, who was working on evolving a full-fledged written language, had begun to show signs of success even before Bharat retired from the office of karkarta. Muni Manu had begun this task nearly fifty years ago, but along the way he had also worked on a number of other fields, notably astronomy and mathematics, including equations for minute divisions of time, starting with heartbeats, and later extended to bodies falling to the ground with a co-relation of weight, speed and distance. Not all these were entirely theoretical applications and apart from other processes, these came to be used to compare competitive performance in sports and races—of men, animals, carts and chariots. Later, Yadodhra joined Muni Manu and together they worked on calculating the age of ancient trees, earth, mountains, and rivers, and on concepts of time and space.

It was in Nandan's time that Muni Manu finally completed the alphabet and signs and symbols to go with it, in order to clarify sound, intonation, emphasis, sex, number and other distinctions. Bharat, Nandan and others were very impressed when they had first seen a preliminary presentation of the written language.

Nandan was now delighted with the final presentation and remarked, 'It has the precision of arithmetic and the expanse of a storyteller.' Along with 'words to be seen', also came advice about materials on which, and tools with which, the alphabet could be written, sculpted, etched or painted—and how the bark and leaf could be treated, depending on whether the written word was intended 'for the time being' or was a record for 'generations waiting to be born'.

The presentation was made by Manu's granddaughter for he had lost his sight by the time he completed the last sign and symbol. According to legend, he had begun losing eyesight in the midst of his work and would have turned totally blind, leaving it unfinished, but for 'the prayers of his granddaughter Kriti who asked the gods to take away her sight and give it to Muni Manu to complete his life's work'. It was believed that when Muni Manu completed his work, Kriti's eyesight was restored and Manu lost his.

The written language did not become popular overnight. It spread slowly. It had earlier taken effort on Bharat's part to overcome opposition from the teacher's guild to include it as a compulsory subject in schools in the future when Muni Manu would complete his work. Nandan encouraged it strongly and it began to gain ground as more and more people saw its advantages. The poets were assured that their songs would remain, for though human memory would fade, the written word would render their poetry immortal; lovers could send messages instead of having them shouted by irreverent messengers to their sweethearts; and everyone came to recognize the superiority of the written word in matters of everyday trade, buying and selling on credit, money-lending and banking.

Nandan took pains to learn the written language. As a council member under Bharat, and as the council head under Dhru, he supported every move to encourage it. He agreed that 'the written word is far above any human invention and shall represent the very essence of our sanskriti to unite people'.

And it was truly so. The spoken languages of the various

peoples in the Sapta Sindhu region differed in many ways. Yet, with written language, a synthesis began to emerge, where the words came to be adopted as synonyms and alternatives to express the same thought. The written word, thus, began influencing spoken language and the emerging common language became richer, more expressive and highly versatile. And certainly, the synthesis brought people closer to each other emotionally and culturally.

There were some who complained that when new words from other regions were absorbed into a language, its purity was lost. But a poet retorted, 'Only the unborn and the dead are pure, and so it is with the language. And the purity you seek is illusory.'

Nandan supported the written language from public funds in schools and outside. He kept insisting that the written word would bind the culture and civilization of the land of the Hindu.

～

At that time, also, a physician was regarded as an important member of the community. His job was to prevent sickness, not merely to cure it. Sage Dhanawantar and his wife Dhanawantri made considerable contributions to advancing the system of medicine and surgery in that ancient era.

As karkarta, Nandan provided generous assistance to physicians, particularly to Sage Dhanawantar. The sage gave his disciples two main guiding principles:

The health of your patients and their recovery is of paramount importance, even at the cost of your own health. You do not choose patients. Their pain and agony calls to you. Do not pass it by—be he a master, servant or slave, rich or poor, man or animal.

By all means, pray for and with your patients, if you wish.

And surely, if your prayers have no effect on your patients, they are at least good for your mental health and to guard your soul.

Sage Dhanawantar described six 'winds' which cause bodily functions—udana, from the throat responsible for speech; prana, from the heart for breathing; somana, fanning a cooking fire in the stomach to separate digestible food; vyana that caused bloodflow to and from the heart; ojas, a diffused wind throughout the body producing energy for bodily functions; and apana that produced semen for sex and procreation.

The sage explained how food is digested and how blood, bone marrow and semen are formed. He listed the functions of the spinal cord, and located eighteen centres in the brain which were the seats of learning, memory, the nervous system, psychic energy and other impulses. Dhanawantar's views on the relationship between the brain and heart were, later, criticized. For instance, he speculated that there was another diffused 'wind'—the 'inner voice'—which measured, weighed and assessed all that the brain wanted to do, and sometimes, it encouraged or even opposed what the brain contemplated, though the brain was the commander and could reject or accept what the inner voice whispered. Many found his views on the adverse effect on the individual's health as a result of the brain rejecting the advice of the 'inner voice' unacceptable. They simply believed that the brain considered all options and finally selected, unopposed, the course that appealed to it.

The sage's wife, Dhanawantri, was also criticized for some of her theories. She conceived three main stages of the functioning of the human brain. In its first stage, the brain received and interpreted outside signals (such as by eyesight, sounds, the sensations of touch or smell). In the second stage, processes took place to analyse those signals and to evolve a plan of action, and in the third stage, the brain issued commands to the body for movement, speech, or any other action or inaction. None objected to these views or to her view of the two organisms of the brain—the 'Stream of the Conscious' and the 'Stream of the Unconscious'. But she was criticized much when she went far afield to speculate that the 'Stream of the Unconscious' had another current, which possibly arose before one was born and remained after one died and that much of its content came from one's past lives and would go forward to one's next series of lives, 'enriched or seasoned by experience of our sojourn in the present'. This hidden, undying 'current', according to her, could be tapped by the wise, for its knowledge of the 'infinite unknown' and 'the memory of what happened before one was born and possibly a preconception of what may happen after one died'. She gave the instance of infants finding music and lullaby soothing, even before they could understand anything else, for it was the familiar sound heard by them for countless past generations.

Their critics complained that the sage and his wife often forgot the line between scientific study and philosophy, but Dhanawantar always held that one led to the other and cheerfully accepted any criticism. To his students, he said: 'If only my ignorance equalled my knowledge, I would know a trillion times more. So be sure, dear students, to question all that I say and investigate everything yourselves.'

Priests disliked Sage Dhanawantar—except when they were sick themselves and needed his attention—as he was suspected of performing dissections on dead bodies. They held that the body served as the temple of the soul and had to be respected even after death. It was entitled to prayers and cremation, and had to be kept whole. Some asked the sage if he had actually dissected bodies, but his reply was, 'A physician never betrays a patient's secret; is he not to guard his own secret!' Dhanawantar always declined to confirm or deny any questions about his personal life or even his charities and when pressed, he would say, 'God and my wife know all my secrets. Let that be.' Since he refused to deny the charge, many assumed that he had performed dissections, especially when they saw his drawings and descriptions of the functioning of the human body; such intimate knowledge was impossible to come by without dissection.

A furor arose when the hermit Dhrona 'willed' that after his death, his body be given to Sage Dhanawantar for dissection. Dhrona had become a hermit at the age of twenty-eight. He was healthy, strong and as he was expected to outlive Dhanawantar, no one took his will seriously. But Dhrona died after a brief illness at the age of forty-four. Purohits approached Nandan, saying that Dhrona's will was unlawful. 'Ashes to ashes, let it be, and neither desecrate nor abominate what once was the dwelling of God's soul,' they argued. Fortunately for Nandan, Dhrona's family quickly rushed to cremate the body, assisted by several purohits who were paid handsomely for performing the last rites at such short notice.

After Dhanawantar's death, his wife Dhanawantri went to Avagana—modern-day Afghanistan—where she remained with Vaid, a physician from the Sindhu region who had been nominated by Karkarta Dhru as headman and chief administrator of Avagana but had since retired as a hermit. It was believed that Dhanawantri and Vaid got married. It was in Avagana that Dhanawantri developed a comprehensive system of surgery. The taboo on dissecting dead bodies had not found its way into Avagana; battlefields there gave her the opportunity to improve the surgical training of students, who became experts in plastic surgery, far beyond anything known at that time; they could repair fingers, noses, ears and lips injured and lost in battle.

∽

Nandan thought of the achievements of his people in agriculture, housing, shipbuilding, language, medicine and surgery, and his own part in facilitating all this progress. Nothing can hold us back, he said to himself. He thought of the vast vacant lands along the route to the source of the Sindhu river that he would acquire for his clan. Nandan allowed his mind to dwell on his ancestor Brahmdas who had discovered the confluence of the Saraswati and Sindhu rivers and vast vacant lands on the route and beyond.

THIRTEEN

SARASWATI RIVER AND SOMA WINE

5068 BCE, with recall of earlier events

Bharatjogi's mind was on pictures and images of the past.

Always, Bharat had been fascinated with the Sindhu river, right from his childhood days. Another river which held his life-long affection was the Saraswati. Ekantra along with his son Yadodhra had once taken Bharat and Suryata to the confluence of the Sindhu and Saraswati rivers. Bharat was then fifteen years of age. The objective of the trip was to locate certain trees in the forests beyond the confluence which could yield ideal wood for making lighter and better-balanced spears for combat against tribal raiders.

To Bharat, more than the awesome sight of the confluence was the feeling of reverence and affection for the Saraswati river, which he came to regard as the 'pure, sacred river of the waters of life'.

Ekantra had told the youngsters the story of Brahmdas who had discovered the confluence of these two auspicious, life-sustaining rivers.

Brahmdas, in 6010 BCE, had become Rishi Vaswana's disciple, at the age of eighteen. He sought spiritual enlightenment as a lifelong brahmachari. But, after eight years, he felt his spiritual strength deserting him. The rishi's daughter, who came to the ashram every spring, became the centre of his dreams. Her stolen glances, answering smiles and shy, whispered greetings assured him that she, too, regarded him with fondness.

As Brahmdas meditated on love's ecstasy, a feeling of inconsolable woe came over him. He knew he would be unable to utter the words in his heart. His soul cried out with the despair that men feel when startled by their inner weakness. He had come to the ashram for enlightenment, to be away from turmoil, lust and attachment. Why was he then being drawn by some strange, irresistible force? Why was he a prisoner of destiny unknown?

All night, Brahmdas would toss restlessly. When at last he slept, he saw her in his dreams, her breast pressed to his face, her naked body merged with his, as together they went on an enchanted journey ending in an eruption of thrill and the glow of release. He would wake up immediately after, tormented with questions: What can I offer her? Nothing but pain and anguish!

Brahmdas feared the fall from grace. God was not in his heart; he could not concentrate on meditation. He counted his sins. He had violated his vow of brahmacharya. His heart was no longer pure. Worst of all, he had allowed the shadow of his unholy desires to fall on a girl whom every ashram disciple considered a 'sister', for she was the daughter of the rishi, their spiritual father. Was it not moral incest that he contemplated! Brahmdas felt he was committing an outrage. 'I am not fit to remain! I must leave!'

Brahmdas left in the dead of night. No one explains why he took the route to the eastern desert. Poets simply speak of his going on and on, plodding wearily, day after day, but not of how he lived in that vast, barren desert that had no edible plants but only thorny bushes and scorpions. Little is known of his journey, except that at times violent sandstorms whirled around him. But then, the storms raging in his heart were far more terrible.

Suddenly, Brahmdas heard a thundering noise, as if two

hurricanes were battering each other. As he gazed ahead, his view of the setting sun was blocked, and it seemed that howling winds had formed themselves into a solid mass rising high up and shimmering in the flaming light of the setting sun! As he ran forward, his body feverish and mind clouded, drops of water fell on him. He looked at the immeasurable sky above. It was clear, cloudless, with no trace of rain. He felt blessed. He knew of the custom of sprinkling water from the Sindhu in the last moments of a person's life. It seemed, in the vast, lonely desert, Someone was looking down from the heavens and sprinkling drops of auspicious water on him. The cry in his heart stilled. He felt forgiven. The vision of the girl he had left behind rose before him, smiling. They embraced each other, for the past, for the future.

He raced faster to meet what he thought were battling storms, to end his life. But he stopped when he saw the dazzling sight below. It was a magical place where two rivers met. He had never seen a confluence of rivers before, and he gazed upon it, fascinated.

Later he would learn that one of these two rivers was the same Sindhu which flowed through his own town. The second river came to be named the Saraswati (due to the constant presence of the swan who is reputed to serve as the chariot for Goddess Saraswati; a poet explains 'It is possible to see a swan without the goddess Saraswati riding on her, but impossible ever to see this goddess without the swan, for never would the goddess venture out without riding on a swan'). The continuous roar he had heard was not of storms locked in battle; it came from the waters of the two rivers rushing headlong to greet each other, the spray rising high as they met. And thereafter, they flowed as one to merge with the Sindhu Samundar.

No one knows how long Brahmdas stood there, transfixed, gazing in awe at this confluence. He saw birds swooping down, but his weak eyes could not discern the small fish they preyed upon. Nor did he see, far beyond, the trees, plants and flowers that the two rivers nourished. Slowly, as though in a trance, he walked into the confluence to end his life but as the waters leapt over him, he felt at peace as never before and he rose refreshed from the waters with the desire to live and love.

On the bank, he meditated and the gods seemed to agree with him that there was no sin in his love. When he opened his eyes, instead of the assembly of gods he expected to see, all he saw before him was a lone swan in the river. He greeted her cheerfully, 'Good morning, fair lady, are you also as lonely and lost as I was?' It seemed that the swan nodded in agreement.

Brahmdas wanted to return, but felt too weak. His sole, silent companion was the swan who came to sit in the water opposite him. Even when he moved and chose a different spot to sit, the swan would fly to take her position in front of him. She knows my sorrow, he thought, or perhaps I should know hers. And he wondered, has she too lost her loved one? Has she been passed over by Goddess Saraswati? He forgot his sorrow and prayed for the swan and, in his daydreams, he saw the goddess riding on the bird, but the face and figure the goddess assumed was of the rishi's daughter.

Eventually, the love story of Brahmdas had a happy ending; he and the rishi's daughter joyously met, and the rishi himself blessed their marriage, saying: 'Nothing should hinder you from loving each other. Why should anyone live without love when the gods themselves cannot? Has anyone heard of a god without his consort?'

Brahmdas begged that his marriage should take place at confluence of rivers. He wanted to marry at the spot where the swan had comforted him in his misery and isolation, though he was not certain if she would be there to witness his marriage. But the swan was there, and many even claimed that Goddess Saraswati was there, too.

BHAGWAN S. GIDWANI

'Though we beheld not her face;
The goddess was there too, yes;
Oh she, Saraswati of ineffable grace;
Herself, yes, herself, came to bless.'

With reverence and homage, then, the river, associated with the swan and its goddess, inevitably came to be known as the Saraswati, and to people all over the land of the Hindu, it came to be regarded as auspicious and sacred.

Rishi Vaswana had a large cottage built beside the confluence where Brahmdas and his wife would run an ashram, not for brahmacharya but for yoga, agriculture, horticulture and irrigation, for the rishi considered brahmacharya only one of the many paths leading to grace.

Lured by the thrill of discovery and the prospect of more land, people moved into the region towards the confluence. Largely, it was a desert though, with huge boulders in many areas washed down by floods through the centuries. Trees, if they ever grew there, were washed away. Only thorny bushes flourished, with weeds so deep that it required extraordinary effort to remove them. Still, people came and settled in this forbidding region. Many ashrams were established; devotees and hermits came in large numbers, attracted by the feeling of holiness in the confluence of the two rivers, all fired with the ambition to plant innumerable trees and plants. The desert was desert no more, with oases flourishing everywhere. In the decades to come, it was green, fertile and prosperous with vegetation, fruits and forests.

Bharat was glad that after assuming the office of karkarta, he had thought of requesting the once-blind singer and others to compose memory songs about the confluence of the Sindhu and Saraswati rivers and of the continuing efforts to improve the land around and beyond. Sipping his soma wine from the jar which his wife had sent him in the last boat-load, Bharat's mind went to the most famous entrepreneur of that region—

the inventor of soma wine—whose story was not totally unrelated to the discovery of the confluence.

∾

Around 6010 BCE, Kripala, an explorer, was given some money, goods and a large land grant by the Sindhi council of chiefs—the institution of karkarta had not been established then—for an expedition. However, the funds given to him for the expedition were inadequate and so, with the honest intention of supplementing the finances, Kripala played a game of dice, but unfortunately lost everything. Disheartened, he went to a faraway farm in hiding, got married there, and returned nine years later, claiming that there was nothing in the region he had been sent to explore except a barren desert where nothing edible would ever grow, an that it was full of thorny bushes, scorpions and snakes.

In those nine years Kripala had developed a new, exquisite wine from mushrooms, flowers and other ingredients, which he now started promoting. He appointed singers and poets to sing of the qualities of his wine, which he called soma in honour of his wife—Soma Devi. He distributed free jugs of the wine to hermits, sadhus and others to popularize his product.

He also appointed many workers and engaged them in spurious tasks of mixing certain flowers, seeds, honey, nuts, and other ingredients which were not needed to make soma so as to hoodwink his competitors who had hired spies to discover the secret behind the wine. There was also chanting of music from dawn to dusk near the wine-casks as Kripala had announced that such music increased the maturity and aroma of soma.

Soon, however, a cloud came over Kripala's growing reputation, when Brahmdas accidentally discovered the confluence of the Sindhu and the Saraswati in the very region that Kripala had reported was a barren desert. It now became clear to many that he had never gone into that region and had been lying all along for if he had explored that land, how could he have failed to discover the magnificent confluence of two rivers!

Kripala simply explained that the Saraswati had not been flowing through the region when he had visited it. And the Sindhu, people asked, how did you miss that! The Sindhu was not there either, he replied. Wasn't Mother Goddess Sindhu free to change her course, he argued unconvincingly.

Kripala, thereupon, became even more anxious to salvage his reputation. He was now wealthy from the popular soma wine. He engaged in tremendous campaigns to promote and publicize himself and his wine. He also commissioned the building of ashrams, cottages and huts in that region, and donated horses and mules to aid with clearing and irrigating the land for farming and planting trees, and goats to eat through the hardy weeds, thus clearing many areas for healthy vegetation. Without waiting to be asked, Kripala generously gave to the council of chiefs whatever was needed to clear land and build canals and reservoirs for irrigation and drinking water as well as water troughs at selected spots for birds and animals.

In time, any talk of his having lied ceased completely; how could anyone misjudge a man of such extraordinary virtue and unbounded generosity!

Kripala realized the importance of image and publicity, and surrounded himself with song composers and poets, whose task was to sing of the heavenly qualities of soma. These singers went to marketplaces, piers and assemblies where their rousing hymns in praise of soma were heard all the time. Kripala also began organizing special functions for soma poetry with public contests and magnificent prizes. Quickly, it became a fashion of the times to sing songs extolling the virtues and splendour of soma, and to invest it with qualities of the divine.

Kripala fanned the flames of soma's roaring success as though his soul's salvation depended on it. All his life he had craved for recognition. It had eluded him. He had failed in his profession as an explorer. Now at last, fame came to him as the creator of soma, and he wanted more of it. Whether or not Kripala had intended to leave such a lasting impression on future generations, his efforts to salvage his reputation did precisely that.

Certainly, everyone was charmed with the songs about soma—their lilt, imagery and fine phrases. Kripala's sons, Som Kavi and Som Bhakt, born and brought up in the midst of soma poetry, became renowned poets themselves and fathered a generation of singers, lyricists and composers who thence sang of soma for many years.

However, in fairness to the later Rig Vedic period, and even to earlier pre-ancient times, it must be emphasized that soma poetry is largely allegorical, and soma achieved status and recognition largely in song and literature and not so much in the hearts and habits of people. In day-to-day life, it was not so highly esteemed; women in any case did not fancy it so much, and even amongst men, except for festive occasions, it did not reach the level of importance that later poets assigned to it. However, in the Vedic period it did achieve a great degree of acceptance, particularly with priests who were unhappy with mere offerings of fruits and flowers to the gods—for fruits and flowers did not command so high a price. Priests found it profitable to recommend soma as an offering to the gods, and even if the priest himself did not drink soma, he could sell it to the next devotee and encourage him to make that as his offering to the gods, and, as a poet who perhaps knew accounts more than poetry, said, 'Thus a single jar of soma often was multiplied by twenty-two'!

To the nagging question that was still being asked, though

by very few—how could the great and generous philanthropist Kripala have skipped his bounden duty to explore the region—Sura, the dramatist who later became a hermit, said:

'In each heart, a deep dark forest
Where worst resides with the best
Count! for all mistakes he made
Has he not fully, finally repaid?'

And then perhaps to emphasize, that all humanity, himself included, is connected with the same kind of heart and soul, he recited:

. . . And hear my secret before I die
For none knew it—and not even I.
I saw God, alone, up and high,
And Devil, down, with triumphant cry,
And a child suckling a mother's breast,
A wolf stealing a bird's nest,
A priest robbing a temple chest,
A youth rushing nowhere in haste;
I saw a widow weep, a maiden sigh,
And a singer, who knows not how to lie.
But then as I wondered Who, How, and Why,
The Truth came to me by and by,
That each one I saw, on earth and sky,
Was none other—Yes, it was I.

Despite these reservations, there is no doubt that soma wine, developed in the pre-Vedic times, was superb and Kripala's sales strategies were highly successful in making it tremendously popular, leading the way for the emergence of Soma, the deity. In fact, the Rig Veda, out of ten mandalas (books), devotes one entire book to the praise of the god Soma.

Clearly, however, most invocations of Rig Vedic poets are to Soma the deity and not to the wine as such.

FOURTEEN

TO FAR FRONTIERS

5051 BCE

Karkarta Nandan thought of the vast land that became available to the clan as the result of the discovery of the route to the confluence of the Sindhu and Saraswati rivers and far beyond. That land was made lush and green with the labour of centuries. Even so, Bharat and, after him, Nandan had poured every effort to make that land even more productive. The treaties of friendship which Bharat had achieved with the tribals had brought far more land under the control of the clan. But Nandan wanted still more.

Nandan's instructions to the contingents, which he sent out to discover new lands, were to avoid quarrels and not to occupy forcefully the lands held by others. Initially, at least, he preferred peaceful occupation. But disputes often arose and several mistakes were made, and though some were genuine, most were by design. Nandan received complaints, but he was not too worried about what he considered minor injustices. He was more concerned with his vision of the future.

It was always the others who suffered whenever hostilities arose. Nandan's contingents were well armed and ably led. The spoils of victory often included a new harvest of slaves. The tribal chief, however, was never displaced; his authority over his people was left intact. He was expected to keep the peace, provide slaves in the future, and to assist in pacifying other tribal areas. The tribals had their own slaves, gained from their own infighting; they found these newcomers reasonable in demanding not too many slaves, and never their goods and women.

The tribal chiefs were given gifts and honoured with invitations to visit the Sindhu–Saraswati region. The visiting chiefs were dazzled by the region's wealth and brilliance. They were amazed by the condition of the slaves—their comfortable living quarters, the good food they were given, including wine on festive occasions, and the leisure time they were allotted for amusements. A chief remarked, 'Your slaves live better than all our free people!'

A visiting chief told another chief named Jalta about the gifts he had received and how well the salves were treated there. Jalta, unimpressed, said, 'Fear them the most, who treat their conquered with gentleness, and fear them even more, when they offer gifts.'

Jalta was chief only in name and prestige. He had distributed his lands among his three sons and now passed his time in sport and hunting with his friends. When one of Nandan's expeditions reached the hunting grounds where Jalta was camping, he refused to let the expedition pass into the lands that lay beyond, for they belonged to his sons. With his eighty men and women, he stood to oppose the much larger contingent of the Hindu clan. He was soon unhorsed and overpowered. Nandan's men demanded three slaves from him, for foolishness in denying passage and opposing them.

'We have no slaves,' Jalta responded.

'Then let three of your free men become our slaves.'

'Take me. I am equal to three of them,' said Jalta.

'No, you are the chief. You cannot be touched.'

Jalta argued. No, he was told. Give us three slaves, or we imprison everyone and occupy the land. He argued no more.

Jalta went to his group and spoke to them. Three of his men volunteered, and Jalta grudgingly led them to be enslaved. Courteously, the leader thanked him and offered gifts. Nandan had instructed his men to give lavish gifts, invest in goodwill, and leave no enemies behind, perpetuating the myth that the slaves were offered freely in exchange for gifts.

Jalta asked, 'Am I free?'

'Yes, of course.'

'Then I am free to accept or reject your gifts.' He turned away, leaving the gifts behind.

Nandan's contingent camped there for the night. Sentries were cautioned to watch lest the hot-headed chief resorted to foolishness.

The sentries watched Jalta's people chanting. Jalta, alone, was in ceremonial robes. He collected firewood in three piles and lit them. Flames erupted.

The chanting grew louder, laden with sorrow and inconsolable, torturing grief. The sentries woke up the camp, and they all watched, wondering what was happening. Suddenly, the chanting stopped. Was it a prelude to a sudden attack? It was not.

In the glow from the flames, they saw Jalta approach the first fire, his arms raised high, and step into the fire. If he cried in agony, no one heard him. With his robe and hair burning, he leapt from the first fire into the second, and with his entire body engulfed in flames, he leapt into the third fire and collapsed, allowing the fire to consume him.

'Why?' the leader of Nandan's contingent asked, aghast.

The tribal priest explained, 'For his three sins in leading three men to slavery. He chose to burn in three fires here, rather than in hell everlasting.'

'But the sin was not his! We took the slaves.'

'Then you too will burn, everlasting, in three fires of hell,' the priest replied.

The leader released the three slaves. He also decided to avoid the hunting grounds of the dead chief and took another route. Whether it was compassion, remorse or superstition that led him to this, remained a mystery. Shortly thereafter, he resigned and died in his hometown, when his cottage caught fire at night. Though some said that he had set the fire himself, not many said so openly for they remembered the Law of the Ancients which decreed that the soul of he who took his life would be condemned for one kalpa—12,000 lunar years—during which it could not take a body, and would have to start life all over again, from the lowest level of the evolutionary ladder, and wait for a 1000 kalpas before taking on a human form again and entering the cycle of birth, death and rebirth, a cycle to be broken only by moksha through good karma.

∾

Nandan's heart swelled with pride at new discoveries of lands in all directions. As the clan's wealth and land grew, he generously increased the rewards for commanders who acquired more land and slaves, thus encouraging greater competitiveness and aggression amongst them. Tribes, near and far, trembled in fear. The commanders returned from time to time to the karkarta's headquarters to report on their success to the council, with Nandan presiding.

Appalled by their reports of carnage, the council chief Gidu resigned from the council, saying, 'Surely we go to seek God's earth, but not to battle with its inhabitants.'

Another council chief also resigned later, followed by two more. Nandan felt sorry for those simpletons who did not share his dream of the clan's greatness. He was sure though that in time, they would view him and his actions with understanding and even affection. To the commanders, he gave clear instructions to go forward and complete their appointed tasks. He also arranged schedules such that the commanders visited headquarters when the council was not in session so they could report only to him. Orders were given for slaves from the tribal areas to remain with the tribes, working under supervision, to design, produce and plant enough to feed and clothe themselves decently and send the rest of their produce to the clan.

FIFTEEN

THE TRIBES STRIKE BACK

5049 BCE

Eventually, deep in the eastern territories, resistance broke out and Nandan's advancing expeditions were halted with casualties. Lured by rewards and Nandan's constant urging, the commanders had ventured too far. The tribes struck at night, springing from trees, bushes, boulders and rocks. If they came into view during daytime, it was to hit and run after an ambush, and as time went by they grew bolder.

It was all so senseless, thought Nandan. He had no wish to occupy by force any territory that belonged to another. His strategy simply was to occupy as much vacant and uncontested land as possible, and, for the time being, leave isolated pockets in tribal occupation. But he had rarely bothered to ask the commanders how and whose land had been acquired. Unknown to him, his contingents had continued to penetrate deep.

The surprise attacks against Nandan's forces were followed by the sudden appearance of the army of a strange eastern tribe at the clan's borders. It came far from its own territory to harass and molest Nandan's teams. They stole nothing, looted nothing, but if they caught any of Nandan's men, they killed them instantly, swiftly, without cruelty, but also without mercy. A vast number of the tribals died in frequent battles. They wore no armour and were easy targets if found in the open. They had long wooden stakes, wooden spears and short-range arrows, but no shields. They mostly attacked on foot, so it was not surprising that so many perished. But still, they kept coming. It was easier to kill than to capture them, for they never surrendered and had to be overpowered by force. Even when swords and arrows flew thick and fast against them and they were cornered on all sides with nowhere to run, they fought on, ready to face death rather than capture.

Strangely, they spoke no language. They could not formulate a single word. Sometimes, they would yell when they attacked, or cry triumphantly when they retreated after inflicting losses. But mostly, they came silently, killed silently, and left silently. If they were captured and wounded, they wept and uttered a guttural cry, but never a word. Even Sage Dhanawantar could not explain how, in the evolutionary process, the vocal chords of this tribe had been suppressed. Undoubtedly, among themselves, they understood each other perfectly with sign language and signals. How else could they organize well-coordinated attacks!

Though they were mute, their ears and eyesight were sharp. Yet they would react neither to gestures nor shouts. When provoked, they would assault their master, but never his wife, child or slave. They could not be tamed or moulded. They were forever tearing off their clothes and walking around naked, as they wanted to wear only animal skins, and not woven cloth, regarding it as a badge of slavery.

In captivity, their behaviour was strange. They would not move and had to be dragged. They would not eat or drink while their hands were tied and chose to starve. But never was it feasible to take off all their chains, for although they saw spears trained on them, they tried to flee, resulting sometimes in injury or even the loss of life. Their captors were not harsh with them, but even so, many died on the march, for the will to live seemed to abandon them during captivity. Those who survived proved to be unsatisfactory slaves, impossible to train even for simple tasks.

As slaves, they were an embarrassment; certainly, they were a terrible example to other, docile slaves. Nandan repeated his orders that no slaves should ever be brought to the clan's region but must remain in tribal lands or in distant outposts under supervision.

~

Nandan had no wish to be involved in long-drawn-out engagements. He ordered his forces to regroup. But the tribes became even bolder, and their attacks increased.

Many faraway tribes witnessed the discomfiture of Nandan's contingents. Jalta's three sons came with their warriors even though Nandan's men had avoided their lands. Yet they marched through treacherous routes to reach within striking distance. They waited till the eastern tribes attacked Nandan's forces, and then they rushed forward, yelling like rabble, without attempt to maintain formation, hoping to make short work of the enemy. But Nandan's troops struck back after losing many in initial surprise, and any tribesmen who were not instantly killed or wounded withdrew in disorder. Among those captured was the fifteen-year-old son of chief Jalta, known as Jalta the Fourth.

Again, rumours spread far and near of this battle. But then, a rumour has many voices, and a story depends on who tells and who hears it. Some spoke of tribal heroism and total devastation in Nandan's camp. Others told truer tales. But the fact emerged that Nandan's troops were not invulnerable. Their losses were heavy.

Withdrawal, Nandan knew, meant the loss of face and renewed attacks now that their aura of invulnerability had vanished. Farther advance was dangerous. Reports of casualties were reaching his clan from returning, wounded soldiers. Nandan decided his troops should neither march forward nor return. Instead, a ring of forts was to be established in the eastern region, where, safe from attack, his contingents would control areas around. Construction of the forts began in earnest.

Some reminded Nandan of the Hindu parliament's earlier decree that the exploration and discovery of lands was for a 'moral and spiritual bond with the earth, not to dispossess the land of another or to hold anyone in captivity', and that no slave is acquired in 'discovered lands, except to set him free'. But theirs were voices in the wilderness. Others chose to remain silent and looked away to brood on different matters—their own future, their privileges and their well-being. Their minds and conscience darkened.

A lone poet cried out in despair:

There is guilt in silence, surely not of cowardice alone
But of sharing another's evil karma as your very own
For silence gives sinners renewed strength and courage
To keep repeating the same ugly, ungodly outrage.

SIXTEEN

A GOD ON THE MOVE!

5054 BCE

Meanwhile, the years passed pleasantly for Sindhu Putra at Muni's Rocks. There was laughter, mirth and games with Muni and Roopa's children. As teachers, Muni and Roopa were not demanding. Their training came not like an avalanche but gently, through stories and tales, verse and song. They sought to implant ideas of right and wrong, truth and virtue and belief in the One-Supreme, but more so, they wished to instil in children a thirst for knowledge, a philosophical outlook, a compassionate heart and a mind that questioned. The serene environs of the Rocks encouraged contemplation as Muni guided the young boy through yoga and meditation.

Sindhu Putra was to remain there till his eleventh birthday, but he was not keen to leave. Nor did Muni and Roopa wish to part with him.

'If it is his wish and yours,' Bharat told them, 'so be it, for another year.'

This went on till Sindhu Putra's fifteenth birthday.

'This time, Sindhu Putra should leave,' Muni told Roopa.

'He loves to be with us. I am sure Bharatjogi would agree.'

'Perhaps. But now, he must leave.'

'Why?' Roopa was puzzled by Muni's firmness.

'Because I have seen hunger in his eyes,' Muni replied.

'Hunger! Hunger for what?'

'For your daughters,' Muni responded.

Roopa smiled. Happily, she asked, 'Which one?'

'Both,' Muni replied evenly.

'Both!' she said, in surprise. Muni nodded. Roopa's smile deepened, 'He is young. They are young. One day, he can marry one of them.'

'Meanwhile, he should go,' Muni countered.

But Roopa objected, 'He belongs to us. If he leaves, he may not come back.'

'If he belongs to us, he will be back. Those that do not come back, be sure, they never belonged to us.'

❧

'God will guide his footsteps,' Roopa said as Sindhu Putra left but Muni rejoined, 'God guides no man's footsteps. That will and choice belongs to man.'

A feeling of loneliness grew upon Sindhu Putra as he left the Rocks to live in Gatha's village. He had a cottage in the temple compound where he was surrounded by adoring crowds. Why then this feeling of isolation and fear that he faced the world as a stranger! At times, a vision of the two beautiful girls at the Rocks rose before him, but when it disappeared his spirit was overwhelmed with sadness again. People clamoured around him, seeking his blessings, and wordlessly he would give it by raising his hand. Often, he did not know how to reply to questions, and simply smiled tenderly, as if that was response enough. It was. But if the questions persisted, he asked them to look into their hearts for answers and follow the path of 'sat chit ananda'. Clearly, he felt Muni was right when he said that each man must answer his own questions and arrive at his own decisions. Decisive issues lie in the heart where battles between right and wrong are fought hourly and daily until man is fully aware of his purpose in life and the direction he must take. When the questions grew, he went into a prolonged silence.

Was it because he could not answer or was it that he was seeking answers within?

The crowds around him grew. People came from far and near, many with cries of pain from some nameless torment. But once in his presence, their panic disappeared, and they seemed to find solace and a calm strength.

'They heal themselves,' Sindhu Putra replied, when many praised his healing presence.

'How? By what miracle?' they asked.

'By the miracle of their own faith,' he replied.

He preached no sermon, chanted no prayers, spread no gospel, established no idols, invented no new faith and everyone felt comforted, for if he supported none, he also opposed none. When the preachers muttered that 'Sindhu Putra says nothing because he has nothing to say,' they were met with contempt. But Sindhu Putra heard of their remarks, and said, 'They are right.' The crowds bowed reverently, 'What humility!' they said.

Sindhu Putra never believed he had in him a divine spark— except that which is present in every human being. He was no god, he knew, though the more he said so, the more it was attributed to his humility. 'How modest he is!' many said.

Yet in Sindhu Putra's heart, there was depression that found no relief. Many saw sadness in his eyes, and said, 'Those gentle eyes reflect all our sorrows!'

A singer explained Sindhu Putra's dilemma:

Godhood was thrust on him, yet he sought only human affection
He sought to live by divine principle, but not be divine himself.
His words!—Were they from his heart, from deep within?
His words! But they were strange to him! Who planted them?

Whose part am I playing? he asked. Why do I say what
I say!
And he longed to be true to himself . . . and chose silence
But silence leads to a bigger lie
For they invested his silence with the message of the
divine.
And he asked—why am I unable to utter the words in
my heart?
Why do I not advance beyond the bonds of this spurious
image?'

∽

Desperate to belong, Sindhu Putra moved from Gatha's
village to Bharatjogi's retreat. After all, he regarded
Bharatjogi as his father.

The Retreat was no longer silent. Everyone knew the
hermit there was the great karkarta Bharat. Many came to
visit him, out of affection and curiosity. As the number of
visitors grew, Gatha had to lay down the law about who
could visit and when, and even erect barriers so they could
not disturb the hermit.

Bharat's wife, Mataji, said, 'The hermit is a hermit no more.
The archaic custom of not visiting a hermit has been put to
rest,' and she visited the retreat, often.

Now that Sindhu Putra was staying with Bharat, Gatha
became even sterner with visitors. He was able to enforce
restrictions only because Sindhu Putra agreed to visit the
village temple daily.

Sindhu Putra loved Bharat. But initially, he hardly
understood him. Bharatjogi spoke against slavery, but Sindhu
Putra, who had never seen a slave, did not understand what
that meant. He knew Gatha had been a slave once, and asked
him, 'Were you treated badly?'

Gatha, aghast that anyone could think that he had been

ill-treated at his karkarta's household, said, 'Oh, no! Never! The love I received there is given to few.'

Also, could he grasp Bharatjogi's concept of unity? His world moved—from Gatha's village to Bharat's Retreat and thence to Muni's Rocks. Were they not all united in that tiny world of his?

Bharatjogi spoke of the land of Hindu—of the majestic mountains of the Himalaya and the idols of Rudra and Brahma that Hindu explorers found there. He spoke of the Sindhu river's source at Tibata, of the mighty Sindhu Samundar, of the land of Sanathana and Sanatan Dharma, of rivers, forests and habitations beyond. 'We were all together, once before,' he said. And even though he feared that such a concept was beyond the fifteen-year-old boy's comprehension, his urge to speak was uncontrollable.

Bharat was wrong to assume he was failing to excite the lad's imagination. However, it was not only the concept of unity that led the youth's mind to distant lands. He longed to know where his mother had come from.

Bharat showed him where his mother's boat had been found—and lost. He saw where Bharat had scattered white flowers for her. But his questions—from where did she come, where was she going, and why—remained. Perhaps some day, he thought, I shall travel far and my feet shall touch the land on which she walked.

The boy did not fully comprehend the shape, size and dimensions of Bharatjogi's perception of the land of Hindu. He understood that on one side stood lofty mountains and on the other a deep ocean, while between them the land and rivers spread out in all directions. He had never seen mountains or the sea and Bharat's rough sketches of land masses and waters were hardly illuminating. Sindhu Putra wondered aloud, 'Surely, someone should attempt to make a chart!'

'Someone has!' Bharat said triumphantly. He spoke of Sage Ekantra, his mentor and father of his dear friend Yadodhra.

Bharat added smilingly, 'They call him Sage Yadodhra now. I do not know how Ekantra unearthed so many charts. Most were disfigured with age and the markings had almost disappeared. He studied them all to prepare fresh charts. Yadodhra had inspired our trans-Himalayan expedition to the Sindhu's source in Tibata with the aid of those charts. They led us to the Sindhu Samundar and our journey was sure and swift and truly rewarding!'

∽

With the arrival of Mataji, Sindhu Putra acquired yet another mother. He had never met her, but he knew she was expected, and bowed respectfully. She recognized him from portraits displayed all over the village. She teased: 'You are Sindhu Putra, honoured as son of Mother Goddess Sindhu!'

'My mother was a nameless woman who died in the lap of the river. My honour lies in having Bharatjogi as my adopted father.'

Mataji heard the distress in his voice and, sorry to have spoken thoughtlessly, she hugged him and said, 'How can a son of my husband not be my own son! Will you not accept me as your mother?'

Wordlessly, the youth nodded and she hugged him tightly.

Later, Mataji said of Sindhu Putra, 'Every woman would love him as a son or a sweetheart, depending on her age.'

'You reside in the shadow of a god who calls you his father. Every day, Kanta and other women come to minister to your wants. What kind of hermit are you!' she said to Bharat in mock sternness.

'One of a kind,' he replied. 'But why don't you come to live here?'

'Who will look after our children, then?'

'Our children are grown up, well settled and so are their wives.'

'And our grandchildren?'

'Their parents will look after them,' Bharat responded.

'Parents cannot look after children. Only the children's grandparents can.'

'I thought we did a good job of raising our children.'

'Times change. Parents no longer have our wisdom.'

Nevertheless, Mataji decided to spend six months each year with Bharat.

'Why do you keep Sindhu Putra cooped up here?' she asked him.

'Because the villagers surround him, convinced that he is a god.'

'Then why not send him away? To see, learn and grow!'

'He will be recognized everywhere,' Bharat said, 'and be surrounded and hounded.'

'Why not to Yadodhra? You keep telling him of Ekantra's charts! How can the boy understand, unless he sees them?'

Bharat nodded in agreement, 'Yes, but Yadodhra will be furious. Hundreds will invade his ashram to greet Sindhu Putra.'

'Yadodhra! He can silence a thousand shrieking devils with a single command. No one would dare approach his ashram if he forbade it.'

'Really! He still shouts as he used to? He is my age, you know!'

'Yes, I know. He is young—like you, though not as handsome.'

'Only the eyes of love will view an old man of eighty as handsome!'

They discussed the plans for Sindhu Putra's travel. 'The singer,' Mataji suggested, 'can take him to our house. Let him meet the family. They will give him all he needs. He can have one of our best horses.'

'A horse! Why?' Bharat asked.

'Because I have never seen a god riding a donkey,' Mataji said.

Bharat smiled, 'Have you seen a god riding a horse?'

'Yes, when you came riding a white horse to marry me.'

Bharat laughed, 'I doubt he learnt horseriding at the Rocks.'

'Then my grandchildren will teach him what Muni neglected.'

〜

'Will Sage Yadodhra show me those charts?' Sindhu Putra asked.

'Yadodhra will do all you ask in my name,' Bharat smiled. 'But if he hesitates, tell him you know the story of the voice in the jar.

'It is the story of Yadodhra's very first experiment, when he was seven years old,' Bharat explained. 'Ekantra had told him that sound is carried by air waves. So if air did not exist, sound could not reach others. Thus, sound transmission came from a sound-producing source only on motions of air. Yadodhra, certain that he understood it all, concluded that if he spoke into a jar and closed it immediately, covering it on all sides, his voice would not travel due to absence of air, and the jar would retain his voice, and later when the jar was opened, the same imprisoned voice would be heard as it would then be free to travel on the motion of the air around it. Yadodhra collected many jars. In each, he spoke his name and described his own greatness. Then he covered them tightly with cloth to prevent the air from escaping with his voice.

'He had already announced that he would, on a certain day, perform the greatest magic feat of all time. Crowds gathered on the appointed day and the jars were opened. But alas! There was no sound. Yadodhra was heartbroken. His anguish moved me to pity. Quickly, I assumed the responsibility, saying I had carelessly dropped Yadodhra's magic powder, which was promptly eaten by pigeons and squirrels and hence Yadodhra's magnificent feat was ruined.

Everyone blamed me. For Yadodhra, they had praise as he gave them all many rides on his father's elephants. Later, Yadodhra had put his arms around me and promised that whenever I asked for anything, possible or impossible, he would do it for me.

'So,' concluded Bharat, 'remind Yadodhra of that promise, if he hesitates to show you the charts.'

Sindhu Putra smiled, 'Your debt is for you to collect. I cannot hold that experiment against him.'

'Indeed,' Bharat said, 'one can only honour him. Even at the age of seven, he tried to uncover a secret of nature's process. Since then, all his life, he has been striving to discover the unknown. For him, no question is useless, no theory impertinent, no experiment a failure, and no myth sacrosanct—everything must be tested, verified, proved or disproved. Only now,' Bharat smiled, 'he makes no rash pronouncements as he had when he was seven years old. He waits, with unending patience, to unveil a truth of nature.'

'And he succeeds, does he not?' Sindhu Putra prompted.

'That he does, but he also knows that mysteries multiply with each discovery. Every tantalizing clue is surrounded by fresh problems and paradoxes. Perhaps, it will always be so and the eternal mystery will remain incomprehensible forever.'

༺

'Thieves and gods will always hide themselves,' sang an irreverent poet to describe Sindhu Putra's departure for Yadodhra's ashram. Unknown to the villagers, he was seen off only by Bharat, Mataji and the dogs who barked sorrowfully.

Yadodhra welcomed Sindhu Putra warmly with a hundred questions about Bharatjogi. Delighted that Mataji was with Bharat, he said, 'He is no more a hermit then! I shall visit him.'

'He will be delighted,' Sindhu Putra responded.

'Delighted! He will jump with joy; he will dance with glee; his heart will sing,' said Yadodhra, adding, 'Oh, but not for my sake!'

'What else!' Sindhu Putra asked.

'For the treasure of knowledge my students have unearthed and to see the charts which, at last, we have corrected and updated. He sent you to see them, yes?'

'I hope to see them, if you permit.'

'Do you know what those charts depict?' Yadodhra asked.

'I believe they indicate lands of the ancient Hindu, the people of Sanathana and Sanatan Dharma,' Sindhu Putra replied.

'And who were the Sanathana people? Men from another planet?' the teacher in Yadodhra demanded to know.

'No, they are from our world. Sanathana were our own ancestors. From them emerged Sanatan Dharma, which itself led to us—the Hindu.'

'Bharatjogi schools his son well,' Yadodhra responded. 'But I suppose you know everything in the charts.'

'I do not,' Sindhu Putra replied.

'No! But I heard a claim that you are a god.'

Sensing the youth's sorrow, Yadodhra added, 'I know you do not claim it. After all, it is only at the end of one's life that one can say if someone was a god. A person's karma alone determines that. Gods are not born; they are made through effort, passion and commitment.'

'I am an orphan whom Bharatjogi found in a storm-tossed, battered boat. I am certainly no god.'

In a swift change of mood, Yadodhra put his arm around him, 'You are my dearest friend's son and surely that places you above any god.'

~

Sindhu Putra pored over the maps, drawn not on bark and leaf but on a huge, wall-like structure, four times his height. By its side were smaller wall-sections, with charts. Yadodhra explained, 'My father tried to preserve the original charts, but they kept deteriorating. So, he made copies on larger pieces of bark, and preserved them with wax to protect them from the elements. They, too, deteriorated, even faster than the ancient originals. That danger is no more. The charts have now been reproduced on this massive stone wall with a protective canopy on top.'

Sindhu Putra went up and down ladders to study the maps while Yadodhra shouted explanations from below. Many lines were in various colours, some inlaid with beads, others overlaid with broken stones. Yadodhra clarified that these maps portrayed all the information from the ancient charts, depicting lands where the ancient Hindu had lived successively from the age of Sanathana, including lands abandoned because of droughts, or the lure of abundance elsewhere, and even for safety from tribal attacks.

Yadodhra added: 'My father's difficulty was that he had not seen the Himalayas or the Sindhu Samundar, but the charts that he had seen in caves convinced him that they were waiting to be discovered. We were fortunate enough to travel beyond the Himalayas, into Tibata, and also touch the Sindhu Samundar.'

Sindhu Putra had doubts, 'What kind of a chart or drawing can show a mountain as great as the Himalayas! Could it not be the depiction of any small mountain?'

'True,' Yadodhra answered, 'but see the evidence. First, there are sketches of a mountain. Second, to the right of these sketches is a column with drawings of men. Each man stands on the shoulders of one below him, and as the right column rises, the figures of the men become progressively smaller and are ultimately represented by dots. It was difficult to count the dots, for they often overlapped, but clearly there were thousands of them. It was simply to show that the mountain peak was higher than the combined height of five thousand men. Third, in all such repetitive charts found in many caves was a box in the left corner in which there was a sketch of a pyramid. Apparently, ancient route plotters and explorers had agreed on a common code—that all drawings of the Himalayas would have a pyramid to distinguish them from others. Do you see the advantage of this now?'

Sindhu Putra asked, 'What advantage?'

Yadodhra explained, 'The advantage of providing a link to identify a number of drawings on the same subject. My father found so many charts and drawings in different caves. Some were repetitive, while others differed in certain aspects. But he soon realized that all drawings with a pyramid in the corner related to the Himalayas—a mountain range that he had not seen, but which existed, somewhere.'

Yadodhra saw Sindhu Putra's puzzled look and added, 'Perhaps I go too fast. The fact is that there were many drawings in those ancient caves, some depicting streams flowing through mountainous terrain and then coming together to form rivers that flowed over land and finally reached one large body of water.'

'The Sindhu Samundar?' Sindhu Putra asked.

Yadodhra nodded, 'Yes, even the drawings of the Sindhu Samundar had their own distinctive symbol—a fish with the face and breasts of a woman—to make it clear that they pertained to that body of water, and not to any river or stream, which had their own distinctive symbols. Similarly, the drawings of the Himalayas also could not be confused with sketches of other mountains as they too had their own distinct symbols.' Yadodhra led him to a distant wall, 'Now, see this copy of an earlier drawing.'

'But there are three symbols on this!'

'Yes—the pyramid for the Himalayas, a dancing girl for the Sindhu river, and the fish with the woman's face and breasts for the Sindhu Samundar.'

A chart with multiple features had symbols for each feature. Later, Yadodhra explained many charts and consolidated maps.

'How many rivers are shown in these various charts?' Sindhu Putra asked.

'Far more than we have discovered,' was Yadodhra's reply.

'Is it not possible to conceive that the ancient Hindus merely saw the Himalayas from a distance? Where is the proof that they actually went in, climbing high and deep into the mountains?'

'How else did we find idols of our gods in the mountains? Our explorers there saw images of Rudra, Brahma, Vishnu and other deities.'

'Yes. Bharatjogi told me of that,' Sindhu Putra said. 'Were there no similar paintings or carvings—for instance, of mountains—on cave-walls?'

'Paintings on cave-walls, yes, but not similar. The paintings on cave-walls were imaginative, captivating. There was one carving and painting, combined, of a mythical 420,000-mile-high mountain, Mount Meru, known in all our children's stories as the place where the gods dwell. It is a marvellous work of art, with its flowing streams and beautiful golden houses inhabited by devas, attended by gandharvas and apsaras, while the mountain itself, rising from the centre of the universe to the heavens, is surrounded by concentric rings, around which are the moon, the sun and the planets, with the earth between the seventh and eighth rings. The artist creates an impression that the mountain top is studded with brilliant sapphires radiating the colour blue all across heaven. Other realms are similarly covered with glittering rubies, yellow and white gems, with a dazzling interplay of colours. No one who has seen this painting can take his eyes off it. Yet, this masterpiece simply captures a charming myth, not a real mountain waiting to be discovered.'

BHAGWAN S. GIDWANI

Yadodhra continued, 'But charts or sketches that identified the physical features of the terrain were made by prosaic explorers with no art or aesthetics, focused only on the details essential to reach or identify the place, to excite us and lead us on a voyage of discovery of the paths that the ancients had taken before us.'

Sindhu Putra asked, 'But what compulsion did the ancients have to communicate with coming generations?'

'Why did your father encourage memory songs? We all wish to belong—to the future and the past. But we can do much more. The ancients had no leaves or pieces of bark large enough, so their charts had to be in several sections. Often, the glue came off and the symbols were obliterated. Distances kept ancient chartmakers apart and consolidating information was nearly impossible. But, we have fewer problems. Our walls here can depict all charts. I shall build many more, as we keep discovering more charts in various caves. The future must never be robbed of its past!'

༄

News went round among Yadodhra's students of Sindhu Putra's visit. His name was well-known as the son of Mother Goddess Sindhu. And though they did not believe it—for Yadodhra had trained them to be sceptics—they were curious. When all the students gathered for prayers, Yadodhra introduced Sindhu Putra.

'He is no god, nor son of Mother Sindhu,' he stressed, 'but the son of my dearest friend, Bharatjogi, the most illustrious karkarta that this land has ever had.' Then, Yadodhra joked: 'But, boys and girls! If ever you are in frantic search of a living god and if you are at my ashram, I alone must be regarded as that living god!'

SEVENTEEN

BHARAT VARSHA

5054 BCE

For days, Sindhu Putra pored over charts. His wonder grew, and wanderlust made him restless. He discussed with Yadodhra his plans of travelling to the caves that Sage Ekantra had discovered along with their treasures of paintings and charts.

'Dress as a muni or sanyasi,' Yadodhra advised. 'No one will bother you.' Seeing Sindhu Putra's hesitation, he added, 'Your youth is no obstacle to donning the saffron robe. The four stages of life—child, student, householder and hermit—are simply guidelines. Our land is full of hermits and ascetics who skipped the student and householder stages to pass life in meditation with no earthly ties. The Muni of the Rocks became an ascetic at the age of twelve.'

'I lack the knowledge of a muni,' Sindhu Putra said.

'You have the gift of silence, at times more mature than knowledge.'

'Yet to go in a garb that does not belong to me!'

'Would you rather travel like the god you are supposed to be? Out of a hundred wanderers clothed in saffron, at least ten wear it to cheat or to protect themselves from robbers.'

'Do robbers respect the saffron robe?'

Yadodhra shook his head. 'But they are superstitious. What will it profit them to molest a wanderer in a saffron robe?'

To Sindhu Putra's reservations about travelling on horseback, Yadodhra asked, 'How far will you reach on weary feet?'

'But do ascetics travel on horseback?'

Yadodhra laughed, 'My father travelled on elephants. You are not that elevated. A horse will do for you.'

～

Sindhu Putra was lost. Although he had discussed with Yadodhra the routes he would take, he was tempted to deviate and pass through towns and villages to see how people lived and worked. No one recognized him—with his shaved head, ash-smeared forehead, and saffron garb he was merely another ascetic passing through. Everyone made way for him; some offered him food, others sought blessings.

After weeks of wandering, he thought that by turning eastwards he might be able to join the route he had intended to take. Far from a town, in the midst of the wilderness, he reached a large plantation. It was after dusk, when work normally stops in fields and farms. Yet, he saw many labourers still at work. He smiled, recalling Sage Yadodhra's words to students, 'God may not respond to prayers but certainly His bounty and blessings flow to those that work harder—and when a man, weary from work, falls asleep without praying, God guards him through the night, and prays for him.'

However, his smile disappeared as he neared the plantation—the labourers were slaves, acting under sharp, curt orders from a foreman. No one paid attention to Sindhu Putra since ascetics and sanyasis often sought food and lodging there. The foreman simply pointed to a hut provided just for that purpose.

Sindhu Putra asked, 'Why are the slaves working at this hour, on a full-moon evening, when no one is supposed to work?'

'Because there is work that remains to be done,' the foreman replied. He was in no awe of ascetics; they came and went, always seeking, never giving anything in return.

Sindhu Putra looked at the slaves. Among them was a young woman, busy at work, with her back to him. He saw her hair, adorned with a white flower. Was it the same kind of flower his mother had worn? He moved forward to see.

The foreman grinned; perhaps this ascetic was not after food or lodging after all. He had met ascetics who loved the 'human touch'. Well, he would send him away forthwith. Meanwhile, Sindhu Putra went near the woman and realized it was the same kind of flower. He touched it lightly. The woman turned around, startled, then smiled hesitantly when she saw it was a sanyasi. She had always prayed silently whenever ascetics passed by, hoping that they would hear the prayers in her heart and carry them to Him. She bent to touch his feet, but he moved back.

'God bless you, mother,' he said, his mind on the woman with white flowers in a boat, who had given him life and then left for nowhere. In a daze he wondered: 'Was my mother also a slave, like this girl with the white flower!'

The spell broke as the foreman rudely shouted at the girl to attend to her work. Sindhu Putra faced the foreman, 'When did they begin to work?'

'At dawn, last night, last year—how does it matter to you?'

'Is there not a law that slaves do not work on a full-moon day and that work stops at dusk every day?'

Bharatjogi had told him about the laws he had introduced, as karkarta, to reduce severity on slaves. But it seemed that under Karkarta Nandan, no one remembered them.

Derisively, the foreman asked, 'Whose law is that?'

'My father's!' Sindhu Putra impulsively responded, stung by the foreman's tone, and immediately realized that he may have inadvertently revealed his identity.

However, the foreman misunderstood Sindhu Putra's words, certain that, like many ascetics, the youth was referring to God, as his divine, universal Father.

'Your Father's law is honoured only in your Father's land. Not in this land of sin and sorrow.' Spurred on by the memory of some old wound, he added, 'There was a time when your Father—the divine, universal Father—created the earth and established His law. But man has moved away and created his own law to banish God. Your Father exists no more and this is not His land.'

Sindhu Putra glared at the foreman. Was this odious, godless man denying God? In his heart there always was silent loneliness. He found solace in those around him who loved him. Yet invariably, he felt the presence of Another whom he loved all the more. Now this evil slave-driver was trying to shatter his faith!

'This is my Father's land!' he shouted angrily, and then stopped. For him, anger was a new experience. He had never raised his voice to someone before this.

Surprised by the ascetic's vehemence, the foreman took a step back. Obviously, this was one of those lunatic ascetics who turned violent if crossed. He could hold him back with a single blow. Still, the plantation owner would disapprove of his hitting a sanyasi.

The effect on the slaves was magical. They heard the sanyasi's shout and saw him shaking with anger, but he seemed no different from a holy man in a trance, deep in the midst of powerful vision. The girl with the flower in her hair came closer and asked, 'Who are you, sanyasiji?'

All thought of hiding his identity left Sindhu Putra. He could not lie to a girl who wore the same flower that his mother wore on her last, fateful journey. Nor could he deceive these simple slaves.

'I am Sindhu Putra,' he replied simply.

Sindhu Putra! The slaves stared in astonishment. They all knew of the One who was destined to walk on the earth as a god. 'The son of Mother Goddess Sindhu!' they chanted and moved forward to touch his feet.

Sindhu Putra raised his hand, determined to avoid the mantle of divinity. Quietly, he announced, 'I am the son of Bharatjogi. That is my highest honour. No more, and no less. I neither possess nor seek a higher honour.'

His words silenced them, but did not stop them from kneeling before him. He raised his hand again and commanded, 'Let us all stand and silently pray.'

❧

When the prayer ended, Sindhu Putra caressed the flower in the girl's hair, moved his lips, as if planting a distant kiss, and then mounted the horse and rode out in a tearing hurry.

Thereafter, every wandering minstrel and visitor to the plantation was told the story of Sindhu Putra's brief visit and his soulful cry that all this land around was his father's—and that he had unmistakably spoken of Bharatjogi, the once great karkarta, as his father. Many came especially to listen to the songs and stories of slaves that made it clear that Sindhu Putra himself had proclaimed that the entire land be known as the land of his father, Bharat.

And that is how, eventually, the land came to be known as Bharat Varsha.

EIGHTEEN

MASK OF A GOD? A GOD WHO PRETENDS TO BE A GOD

5054 BCE

Thunder and lightning rent the air as Sindhu Putra rode away from the plantation. To the slaves, this was a heavenly omen, to mark the visit of a god. But Sindhu Putra was in a bewildered daze. How foolish I was to get into a rage, he thought. Did it matter if the foreman disbelieved in the One-Supreme? Did not Muni say, 'Conduct and morals are the basis of karma, not the irrelevancy of faith?' And did not Roopa sing, 'The Real is in us all, whether we know it or not . . . ' Also Yadodhra had said, 'If the Reality of the One-Supreme depended on people's acceptance, it might as well cease to exist. God is not like a headman seeking re-election. *God is.*' Even Bharatjogi had said, 'A tree gives shade to the believer and non-believer alike.' How foolish to reveal my identity! Why—he asked himself—to be treated as god! My only sensible action was to leave quickly, before they knelt to me. His mind tossed from his conversation with the foreman and the condition of the slaves, to the white flowers of his lost mother.

Suddenly, the thunder gave way to a gentle rain. Rider and horse were thirsty and welcomed the rain as they rested under a rocky ledge.

When he woke up, in sunlight and warmth, Sindhu Putra felt his mind caressed. Last night's questions ceased; instead, came the stirrings of a new emotion. He recalled Bharat's words on the slaves' plight; when he had first heard them, slavery was an impersonal, distant concept, but now he understood those words clearly.

Day after day, Sindhu Putra continued on his journey till he spotted a distant hilltop that looked as if there might be a human settlement. He reached the hill after an arduous journey of four days through overgrown paths and discovered that a fort was being constructed there. It was one of the many forts that Karkarta Nandan had decided to establish at strategic points to control the areas around.

Sindhu Putra's approach surprised the sentry on the hill. No one ever took this treacherous route. 'Who goes there?' he challenged, ready with spear.

Sindhu Putra replied, 'A traveller in need of water, food and rest for his horse.'

The sentry's doubts vanished; a tribal would have yelled, fled or attacked, but this man spoke his language and was clearly educated. 'Welcome, sir. Approach,' he said.

Gratefully, Sindhu Putra and his horse drank their fill of water. The sentry saw his tattered saffron robe, and beat on his drum to summon some men. Sindhu Putra was escorted not to the hilltop but to the township. The headman welcomed him to his cottage where his wife gave Sindhu Putra herbal water to wash his bruises. He declined the wine they offered, but accepted juice and wheat rolls. He was given white garments to wear, while his robe was mended. 'It will be as good as new,' the headman said. 'My wife is an expert.'

The wife smiled to say, 'I shall mend your robe, but it may not last. Let me also make another robe.'

Meanwhile, in response to the headman's questions, Sindhu Putra told him that he was looking for Sage Yadodhra's caves but had lost his way. The headman realized that he must be a sanyasi of quality as he came from the reputed Sage Yadodhra's ashram. The headman escorted him towards the cottage reserved for honoured guests. On the way, he pointed to rows of cottages for soldiers and workers. New housing, the headman said, was being built near the fort. 'Our contingents shall then be invulnerable and ready to strike terror amongst those who seek to terrorize us.' Proudly, he pointed to gardens carpeted with flowers and trees, ignoring a large area peppered with tattered huts whose walls were crumbling and roofs were broken. Those huts housed the slaves.

The moon was riding high in the cloudless sky at midnight when Sindhu Putra awoke from sleep in the guest house. He noticed the glow of torches at the site of the fort and asked the sentry outside, 'How long do they work?'

The sentry replied, 'From sunrise to midnight. But the fort has taken too long to build, so now they work past midnight.' A little later, Sindhu Putra heard countless footsteps. The sentry enlightened him, 'They are back from the fort, but in five hours they will march back to work.'

Sindhu Putra went back to sleep and, in his dream, heard a sad, haunting melody coming as though from the bosom of the night to sing of the unspoken despair of the heart. When he woke up at sunrise, he heard noises outside. Obviously, the workers were marching to the construction site. He, too, wanted to accompany them, but as he was leaving, Mithali— the thirteen-year-old daughter of a maid-servant in the headman's household—came with his robe that had been mended and a new robe. He waved off her apology, saying he was simply going to the construction site, and, since he did not know the way, he intended to follow the workers.

'The fort is easy to find,' Mithali said. 'Besides, the headman can always take you there.'

'The headman, I am sure, is busy,' Sindhu Putra said.

'The headman is never busy. He keeps others busy,' Mithali replied to his amusement.

The headman came to meet him, flustered. He had just

received word that Karkarta Nandan would be visiting the town in three weeks and he had to complete ten thousand things before that. Even so, the commander at the fort wished to welcome the sanyasi.

Mithali escorted Sindhu Putra to the fort. The headman had said that the commander would receive him at the entrance to the fort, but, on hearing of Karkarta Nandan's impending visit, the commander had rushed out to inspect distant outposts.

Many came to greet the sanyasi, but his eyes went to an area where many half-clad men were tied to posts with long ropes, slaving under the watchful eyes of the sentries. A slave—hit on the chest by a stone block—had fallen and his prone body was hindering the work of the other slaves around him.

Cursing the sentries for not removing the fallen slave, a man walked authoritatively over to the huddle and cut the rope that tied the injured slave. He pushed him away roughly, unmindful of the jagged stones and boulders, barking orders at the rest of the slaves to continue work. This was Daspati—the supervisor at the construction site. It was widely said that he had a cruel streak that was kept in check only when the commander was nearby. But the news of Nandan's impending visit had spurred Daspati into a merciless hurry to get the work completed.

The sanyasi ignored Daspati's greeting and went to help the injured slave. As he lifted the wounded man's head on to his lap, blood stained his robe. He tore a strip of cloth from his robe to tie around the wound, but first, he wanted to clean it free of dirt. He cried out, 'Mithali! Water, please, water!' Many heard him, but no one offered to help, afraid of Daspati.

Mithali ran to the water pots. They were too high, and she had to jump several times before she could grasp one. Unfortunately, it shattered against the wall; her clothes were drenched, but she had no water. With tears, she ran back to the sanyasi, and sat beside him. He lifted the slave's head from his lap and placed it on hers, and cleaned the wound with her wet shirt.

Daspati glared at the sanyasi in fury. The man was obstructing work. With no room to manoeuvre, the slaves around him had stopped while others watched. Daspati's own diseased mind was warning him to avoid a quarrel with the sanyasi. Not that he cared for the saffron robe, but this sanyasi was the headman's guest, and even the commander wanted to receive him with honour as he was from Sage Yadodhra's ashram.

Daspati's anger kept rising, but he did not know what he could do to teach the sanyasi a lesson. And then his gaze fell on that chit of a girl. Mithali, a servant's daughter, had dared to sit by the sanyasi, and tend to the injured slave! She would pay for her impudence as a lesson to the sanyasi who had encouraged her. With a grim smile, Daspati strode forward and grabbed Mithali's long hair, determined to drag her away. But he could not. The sanyasi held Daspati's offending arm in a tight grip and twisted it. His left hand shot forward instinctively to strike, but the sanyasi held that too. All the strength in Daspati's arms drained away.

Dasapati was a big, powerful man, known for ruthless violence. How could this slender sanyasi hold this powerful man rooted to the spot! His face turned purple with anger and then terror as he struggled to wrench himself free. At last, with a purposeful jerk, the sanyasi released him.

Daspati glared at the sanyasi malevolently. He gripped the dagger in his belt and said in a grim voice, 'You have abused the hospitality of this place.'

'And you have abused the hospitality of God's earth,' the sanyasi replied.

Daspati's rage exploded. He grasped Mithali's hair and shaking his fist, dagger held high, right in the sanyasi's face, asked, 'You lunatic! Who do you think you are?'

A crushing uneasiness took possession of the large, silent crowd. No one knew who was in greater danger—the sanyasi or Mithali.

Quietly, the sanyasi spoke, 'Who I am, you ask! I am Sindhu Putra.'

Sindhu Putra! A murmur went through the crowd, and rose to a cry, a roar, a chant. Was there anyone in the land who did not know of him! Many moved then, daring at last to prevent Daspati from committing a grievous, heinous sin. But their intervention was quite unnecessary. Daspati himself was immobilized by shock. The slaves, too, were quiet. They understood nothing, their eyes on their wounded comrade.

Sindhu Putra lifted the injured slave in his arms. A mournful cry came from the other slaves, who feared he was being taken to be slaughtered. Sindhu Putra walked into the midst of the slaves and gently lowered the injured man. He took off his robe, tearing off strips to bandage his wounds and placed the rest under the slave's head as a pillow.

The injured slave was the fifteen-year-old son of chief Jalta, named Jalta the Fourth, who had been captured by Nandan's troops. A slave girl—the young Jalta's wife, who had rushed headlong into the battlefield when her husband was surrounded and had been captured too—gently caressed him, hoping to revive him. They were married when she was a year old and he was sixteen months, by their parents, according to tribal custom. Their marriage was not consummated, as the appointed time arrived when both were in captivity. The girl was chanting a soft, mournful tune as she sat by her husband's body; perhaps it was the same melody Sindhu Putra had heard in his dream the night before.

Sindhu Putra walked away from the slaves to face the crowd of free, skilled workers. Some sought his blessing, others knelt before him. He pointed to the injured slave and said, 'Go, touch his feet against whom you have sinned.' Suddenly, his trembling voice rose, 'Go, free all slaves.' There was no movement; his voice rose higher, crying out, 'This I ask you, in the name of my father.'

Sindhu Putra's repeated references to his earthly father—Bharat—reinforced in many minds the notion of Bharat Varsha—the land of Bharat.

Sindhu Putra and Mithali were leaving the construction site. Everyone wanted to follow them, but Sindhu Putra stopped them. 'Do not follow me *until* you have followed my will,' he said and pointing to the slaves, added, 'let them go free.'

As he was about to leave, his eyes went to a woman; a white flower had fallen from her hair amidst the jostling crowd. He went closer, picked up the flower, caressed its petals and carefully put the flower back in her hair, making a movement with his lips, though nothing was heard. Pointing to the ground where the flower had fallen, he said, 'This earth is sacred,' he said. And pointing to the slaves, added, 'Do not smear it with their blood.' Then he left.

Daspati was sitting on a high boulder, his mind in a whirl. He knew something terrible had happened to him in the encounter with the lad who called himself Sindhu Putra. But what? Why did my heart freeze in nameless terror? Why was my arm numb, unable to strike? Even now, he felt a sensation of helplessness coursing through his arms! At last, he had the answer. He recalled stories of yogis who, by meditation and austerities, had acquired the power of black magic to dominate others' will. Yes, I was subjected to such 'will-domination' by a manipulating charlatan who knew this art, he concluded. Yet the one who did it was a mere boy! But then this boy had been immersed for years at the Rocks with the Mad Muni, and learnt the mysterious art there. Still, this did not console Daspati. He felt bitterly mortified and humiliated, but at least he understood how he had been tricked.

The workers went to Daspati, demanding that the slaves

be freed. He thought, these simpletons were duped even more than me; I understand how that deception arose, but they are still under the spell. He barked, 'Go back to work.' The crowd did not move. Daspati explained, 'I did not hurt that lunatic out of respect for his saffron robe, however unworthy he was to wear it. No wonder he himself felt the need to tear it, and walk out, half-naked, like a slave. Even then I forgave him, for he is known as the adopted son of a former karkarta. Besides, Karkarta Nandan would not have appreciated my harming an ascetic. But do not misunderstand my forbearance.' It was an excellent explanation; no one would ridicule him for weakness.

But the workers remained where they were. Daspati glared. Someone said, 'Free the slaves. That was his will.'

Daspati retorted, 'That I shall not. Before I do that, I shall kill all slaves. Yes, I shall, upon my soul and yours, if we have a soul.'

Blasphemy of his possible denial of the soul would normally have led to discussion. But now, all were silent. Daspati smiled grimly and said, 'Let us resume work.'

Kaka, an old man, said, 'You do not have the right.'

Daspati was startled. 'What right?' he asked.

Kaka clarified, 'The right to kill slaves. You said you would. Karkarta Nandan does not have that right, either. No one has that right.'

'I have no intention of killing them,' Daspati replied. 'We need them for work. My friend, go back to work.'

Kaka stood his ground, 'The slaves must be freed.'

'Go, old man,' Daspati said. 'Go and follow that stupid sanyasi. I don't need you. I need younger men to work here. Go!'

Mournfully, Kaka replied, 'I cannot.'

'Why not? Do you need wages so badly?'

'He said that we cannot follow him, until we have obeyed his will to free the slaves.'

'Who will free the slaves? You!'

'I am hoping you will,' Kaka said. Daspati looked as if the old man was insane. 'He is the son of Mother Goddess Sindhu.'

'If he is a god, why did he not free the slaves himself?' Daspati shouted. 'Why did he run off with a servant girl?'

'He knows what he does. He knows what we do.'

Daspati was frustrated; clearly, the same madness had affected them all. He changed tactics, 'You know, Karkarta Nandan is coming soon. Maybe he will free the slaves, if our work progresses fast.' He scanned the unresponsive crowd to add, 'There will be another bonus too when he comes. Why miss that opportunity!'

'It is good of you to increase our wages,' Kaka said.

'So,' Daspati cut in, 'get back to work right now!'

Kaka looked at his co-workers, sadly realizing his failure as spokesman. Another spoke, 'It is not a question of our wages. The slaves must go free.'

Surely, in this devil-ridden multitude, there must be someone with sense, Daspati thought. His eyes fell on the woman who wore the white flower in her hair. After her son had been killed in a tribal raid, she had started work at the construction site, not for the wages, for she was well off, but to do her bit against the tribals in memory of her son. While the other workers were sympathetic to the slaves, she had no such feelings.

'Speak, Sarama, speak,' Daspati invited her. 'Cut your cackle and listen to Sarama,' he told the others. Silently they watched Sarama, unaware that as he had placed the flower back in her hair, Sindhu Putra had seen a vision of his lost mother, and she of her son. When she saw his soft smile, and heard him say 'Mother!' and watched his lips move as though to kiss her from a distance, through the mist in her eyes, she saw not the youthful sanyasi, nor Sindhu Putra, but her own son who had picked up flowers when they fell from her hair and kissed her. She had felt the touch of his golden hand as he put the flower in her hair and a feeling of tremulous joy passed through her heart. In that moment, she had stood before her child, and he asked her for something. As she saw him leave, there were tears in his eyes. She saw the other workers were ready to do his bidding, to free the slaves, but she—alone— had stood speechless. Her anguish at not having clasped her son to her bosom manifested as tears that cleansed all bitterness for eternity, leaving her pure and beautiful. She struggled to find her voice and at last, with trembling lips, she said, 'Deny him not! Let the slaves go free.'

Everyone heard her, amazed. Her calm, gentle look of sweetness disturbed Daspati even more. 'There are penalties for stopping work,' he said. 'This fort is to make us strong, invulnerable against tribal attacks. What you contemplate is treason.' He sensed their unresponsiveness and pleaded, 'I do not have the right to release the slaves, nor does the commander. Only Karkarta Nandan can authorize that. Do you understand that I do not have the right?'

The question was fair. Indeed, Daspati could not free slaves. But surely, he could stop their work forthwith while awaiting the karkarta's decision. Respectfully, Kaka explained this alternative. But Daspati rejoined, 'I have no authority to stop their work. The slaves are at my disposal for work, not to be released from work.'

'You must do what you must. And we must do what we must.' Lines were now rigidly drawn. The workers refused to resume work unless the slaves were released.

Daspati thundered, 'I shall put the slaves to work. You go where you have to go.'

But they said they had nowhere to go, for they could not follow Sindhu Putra until his bidding was done; they had to remain at the fort.

'For how long?' Daspati asked, and they said, 'For as long as it takes!' Daspati asked, 'Who will give you food here?' But they seemed unperturbed—'He will provide.'

BHAGWAN S. GIDWANI

This was perhaps the first threat in the land of a strike, but what could one do to free people except threaten their wages! Enraged, Dasapti ordered his assistant, Tahila, to put the slaves to work instantly, sparing neither the rod nor the whip nor the lash. But mild-mannered Kaka intervened, 'Give up on our working for you ever, even for a moment, as long as we live. This I swear. And Tahila, that goes for you too.'

Tahila whispered to Daspati, 'Nothing good can come out of this. Let the commander take responsibility. He is to return in three days, but why not recall him earlier!' Daspati agreed. Tahila raised long poles with polished, shining shields tied to the tip—a signalling device to be repeated by guards posted on various hills at short distances from each other.

The headman, too, was summoned. The commander arrived after sunset and went over each detail, questioning everyone. He had interfered at times when Daspati had ill-treated the slaves. He always felt that Daspati's cruelty arose from basic insecurity. Even so, it puzzled him that the protest now came not from slaves, but from the free workers, and that too for the slaves' freedom. He dismissed Daspati's claim that the sanyasi's black magic had dominated the others' wills. Also, he brushed aside the headman's view of Sindhu Putra's godhood. He did not believe that a living god could walk on earth. Yet he could appreciate Sindhu Putra's feelings on seeing a slave wounded by Daspati's callousness. Undoubtedly that was what had led to all this.

'Where is Sindhu Putra now? In the guest house?' he asked.

'No. Mithali said that he went straight to the slave-quarter,' the headman reported.

'Alone?' the commander asked. The headman nodded. The commander kept his fear for Sindhu Putra's safety to himself. The slaves might not distinguish between a friend and a foe from an alien race. All the slaves were at the fort, except those who were too sick to work, but when driven to extremes, even the sick could cause hurt. How would they know of

Sindhu Putra's help to the slaves at the fort!

The commander began thinking of a solution. Half of those working there were slaves and the rest were free, wage-earners. The slaves worked till midnight and the wage-earners till sunset. If the slaves were let off from work, it simply meant that the wage-earners would also have to do the work allotted to the slaves. The wage-earners agreed—both for long hours without payment and to do the unskilled, back-breaking jobs normally assigned only to the slaves. Kaka—the commander decided—would see to it that they all held their honour in forfeit if they failed to do what was expected of them. The commander made no threats but challenged that there would be a strict accounting by Kaka, and on Kaka, every day.

'Surely, Kaka is not in charge!' Daspati objected.

'No, I am,' the commander replied sternly, annoying Daspati even more.

The commander saw the intense light of faith in the workers' eyes. They had not asked for extra wages for the additional work but the commander mentioned Daspati's promise of increased wages.

Daspati protested, 'That was said in a different context.'

'Did you say the karkarta has authorized the increase?'

Daspati explained that he had the authority to increase the hourly wage by 22 per cent during the day and 44 per cent at night, if circumstances so warranted.

'Good,' the commander responded, 'I am glad you exercised that authority to increase the wages this morning onwards. I cannot permit anyone to dishonour the karkarta's orders.'

Now that all was settled, the commander ordered that the slaves return to their quarters. 'You all may also leave,' he told Kaka, 'but after midnight.'

Happily, they remained and worked with energy and zest, as never before.

༄

On their way back to their quarters, the sentry, Hardas, who could speak the language of the tribals, told them what had transpired during the day.

Four years ago, Hardas had been part of the Hindu contingent that had attacked the tribes. The tribals had taken shelter behind their huts, but the Hindu soldiers had set the huts on fire with flaming arrows. Hardas had heard a scream from a hut on fire and rushed in. When he came out, with searing burns over his face and body, he bore in his arms a tribal child. Faint from exhaustion and pain, instead of returning to his troops, he went in the opposite direction, towards the tribals, faltering, falling, slipping, but all along protecting the child. Both sides stopped shooting their arrows, lest they hit their own. At last he reached the tribals and fainted in their midst. The tribals cared for him and tended to his wounds. Six months later, when he was ready to leave, they asked him to remain with them as a member of their own tribe. Their chief, however, rebuked them: 'Just as you would not wish to forsake your own tribe to join another and still be considered honourable, why ask another to do that, unless you consider him without honour? What benefit is a dishonourable man to you! To himself! To the gods!' But the mother of the child Hardas had rescued said that she would marry him, and a husband of a tribeswoman could not be ordered away. However, Hardas explained that he was already married and as a Hindu, unable to marry another. At a solemn ceremony, attended by tribal priests, the woman tied a bracelet around Hardas' wrist and adopted him as her brother, acknowledging his vow to accept her as his life-long sister. The tribals offered Hardas gifts as they parted. The chief had sent a message to the supreme chief, who sent back an impressive gold ring as a gift for Hardas. No tribal would ever harm a person honoured with that ring. His own contingent did not receive Hardas effusively, for he refused to fight against the tribals, claiming that amongst them was his adopted sister. The commander had reassigned Hardas to the lowly position of sentry.

Now, as Hardas marched back with the slaves, his one thought was to speak to them about Sindhu Putra. These slaves were hardened by cruelty and abuse; they expected only evil from those holding them in bondage. Some were impressed with what the man in the saffron robe had done for the injured Jalta, but others suspected it was simply an attempt to revive him and put him to work again.

Hardas had seen the commander's apprehension when told that Sindhu Putra was in the slave-quarter. Hardas, too, feared what the slaves might do to Sindhu Putra and spoke eloquently of him to the slaves. Jalta, now recovered, asked, 'Can a god of such goodness be born among people of such great evil!' But the slave-girl answered, 'It is only amongst people of great evil that gods manifest themselves. Where else are gods needed more, except among the damned and the doomed, where the devil rides high? And did you see how their god went back, in defeat and disgrace, with tears flowing, but not a single follower, except a little girl?' Hardas listened sadly, but perhaps she had said the right words. Even in their own abject misery, the slaves still had room in their heart for sympathy for a god; they would not bow to that foreign god for he belonged to those wicked, wanton people, but they were kind-hearted enough to wish him no hurt or harm.

Meanwhile in the slave-quarter, Sindhu Putra was trying to pray. But he could not. Like footprints washed away by waves, his earlier exhilaration had disappeared. What folly tempted me—he asked himself—to reveal my identity as Sindhu Putra! But what is wrong with that—he rationalized —surely that is my name! Did I lie? He recalled his own nameless terror when Daspati had confronted him. Yet, when the hated man was subdued, he had felt a strange surge of triumph, and to a question that could easily have been ignored, he had announced himself as Sindhu Putra! What

BHAGWAN S. GIDWANI

was I thinking at that moment—to stand out flamboyantly as a god so that all may worship me? Yes, I stood there, preening myself, masquerading as a god I am not, demanding that they do my bidding. Again he sought to find an excuse— 'But did I really lie?'

He had seen violence against a slave and felt as if the blood of the slave was his own. When he saw Mithali being threatened, he was frightened, and had impulsively blurted out his name, lest Daspati renewed the violence. But he could not reconcile this with what had happened thereafter. He had glowed inwardly, seeing the effect of his name on everyone, and when Daspati stood paralysed and others gazed, fascinated, he had felt an exhilarating sense of triumph. He was confident that he had only to lift his finger and they all would do his bidding. The lie, then, was not in his words but in his manner—acting, behaving, gesturing, even strutting like a god!

This self-analysis only increased Sindhu Putra's anguish. He thought of the days ahead, amidst people in the township who would want to worship him—and he shivered. He must run and hide—but where? Mithali had spoken of the dreadful slave-quarter which the townspeople never entered. He had decided to go there. Mithali wept for she wanted to go with him, but he went alone.

∽

The slave-quarter was dark when the slaves marched in. They watched Sindhu Putra curiously—but without hatred. Even so, they found it impossible to believe that this half-clad youth was a god. He had neither venerable age nor the splendid adornments of their imagination. 'Is he really a god?' the slaves asked Hardas. 'Why does a god have to pray? To whom does he pray?' Sindhu Putra heard them speak but did not understand what was being said for Hardas did not translate. His mind was on his own questions that were tormenting him. A new fear assailed him—has my posturing deluded these simple slaves into believing in my godhood! I must erase such thoughts from their minds.

'I am no god,' he addressed them. 'I never was a god and I shall never be. But I wish to devote myself to search for the eternal rhythm of God's spirit, to hear the precious echoes of God's voice and to understand the mystery of divine reality. Those that call me a god are in error. I pray, but I do not even know the pathway which a seeker must choose. For the rest, my brothers and sisters, I am like you, and I pray to the God that lives in all of you.'

Hardas translated. The slaves wondered how Sindhu Putra had understood and addressed their questions. To Hardas, it was no mystery—how can a god fail to understand! Jalta asked, 'When your god says he is no god, do you believe him to be a liar? Do your gods always lie?' Yet they wondered— how had he understood them? But then, he had not answered their questions, only the torments in his heart.

Their wonder was perhaps even greater that he denied his godhood! Their own gods came forth in a shining blaze of glory, roaring and thundering, with claims that they were the first and the last, the origin and the dissolution, and that all must take refuge in them or else they would be punished with destruction everlasting and forever be denied the glory of Their power, and only those that believed in them would be saved. Some lesser gods had some modesty and chose not to call themselves the All-mighty God who created the universe, but simply His Viceroy on Earth, or His Son, or His Prophet, or Messenger, or First Chosen Deputy to speak to His chosen people.

But this god! He denied all such claims for himself!

Sindhu Putra closed his eyes to pray. The slaves saved a portion from their scanty food rations and kept it by his side.

A silver half-moon was shining. A woman in the slave-quarter sang. Was it the same melody he had heard in his dream, Sindhu Putra wondered. But it was no longer the plaintive summoning cry of the night before. He asked, 'What does the song say?' Hardas translated:

In the desolate desert of lost hopes untold
Where wind cries, moon shines, unseeing, cold,
Where stars twinkle, only to sneer and mock,
At unmoving gods we made of clay, sand and rock
Where Death stalks with ghostly steps by day
And the Devil laughs, all night, all the way
Amidst the caravan of the Defeated and Damned
Where all pathways are closed and doors slammed,
A stranger comes, softly by an unseen way,
With soft, silent steps—a golden day—
He comes, He comes, Ever He comes.

Sindhu Putra repeated the last words—'He comes, Ever He comes', and said, 'We too have a song that begins and ends with these words.' Actually, it was the song which Muni of the Rocks sang when Kanta parted from him after the death of her child, celebrating God's love and compassion.

'Many of their songs,' Hardas said, 'are almost like ours. The words differ but the meaning is the same.'

Sindhu Putra thought, Bharatjogi is right; everyone, everywhere has one soul, one aim, one goal. The bond may be invisible, yet it exists.

∽

'The slaves were freed early tonight! How?' Sindhu Putra asked.

'Such was your will, master,' Hardas replied.

'You think it is possible that they would free the the slaves?'

'Everything is possible for a god,' Hardas replied.

Sindhu Putra tried to pray, but his mind wandered. He thought of Bharat's dream to free the slaves; of Bharatjogi's prayer when he sent him to Muni's Rocks—'God, give Sindhu Putra the vision to walk as my son should, to unite our people!'

His mind then leapt to what the singer had told Bharatjogi, 'We have gone too far downhill. For unity and freedom, now, we need *not* a new karkarta. We need a god.'

Bharatjogi had laughed, 'Do we not already have enough gods? The strong in spirit find God in their deeper selves, and the rest find gods in water and fire; in images and idols of wood, metal and stone. And yet you seek a new god!'

The singer had replied, 'I seek no new god. But I wait for a god to reveal himself—even to himself!'

Yes—said Sindhu Putra to himself—the singer is right. A god is needed to recapture Bharatjogi's vision of freedom and unity. Let me be that god! Let me be as I was today at the fort, and if they honour my word as the word of a god, then so be it. Let it be their solace that I have come.

But another wave of feeling came flooding into his mind. I will be living a lie. By what right do I degrade godhood and pass myself off as a god? Are the foundations of freedom, justice, unity to be based on a fraudulent lie? There is God above us all, and He shall see to it that the dream of freedom and unity shall one day be fulfilled. Yet, he remembered Muni's words, 'Evil grows to rise like a flood. It may not subside, for God does not choose to interfere with the world of man. Man moves his world, by his own actions, by his own will and by his own karma.'

Karma? What kind of a karma would it be to pass myself off as god! Did not Yadodhra say that *only a trickster or a lunatic would like to be known as a god while he lives.* Do I then live the life of a trickster or a lunatic and be forever damned, condemned and scorned for this grievous sin, before God, who sees all! Is this to be my karma—when all I wanted was an opportunity to devote my life to truth and piety, hopefully on my way to moksha? Why then am I drawn by this strange, irresistible force? What is it telling me—to live the life of a lie? And what of my moksha then? What use will the soul of God have for a dishonourable trickster who falsely wears the garb of a god on earth? But does it matter if my own moksha is unattainable, by taking on others' sorrows? How can I think of my own salvation, when others are suffering!

His mind went again to Muni who had said that God does not interfere with man's actions. Obviously then, it is through man that human suffering can arise or cease. Is it not man's duty, then, to intervene? Surely, it is not enough that a devotee surrenders himself to the Divine simply in prayer, piety and meditation. The doctrine of grace and salvation should mean much more—that anyone who gave up his duty, to pass his time merely in prayer or to proclaim the Lord's name, but devoted not his energies to protect righteousness, was a sinner. How can anyone lose himself in inner piety alone while hearts heavy with sorrow cry out for help when they are being maltreated and humiliated! Thus, prepared though he was to exalt a life of contemplation, he was convinced that man could not make himself a perfect instrument for His use or attain the highest spiritual wisdom unless he sought out action and adventure to fit God's transcendent pattern, purpose and will; man's purpose was to live on earth and save it.

Thus Sindhu Putra kept unburdening his heart to himself. Perhaps that alone served to erase his doubts. His mind began to resolve itself. His decision was made—yes, I will take on the burden of giving shape to Bharatjogi's dream of freedom and unity; I shall not proclaim myself as a god, nor shall I deny it. If suppressing the truth is worse than an outright lie—so be it.

He silenced the voice that cried out within him that questionable means cannot achieve honourable results. As to his own moksha, he renounced all aspirations to it. He was, he realized, setting out on a path of falsehood to hold himself out as a god—if not by words, at least by silence and conduct. Moksha shall not be mine—he told himself ruefully. But renunciation of his own moksha no longer mattered to him. He thought of the simple, frightened men and women in bondage. Surely, on God's good earth, with its endless series of lives, they too counted for something—and if my moksha is the price, so be it.

NINETEEN

GO! TAKE YOUR PEOPLE AND GO!

5054 BC

Nandan glared at Daspati, the headman and the commander. He had summoned them to his headquarters. The commander's message had mystified him. Clearly there was a revolt brewing at the fort-site. But for what! To work endlessly, instead of the slaves who must be freed! A revolt instigated by Sindhu Putra!

Nandan wondered how the scoundrel had found his way to this godforsaken land that even his father Bharat had never seen! And what made him incite a revolt, so far from his own temple, his land, and his people! Was it some deep-seated conspiracy by Bharat for his ill-begotten, adopted son to win laurels in a faraway land! Why? So he could return like a conquering hero and begin nefarious activities here?

Nandan heard Daspati's explanation with contempt. How could he accept that the boy had dominated the wills of all those present through black magic! Even Sage Dhanawantar had said that a person's mind could be put to sleep only if he willingly subjected himself to that will. This thick-skulled bully, Daspati, who caused such terror among the slaves, must be a weakling at heart, Nandan concluded. His assessment of the headman, who said that Sindhu Putra spoke with the voice and heart of a god, was not very different. Nandan wondered why he had not realized earlier how soft in the head this man was! Only the commander was objective. He reported that work at the fort was progressing well—ahead of schedule—despite the absence of the slaves.

'The slaves, then, seem unnecessary,' Nandan remarked. 'You think they should be sent elsewhere under Daspati?'

'No, I think Daspati has served his purpose,' the commander replied.

Nandan flared up, 'What purpose has he served? Except to create this fiasco!'

The commander was thinking: tyranny itself serves the purpose to inspire the cry for freedom.

'Surely,' Nandan began, 'we can send the slaves elsewhere under someone else who will know how to handle them!'

'That will serve no purpose. Our skilled workers are demanding that the slaves be freed and allowed to go back to their own land.'

'Are we so dependent on them? Why not dismiss them?'

'We can appoint new workers to replace them,' the commander agreed. 'But the present workers are determined to remain at the construction site until their demand is met. Hiring new workers might lead to a confrontation. The new workers might even be influenced into joining their cause and making the same demand. This new, sudden wave has affected the townspeople, too. Bhavnan, the merchant, has joined hands with Lekhan, the horse-trainer, to donate large sums to set up a food-kitchen for the slaves.'

'Why! Have we denied food to the slaves?'

'No. But Sindhu Putra refused the food that was sent for him. He would eat only what the slaves eat. The townspeople now send the best food for the slaves.' The commander looked at the headman pointedly, but did not tell Nandan that the headman's wife was in charge of running the food-kitchen.

Daspati, wilting under their contempt and neglect, now spoke firmly, 'All that is required is to arrest that rascal Sindhu Putra.'

The headman's face turned pale. The commander looked at Daspati pityingly. Nandan simply shook his head. Arrest Sindhu Putra! Such an action would have unexpected consequences throughout the land! He asked the commander, 'Your advice then is that these slaves be freed?' The commander nodded in response.

Karkarta Nandan realized that the situation in the township had to be contained before news spread and the ill-wind from the township turned into a chilling whirlwind that infected the entire land. There was no sense in allowing an isolated issue to turn into a major disaster.

Nandan gave his instructions to the commander. 'Let the slaves at the fort be freed and allowed to return to their tribes. Sindhu Putra shall lead them to their lands.'

'I shall send soldiers to escort them out,' the commander said.

'No, I don't want our soldiers at risk. The slaves are under Sindhu Putra's protection. Let them so remain.'

Their eyes met. Nandan was calm, unwavering, and decisive. The commander, however, was concerned: their slaves belonged to two different tribes, but once free, they would have to travel through lands infested by other hostile tribes. It was impossible to hope that these slaves would reach their homes unmolested. And what would happen to Sindhu Putra, alone, amidst these slaves! Would they not turn their ferocity against him, in their first flush of freedom from the hated captors of his race?

Nandan shook his head, 'Our soldiers shall not escort them.'

The commander understood, but said, 'They face the danger of deadly attacks from other tribes. I shall give them a few weapons for self-defence.'

Nandan said, 'No. They go with nothing. If such weapons are used by them against Sindhu Putra, we shall be accused of arming them to harm him.'

'Would it not be said that we led them, along with Sindhu Putra, into an ambush, unprotected and unarmed?'

Nandan smiled, 'Such an accusation would be unjust. Does a god need protection! How can I act from want of faith! I leave the task of escorting the slaves to Sindhu Putra because I am led to believe that he is more than a mortal man, who controls the weaponry of the gods.'

TWENTY

NAMASTE!

5054 BCE

The entire population of the township lined up to bid Sindhu Putra farewell. Sindhu Putra then did what surprised them all. Looking at the headman's wife, he joined his palms and raised his hands to his forehead; it was the gesture of a slave and no free man would have dreamed of demeaning himself by adopting such a gesture. Captors of newly captured slaves always insisted that the slaves march with their hands tied and raised so they could not carry a concealed weapon. Eventually, the slaves were expected to voluntarily greet free men and women with this gesture—the only difference was that their hands were no longer tied. It was a badge of dishonour, imposed on the insistence of free, wage-earning workers who did not wish to be mistaken for slaves.

It was this gesture of the slave that Sindhu Putra made as he faced the headman's wife. Involuntarily, her hands moved, though not to greet him in the same fashion, but simply to touch his hands. Sindhu Putra walked past other townspeople, greeting them with the same unvarying gesture of the slave.

Everyone seemed nonplussed. Many bowed; the closest that some came to repeating Sindhu Putra's gesture was to hold his folded hands in their own. Many saw his lips move, but could not hear what he said.

Eventually Sindhu Putra came to face to face with an eight-year-old girl carrying a two-year-old in her arms. Sindhu Putra smiled at them and as he began to move away, the girl said,

'Baba, will you not bless my little brother and say for him what you said for all?' Sindhu Putra stopped and looked at the two children. To each he said, 'Tat tvam asi'—Thou art that.

The words were silent no more. Each person heard them distinctly—'Tat tvam asi.' What did it mean? Many knew and understood that he was simply holding himself out as a slave to the God within everyone, as his submission to the Ultimate. The urge for the same humility came over them. They, too, raised their hands, palms pressed in the same manner, to reciprocate Sindhu Putra's greeting while chanting 'Tat tvam asi' soulfully. Whatever their earlier doubts, they were now convinced that facing them was a youth who had found fulfilment in the heart of the Eternal. Others, whom Sindhu Putra had passed earlier, rushed forward with their belated greeting, as the chant filled the air.

Sindhu Putra, at last, walked towards the slaves. Here, too, he greeted them similarly. It was Jalta's young wife who raised her hands to make the same gesture. And the chief of the Silent Tribe—and then his men—followed her example.

But Jalta's fists were clenched. Anger re-entered his heart: why must I suffer the ignominy of raising my hands in a slave-gesture? Even during his captivity, he had told himself, 'I am a slave not when the rope ties me, but only when I *think* I am a slave.' He glared at Sindhu Putra. Maybe he is truly a god—but then he is a god of that hated race—not ours! What is his purpose? To make us slaves forever! In body and spirit! Never! In defiance, Jalta raised his fist at the townspeople in the distance. The slaves, next to him, also raised their fists with a mighty roar, in a show of solidarity. Many townspeople saw the slaves' raised fists and heard their shout, and misunderstood. They saw it not as defiance, but an invitation for a rallying cry—and their own cries went up, loud and clear—'Tat tvam asi!'

It was Jalta's turn to ask Hardas, 'What are they saying?'

Hardas explained, 'They say there is God in you and to Him and to you, they salute.'

Jalta misunderstood. He pointed at Sindhu Putra to accuse, 'Yes, there is god among us. But he is their god, not mine!' His accusing finger was still pointing at Sindhu Putra. Silently, his wife grasped his hand and kissed it.

Hardas explained, 'The God in you . . . He that resides in you . . . He whose divine flame ever burns in You . . . You whose soul is the same as that of God's own . . . '

First, they make us slaves, Jalta thought in disgust, then they make us gods; first they are treacherous and callous, then they are stupid and dazed. But he wavered as he noticed the lips of his wife resting on his hand. Perhaps it was her plea of love that overcame his resistance or maybe it was because Sindhu Putra came to stand before him just then, but his hands rose in a silent, spontaneous salutation just as fervent as Sindhu Putra's.

All the slaves raised their hands in the same salutation, but it was no longer a gesture of the slave, and as they repeated 'Tat tvam asi,' they saw with the eye of their own inmost heart, the unique splendour of One-ness, of atonement—and thus it became the salute of the liberated and the free.

TWENTY-ONE

THE LONG MARCH

5054 BCE

The slaves were slaves no more. As they marched to freedom, they wondered about Sindhu Putra, this god of their oppressors marching with them. Was he their god too?

They heard Jalta's wife, as she haltingly explained Hardas' translation of 'Tat tvam asi', in her own words, simplified, in their own idiom. She spoke of the majesty of all mankind and the concept of God as the ultimate cause from whom we were all born, through whom we lived, and unto whom we returned and merged.

But what about hell everlasting, they wondered as they recalled their own ancient myths. What about the mistake of God's first servant, steeped in original sin, whose hands trembled as he fashioned them all—and who took refuge with the Devil! And their exile, then, from deathless heaven to this desolate earth for their failure to be fitted into the God image by that mistake? Was this youth the promised Redeemer? Was he the one prophesied to slay the banished first servant, whose legion of a thousand devils and ten thousand serpents guarded the route to the gate of heaven!

But then, Jalta's wife explained Sindhu Putra's views as Hardas had related them.

'As a Hindu, how can I believe in hell except on this earth itself? Would God, whose attribute is compassion, really create hell or a place of eternal torment? Does it not presuppose a place where God is not, where there is a being in control, uncreated by a merciful God, who torments all in defiance of the compassionate God?'

They marched with diverse thoughts, many wondering why their hearts felt cleansed of hatred against the people who had held them captive.

Jalta, though, was more concerned about sudden attacks from hostile tribes on the route. In their exhilaration, they had overlooked that danger. They had no weapons, no protection and far too many dangerous tribes to face. At his bidding, everyone stopped to collect jagged stones. It would be a poor defence, but it was better to die fighting than be slaughtered or enslaved again.

Hardas took out the weapons he had brought on two mules—an axe, six swords, some daggers, short spears and knives. He began making new spears from tree branches and encouraged others to do so, lending them his axe.

Everyone saw Jalta's sadness. He and his wife had been unable to consummate their marriage while they were in captivity even though the time had arrived. Now, though they were free, there was no priest who could perform the ceremony to sanction consummation.

'I am the upholder of law in my tribe,' he said. 'How can I break the law!'

When Hardas told Sindhu Putra of Jalta's sorrow, he held Jalta and his wife's hands in one of his own, and with his other hand he pointed to his breast, then at the heavens and finally at everyone present there. All he meant was that he, the God above and everyone present were witnesses. But to Jalta and his wife, it was as though he said—I am the one sent from heaven to lay down Law for all. Do you disbelieve a god who seeks to fulfil your heart's desire! If Jalta had lingering doubts, the Silent Chief said in sign language: why stop the rhythm of your heartbeat and the urge in your body, to wait for the senseless chant of old priests!

Blessed by Sindhu Putra, Jalta and his wife went behind a

grove of trees and lay down on the soft, cool grass. They said little to each other, their thoughts wandering to the dreams of their past, rediscovering them in the beating of their hearts and the warmth of their bodies. Gently, unhurriedly, they moved and together they stitched an unbroken tapestry of love and fulfilment, culminating in their first mingled cry of joy, pain and ecstasy.

Later, when the march recommenced, Jalta realized that he would meet criticism from his people back home for abandoning the time-honoured custom of having a priest sanction consummation. Surely they would say that the god who had blessed their union was not a god of their tribe. What would he tell the priests in response? He thought of the long, treacherous journey ahead, fraught with danger. Many would die if they were attacked. Perhaps he himself would fall. But he prayed for his wife to survive and for a child to be born from their union and become the chief of his tribe.

To his wife, Jalta said, 'No one must doubt the sanctity of our union, nor question the right of our offspring to be the chief.' She simply smiled. He gazed at Sindhu Putra and continued, 'I shall declare him a god. No one will be able to question the validity of our marriage or the legitimacy of our child then. I shall call on all tribes to accept him as a god from now on.'

'But he always was and is a god,' his wife said, simply.

Jalta walked to the silent chief who readily agreed. The march was halted for Jalta's announcement. He declared Sindhu Putra as god of all the tribes from end to end, for all time, from the first arrow of time, to time unending. Appropriately, the Silent Chief repeated the declaration in sign language. Jalta knew that tribal custom did not permit him to anoint a god; it was the privilege of tribal priests, and only done after years of deliberation. Jalta had wrestled with this problem and concluded: If I live, I shall fight to justify my declaration. But if I die on the march, I will be sheltered, and no one will question the sanctity of my marriage or the legitimacy of my child. The dead, he knew, were treated with respect and much was forgiven them. His brothers, too, would fight to protect his honour and memory.

Jalta watched his motley army carrying sticks and spears, freshly hewn from trees. They would frighten no one. They marched, day after day, with their pitiful weapons, wondering if the hooting of an owl or birdsong they heard were signals of enemy lookouts, calling their tribes to attack. In valleys and gorges, they looked up fearfully, wondering if boulders would be hurled on them, as a prelude to furious assaults. As they traversed dangerous passes controlled by hostile tribes safely, the enemy's inactivity surprised them. Looking at Sindhu Putra, they wondered: is this god really guarding us? The Silent Chief simply nodded. But even he looked concerned when they reached a pass deep inside enemy territory. However, nothing happened; they passed unmolested. Their relief was immense.

One more treacherous pass still remained—dominated by a murderous enemy tribe which would never let them pass unharmed. The terrain was such that they would be frightfully vulnerable even against a small number of attackers, but that tribe always had huge forces. It was unthinkable that their lookouts would not be watching. The tribe's lands were rough and barren, but they had not always been so. There was a time when everything was lush and green. But over centuries, the tribe had violated mankind's ageless oath to protect wildlife, and started slaughtering animals and birds for sport. Perhaps it was the effect of their actions or the just wrath of the gods, but their forests were dwarfed, and now they relied on warfare to catch slaves and sell them to other tribes. The wounded among their prisoners often served to feed the tribe itself. Jalta and the Silent Chief realized that whatever their good fortune so far, there was little hope that they would escape unscathed. Even now they could hear the noise of drums in the distance, no doubt to call the tribe to arms!

Jalta ordered his men to stand in a zigzag pattern, so the enemy onrush would not wipe them out in a single sweep, giving some of them the chance to hit back or escape. The Silent Chief asked twenty of his men to form a circle around Jalta's wife.

'Why?' Jalta asked, grateful and surprised. The chief gestured that he had adopted her as his daughter, and the child in her womb had to be safeguarded.

The drumbeats were becoming louder. Clearly, an attack was imminent and the enemy was on its way, ready to slaughter or enslave them. But nothing happened; no one blocked their way. Even so, they said, 'Let us help the miracle,' and they ran through the pass. When they emerged safely, their hearts pounding, they all had but one thought and they gazed at Sindhu Putra, certain it was a god who was guarding them.

With a sigh of relief, they neared the village of Jalta the Third. The lookouts recognized Jalta the Fourth. The reunion was joyous; the drumbeats announcing his return were louder than any heard in that village before.

∾

How did this miracle occur? Were the thirteen hostile tribes on that perilous route in a stupor, or had they suddenly become compassionate? Or was it really a miracle wrought by Sindhu Putra?

According to legend, when Sindhu Putra marched out with the slaves from the fort, the commander felt compelled to move with his troops into the eastern region to block the routes the hostile tribes might take to attack the slaves.

He had obeyed Karkarta Nandan's instructions that Sindhu Putra and the slaves not be given any weapons to defend themselves on their journey. It occurred to the commander that perhaps the karkarta desired that Sindhu Putra and the slaves would be slaughtered by the hostile tribes.

It was the commander's duty to occasionally make a show of strength and carry out selective sorties against hostile tribes. Now, he decided, was the right time, and so, with full force, he chose as his target the thirteen tribes that posed a threat to Sindhu Putra and the slaves. He made no frontal attacks, simply blocking the routes and preventing the movement of the hostile tribes towards the passes through which Sindhu Putra and the slaves marched.

However, hostilities did break out between the tribes and the commander's troops. The last battle was fought in the area where Sindhu Putra and the slaves had heard the drumbeats. It was a bloody and fierce confrontation; the tribals were beaten back but the commander lost his life when an enemy arrow pierced his chest. Some say he died instantly. Others claim he whispered 'Tat tvam asi,' and raised his hands in the gesture of a slave before dying.

The miracle, then, was not that none of the hostile tribes chose to molest Sindhu Putra's march—how could they, with the solid wall of the commander's troops standing in their way—but that a change came about in the commander's heart. *'A fire was lit in the heart of the non-believer that consumed him quite; And the Believer then emerged to go forth with all his might.'*

The freed slaves, who marched with Sindhu Putra, knew nothing of the commander's push in the eastern region. To them, the failure of the tribes to attack was simply Sindhu Putra's miracle. When they told the tale to their own tribe, there was rejoicing for they had walked through the valley of death, defied the devil, and reached unharmed and safe, because a god escorted them.

When Jalta the Fourth guided his blind mother to Sindhu Putra, she hesitantly embraced him, wondering if her greeting was too familiar. Sindhu Putra hugged her tightly. He guided her hand to his face so that she might touch his features and 'see' him. Through tears of joy she said, 'If you were not a god, you would be my son.'

Jalta the Second, her eldest son, laughed, 'Mother, be careful, you have three sons already as chiefs, and there isn't enough land to go round for another son to be a chief.'

She turned to the tribe with her sightless eyes and said, 'You will call him chief! He is the chief of all chiefs! Nobler, mightier, greater than all. Honour him then, all of you.'

TWENTY-TWO

OM! THE FIRST WORD OF GOD!

5053 BCE

The chief of the silent tribe and his men were honoured guests in Jalta's land. A messenger was sent to the chief's homeland with news of their safe return. The chief's brother, Rohan, who had acted as chief in his absence, rushed to Jalta's tribe with priests to escort his brother back. But the chief said he would not return to his land, that he would henceforth serve Sindhu Putra. He wanted his brother to be chief. The priests explained that the chief could not resign without his people's consent, and nor could he appoint his brother as successor without their consent. And in order to get that consent he had to appear before his people, or his resignation and the successor's appointment would both be illegitimate.

When asked why he wanted to resign, the chief explained, 'He who leads his people does not have to be a total scoundrel. But nor can he afford to be too godly. At times, he must serve the devil also. A chief may sacrifice an individual to serve the larger greed of the community; or he may declare a war that the gods consider unholy. How can I then serve a god and yet be a chief? From a chief, his people expect courage, but a god may demand honour. How then is it possible for a person to be a people's leader and yet serve god! And when that inevitable conflict arises, whom does he abandon—his people or his god? It is easy to abandon god, but not so easy to give up power!'

Rohan, his brother, was mystified by the chief's reluctance

to visit his homeland, even briefly, to resign. If indeed the chief's decision to abdicate was firm, Rohan wanted his succession to be regularized so that no one could ever question its legitimacy.

Rohan went to Sindhu Putra and, using gestures, begged him to accompany them to their land. Sindhu Putra readily agreed. Rohan went back to interrupt the discussion between the priests and the chief and, with a dramatic flourish, announced Sindhu Putra's keen wish to travel to their land, effectively ending the argument. The priests smiled, the chief nodded sombrely.

True, the chief wanted to remain by Sindhu Putra's side, but his reluctance to visit his homeland arose from the fact that his land had slaves and his new god, he feared, would demand their freedom. How would he pit himself against his people to remove slavery? How would he remain true to his new god? All tribes had practised slavery since time immemorial. The only exception was Jalta's tribe, which had not descended from the sun or moon or heaven. Whatever changes time had wrought in Jalta's tribe, their principle of 'no master, no slave', had remained unbroken and sacrosanct. But, for his own tribe, was it not an impossible dream to abolish slavery? How could he compare his ancient tribe, which prided itself on its customs rooted in antiquity, with Jalta's tribe? He feared that he would simply be ridiculed if he suggested that his tribe free their slaves because his new god said so. Surely, they would ask, what has this new, foreign god done? True, he had secured their freedom, but then the tribe had often entered the territory of other tribes to free their own people from slavery; no one thought of conferring godhood on those men. Why, sometimes they even released their own slaves when they served them well. Did that make them gods? Priest Jarasanda had freed his slave Arundhati because she bore him a child. Did that make him a god? And what about Pitamana, who had liberated three of his female slaves whom his grandsons were trying to seduce. Was he a god too? And if he made too much of their safe journey through the territories of the hostile tribes, would they perhaps point to Khashan, the old priest, and ask: 'Do you know how many journeys the old man has made over the last thirty years to lands near and far? And was he ever attacked?'

No, they would simply mock him, the chief told himself. The task of freeing the slaves in his homeland was beyond him. With a heavy heart, he went out into the open to be alone with his melancholy thoughts. Suddenly, his gloom vanished as he saw someone familiar in the distance. It was his cousin Narada, his dearest friend, riding out towards him. Narada and the chief were devoted to each other. The chief ran forward, his arms outstretched, to greet his friend, almost colliding with the horse. Narada dismounted and they embraced each other.

'Why were you trying to kiss my horse?' Narada gestured to his cousin.

'Why not?' the chief replied. 'He is the one who has brought you to me.'

Outwardly, there was nothing impressive about Narada except that he was older than the chief, but looked ten years younger. He was used to saying, 'I am too young to be old and too old to be young; so neither the young nor the old want my company.' But actually, he was welcome everywhere. He was respected as a dreamer and visionary. He himself had little time for others as he was busy studying stars and planets. His father had been the chief of the tribe, and he was nominated as the next chief, but he declined. When the tribe protested, he insisted that he had received a vision 'from above' that the office must go to his first cousin who was next in line—and that is how the present chief was appointed. Narada had also refused to serve as the chief priest. He wanted to remain free to lead a life that was totally free. He had only two close friends—the chief and Khashan, the old priest.

Narada touched the chief's hair and then his heart, as if to say, 'Your hair is whiter, your eyes sorrowful, and your heart heavy with grief.'

The chief nodded sadly and Narada smiled. 'Then I was right in refusing to become the chief?'

'Is my sorrow not yours too?' the chief retorted.

Narada embraced him again to sympathize with the chief's suffering during captivity. The chief shook his head and poured out the anguish in his heart—he was about to betray his new god. 'How can I face my people and demand that they free their slaves!'

Narada was pitiless. 'But you have already betrayed your god by deciding to resign and staying away so as not to direct your people to carry out your god's will. And now the fear in your heart is that your god will discover your betrayal when you fail to call on your people to free their slaves.'

The chief nodded; Narada was right. True, the seed of his guilt lay in trying to shirk his responsibility. But this realization only increased his gloom.

Narada laughed and thumped his own breast. 'Here I stand before you, my dearest friend! I, the greatest shirker in the tribe! I, who escape all responsibility and accept no duty— neither from man nor from the gods! Why this grief then? What is there to fear?'

The chief's depression grew. 'You made me the chief to escape responsibility yourself, while I remain rooted to it. How does that help me?'

Narada smiled, his finger raised high as if to remind his friend of the common belief that the sky sent visions to him. In spite of his gloom, the chief smiled too, knowing that Narada saw no such visions. Narada's smile grew wider. They sat for hours while Narada asked the chief about his time in captivity, those that died, how they were freed, of their long march to Jalta's lands.

BHAGWAN S. GIDWANI

Why so many questions, to what end, the chief demanded, but Narada continued his relentless inquiry, until there was nothing left to add or clarify.

Narada had one more surprise. Instead of going with the chief to Jalta's village, he mounted his horse and turned back. 'No one must know that I was here or that we met,' he warned.

'But everyone must know that you left to come here. Then how could we not have met!' the chief protested.

'You think if they knew I was coming here, they would allow me to travel alone! No, they still think I am holed up in my study.' They embraced. Narada's final advice was, 'Enter your land on a full-moon day, and you must demand a sacrifice to the gods.'

'Why must a horse die?' the chief objected, referring to the fact that a sacrifice involved killing a horse. He knew that like him, Narada hated that anything living should be sacrificed, but they both were powerless to stop this age-old custom.

'No horse shall die,' Narada assured him. 'The lie shall lead to the truth, as the truth often leads to a lie . . . ' and then he faltered, 'maybe your god, be he a true god or false, maybe he would be pleased. But the true God of all . . . who knows! Who knows!'

∾

A week before the full moon, Narada emerged suddenly from his retreat, dishevelled and distraught, and ran towards the chief's house, drawing maximum attention to himself. Many were there, waiting for the chief's arrival. Narada announced that the chief would arrive on the day of the full moon and would demand a sacrifice. No one asked how he knew; was anything ever hidden from the man who conversed with stars and had visions! Nor did they ask the nature of the sacrifice.

Obviously, a horse would be sacrificed, for that was the most auspicious omen. As the crowd grew, Narada saw the six men and two women he was searching for. With tears streaming from his eyes, he then indicated the names of those who had died in battle and later in captivity at the fort. There were tears now in everyone's eyes, for they had not known till that moment who had died and who lived. Narada then spoke of the survivors—their sorrows and suffering in captivity. He made it clear that all of them would have died but for their heroic chief, who not only looked after his people constantly, but summoned the spirits of their tribal ancestors with his willpower and meditation. Yet, the tyrants who had held their people captive were too powerful. Even so, the chief never gave up hope. He dissociated from the powerless gods of his own tribe and asked the God of All for a new god. The spirits of the dead had told him that the danger was not only to the captives, but the entire tribe. An ancient curse would come to pass and the fate of the tribe would be more terrible than death.

With the undivided attention of the crowd focused on him, Narada added, 'The chief himself died a thousand deaths as he foresaw the tribe's awesome fate. He continued practising austerities. But enough of this . . . ' He pointed then to the men and women he had selected, and promised that they would announce fully the successful outcome of the chief's efforts.

Narada then simply made short points in sign language to indicate that the God of All could not resist the chief's devotion and demand, and had sent a new god. The chief had offered his tribe's allegiance to the new god and promised a personal sacrifice and another by the entire tribe in his honour. Thereupon, the new god had secured freedom for the chief and his men, and boldly escorted them through the lands of the thirteen hostile tribes. He raised a screen of unseen smoke so that no one could see or attack them as they passed through those valleys of death. At times though, the smoke disappeared, for some of the chief's companions doubted this new god, and gods cannot exist without faith. But this god was too powerful. His deadly arrows flew invisibly and the enemy was paralysed. After a long pause, he added, 'The new god shall come soon and the chief shall demand a sacrifice to save the tribe. Are you ready?'

'Ready? Of course!' everyone said. 'Why just one horse? Two, three, ten!'

Narada shook his head—no, not horses.

'What then? Surely not a goat or a sheep! The occasion is too great for such a lowly sacrifice!'

Narada explained: the chief's personal sacrifice was to resign and leave the office to his brother. That is what the new god demanded. They felt sad. Now that Narada had revealed all, their love for their chief had grown tenfold. Still, who could stand in the way of his promise to a god! As for the tribe's sacrifice, Narada gestured haltingly, building up the effect artfully, to say, 'Not the horse. It has to be a human sacrifice.'

'Human sacrifice!' They were aghast. Surely the gods were not bloodthirsty. They knew other tribes performed human sacrifice, but it had never been done in their own tribe. Sadly, they wondered who and how many would have to die among them. Narada reassured them—nobody from the tribe would die. Who then, they wondered. Do we go to war with other tribes to capture victims for human sacrifice?

'No wars, no capture, no blood. Only our slaves.'

'Our slaves! Why does the new god want them killed?'

'No, the slaves shall not be killed.'

'What then?'

'Simply to free them. The slaves shall be slaves no longer.'

'Why?' the question echoed through the crowd.

'Why!' Narada looked towards the clouds. 'Because the new god reached a covenant with the God of All that if the chief and our people were to be freed from the fort and the entire tribe was to avert catastrophe, they must liberate all the slaves.'

'How many slaves have to be freed?' they asked.

'All,' Narada said firmly. 'And never must we hold a slave again.'

Their questions ceased, but their doubts remained.

'The tribe must honour the chief's promise if it is to be saved,' Narada continued. 'But some among us might refuse to part with their slaves. Think about how this god unleashed his deadly arrows against the thirteen tribes. Is it wise to incur the wrath of such a powerful god? He may choose to wipe out only those who defy him, or he may sanction that the entire tribe be destroyed. Do not, I beg of you, invite his wrath by retaining your slaves. Save the tribe, save yourselves, your loved ones, your children.'

All heads were bowed. Only one man challenged, 'What about your own slaves?'

'They were freed, this morning, before I came here,' he replied, speaking of the slaves he had inherited, and were more like his friends.

A few raised their hands to gesture that their own slaves were also free forthwith. But many remained undecided—they were afraid to affirm and yet terrified to refuse. Perhaps Narada's vision would be false; they scanned faraway paths, hoping to see the chief arrive before the full-moon day.

Away from Narada, they consulted each other. Unfortunately, the priests were absent as they had left to escort the chief back. At last one priest returned, two days before the full moon. It was old Khashan. News of his arrival spread. He went straight to his hut where his daughters and slaves gathered round him. He informed all his slaves that they are free forthwith. The slaves protested, 'We belong to you.' Khashan shook his head, 'We all belong to God, and He belongs to us all.'

Later, many of the tribesmen spoke to Khashan, but he

did not know when the chief would arrive. Strange, they thought, he comes direct from the chief but knows not. Yet Narada's 'inner vision' knew it all! For the rest, Khashan confirmed to Jabli that her husband was alive and with the chief; and he also disclosed the names of all those alive. But he could not give the list of those who had died in captivity. His information matched what Narada had seen in his vision, but the latter had revealed far more, including the names of those who had perished in captivity or earlier in battle. Khashan's actions provided the proof the tribe needed to believe in Narada's vision. Many went, with heavy hearts, to free their slaves. Having done so, they fanatically tried to convert those who still vacillated. The danger, they urged, was for the entire tribe if even a single slave remained.

Meanwhile, the six men and two women whom Narada had called moved into action. They were the *Itihasa* group, and acted as keepers and guardians of tribal knowledge. Like the memory singers of the Hindu clan, their task was to keep alive past and present knowledge for future generations. They repeated throughout the tribe what Narada had said and narrated Khashan's actions. They presented the tale of the superb heroics of the chief and his men; of how they had fought valiantly when the tribe was threatened; of the amazing spirit of the chief who, in the midst of his captivity, lost neither his dignity, nor his love, nor his faith in the values he cherished; his meditation and austerities that had compelled the God of All to send a new god to assist him; the chief's promise of a sacrifice—both personal and tribal; how he had secured the freedom of his people, and the dramatic march through the lands of the thirteen hostile tribes; how the new god had protected them; how perilously close they came to disaster when some doubted the new god; how the new god had set into motion a whirlpool of destruction that swept into the thirteen tribes so that their blood-chilling screams rent earth and sky; and finally, how, unharmed and in a blaze of glory, the chief was expected to arrive on a full-moon day, accompanied by the new god.

'Render unto this god, then, what is promised unto Him. Deny Him not.'

❧

The chief and his men planned to leave soon with Sindhu Putra.

Jalta's mother told him, 'The chief escorted you to your land, now be courteous yourself and escort him to his.' She added, 'Let all, far and near, be our friend—always.'

His brother, Jalta the Second, intervened, 'All! You want friendship even with those who caused our father to burn and enslaved our brother, his bride and our people!'

'Yes,' she retorted. 'Are they not also from the tribe of the god Sindhu Putra? There is evil in us all, and goodness in us all—in the universe—among tribes, among individuals. There is virtue and there is vice, wisdom and folly.'

'But you are all wisdom, Mother,' Jalta the Fourth said.

'Yes, but I have foolish sons!'

❧

When the chief and his party arrived at his lands, the entire tribe was there to greet them, and above all, Sindhu Putra, whom they had already accepted as their own god, sight unseen. The elders in the tribe had schooled them on how to greet their new god.

Respectfully, their hands were joined and raised in 'Namaste'. Then the tribe's silent song of welcome began. It had alternating moods, with overtones of past sorrow, and joy of the present, and accompanying it were rhythmic hand gestures, though only those who understood sign language could listen to the song. Legend is that, with his inner ear,

BHAGWAN S. GIDWANI

Sindhu Putra could hear the song of the silent people, in all the richness and the beauty of its melody.

The ancients had no problem in accepting that a song could be sung without formulating words and yet carry a tune, rhythm, melody and lilt. Many believed that a song was not simply a function and result of words, but could be independent of them. Sindhu Putra did not know how and why the people of this tribe found it impossible to articulate words. It was not as though they lacked voice altogether. They could yell and even laugh, express elementary exclamations to indicate joy and anger. But they just could not form words either to speak or sing.

Sindhu Putra went through the crowd. From Devita, he had learnt how to express 'tat tvam asi' in sign language. He greeted each person with Namaste and 'tat tvam asi'. And though many did not grasp the significance of 'tat tvam asi', faith had overtaken the frontiers of knowledge, and it seemed that all their questions were answered, unasked, and that their life had become purer and nobler. Yet, there was longing in the hearts of many who remembered an ancient prophecy, handed down from generations, which said:

'Then the Lord God shall send forth this command and you shall hearken and obey, that he might reveal unto you His First Word that you yourself shall utter, and having uttered it, it shall be yours as it is God's and you shall then know that the First Word was always there within your reach and grasp, waiting to be uttered, except that you shall not come upon this inheritance unless the Lord God Himself sends down the Witness and the Source.'

Was Sindhu Putra then the god foretold in the prophecy? Was he the Witness and the Source? Did they dare ask? An old woman, however, was undaunted. She was too frail to raise her hand for sign language and kept nudging her son to ask, but he refused by shaking his head. A priest was furious to see the youth shake his head. With enormous pride in his own importance, the priest asked the youth, 'Are you denying Sindhu Putra?' The youth waved his arms to refute the charge, while those surrounding him stared at him as Sindhu Putra approached. Finding his own explanation inadequate, the youth knelt at Sindhu Putra's feet. Devita questioned the youth and explained his gestures to Sindhu Putra, 'His mother waits to hear from you the First Word of God so that she might utter it herself.' Devita was not clear what it all meant or what the First Word was, for she knew nothing of their ancient prophecy.

Sindhu Putra, however, was lost in thought. Then, looking at the eager, expectant face of the old woman, he simply raised his hand to the sky and placed it on his heart in humility, to suggest that 'God's Word resides in every heart.' But the effect of his gesture was magical. It was as if he promised that he would be the one to receive the First Word of God and communicate it to them.

The old woman was in tears, but they were tears of joy. Those nearby shared her ecstasy that the ancient prophecy was to be fulfilled. They were quick to transmit it to others through hurried sign language; and with each repeating, the hope grew into certainty, till in everyone's hearts was the exalting, exulting assurance that God's First Word would be revealed to them and they would utter it.

Later that day, Devita learnt more about the prophecy, and Sindhu Putra understood the enormity of the hopes he had raised. It was easy to claim knowledge of the First Word of God—many in the past, some guided by faith, others for motives of their own, had tried to communicate the First Word to mankind. But how could he make those who had never articulated a single word utter the First Word? He now understood clearly what these simple people expected. Here is the largest tribe in the eastern region, he thought, willing to surrender their slaves for their faith in me! Must I continue to betray myself and pose as a god, simply for the slaves?

But his decision had already been made. He was committed to the cause of freeing slaves everywhere.

Instead, he searched for the secret behind the ancient prophecy. What was the First Word of God? His thinking led him nowhere. He feared that First Word of God would never come within his grasp. What would be the consequence of his failure? Perhaps the priests would kindle in the hearts of these simple people resentment against a false god who makes promises but cannot deliver, and yet seeks to deprive them of their cherished slaves. Sindhu Putra almost smiled; he would then be free, released from the burden of godhood. But his happiness was shortlived, for he realized his mission to free the slaves would then fail!

The silence around Sindhu Putra was unbroken. Everyone expected him to speak. But he seemed in deep meditation, so they left quietly to wait outside the hut. Actually, Sindhu Putra's mind was filled with a maze of confused thoughts. He went deep into the past, searching for clues to discover God's First Word, wondering at his own arrogance in aspiring to discover the Word that no one had found before. What was his claim to such knowledge and illumination? And even if he did discover the First Word, how was he to find a way for the mute tribe to utter it? A feeling of helplessness assailed him and he heaved a deep sigh—it was more a groan than a sigh. He was not even sure if he heard the sound of his groan. But swiftly, his soul was on fire, and he leapt up. It was as though he had heard an echo from a long-forgotten age.

His eyes were wide open, and his heart was filled with tumultuous excitement. Instead of turmoil, he experienced the radiant joy of blissful fulfilment though all he could have heard was his own whispered groan and a sigh. Yet his mind had reached deep into the limitless past where the gates of perception were opened wide for him and he could see all.

He swayed unsteadily, as though intoxicated, and uttered a sound similar to his own groan. He tried it again. He felt an overwhelming emotion and was filled with it to bursting. Tears came to him but they were tears of thanksgiving and he knelt to pray.

Well before dawn, when the silent chief and some others peeped into Sindhu Putra's room, they found him kneeling in prayer. Those who approached him felt there were tears flowing from his eyes. They tiptoed back out, where a sea of people had collected. Many asked what their new god was doing. The chief gestured, 'He prays.' But others added, 'He weeps.' They asked, 'He weeps! For whom does a god weep?' 'For us, who else!' For no reason at all, tears came to the eyes of many.

The sun had risen. The crowd waited in silence. Only the twittering of the birds and the murmur of the breeze could be heard. Hours passed. The setting sun was still gleaming in a far corner when Sindhu Putra emerged. He walked through crowds, his steps sure and firm as if he knew exactly where to go in this unfamiliar village. They all followed. He turned to the valley ringed by hills, stopped and sat down on a stone. It was not a comfortable seat, but he looked calm, serene, rested. His eyes were closed. Was he listening for a voice from within, the crowd wondered. A vision? An illumination? Many were afraid even to blink lest they miss something! Then, suddenly, it began. Sindhu Putra emitted a sound, emanating from the base of his throat, though the crowd was certain that it came from his heart. It was a long inarticulate sound and some would swear that it began like an *o*, while others were certain that it sounded like *au*. Gently Sindhu Putra closed his lips, while continuing the sound, and without any apparent effort on his part, the sound changed into an *m*—together the sound was heard as *aum*, or more clearly, *om*.

There was silence as Sindhu Putra uttered the mantra. But the hills were not silent and they echoed the sound. The crowd listened in awe and wonder as Sindhu Putra repeated the sound. Again, the hills reverberated. No one knew at what stage the crowd joined in the chant. Perhaps, they all were moved to join in, all together.

Om! It was like modulating a singing note, an inarticulate, universal sound, uttering which required no effort from the mute and speechless. Anyone who could utter any sound could easily chant *om*; and the silent tribe chanted it easily, effortlessly and worshipfully.

Om! Was it the symbol, the name, the essence of the Infinite and the Imperishable? Was *om* everything? Was everything from *om*? Did *om* identify God in all His fullness, in His transcendence and immanence? Those questions would come later. For the moment, there was only one realization in their minds, as they came under the enticing spell of this mantra which they recited again and again—indeed *om* was the very First Word that the God of All had uttered.

As they chanted, deep within their beings they felt a cosmic vibration—mystical and radiant! It was like the flowering of spiritual consciousness, bringing with it a vision of reality combined with humility that the transcendent truth is yet to be discovered and the eternal search must continue. A golden mist descended from the sun on the green hills around them. The chant continued, and their hearts soared in the ecstasy of love and beauty. With each chant, they came more under the magical spell of, what was to them, a truly sacred utterance of utmost power and mystery.

And they wondered: did the universe itself arise from this word—*om*?

Later, for centuries, even up to the modern era, scholars would analyse, examine and interpret the sacred symbol of *om*. The silent tribe, however, needed no explanation. They readily recognized *om* as a natural symbol, nature's word, a pure genuine impulse of the heart distinct from knowledge arising from the mind. Surely, then, it was nature's own mantra, their very own mantra, a part of their being. No wonder it produced harmony, peace and bliss in their hearts. With it came also the realization that since they had patiently waited for a god to manifest himself as 'the Witness and the Source', this sacred utterance was always within their 'reach and grasp', as foretold in the prophecy.

The people from the silent tribe, who soulfully chanted *om* with Sindhu Putra, would remain unaware of the rich and colourful analysis which succeeding generations extended to this mantra. But they needed no such analysis. The feeling in their hearts was of radiant joy and pride at the revelation to them of the First Word of God. That they could even utter the Word was, for them, the height of bliss. Nothing that later scholars have said to extol and exalt the magical utterance of *om* could ever match their own indescribable feeling of bliss and fulfilment.

TWENTY-THREE

MESSENGERS FROM A GOD

5052 BCE

The belief in Sindhu Putra's godhood was deep and abiding in the silent tribe, Jalta's people, and many of the surrounding tribes, and spreading fast in the land of Hindu and elsewhere. Even those who found it difficult to accept that Sindhu Putra was a god were ready to acknowledge that he was fired by godlike vision to free the slaves and achieve unity. A poet sang:

'More he did than what a god would
No less than what a real god should.
Go! Blame then the real gods that failed,
Why curse this lad to godhood nailed!'

Still, there were those who were intrigued by this god's reluctance to proclaim himself as a god, and sang:

'He was a god but he knew it not
So, to pretend godhood was his lot,
To do Father's bidding, his sole thought
Nothing else but nothing else he sought.'

These people were dismissed as thoughtless. How could a god not know that he was a god!

❦

The slaves of the silent tribe were free. Many wanted to return to their own tribes. But some had nowhere to go: 'We have lost links with our ancient tribes. This is our home now.' And

Sindhu Putra said to the tribe, 'They are yours now and your tribe is theirs.' Who could deny him! Readily, the slaves were accepted by the tribe as their own free people. Those slaves that left for their own lands were promised that if their own tribes rejected them, they could return to the silent tribe.

Jalta the Fourth told the chief of the silent tribe, 'My mother says our tribe and yours are brothers and must unite. Such is also my brother's wish and mine.'

Hardas translated for Sindhu Putra, who said, 'Unity! Yes, such is the wish of my father too,' thinking not of the Divine Father but of Bharatjogi, who sought unity—unity of Hindu with tribals and unity among tribals. Yet, as usual, many misunderstood him.

Soulfully, the chief said, while the priests and Rohan applauded, 'Our tribes and Jalta's people are one—truly as brothers.'

Jalta's wife spoke to Rohan, 'You speak of brothers only. May I speak of sisters?' and added that she would like Rohan to marry her sister.

The priests were tempted to interrupt: 'How can our new chief marry outside his tribe?' but immediately remembered their new bond of unity.

Rohan responded, 'With pleasure, if my elder agrees,' and pointed, not to his elder brother, but to Sindhu Putra, who was much younger than him. Sindhu Putra nodded his assent and hoped that boys from Jalta's tribe would also find wives from the silent tribe.

'Why not!' Hardas whispered to his wife. 'To marry a girl who shall not speak—that is my idea of heaven on earth!'

As it is, inter-tribe marriages became fashionable, and a popular belief took root: God comes to you, but to seek a wife, go far out.

Om—the First Word of God had been revealed to the silent tribe, and been uttered by them. But much more was to come to them. Eventually the men and women from the tribe married the freed slaves, which, coupled with the frequent marriages with people from Jalta's tribe, almost ended their inbreeding. The result was miraculous—their newborn children were not mute.

The silent tribe knew nothing of Sage Dhanawantar's discourse on 'Evolutionary Process and Hereditariness of Defects'. So the credit for the miraculous transformation from a silent to a speaking tribe went to Sindhu Putra and the *om* mantra. True, it took years, but some said, 'If only all of us had uttered the *om* mantra more often, and with total faith, it would have occurred much sooner.'

∽

Not only was the silent tribe the largest in the region, it had also the largest number of slaves—greater than its free population. As the slaves were leaving, they sought Sindhu Putra's blessings. To them, he said: 'Go in freedom; remain in freedom. Never be a slave, never a master; never permit it and be not a witness to it.'

Was Sindhu Putra charging them with a heroic mission— *Let none be a slave; never permit it, and be not a witness to it*? The slaves thought so.

Afraid to venture out in small groups lest they be recaptured en route, the slaves banded together to travel to their homelands. When they left, it was an army on the march. Remembering their heroic mission, they struck at various tribes on their way, often without provocation, if only to free the slaves and swell their numbers. There was a tragic randomness about it, accompanied by brutality and slaughter. And a question would be heard across centuries: did Sindhu Putra, the prince of peace, sanction all this? This violence? This bloodshed?

Yet Bharatjogi's dream to abolish slavery was being fulfilled, at least in tribal lands—not so much by a change of heart as by the murderous violence of militant slaves on the march; and the innocent died along with the guilty.

The slaves on the march overcame many tribes. They would establish a new order in those lands. Initially this new order led to chaos. More blood flowed. Lines of command were blurred; men, women, children fled, while the slave-armies tore across the land freeing many, and wreaking vengeance on those that opposed them.

When the tribes retaliated, the slaves fled. However, the tribes ignored the fleeing slaves and attacked the silent tribe instead, knowing that the trouble had been caused by the slaves unleashed by that tribe. But the silent tribe was strong. Its unity with Jalta's tribe made it invulnerable. Enemy tribes were routed. Badly shaken, they fled, leaving their dead behind, only to be attacked by the slave-armies again. A scream of anguish rose throughout the land. But in all this turmoil, more and more slaves were being freed.

The chief of the silent tribe resigned. Rohan, his brother, was appointed as chief, but he was killed while leading his forces against a fierce attack by enemy tribes. Rohan's wife was in the seventh month of pregnancy, and was appointed as acting chief until the child to be born to her crossed the age of sixteen, when he or she would assume the office of the chief.

Never before had a woman been appointed as the chief. Yet, Sindhu Putra had already blessed the glorious seed in her body. What greater qualification could one seek from a chief! However, tradition was preserved, when Rohan's widow gave birth to a male infant. Nevertheless, the tribe became attuned to the idea of a female chief.

∽

Forty of the freed slaves were from Hindu contingents, captured by the silent tribe after Nandan's forces began their infiltration to the eastern region. To them, Sindhu Putra spoke directly to spread the message of freedom and unity on their return to the land of Hindu. There was no call to arms or violence, for the land of Hindu was much too large and far-flung, its armies too powerful and vigilant, its abhorrence for avoidable war far too pronounced, and its system much too constitutional. If a change was desired, it had to be achieved through the hearts and minds of people and not by violence.

There were two among the freed slaves, father and son, from far-off Daksina. They called their land Dravidham, and themselves Dravidas. They were explorers. They had been travelling, when they were caught in the silent tribe's land where no outsiders were allowed. They were enslaved, though treated benevolently as their master, Khashan, was a kind man.

The two slaves would not eat meat, nor kill a living thing. Many wondered how they had travelled for all these years through forests, deserts and barren lands, and yet remained vegetarian. Maybe only grass grew in their homeland, with no animals around. Not so, they said and spoke of the contract between God and man, whereby birds and animals would remain protected. However, they added there was no contract between masters and slaves and it was a slave's duty to escape. Khashan agreed wholeheartedly. They had been planning their escape when Sindhu Putra arrived in the land and all slaves were freed.

The Dravidas explained their darker complexion by saying that the sun shone more brightly in their land, that they worshipped the sun and constantly bathed in its light, and their temple tops were so designed that each change in the sun's position illuminated their fine texture in new ways, as though flecks of gold and multicoloured jewels were dancing on them, in the vivid motion of light. No wonder many thought that these two strangers were story-tellers, with their tales of magnificent temples, towers, art and sculpture in their land. They spoke of gracious rivers and mighty seas, myths and legends, songs and poetry, and of the respect of man for man, of man for God, and of man for all creation.

There was another batch of twenty-six among the freed slaves from the Ganga civilization—a civilization as yet unknown to Sindhu Putra and his people. The day was not far off when the people from the Sindhu–Saraswati region would meet the people of the Ganga and marvel at their vitality and grandeur, the clarity of their language, richness of their minds and vigour of their thought. They would meet thinkers from the Ganga, some with an intense sense of individuality, and others immersed in their heritage. From them, they would learn much of cultural continuity and depth of philosophical thought. Above all, the Ganga would offer something new, something fresh, something vital, something vivid to assist all those seeking answers to the eternal question in their hearts. But that meeting of the people of the Sindhu–Saraswati and the Ganga was yet to take place. Meanwhile, Sindhu Putra was lost in wonder as he spoke to the twenty-six freed slaves from that region. He was able to understand some of their words, and discovered that some of their thoughts were also close to his own heart. They called themselves Sanathani. He wondered if it was the same as Sanatan Dharma? Or Sanathana? They nodded when he spoke of karma, and bowed when Brahma and Shiva were mentioned, though they did not react when he spoke of Rudra, the other name of Shiva. They spoke also of worshipping Shiva in various forms, even in the form of linga. Was it at all different from the lingum to which the Dravidas had referred in the land of Daksina, though they had also mentioned yoni, the female counterpart of the lingum which symbolized regeneration? Was it any different from the Rudra linga in the land of Sindhu–Saraswati?

With a thrill, Sindhu Putra asked, 'Have we been there

before?'

Some wondered why Sindhu Putra spent so much time with the freed slaves from Daksina and Ganga. Why was he drawing charts to understand routes to their lands? Surely a god knew all!

Sindhu Putra realized that Yadodhra's dream of lands faraway was real, and if men from Daksina and Ganga had found their way here, surely those lands were not beyond the reach of the Hindu clan.

Maybe, one day I shall go there and see for myself if they too were once the lands of Sanatan Dharma and Sanathana, at the dawn of civilization!

☙

The father and son from Daksina refused to go back to their land. They told Sindhu Putra, 'We are explorers and will follow you to the ends of the earth.'

'But what happens when I wish to go to your land?' he asked.

'Then our land will be refreshed anew, more glorious than ever before, and we shall follow your footsteps there.' Thus, they remained.

Of the twenty-six from Ganga, ten stayed with Sindhu Putra.

The forty slaves from the Hindu contingents returned to their land, entrusted with the mission to spread the message of freedom and unity. Two of them reached Bharatjogi at his island retreat. The time was ill-chosen as Bharat was ailing. But as he listened to the tale of what Sindhu Putra had done, he let out a joyous cry that was heard far and wide. Suddenly, he felt recovered, refreshed.

From Bharatjogi, these two visitors went to Kanta. The temple bells were rung to call in the faithful and the two emissaries addressed the crowd from the temple podium. The heat with which they spoke was not Sindhu Putra's, but to these simple men, a god's wish was a command to be obeyed in all earnestness. Their wrathful words hung over the crowd like a curse, burning in the consciousness of the listeners: 'Release your slaves lest you offend God and be yourself mortally wounded.'

Kanta announced that the temple would remain closed to those who still denied and defied Sindhu Putra by clinging to their slaves.

But Bharatjogi put his foot down, 'How can temple doors be barred to anyone! A devotee or sinner or doubter or even a blasphemer has the right and, surely, his need is greater.'

Kanta withdrew her decision. But the damage was done, for others challenged, 'Let the slave owners enter the temple and be cursed by the gods directly.' And when slave owners began to visit distant temples, a shrill cry came from many, 'God's arrows reach everywhere and the farther they travel the faster they become—and more potent.'

Bharatjogi urged, 'Persuade with love,' but in moments of passion and frenzy, no one would listen to the voice of reason, even from the most exalted!

Those who freed their slaves were honoured with garlands. The few slaves that remained in the village were quietly purchased by Kanta and freed. How could she deny her son's wish! The slaves did not come cheap, for unknown to her, Mataji was also buying the slaves to liberate them, and with the two of them bidding, the price went up. Gatha's village was now entirely asudra, with not even a single slave. And not only Gatha's village! The movement spread all over. Thousands joined the forty emissaries of Sindhu Putra to demand obedience to his message.

A preacher went through twenty-seven villages, freeing his slave in each village, and earning respect and donations. Unfortunately for him, he was caught in the twenty-eighth village, where it was learnt that his 'slave' was actually a hired hand, falsely 'released' twenty-seven times. Angry villagers confiscated his two horses and moneybags to buy twenty-seven slaves, each for a village he had cheated, and freed them forthwith. But there were hundreds of honest people who went from village to village to cajole, coerce, beg and plead with slave owners to comply with Sindhu Putra's wish. Some even imagined that all slavery was ending. But, more than half the slaves, in public works, were the property of the clan and only the karkarta could free them. And Karkarta Nandan had no such intention.

Nandan felt as if he was under siege. Even those who owed their success to him began to urge respect for Sindhu Putra's wishes. But Nandan was firm; he would not release his slaves, nor would he integrate with the eastern tribes. He shunned all such advice. However, when a deputation came he dared not refuse to meet them for it was led by Bharatjogi.

Nandan's eyes were cold and glittering, his smile mocking as Bharat asked that the slaves be freed and the land united.

'How is a hermit interested in the affairs of men?' Nandan asked.

'Affairs of men? Are they divorced from God's affairs?' Bharat asked.

'You were karkarta yourself. You were ahead of your times, always in a hurry. Some even joked that you moved so fast, you might overtake yourself. Yet you did not abolish slavery!'

'Times change and one must move with the ever-changing stream of life. In my time, the idea of freeing the slaves met with intense opposition, led by you. Today's demand is to abolish slavery, and the time for action is now.'

'That is not an enlightened view. And only held by your son, Sindhu Putra. He is your son, is he not?'

'Yes, not through blood, but love.'

'But to whose bloodline does he belong, then?' Nandan asked, his voice silky.

Bharat realized that Nandan wanted to trap him into an admission or a lie. 'I know as much as you do, or they,' he replied, pointing to his companions.

Nandan saw everyone's eyes on him. It was clear they wondered how it was possible for him to be unaware that Sindhu Putra was the son of Mother Goddess Sindhu. He changed tack. 'You do know that a karkarta cannot abolish slavery on his own volition. It would call for action by the council and the assembly, and the people's vote.'

'Of the people's vote, I am assured,' Bharat said. 'And if I have your permission, I can address the council and the assembly.'

'That right is not yours, Bharatji!'

'I know. That is why I ask you to do it.'

'I was elected as karkarta to honour our age-old customs. You, who are no longer a karkarta, find it easy to toy with people's emotions. But even you must realize that all traditions would be in jeopardy if we were to disown our customs.'

'As Sage Yadodhra explained to you, Humanity is more ancient than slavery.'

'Maybe. But I also believe in progress and enrichment, in going forward instead of returning to poverty and decadence. I am not against freedom or unity. I believe in freedom for the Hindu and unity among the Hindu.'

'God conceived man as man, not as Hindu or tribal.'

'And you perceive no difference between a Hindu and a tribal!'

'As I see the difference between you and me—your short stature, your handsome features, your wealth, your commanding personality that are all so different from mine. Do these differences make you or me less or more Hindu? Or human? Is a Hindu to carry out the will of the Transcendent by freedom only for himself and unity solely within his clan?'

'Yet that unity in our clan is what you seek to break! To set up the slaves as our equals! To bring to us the corrupting influence of union with the tribals! To tear apart the oneness of our fabric! And your seditious son! By what right does he consort with enemy tribes? By what right does he seduce our soldiers and send them out to spread his treason? By what right, I ask?'

Bharat watched Nandan's rising anger in silence. He waited for Nandan's temper to cool. But his companions were furious. They mistook Bharat's silence for weakness. One of them, the singer, rose and asked, 'And by what right do you dare to shout down God's voice? The entire clan has heard Sindhu Putra's message and demands freedom for the unfortunates and unity with the tribals. Will you dare turn him down when he comes to confront you?'

Nandan was livid. With Bharat, he could have continued to trade blows. Bharat was an equal, a former karkarta. But the temerity of the singer infuriated him. 'He shall not confront me!' His voice rose, 'He went to enemy lands in violation of our laws, and continues to violate the law by remaining there. He contrived escape of the slaves, repeatedly. He spreads sedition against the clan. No! He shall not enter this land. Never!'

Everyone froze as Nandan finished speaking, even the council members. Bharat watched the karkarta pityingly. What is it, he wondered. Frustration? The ravages of age? Yes, it was eminently sensible for people to retire as hermits at sixty, before their minds become warped.

'Karkarta Nandan,' Bharat said softly, 'that right is not yours.'

'Why? Because it is your son who pretends to be a god?' Nandan asked furiously.

'Because he is of the rya. No one should demand that a rya be made an arya. It is not dharma to even contemplate such an action.'

'Allow me to be the judge of my own adharma and dharma.'

Bharat rose and said, 'Then there is little to discuss. I must leave you to discover what dharma is and what dharma is not.'

Bharat and his companions left before Nandan could declare the audience at an end.

BHAGWAN S. GIDWANI

TWENTY-FOUR

DID GOD FLY AWAY?

5052 BC

Nandan's emissary, Chautala, reached the eastern township to meet the new commander. The karkarta's orders were clear—Sindhu Putra is not to enter the land of Hindu.

'Why?' asked Vashita, the new commander.

'Orders are orders,' said Chautala, but smiled.

Vashita was a dear friend who was to have married Chautala's sister, but she had died before the wedding could take place. Vashita had chosen to remain a bachelor as a sign of his lifelong devotion to her. To Chautala, he was like a brother. Vashita, unknown to himself, owed his promotion to commander to Chautala's influence as a council member and Nandan's trusted advisor.

Chautala explained, 'Sindhu Putra heads enemy armies and creates mischief here.'

'What mischief?'

'Did you not report that he united the silent tribe with Jalta's people and the two together caused havoc for other tribes?'

'Yes, but after those deadly battles and bloodshed, there has been peace; no more hostilities. Slavery is virtually over and all sixty tribes in the east are united under Sindhu Putra's banner. Where is the mischief against us?'

'You amaze me! Sixty tribes united under Sindhu Putra, and slaves who are slaves no more! And yet you see no danger!'

'Then my reports are at fault. When I spoke of tribes uniting under his banner, I meant in the spiritual sense. Not to command armies, or pose a threat to us, but to seek freedom for the slaves and unity amongst different tribes through moral force.'

'And is that not a threat? Instead of sixty weak, divided tribes, warring with each other, we now face one huge force—formidable, united, single-minded—on our borders.'

'But the threat begins from us. They will not attack us unless we move into their land. Even now, with all their united strength, they are no match for us.'

'So we sit back till they get stronger and gather more support?'

'Even our own men who came back said Sindhu Putra's aim is friendship and unity.'

'Unity! To be submerged in a sea of sub-humanity! And I suppose you would like to give up your slaves!'

'That would be an inconvenience,' said Vashita with a smile.

'Then, my friend, to avoid that inconvenience, keep Sindhu Putra and his people from entering our land.'

'But suppose he enters alone, without the tribal army?'

'Then it will be all the easier to stop him, without fear and fuss.'

'On what grounds?'

'His crimes against our land are many.'

'Then why not let him enter and try him for those crimes?'

'You must really be a great soldier and a great commander!'

'How so?'

'Because so much in you is so impractical. How can we try Sindhu Putra in our land when thousands upon thousands regard him as a god?'

'And you think they would applaud our stopping him from entering his own land, even when he comes alone, without an alien army!'

'Hearts do not grieve over what the eyes do not see and what the ears do not hear. Given the remoteness of this region, who will know if he came alone or with an army? Who would know that he was turned away? If complaints mount, there are always explanations and, if needed, mild reprimands followed by promotions to higher positions. But why are we arguing? As I said, orders are orders, so let it rest on the karkarta's conscience, not on yours.'

'Did not a former karkarta say: question an order that is immoral or unlawful?'

'We are not in Bharat's times.'

'Yet the wrongful act shall be mine in obeying an unlawful order of my superior.'

'No one shall call upon you to explain . . . '

'Yet I must explain my actions to myself,' Vashita interrupted.

Their discussion continued. Chautala pleaded, but Vashita was unmoved. Finally, Chautala spoke of his efforts to get Vashita the command of the region.

'I did not know that,' Vashita said. 'You have given me yet another reason to resign, for I cannot pay the price you seek.'

Chautala felt stung. 'Price! It was not to seek a price, but out of love for you, for my sister . . . '

Vashita was touched, 'That love shall always remain, whatever your path and mine. But I must request you to relieve me of my command.'

'That I shall not. But I accept your request for a long sick leave.'

'I made no such request. I am not sick.'

'Don't make a liar of me,' Chautala laughed. 'And as to being sick, we are brought up to believe that anyone who disobeys Karkarta Nandan must be sick—in mind, if not in body.'

It was a way out of their predicament. Vashita smiled, 'So be it. I request sick leave.'

'Granted!' Chautala said. Both left together, after Rochila, who did not suffer from Vashita's scruples, was installed as the commander.

Yet, it was Nandan himself who queered the pitch for Rochila. In unthinking rage, he announced publicly that Sindhu Putra would not be allowed to enter his own land.

Hundreds of people, not just from Gatha's village but from all over the land, marched to the eastern township to challenge those who would dare obstruct Sindhu Putra. Kanta remained behind with a heavy heart—she could neither desert the temple nor abandon Bharatjogi who had fallen seriously ill after his meeting with Nandan. Yet, she kept supplying carts, horses and provisions to those that marched. Gatha, with the help of the other headmen and support from Mataji, did the same.

Did all these thousands march for the love of Sindhu Putra? Many, yes, but some went for sheer enjoyment or the chance to get a free horse and provisions. They were the ones who shouted the loudest. Of them, a few became fascinated by their oratory and soon enough began to cling to Sindhu Putra's cause in faith.

But some marched, unconcerned with Sindhu Putra personally. What concerned them was the violation of a principle. How could a rya be refused entry into his own land and be made into arya? Sindhu Putra's godhood was irrelevant to them. If he is a god, they asked, then how can his entry be prevented by man—even by the karkarta? It is because he is *not* a god that we must move to protect his right as a man—a rya in his own land.

Rochila was furious when the vanguard of protesters arrived. His orders to them to go back were of no avail. 'What will you do if I prevent Sindhu Putra's entry? Will you kill me?' he demanded.

'No, we would rather kill ourselves than allow you to kill

your own soul,' they said, with neither fear nor defiance.

This was the first time that the eastern township learnt what was going on. Obstruct Sindhu Putra! They stared accusingly at the headman, but he had known nothing. Immediately, he took on the task of looking after the needs of the protesters, for they arrived in droves. First, he spent his own funds, and when his funds ran out, he used official funds earmarked for visitors to the township. Protestors or not, they were certainly visitors!

As soon as he found out, Rochila dismissed the headman. That raised the headman's prestige sky high. At his request, many vacated their huts to accommodate the new arrivals. His wife gave up meals on alternate days, and the township followed her example to conserve food for visitors. They felt relieved when Vassi arrived with Kanta and Gatha's cartloads of provisions.

Rochila turned to Vassi and expressed his displeasure in no uncertain terms. An undaunted Vassi asked, 'When has it been unlawful to bring food?' Their shouting match continued till Vassi said, 'I have faced thugs like Jhadrov, Ranadher and Ghulat, and lived in whorehouses all my life. Do you think I am afraid of you?' Looking at his disfigured face and hearing those infamous names, Rochila thought, My god! This Sindhu Putra has both gangsters and saints on his side! He ordered that all newcomers be searched for weapons. They had none.

It bothered Rochila that his own soldiers were whispering, muttering, complaining. Some were asking to be released from the army, others sought sick leave, and a few disappeared. He moved his contingents two yojnas away to keep them away from the influence of the township and newcomers, and so he could face Sindhu Putra away from their gaze.

Rochila knew that if the tribes were to send an army with Sindhu Putra, there was only one route they could take. He occupied a commanding position on that route, and sent out spies to discover if the tribal army was marching. The battle, he was certain, would be quick and intense and the tribal forces would be crushed. But what of Sindhu Putra, he wondered! Rochila decided that weapons would not be aimed at Sindhu Putra directly, but one could never predict the course of a battle! Rochila's only concern was that Sindhu Putra might creep in, quietly and alone, under the cover of night, without an army, undetected. But why would Sindhu Putra sneak into this land like a thief in the night, when he commanded the armies of sixty tribes, including the dreaded silent tribe and Jalta's people! Even so, Rochila decided to send out spies to find out.

Mithali, the girl who had accompanied Sindhu Putra to the construction site, followed Rochila's contingent on her mule. She took on the task of serving water to the troops. The commander was pleased; at least someone from the township, albeit a child, had a sense of duty. He patted her and she gave him winning smiles. He did not notice her absence after they had rested at their commanding pass. Her mule had been left behind; his own fleet horse was missing.

Far away, Mithali was caught in a tribal village. The village chief thought she was a spy. The language barrier prevented conversation. The village chief finally relaxed his hold on her hair when she sobbed piteously, 'Sindhu Putra! Sindhu Putra!'

'Sindhu Putra?' he asked. She nodded through tears.

Still, she could be a spy, he thought. He took her to a tent occupied by an administrator sent by the silent tribe. The administrator was annoyed at being woken up so early, but when he saw Mithali, he embraced her. He had been one of the slaves at the fort and had seen Mithali with Sindhu Putra. Her gestures and tears convinced him that it was vital to reach Sindhu Putra who was in danger. The administrator commandeered two fresh horses for himself and Mithali, grabbed food that both could eat on horseback, and departed.

When Mithali was overcome with sleep, he would snatch her from her horse and they would both travel on one horse. For himself, he needed no sleep if Sindhu Putra was in danger. They stopped only briefly at villages to secure food and horses. After days, they reached Jalta's lands. Sindhu Putra was there. But Mithali was asleep when they arrived.

'Let her sleep,' he said.

But soon she woke up, with tears of shame, and told Sindhu Putra of the danger facing him in his own land, with the army waiting to block him—to wipe him out, if he came with a tribal army . . . and maybe, even if he came alone.

Sindhu Putra had no intention of marching with an army. At best, Hardas and Devita, the Dravidas, and two more people from the Ganga civilization were to join him, though hundreds were determined to escort him until the last frontier village. He decided he would go openly. He saw their anxious faces and said, 'I am a Hindu, entering my own land of Hindu. Who can stop me!'

Everyone's fear vanished and they felt, 'Indeed, who can stop a god for going anywhere at his will? Who indeed!'

Jalta's mother, however, was fearful. Her ancestral memory told her that gods came to earth in order to save mankind, not themselves. They could protect others, but were they protected against man's onslaughts? Yet, how could she say this and incur everyone's displeasure for want of faith in this new, mighty god! Yet she spoke, 'A sin it is for them that seek to prevent you. And in their misguided attempt, how many innocents may lose their lives! But, there is a way to avoid that temptation to them and save them from committing that heinous sin. It is so easy to cross into your land from various passes! And since you cross with no army, who would detect your entry with only a few companions? But if you go openly and someone dares to stop you, imagine the friction between your clan and our sixty tribes, when all you really seek is unity and not division.'

Many were annoyed that she dared lecture a god! Quickly she added, 'Forgive me if love tempts me to speak like a mother to her son.' This was perhaps the best thing she could have said to a motherless youth for Sindhu Putra responded, 'Mother, I shall do exactly as you say,' and left discreetly with a few companions.

Certain that Rochila would have sent spies to track them, Jalta's mother had suggested sending a decoy, and accordingly a huge tribal army marched towards Rochila's camp, under Jalta the Fourth and the silent chief. Slowly, noisily, this army lumbered along, resting, frolicking on the way with seemingly no care in the world. Viewed from a distance, but hidden by tall companions and shielded by banners of escorts, it seemed that Sindhu Putra himself led the army. This look-alike had the same build and height as Sindhu Putra. His hair was dyed and cut to match, and colour applied to his face. 'How can a mere man look like a god?' Jalta the Fourth had protested, but his mother asked, 'How does a god look like a man?' She gave in to theatrics and made the look-alike wear a light crown of gold, though Sindhu Putra never wore such adornments. A decorative umbrella, with long tassels, was held over him throughout the march, preventing a clear view. At each stop, his tent was the first to be set up, and the tribals would bow to him as he walked in their midst.

Rochila's men 'saw' Sindhu Putra heading a huge army, with Mithali riding next to him, and did not bother to look any farther. When they reported back to the commander, he was delighted at the 'sightings', not only of Sindhu Putra and his army, but also of the 'horse-thief', as he called Mithali. Soon they would be trapped. Pity, they were moving so slowly, but what else could one expect from undisciplined barbarians led by a mere boy!

Sometimes, however, even the best-laid plans go awry. Jalta's mother had told the decoy to return once Sindhu Putra had crossed into his land. A tribesman, who had guided Sindhu

Putra through devious paths, reached the tribal army to report his crossing into Hindu land, undetected. The silent chief and Jalta, however, decided to continue the masquerade. They feared that the people who could contemplate obstructing Sindhu Putra's entry in his own land, were also capable of harassing him there and it was essential that he reach the safety of his temple. Until then, it was decided, the masquerade would continue. And so the tribal army quickened its pace.

Rochila was delighted to hear of the tribals' speed from his spies. The terrain was rocky and it would take a day to rush at each other's throats, but Rochila was in no hurry. They were the ones who marched hither. They were bound to move to escort Sindhu Putra onwards. Let those lunatics rush to their doom. Why sacrifice a single life to march to the guarded position of the tribal army! But as the days passed, Rochila became impatient with the tribals' inaction. Were they waiting for more reinforcements?

Meanwhile, as the tribal army prepared to depart from the hill where they had set up camp, the look-alike astounded the silent chief by saying, 'Let our entire army return. I shall go forward alone, unattended, towards the enemy. Let them block my entry. I shall rush back to catch up with you. And if they kill me, so be it. Their hunt for our real God shall cease. Our God can then reappear, mysteriously. He is the Master. He alone shall will what He must will.'

The look-alike dismissed the chief's warnings of certain death: 'Would you not die to protect a single hair on His head? Then why is the privilege of dying for Him denied to me?'

The look-alike had been a good-for-nothing lad, dismissed from his last job of mixing wine for drinking more than he mixed. Until now the tribals had bowed to him to fool the enemy spies, but now they viewed him with deep respect.

The next morning ushered in a beautiful sunrise. Rochila saw the lone horseman—Sindhu Putra—on the crest of the hill. Everyone in the tribal army was bowing to him and mounting their horses. Surely an attack was imminent. But the tribal army moved off in the opposite direction. Rochila smiled— obviously a petty trick. The tribals would no doubt hide behind the hill to tempt him to rush towards the lone Sindhu Putra. Then he saw that even the tribals who had been holding banners and the umbrella over Sindhu Putra's head had disappeared and their God stood alone, unattended. Sindhu Putra waved back, as though in farewell to the retreating tribal army. Rochila smiled again at this obvious pretence.

An hour passed and the lone horseman began his slow descent towards Rochila's contingents. Rochila's men climbed up long poles and saw that the tribal army was truly retreating. The day wore on. Rochila waited, certain that the tribals would double back.

Certain now, that the retreating tribal army was beyond pursuit, the horseman—the look-alike—increased his pace.

Rochila watched, his javelin at the ready though he had no intention to hurl it at Sindhu Putra. That task belonged to his men. Not that he had moral scruples, but he was too high up the chain of command and the karkarta might be blamed for his actions. Let the deed be anonymous, so no one would know whom to blame for losing his head in the heat of the moment. As the horseman drew nearer, Rochila saw he rode the horse Mithali had stolen—another reason for him to die.

A line had been drawn where Sindhu Putra was to be stopped. Rochila's voice boomed, 'Sindhu Putra! Set not your foot on the line. This land is not for you to enter—ever. Go back!'

The look-alike wanted to reply, 'Are you preventing me, a Hindu, from entering my own land of Hindu?' for it was what Sindhu Putra himself had wondered. But how could a mute say all this? So, loudly, he uttered the First Word of

God—*om*—and with his hands folded in the gesture of Namaste, urged his horse forward, crossing the forbidden line.

No one knows what moved Rochila's men to drop their javelins on the ground despite clear orders to hurl them at Sindhu Putra! As for the look-alike, he had been afraid to cross into the alien land, but now he surged ahead with no fear. Let the First Word of God—*om*—be my last word when I die, he prayed. When he saw weapons aimed at him, he softly intoned a long-drawn *om*, certain that it was to be his last breath. But in the hushed silence that followed, Rochila's men dropped their weapons and moved closer to him, not to arrest him, but to form a guard of honour.

Rochila glared, furious at his men's cowardice. He flung his own javelin directly at the horseman. Had the horse seen the danger that hurtled towards his rider? Without warning, the animal pricked his ears and raised his forelegs high in the air and caught the javelin in his chest. Rider and horse lay side by side on the ground. Within moments the writhing agony of the horse stopped, and the brave animal died.

Suddenly there was a cry, and Rochila died, too, with a javelin through his breast. No one ever admitted to hurling it, but there was lots of speculation. It was a thunderbolt from the gods, some said. No, others remarked, the horse took out the javelin from its body and hurled it at Rochila. Realists questioned: how then did the horse still have the javelin stuck in its breast?

No one would ever know why and at what precise moment Rochila's men had decided to rebel against their commander. Whatever the truth, the fact is that the horse and his old master Rochila breathed their last at the same moment, and only one of them was mourned.

Escorted by Rochila's contingent, and even by Rochila himself—for his dead body was carried on a stretcher—the look-alike reached the township. A cry of agony rent the air—

was it Sindhu Putra on the stretcher? The look-alike stood up on a horse to see the crowds. My God! everyone cried. Blood on Sindhu Putra's face and body! But it was the blood from the horse that had died to save him.

Many came to the look-alike with questions. But how could a mute answer them! The townspeople respected his silence. They wanted to take him to the guesthouse. He shook his head. With frantic gestures, he moved the crowds back and drew a circle on the ground, with a radius of 300 feet, making it clear that he would remain alone there. Then with his head bent, eyes closed, face shielded by Namaste, he sat in meditation. No doubt he did not want anyone to see him up close, lest they realize he was not Sindhu Putra. The headman begged to enter the circle, but the look-alike raised a forbidding hand. Clearly, he was in communion with the Divine Father; no one dared disturb him.

But Mithali, who had hidden behind a rock when the tribal army retreated, emerged. She had followed the look-alike at a distance and had witnessed the drama. Mithali reached the fringe of the crowd. The headman knew she was the one who had run off to be with Sindhu Putra. He lifted her onto his shoulders and she cried out, 'My friend! My friend!' Foolish girl, everyone thought, what a way to address a god! But the look-alike glanced up and with a gesture invited her to come into the circle. The headman rushed in with her on his shoulders, but was stopped by a look. Alone, Mithali ran to the look-alike and they embraced.

No one understood what they said to each other with unmoving lips and elaborate gestures. But soon Mithali came to the crowd outside the circle and said to the headman, 'He wants silence, with everyone back in their homes. If he walks, he does not want anyone to follow him, neither with footsteps nor with their eyes. He is in communion with his Father and shall obey his Father's command. Obey him yourself and see that all do likewise in all he asks!'

Many wondered at her temerity in speaking thus to her master! But she touched the headman's feet, 'These are not my words, master!' Everyone was touched. The headman asked, 'Should I send food for him?'

Mithali agreed, 'Yes, please. And mattresses and twelve horses.'

'Twelve horses?' the headman asked, astonished.

'Yes, with feed for them and poles to tether them. He wants to speak to the twelve horses of the death of the horse that brought him here.'

'Yes, of course,' the headman said.

Later, many came to believe that Mithali invented these requests. The look-alike wanted only one horse to escape, for judging from this affectionate reception, he realized that there was no danger to the real Sindhu Putra. The sooner he escaped the better, lest his identity be discovered.

Twelve horses, food, pillows, bed sheets and mattresses arrived. On one of the horses, Mithali rode through the crowd commanding everyone to retire. The silhouette of Sindhu Putra could be seen, even on that moonless night, and if some saw a glow on his face, it was simply a reflection of the glow in their own hearts. Even when everyone had retired, Mithali kept circling on her horse, as though to keep people from returning.

On one of her rounds, the look-alike jumped onto her horse, while the remaining horses blocked the view. If anyone had bothered to look towards the circle, they would have seen the silhouette of the sleeping Sindhu Putra, when in fact it was actually the mattresses and pillows roughly shaped together. But the townspeople assumed the sound of the hooves meant Mithali was busy with her task of keeping people away. But now, she and the look-alike, mounted on a single horse, were headed elsewhere. They crossed the township into no-man's land.

Suddenly, the look-alike pulled up the horse, on hearing a

shrill hoot from a short tree. It was not a tree, but a tribesman covered with bark and branches, watching for the look-alike. He took the look-alike to horses tethered nearby and together the two men rode away. Mithali went back to the circle in the township, but not directly; she kept going in many directions, as though still on her task of keeping all away.

At the first light of dawn, the townspeople saw Mithali alone, sleeping peacefully. 'Where is Sindhu Putra?' they asked.

Mithali replied, 'He flew away to meet his Father.' Yes, what else could it be! All twelve horses were still tethered inside the circle. Surely he could not have ridden out!

It was a memorable day for the township. And equally so for Gatha's village, for it was on that day that the real Sindhu Putra reached Bharatjogi.

When word spread, everyone was astounded that Sindhu Putra was present at the same moment at two different places, removed by a journey of many days! But had Mithali not said that Sindhu Putra flew away! Surely the gods can do what no man can!

therein.

Deeply moved, Bharat half rose to embrace Sindhu Putra. He looked at the doorway and said, 'My son! He shall liberate the slaves—all the slaves, everywhere! He shall unite our land!' But, through his joy, a troubling thought came to Bharat, 'How will I remember all the names you tell me of the sixty tribes that you united?'

'Those names exist no more. They are all known by a single name—Bharat Varsha.'

Bharat lay back on his bed, a wave of happiness washing over him. But again he asked, 'Why Bharat Varsha? Why not your name?'

'It was not my decision, father. They took that decision.'

'How? Why? When?' Bharat asked.

'I simply spoke of my father's wish that this land be free of ery, and united.'

Bharat laughed, and spoke to the empty doorway, 'Forgive father, if my name got mixed up with yours. And forgive r being happy about it.' He laughed again, and then 'How did you enter? Were they empty threats then?' h so many people surrounding him, Sindhu Putra did h to say anything that might endanger the safety of alike and the tribal army. Sindhu Putra bent forward pered in Bharat's ear. It could not be a secret of Bharat was laughing, the hearty laugh of a young ng with vitality—and his laughter would not stop. at spoke, 'Life is beautiful.' He looked again at orway, 'And greater beauty is yet to come.' harat tenderly held Mataji's hand. One by one, e forward to clasp his hand, and then, except Sindhu Putra, they all left, keeping a vigil Mataji washed Bharatji with water from the sed him in a new robe.

and asked, 'Am I presentable to go where I

TWENTY-FIVE

FAREWELL, BHARAT!

5051 BCE

Bharatjogi was gravely ill. Sindhu Putra touched h'
kissed his forehead. For the first time in many
opened his eyes and looked into the distance as
someone else, 'My son has come! Yes, I shall

To Sindhu Putra, he said, 'I knew you
son. Who could prevent your coming?' He
but it ended up being a terrible cough. Ev
Only Mataji dared to tell Sindhu Putr
to speak. Sindhu Putra placed his hea
his cough ceased. Bharat smiled. F
bathed in a ray of light; his pain d
of well-being. He asked in a fir

Sindhu Putra's eyes were m
'No, son, no need for tears,
His gaze shifted to the door
continued, 'He kept vi
homecoming. Let us no
more. Thank him for

Sindhu Putra gaz
hands in the gestur
back to Bharat ar
of how the slav
the abolition
between Jal
tribes had been

sla
me,
me f
asked
Wit
not wis
his look
and whi
gods, for
man burst
At last Bha
the empty d
Quietly, E
everyone cam
for Mataji an
outside the hut
Sindhu and dres
Bharat smiled
am going?'

She smiled through her tears, sprinkled water towards the sky, and said, 'Wait awhile. Give them time to be presentable to receive you.'

Their eyes closed, they held each other's hands, silently speaking to one another. When they opened their eyes, Bharat turned to Sindhu Putra, 'Tell me the last word again.' Actually he meant the First Word of God. Sindhu Putra intoned *om*. Then holding Sindhu Putra and Mataji's hand, Bharat looked at the doorway and quietly said, 'Thank you for waiting. I am ready now.' Mataji and Sindhu Putra saw his smile and heard a long-drawn-out *om* from his lips.

And then, quietly, Bharatjogi died.

∾

'As for me, the battle is over and lost,' Nandan said. There was much he did not understand. A reliable eyewitness had reported that Sindhu Putra, with his army, was facing Rochila's contingent and soon the tribal army would be wiped out. Another eyewitness, equally reliable, said that Sindhu Putra was at Bharatjogi's deathbed. The first report was sent four days earlier and the second report only the day before. Nothing made sense. It was impossible for Sindhu Putra to reach Bharatjogi in such a short time, even if Rochila was mad enough to escort Sindhu Putra on his fleetest horse himself. Nandan had yet to hear about Rochila's mysterious death and the disappearance of the tribal army.

Only one thing was clear to Nandan—he had chosen the path of his own destruction. How could I be mad enough to announce that I would prevent Sindhu Putra from entering his own land? Now he is with his dead father and I shall be laughed at forever! Nandan realized that a leader could recover from any disaster except ridicule. At the next election, he wondered, will they vote for me or laugh at me? With this one false step, all his carefully laid plans had gone awry. He worried not so much about himself, but about the future of his clan, and his son Sharat. He had done away with the odious law that said a son could not succeed his father as karkarta. Ably, his friends had argued: why should we place such a limitation on the people's choice? Does it not offend against the right of a rya to stand for election, and against the collective right of all ryas to elect anyone they choose?

But who will wish to elect my son! He now carries, not my legacy of greatness, but my taint of ridicule. And who will stop the floodtide of freedom for the slaves, when this Sindhu Putra is thrice blessed—with the image of a god, with breaking barriers to block his entry into the land, and now with the people's tears and sympathy over his father's death. 'My sun has set,' Nandan said.

'There never was a sunset that was not followed by sunrise,' Sharat said. 'Your sun will rise; even your son will rise.'

$$\sim$$

Sharat rushed to Gatha's village, leaving word for the others to follow.

Bharatjogi's body lay in state. Lovingly, men skilled in the art had prepared Bharat's body for its last journey. Its countenance retained the vigour and dignity which had marked the great man during his lifetime. Mataji closed his eyelids and kissed his lips which still held a faint trace of his last smile.

Sharat bowed to Mataji and Sindhu Putra and said, 'My father prays that Bharatjogi be cremated in the karkarta's town.'

The singer intervened, 'Why?'

Sharat said humbly, 'It is the clan's main town and Bharatji was our most illustrious karkarta. The clan reveres him, mourns him.'

'Everyone mourns him in this village too,' the singer retorted.

'Of course! He belongs to this whole land which is beginning to be known as Bharat Varsha. My father wishes that he be escorted in an open, decorated carriage for all the villages to see him and pay their respects.'

Mataji and even Sindhu Putra wondered why the singer was against their beloved Bharatjogi being accorded such an honour. Mataji simply said, 'Yes, I agree and thank you for the thought.' Sindhu Putra, too, nodded his acquiescence. Soulfully, Sharat thanked him.

Although Sharat had many men, he himself slaved to make a single cart by joining many together, and decorated it with flowers and gold-threaded cloth. One hundred and eight horsemen were to precede the cortege, five hundred to follow.

Muni and Roopa reached Gatha's village before the procession could leave. Muni bent to kiss Bharat's cold brow. He commented on the lavish arrangements, 'So much for a hermit.'

But Sharat said, 'He was more than a hermit,' and everyone agreed. He asked Sindhu Putra, 'Will you join Bharatjogi's journey?'

'Yes, of course. He is my father. He guided me through life.'

'He is the father of the entire clan,' Sharat said. 'My father, though too ill to come here, will honour your father in a special way.'

'How?' Sindhu Putra asked. He was beginning to like Sharat, but suspicion still lingered for was it not Nandan who had tried to prevent him from entering his own land?

'He will release the slaves and abolish slavery,' Sharat said simply.

'What!' Sindhu Putra exclaimed, unable to believe his ears. 'But how! When? I thought your father opposed it!'

'Bharatjogi's inspiration convinced my father.'

'Yet everyone says that the karkarta firmly rejected my father's ideas.'

Sharat smiled sadly, 'What was my father expected to do! If he had announced his intention to abolish slavery in front of everyone, can you imagine the storm of protest from those who favour slavery and oppose unity! Your father had the same difficulty when he was karkarta, even though he was more popular than any karkarta could ever hope to be.'

'But your father also decreed that I could not enter our land.'

'True, but only to protect you. Not from the tribes, but from those, here, who insist that slavery must remain. Once they knew that my father was going to keep you from entering, they had nothing to fear. Otherwise who knows to what lengths they would have gone to stop you!'

Sindhu Putra remembered what Bharat had once said: to lead people, a leader must sometimes appear to be sincere without being too honest. He felt sad for having misjudged Karkarta Nandan. 'It will be an honour to meet your father,' he said.

Sharat responded, 'Thank you. But no one must know of his intention to abolish slavery. Otherwise, the entire campaign might be defeated.'

'I understand,' Sindhu Putra said. 'But tell me, do you think he will also agree to unite with the sixty tribes of the eastern region?'

Sharat laughed, 'Strange! You speak of precisely what is in my father's heart. He wants to request you to arrange a meeting with the eastern tribes to discuss unity.'

A happy smile lit up Sindhu Putra's face as he remembered Muni's words—the life of every man is a deep, dark forest—and realized how wrong he had been about Nandan!

Later people said that surely Sindhu Putra was no god, for he was fooled so easily! But others argued that only man understands man's villainy and duplicity, not a god; a god trusts.

Nandan was one of those who carried Bharatjogi's body to the funeral pyre. Everyone knew he was unwell and admired him for the effort. Later, at the memorial service, Nandan said, 'Whatever we do to honour Bharatji is less than what he deserves. Yet, what is it that we can do? Confer on him a title—"Foremost amongst us all" or "The shining light of Hindu"?' The audience applauded, but Nandan ignored them and continued, 'No, Bharatji coveted no empty titles. He had a mission, a dream. We must translate that dream into reality. That will be a lasting memorial to him. For this, my son Sharat and I shall consult Bharatji's son, Sindhu Putra, and I hope you will all agree with our joint decision.'

But, of course, everyone said: a joint decision between a karkarta and a god! Who would dream of opposing such a combination!

∽

At Sindhu Putra's meeting with Nandan and Sharat, Nandan said, 'What I have to say is for your ears only.' Sindhu Putra nodded.

Nandan continued, 'Keeping before me the views of your illustrious father, it is my wish to release all the slaves under my charge on behalf of the clan. This right I have in consultation with the council. Second, I would like to request—as I cannot demand—that all private individuals should free their slaves. Third, I want to appeal to the parliament of Hindu to approve legislation to abolish slavery in the future. Fourth, appeal to the people to approve parliament's legislation, as it will require a direct vote by the people of the clan. Fifth, by virtue of that approved legislation, I want to ensure that all who still hold slaves are obliged to let them go. Sixth, grant compensation to those needy or handicapped persons who are particularly hurt by releasing their slaves. And seventh, to consult with you on how best to achieve unity with the eastern region which now consists of a single tribe instead of sixty.' Nandan paused, and then continued, 'I would wish that this seven-point programme, when implemented, be known as the Bharat Programme. But I must ask you if you agree or if you have any reservations about any of these points?'

'I? Karkarta, yes, I agree, fully. My father could have asked for no more!' Sindhu Putra replied.

'Good. We will go ahead with the first six points, and tackle the seventh later.'

Sharat intervened, 'Why, Father? I thought you were keen on uniting with the eastern region.'

'I am. But some oppose the abolition of slavery and others oppose unity. I do not want the two groups to join together and defeat us. And suppose we are defeated on the question of slavery. Of what use is unity if we end up subjecting the eastern region to slavery again? What do you think?' He looked at Sindhu Putra, who responded, 'You are right, karkarta. But the question of unity is also paramount.'

'Of course. That is why I want you to create a strong atmosphere in support of unity. Don't forget, I have no more than six months as karkarta. The election of the karkarta takes place in six months. Surely, I cannot stand for re-election.'

'Why not?' Sindhu Putra asked. How could a seven-point programme be implemented in so short a time, he wondered.

'In order to ensure the success of these measures, it will be better if I am away from the fray and able to take a principled stand, rather than make these a part of my re-election platform. You see my difficulty?'

Sindhu Putra understood nothing and asked, 'But what if matters drag on beyond six months and the next karkarta favours slavery and opposes unity?'

'That is a risk, of course.'

'Who is likely to be the next karkarta?' Sindhu Putra asked.

'Who knows! I hope not Kulwant, Prakash or Bhardawan. They hate the tribals and favour slavery. They were not inspired by Bharatji's dream.'

'But surely there must be some who support us,' Sindhu Putra asked.

'Oh yes, apart from Sharat, who is seniormost in the council, and of course deeply committed, there are some other members, not well-known but . . . .'

'But why not Sharatji?' Sindhu Putra interrupted.

'Me!' Sharat interjected and broke into a laugh.

Nandan's expression was thoughtful as if he were pondering over this suggestion. At last he said, 'But yes, Sharat, my son; why not!'

Sharat laughed again. Nandan silenced him, 'I begged Sindhu Putra's presence, so that he may advise us, guide us. He makes a suggestion and you laugh, without even considering it. Surely we owe him that courtesy. What is your objection?'

'I am your son,' Sharat weakly responded.

'Do I need to be reminded about it?' Nandan asked, frostily.

'I am not fit for the job.'

'I know that. No one is fit to be karkarta. But when a person achieves that position, he grows to be worthy of it. God guides him.'

'I don't like the job,' Sharat argued.

'So take it and resign after the Bharat Programme is fulfilled.'

'What makes you think I shall be elected?' Sharat argued.

'There is much in your favour,' Nandan argued. 'You are my son. That entitles you to respect. You are seniormost in the council. You are committed to Bharatji's legacy. There is an overriding reason, too—Bharatji's son, Sindhu Putra, is asking you to do it.' Nandan looked directly at Sindhu Putra.

Sindhu Putra spoke, 'Yes, Sharatji, yes, I request that you accept.'

Sombrely, Sharat looked at Sindhu Putra and saw the appeal in his eyes. 'Yes, I must. I shall not deny you; I accept.' He looked thunderstruck, but in his heart surged a wave of happiness.

'It is not enough that you accept the position,' Nandan said. 'The people must accept you. Consult Sindhu Putra on how to proceed. You are his nominee for the election, not mine.'

'No, father, I am doubly blessed. I am his nominee, but yours, too, I hope.'

'Yes. But let Sindhu Putra be the first to press for your election.'

Sindhu Putra nodded, though not certain what he had to do.

Nandan took charge of the situation and said, 'Next week, I shall announce my programme to abolish slavery, as well as my decision not to stand for re-election. Then, you, Sharat, can announce your intention to stand for election. Or maybe . . . ' he paused, 'no, let it not be you. Let Sindhu Putra announce you as his nominee. Then we are closer to the truth, as after all he was the first to suggest it today.'

Sindhu Putra nodded in agreement.

TWENTY-SIX

FREE, FREE AT LAST!

5052 BCE

At a specially convened session of the Hindu parliament, Karkarta Nandan announced his commitment to abolish slavery and hinted at uniting with the eastern region. There was loud applause from the spectators' gallery. Some claimed that the people came from Gatha's village to create the illusion of massive support. But that is doubtful, for on that very day Sindhu Putra was to appear in the temple, and who would leave the village to witness a mere parliament session!

However, there were many who resented Nandan's announcement. He heard the rumble of thunder in their questions and, when the din subsided, Nandan announced his retirement. The parliament was stunned. Nandan chose to ignore all their questions, except the one about his choice for the next karkarta. He said, 'Each one of you here is my favourite.' But this was no answer. A retiring karkarta always recommended a candidate, though the final choice remained with the people's vote. Questions came, but Nandan ended the session, smiling with ineffable contempt.

Why did Nandan have to retire? Perhaps the poetess Papu (5010 BCE) is correct. She says, Nandan promised Sindhu Putra that he would move to abolish slavery and unite with the tribes; but he was determined to never truly implement that pledge. So he asked himself: do I wish to be remembered as the karkarta who violated his pledge? Why not leave the field to another karkarta, then? My own son. But is not a son bound by his father's pledge? Yes, but surely a karkarta is not bound by the promise of another karkarta, and so my son shall face the people not as my son, but as karkarta in his own right, uncommitted by any pledge I make.

The temple was overflowing when Sindhu Putra appeared. Normally, he blessed all with Namaste, but today he expressed his hope that Karkarta Nandan's office would pass to his son, Sharat. Some wondered why he spoke of so distant an event, but soon reports came that Nandan was retiring. While many grappled with this miraculous coincidence, some felt that gods should be concerned with the salvation of men's souls, and not their worldly ambitions.

There was resentment in some quarters that Sharat wanted to be elected as karkarta. When the law had been changed to allow blood relations of the karkarta to aspire to that office, there was an implied promise that it was intended for future generations, not to benefit Nandan's family.

How could Nandan confide to anyone that the only way to salvage his reputation and secure the future for his son was by joining with Sindhu Putra!

The opposition to Sharat's election did not worry Nandan. Armed with Sindhu Putra's support, no one could defeat Sharat. It is good, he thought, if there is some opposition to Sharat, for undoubtedly he shall win, but that opposition will be the excuse later for Sharat to distance himself from the Bharat Programme, and even from Sindhu Putra. When Nandan's friends complained bitterly against the programme, but said they would be silent out of regard for him, he said, 'It would be a disservice to your conscience. Speak as you should.' And they spoke. But theirs was a cry in the wilderness, against the avalanche unleashed by Sindhu Putra.

Nandan's plan was flawless. He encouraged Sharat to have private meetings with Sindhu Putra lest he be goaded into making a public commitment. 'Do not let your words return to haunt you as a broken pledge!'

'Yet, Sindhu Putra may object if I make no public statement.'

'No,' Nandan said, 'he understands that you must not antagonize anyone. He believes in your commitment. Gods always trust—yes, gods and simpletons.'

But some, who were neither gods nor simpletons, distrusted Nandan. The singer went to Sage Yadodhra who laughed at his grief over Sindhu Putra's involvement. 'But he will be betrayed!' the singer complained.

'Then he will be wiser next time; or do you think gods need no wisdom?'

Sadly, the singer said, 'After the elections, Sharat is sure to abandon the Bharat Programme.'

Yadodhra advised, 'Commit him, then, fully! Or let him deny it and be exposed!'

Overnight, the singer became Sharat's strongest supporter. His group of singers went to villages across the land, singing of Sharat's deep commitment to the Bharat Programme. The singer himself regaled people with songs, and though his words varied, he always sang of how Sharat's mind, heart and soul, all his hopes and aspirations, were centred on the success of the Bharat Programme. Soon, new slogans were heard from his sixty-six singers that if the programme was not implemented soon, Sharat would retire as a hermit.

Who could blame Sindhu Putra if he thought that the singer had learnt it all from Sharat himself! And who could blame Sharat if he thought that the singer was the mouthpiece of Sindhu Putra, to commit him to the cause! My father is wrong to consider Sindhu Putra a simpleton, Sharat thought. Yet do I dare deny him?

Sage Yadodhra also said, 'The call to become a hermit springs from the heart, without conditions, but Sharat has vowed to retire *if* the Bharat Programme is unfulfilled in half a year! Yet a dreamer or a visionary must sacrifice, supremely, for his dream and vision. Truly, therefore, I honour Sharat's commitment that has led to his irrevocable vow to retire as a hermit, if . . .'

Who could ignore the sage's words! Everyone knew that the Bharat Programme was Sharat's brainchild. And Sindhu Putra always gave him credit for inspiring it.

Sharat was elected the twenty-second karkarta of the Hindu clan. There was some unhappiness over Sharat's victory, but no one was as unhappy as Nandan. God, he felt, grants our wishes and prayers only to defeat us! Nandan's hopes were shattered; his son became a stranger. Was it, Nandan wondered, an aberration in the first flush of pride at being elected karkarta! No, he feared that Sharat had truly committed himself to the Bharat Programme.

Had Sharat been out-manoeuvred by the singer and Yadodhra? Not so. As he had spent more time with Sindhu Putra, Yadodhra, and a few of the slaves freed by the silent tribe including the Dravidas and those from the Ganga civilization, and heard their glowing descriptions of green, fertile lands, rich in material, spiritual and artistic attainments, many of his old ideas began to drift away. He started realizing that there was a vast world outside, and he saw a clear vision of the future. But was that future attainable without Sindhu Putra's help? Who held the key to the lands of the sixty tribes and beyond? Who would lead him there?

Sharat began thinking: even if I can break free from the shame of abandoning my assumed vow, will I ever be permitted to move into tribal territory without battling every inch of the way? How and when do I then reach the lands beyond! And who will protect my flank? Is slavery really such a dire necessity for my land? And uniting with the tribes? Surely, the vacuum created by the abolition of slavery can be filled by cheap tribal labour, and their lands will then be open to create wealth for my own clan. Not only that, they will serve as gateways to lands far away.

Though he is wrong in all else, my father is right in one

thing, Sharat thought. When a person becomes karkarta, he begins to see everything afresh, without the blinding mists of the past. Sharat now saw the Bharat Programme in a different light, not for the principle behind it, but for the profit it could bring; and he thought only a fool would run after a principle unless there was profit in it.

Sharat put his heart into successfully implementing the Bharat Programme. Slavery, he said, was a crime against humanity and a sin against God; he urged that the unity and brotherhood of man must remain the clan's ideal, as it had been under the ancient Sanatan Dharma, which never entertained different levels of humanity.

The singer felt ashamed for having doubted Sharat. Nandan begged and cajoled his son to stay away from this dangerous course, but Sharat said, 'Times change and we have to move with the ever-changing stream of life.' Sharat could not have used more brutal words, for these were the very words that Bharat had uttered at his last meeting with Nandan. He argued no more. Sharat was pleased. All his life, he had been controlled by his father. Finally, he was his own man.

As for Nandan, he did what a retired man does when he feels he no longer matters and is unheard, unloved, unwanted. He died. But he was wrong to feel unloved, for Sharat was desolate and Sindhu Putra wept at his passing, for it was Nandan who had first inspired the Bharat Programme. The entire clan went into mourning for their former karkarta.

At Nandan's funeral, Sindhu Putra, pointing to Sharat, addressed all: 'For his father's sake who is one with my Father, hear him in your heart.' They heard. It is not easy to ignore the voice of the dead. Slave owners halted their campaign against the Bharat Programme, which was due to be voted on by the people in seven days. And later, many would say that even in death, Nandan served his clan.

The Bharat Programme was approved. Slavery was abolished in the land of the Hindu, in law and in fact.

TWENTY-SEVEN

MAHAKARTA

5050 BCE

Jalta's mother was nominated by the sixty tribes as their plenipotentiary to negotiate terms of the union with the Hindu clan, although many thought it strange that an old, blind woman was chosen to speak for them! What would she know!

Sharat's men received Jalta's mother at the border, to escort her to the karkarta's town. She asked, 'Will Sindhu Putra be there?' When she was told he would be in Gatha's village, she insisted on going there first. The men reminded her that she was already late and the council meeting to approve the union was to take place very soon. So she suggested, 'Why don't you hold the meeting in Sindhu Putra's village?'

At their objections, her native distrust of outsiders rose. Why were they avoiding meeting in Sindhu Putra's presence? Actually, she was being unjust. They were simply thinking of the custom of holding council meetings in the karkarta's town. But now that her suspicions were aroused, she insisted that the meeting must take place in Sindhu Putra's presence, or not at all. She went to Gatha's village, with her entourage of sixty. Both she and Sindhu Putra touched each other's feet, for she was the mother and he a god; thereafter, they embraced.

When Sharat heard what the old woman had demanded, he said, 'So what! Let the meeting be held in Gatha's village.' At least one thing was certain—she would readily agree to everything in Sindhu Putra's presence and create no problems.

Many people along with the council members gathered in Gatha's village, for this was a historic occasion—the first council meeting outside the karkarta's town and in Sindhu Putra's presence!

Gatha made impeccable arrangements. He gave the seat of honour to Sindhu Putra. And he even stationed 'repeaters' at strategic points in the crowd, to repeat what was being said on the dais, so that the audience, even in the back row, was informed of the proceedings.

Sindhu Putra blessed the meeting with '*om*', and blessed everyone seeking unity and union. Karkarta Sharat then welcomed Jalta's mother and her sixty companions, explaining that the purpose of the meeting was to unite the clan of the Hindu with the people of the sixty tribes.

The old woman should have waited for Sharat to conclude, but she objected, 'We are not sixty tribes, but a single tribe.'

Some then wondered if she was representing only the interests of Jalta's tribe? Sindhu Putra explained that all sixty tribes were now united as a single tribe, and a reference to sixty tribes was a matter of itihasa and did not reflect the present reality.

Graciously, Sharat resumed his address to say that the purpose, then, was to unite the Hindu clan and the people of the eastern tribe. But again Jalta's mother rose to correct him and said, 'It is the union of Hindu with Hindu.' Here the interpreters failed. Doubts arose. Was she claiming that all this would benefit only the Hindu clan? She clarified, 'You spoke of a union between the Hindu and our people; but our people are Hindu too!'

Sharat turned to Sindhu Putra to ask, 'Are they Hindu?' Sindhu Putra nodded. Sharat echoed the question in everyone's mind and asked, 'Since when?' Sindhu Putra's glance rested on Jalta's mother. Quietly, he said, 'Always.'

Always! No one asked Sindhu Putra to clarify. The fact was that these tribals had begun to call themselves Hindu

after Sindhu Putra came into their midst. But, Sindhu Putra's mind went to the ancient past of which Bharat had spoken—of the days of Sanatan Dharma and Sanathana—and he was convinced that tribals belonged to the same common root. In any case, the tribals had profound and indissoluble respect for the ancestral link, and after a prolonged ceremony and prayer session that had lasted for three days and nights, the priests had assured all the tribes of their ancestral blessing and approval for their being Hindu, always.

Sharat gave up his idea of a long speech and said, 'We are already united in our hearts. All that remains now is to formalize steps to make our ties stronger, and bring us all closer in our relationships, movement, travel, trade and land-use.'

Jalta's mother heard him attentively thereafter, merely nodding vigorously to agree with each item, and there were many, that Sharat proposed—free movement of people in and out of each other's regions and beyond; free trade and movement of goods; freedom to purchase land when buyer and seller freely agreed; respect for each other's customs; attack on one region to be treated as an attack on both; joint action against raiders; arrest of criminals who ran away to other regions; assistance in exploration of new lands; guild membership; representation in the council and the assembly; voting rights . . .

The list went on with assenting nods from Jalta's mother. Finally, as Sharat concluded, she spoke, 'All you said is near to our heart and we agree. Yet you did not speak of what is also near to our heart—no master, no slave!'

Sharat quickly replied, 'But we have abolished slavery!'

'Yes,' she said. 'For in the kingdom of God, there is no higher or lower . . . And there is only one class, even as there is only one God . . . ' Everyone applauded, for obviously she quoted from the *Song of the Hindu*.

Sharat nodded, as if it was not necessary to say anything

in repsonse. But softly Jalta's mother challenged, 'You spoke of the past and the present. But should we ignore the future? The future may then ignore us too. That is why our people have sworn that even in the future slavery shall not come into our land. Is that your pledge too, binding to all who come after you?'

Sharat nodded lightly, but it did not matter, for she gave words to his nod and said, 'I am glad that it is your sworn pledge, too. Then we are agreed on this, and on all else, with no reservations.'

Many people were puzzled when they heard Jalta's mother. They marvelled at the intelligence of this tribal matron and wondered at their own absurd beliefs that tribals were primitive and that every person with different values, language and customs, was a barbarian.

Sharat now came to his final question, 'Who will be the chief or karkarta of your land?' Secretly, he hoped they would not nominate the woman before him, for she disconcerted him. She may have a big heart, but she has a bigger mouth, thought Sharat.

But her unexpected answer delighted him, 'Of course karkarta, you shall be our karkarta. How can there be two karkartas if we all are one clan?'

Sharat felt thrilled, but he was not alone. The council members, headmen, audience shared his elation. Gracefully, Sharat bowed. But Jalta's mother had more to say, ' And for us, and I am sure for you too, Sindhu Putra shall be mahakarta.'

Mahakarta! The word was new, but the meaning was clear. The old woman had used Sharat's language to invent a new title—Mahakarta—the Great Leader.

Sharat tried to smile, though his heart froze with dread. How was he to react to this absurd woman's impossible suggestion that someone be superior to him! How could he discredit the very institution of karkarta and submit to the higher authority of an unelected mahakarta!

However, her subsequent words gave him, if not comfort, at least an escape, for she said, 'He shall guide us all in spirit, and when troubles come or problems arise, he shall be the one to resolve our doubts and bind us together—'

'Of course,' Sharat interrupted, intending to stop her from saying anything else that would bind him even more. But his sudden, shouted enthusiasm was seen as his wholehearted acceptance of the office of mahakarta. Already many were chanting 'Mahakarta!', delighted with the new title for Sindhu Putra. The meeting after all was being held in the heart of his homeland, in his temple compound, and his devotees in the crowds outnumbered the rest.

Sharat continued without a pause, 'I thank you all. Now that there is a meeting of minds on all main issues, our people shall meet again to fill in the details; and all that remains is for us to seek Sindhu Putra's blessings to end this meeting.'

Jalta's mother nodded and it was amidst the crowd's repeated cry of 'Mahakarta!' that Sindhu Putra rose to bless all.

Later, Sharat consoled himself with the thought that titles meant nothing. All pretenders to godhood were invested with all kinds of titles—'merciful', 'divine', 'all-powerful', 'wise', 'prophet', 'son of God', 'God's messenger'—but they were empty and meaningless in terms of earthly power. Let them chant!

Much later, when the resolution of the union with the eastern region was moved in the Hindu parliament, there were some who raised the question that the resolution did not mention 'mahakarta' anywhere. Sharat was ready with his answer: 'Mahakarta, as we call Sindhu Putra, guides our spirit, our aims, our goals, our quest. But ask me not to include him in this resolution. Never shall I expose the Mahakarta to any such indignity. No, he remains out, above and beyond any questions and criticism of imperfections in our resolutions.' This puzzled many, but Sharat added, 'In the past, in our countless resolutions, we never suffered from the temptation to say that they were inspired by the One-Supreme or divine authority. The reason is simple—our thoughts, ideas, words, actions remain imperfect. It would be arrogant to claim that we have encompassed the Perfect Himself, within the ambit of our resolutions. We have a long way to go.' Then he quoted Hindu thinkers who held that truth, as ultimate reality, had to be eternal, imperishable and unchanging, but that such infinite truth could not be captured by one's finite mind, conditioned and limited as one was by time and space, and above all, by ignorance. And then he quoted from the *Song of the Hindu*, as Jalta's mother had done: '*A Hindu must learn to refine everything through continuous testing and experiencing . . . to reach the ultimate awareness . . .* '

Even from the special gallery, reserved for special invitees, Jalta's mother, Jalta the Second and Jalta the Fourth nodded. They were guests now. Later their people would take their place in the expanded parliament of the Hindu, once the resolution of union with the tribes of the eastern region was adopted.

TWENTY-EIGHT

VISITORS TO GANGA—
MAHAPATI SINDHU PUTRA

5046 BCE

Inspired by Sage Yadodhra's charts and assisted by the slaves from the Ganga civilization who were freed by the silent tribe, Sindhu Putra reached the land of Ganga. Thousands followed him as he travelled by horse, mule, camel or elephant, and occasionally in a litter. There were times when he moved fast, but often the terrain remained impassable for hours.

It was a glorious journey through shining streams and beautiful forests, murmuring brooks and the scent of wild flowers, and splendid snow-clad mountain peaks. But there were also barren lands and treacherous passes, tracks that led nowhere and detours that took days yet only covered fifty feet. The travellers saw magnificent works of art—in clay and stone—in the midst of lonely landscapes, and paintings and carvings in caves along a myriad lakes, though clearly there had been no one around for centuries.

At many places, crowds waited to greet Sindhu Putra. As people had migrated from one region to another, his fame had spread far and wide. And if there were isolated spots where he was less known, the entire population would hear from those who reached ahead of him of a god who was to arrive in their midst.

Sindhu Putra himself said little to those who came to greet him. He simply blessed them with *om*. Many from various villages joined the march. Sometimes, entire villages would join in and the vast procession continued. It rarely occurred to them to ask themselves the purpose of the long journey; they were simply following a god.

Only once did Sindhu Putra intervene when an entire village gathered to join his march. From a distance, two emaciated boys and a girl watched wistfully and Sindhu Putra asked, 'Whose children are these?'

They were orphans, he was told; the villagers fed them, but the children did not belong to anyone. A poet described what happened next:

'He looked into the eyes of the orphans and saw what lay behind them. He said, "Come, be with me," and their eyes were sad no more; and he asked if there were any more children unattended. And they told him of an unwed mother who lay dying, with her infant just born, and an orphan girl who waited on her; and like a hurricane, he ran to her hut, though no one knows how he knew where the hut was. Or maybe he guessed it from their gesture . . .

'But then even gods do not always run faster than Time . . . and the mother was dead when Sindhu Putra reached, or maybe it was willed that she live only till he arrives . . . and even through his tears, Sindhu Putra saw all and heard the infant's cry; and he saw a vision of his own birth, merged into living reality, as though the infant and he were two lives that moved together, inseparably tied to one another and yet apart . . .

'And he prayed for the dead woman and called her "Mother", and kissed her hair which held no white flower and he wondered why and where she lost it . . . '

The poet goes on to say that Sindhu Putra picked up the infant and led the weeping orphan girl out to where the crowds waited patiently, ready to march with Sindhu Putra. But the procession was delayed for Sindhu Putra waited 'to gather firewood to cremate the woman he had called "Mother", and her ashes he kept, to immerse in the holy river called Ganga, still far away.'

Sindhu Putra walked the last stretch of the journey to the land of Ganga. Couriers from Gangapati XIII had already reached him, with fresh horses and a cushioned carriage to escort him. He rode briefly to show his gratitude for the courtesy, but then walked. For him, it was a pilgrimage to Ganga mai.

With a huge crowd waiting behind him, Gangapati received Sindhu Putra. There was disappointment in the ruler's heart as he viewed the pale, fragile youth before him who looked even younger than he actually was. Certainly, he did not look like a god, or even an ascetic or a dreamer. The youth's words had no flourish, no fluency, even taking into account the language barrier.

The Ganga and Sindhu regions had quite a few words in common, and Sindhu Putra had learnt many new words during the journey from the men of Ganga who accompanied him. Even so, in response to Gangapati's eloquent words of welcome, the youth merely mumbled a few words—Tat tvam asi—and joined his hands together in Namaste like a mendicant. Yet, this boy is known as a god in the land from which he comes, Gangapati marvelled. And he knew, better than many, of the turmoil that this lad had caused not only by freeing the slaves, but by sending them out everywhere, with the mission to free others; and the ways of these freed, missionary slaves were not always peaceful or godly. They moved in armed bands, conducting murderous raids and even risking enslavement themselves. Already, they had created havoc in the First Tribe and elsewhere. Some said that Sindhu Putra had never sanctioned such himsa. But so what? What kind of god was he if he was unable to control his men!

As it is, Gangapati had never believed that Sindhu Putra was a god. Would a god waste his time on just the insignificant issue of slavery! Gangapati himself regarded slavery as a

necessary evil of a temporary character and not something that would last eternally. It was the same as 'enslaving' animals—horses, asses, camels and elephants—to use in the fields, for personal transport or as beasts of burden, though he did wonder if there was a divine spark only in humans, but not in dumb animals. In any case, he foresaw an era in which a vehicle would be found to ply on land, in much the same way as a boat sailed on a river without the aid of animals. Meanwhile, the 'slavery' of the animal was as necessary as that of humans—'though it too shall pass away in time'.

Gangapati believed that if ever a god walked on the earth, he would concern himself with the greater problems of humanity—of life, the afterlife and moksha (salvation). Why would a god need to unleash armies of slaves to create disorder and division? How then was he different from a chief seeking power for himself? Is that what he is after? Yet, the lad did not appear as someone aspiring to be a chief either; he was simply a bewildered youth.

In any case, Gangapati XIII had no serious worry on the question of slavery. Long before, during the time of his ancestor Gangapati IV, Dasaswamedha's great-granddaughter had gone on a fast to prevent slaves from entering the land of Ganga. It then became an established practice never to permit slaves to enter. What Gangapati IV had then done was to have huge areas ceded to him in the lands of the First Tribe and other tribes. The slaves were kept there to work under the supervision of Gangapati's men; and their produce was exclusively for the benefit of Gangapati's lands. Subsequent Gangapatis perfected the system, expanding the slave areas in tribal lands and increasing the numbers of their slaves. The slaves were far too well-guarded to suffer from encroachments or rebellion.

Gangapati XIII shrugged and put away his passing thoughts. He was about to introduce Sindhu Putra to his wife and to the entourage of sixty men and women standing well behind him.

Several people speak long and lovingly of what transpired next; many call it a miracle, while others go further to say that this miracle arose from a heart full of faith that moved the heart of God! But there were some who simply called it a coincidence, even though, at times, they marvelled at it too.

Even before Gangapati XIII introduced Sindhu Putra to his wife, Sindhu Putra had been staring at her, fascinated by the white flower she wore in her hair. His eyes seemed vacant, thoughtful, wrapped in the emotion that always flooded over him whenever he saw a woman's hair decked with a white flower. Although Gangapati found it rude and impertinent of Sindhu Putra to stare, his wife looked at the young man, doubt and faith alternating in her heart—would this god be the one to answer her constant prayer for a son? As he stared at her, straight and direct, her will gathered itself into a silent cry of faith; it was as if a door was opening to receive her prayer, and a soft voice was telling her, 'Come in, dear child!' But when she drew nearer, Sindhu Putra simply said, 'You have the same flower that my mother wore.' All she heard or understood was the word 'mother', and she said, 'That is what I long to be—a mother.'

Maybe, the waves of her passionate yearning reached him, or perhaps someone translated her words. However it was, Sindhu Putra understood that she was childless. Without saying anything, he turned and went into the throng of his own people, and brought out the motherless infant he had picked up from the village. He startled everyone by placing the child in the waiting arms of Gangapati's wife and said, 'Be you then the mother of this babe.'

This was not what the lady had hoped for. She was praying for a son to be born from her own womb—not to adopt an unknown child brought from some faraway land. But as she held the soft, warm body, so light and so lovable, she felt she was holding the very future, the earth and the sky, the sun and the moon.

Gangapati was seething with anger. If adoption was the only choice open to them, he already knew whom he would adopt as his son. He did not want his wife to be enchanted with a strange, stray, nameless infant from nowhere. He steeled himself not even to look at the infant in his wife's arms. But as she brought the infant near his face, a vague suspicion struck him. He moved the sheet around the infant's waist. It was a girl!

A girl! Gangapati was too furious to speak. He wanted a son, to be the next Gangapati, and this clueless clot had foisted a baby girl on them!

Even Gangapati's wife cried out, 'But I wanted a son!'

Her vehemence troubled Sindhu Putra. Quietly, he said, 'God will give a son too,'—a blessing, not a prediction.

'When?' Gangapati shouted fiercely, voicing years of pent-up frustration rather than just his anger at the youth.

Now, Sindhu Putra was truly bewildered. He pointed a finger heavenwards and said, 'As soon as God wills it. What can I do? Who am I to say when that shall be? It is in God's hands.'

Sindhu Putra had partly raised his hands as he spoke in utter helplessness, his fingers slightly parted, palms facing outward. The young daughter of the chief of the eastern tribe, who was in Gangapati's entourage, had her eyes riveted on Sindhu Putra's hands. She was an accomplished dancer and, to her, hand gestures meant more than words. She shouted excitedly, 'Look! Look! Ten fingers! He means ten months! Did he not say, it is in God's hands?'

Nonsense, thought Gangapati. But pitifully his wife asked Sindhu Putra, 'God, do you mean ten months?' Sorrowfully, Sindhu Putra pointed towards the sky once again, hoping to convince everyone that he was leaving it all to God above.

But even for days and weeks after Sindhu Putra was escorted to the guest-house, rumour, hope and faith combined, and many believed that a prediction had been made by the new god that Gangapati's wife would give birth to a son in ten months.

'Utter and absolute nonsense!' said Gangapati, firmly and furiously, keen to spare his wife cruel disappointment. But he did not stop his wife from keeping the infant. He had seen the glow on her face as she held the child. There is no harm, he thought, in adopting her. Later, he would adopt a son, fit to be Gangapati after him. He thanked his lucky stars that this crazy new god had not palmed off a boy on his wife. That would have complicated his adopting a son later to succeed him as Gangapati.

During the next four months, two maids who worked for Gangapati's wife became pregnant. But the lady herself did not. Yet she was happy, fulfilled, as never before, with her 'daughter'.

Many looked on Sindhu Putra as a god that failed. But at the end of the fourth month, Gangapati's wife felt something was happening. It gave her a ray of hope. Next month, she was certain. Her son was born twelve months and twelve days after she first met Sindhu Putra. Almost everyone thought of the birth as a miracle wrought by Sindhu Putra. A few saw it as a coincidence, but even for them, it was much too marvellous.

One poet, though, argued that Gangapati's son was born not through a miracle but simply because when Gangapati's wife became a mother to the infant girl, the birth juices in her body flowed. This, he pointed out, had happened in innumerable cases, where a childless woman adopted a baby and then something happened deep within her to stir her and she gave birth soon after.

'Nonsense!' said many to the poet who sought to give this simple and prosaic explanation. But even so, some argued, 'Whose miracle was it then to give an infant girl to Gangapati's wife?'

The poet agreed that indeed it was a great coincidence, as

without the infant constantly in her loving lap, nothing could have stirred the movement in the lady's womb. Another said, 'Yes indeed! The miracle maker presents a miracle and yet forgets not the physical law.'

But one question was raised, 'Did not Sindhu Putra promise a birth in ten months? And yet it took twelve!'

The answer was simple. 'Oh yes, but did he not twice raise his finger heavenwards, too? Much have I forgotten what my teachers taught me in my childhood days but I still seem to remember that ten plus two comes to twelve.'

Meanwhile, Sindhu Putra was hardly aware of the ups and downs in his esteem during the first year that he was in the land of Ganga. He did not even know that Gangapati had initially regarded him as a fake god and that many had laughed at him. If he heard or saw them laughing, he believed they were laughing *with* him, not *at* him. Those of his followers who suspected that their god was being laughed at only huddled around him all the more protectively. A few wondered how a god could be so untouched by disrespect from some. Others saw it simply as a godly virtue.

If Sindhu Putra was touched by something, it was by the magnificence of the land. Nature had been generous, but it was the miracle of man's toil that impressed him. When he looked at the distant fort in the moonlight, it looked like a golden mountain squared off in straight lines. At first, he thought it must be Gangapati's palace. But Gangapati had a humble home, less conspicuous than the homes of rich merchants. In fields and farms, he saw oranges and lemons, grains and cereals, trees and plants which provided wells of oils, grapes for wines, oceans of onions, tomatoes, cauliflowers and eggplants. Everywhere, he saw jars and clay pits in which to stock grain for lean periods and innumerable basket-lined silos for grain storage. Their fabrics were as fine and attractive as those woven in the Sindhu–Saraswati region, though they were more conservative. Many were at work, smelting and casting weapons and ornaments of high quality and making distinctive tablets and seals. He admired their filigreed silver, glazed pottery, shining metal ware and intricately carved statues. Their houses were designed for comfort and their public baths, temples and meeting places were erected with every convenience in view. He saw marvels of their irrigation and engineering skill, their broad streets, well-built houses, elegant temples, granaries, chariots, gardens and fountains, and he felt that there was much they could teach, and learn from, the people of Sindhu.

More than the magnificence of the art and architecture there, for Sindhu Putra it was the Ganga river itself that held the greatest fascination. In the murmur of her waters, he could hear the voices of the ages long gone by, as though he had himself been there before. He found peace and solace there —for whirling in his mind were the questions that many had asked, and to which he had inadequate answers.

Though Gangapati XIII had no questions—he had been cold, but always polite to Sindhu Putra during the first four months—there were others who crowded round him, some to learn, but many more who simply wanted to find flaws in order to feel superior themselves. Sindhu Putra's mistake possibly lay in trying to answer all their questions. Sometimes the questions he was asked were foolish and absurd. But in his humbleness of spirit, he would reply. Yet anyone could find flaws in his replies.

How did he know of the existence of God, he was asked. I feel it in my soul, he replied simply. When I see the multitude of trees clinging to the Ganga and the vastness of the infinite sky with thousands of beckoning, luminous stars and planets, all pulsating with life and light, how can I doubt that God exists!

What is man's duty, some wanted to know. Conduct that is pure and includes a striving for unity, justice, harmony and freedom, was the answer. He who seeks salvation shall not permit another to be held a slave.

Will a man who acts towards these goals achieve bliss, others asked. Maybe not, Sindhu Putra replied, but his purpose is not to seek bliss. Only to assume the sorrows of others to free them from grief.

But what about those that only pray and meditate? Truly, he said, they honour God and God honours them. But maybe they do not do God's work. They are born in life but they do not participate in it.

And what about those who do not believe in God, came the rejoinder. God is always with us, even if we are not always with him, Sindhu Putra answered. He will judge the believers and non-believers alike—by their intent and conduct. Disbelief in God may itself be the starting point of a relentless search for truth.

Then you see no difference between believers and non-believers, people persisted. Sindhu Putra smiled: Believers and non-believers, they all spring from a fragment of God's splendour. It is possible for a man to be deeply spiritual without believing in God, just as it is possible for a believer to commit ungodly acts.

Can you describe God, he was asked. Only in my heart, in silence, where there is no utterance and the definition is unknown.

Why do people die? Because they are born. Death is their birthright. For some, it is the end of a journey into the bliss of moksha. For others, it is the start of another. Each generation dies so that the next generation can be born.

Like us you speak of karma that leads either to rebirth or to moksha, but what about a totally evil man who, through all his successive births, commits only evil and never obtains salvation? That would be God's failure—and God does not fail, Sindhu Putra said.

How would someone who is totally evil, ever journey towards salvation, he was asked. Because his soul is pure.

Like the journey of the Ganga to the sea, or that of the sun, moon and stars as they wend their way through the infinite, the soul knows of its ultimate pilgrimage to salvation.

But, the waters of the Ganga go to fields, they quench the thirst of animals and people, and some water even evaporates in the sun. Then how can you say all of it reaches the sea? Water turns into water, Sindhu Putra replied. That which evaporates becomes vapour and comes back as rain, and that which is consumed in the fields or by people and animals returns as water to find its way into rivers and the sea.

But how does karma operate on the day of judgement? Are all the good and evil deeds of a person counted to determine if a person is to be granted moksha? If not, how is his position in rebirth determined? Sindhu Putra thought for a moment, and then said, I do not know. But I have heard of a dance-drama which shows that an angel interceded successfully on behalf of a sinner to plead that his saving an injured bird and bringing it back to life must be counted in his favour as good karma to determine his position in his next rebirth.

How ridiculous, the people thought, to rely on a dance-drama to answer such a weighty question! But then there was no holding back Sindhu Putra from quoting from the dance-dramas that Roopa had narrated to her children and him.

But surely, the questions continued, *God can deny moksha to a person who defies him by neither praying to him nor by pleasing him!* I doubt it. My belief is that a person may be an atheist and may deny the existence of God but so long as he shows goodness to all around him and leads a pure, sinless life, he cannot be denied salvation.

'No man is above the Law;

Not even Him that made the Law;

Verily God cannot destroy him who conquers himself;

For he who conquers the self is the very Self of God;

And God and he are One;
Where is the duality then, when they are One!
Yes, One—without the Second;
And how can God destroy him without destroying
Himself?
He can but he cannot . . . '

You mean that there are things that God himself cannot do and there are limitations on his competence? No, not at all. At best, you may consider it a self-imposed limitation by God. But really, it is no limitation at all. God recognizes that a man of goodness and purity becomes a part of him.

'Then God looked in wonder and awe at the spirit of the man who had conquered his Self, and Rudra asked God: "Is he then a God like you?"

'And God said, "No, he is not a God like Me. He is Me!"'

Again, Sindhu Putra confessed that he was relying on the stories he had heard from Roopa. To his audience, it was strange that this man, regarded as a god by some, should be quoting from fanciful stories for children culled from dramas!

We notice you show so much respect for the cow. Why? Because respect for the cow is traditional in my land. My mentor, Muni of the Rocks, told me that veneration for the cow started over 2000 years ago when 108 tribes reached the river-village of Sindhu after a long, gruelling journey during which many lost their lives. The river people saw the frightened faces of bruised and wounded men, women who could hardly stand and emaciated children. Clearly, they realized, there was suffering here, and hunger, thirst and dread. They rushed to bring buckets of water, fruit and food. Cows were ushered in so they could be milked right there to serve first the children, and then the adults. And when a tribal woman said to a child, pointing to the cow, 'She is the mother of us all and gives milk to our children,' the leader of the tribes heard her and pledged, 'She will always be the Mother

to our tribes.' Over the long centuries thereafter, respect for the cow has been reinforced.

Did God create the universe? Yes, but perhaps before Him was She—the Mother.

You often recite from the Song of the Hindu *composed by Bharat or quote Muni of the Rocks. Are they the founders of your faith or its prophets?* No, Sindhu Putra replied, not at all. Hinduism has no founder and no prophets. Hinduism is a movement, not a dogma; it is not a mere protector of present knowledge or a preserver of custom. It is a growing tradition, not a fixed revelation, and its aim is to achieve perfection through growing knowledge that refines everything, through continuous testing and experiencing.

Many felt that the answers Sindhu Putra gave had no depth. And to many more questions, his answer simply was, 'I don't know.' In Gatha's village, people simply sought his blessings. Here, they were trying to test, even to trap him. There was no poetry in his words, no fine phrases, no eloquence, no flourishes. His replies were slow, halting, diffident, as though he himself was searching for answers. Often he would quote Yadodhra or Muni, Roopa, and Bharatjogi; people would ask, 'Are they gods?' No, they were his teachers. Teachers! Then he was not divinely inspired!

Sometimes, he failed to give a conclusive answer to a question, groping and even contradicting himself in the process. Yes, he said, the Ganga is a place of pilgrimage. But so is the Sindhu and also the Saraswati, and so is every river, the sea and all of God's good earth, every place of work, even a cow-pen. A temple? It does not have to be erected. No, you don't need a sacred fire, your prayers can rise as an auspicious flame.

One of the places where he fell short was in expressing the ultimate reality of God. He was infinite, eternal, imperishable and unchanging. But then, he pleaded, how could something infinite, eternal, imperishable and unchanging be

fully understood by our finite and limited minds! They asked if God was unchanging. If He was the first seed, was it not possible that like a seed it transformed itself into a tree? If the progress of humanity was continuously in motion, why should it not be assumed that God too progressed in the same fashion! Was humanity not in His image? Did our duties not change—there was no slavery a thousand years ago! If a man must move to meet a new challenge, why must it be assumed that God remains unchanging?

He could only answer with silence, though his faith never wavered. But he did speak of one certainty in his mind. It was man's duty to live without sin and to achieve unity, harmony, love and freedom.

Some sneered, 'You speak so much of man's duty to man, of the abolition of slavery, to prevent hurt or harm to people, rather than of man's duty to God. Why do you not begin a new faith under a new god, away from what our ancestors said when they established our order of Sanathani and away from your ancestral order of Sanatan Dharma, to spread your ideas of man's duty to man?'

'I know not who my ancestors were,' Sindhu Putra replied. 'But I tread the same ancient path that my teachers followed. Whatever I know, I learnt on this path. And the path renews itself with fresh flowers of new knowledge and higher thought. What will I achieve elsewhere? A good Sanathani is a good Hindu, and a sinless tribal is both a good Sanathani and a good Hindu—is there a difference? Whatever god you worship, He is That God and Dharma is His Will.'

Sometimes priests, learned men and even Gangapati's courtiers who questioned Sindhu Putra carried an echo of his insufficient answers and self-doubts to rishis and sages in the forests. They listened in silence, then some said, 'A god he may or may not be, but perhaps he may yet achieve the goodness of a god.'

But not many took these rishis and sages seriously. These

forest-dwelling hermits, they knew, were always generous, even to the mosquitoes that drank their blood or the wasps that stung them.

But man is fickle. As news of Gangapati's wife's pregnancy spread, those who had scoffed at him before now clustered around Sindhu Putra worshipfully. Sindhu Putra himself remained unaffected, for he did not seem to know that many of them had ridiculed him earlier.

∽

When Gangapati XIII was told of his wife's pregnancy, he had vowed to himself, 'I shall release all my slaves if a son is born.' Later, as the pregnancy progressed, he said, 'At least half the slaves.' Then, he said, 'Many.' In her eighth month, he said, 'Some.' As his wife went into labour, he said, 'All, yes all.'

Finally, when his son was born, how could he remember, among so many vows, what he had promised! But, in gratitude, he went to Sindhu Putra. Thousands followed him. Many more joined him on the way. Everywhere, Gangapati heard the same cry, extolling Sindhu Putra as 'mahapati'— the great protector. It was a new title, but why not create a distinct title of their own! Was he not the one who had protected the land of the Ganga by providing a continuity of succession? Was he not their own then! Gangapati bowed to Sindhu Putra, addressing him as 'Mahakarta Mahapati,' combining the titles of both the Sindhu–Saraswati and the Ganga regions.

Sindhu Putra asked for nothing and Gangapati felt relieved. When Gangapati returned home all he wanted was to look at the magic and wonder of his infant son, but his wife asked, 'Did you deny him?'

'No,' he said, 'I called him *mahapati*, and so shall he be addressed henceforth.'

BHAGWAN S. GIDWANI

Again, she asked, 'But did you deny him?'

'No,' he replied, 'he asked for nothing.'

And she said, 'Then you did deny him!' and her eyes went to her infant.

Miserably, Gangapati said, 'I shall release some of the slaves,' and gave the order releasing 900 slaves held in an eastern land.

He returned to find his wife still plunged in melancholy, but attributed it to the exhaustion of childbirth at her age.

It was some forty days later that fear set into Gangapati's heart. Even in his sleep, the infant used to smile, charming his parents. But suddenly, his mother saw that smile turn into a grimace and then a twitch. The next day, the infant was unable to breastfeed and had fever. The vaids said it was not serious, but the fever persisted. The infant's tiny body shivered. There was an icy dread in the mother's eyes as she gazed at her infant, a beseeching look when she spoke to the vaids, and unveiled accusation when she glanced at her husband.

Suddenly, Gangapati said, 'I shall go to Sindhu Putra. I shall promise that I will release all the slaves if he cures my son.'

She turned coldly on him, 'Do not bargain with a god! Release your slaves! Then go to him!'

Gangapati shook his head. His wife was asking for the impossible! Dozens of messengers had to be sent to release all the slaves in captivity in the scattered areas of the eastern tribes and the First Tribe. Besides, many arrangements had to be made. But he swore on the life of his infant that he would release them all.

He rushed to Sindhu Putra who had gone far into the forest. He found him and begged, 'Pray for my son.'

Sindhu Putra said, 'We shall pray together.'

Gangapati returned home in the morning.

Coincidence, chance, fate, destiny—call it what you will.

Some said there never was any real danger and it was just something that all infants went through. Others said the change of medicine prescribed by the vaid had worked wonders. The child was sleeping peacefully, and the fever was gone. Gangapati and his wife thanked the vaid profusely, but in their hearts they knew it was the miracle of god, not of man or medicine.

All the slaves held across the land were freed. With hundreds to help him, they were placed in Sindhu Putra's care. He asked to feed, clothe and transport them, to repair their broken bodies and spirits and even to send those who wished to their homelands! Nothing was denied to him. The freed slaves wanted to distance themselves from the people who had enslaved them, and began calling themselves 'Sindhu Putra's slaves'.

'Slaves you are not and never shall be!' Sindhu Putra told them firmly.

They called themselves 'Hindus' and believed that a Hindu could never be a slave.

༄

Eventually, Yadodhra arrived in the Ganga region. He spoke with the magnificence of a sage. He told the people of the era of Sanathana and Sanatan Dharma. He said that every Hindu in the Sindhu–Saraswati region was also a Sanathani Hindu, like the people of Ganga. He spoke of the glorious heritage of 'togetherness' of the two regions, with 'pride in my heart and yours'. Some people called Yadodhra a 'modern', in the sense that where his knowledge of itihasa deserted him, the bold stroke of his imagination replaced it.

With a dramatic gesture, Yadodhra escorted Sindhu Putra to bless the infant son of Gangapati, who later was to be anointed as Gangapati XIV, as the 'First Sanathani Hindu who was always a Sanathani Hindu for all generations'.

It did not take too long—perhaps a few years, or maybe a decade or two—for everyone in the land of Ganga to be called a Sanathani Hindu, and later, simply a Hindu. Even Sindhu Putra said, 'Call yourself a Hindu by all means, if it pleases you. There are no compulsions. The eternal guarantee of God's love is with you, whatever you call yourself. And remember, God's gracious purpose includes everyone and in his kingdom there is no higher or lower. The passion for perfection burns equally in everyone, for there is only one class as there is only one God, who is all-loving and universal.'

～

Sindhu Putra, along with Yadodhra visited the sangam, the confluence of Ganga, Yamuna and Saraswati rivers, and rested leisurely by its side. There he learnt of how the source of the Ganga and Saraswati had come to be discovered and a little bit also about the history and antiquity of the region: The great-great-grandfather of the present Gangapati, thirteen generations ago, came to be known as The First Gangapati or Gangapati I. Before assuming that title, he was simply a visitor to the Ganga region but due to his extraordinary and selfless services to the people of Ganga and for protecting them against invaders, he became their leader. He went by the name of Brahmadatta (not to be confused with Brahmdas who discovered the Saraswati river's sangam with the Sindhu. Unfortunately, this similarity in names has caused confusion amongst poets of later eras).

Brahmadatta and his wife Kashi were wandering in the Himalayas. None knows what catastrophe or curiosity drove them there (though much information about them and the Ganga region in ancient times is given in the book *Return of the Aryans*). But they are known to be the first to witness the glacial ice-cave at an altitude of 12,770 feet in the Himalayas, which later would come to be known as Gai-mukh (Mouth of Cow). From the belly of that ice-cave flowed two torrential streams, crashing against each other and throwing up their foam, white as milk, and thence parting, each rushing in a different direction. Brahmadatta and his wife chose to follow the path of one of the two streams. They did not know then that it was the Ganga river itself, for initially it appeared like any other mountain stream, no more than 20 *angulas* (approximately, 40 cms or 15 inches).

They simply called it Kshira-subhra (white as milk), as that seemed to be the colour of this rushing icy stream. The other stream, which they did not follow, turned out to be the Saraswati. Thus both the Ganga and Saraswati rivers flowed from 'nipples' of the same 'divine cow' in the glacial ice-cave in the central Himalayas and thereafter each followed a different course to sustain life along its route.

Slowly and painfully, through trackless passes, formidable peaks and deep gorges, Brahmadatta and his wife followed the course of the river and at last they reached the plains where the Ganga finally breaks through the last outriders of the Himalayas to enter the plains at Hari Hara Dwara (literally meaning the home of the gods Vishnu and Shiva, now known as Haridwar). According to Brahmadatta's reckoning, they travelled only 60 yojnas or 300 miles from Gai-mukh to Haridwar (including detours where the terrain was impossible)—but the journey took them nearly a year. All along the way, they met no one; but at Haridwar, suddenly, they saw a number of people along the riverbank.

The local people viewed Brahmadatta with caution as he limped towards them, carrying his wife on his shoulders. Obviously, he was an outsider with his garb of animal-skins, a wild look in his eyes and strange way of speaking; but some of his words were familiar though he spoke with an atrocious accent and pronunciation. However, obviously he meant no harm and needed to rest himself and his wife. They were fed, their wounds washed and a hut given to them to rest.

Later, neither his strange speech nor his wild appearance mattered, once the people of Ganga learnt that he had witnessed the source of their holy river. He drew sketches of the glacier and the icy cave and described vividly the two milky-white streams, one of which was their Ganga. In those sketches, people clearly saw figures of the divine cow from whose nipples flowed two milky rivers—the Ganga and Saraswati.

Brahmadatta led an expedition down the Ganga from Hari Hara Dwara. It was not an uneventful journey as they crossed exciting rapids and waterfalls in lovely though lonely country. Sudden attacks came from tribesmen hiding behind dense groves of reeds and grass. Fortunately, the attacks were ill-organized and Brahmadatta's team suffered no mishaps other than minor injuries. The attackers belonged to new tribes, which had moved in to displace earlier inhabitants. They were sullen, under-nourished, wretchedly emaciated, and initially refused gifts from Brahmadatta. Cautiously, Brahmadatta's contingent moved, day after day, surviving sixteen fights on the way—none of them had serious consequences except for those who attacked them.

Suddenly, they stopped and looked about in wonder, as if seeing the earth for the first time. There was not just one river. There were three! Here was the milky-white Ganga river they were following. Here was another river, blue, glistening with flakes of silver in the brilliant light of the sun! And here was yet another, shimmering like gold! Where did they come from? Did they rise up, unseen, from the earth!

They walked slowly, as though in a trance. But the spell was broken when they heard a roar. Another attack? They readied themselves to meet the enemy. But there was no threat. It was the sangam of the three rivers—the Ganga, Yamuna and Saraswati. And they saw the Yamuna, a river of blue water, becoming one with the Ganga, as they both flowed together, united and strong; while the Saraswati, the river with ripples of gold, rushed through to chart a separate course, as though it came simply to embrace the two rivers and also say farewell at the same moment. (A later poet had this to say of the Saraswati river at the confluence— 'Saraswati, impetuous as always, rushed headlong through the confluence, as though to meet and part in the same single moment; and it greeted and was gone in one breathless heartbeat, leaving a little of its waters behind, but taking no less from the Ganga and Yamuna to flow in a different direction to embrace the far-away Sindhu River, and thence both the Saraswati and Sindhu flowed, as one single river,* to their own Sea—the Sindhu Sea.) For many long centuries, since then, the Saraswati flowed broad and strong. It is frequently mentioned repeatedly and glowingly as an auspicious river in the Rig Veda and other ancient Hindu literature. The Saraswati is now no more, having lost itself in the deserts of Rajasthan. (A poet adds, maybe too fancifully, that the Saraswati river went underground, and somehow that occurred when tribals began sacrificing bulls and eating their flesh.)

Gangapati I and his companions watched fascinated the picturesque dance of colours as the three rivers met to rise in foam of pure white. There was no need for words as they gazed at the sangam. Some poets assert that while 'sangam' is a popular word for a confluence of rivers, this particular confluence was called Sangayam, to represent the meeting of the Saraswati (sa), Ganga (ga) and Yamuna (yam)— in silence. It was as though the waters spoke in the language of the sky. Slowly, they moved to bathe in the waters of the sangam. But then suddenly, viciously, came an attack from the riverbank. Gangapati's shout rose to call his men to arms.

---

* The Saraswati joined the Sindhu River possibly well below the confluence of the Sutlej with the Sindhu, and united, they flowed to the Sindhu Sea (now, the Arabian Sea.)

BHAGWAN S. GIDWANI

Lifting Kashi, he rushed to the bank, followed by his people, while arrows flew around. But the attackers did not remain to fight. They ran.

Gargi's arm was bruised from an arrow; eighteen men of Hari Hara Dwara were injured, but only slightly. Kauru alone, with three arrows in his chest, died in the waters of the sangam itself. He smiled before he died and pleaded that they not move him away from the sangam, but only help him to remain afloat. They held him and saw around him a colour that was not in the sangam earlier—the red colour of his blood. He was looking at the immeasurable, impassive sky. Above him, a dark cloud moved. He smiled. Then there was stillness and peace. He was dead.

And many wondered over Kashi's words about Kauru— 'He died sinless—always sinless.' Imagine calling a man like Kauru 'sinless'! He who was well known as a scoundrel and a slanderer of innocent, blameless women. But poets said Kashi was right—and they began to convince themselves that he who dies at the auspicious sangam, 'sinless he is and sinless he always was', because 'the sangam is the source of redemption . . . be it a billion of his births and the billion of his sins, sangam washes them all . . . there is pardon for all faults, if one breathes his last at the sangam . . . ' and 'if sinless you are at the moment of death, does it not stand to reason that sinless you always were!'

Perhaps all that Kashi meant was that Kauru died with the clan and for the clan; that if he had not been there, arrows aimed for him would have found another, worthier target and therefore all his past was forgiven because of this final sacrifice.

Yet, Kashi's characterization of Kauru as 'always sinless', when he died at the sangam, encouraged many in later generations to believe that all their sins would be washed away if they died at the sangam.

The sangam (where the Saraswati, Ganga and Yamuna

meet) came also to be known as Prayaga or the place for sacrifice—as Kauru lost his life there and nineteen people were wounded—*pra* signifies extensiveness or excellence; *yaga* means sacrifice. A later poet ridicules the idea that so small a sacrifice should be considered 'extensive' or 'excellent'. But then, life was not so cheap in Brahmadatta's times and battles did not involve so many injuries and deaths. Incidentally, later, with the emergence of foreign tribes, Prayaga was often polluted with the sacrifices of animals, including magnificent horses. But people of Brahmadatta's time, totally unfamiliar with such 'blood sacrifices', would have regarded them as inauspicious, inhuman and ungodly. Presently Prayaga is known as Allahabad (place of Allah or God) in Uttar Pradesh, India.

Brahmadatta, moved by Kauru's death and the injuries of the others, swore that he would make the route from Hari Hara Dwara to the Sangam so safe that even 'our dogs shall walk unmolested by tribal arrows and assaults. Enough have we sacrificed already!'

Brahmadatta's return journey to Hari Hara Dwara was less perilous with only seven skirmishes and no casualties.

Everyone in Hari Hara Dwara heard of the enchanted, magical Sangam, and many sought to rush to it but held back, as they heard stories of perils and bloodshed on the route, magnified a hundredfold by those who had returned.

A legend was already growing around Brahmadatta, and people told stories of him as they tell stories of legendary heroes—how he could deflect enemy arrows to render them harmless, how unerringly he took his people to the Sangam, how his followers could come to no harm! But there were questions. How could he not protect Kauru? Kauru! Do you not recall Kauru's insult to his wife Kashi! But Kashi had forgiven the insult.* So what—why would her husband forgive him? Yet did he not declare Kauru to be sinless? No, Kashi did that. Nonsense! Does Kashi speak with a voice different from her husband's?

BHAGWAN S. GIDWANI

But questions ceased as they all heard Brahmadatta's grim resolve to clear the route to Prayaga (Sangam). Truly, they realized, he was inspired. Many volunteered to assist. None, he ordered, can leave for Prayaga until the route was cleared. This was for their protection but he wanted their single-minded attention to clearing the route, not only of hostile tribes but also of rocks and boulders; to level the terrain, make tracks for men, mules and horses to pass; to build rope-bridges and even plant trees.

Only one man defied his order and moved to Sangam. It was Tirathda. He glared at Brahmadatta who let him pass with the traditional blessing, 'Go with God.' Later, Tirathda was not found at the Sangam. For two decades, no one knew where he was. He was seen at last near Ganga Sagar, in the Bay of Bengal where the Ganga divides herself into several streams—some said 108 though now there are fewer—to complete her incredible 1,560-mile journey.

Thousands worked for Brahmadatta to clear the path to the auspicious spot where the waters of the Ganga, Yamuna and Saraswati mingled, 'with colours more than seen in a rainbow, as though diamonds and sapphires, rubies and emeralds and threads of gold and silver dance to meet the sunlight as it breaks into a myriad hues and tints, passing through each drop of water.'

The route from Hari Hara Dwara to the Sangam became safe, secure and free from hostile attacks. Poets speak, not of the cruelty of Brahmadatta's men, but of how Kashi moved

---

* Kauru had once spread a malicious rumour that Kashi was unfaithful to Brahmadatta. Verdict of Hermit Parikshahari was that a woman, whose virtue or chastity is questioned, must walk 10 steps through fiercely burning fire to prove her innocence, but *only after* the slanderer had gone 30 steps through fire to show that he had honest grounds and honorable motives for making such a charge. Kauru begged not to be consigned to flames and confessed that he had lied. Kashi forgave him and thenceforth, he always addressed her as 'Mother Kashi'.

'with boundless compassion, to wipe a tear from every eye, for she said that they too were children of the Ganga and then "hostiles were hostile no more, bubbling with friendship and fellow feeling", and when Brahmadatta was around, they bowed, in remembrance of their fear of him, and called him Gangapati (Protector of the Ganga)'—a title which the people of Ganga adopted, lovingly, for Brahmadatta.

❦

Back from the rest and recreation at the Sangam, Sindhu Putra pleaded with the chiefs of the eastern tribes and the First Tribe to release their slaves. But, much to his disappointment, each offered to free only 500 slaves. What he possibly failed to realize was that the chiefs had no centralized command like Gangapati, who could with one stroke release all his slaves. These chiefs had many smaller chiefs, warlords, priests and prominent and leading figures who had their own slaves. Demanding that they all free their slaves was likely to incite rebellion!

But what a god cannot do, his lieutenants and followers sometimes can. The freed slaves marched as an army to free other slaves, leaving turmoil and massacre in their wake, which even Jalta and the silent chief, who had accompanied Sindhu Putra, could not control. Thus, while many more slaves were freed, the number of bloodbaths multiplied, too.

Did Sindhu Putra worry? Some said that he had already left for faraway lands. But others said he had cried, 'I am beyond redemption.'

'How could a god be beyond redemption when redemption is denied to no man?' many asked. At which a learned man said: 'Be it man or god, the rita—the moral law of the universe—is the same. Gods live and die and are replaced, like stars, some are springing anew, while others splinter into lifeless fragments.' The argument went on until the learned

BHAGWAN S. GIDWANI

man concluded that it was better to share one's knowledge with trees in the forest than with ignorant men.

From the First Tribe, the slave armies moved to other tribes, and then, along wayward paths, to Gangasagarsangam, always swelling with new recruits, till the entire land was the land of Hindu, with not a single slave in sight.

Within a relatively short time, the slave armies were in control of the route along the Ganga to Gangasagarsangam, though battles to secure commanding positions in the lands around and beyond continued to rage. Later, some contingents which had branched off to strike out in different directions extended themselves and went as far as Bhutan's border with Tibet and to Burma's border with China and Thailand in the east, not only to free the slaves but also to settle them in new lands.

Meanwhile, Sindhu Putra was already on the move to Daksina. He had with him the father and son duo who had been freed by the silent tribe. They were joined by seventy-eight other slaves freed by the land of Ganga, whose roots were in Daksina. And thousands followed, not because of the lure of Daksina but to be with Sindhu Putra.

Gangapati XIII himself visited the land of Sindhu, escorted by Sage Yadodhra. He called it a pilgrimage, but some say it was with a hope that one day his newborn son would rule over the united land of Ganga and Sindhu–Saraswati.

TWENTY-NINE

TO THE LAND OF TAMALA

5044 BCE

Sindhu Putra moved from the land of Ganga to the south with thousands, and though some called it an army, they were quick to clarify that it was an army of pilgrims. The father and son duo of explorers and the slaves from Daksina regaled everyone with tales of the beauty and poetry of the south. But the main task they undertook was to teach everyone their own language. When asked why, the father replied, 'So that you may not only see the exquisite beauty of my land, but also learn to sing its great songs.' Sindhu Putra had also advised everyone to try to learn the language. The old explorer would shout out numbers, words, odd sentences in order to teach them, though often he would recite poetry and sing songs.

'Are all your people as dark as you are?' someone asked.

'Not all my people are as handsome as I am, but yes, most of us are dark,' he answered.

'Did you then come from some other planet from a dark sky or from the sea on a moonless night?'

'No. The songs of our itihasa say that we came not from a planet or the sea, but from a tamala tree of dark leaves and bark which hold a promise that the darkness in man's mind shall one day be dispelled by devotion to truth.'

'How can man spring from a tree?'

'It is a myth, my friend. Only to demonstrate that in the beginning there was a tree, and then, slowly, came the life that evolved from that tree. But don't be surprised when I tell you that my earliest ancestor was born, if not *from* a tree, at least *under* a tamala tree, for in those days the sun shone even stronger on our barren landscape and women often gave birth under a tree.'

'But then why don't you call yourself the people of Tamala?'

'Our legends also say that while the first man came from a tamala tree, our first woman came from a silk-cotton tree, whose deep scarlet flowers bloom at the onset of spring. Besides, our first priest sprang from the sami tree, as it is said to hold within itself the radiant fire of the Lord. And then our first yogi came from a pipal tree, and the first hermit from a banyan tree, which lives and renews itself through centuries, offering shelter to birds and their nests and even solace to hearts burdened with sorrow or minds seeking wisdom.'

'When did it all happen?'

'My friend, I told you, it is a legend, a myth. It arose in the mind of man before man came into being, like a dream-song, a rhythm, a feeling for poetry.'

'How could the mind of man exist before he came into being?'

The old man gestured to the sky and said, 'Nothing and all things come from that which is not; and nothing and all things go into what is not! Man's mind? It is not all matter. The largest part is spiritual. Then there is also the will that evolved man into being.'

'Where did that will come from?'

'From the heart of all spirit, desire, atoms, cells, elements, non-beings and beings from which man successively evolved.'

'How much of man's mind is then physical matter?'

'I shall take you to the ocean. There you will see, at times, a huge wave, foaming white, riding on the crest in a vortex of ceaseless activity. That much of our minds is matter. The rest of the vast ocean is comparable to the unseen, unperceived spiritual portion of the mind.'

Someone laughed, 'Then we who live are really bigger than we are!'

'You are bigger than you are, dead or alive,' the explorer replied. 'Only the physical matter of your mind dies with death but the larger, spiritual part is indestructible and changeless.'

'Good! Then we never really die! Is everyone in your land immersed in matters of the spirit?' they teased.

'No,' he said. 'Some sing, others dance or tell stories, some try out new herbs and medicines. Others seek to discover physical laws of nature, to find unity in diversity. Many dig wells or build reservoirs, granaries, huts, cottages, make water clocks, cloth looms, boats, toys or work in fields and farms.'

'So many earthly, material activities, then?' someone quipped.

The explorer laughed, 'All these are essential fragments of the human pursuit to eat, drink, live, dress and travel. Can man plunge into a spiritual ocean before his basic needs are met? Perhaps a thousand years from now, when all knowledge is available to discover unity and balance among physical laws . . . '

A thousand years! Some laughed at this enormous stretch of time, but he thought they ridiculed his hope for such quick results and said, 'Maybe it will take two thousand years or five, but then the physical laws of the universe are, as I said, like a tiny wave in a vast expanse of ocean. We will still have to see where God's finger points, to hear His voice and know His Mind, why He brought the cosmos to us and us to the cosmos, why there is a universe and why we are here!'

Again, they delved into the question of human origins in the north and south, and asked why the physical characteristics of his people were different. 'I don't know,' the explorer smiled. 'The people of the south came from beautiful trees, but I think, maybe, except Sindhu Putra who undoubtedly sprang from a lotus, the rest of you originated from a tree in which a dark-brown monkey lived with a pink mate. Hence your brown skin.'

But he added, seriously, 'I shall take you to our rishis who study man's evolution. They will explain how ancestry, mountain air, climatic change, proximity to sea, and inter-marriage affect man's appearance and complexion. It may even depend on when your first ancestors evolved into man and through what creatures and how long they have been on earth under the bright sun.'

He explained that those who originated from the earliest tamala tree were darker than those that came later from the banyan tree. What was the time frame, he was asked. He did not know. All he could give them was his ancestral knowledge that plants came to earth some 555,000,000 years ago, and the tamala tree evolved about 333,000,000 years ago, while the banyan tree came 222,000,000 years ago. Other creatures evolved around the trees, on the earth and in water, and from them evolved man, at different stages, though not through the same creatures.

'How could different creatures bring out the same result?'

'It was the energy of spirit and will that caused man to evolve; and not the creatures through which man came. Perpetual movement there may be, for nothing stands still—be it atoms or stars—but perpetual repetition there is not.'

They asked, 'What was there before trees, before plants?'

'Perhaps it was ice all over. All I know is that you and I were not here. Or maybe we were, since the spirit is ever present. But in physical terms, maybe there was nothing. Only the spirit persisted. Then came space, and atoms, and the will of the spirit and atoms to form, combine and evolve. That is how physical creation is continuing, and that is how you and I are fated to meet and talk today, till we meet to merge with each other and be One.'

'Does the tamala tree of your ancestors still exist?'

'It does and it does not—like a river, with its waters changing every moment. We have thousands of tamala trees in place of that mythical tamala.'

Every question he answered raised a thousand. He promised that thinkers and sages of his land would answer them. But he startled them by saying that his land had a banyan tree which was 5,000 years old. The glorious canopy of this tree had a circumference of eight acres and could shelter over 100,000 people; it had thousands of prop roots, developing into secondary trunks to support the widespread, constantly extending branches. The explorer tells tall tales, they thought. But, later, they found that the tree was even larger than he had described.

Sometimes the explorer would break into a song:

'I am from Dravidham, Dravidham,

But Brahma idam visvam (But this whole earth is Brahma).'

His companions laughed, and his son and many others joined him. Again, he sang:

'Soham, Soham, Soham (I am He; that I am)

From Dravidham, Dravidham!'

Many joined in the laughter and revelry. Their songs were many, and some of them became their marching songs:

'We go to Dravidham, Dravidham,

With satyam sivam advaitam (with tranquil bliss, undivided).'

Sometimes, Sindhu Putra, too, joined in their frolic and rollicking songs.

Poets speak of slave armies far ahead and of the cry of slaughter when the slaves were being freed. No one mentions that Sindhu Putra was aware of the cry!

At last, when they reached the fragmented Deccan interior, they felt that they were really in the land of Dravidham. The entire region had never had slaves at any time. The old explorer also explained that there was no precedence of one group or class exercising superiority over others. Priests? They were appointed by the head of the family. Family? It meant everyone—a thousand or more—in the village. The

BHAGWAN S. GIDWANI

head of the family? Often the eldest woman—mother or grandmother—advised by a group of ten other women and two men, usually the priest and the vaid. They were perhaps the most 'responsible' men in the village, as they were held accountable for much that went wrong. The priest was blamed if anyone in the village misbehaved, and the vaid was blamed if anyone fell ill, for his job was to prevent sickness, not merely cure it.

Ten or more villages would join to form a common unit, called nagara. The head of each village would be represented on the nagara council.

Each village had parks where it began and ended. Every nagara prided itself on its landscape, gardens, architecture, fountains, public squares, bathing pools, drainage system, statues, idols, frescoes painted in caves and figures cut into rocks.

Each sub-family—wife, husband, their unmarried sons, daughters, sons-in-law, grandchildren—had a large house, with a veranda, behind which were living quarters and bathrooms. Married sons, often, moved in with their wives' families. No one could have more than one living spouse. Widows and widowers were encouraged to marry if they were below thirty-six years of age.

Each house had its own temple, apart from the large village temple where the villagers and the gods met. There were no theatres; song and dance performances were held in the public square or in the temple. Performances at the temple were devotional or classical while those at the public square were for casual entertainment.

Sindhu Putra felt at peace among the Tamala people. He found them gentle and thoughtful, even as they sat enjoying their discussions or watching the many performances—some depicting passionate love between men and women, others the unity and balance in nature, attributing divinity to each element of nature. There seemed to be no bafflement and brooding in their songs and dances. Instead, there was faith that was both intense and joyous. But not all their performances were concerned with serious subjects. Many sang simple folk songs about heavenly lovers and earthly mistresses or about idle husbands and autocratic wives that left the audience laughing. Then there were duets and choruses where men complained that they were loved only for their bodies and not respected for their minds and women quickly retorted that they could not respect what did not exist! And then a newly married daughter would enter to complain that she ate very little because her husband ate too much and the other women would clamour:

'Oh feed him, feed him well, for a body is all he has got:
How else do you think, you have a mind, and he has not!'

There were songs about henpecked wives, as well as those that poked fun at family heads and even the head of the nagara council, all of whom were women.

Sindhu Putra enjoyed the music, songs and dance of the Tamala people, or Dravidham as his own people called them. But most of all, he loved their 'mood music', with its different tempo and rhythm for different occasions. From the temple courtyard would float the strains of devotional music, inspiring those who approached to empty their minds of stray thoughts and concentrate on the Divine. In fields and farms, the music would be sprightly to encourage the tempo of work; on the riverbank, before a class started in yoga or meditation, the music would be soft, peaceful; where people sat around village parks and fountains, the music would have an entertaining lilt, working up to a climax of rapid ornamentation; and beyond the fringe of the forest, or on the riverfront where men went to walk and think, the calming rhythm of the music would aid reflective thinking. For sportsmen and athletes who trained and jogged, the music would keep time to their movements.

'Do these people do anything without music?' asked some

who had come with Sindhu Putra.

'Music is humanity's earliest heritage,' the old explorer answered. 'It was there before language, before thought. Perhaps it evolved before man finally emerged, in his uniqueness, to walk on two legs, distinguished from the rest of his ancestry. Maybe it arose when there was only a sensation and impulse in the mind of our earliest ancestress as she sang a lullaby to her first child. That is why, even today, before it can hear or utter a sound, an infant is soothed to sleep by music or a tune or a lullaby. For it is a familiar sound heard for countless generations long before he was born.'

Many laughed at his impossible explanation and teased the explorer, 'How do you know so much, old man?'

'It is because I am old that I know so much,' he replied. 'But go, listen to our songs of remembrance, and you too will know.'

'And these songs of remembrance? Do they tell the itihasa of music?'

'Not just of music, but much more.'

More than the wide range of musical instruments, what impressed the newcomers was the fact that the singers treated the voice itself as a musical instrument. They would sing softly, performing long, complex variations on a simple, wordless melody. They often sang as an accompaniment to a dance or at a wedding or funeral or an invocation to the gods; the voice would then be neither loud nor throaty, but as though it floated from a remote distance, passively, never intruding, never drawing attention to itself, but only to the event that it accompanied. A song, normally, would arouse an emotion, but this kind of song, that stood by itself without any musical instruments, was more for creating an atmosphere that was calm and tranquil, like the gentle, unobtrusive air around us, while every eye and ear, and every feeling and emotion was focused on the event that it accompanied. An accomplished Tamala singer could achieve even more than merely creating an impersonal atmosphere, for his singing could uplift the feeling to an ineffable, aesthetic sensation, obliterating the grief of the sorrowing parents at the funeral pyre of their child, and bringing the certainty that the child would always live in their hearts, as a part of the universe, and in the lap of the Divine. The grief transformed itself into love and faith, and that moment would have the *dhvani*—the reverberation—that the stream of life must go on with that love and faith forever.

The newcomers were equally fascinated by the dance of Dravidham, with its forty-four movements of the eyes and eyebrows, eighty-four of the hand, eight of the neck, nine of the feet, six of the breast, four of the torso, and hundred and eight of the fingers, with every gesture controlled and significant, depicting an emotion, feeling or object. There was grace and artistry in their body movements and facial expressions as they danced to present various emotions like love, surrender, mirth, terror, devotion, surprise, wonder, awe and pity, as well as the beautiful but complex code of mudras—hand gestures—to depict gods, animals, flowers, sweethearts, lovers and demons. The newcomers, though, found it easier to participate in the folk dances, which were many, and largely required vigorous use of arms, legs and body without subtle gestures or complicated poses.

Some say that Sindhu Putra's feeling of peace in Dravidham came from the beauty of the land and the love of its people for simplicity, justice and equality. But others said that Sindhu Putra's enchantment arose from his triumph of freedom—in Sindhu, everyone bowed to him as a god, sought his blessing and called him 'mahakarta'. In the land of Ganga, too, he was honoured as a god and a miracle worker, and they called him 'mahapati'. But here in Dravidham, they respected him, honoured him, yet they sought no miracles from him. Gods, they felt, came to purify the world, not to perform conjuring tricks. They honoured him all the more when they listened to his mantra—*om*, and they recognized its power and mystery. They had hundreds of mantras of their own—some to bring peace of mind, others to eject evil thoughts and some even to cure mental illnesses.

'Do your mantras work?' someone asked the old explorer.

'Each one of them works—until it doesn't,' replied the explorer.

'Namaste' was adopted as a part of the repertoire of the Tamala dancers, in a series of hand gestures. It did not take too long for Dravidham to accept this as a form of greeting, as well. *Om* became their very own mantra and began to be celebrated in their classical performances.

Did the people of Dravidham treat Sindhu Putra as their own god? The old explorer had difficulty in understanding the question. Where is the question of your god, my god, their god, and our god, he asked. Is not a god of one the god of all, and is not the god of all the god of one? How do you own a god? Or limit and confine him? Besides, in Dravidham, a god was not required to show magic potency, to lift mountains into the air and crumble them into dust. In fact they believed that a god who walks on earth conforms to the pattern of the earth. How could they believe otherwise, when they treated a tulsi plant, a tree and a cow as gods! Different gods were simply symbols and pathfinders, and even temples and statues of gods or idols were merely inspirations in the approach towards salvation to reach the Supreme. Did Dravidham believe that the efforts of various gods could lead them to salvation? 'No. For that, the individual has to strain himself. All a god can do is point to the path tempting many, but force none to follow it.'

There were some who said that the philosophical conceptions of Dravidham were beyond Sindhu Putra's comprehension. Others disagreed: how can the 'Knower' not know all!

There was much that Sindhu Putra found different in the mentality and atmosphere of Dravidham. Certainly, their minds were introspective and drawn to the niceties of philosophical and metaphysical discussion and yet there was such a passionate, devotional abandon in their worship. It arose simply from meekness in utter humility of self-surrender to the abiding will and grace of God.

When a wise man among the newcomers remarked, 'Surely with so much worship, these men are seeking something,' the explorer disabused him, saying, 'How nice it would be if God were a shopkeeper with a weighing scale to offer so many boons for so much worship. But he waits neither to give nor to receive. He judges you by your good deeds, not by how much you pray.'

'Then why pray at all?'

'To fill your heart and mind with devotion so that your thoughts and actions remain pure.'

And the gifts placed before idols during worship? How insignificant they were in Dravidham! Often a flower, sometimes a banana and at times water from the Kaveri, the holy river. In the Sindhu and Ganga regions, offerings would be soma wine, mountains of fruit, thousands of garlands, and the priests there called for far more generous gifts to gods. No wonder in Dravidham, they called worship pujey or puja— where 'pu' meant flower and 'jey' was to give.

For Sindhu Putra, the Tamala idea of oneness and social equality had its own fascinating and even practical appeal. Of the thousands who followed him, many were freed slaves. Yet, even though they were slaves no more, they did not instantly earn the respect of others, often encountering contempt instead. Solace came to them when they clustered round Sindhu Putra, but they never felt as though they belonged anywhere until they reached Dravidham. Now, the memory of their crushing hopelessness was gone and they walked erect and proud, unafraid to look anyone in the eye

BHAGWAN S. GIDWANI

as equals in a land whose people regarded equality amongst the essentials of the supreme moral law.

The old explorer even carved for himself a new, though unpaid profession as a match-maker, finding brides and grooms for these newcomers, slave and non-slave alike.

Sage Yadodhra arrived in Dravidham long after Sindhu Putra had reached. Accompanying him were the silent chief and also three children who were known as the sons of Manu of Tungeri. Manu of Tungeri was a celebrated sage who lived alone in an isolated part of the forest, separated by mountainous terrain, near the Tungabhadhra river. It was to meet him that Yadhodhra had come. So rocky and rough was the way that many waited on the main route while Yadodhra took a different path, with a few of the hardiest among them, to meet the sage.

But Manu of Tungeri had died just before Yadodhra reached. Manu's last words of solace to his three children were, 'God shall come to claim you as his sons.' When the children saw the venerable Yadodhra descending from his litter, they were certain that a god had come, but he told them, 'I shall take you to Sindhu Putra, who is a god greater than I.'

Sage Yadodhra presented the three children to Sindhu Putra who gently raised the children to kiss them on their foreheads, and accepted their homage as a father. Thereafter some started calling them the children of Sindhu Putra, but he asked that they be known as sons of Manu of Tungeri. It would be disrespectful, he said, to forget that Manu of Tungeri was their father.

While it was the heart of Dravidham that had touched Sindhu Putra, it was the mind of Tamala that fascinated Sage Yadodhra. Certainly, the yoga of Dravidham was far more advanced than that of the Sindhu–Saraswati, even the Ganga region. The Tamala people laughed more easily and yet worked harder. The language of Tamala was rich and abundant, with a wonderful structure, and yet exquisitely refined! And it was so poetic in its content and so rich in its philosophy, that Yadodhra often found it difficult to translate the words and phrases into his own language. Many thought that Yadodhra was being unfair to the languages of Sindhu and Ganga. But this was not so. He spoke of the language of Sindhu and Ganga too, as being full of beauty, imagination and deep thinking. His reverence for the language of Tamala was explained by the fact that it followed a different discipline and he was actually astonished to come across a language of such strength and dignity which, apart from its vitality, had such a romantic, devotional approach. The Tamala script was equally advanced—rich in consonants and vowels that give it a crisp character, distinguishing it from the scripts of the Sindhu and Ganga regions.

What impressed Yadodhra most about Dravidham was how far advanced their system of mathematics was. It was Lilavati, a Dravidham woman, who, around 6000 BCE had pioneered mathematical lore among the pre-ancient Tamalas who later came to be known as Tamils. Her work had led to the development of the decimal system. Later, the decimal notation and mathematical lore of Dravidham would be learnt by the people of Sindhu and Ganga. Somehow Yadodhra, long after he was no more, would be erroneously credited with developing the system.

Yadodhra was convinced that the people of the Sindhu–Saraswati and the Ganga were once linked with the Tamala people of Dravidham though he could not say how, why or when they parted for these long centuries. His belief in this ancient togetherness arose from what he saw was a common heritage with a single family of beliefs and cultural affiliations, and if he did not see total uniformity, it delighted him for he believed that unity lay not in duplicating sameness, but in harmony that accommodated diversity. Yadodhra could point to a number of common links that the Tamala people had with the rest of Bharat Varsha—the belief in the infinity of the soul; in karma to affirm the presence of the past in the present, and the opportunity to work towards salvation; in the concept of dharma that is changeless, and the virtues of ahimsa, showing compassion for all creatures; auspicious thought, purity of conduct, and earnest endeavour; the belief in the universality of the One-Supreme; and the concept of moksha—freedom from the cycle of death and rebirth.

As Yadodhra discussed the sacred law of Dravidham with Tamala sages and thinkers, he was convinced that with its concepts of dharma, ahimsa, karma and moksha, it was simply a purer and more pristine reflection of Sanatan Dharma or Sanathana or Sanathani of the Ganga. In all its essentials, he could see no basic difference between the Tamala sacred law and the Hindu dharma.

Was it wishful thinking that led Yadhodhra to conclude that somewhere, sometime, his people and the Tamalas had co-existed? The fact was that he was not the first to voice that view. It was a spontaneous reaction of Tamala thinkers as he spoke to them of the precepts of the Hindu. True, the concepts of the Tamala sacred law were more refined and sometimes more demanding, but the differences in conception and approach, influenced by local colouring and social adaptations, were inevitable in a liberal faith that tolerated, and even respected, all views, without regimentation or dogma of a single monotheistic, inquisitorial belief.

As they travelled from one nagara to the next, Yadodhra occupied himself with Tamala philosophers and thinkers, focusing on the triumphs of the Tamala intellect, their sense of social justice, freedom and above all, unity. And though he agreed with Yadhodhra's thoughts, Sindhu Putra was happy to pass time with the ordinary folk for unlike Yadodhra, he was not curious about the intellectual and spiritual. As he interacted with them, he noticed that the lives of the Tamala people were never empty. They had deep affection, a sense of great value for love, friendship, family attachments and human relationship. There was a spark of poetry in their beings and an abiding faith in the unseen reality and respect for others which gave them a sense of exaltation in companionship, even with strangers.

But the silent chief gestured that the land lacked unity, pointing to vast distances that separated each nagara from the next, with a terrain so difficult to negotiate that it was often impassable in certain seasons; in fact, it was considered a significant achievement if as many as four nagaras could join together for a spring festival and dance. Even Tamala proverbs and stories lamented over lovers staying five nagaras apart: 'Who will ask in vain/ Where or when/ Shall we meet again!'

Yadodhra laughed at the chief for this was not the kind of unity he had in mind. But Sindhu Putra was impressed; he had already been wondering how to occupy the time and energies of the vast multitude that had followed him from all over.

'You shall be the pathfinders, bridge builders, and terrain levellers,' he told his followers. And the silent chief assumed leadership of the project.

Eventually, this effort to build paths and tracks to connect all the nagaras began to yield results. Thereafter, the bountiful produce of one nagara never withered away, but reached the other nagaras where it was needed, well in time. Everyone saw the fascinating possibilities of this new beginning, even though they had thought it was intended only for people to move, meet and mingle, and not so much for economic prosperity.

Blessed by Sindhu Putra, extolled by Yadodhra and supervised by the silent chief, the route-building enterprise continued unhindered. Thousands more poured in from the silent tribe in answer to their chief's summons to assist with the work. For their silence, and devotion to work, they were

BHAGWAN S. GIDWANI

compared to the silent ascetics of Dravidham who were known as Aravalu, a name that lingered for centuries, even though the muteness of the silent tribe vanished altogether in a few generations as the result of their intermarriage with people of the Ganga, Sindhu–Saraswati and Dravidham regions.

Yadodhra's health was failing. Sindhu Putra wanted to escort him back to his home in Sindhu. The sage was his last link with his father, Bharatjogi. But Yadodhra declined, 'Sindhu, Saraswati, Ganga, Yamuna, Kaveri . . . He is manifest in all waters.'

Upon his death, Yadodhra was cremated by the side of the Kaveri river. Sages, philosophers, thinkers, mystics, ascetics from all over Dravidham travelled to pay their respects to him. The foremost among them, Tirukavi, said, 'Thus him we salute, the illustrious Hindu who was from the ancient root of Sanathana, Sanathani and Sanatan Dharma, but also from the ancient root of the sacred law of our people of Tamala . . . yes, we Hindus all.'

Few understood Tirukavi, for she spoke with a rush of emotion, through tears. Yet it was the first declaration in Dravidham that the Tamala people regarded themselves as 'Hindus all'. Not that it was such a dramatic or revolutionary declaration! From the Dravidham point of view, the name of one's faith, even the name of God, and the form of its expression were relatively unimportant.

Tirukavi maintained, 'Every name is of One Name;/All names speak of One that is the Same.'

To the Dravidian mind, Shiva was Vishnu and Vishnu was Rudra who was surely Brahma, and verily they all manifested that One Atma. This was no different from the Sindhu belief in 'tad akam' or That One—She that is universe but more; She that is heaven but more; She is the mother, father, son, all gods, the whole world but more; She is the creation and birth, but more . . . She is the atma—the soul.

Even so, Tirukavi's soulful declaration of 'Hindus all' had a stirring impact on the Tamala people and those who had come from Sindhu and Ganga and on the freed slaves who had followed Sindhu Putra. Their sense of 'belonging' and 'acceptance' grew, for this was what they had dreamt of in captivity—a land without a master or a slave. And it was as though they were now reunited with their dream in a land that was theirs and with people who were their own.

They were determined to work harder and for as long as it took to build the paths and tracks that would connect the nagaras of these people whom they regarded as their own. As it was, each day the plan became more ambitious than simply levelling and clearing routes. Little townships were set up to provide homes for the newcomers in barren lands cleared for the purpose. This involved planting trees and crops, diverting streams, and digging more wells and reservoirs of enormous sizes. The townships grew, each with a small temple—and the deities there were modelled on the available idols of Dravidham.

Work went on furiously to ensure that the 8400 nagaras of Dravidham were one, from beginning to end, as Sindhu Putra had willed.

The prosperity of Dravidham grew. Their feeling of oneness with the people of Sindhu Putra grew. Tirukavi's declaration of 'Hindus all' seeped fully into the mind of Tamala, especially when they saw the temples that the newcomers had built to honour the gods of Dravidham. Far greater was their admiration for Sindhu Putra—this god of the newcomers who had no aim other than to serve them and sought nothing in return! To them, he came to embody the highest ideal of Tamala goodness. Yet, when the foremost Tamala artists wanted to sculpt a statue of Sindhu Putra to be kept in a temple, Sindhu Putra demanded that no one keep his statue in a temple.

'Not even at the foot of gods, for god I am not;

Nor among noble worshippers, for that I am not;
The road I travel is the one that I sought;
Another life, to atone, has to be my lot . . . '

This denial of his godhood actually endeared him to many,
though some wondered why he felt that he was not amongst
'noble worshippers', and why, with a life so auspicious, he
thought he would be denied moksha and be subjected to
rebirth and another life! Yet he was firm and no statues were
erected, nor images carved.

For the six years that he was there, Sindhu Putra threw
himself, body and soul, into the concerns of Dravidham—for
its health, happiness and prosperity—and the results, as
everyone could see, were spectacular.

The widely scattered nagaras of Dravidham and several
dispersed areas came closer to each other, bridged by
townships, separated no longer by impassable ravines, while
gardens sprang from wastelands. Commerce began but not
just between the nagaras of Dravidham. A caravan left for
Sindhu, to the village of Gatha, carrying sandalwood, oil,
cosmetics, painted pottery, garments, toys and ornaments of
gold and silver, with a request from Sindhu Putra to Gatha to
encourage the guilds and the merchants of Sindhu to come to
Dravidham and trade for 'they would find in Dravidham the
same abundance and yet so different and charming.'

The people of Tamala began to call him 'periyar'—the
great one. He was their bridge to lands unknown. He criticized
no one and nothing—neither an individual, nor a custom,
nor a ritual, nor a doctrine. He had no message of
enlightenment to offer and prescribed no rule of conduct or
way of life. Still many chose to see much, not in the words he
uttered, but the life he led, and the attention he gave, unasked,
to their welfare. The one emotion they recognized in him,
clearly, was his love for them that arose from a gracious
mind and a tender heart. And that impressed them more and

made up for the absence of flourish in his words and his refusal to engage in discussions on the nature of infinity. 'That discussion,' he would say, 'may take all eternity, but meanwhile much work remains to be done.' And clearly, they saw that his heart was set on spending every moment in the service of Dravidham and its people. In return, the people gave him their love in abundance and found comfort in his presence and were thrilled to claim him as their very own periyar and themselves as his people—Hindus, all.

THIRTY

HINDUS ALL—SVASTIKA AND THE FRONTIERS OF BHARAT VARSHA

5058 BCE

Thousands wanted to join Sindhu Putra as he left Dravidham to go to the Ganga, but he held them back. 'Your work is not finished here,' he said. That was obvious. The work plan, as it had ambitiously evolved, would take more than a generation to build paths and bridges, dig wells and reservoirs, plant gardens and divert waters.

Even so, he left with huge groups which included the silent chief, Manu—one of Tungeri's three sons, the old explorer and his son and many Tamala men and women. Sindhu Putra left his vast workforce in Dravidham with Dharmdasa, the speechless Aravalu, a remote cousin of the silent chief, in charge.

No one knows if in Dravidham or even on his journey back, Sindhu Putra heard the roar of battles raging in the far north and west, fought by the commanders acting in his name to free the land and the slaves from warlords. Many believed that Sindhu Putra knew nothing of the bloodshed, for no one burdened him with the knowledge, and each time messengers reported freedom he blessed them and thrice-blessed those who achieved it.

When he reached Ganga, he heard the sad news that Gangapati XIII was dead. His little son, now eight years old, was anointed as Gangapati XIV with Sindhu Putra's blessing. Sindhu Putra also blessed the regent who would look after the land and train Gangapati XIV until the child came of age. He was nominated by the assembly and approved by the young Gangapati's mother.

Sindhu Putra caused confusion by blessing two girls as prospective brides for Gangapati XIV, without indicating a preference for either, obviously leaving the final choice to the mother. Of these two, one was the regent's five-year-old daughter and the other was Sindhu Karkarta Sharat's two-year-old granddaughter. Some felt that Sindhu Putra should have made the selection, blessed one and not both; but others said that Sindhu Putra always blessed everyone and everything, sometimes without even knowing who or what he blessed!

From the Ganga, Sindhu Putra reached the Sindhu. Muni and Roopa had died two years earlier within a few days of each other. Roopa's father, the singer, was still alert and active despite his advanced age. Some said God had granted him extra years on earth to compensate for his early years of blindness.

To the ailing Gatha, Sindhu Putra said, 'You are the only father I have left.' Gatha died in ecstasy. Sindhu Putra wept.

Sindhu Putra would sometimes sit by the side of his two mothers—Kanta and Sonama. He would then feel at peace, while Kanta brushed his hair. He wondered at their uncomplicated lives full of faith! But those moments of peace were few. Everyone in the village and thousands beyond came to be near him, cheer him and be blessed. They no longer wanted miracles from him. *He was their miracle!*

What, then, was the burden in his heart, he wondered. He remembered that moment of elation when he had reached the Ganga, where every chief, from far and near, including Karkarta Sharat, had gathered to witness the anointment of Gangapati XIV and had all bowed to him in utmost reverence.

BHAGWAN S. GIDWANI

Everyone had thought it a miracle that he had arrived on the very day of anointment, especially since Gangapati's mother had prayed that Sindhu Putra might come to bless the ceremony.

'This god hears prayers, across vast distances,' they said, when he appeared.

All the chiefs and rulers had touched his feet and kissed the hem of his garment and he had felt ecstatic. But he forgave himself for that thrill. It was, he rationalized, nothing personal and in their exaggerated respect he simply saw their assurance that they would never revert to the old ways of slavery and disrupt freedom and unity. That feeling of elation had continued as the crowds cried out: 'Mahapati!' 'Mahakarta!' 'Periyar!' 'Maharaj!' And again, he forgave himself, thinking that the people's love for him was a guarantee that they would never again permit slavery. Even so, his feeling of guilt remained for posturing as a god, which he knew, he was not.

∽

As the crowds around him grew, so did Sindhu Putra's loneliness. He had no privacy, and decided to go to Muni's Rocks. That would be his retreat. The less people see of me, the easier they will find it to forget me, he thought. He was wrong. Hundreds of boats would line up in the river along the Rocks with people eager to meet him and seek his blessings.

The singer lived at the Rocks with his two granddaughters.

'Man sees little and grieves much; surely a god who sees all, will grieve all the more,' he said. 'Remain at the Rocks in peace,' he advised Sindhu Putra. 'The thousands who line up at the river seek nothing. A simple blessing, a distant nod, a mere raising of the hand, is enough. Once a week, we can allow them to enter the Rocks at a prayer meeting.' The singer was right, he thought. They seek nothing—simply to be blessed. That spiritual solace was enough.

None of the high and mighty came. They had bowed to him at the anointment of Gangapati XIV, and when he first arrived in their lands. Often, they sent gifts, big and small. That surely was enough, as his titles—Mahakarta, Mahapati, Periyar, Maharaj—were simply spiritual and had no power over them. In public if the high and mighty had to speak of him, their words were laced with honey, but privately they felt it was good that he had shut himself away at the Rocks and did not venture out.

However, the people had their grievances too and hopes and aspirations far beyond spiritual solace. How could one have a god around and seek only a blessing! A wit even asked, 'Would not the gods feel ignored and insulted if I seek nothing from them?' But it was not easy to gain access to Sindhu Putra. The silent chief would not permit it. It was enough that Sindhu Putra appeared every dawn at the commanding balcony to bless all those gathered outside or greet them once weekly at prayers.

Thus, in peace, Sindhu Putra remained at the Rocks. A large group of the Tamalas, along with the sons of Manu of Tungeri, left to explore the entire Sindhu region. Only the silent chief and a few others remained with him at the Rocks.

Meanwhile, battles continued, far away in scattered, unknown, remote pockets, as the commanders, inspired by Sindhu Putra's message, continued to free slaves. Couriers would reach the Rocks to convey to the silent chief glad tidings of this or that victory won, such and such region freed from old tyranny and names of new chiefs appointed, old chiefs expelled or reformed. There would often also be news of how the freed lands had been amalgamated with Ganga or Sindhu lands or even set up as a nagara of Dravidham under the supervision of Dharmdasa, so that they would function wisely with a proper council. In several cases though, the land would be on its own, under a new chief, committed to the 'freedom wave' begun by Sindhu Putra.

The silent chief told Sindhu Putra only of the lands that were freed, and not of the bloodshed and cruelty, or of the fresh wave of tyranny that the new chiefs unleashed. There were some who felt that Sindhu Putra should have known about the carnage that was taking place in his name, and that the blame for it was his alone.

～

The silent chief listened long and hard to a Tamala explorer who had returned from a tour, and spoke of a huge colony of slaves, freed, but only in name, and forced to work in pitiable conditions, their lot worse than before. He told the chief about raids into Jalta's lands by armed men from forts at the eastern tip; and though those lands were united with Sindhu, Jalta's people were stopped and harassed if they crossed over to pursue offenders. The three Jalta brothers were away, fighting battles in Sindhu Putra's cause, in distant regions. Alone, ailing and sightless, their mother grieved over the plight of her people.

The explorer was instantly taken to Sindhu Putra who was told the grim tale. The reference to Jalta's mother affected him deeply. 'She is my mother,' he said. But his faith in Karkarta Sharat was unshaken. 'He is a man of honour. These atrocities are taking place without his knowledge and against his wishes.'

When told that the new colony of slaves was too large and the raids on Jalta's lands too well-organized for the karkarta to remain unaware, Sindhu Putra felt hurt at this lack of faith. He reiterated, 'I trust Sharat. Conscience is his best friend.' He turned to the silent chief, 'Go, place the facts before him and he will instantly set everything right.'

The silent chief left with the Tamala explorer who was to

act as his interpreter.

Jagasi, who acted as the karkarta's secretary, insisted on knowing what the message was.

'It is for the karkarta's ears only,' the chief replied.

'But I am the karkarta's ears! And eyes too!'

'I am sure the karkarta still retains his ears for messages sent by Sindhu Putra.'

'Sindhu Putra! Of course, to hear him is to obey! I shall soon send for you.'

When two days passed without any summons from the karkarta, the chief went storming in. Jagasi apologized. 'The karkarta has been so busy,' he said. 'Why not meet him any morning when he is at the Raj Garden, listening to all who wish to meet him?'

The next morning, the chief and the explorer were in the garden. It was besieged by throngs of petitioners, making it impossible to catch the karkarta's eye.

They saw Jagasi again who was as cheerful as ever. 'All good things come to those who wait. I promise you a meeting in a day or two.'

But the chief, resolved now on a different approach, said, 'Thank you, but I cannot wait. I have to leave now for Jalta's lands.'

'Well, suit yourself. But do see me on your return.'

'Of course, though I wanted to see Karkarta Sharat before discussing with Jalta's mother the problem of her becoming karkarta.'

'What!' Jagasi's eyes popped out, but the chief and the explorer walked out. They did not seem to hear Jagasi calling them back. But messengers ran to halt them.

Karkarta Sharat received them graciously. 'What is this I hear about Jalta's old mother aspiring to be karkarta?'

'It is a high position, high honour,' the chief replied.

'But at the time of the union, she openly declared that she wanted me to be karkarta.'

The chief nodded sympathetically, 'Maybe she has heard that the office of karkarta is not a lifelong position, but an elected term of seven years.'

'What chance would she have of winning?' Sharat asked. The chief simply shrugged. Sharat continued, 'What does Sindhu Putra think?'

'How can I speak for my master? All I know is that Sindhu Putra regards Jalta's mother as his own mother. She accepted his plea for union with Sindhu. He owes her much! Maybe he can deny her nothing!'

Just as the silent chief had concluded that spiritual power by itself was not enough to command men of power, Sharat realized that earthly power itself had limits. Jalta's mother might be blind, old and stupid, but what would happen if Sindhu Putra openly favoured her? Sadly he realized that if Sindhu Putra decided to put up a dead donkey to fight an election, there would be many who would lend their support. Maybe she wouldn't win. But who knew! And the disgrace! He did not want to be challenged. He wanted to remain the karkarta till his death, and pass on the office to his son. He pasted a gracious smile on his face and asked, 'But why this sudden, insane ambition? Does she know the problems a karkarta must face?'

'I don't think she knows. Maybe she is not really interested in all the great things that a great karkarta can accomplish. She's probably worried about one or two things such as incursions and raids from Sindhu forts into eastern territory, and hopes to set them right.'

'These incursions and raids shall stop, forthwith,' Sharat thundered. 'Sometimes our commanders act as criminals. There will not be a single incursion again, I promise.'

'I suppose she is also worried about all that has already been taken away from her land . . . '

'That is a small matter. The criminals will be punished.'

'That will certainly give her comfort, but she will still wish to regain what they have lost.'

'Of course, there will be restitution. Not just that, she will get more than they have lost.'

The chief nodded, obviously impressed with Sharat's generosity, 'Yes that will be the best, for sometimes her people exaggerate their losses. There's just one other matter in which she hopes to make a difference—the colonies of former slaves.'

There was concern in Sharat's eyes as the explorer translated the chief's gestures, 'Since Jalta's lands have no burden of past slavery, she may think it is easy to dismantle colonies, newly established, to herd the former slaves, where these unfortunates are forced to work in poor conditions. Maybe she feels that they can immediately be helped to rise to the level of rya.'

With a sweep of his hand, the chief seemed to suggest that such colonies existed all over, though the explorer had reported only a single colony. Slowly Sharat replied, 'Such colonies must be done away with, and surely the former slaves must have the rights—equal and indivisible—of the rya. More, in fact, to compensate for their past suffering. I will see to it myself. Too long have I relied on others.'

The chief mentally noted that Sharat's reply gave away that there were many such colonies. Quietly Sharat asked, 'Is there anything else Jalta's mother is concerned about?'

'I doubt it. She is not a person with many ideas and she will be happy if these few matters are addressed. Of course, just words may not satisfy her.'

'No,' Sharat interrupted. 'Positive proof is what she shall have.'

'What more can she ask for?' the chief graciously conceded.

'And her ambition to be karkarta?' asked Sharat.

'I shall persuade her to relinquish such a foolish ambition once she has proof that her real concerns have been met.'

Sharat liked this turn in the conversation, even though the chief's gestures and their interpretation by the explorer made it a little tedious. He had already played out the farce of shouting at Jagasi for keeping such important visitors away from him for so long. Now, graciously, he invited them for a meal.

All the while, Sharat wondered how that stupid, half-witted, blind old woman had seen or heard of their slave colonies in remote areas, well hidden and guarded! An awful thought struck him—was it that woman's dream to be karkarta or was Sindhu Putra supporting her candidature! This man sheltered at the Rocks was not, then, a mere dummy! Sharat decided to subtly question the two simpletons before him.

Unfortunately, the subtle interrogation brought him no joy, though the chief and explorer were both forthcoming in their responses. Sharat expressed happiness that Jalta's mother had learnt about the slave colonies and brought the matter to his attention to rectify it. Then he casually asked, 'How did she come to know about the colonies?'

The chief said that it was actually a discovery made by the explorer who was a rather talkative person and could keep nothing to himself. But he had been instructed not to blabber to anyone, and report only to Sindhu Putra in the future.

Concerned, Sharat remarked, 'I thought your friend the explorer and the Dravidham team travelled for pleasure.'

'That too. But they must go from place to place and report all to Sindhu Putra. After all, he is mahakarta and he realizes what he owes to that position.'

Sharat could have told him that mahakarta was only a title of honour, with no rights, no powers and no duties. Instead, he said, 'But what would these men from outside know about what happens in our land of Sindhu?'

'Exactly my thoughts, Karkarta! But just as there are teams from Dravidham and the Ganga here, there is a Sindhu team in Dravidham, and Dravidham teams in the Ganga, and

Sindhu teams elsewhere. I don't see much merit in that but mahakarta seems to think it is good to avoid local influences in fact-finding.'

My god, Sharat thought, Sindhu Putra's teams were on the prowl everywhere then! Waiting, watching! Why?

'Perhaps I am wrong,' the chief continued. 'Mahakarta always tells me that people from Dravidham, the Ganga and others are not outsiders. To him, like the people of the Sindhu, they belong to Bharat Varsha—Hindus all—though they may be governed separately, under the karkarta in the Sindhu or the Gangapati in the Ganga. But then, here, there, everywhere, they are one, for he remains the single, common link as mahakarta, mahapati, periyar, maharaj for all Bharat Varsha.'

Sharat fumed silently. So I serve under this mahakarta! But the chief's next observation assuaged his anger. 'Of course, the mahakarta is not interested at all in the affairs of men. In two years, he will retire totally as an ascetic, unconcerned with matters of earth. Even now he would have, but for his promise to eradicate slavery all over the land and uplift former slaves to the level of rya.'

So, the imposition is for two years, Sharat thought hopefully. 'Do you think all this can be achieved in two years or less?' he asked.

'Why not? He can only pave the way, not resolve everything. Maybe he will increase his teams so that things progress quickly.'

'His teams have no difficulty in gathering information?'

'Who will deny them information? They carry mahapati seals in the Ganga, periyar seals in Dravidham and mahakarta seals here.'

'Mahakarta seals? What are those?'

'Oh, only to indicate that the team is on the mahakarta's business, so that everyone cooperates.'

'May I see the seal?' Sharat requested. But the chief said

he had not brought it with him to this meeting. However, he would send it soon to him.

Once the meal was over the chief and the explorer took their leave. Outside, the explorer said, 'Our periyar, Sindhu Putra, told us that conscience is your karkarta's best friend!'

'The karkarta's dog, too, is his best friend. But did you not see how roughly he spoke to it when it barked, and the dog went into a corner, its tail between its legs?'

'Your own conscience did not impress me, either.'

'Why? You are the one who told all the lies!'

'Under your corrupt manipulations.'

'Yes, I realize, you are not an original thinker.'

'May God save me from such original thinking!'

'Why? Think, old man. Think! The slave colonies will be disbanded! The promise to treat them as rya will be honoured! The raids on Jalta's lands will stop! They will even be compensated for the losses. Did you ever achieve that much in your lifetime of truth?'

'Yet to attribute false words to periyar! And to that poor lady!'

'That was a result of your poor skills as a translator. I attributed nothing to Sindhu Putra or Jalta's mother.'

'Is that the impression you left with Karkarta Sharat?'

'The impression given to him was the right one—to follow the right path in the future.'

'For how long? A year? Two years?'

'No more is needed. Once he raises the slaves to the level of rya, how will he turn back? And once the raids on Jalta's lands stop, do you think they will be resumed after the brothers have returned from battle and are able to protect their people?'

'And how will you know if all the slave colonies have really been dismantled?'

'That is your task, my friend. Your teams will go round to see if any more remain. You are the "eyes" of your periyar. Did you ever dream of such a high honour when you were languishing as a slave?'

'In your land! While you were its chief!' the explorer accused.

'That chief was a different man, untouched by God. He that stands before you now is your friend, your brother.'

The explorer asked, 'Could you not at least have told a less outrageous lie? To imply that poor, blind old woman is hoping to be karkarta! You could have used the name of one of the Jalta brothers!'

'But the outrageous lie succeeded! The fact, though, is I really wasn't thinking. It came on the spur of the moment.'

'I know. Others think first and act thereafter. With you, it is the opposite. And what was that nonsense about the mahakarta seal?'

'Merely to anticipate events. You will soon have your mahakarta seal.'

∽

In a town not far off, a well-known seal-maker was found. 'I work where I work,' he said when the silent chief's emissary tried to entice him to go to the Rocks.

'You will have the honour of working for Sindhu Putra.'

'Honour! Does it mean I will not be paid?'

'No, it means you will be paid twice—once on earth and in the hereafter.'

'I prefer being paid twice on earth.'

'So be it,' the emissary agreed.

The terms were settled and the artist left for the Rocks, with mules to carry his equipment. When he arrived, the chief demanded ten seals in a hurry—it didn't matter if they were not too artistic.

'Then you should hire a brick-layer or a barber. An artist can only create art,' the artist retorted, and agreed to produce one seal per week.

What would the design be?

'Why not depict the map of Bharat Varsha?' the explorer suggested.

But the chief said, 'The frontiers of Bharat Varsha advance every day, in every direction. As Sage Yadodhra said, all who were once together are coming back together.'

'How about a circle to show that all those who were apart have come together?'

But the artist asked, 'Those who were apart . . . have they *all* come together?'

The chief drew a cross to symbolize the expansion of Bharat Varsha in all four directions. The artist shook his head, 'It looks like a wooden frame my brother makes for hanging his scarecrow in his field.'

The chief drew another figure—a straight line, with the top branching into a number of lines in all directions. The artist said, 'With fewer lines on top it could look like a pitchfork; with more lines on top, it may look like a broom with which my mother sweeps floors. Now it looks like a plant with needles but no flowers.'

'Since you are such a great artist, why don't you think of a better idea?' asked the explorer.

'No, the chief's idea is sound. I will work on his lines,' said the artist. He drew an unfamiliar figure. Later, this figure would be known as the auspicious svastika design. It was in the form of a cross with equal arms, each arm having a limb of equal length projecting from its end, and pointing in a different direction.

The chief approved, 'It points in all directions, suggesting movement, strength, unity, equality and togetherness.'

'Yes,' said the explorer. 'Togetherness, but also diversity without offending its wholeness.'

When Sindhu Putra saw the artist at work, the chief explained, 'So many seek tokens of your affection. These seals will serve that purpose.'

Later, when he saw the seal, Sindhu Putra was delighted,

'I like it. It shows flow, movement in all directions, strength, unity, equality, togetherness and diversity.'

Sindhu Putra tried his hand at cutting steatite to try to make a seal, but could not. Nor could he carve. The artist laughed, 'It is easy to be a god, but it takes time to be an artist.' Sindhu Putra laughed too. 'I am neither,' he said.

The chief wanted all the seals to be the same, but the artist said, 'I do not copy. I will send my cousin to you. He cannot create, but he copies beautifully.'

He made fifteen seals, taking only five days per seal, 'I would have finished earlier but for your god hindering my work.' When he left, he demanded, and received, wages also for two additional days to reach his town. Later, his cousin came to work. He brought a gift from the artist for Sindhu Putra—a svastika carved in gold with a slight silver content. The chief was mystified, 'How demanding he was about his wages! And yet he sends a gift of gold that costs far more than his wages!'

The explorer left with a few seals to rejoin his team. Couriers from the chief were scurrying all over to assemble four new teams. Their task? To act as Sindhu Putra's 'eyes everywhere and report'. Each team carried Sindhu Putra's seal. Crowds would gather to touch the seal, pray and even shed tears.

There was no secrecy in the movement of the teams. The svastika seals with them simply made them inviolable and encouraged everyone to open up to them. If injustice was persistent or widespread, the team was to send reports to the silent chief. The teams could not redress grievances, nor intercede—only report. But often, their mere presence goaded administrators to remedy matters. Communication was inadequate, the teams far away and reports often did not reach. But the teams gave hope to all.

People put up large metal tablets in villages, the svastika etched on them, with its message of the oneness and unity of

Bharat Varsha emerging clearly in their minds. Even clearer was the message that far above those that ruled them was their overlord Sindhu Putra, who cared for them and would move to redress their grievances. The message to the karkarta, Gangapati's regent, and other mighty lords was clear too: Sindhu Putra is watching. Deny him not!

Jagasi arrived with boatloads of gifts for Sindhu Putra. The chief suppressed the impulse to tell him that he should seek his chance to meet Sindhu Putra on full-moon day when he mingled with visitors.

Jagasi presented Sharat's gifts to Sindhu Putra and thanked him for the information about the raids on Jalta's lands. 'The criminals have been punished. This will not happen again. Chief Jalta's mother is delighted with the caravans of gifts sent to compensate her.' He added, 'The slave colonies have been dismantled as well. Every slave is now rya.'

Sindhu Putra was pleased and told the chief, 'See! I told you the moment Sharat hears, he will spring into action.'

Jagasi added, 'The karkarta seeks to serve you. He can do far more when family ties are established with Gangapati and a true unity of hearts is achieved between the Sindhu and the Ganga regions. Why, the karkarta would even assume the regent's responsibility so both the Ganga and the Sindhu move together towards unity, freedom and justice.'

Jagasi sought, and was granted, Sindhu Putra's blessing for the marriage of the karkarta's granddaughter with the young Gangapati. But he was also told that the blessing granted to others must remain as well. More would have been said but for the timely interruption already arranged by the chief.

❧

The teams increased in number, size and even function. They were fact-finders who were to observe and spread the message of the oneness of Bharat Varsha under Sindhu Putra, but sometimes they took up issues with local lords, chiefs and headmen, ignoring the excuse that the orders came from the karkarta or Gangapati. The question was: did they conform to the higher order of Sindhu Putra?

Slowly, spiritual power was transforming itself into earthly power as well. Much later, Nandan's eighth great-grandson blamed the chief of the silent tribe and said of Sindhu Putra and the silent chief: 'Always a pawn . . . this Sindhu Putra . . . son of an unknown, an orphan from nowhere, with the mind of a goat, was first manipulated by Bharatjogi who put a false mask of a god on him. And then came this cold-blooded, silent, tribal chief, with teeth of iron and the mind of a monster, thirsting for the power that rightfully belonged to the lords of the land . . . '

∼

Gangapati's regent was livid. 'How dare he send his prowling teams here!'

Gangapati's mother was horrified to hear him, 'He is the mahapati. It is his right.'

The regent saw Sindhu Putra's teams welcomed everywhere. He vowed to put a stop to it. He was determined to even ignore Gangapati's mother. She enjoyed respect, but he was the regent, with complete power over all that happened in the land of Ganga.

However, there was something that he lacked. The power to go against a mother's right to accept or reject marriage vows offered for her minor child. And his one overpowering ambition was to see his daughter marry Gangapati XIV and rule the land. He was amazed when Gangapati's mother hesitated when he offered his daughter's marriage-vows. Sweetly, she mumbled something about Sindhu Putra, but he said, 'Sindhu Putra has blessed them.'

'He has also blessed Sharat's granddaughter and others,' she replied.

'How can he bless so many vows?'

'Why not! It means that whosoever my son marries, the union shall be blessed.'

'Then why not my daughter,' he pressed.

But she said, 'Sindhu Putra must decide; he must choose among those blessed.'

The regent went with gifts to sway Sindhu Putra, but found him as indecisive as ever. 'How can I choose one over the other? That is a decision for the mother.'

The regent emphasized the need to choose a girl from the Ganga region, otherwise outsiders would nurture ambitions of ruling the land. Still, Sindhu Putra was unmoved.

The regent's only comfort came when Sindhu Putra embraced him and said, 'All will be well. Wait and see.' Even the silent chief nodded.

As he bade farewell to the regent, the silent chief gestured, 'Sindhu Putra favours you. It is foolish to think otherwise. Did you not hear his last words! Wait . . . All will be well.' This was no assurance either, but as near to it as it possibly could be.

Back in his own land, the regent ranted over Sindhu Putra's indecisiveness to his wife. But she simply said, 'Men decide quickly; gods wait.'

Distressed by how openly Gangapati's mother welcomed Sindhu Putra's teams, the regent exclaimed, 'Really, if Sindhu Putra wished to take over Gangapati's position, no one would even question him!'

'Of course, but why would the mahapati descend to the lowly position of Gangapati!' the lady replied.

'Mahapati! Mahapati!' the cry rang through the populace as Sindhu Putra's team walked among them. Later, the team met the members of the assembly and drew their attention to various issues, as though they had the inherent right to demand redress. From the regent himself, the team demanded nothing. Yet his own people kept reminding him of concerns voiced by the team.

The regent's heart froze. Swiftly, surely, the realization dawned on him—as it had on the karkarta of the Sindhu and on many mighty chiefs—that Sindhu Putra was not only a spiritual power but an earthly power as well.

Everywhere the team went, people wept as though Sindhu Putra's hand had reached out to touch them. They felt the thrill of his nearness. No longer would they feel alone, for he who commanded all the rulers and chiefs of Bharat Varsha was with them. The chiefs and rulers fumed. They felt diminished, numb.

❧

Jalta the Fourth came to the Rocks. Battles on the eastern front had died down. He and his brothers had won decisive victories and he could now look forward to an era of tranquillity. He embraced the silent chief, then asked, 'What do you mean by sending your teams of spies?'

'Did they offend you?' the chief asked.

'Not me. But they annoy the chiefs whom I appointed.'

'And your heart grieves over their annoyance! Are those chiefs very honourable?'

'No, some have become scoundrels. But I should be the one to question them.'

The chief put his arm around Jalta's shoulder. 'You and I were slaves together. What does that say to you?' he asked.

'It says that you and I are brothers and we shall never be slaves again.'

'No,' the silent chief gestured. 'It says *no one* shall be a slave and we are all brothers.'

Jalta nodded.

'There will be justice for all, if we can help it. And the

chiefs you appoint are not intended to replace one form of tyranny with another. They are the ones who must bear greatest scrutiny. For no one must say that you, my brother, let your cause down.'

Jalta nodded, but the chief had not finished. 'And those you appoint are not there to serve you, but the higher cause of him whom we have sworn to serve. Tell me, am I wrong?'

'No brother, you are not wrong. But if you were, would I ever say so?' After a pause, he added, 'And this I promise you—the thoughts you have expressed today shall guide me forever.'

Smiling, they went to Sindhu Putra together.

~

The message to people everywhere was clear—the old fears, animosities and hostilities are no more. March to the music of Sindhu Putra. Take refuge in him; His mission is timeless. He holds the promise of Bharat Varsha. Rejoice!

And what of the mighty chiefs and lords! Their power was slipping. It was as if they retained their positions at the will and pleasure of Sindhu Putra.

What does the future hold for an oppressor when the oppressed cease to fear him and look to someone else for hope and healing? Those chiefs had been powerful once, and greatly feared, but with fear gone, the very foundation of their tyranny was disappearing. People would hide their faces no more, warmed by the realization that far beyond the insolent might of their chiefs was the greater, more awesome power of him who watched from the Rocks.

However, most chiefs were not removed from their positions. Emphatically, in Sindhu Putra's name, the silent chief had ordered the teams: 'Change not the chiefs, change their hearts. Give them your love, seek their love. Go, re-elect them as your own and so shall they be your own, and let every action of theirs be for your good and for the good of Bharat Varsha.'

Much later, though, Nandan's poet–great-grandson would say: 'This widely scattered, far-flung, never-ending land that they called Bharat Varsha was built on the tears and ruins of rightful chiefs and rulers . . . And beggars became tyrants and uprooted lawful masters . . . and everywhere these new, arrogant upstarts wielded the swords of Sindhu Putra that were pitiless, indiscriminate . . . Ruthless also was his rod of authority held by a single puppet-master, who could speak not, whose face was dark, but not as dark as his black heart and whose eyes glowed with fires as in the deepest pit of hell.'

How far one accepts this statement is open to question. However, he also took pains to describe with sadness, each and every region throughout the land, where various chiefs were displaced, disciplined or subordinated by Sindhu Putra's 'legions'. His description confirms the length and breadth of Bharat Varsha, 'where many chiefs remained, though vassals they were, fearful of their position and subordinate to the shadow of Sindhu Putra, who alone, unchallenged, commanded this vast land of Hindu.'

And yet the description of Bharat Varsha provided by Nandan's great-grandson, who was always hostile to Sindhu Putra, conforms with that of Sindhu Putra's contemporaries. In modern terms, Bharat Varsha, extending from the Sindhu and the Ganga, included the entire territory of present-day India, Pakistan and Bangladesh. Additionally, in the north, the territory went beyond soaring peaks and plunging valleys to reach Lake Manasasarovara (Mansarovar), Mount Kailash, right up to the source of the hallowed Sindhu River in Tibet and beyond, by sixty yojnas. Bharat Varsha also included Avagana (Afghanistan), where everyone called himself Hindu, since the time of Sadhu Gandhara, father of Dhru, the twentieth karkarta of the Sindhu region. Farther west from Avagana, Bharat Varsha intruded into parts of Iran, beyond Lake Namaskar (Namaksar), where several Hindu hermits congregated. Towards the east, Bharat Varsha included the land of Brahma (Burma) and beyond. Additionally, the land of Newar (Nepal) too became part of Bharat Varsha, not because the legions of Sindhu Putra inspired it but because Rishi Newar himself so declared it, for he, a Sanathani from the Ganga region, knew that all pre-ancient streams of Sanathana, Sanatan Dharma, Sanathani and the sacred Tamala tradition had all come to merge into a single gracious unity—the Hindu! In time, Bharat Varsha also came to include the entire territory of Kashmir, Bhoota nah (Bhutan), and the land of Vraon (Sri Lanka).

It was faith that moved millions across the land and fired them with enthusiasm to regard Bharat Varsha as a cultural reality—Hindus all. Soon, it would emerge as much more than a simple cultural entity, for the entire land was stirred by the diverse cry of Mahakarta, Periyar, Mahapati, that was replaced by the common overriding cry of 'Maharaj . . . Maharaj!'

Thus, far beyond a common consciousness and ideology, there arose a triumphant understanding that this land of Bharat Varsha was one indivisible entity from end to end, with Sindhu Putra at the helm, to guide them—Hindus all.

THIRTY-ONE

THE LORDS OF GANGA
AND SINDHU

5032 BCE

Years passed.

'Sindhu Putra will outlive us all,' Karkarta Sharat said to his son. He was ailing, but he found some comfort in the knowledge that Sindhu Putra had blessed his son Sauvira's election as karkarta in the event of his death, though the fact that he had had to seek Sindhu Putra's blessing was galling. Yet there was no other way out. The law prohibiting a karkarta's son from succeeding his father to the office had been abolished in his father Nandan's time. But even so, when Nandan retired, Sharat himself would not have been elected without Sindhu Putra's blessing. Since then, Sharat had won the people's love and respect—not only in the traditional land of Sindhu, but also in the new lands in the union.

He had been especially generous to Jalta's lands ever since he heard of Jalta's mother's aspiration to be karkarta, and more considerate towards the former slaves. He had secretly cherished the silent chief's assurance to Jagasi that Sindhu Putra would soon retire, closing his eyes and mind to the affairs of men, but it was not to be. Instead, Sindhu Putra's teams, armed with the svastika seal, continued on the prowl. And he felt compelled to welcome them with a smile.

But then gods have their uses too, Sharat realized. When he fell ill, he was consumed by the desire to see his son,

Sauvira, succeed him as karkarta. As soon as he heard that some people, with ambitions, were muttering that the karkarta's office should not be degraded to a hereditary office, he sent Sauvira to seek Sindhu Putra's blessing to become the next karkarta. Readily, Sindhu Putra gave the blessing.

'And did you ask Sindhu Putra to bless your daughter's marriage to Gangapati?' questioned Sharat.

'I asked, but he said one thing at a time,' Sauvira replied.

'Did you ask for anything else?'

'No.' Sauvira saw his father's sadness, and wondered if Sharat, in the sunset of his life, was beginning to believe in Sindhu Putra's divinity. Had his father expected him to show concern for his health by begging Sindhu Putra to cure him? Quietly, Sauvira added, 'Father, I inherit my intelligence from Grandfather Nandan and you. If I suffered from the slightest belief in this false god, I would have washed his feet with my tears to seek his blessing for your health.'

Sharat embraced his son, proud that his son understood his unspoken question.

Svastika teams went around announcing that Sindhu Putra had blessed Sauvira to succeed as karkarta. It surprised everyone. How premature! The elections were far away! And surely Karkarta Sharat would not retire in the middle of the term to impose a new election! Hardly anyone knew the condition of his health and the few that did were silent. Jagasi, as always, was wreathed in smiles. Sharat was said to be touring eastern lands, though he was actually in his ancestral family home, far from the karkarta's town. Sauvira, as a senior council member, was fulfilling the karkarta's duties in his absence. Surely, if the karkarta was unwell, the son would be near the father! Why this untimely announcement then that Sauvira would succeed Sharat!

The news of Karkarta Sharat's death, then, came as a sudden shock to everyone. But their sadness was overshadowed by the widespread wonder that Sindhu Putra had known what was about to happen! That Sharat was going to die soon!

And to those who asked, 'If he knew, why did he not prevent it?' the answer was simply, 'Why would he delay Sharatji's moksha!'

Sharat's body, preserved for his final journey, was brought to the karkarta's town in horse-drawn carriages. People grieved, but also believed that 'it was meant to happen when it did, for had not Sindhu Putra already blessed his son as karkarta?'

Sauvira fumed in silence, for he could not admit that he himself had sought Sindhu Putra's blessing! After that meeting, the silent chief had offered to send out svastika teams to announce that Sindhu Putra had blessed his election as karkarta. Sauvira demurred; was it not too early? But the chief smiled. 'Teams move slowly, they take time to reach people.' Was there a hint in the chief's smiling words that it was better to commit Sindhu Putra immediately, lest he blessed some other aspirant later? For everyone knew that he withheld blessings from no one, so why not bind him with an open, public announcement! Sauvira agreed instantly, and svastika teams were dispatched to make the announcement.

Sindhu Putra reached the karkarta's town to pay his respects. This was the first time in years that he had left the Rocks. But he had felt he must. His love for Sharat was immense, for Sharat was the one who had first freed the slaves in Sindhu, and united with tribal lands, and worked tirelessly thereafter to raise the former slaves to the level of rya, and always sent timely aid and succour to Jalta's mother and her people. He was the moving spirit behind the Bharat Programme. He was the one who called the land of Sindhu and the lands beyond 'Bharat Varsha' to honour Sindhu Putra's father, Bharatjogi.

Sindhu Putra did not share the doubts of the silent chief and other people who had seen ulterior motives and deceit in

BHAGWAN S. GIDWANI

Sharat's words and deeds. To him, Sharat was a man of goodness, honour and integrity, whose achievements in furthering freedom, unity and justice were far greater than those of anyone else.

There were tears in Sindhu Putra's eyes at Sharat's cremation. Sharat's mother, old and limping, came to him, and with tears, she begged, 'Master, bless my son.' And Sindhu Putra replied, 'Mother, I seek his blessing. He is greater than all of us here. He is with God and he is God.' And he folded his hands and began to pray near Sharat's body.

Sauvira's election as the next karkarta was a foregone conclusion; there was no opposition. However, before the elections, Jagasi travelled to the Rocks with gifts, not for Sindhu Putra, but for the silent chief, and suggested that as Sindhu Putra had blessed Sauvira to be karkarta, why not recommend doing away with the seven-year term and make Sauvira karkarta for life. Elections, after all, cost a great deal and so much effort was wasted in them. And if Sindhu Putra were to make this suggestion publicly, who could deny him! He was after all the mahakarta!

The silent chief was sympathetic, but sadly reported that though Sindhu Putra loved Sauvira, he felt that the people must have the opportunity to demonstrate their lasting love by voting for, and re-electing, him time and again. It seemed the chief disagreed with Sindhu Putra, but then as if to rebuke himself for daring to disagree, he said, 'He knows what he is doing; he is the mahakarta. He alone decides!'

Mahakarta Maharaj! News spread that Sindhu Putra had rejected the plea to end elections. 'Pity!' admitted the silent chief. 'It was a confidential request, but then so many are so garrulous!' Yet the message was clear—the mahakarta decides all . . . he is supreme.

Sauvira, twenty-third karkarta of Sindhu–Saraswati, glared at the distant Rocks with a hatred that he neither named nor described.

Gangapati's mother had died four years ago. There had been increasing pressure on her, during her sickness, to choose a wife for her son. It would be wrong, said some, for Gangapati XIV to grow to adulthood without his mother having fulfilled her basic duty. She heard the criticism and exercised her right to attend the next assembly meeting. Her voice was weak, but the message was clear: Sindhu Putra alone would decide on the marriage vows of her son. When a voice requested her to beg Sindhu Putra to give his decision soon, she simply said, 'He will decide when he decides. He is mahapati maharaj.'

Why did Gangapati's mother choose to leave the decision to Sindhu Putra? Some said it was an act of faith. Others said she needed time to see which way the wind was blowing—if Sharat's son eventually did become karkarta, she would prefer her son to marry his daughter; otherwise the regent's daughter was acceptable.

The regent, meanwhile, was on his best behaviour lest Sindhu Putra fling his daughter's suit in his face. He was fascinated by the concept of one people and one land of Bharat Varsha. The idea of unity and togetherness appealed to him, but what he disliked was that Sindhu Putra should be regarded as its supreme leader. That right and title, he felt, ought to belong to Gangapati. He recalled the glory of past Gangapatis, and their victorious cry—Har Har Gange! Har Har Gange! It was a cry of faith in the Ganga and in the legendary force of Gangapati, heard over centuries all the way from Hari Hara Dwara (Hardwar) to distant lands. It was galling that the descendant of the illustrious Gangapatis should be viewed as subordinate to this false and fake god!

There were not many to whom the regent could bare his heart. But the one listener that he did have was young Gangapati XIV. No one showered as much love and attention on the boy as the regent himself. If he had succeeded in distancing the boy even from his own mother, it was not so much the result of a command as of his affectionate and indulgent approach with the boy. He had carefully selected the people who surrounded the boy, and always took him on journeys, making sure that his every whim and wish, every comfort and convenience was met. After Gangapati's mother's death, they became even closer.

The regent was Gangapati's real mentor and the training he imparted was gentle and yet persistent. He described the past glory and greatness of the Gangapatis and helped him nurture a dream for the future. The regent employed singers and poets whose tales and anecdotes filled the boy's mind with a thirst for glory that matched the greatness of his invincible ancestors. The rigours of higher and more intensive training for the young Gangapati were yet to come, but even then he was learning that the sword was mightier than the spirit, and there was no power greater than the Gangapati. It was as though the inscrutable wisdom of providence and the inexorable process of historic destiny had so ordained.

However, the more important lessons that the regent wanted to teach the young Gangapati were that power could be elusive unless wielded with finesse; that the sword must remain sheathed until ready to strike; that speech was not always intended to reveal thought, but often to conceal it; that the words one uttered were not necessarily linked with the action one wished to take; that the powerful had no friends, but only allies and dependents, and that they must all be watched lest their loyalties waver; that to regain lost power, one had to retrace a step or two, to run faster forward; and that power must grow, lest it stagnates and disappears.

The annual spectacle of athletics, sports, song, dance and drama initiated centuries earlier by Gangapati II had continued, becoming more magnificent year by year. With Gangapati as the host, it continued to draw every chief from far and near. Gangapati XIV understood the dislike, even hatred, the mighty chiefs and lords felt towards Sindhu Putra. But though little was expressed, the hints were subtle and their protestations of reverence for Sindhu Putra were profuse. Clearly, there was no connection between their words and their feelings.

The regent pointed to the vast territories to the south of the Ganga that Sindhu Putra had passed through to reach Dravidham. Earlier, many of them were barren wastelands with a limited population in scattered pockets. Since then, many displaced former slaves and others had settled there, and the lands were now fertile and prospering. But instead of bringing them under Ganga, the silent chief and Sindhu Putra had conspired to make them separate, independent entities! 'Yes,' Gangapati XIV softly responded, 'and it is all Gangadesa.' The regent was thrilled. He had no more doubts. The lesson was well-learnt—this boy would always be a man of Ganga and the entire land would be Gangadesa.

Only a few months remained for Gangapati to come of age. Sindhu Putra had not yet selected anyone's marriage-vows for him. Obviously, the question of marriage-vows in the traditional sense would lapse as soon as Gangapati was an adult. By and large, everyone deferred to parental wishes when choosing a marriage-partner, but Gangapati's parents had never chosen for him.

'You are my teacher, my mentor. You are more than my father and mother to me; always be with me, to guide me,' he had told the regent whose heart warmed at such words of love and gratitude from the boy who was normally so reserved and reticent with others.

The regent suppressed the impulse to extract a promise from the boy to marry his daughter, for he knew how inauspicious it was to take up with a minor the question of choosing his bride. I shall wait, the regent told himself. He did not doubt the love and trust always reflected in the boy's actions and on his lips. If at all, his anger was actually against his own daughter, who foolishly, rebelliously and repeatedly sought to join Sindhu Putra's ashram—as the Rocks had come to be called. Many in faith, and some with despair in their hearts, had found permanent refuge in the ashram.

At first, when the regent heard his daughter's plea, he was proud and impressed. Obviously, her move was calculated to secure Sindhu Putra's blessing for her marriage to Gangapati. What else could the brilliant daughter of a brilliant father think! But as he heard more, his mind exploded. She was moved by faith, she insisted. He came as near to hitting her as any father possibly could.

On reflection, however, he felt that it was her frustration at the delay in her marriage, when all her friends had had their marriage-vows accepted years ago, that had tempted her to seek an escape. In a rush of feeling, he put his arms around her and said, 'A great prize, a great dream, a great ambition takes time to be fulfilled.' She saw hope in his words; he saw hope in her smile. But their hopes were different.

The annual spectacle of sports, song, dance and drama was two days away. It was preceded by a momentous celebration to mark Gangapati's coming of age when he became undisputed master of the land of Ganga, in law and fact. The regent was regent no more, but he basked in the glow of a job well done and in the sure hope of greater laurels in the future.

The lords and chiefs of many lands had gathered. Sauvira, the twenty-third karkarta of Sindhu, saw the glow on the former regent's face and abandoned his idea of pursuing his daughter's suit with Gangapati.

After the ritual ceremony, it was Gangapati XIV who went to Sauvira and, untroubled by the presence of many, said, 'Karkarta, I have always felt a special friendship for you. Would you and your daughter object if our friendship became even closer?'

It was an odd, direct, frontal way to propose marriage, but Sauvira gratefully said, 'For me, Gangapati, it would be an honour which my late father and I always wished for, and for my daughter it would be an honour beyond her dreams.'

Gangapati pointed to the former regent, 'He has always been like a father to me. He will speak to you about whatever arrangements are necessary.'

Although the former regent was secretly heartbroken, he gave his complete attention to the wedding negotiations. He resolved matters of the union between Ganga and Sindhu, the rights of succession in the event of Karkarta Sauvira having no male heirs, or if Sauvira had a son, but Gangapati did not; the action that would be taken on frontiers against raiders; the common approach to outsiders, joint exploration, discovery, resource-exploitation, and so on and so forth.

The former regent died shortly after the wedding. Gangapati ordered a state funeral and mourned him as a son would. Everyone seemed to agree that the regent died of a broken heart, deceived by Gangapati whom he had loved liked a son.

It did not take Karkarta Sauvira and Gangapati XIV too long to understand each other perfectly. If the karkarta had thought that he would have to brief his son-in-law a great deal, he was mistaken. The young Gangapati had forgotten the regent, but not the lessons he had learnt. He knew who the real enemy was: it was Sindhu Putra. He was the one who was out to rob Gangapati of his heritage. It was clear to him that the entire itihasa of the great and glorious Gangapatis was being mocked by the odious charlatan who claimed to call himself mahapati and maharaj. Taken in by his fraudulent act, the people had come to regard him as superior to Gangapati, and even accept that his would be the law to prevail over the wishes of Gangapati. That this son of a nameless father and an abandoned woman, from nowhere, through the scheming of Bharatjogi, would arrogate to himself a position far above thirteen of his illustrious ancestors who had nurtured this land of Ganga with their love, blood, sweat and sacrifice . . . it was insupportable.

The two men parted with a mutual understanding and a clear resolve.

Gangapati XIV and Karkarta Sauvira were not the only ones with hate in their hearts. Even more savage was the hatred of the influential lords and chiefs who had once held the power of life, death and liberty over their people, but were now being subjected to scrutiny by the teams sent out by the silent chief from the Rocks. Some of them were even thrown out of their positions! Maybe one day, the man from the Rocks would ask beggars to mount horses and take up the rod of authority!

Meanwhile, Sindhu Putra gave up much of his isolation and often came out to meet crowds at the Rocks. The wisdom he had sought in silence and loneliness had eluded him. Prayers and meditation gave him no answers to the riddle of universal mystery. To the many wise and learned who congregated at the Rocks, he could say little except that dharma controls the universe, that it is the laws of karma that rule individual emancipation and not blind chance or destiny, and that human will and effort help reshape man's environment and future.

The wise and learned were unimpressed by such commonplace utterances which they had learnt as children in their parents' lap or at the feet of their first guru. Sindhu Putra's silence on nature and the identity of the universal spirit and the ultimate reality behind the phenomenal world startled them even more. But if the wise learnt little from him, he perhaps learnt even less from them.

'Why don't we all simply admit that we don't know and perhaps never shall!' he was driven to say. Often, he would point to a snail or a worm in the Rock garden and remark, 'The smallest of God's creatures possibly knows as much about the universal spirit as I do—or maybe he knows more.'

He was glad that he said so, for later he found some walking carefully in order to avoid treading on worms in the garden.

All he was sure about was that the universe was alive, the earth was holy and that all life was a part of an eternal and infinite process. But if the wise and learned were disappointed with him, his devotees were not. They had the calm assurance that arises from love and faith. Sometimes, out of reverence, his devotees would look grave as he passed by, but he would pinch a little girl and say, 'Give me your smile and make it a part of me,' and she would smile, and so would all.

Often now, Sindhu Putra left his retreat, not to attend spectacles, weddings or rituals, but to move on dusty paths and lonely routes, to areas where former slaves and others lived in lowly conditions. Thousands followed him. And he would ask that their condition be improved. Sometimes he made demands that were impossible, but slowly, surely, many of them were met, for the people who followed him kept pestering everyone in power.

To him, poverty was a form of slavery. The lords of the lands were answerable to those they governed. They were trustees of the people, and to live better than the least of their fellow men was to abuse that trust. Sindhu Putra believed the weakest must have the same opportunity as the strongest, that God cared for everyone, and man's purpose on earth was to seek out God's purpose and serve those who needed help.

The chiefs, far and near, did not need teams from the Rocks to hear these words. Their own men were at the Rocks, and to them Sindhu Putra's purpose was clear—creating a climate of contempt against them and an aura of sanctity for himself.

∽

The annual Ganga spectacles continued to attract chiefs, but not just to the festivities. There was much to say, more to discuss. An overwhelming sense of frustration assailed the mighty chiefs and lords. The arrogance of their people astounded them. What shocked them even more was the total ingratitude of Sindhu Putra, who accepted all their magnificent gifts, but continued to do everything he could to spread discontent and sedition. Like Karkarta Sauvira and Gangapati XIV, they, too, looked towards the Rocks with bitter hatred.

The people's love for Sindhu Putra grew, as did the chiefs' hatred for him.

THIRTY-TWO

DEATH OF A GOD

5015 BCE

A scream of anguish rose from the Rocks. Sindhu Putra was dead.

Throughout the land, there was a cry of despair, a prayer for mercy, a deafening silence—and each mourned in his own way.

How had that terrible, fateful moment arrived?

∽

It was a day not too different from any other. Sindhu Putra woke up well before dawn and, after a bath, sat for his prayers. Girls entered, with soft footsteps, bringing large baskets of fruit from which Sindhu Putra took some before the baskets were distributed among devotees.

Two girls remained. They chanted, one after another, his favourite hymns. Then one of them began a song he had not heard before.

'Swifter than sound, faster than light, quicker than thought
It came—and came with a motion as if it moved not
Yet it moved all that kept far, asunder, apart
And they sang—we all have the same one heart!'

The song continued, and the second girl joined in with a

soft, delicate tune that seemed to dance around the melody, and the refrain—'We all have the same one heart!'

The voices were captivating. Sindhu Putra liked the thought, particularly when the song went on to say that every heart, whether it belong to man, beast or plant, is the same one heart, that of the Lord of Creation to whom all pathways lead.

Yet the words of the song were a little laboured and it lacked the flow and imagery of the old singer from whom no doubt she had learnt the song.

'When did he sing that song?' he asked.

She blushed, stammered, 'I . . . I composed this song. You did not like it?'

He put his arm round her, 'Like it! I love it. Sing this song for all at the prayer session today.'

'Will you be there?' she hopefully asked.

'Nothing shall keep me back from wishing to hear you again.'

Sindhu Putra never had a precise schedule. Sometimes, he would walk into the evening prayer session in which the people of the ashram and devotees participated. At other times, he would simply stroll in the garden or rest under a pipal tree or move amid throngs of visitors. But there would be days when he would not appear, except to bless the crowd from the balcony. He had no fixed days on which he would fast, nor did he plan his visits outside the Rocks ahead of time. 'As the spirit moved him, so did he move.'

How different he was from the silent chief who was precise and punctual in all things . . . in all except his time to sleep. Sometimes, the chief would be up all night, talking to returning emissaries, discussing things with teams, planning, thinking . . .

The explorer would laugh at the chief and say, 'Perhaps for your dark thoughts you need darkness.' But irrespective of when he slept, the silent chief woke up every morning at the same time, earlier than Sindhu Putra.

That is why it was surprising that the chief did not arrive that evening. He was always punctual. He had left the Rocks only for four days for a nearby visit, and had even arranged two meetings at the Rocks for that evening itself. Sindhu Putra had intended to drag the chief to the prayer session to hear the song which the girls had sung for him in the morning. He waited, asked others, but the chief had not arrived.

Sindhu Putra reached the prayer meeting late. But since everyone knew that he was to attend, they had waited. He reproached them, 'How can you delay prayers!'

Hymns began, then the song he had heard in the morning—it sounded different, more captivating, but that was not surprising for now it was accompanied by musical instruments and even a chorus of children, who soulfully sang the refrain—'We all have the same one heart.'

When the prayer was over, he walked on the lush grassy path through the crowd towards the edge of the Rocks. Everywhere people lined up, saying 'Namaste' as they let him pass. Some even stood, with children, at the edge where it was slippery. A man in front obligingly took in his arms an infant from someone behind him to bring it closer to receive Sindhu Putra's blessing.

Sindhu Putra continued. It was, as always, a slow, silent walk. Usually, there were three women behind him with strings of 108 prayer beads, but this time he also asked the two singing sisters to join him. Silently, he responded to people's greetings.

Suddenly, when Sindhu Putra was barely three steps away, the man holding another's infant, gently dropped the child in Sindhu Putra's way. The girl behind Sindhu Putra murmured at his carelessness, 'Brother, what have you done?'

Sindhu Putra said nothing, and stooped to pick up the baby. The man said, 'Forgive me,' and he too bent as if to do the same. Suddenly he shot out his right hand, and the dagger concealed in it tore into Sindhu Putra's chest.

'Om!' Sindhu Putra gasped as he sank to the ground, lifeless, his hands frozen in the gesture of picking up the infant, close to each other. Perhaps he intended his last gesture to be 'Namaste'. Instead, they pointed to the sky as though with a question or a complaint to someone above.

The infant, blood-soaked, slept.

No one moved. All eyes were riveted on Sindhu Putra. The assassin dove from the high rock into the river below. No one tried to stop him. He was seen from the boats lined up on the river, but the occupants of the boats did not know what had happened. Some people saw him swim and climb onto a waiting boat with three other passengers. Quickly, they rowed the boat towards the opposite bank, away from the village. Just before it reached the bank, the boat was seen floundering. Later, when the boat was found, the assasin's dead body was discovered within, his face bashed beyond recognition. Apparently, his companions, having done their deed, had abandoned the boat near the opposite bank and left. But a short distance from the boat, in a narrow pass beyond the grassy bank, the bodies of the men and their horses lay, riddled with arrows. The faces of these men had been battered too. Apparently, Sindhu Putra's assassin was killed by the three men waiting in the boat and those three were waylaid by others and butchered.

Whoever was behind it all did not want the assassin or the three men waiting for him in the river to be found alive for questioning, or even recognized when dead.

A few days later, the silent chief and his four companions were found dead. Among them was the old Dravidham explorer. Elsewhere, members of the svastika teams, sent out by the silent chief, were also killed. No one knew who was responsible for their deaths.

❧

Flames from the cremation pyre rose and fell as the fire consumed Sindhu Putra's body.

At the sight of the smoke curling up from the pyre, a mournful cry rose, which subsided as the crowd heard the old singer's voice. Was he chanting a prayer? No. His tearful eyes seemed to focus not on the present, but on the past. He was thinking of the time when he had hastily been summoned to Bharatjogi's retreat where the latter had denied that the three-year-old child was a miracle of God and had said, 'Gods do not come to walk on earth among men.'

The old singer was smiling now, his thoughts locked in that argument with Bharat, and suddenly he raised his hand to point beyond the river to the horizon, as though he saw Bharat there, and he cried, 'Yes Bharat, yes!' and then he began his chant:

> 'He was the one when rock and tree was One
> When air, earth, river, sea was One
> When all below, up, above, high was One
> When stars, moon, sun, sky was One . . . .'

The chant went on, obscurely, to speak of the One who rose from 'blackness of black nights, when nights and days were not; and light and dark were not'; and of Him who sprang from 'nothingness when nothingness and existence were not', and He it was who sent His glorious radiance, here on earth, 'in the darkest of dark nights that was'.

The people around him did not understand that in this moment of overwhelming grief, his mind had wandered into the past, but they did realize that he spoke, not of Bharatjogi, but of the god who had walked amongst them, briefly.

Kanta watched as Sindhu Putra's ashes were immersed in the Sindhu. While everyone grieved for the god who was no more, she was remembering her two-day-old son whose ashes, too, had been sprinkled from the Rocks, the child whom Muni had blessed and who had returned to her as Sindhu Putra. She put her face against one of the trees which Roopa had planted for her son. Her tears fell on the tree trunks and disappeared into the bark. Maybe the trees spoke to her or maybe her heart spoke and she cried out, 'Yes, this is where he began his last journey and this is where it ends. Only to begin anew.' Soulfully, dry-eyed, she spoke, 'He shall come again,' and softly began to hum, 'He comes, He comes, ever He comes . . . '

Some joined her song. But many wept . . . and their tears did not stop.

THIRTY-THREE

WE ARE THE ARYANS! BUT WHY?

5014 BCE

Sindhu Putra, known as mahakarta in Sindhu–Saraswati, mahapati in Ganga lands, periyar in the south, and maharaj everywhere in Bharat Varsha, was no more. Though thousands had followed his footsteps while he lived, in a sense he had walked alone. He left no successor—no one on whom people could pin their hopes and faith. Adored and cherished, his memory lingered in their hearts, but after his tragic assassination there was no one left to guide them.

The silent chief, who had been the administrator of Sindhu Putra's affairs, was slain, too. The teams which he had sent out faded away; many disappeared without a trace and some were suppressed. Those that remained could do little. Their voice was not the same as the voice people had loved and revered; they were shrill and loud. The voice the people longed to hear had been soft and gentle, yet audible above the din and shouting of all, thrilling men and moving the lords of the land. To the weak, he had said, 'Shed your fear.' To the strong and powerful he had said, 'This land is yours, theirs and mine. Make it worthy for us all.' Now that voice was stilled. With no one restraining the lords, the black pall of fear would re-emerge. The hurt that Sindhu Putra had caused to the powerful was great; the poor do not mind when much remains denied to them, but the mighty had not only suffered encroachments on their privilege but also the shame of being regarded subordinate to his commands, and even to the 'advice' of his deputies.

The high and mighty lords smirked.

'They are not mourning Sindhu Putra's absence. They are celebrating his second coming. They're singing, *"He comes, He comes, and ever He comes."*'

Another asked in mock fear, 'How long do you think we have before he comes again?'

'Well, his last coming was after a prophecy that raged for a thousand years.'

'Oh, we have time then!'

'Certainly. Enough time to make his Bharat Varsha fit for him.'

'I hear, they are also singing that his glorious radiance shall arise when the land is in the blackest of black nights!'

'I am glad. Many oil lamps burn in my house and yours at night.'

'Yes, but I think we should burn lamps in the village streets also.'

'Good idea! Let us keep thieves and gods away.'

However, neither Karkarta Sauvira nor Gangapati XIV nor any of the other mighty chiefs indulged in such open glee. Publicly, they maintained a solemn appearance and joined the mourning over Sindhu Putra's passing away. So that the masses did not feel dejected that there was no one to listen to their woes and right their wrongs, now that Sindhu Putra was no more, Sauvira declared that he felt honour-bound to listen to the people in the same way, with the same attention and compassion as Mahakarta Sindhu Putra had done. Soon, those around him began to address Sauvira by a title that went far beyond mere karkarta. They called him 'Karkarta Mahakarta Maharaj'. And many soon learnt that the use of this expanded title made the karkarta more receptive to their grievances.

Similar changes arose in other lands as well; in the Ganga region Gangapati came to be called Gangapati Mahapati Maharaj. Of course, it meant less to Gangapati than to the karkarta, for his title was not subject to the vagaries of elections. But would a mahakarta maharaj also be subject to elections? To those who still harboured the illusion that mahakarta was simply a title of respect, but not of authority, much was said even by Karkarta Sauvira of the power of Mahakarta Sindhu Putra. How these new and various titles would add to the power and prestige of the karkarta and other lords remained to be seen.

In the meantime, armies were on the move everywhere. Sauvira's forces were moving in two directions; Gangapati's contingents were marching into all the lands around; and eleven armies of the other mighty chiefs were advancing on many lands.

And the lands under attack? These were the lands from which petty tyrants had once been dispossessed by Chief Jalta and his men, serving the cause of Sindhu Putra to make those lands slave-free. In most of those lands, new chiefs had been appointed. There were also vast areas that came under no lords and had been abandoned for they did not provide any sustenance for man, animal or bird. Monumental efforts had been made to clear these lands, plant crops, irrigate them and even provide housing and many amenities to resettle large numbers of freed slaves. All these efforts had been personally supervised by the silent chief. Many came, inspired by the god from the Rocks, to help in making these lands lush, green and fertile with their incessant toil. To many rich devotees, Sindhu Putra had said, 'Help me improve that new village,' and some responded by 'adopting' that village. He had made similar appeals to artisans, builders, artists and others. Additionally, many visiting devotees had left small offerings at the Rocks, including ornaments and even ancient family heirlooms. Little by little, but in an almost unending stream, contributions had flowed into the treasury guarded by the silent chief. Some said even thieves, robbers and criminals left a part of their loot in the hope that this pious contribution would wash away their sins. The silent chief had also sold or auctioned little leaves on which Sindhu Putra had drawn *om*. When they had needed greater assistance, Sindhu Putra had merely to appeal to the karkarta, Gangapati or other lords, who had graciously responded despite the hatred in their hearts. Although each such land bore its separate name, all these lands together came to be known as Punya-bhumi—sacred land. In these lands, no chiefs were appointed; instead sabhas were established on the basis of free elections.

As armies marched towards these vast, extensive pockets of Punya-bhumi, some asked, 'But why?'

The reply was, 'To unite. Deep divisions in Bharat Varsha must cease.'

Some still argued, 'But to take Punya-bhumi! These lands were freed from tyranny and established as parts of Punya-bhumi under directions from Sindhu Putra!'

'His aim was unity,' they were told. 'His mission was timeless. On our shoulders falls the burden of his greatness . . . we must pick up the fallen torch, and move forward with faith. Unity is our aim, and if some fall by the wayside, so be it.'

'But Sindhu Putra never conquered with force, fire and sword!'

'No? What about the massive battles fought in Sindhu Putra's name by his commanders to free the slaves and remove chiefs?'

'But where do we go?' the people of a village asked when they were told to leave their land. The commander pointed to the wilderness, far beyond, where their land ended. Again the people cried out, 'There is nothing there!'

'That is what you are! Nothing! Leave this land. It belongs to our people,' they were told.

'We are the rya, the people of the land,' they shouted.

'Leave! You are not the rya!' the commander thundered.

'This land is ours. We are rya!' they insisted.

The soldiers' swords gleamed; the villagers stood unmoved.

The commander had no wish to order his horsemen to charge and cause bloodshed. He pointed his sword at the throat of an old man who was the spokesman for the village and said, 'Listen, old man, you have not many years left to live, but the others do. Leave. Go beyond. You can make those rocky barren lands as green as this one. No one shall molest you there, so long as you set no foot here. By midday, if all of you are not gone . . . '

But the unpredictable happened. The old man's six-year-old grandson suddenly lunged forward at the commander. Both the old man and the commander moved unexpectedly, and the swordpoint went deep into the throat of the old man. Blood gushed.

The old man was dead.

And all that the six-year-old child was now saying to the commander was, 'Let my grandfather go! We are not rya, not rya, not rya!' He only wanted to save his grandfather from the menace and thought that all that the commander wanted was to hear that they were not rya.

The child saw his grandfather fall. He buried his face in his chest and kept repeating, 'Baba, Baba, say you are not rya, not rya.' Somehow he hoped that if his grandfather said that, the commander would restore to him the life that he had taken away.

But then at last a whisper made its way into the child's tiny heart and he stood, his grandfather's blood streaked on his face. Quietly, he said, 'We are not the rya.'

The child no longer said this to gain favour with the commander. There was a deep silence in his heart that he did not understand. All he knew was that he was not the rya of those that struck his grandfather.

The commander moved away with his men. Outside the heat of battle, he had never killed a man. Perhaps he would not have grieved if the crowd had been rebellious and he had been forced to charge, killing many in consequence. He washed his hands in the stream, repeatedly, though he knew the stain was not on his hands, but in his heart. He had no wish to menace these people further. There would be other lands—hundreds—from which people had to be moved.

But the villagers hardly noticed the commander's departure. Their eyes were riveted on the little boy standing next to his grandfather's fallen body. When he had spoken, it was not the voice of a grieving child; there was no emotion— neither fear nor despair, nor hate nor anger—but a simple, quiet acceptance of a reality. *We are not the rya.*

Their thoughts drifted to the time, three years ago, when the boy's father had died while working on a high rope-bridge over a ravine. The child had been in shock, without words, without tears. When Sindhu Putra had visited the village, he took the boy in his arms and asked, 'Would you accept me as your father?'

Rebelliously the boy had replied, 'No, I am my father's son.'

'I, too, lost my father and my mother,' Sindhu Putra told him gently. 'I was younger than you, then.'

The child then had tears for someone who had possibly borne greater sorrow. His hand moved to touch Sindhu Putra and with tears he made a concession, 'You shall be my father-friend.'

Father-friend! It was a new relationship, unknown, unheard of. A respected elder would be called 'uncle'. But Sindhu Putra said, 'Then you will be my son-friend,' and thus a new bond was forged. Sindhu Putra had invited the boy for a visit to the Rocks. But the boy objected, 'My grandfather will be lonely without me.'

'Then your grandfather must come too,' Sindhu Putra had insisted.

Both the boy and his grandfather had visited the Rocks. The boy returned with mountains of toys—everyone there had wanted to give a gift to Sindhu Putra's 'son-friend'.

Ever since his return from the Rocks, the boy had stood apart in the eyes of others. Now they heard the boy: 'We are not the rya.' With an icy chill, the pitiless words echoed in their hearts, and would soon be heard everywhere.

'We are not the rya.'

Yet this was only a tiny village in the vast area that was called Punya-bhumi. In other villages commanders pleaded, in some they roared and in yet others they charged without warning, mowing down crowds, burning their homes and crops. In one village, a commander was unhorsed, which unleashed a reign of terror, with children burnt to death and women thrown into wells.

There were many stories, each with its own tale of tears and pathos. The names were different; heroes and villains diverse; and the villages far apart. Yet, in essence, they were all the same! Everywhere, these stories ended with the same cry born from a desolate realization of their nothingness in a land that had disowned them: 'We are not the rya!'

'Why have you forsaken us and left us anath,' the people demanded of the pitiless gods.

The question—'How can we be the rya of those who caused the death of our "nath" (protector; so "anath" means unprotected) Sindhu Putra?'—burned in their hearts.

'We are arya!' The cry rose, but it was not one of agony. It was the voice of their conscience, encouraging them to distance themselves from their oppressors, to cling to their one certainty of Sindhu Putra in the shifting sands around them.

No one knew who had slain Sindhu Putra. The mighty lords and chiefs had publicly mourned his passing away with unrestrained tears. They spoke of their determination to hunt the faceless, nameless killer. Meanwhile, rumours abounded—it was a demented lunatic; a tribal, angry that his land was united with another; someone whose wife or daughter had become a 'bride of Sindhu Putra'; a drunkard with nothing whose parents had donated their all to Sindhu Putra; it was the devil himself; someone who had sold his soul to the devil. But, in the wake of their dispossession, the oppressed proposed a new theory—all those who were terrorizing them were the real killers of Sindhu Putra. But how could that be? *One* man had thrust his dagger in Sindhu Putra's heart; how could they *all* be responsible? The devil comes in ten thousand forms, was the answer, and single or together, it was he who shed the blood of their 'nath'. The lords creating terror in Punya-bhumi and confiscating their lands were the devil incarnate and they were the ones responsible for the death of Sindhu Putra.

The cry of arya became a badge of honour, giving them a new identity, distinguishing them from those who had shed Sindhu Putra's blood; and they felt the thrill of being 'the chosen ones' who had served Sindhu Putra with their whole heart and soul. And they were certain that as unrighteousness increased, he would reappear and lead them to redemption.

Some people believed that the cry of the arya was widespread, extending across the land and skies of all Bharat Varsha, in one single sweep like a giant crusade. Not so—movements, unled and undirected, are never fast-moving.

Meanwhile, turmoil continued not only in Punya-bhumi, but throughout the heart of Bharat Varsha. With armies on the move, fresh alliances were forming, new spheres of influence were being established, and recently appointed chiefs were being sacked to make way for new favourites. But these developments distressed only a few at the top of the hierarchy. What affected the vast populace was that even the dispossessed, who had been rehabilitated by Sindhu Putra, were being uprooted. Terrified and dazed, they tried to flee and migrate, but they had no place to run to and no place to hide. Every step was a step to nowhere. Their way to Punya-bhumi was barred, and they were being forced to leave for the wastelands beyond.

They, too, cried in anguish, 'We are arya!'

The displaced and the dispossessed were not the only ones who uttered the cry. Moved by the pain and tears of others, some affluent people, secure in their position and threatened by no one, also joined the cry. As their minds dwelt on Sindhu Putra, the feeling in their hearts was that they, too, were victims. There were also those who sympathized with the suffering of others, but theirs was a silent despair for they were fearful of the vengeance of the mighty lords of the land. But in their hearts they heard the echo of what Devdatta and Bharat had often repeated: 'There is guilt in silence. Our silence in the face of injustice to others is a betrayal and a sin. The persecution of others demands a protest from us all.'

Confusion and chaos spread. Yet the cry of arya rose and surged like a whirlwind. The mighty lords of the land laughed contemptuously and said, 'Yes, you are arya, and so must you be treated—landless, homeless and driven away to the barren, infertile wastelands beyond our villages, and driven away again if by your effort those lands become prosperous!'

But to those that banded together to participate in the cry of arya it was like a beam of light that pierced the darkness. Suddenly, they found that they were not alone; thousands had joined the cry. It was a cry of togetherness, of fellow-feeling, of belonging, of comradeship and brotherhood. Troubled in mind they still were, but no longer did they feel lonely and lost, and the realization dawned on them that they were being tyrannized not because of their intrinsic inferiority, but because those who ruled the land were vile and vicious. The realization brought with it a sense of their own dignity and righteousness, and the awareness that they were being hunted because they had chosen to follow the auspicious path of Sindhu Putra.

Thus it was that the cry of arya achieved two different, disparate dimensions:

'Yes, you are arya,' said the lords, with contempt.

'Yes, we are arya,' said the people, with pride.

But how much could faith alone achieve against the mighty lords! The power of the sword, some said, was mightier than the power of the spirit! Fear alternated with faith, and sometimes it overcame it. The people did not fear being driven into inhospitable wastelands as much as being herded in separate, isolated areas. Were they being sent there so it would be easy to pick them up, at will, and enslaved again? Slavery had been abolished throughout Bharat Varsha in fact and in law, yet its memory lingered.

The movement thus began, in fear and faith—fear of the land that had rejected them and faith that the spirit of Sindhu Putra would guide their footsteps towards an auspicious path. They were convinced that the land that had disowned them had also denied their nath, Sindhu Putra. But surely, he reigned elsewhere. And hundreds of songs were sung to radiate this belief. These songs, heard everywhere, fired the imagination of receptive listeners, luring them to 'walk the earth where Sindhu Putra walks', to the 'Land of the Pure'.

However, the great migration did not begin overnight. There was fear that the routes to new lands would be difficult and dangerous, but, they wondered, could they be more dangerous than remaining here? But what if they found no new lands, some asked. How was that possible, others replied. Did Sadhu Gandhara not travel all over? Surely there was land wherever he went! Did Rishi Newar not find the land he was seeking? What of their ancestors who had found the Land of Kosa Karan (China) and brought back quantities of jade? Thus stories of discoverers and explorers were told, of Tirathada who visited every sanctified spot there was, and of brave explorers who had reached the source of the Sindhu and the Ganga, travelling across the Himalayas to Mount Kailash and Tibata and Gai-mukh . . . and to the 108 mouths of the sacred Ganga. Little was said of the intrepid wanderers who died on those journeys from starvation, exposure or in attacks and never returned to tell their tale. Yes, danger there would be, they knew, but the spirit of Sindhu Putra would guide them.

'Escapees we are not, nor vagrants, nor aimless wanderers, but pilgrims we are, in search of God's land, pure and free,' the Aryans—for that is what they called themselves—told each other, suppressing the thought that it was fear that tempted them to flee.

Others were even more positive and said: 'We go not for enticement into the unknown, but with the sure knowledge of being near the blaze of the unfading glory of our nath, Sindhu Putra.'

Some, to gain courage and take the final, awesome step of leaving their land, wrapped themselves with many comforting self-assurances, and cried out:

> *ARYA!*
> *Noble our aim, noble our thought*
> *Rya of house of clay we are not!*
> *ARYA!*
> *Noble our quest, noble our deed*
> *Rya, we of distant noble land indeed!*
> *ARYA!*
> *Where our nath, radiant, untouched by evil is He*
> *There are we rya, noble, pure, free!*
> *ARYA!*
> *So onward in joy!*
> *No tears, no sighs!*
> *And if unseeing, our eyes*
> *Pass that land by,*
> *We will hear love's cry*
> *From earth and sky,*
> *'Come! Here am I!'*
> *And He will bless us then*
> *And we, arya no more, rya again, rya again, rya again . . .*

Great poetry this was not. But as slogans, they gave comfort and cheer to those who were afraid to leave, encouraging them on their way forward. And if an Aryan sought to whisper his fears, another would burst into songs of faith, 'Onward Arya, onward in joy . . . ' And emotions would rise, sweeping past all fears and uncertainties. Thereafter, it was no more a discussion or a dialogue or a debate, but simply a series of songs and declarations, each full of faith in the future.

Later, Nandan's eighth great-grandson asked: 'Where was the need for fear! Did the mighty lords and chiefs, the karkarta and Gangapati and everyone in power, not go out of their way to assist the Aryans? Were the doors of vast treasure-houses not opened to equip the Aryans? Were they not given horses, swords, axes, arrows, and even tents and clothing? Like filthy beggars, these Aryans came, swarming before their lords, and freely and fondly the benevolent lords gave. Are we then so lost to logic, so bereft of reason, so devoid of sense, as to believe that the Aryans fled from those bounteous patrons who gave them such prodigious help?'

It was a powerful argument indeed! And powerfully persuasive! And, by and large, his facts were right, too. Only the conclusion was wrong. The mighty lords gave liberal help to the Aryans when they moved out because the Aryans' desire to migrate to faraway lands was a boon for them. After all, why were they trying to herd these unfortunate Aryans into the deserted lands outside their villages, where nothing grew? One advantage was that their lush and green lands that were being vacated could be given to more desirable citizens—for patronage or sale. But beyond that short-term gain was the hope that these men and women, forced to eke out a living in the rocky, toilsome terrain, would renew the land and make it fertile. Then the lords would take over those lands as well, and send the Aryans out to other uninhabitable areas. After all, the lands from which they were now being displaced were once barren, but these men had toiled and made them green. Why could they not keep repeating the miracle! Besides, in their passion to leave Bharat Varsha and seek out new lands, who knew, some of the Aryans might actually succeed. Surely then, the lords could take over the lands so discovered! True, many of these pathetic Aryans would die in the attempt, but it would all be for a worthy cause. The wealth from those newly discovered lands would be enormous. So why not encourage them, and let them pave the way for us—the lords decided.

Were the lords pinning their hopes on a far-fetched idea? Was it possible that the Aryans might find new lands which the lords could take over? The fact is that not all new lands in the past had been found only by intrepid explorers, intent upon discovery. Everyone knew the ancient story:

A drunkard leapt into the Sindhu to retrieve his half-empty barrel of liquor that had fallen in the river. The current swept the barrel beyond his reach. Before he lost consciousness, he had the sense or good fortune to climb on to a large chunk of driftwood. On that he slept, dead to the world, and ignored by the beasts in the river who stayed away from him because he smelt so strongly of liquor. When he woke up the next morning, though he did not find his barrel, he realized he had arrived at the confluence of the Sindhu and Sutudhri (the Sutlej river in Panchanad—Punjab). He returned, devastated by the loss of his barrel, but was delighted when the council of chiefs of the Sindhu presented him with five large barrels of liquor for his amazing discovery of the confluence.

And so it was not surprising that the mighty lords hoped that these 'faith-drunk' Aryans might succeed in finding new lands in their search for the Land of the Pure, and encouraged them to migrate. From various scattered pockets, small bands of Aryans were helped with mules, horses, camels and boats for transport to join together in larger groups.

The choice for the Aryans was simple—go empty-handed,

unprotected to the raw, rocky, untamed land outside the villages or heed the call of hope in lands far beyond and reach, hopefully, the Land of the Pure. They chose the lands beyond to get whatever help their lords offered. Their lords were generous with their help, even nominating men to advise the Aryans on different routes to follow. The lords hoped to keep the Aryans from focusing on a single route; surely much more would be revealed, if more routes were taken.

Whenever an Aryan group was overtaken by momentary panic at embarking on a journey into the unknown, the men sent out by the lords were ready not only with words of comfort and cheer, but larger aid in stores and equipment. The singers sent out by the lords sang,

> 'Child! Be blessed of one mind;
> Go! His glory seek, and find;
> On and On . . .'

Some groups paused to wonder—if the mighty lords supported their move, perhaps there was something really wrong with it. But was that reason enough to give it up, when the alternatives were so bleak? Instead, greater wisdom prevailed and they spoke of their fear and torments as though they were hesitant, even uncertain, about travelling so ill-equipped into the lands beyond. The lords responded with greater generosity.

Said one Aryan to another, 'How stupid these clever people are!'

The lords were unconcerned with their munificence, for the burden of their largesse fell on the petty chiefs, who, in turn, fumed that so much was being given away to these miserable creatures.

And thus the great migration of the Aryans from Bharat Varsha began, in search of the Land of the Pure, where their god, Sindhu Putra, reigned.

THIRTY-FOUR

THE ARYANS MOVE—TRAVEL ROUTES

5011 BCE

The Aryans initially travelled on twelve routes. They came together from hundreds of points to form larger groups, so as to leave on specific routes from their respective regions. There were bands of varying strengths, following each other at intervals, often joining together, and sometimes parting to go on their own.

The first series of routes, as Nandan's eighth great-grandson said correctly, began from Avagana. According to him, 'The route to Avagana was traditional and presented no danger. For it was there that Sadhu Gandhara had established his first ashram, the large area surrounding which came to be known as Gandhara (Kandahar) in his honour. Thereafter, the sadhu set up his ashram at Kubha (Kabul), named in honour of his devotee who died protecting Gandhara's life. Later all Avagana up to and beyond Hari Rath came under his protection and when he died, the land was left in trust with the headman from the Sindhu region, until his son Kush—born to Sadhu Gandhara's Russian wife—came of age. Then began the glorious reign of Lord Kush, who married the daughter of Dhrupatta's wife's sister's daughter from Sindhu—a union blessed by my great-grandfather Karkarta Nandan, the most illustrious of all karkartas. He regularly sent caravans of goods, artisans and assistance to Kush and his land, which always was and shall be a part of Bharat Varsha. So where was the danger to these wandering Aryan bands travelling through Avagana, when the magnificent Kush was there to assist them! Karkarta Sauvira had clearly requested Kush not to permit these wanderers to remain in Avagana but lead them out to lands beyond, and should any try to tarry in Avagana, to send them back forthwith. It was a pity, then, that Kush misunderstood this request and allowed some Aryans to stay back, choosing those who would be valuable in developing his own land, and others too sick and old to travel. But, honourable as always, Kush sent a message to Karkarta Sauvira, though perchance, the messenger failed to arrive.'

At Hari Rath in Avagana, several Aryan bands congregated. Many parted here, too, to branch out on different routes. Purus, who lived by the side of the Saraswati river, led his bands towards Lake Namaskar.

'We know not if we shall meet again on this earth,' remarked Purus while parting from the other Aryan bands. 'But surely we shall reassemble at the feet of the master in the world beyond,' he said, referring to Sindhu Putra.

'Yes,' said the leader of another band, 'we that saw him live, know that he lives, and so shall we.'

Such cries of faith came, no doubt, from the heart, and these self-assurances served to sustain their hope that somewhere there was a better land where their lost god awaited them with outstretched arms, alive and welcoming.

But consistency belongs only to gods. With humans, each cry of faith is overtaken often by another cry of despair, and even grief dies only to be replaced by another greater grief.

Six scouts of the Aryan band led by Purus were killed at the outset of the journey. The four men and two women were travelling ahead of the rest and were suddenly set upon by a group of roving bandits. But as the large columns of Aryan bands, escorted by Kush's men, came into view, the bandits fled. The gruesome sight of the murdered scouts reawakened the feeling of dread that lay in the heart of every Aryan who marched.

Purus and his bands reached the area around Lake Namaskar. Already, several hermits of Sanatan Dharma had settled down there.

One such hermit adopted the nine children of those who were killed by the bandits on the way. At first, Kush's men insisted that these children could not remain, for Kush had ordered them to ensure none of the Aryans stayed back. Karkarta Sauvira's request had been clear—to send out all of them to lands beyond. Already, Kush had deviated from it somewhat by allowing many to remain behind in Avagana. But the hermit glared at the soldiers, ready to shout. The commander advised his men, 'Look the other way; hermits carry a powerful curse, so beware!' And thus the children, and some adult Aryans too, stayed back with the hermits, though the eldest of the children—a twelve-year-old—ran to rejoin Aryan bands a few hours later.

Purus did not object to anyone remaining behind. 'Your feelings must be your guide. You must follow the faith that calls you. Who knows where the master needs you! Perhaps we, too, may retrace our steps!'

Some viewed this as a lack of faith, as if Purus feared that after all his wanderings, the object of his quest might elude him. But as one person said, 'I know of no man of faith, nor a god, who is untouched by anguish and self doubt.'

It was clear that the Aryan bands did not go out into new lands with feelings of triumph or banners flying. The refrain of 'sanctified terrain . . . far, somewhere . . . elsewhere . . . ' may have been somewhat reassuring, but their journey to lands unknown was not without mournful doubts.

Quietly, they heard the blessings of hermits at Lake Namaskar and did not even smile when the oldest hermit possibly mistakenly addressed Purus and said: 'Go then,

Purusa, take your Aryans. But as you flee from evil, carry not evil with yourself, and even if you are sacrificed in many parts, let your deed be noble in the reckoning of God *and* man. Not by one *or* the other, but in the judgment of both, so that till the end of time, the Aryans shall be known as noble.'

Purusa! Some said the enlightened hermit had made a peculiar mistake indeed; others said it was not a mistake at all! 'Purusa' had an enticing array of meanings. It meant ideal man, but it also meant 'world spirit' to those sages who considered the entire universe an organic whole and various aspects of creation parts of the macrocosmic unity. There were other sages who synthesized all humankind into one being—the Purusa. It also meant the primeval man who sacrificed himself to bring justice and freedom to others.

The lands beyond Lake Namaskar, into which the Aryan bands moved, had no special name. The hermits referred to them as the lands of Hari Haran. Long after the Aryan bands moved in, it began to be called Hari Haran Aryan or simply the land of Aryan, and from this later emerged its present name—Iran.

It was in the isolation of Iran that the Aryan bands rested. Several other bands travelling from Avagana joined them. Purus injured his leg and remained in Iran with some Aryan groups. Other groups moved on in various directions— westwards to modern-day Turkey and Iraq; southward to the Persian Gulf and the Gulf of Oman; and northwards into the erstwhile Soviet Union. The influx into the former Soviet Union had begun not only from Iran. Many Aryan bands from Avagana itself journeyed there, on the routes which Sadhu Gandhara had once taken. Sadly, nine out of every ten who travelled on Gandhara's routes died. Those who went there from Iran and beyond did not fare so poorly, but, even so, less than half survived.

When Purus recovered from his leg injury, he was impatient to move forward. But during his enforced stay in Iran, he had become a key figure in protecting Aryan groups and assisting and equipping them to move out in various directions.

And move out they did, all across the west.

It was also the sea route from the mouth of the Sindhu river that attracted the Aryans. They travelled from all over upper Sindhu and elsewhere to congregate in lower Sindhu. Karkarta Sauvira himself set up comfortable camps for them to oversee and encourage their move to lands beyond the sea—the Persian Gulf and Sumer (modern-day Iraq).

And so the sea voyages of the Aryans began.

Long-distance sea voyages had begun much earlier in the Sindhu region. Bharat, the nineteenth karkarta, had given tremendous help to the boat-building programme, and Nandan, the twenty-first karkarta, had provided generously to the programme so that bigger, faster and safer boats could be built. The seafarers had then touched the Persian Gulf and thence proceeded to the coast of Sumer between the Euphrates and Tigris rivers. But the men who went in those boats were sailors, mariners and seamen, interested in exploring the sea, not the land. A few had stayed back to build their huts along the coast, and even piers and docks for the loading and repair of boats that came infrequently from Sindhu. However, finding no locals nearby, and nothing of real interest to them in the immediate vicinity, their trips inland were never too deep and few and far between.

However, the Aryans who crowded into the boats headed towards the Persian Gulf and Sumer were not seafarers. They were frightened, gentle souls, certain that the winds would tear their boats apart and the ocean would open its depths to swallow them. And then at times, even the song, 'Onward, Noble Arya . . . ' failed to soothe them.

Shipwrecks did take place since the boats were being hastily built in order to meet the large demand. Suddenly, however, all sea-faring activity stopped as the naudhyaksa of the lower Sindhu intervened, demanding that no boat leave,

BHAGWAN S. GIDWANI

until he and his men had inspected it fully.

Karkarta Sauvira himself rushed to the scene. The 'unfeeling' retort attributed by a poet to Naudhyaksa was:

'I care not how many "faithfuls" drown
But how dare they drag my sea-men down!'

Nandan's great-grandson, later, also refers to this, not so much to show that the naudhyaksa was concerned only for the safety of his sailors, and not the Aryans who drowned, but mainly to show how considerate Karkarta Sauvira was, to bring in hundreds of men to assist with building the boats.

Most Aryans waiting to be transported to the Persian Gulf and Sumer were also roped into repairing and building the vessels. Many 'unfeeling' lines have been attributed to the naudhyaksa, but he was not always caustic. He and his men would often sit with the Aryans and explain the finer points of building boats to them. He also demanded that each Aryan—man, woman and child—learn to be a better swimmer. He concentrated on the children, saying, 'Adults have lived long enough, so it does not matter if they drown, though they too should learn to swim if only to save their children, should the need arise, and then they can drown in peace.'

The naudhyaksa also 'persuaded' some Aryans, who became proficient as builders, to stay back. When Karkarta Sauvira's men warned him that the karkarta was against keeping back Aryans, he scoffed at them. 'Impossible! Don't forget, he is the grandson of Karkarta Nandan who helped us to build bigger, better ships. He is the son of Karkarta Sharat whose elder brother was an illustrious naudhyaksa who toiled and died to make a ship of 108 oars a reality, and at whose feet I learnt my craft. You dare tell me that Karkarta Sauvira is forgetful of his ancestry—and so unenlightened—as to object! Nonsense! You insult your karkarta! And you insult the memory of his ancestors!'

The karkarta heard this statement and never objected again.

By and large, however, the 'herd instinct' prevailed, for when asked, 'Why do you desert us cruelly at this moment of parting?' by their fellow Aryans, though most of the Aryan shipbuilders delayed their departure, eventually, they, too, left.

Steadily, one after another, groups of Aryans reached the coast of Sumer. They moved deeper inland, coming across many people and settlements. Later, some Aryan groups would even mix and mingle with the other groups which had reached Iran with Purus.

The Aryans took many routes to the north and east, but not all of them are known. Their paths often criss-crossed, sometimes joining other groups, sometimes separating. At times, groups and even individuals refused to go on, some staying back, and others returning.

However, the major routes to the east were through the Land of Brahma—modern-day Burma—governed by an autonomous chief under the sovereignty of Gangapati XIV. The treks led through modern-day Bangladesh, Assam and Manipur, and thence to upper Burma, from where the Aryan groups moved southwards to Malaya and Sindpur (Singapore), and thereafter to Bali and Sumatra by boat. At Bali, the Aryans would build the first Hindu temple, and later at Sindpur and Cambodia.

Gangapati had also organized boats, just as Karkarta Sauvira had done from the Sindhu Sammundar. Aryan groups worked day and night to build more boats at the Tamralipti port and at ports on the Orissa coast. The boats sailed along the coasts of Bengal and Burma and after crossing the Bay of Bengal reached Malaya, Sindpur, Hindu Chhaya (Indo-China) and Indonesia.

Among the routes to China was also the land route across

Avagana, over the Hindu Kush to Bactria, and thereafter through Central Asia to western China. Another route went through upper Burma to southwest China. Additionally, there were the sea routes from the coasts of Indo-China and through the East Indies islands.

The Aryans were not the first people from Bharat Varsha to arrive in China. Long before the Aryan movement began, a team from Bharat Varsha had visited China (known then as the Land of Kosa Karas). Rishi Skanda Dasa had established an ashram near the source of the Sindhu river in Tibet, which attracted a number of locals. One of them presented the rishi with a treasured possession—a cloth of soft, sleek silk. The rishi was told that the silk, brought by a traveller from the north, was made from the cocoons of domesticated worms. The traveller had been delighted to exchange the silk for the finest cotton made in the Sindhu region. The rishi sent the silk cloth to Karkarta Bharat, and from then on began a series of consultations between the guild of weavers and guild of merchants. The weavers' guild was content with the excellent cotton fibre and textiles they were producing in Bharat Varsha, but the merchants' guild decided to organize a team to travel north with the rishi's help. The team—composed of fifty-four locals from Tibet and six weavers from the Sindhu region—left for the Land of Kosa Karas.

After eight years, fifteen members of the team returned. With them, they brought a group of over 450 men, women and children fleeing the anarchy in the Land of Kosa Karas. They had harrowing tales to tell of the brutality, massacres and incessant warfare everywhere in that land. Yet, they spoke also of the gentleness and compassion of the many ordinary though powerless people. Although the team had failed to find areas in China which domesticated silkworms, its success lay in the fact that the group of 450 had brought large quantities of jade with them. Which was how the proverb—Look for a worm and a treasure you may find—originated, and was current even in Karkarta Sauvira's time.

Of the remaining forty-five members of the team, twenty-one were never heard from again, fourteen died during the journey, and ten decided to stay back in Kosa Karas. One of them, a weaver from Sindhu, took a wife from Kosa Karas. Unfortunately his refusal to accept the local custom according to which all childless women—sisters, cousins, aunts—in the family were considered 'married' to the new husband made him unpopular with his wife's family. He had heard about the custom before marriage, but thought it was a spiritual bond, not a 'body-bond'. It is not known if he resisted temptation or ultimately succumbed to it, but one thing is certain. He prayed to Skanda—the god of fertility—day and night, for a child to be born to his wife, so that she would not be 'married' to any new husband who entered the family fold. Skanda was apparently impressed with the man's prayers for his wife gave birth to twins—a boy and a girl—just two days before another husband joined the family.

Much about the weaver from Sindhu is well-known and is substantiated by many. But later, his story came to be wrapped in myths and miracles. He was credited to have sired eighteen children in eight years of marriage. That is not too difficult to believe, as he may have finally adopted the local custom of accepting all childless females in the family as married to him. But far greater myths about him were born in later centuries, not so much in Bharat Varsha but in Kosa Karas. He came to be known variously as the 'Lord of Grain' or the 'Lord of Millet and Wheat', or the 'Lord of Soil'. These titles of honour came to him not as a lord of the land, but simply as a cultural hero who taught agriculture to the locals. In Kosa Karas myth, he was known as the lord who sprang from below (the south) to tickle the soil of the earth and bring forth grains and fruit. His inventions included boats and oars, common in Bharat Varsha but not then in Kosa Karas. He also taught them how to breed domestic fowls. Finally, he retired to Tien Shan (the celestial mountains) where God Skanda was said to visit him occasionally.

Several portraits and statues of the Sindhu weaver appeared in Kosa Karas, depicting him in a heroic fashion. He was clearly shown as brown-skinned, with eyes and features which distinguished him from the Chinese race and identified him with the kind of statues found in the Sindhu–Saraswati civilization. Centuries later, for social and political reasons, the Chinese removed and modified the portraits and statues of this Bharat Varsha weaver, to show instead a legendary figure with Chinese features.

In Karkarta Nandan's time more teams—better equipped, armed and ably led—were sent to Kosa Karas. These teams found more jade and some precious stones and metals, but were unable to reach the region of silkworms.

Even though several teams were sent over a number of years, it was not as if the route to Kosa Karas or even to Tibet was well-frequented. Only hardy, intrepid travellers would venture on it. Yet the Aryan groups moved there and elsewhere too, fired by the spark of their faith that somehow their god would guide them to the enchanted land where he dwelled. If doubt sometimes crept into their minds, they took refuge in their exulting songs, and there were always singers and poets whose ballads were inspiring, to the point of rapture, reminding them that for those who tread on them in faith, all paths were without danger. Some of those songs referred to them as 'Aryan pilgrims of no land, but God's pilgrims to all lands, everywhere, with a purpose that is sacred and intent that is noble.'

Obviously, there were other routes that Aryan groups often deviated to, sometimes in faith, and sometimes in frustration. Many routes, however, would remain unknown. For instance, of a group of 120 Aryans in the middle of the Gobi Desert, only two survived. The survivors found shelter near a mountain which they called Hari Haran Mountain—Mount Hayrhan. Even this odd incursion, outside any known route, would have gone unreported, except that one of the survivors, a poet, wished to recite the prayer of an Aryan who died in the Gobi Desert.

> *God! Bring me not back as I was*
> *Let me come as a blade of grass*
> *Or a droplet of dew and rain*
> *So this waterless desert blooms again . . .*

The poet went on for 400 more lines to speak of the blessing of the dying man so that the waterless Gobi Desert might bloom again.

THIRTY-FIVE

ARYANS OF BHARAT VARSHA
IN IRAN

5005 BCE

With the distortion of time and memory, some poets have been tempted to go to extraordinary lengths to depict Aryans as warlike, vigorous, courageous, enterprising, overflowing with all the lusty emotions and desires of life, and fired with the passion to explore and discover the world. With superb rhythm, imagery and narrative force, poets have recited not only some of the exploits of Aryans, but even speak of a well-coordinated organizational plan, for how else could they have travelled from so many points, on different routes, to reach so many destinations?

However, there was no aim to discover the world, or to seek adventure. The Aryans left in search of an elusive purity, the Land of the Pure. The assassination of Sindhu Putra had left a scar, but not all were influenced only by that. The feeling went far beyond and affected even those not emotionally involved with Sindhu Putra. They saw decay around themselves and the failure of the land of their birth to protect them from the evil that was growing rapidly. Somewhere else, they felt, a moral order existed, and that was where they had to go.

A well-coordinated organizational plan? True, the Aryan groups moved out from many points. But it had to be so. Obviously, it was impossible to cover the vast distances from one end of Bharat Varsha to another in order to congregate at a single departure point. The varied routes they took—some over land, others over water—were determined often by the point of departure. So where was the question of a well-coordinated plan? They did not choose the path they had to tread. It was simply their faith that led them.

The migration and movement of Aryans from Bharat Varsha continued. They were unaware of shipwrecks, disasters and sudden deaths that overtook their compatriots in foreign lands.

Many who had reached Sumer and Iran would stay there, their feet weary and their hearts heavy with hopelessness, certain they would never find the land of the pure. But many more, fired with faith, went on in different directions, on different routes, and found themselves in faraway lands.

Much of the land through which Purus and his group of Aryans passed from Avagana was unoccupied. Their first contact was with a settlement of people, working under warlords and bandits with the power of life and death over whoever was around them. Possibly, the bandit chiefs could have easily wiped out the largely unarmed Aryan groups when they were first seen. But their sheer numbers were frightening, and the local bandits could never imagine that such a large 'army' came on a peaceful errand. Maybe, the initial approach of the first Aryan band would have convinced them of the peaceful intent of the newcomers. But the local warlord did not wait for that first approach. He did what he had always done whenever a large army came into view. Drumbeats sounded, gongs were struck and the inhabitants of the village were driven out to the hills before the Aryans could reach the settlement.

Three young men, three naked women, and twelve dogs and cats were left, tied and bound, in the village. This was the usual 'peace offering' the bandits left whenever fleeing from a large army in the hope that they would not be pursued or dealt with severely if caught. It was simply a tribute to a conquering force, an acceptance of temporary sovereignty. The six men and women were intended for slavery and the lustful enjoyment of the newcomers, the dogs and cats for their eating pleasure.

From a distance, the Aryans saw the villagers fleeing. It then occurred to them that their walking staffs—and the arrows and swords that some of them carried—had frightened the locals. They shouted reassuring words and even ran to tell them that they came in friendship, but this frightened the bandit chief and his men even more, and they cracked their whips to drive their 'human cattle' faster to the hills.

The Aryans freed the twelve cats and dogs and the six men and women. Their words were foreign, but a common language was not needed to understand their fright and suffering.

Perhaps the first frightening thought that ran through the minds of these six released persons was: 'why are they letting animals go free—are they amongst those bandits that eat only human flesh?'

Purus, the Aryan commander, was not from slave stock. His father was a hermit in the forests of Varanasi, who had been disappointed with Sindhu Putra's inability to offer enlightenment on the mystery and identity of the Universal Spirit. He was even more disappointed with his son Purus, who did not believe in God, but only in goodness. Later, Purus had taken to wandering, but not like an ascetic or a sadhu. He enjoyed a dice game and an occasional draught of soma. He was proficient in yoga, yet he practised it not for spiritual release but for relaxation.

In his wanderings, Purus had visited the Rocks where Sindhu Putra resided, more out of curiosity than faith. And despite what many said, he could not believe that Sindhu Putra was a god. To him, Sindhu Putra appeared simply as a lonely individual, surrounded by many in faith, and by some who were scoundrels. He did not see in Sindhu Putra the glow of inner peace which a god, or even a man of god, ought to have in himself. It was as if Sindhu Putra had lost control over events and wondered if what others did in his name was the right course of action.

Purus, then, had taken up residence beside the Saraswati river. He acquired barges to transport soma wine for sale—'sacred wine on a sacred river'. And in the midst of his lucrative business, he thought no more of Sindhu Putra. But the sudden news of Sindhu Putra's assassination struck him like a shattering blow. That night he tried to drown his despair in soma, and when that failed to comfort him he followed it up with the cheaper but stronger sura liquor. Soon after, Purus dedicated himself to the cause of the Aryans and led the first Aryan contingent to Iran through Avagana. Many wondered why and how this pleasure-loving man, with no affiliation to Sindhu Putra, had joined the cause after his assassination, but some said, 'Perhaps it occurred to him anew, that gods are many, and men who proclaim God's name, many more, but men of goodness are few, and the assassination of a man of goodness diminishes us all.'

Maybe, it was the association of men like Purus with the Aryans which suggested to some that the Aryans were intent on conquest and discovery. Certainly, they said, he was not searching for a god, or the Land of the Pure. The defining moment for Purus came in Iran when he saw the six unfortunates left as slaves by the bandit lord. He realized, with even greater force, that it was futile to search here or anywhere for gods or for the Land of the Pure. 'They are all hidden by heavenly smoke,' he said. 'But it is necessary that as far as man can, he should strive for goodness to make his land pure, fit for the gods to enter.'

'Goodness comes first to the land by man's effort and then only do gods enter,' Purus claimed. 'And gods come not to do man's work, but to bless him, and they depart in sorrow if man ceases his work.'

If his thinking was obscure, his orders at least were clear, as he saw the anguish of the six people left behind as slaves. 'Wherever we go, we shall drive out the bandit lords and set their slaves free.'

Most of their men could look into their own past and easily relate to this order. But some demurred. 'Surely this was not our mission!' Purus was silent, but others answered for him, 'If our goal is to reach a god, and god asks what we did on the way, shall we say that we paused not to do god's work!' Purus merely nodded, for he was not a godly man. Some reported that he had made his Aryan group carry eight barrels from Bharat Varsha, saying that they contained water from the Ganga, Saraswati, Sindhu and five other sacred rivers, and that his men guarded the barrels with their life through steep ascents and treacherous gorges en route, when in fact the barrels contained soma. When the truth was finally revealed, Purus cried out, 'It is god's work, turning water into wine!'

Wayward Purus may have been in regard to his belief in gods, but he became single-minded in his aim to free slaves. The six 'slaves' left by the bandit chief now insisted on joining the Aryans. Guided by them, Purus and his group saw to the release of many along the way. Soon, Purus realized that the task he had undertaken was not to be treated lightly, for the bandits often fought back or attacked them later. Purus had the advantage of numbers with him, but his people lacked the spirit of violence and the skills of warfare. To remedy that, he engaged in battle-exercises to teach his men to fight. The Aryans made arrows, swords, slingshots and poles with sharp, pointed ends, and learnt to wield them all with skill, and to scale up and down trees, and to move in silence to take the oppressor unawares.

The Aryan groups swelled. More and more were reaching from Avagana. The slaves freed by the Aryans in Iran were joining them, afraid to remain in their old settlements for fear of bandits returning to wreak vengeance.

But this degradation was not spread over the whole land. Society, though divided largely between a vast number of slaves and a few bandit chiefs, had men of learning too— mostly ascetics—whom the bandits were afraid to hurt. Those who harmed ascetics were cursed to burn in hell and their descendants would become slaves. And as if that was not enough, the curse also fell on those who associated with such persons and so anyone who hurt an ascetic was treated as an outcaste by his associates, lest the curse affect them too, and thus isolated.

Inspired, Purus began to woo ascetics and build villages around them. The villagers were declared 'disciples' to discourage bandits from attacking them. The locals living there were trained to defend themselves and were named Aryans, so the bandits would know that Aryan groups would seek revenge if the locals were harmed.

Purus set up Aryan camps in coastal regions outside the mountain ring. In these settlements, Iran witnessed for the first time the development of settled village agricultural life. The domestication of animals and plants started, along with tool-making and a shift to sophisticated farming at a number of places including modern-day Asiab, Ali Kosh, Ganj-e-Dareh, Guran, Tepe Sabz, Sialk, Yahya, Godin and Hajji Firuz.

Villages in these new settlements followed a simple rectangular pattern devised by Aryan groups. High walls with towers at corners formed the outer face of houses, which had flat roofs of mud and straw supported by wood rafters. Cattle and fowl were herded inside the walls. It was a far cry from the aesthetic villages of Bharat Varsha, but even there in earlier centuries, the beginnings had been equally modest. In the centre of the walled village would be the best hut, often unoccupied, meant to house the ascetic, who was usually found in the forest under a tree or on a rock. Still, an attack on the settlement was regarded as an attack against his person.

Purus regularly sent teams to visit and check on the Aryan settlements and made sure that the bandits guilty of violating them were punished. He also organized teams along the routes to look after new groups arriving from Avagana and those moving from Iran to Sumer and the Persian Gulf.

Eventually, Purus married a wild girl of the forest. She was supposed be the daughter of an ascetic. When she was three years old, she had been abducted along with her father, mother and several other families by a team of bandits. Normally bandits had no use for children, but this chief was merciful and allowed the mother to keep the child, leaving it to the mother's buyer to decide the child's fate. The abducted group was being driven to a faraway land where they would be sold, when another group of bandits attacked them. The mother saw her chance and ran with the girl towards a clump of trees. As she was fleeing, an arrow struck her, but she still kept running, carrying the child. She fell in the forest and died. Three days later, a wandering ascetic found the little girl. She could tell him little about her people or the town. All that the ascetic could discern was that her people came somewhere from the vast plains of 'Oxus and Jaxartes'. He took the girl along, hoping to leave her with some family on the way. Several months went by before the ascetic finally found a family willing to take in the girl.

Next morning, the ascetic went on his way, happy to be relieved of his burden. When he entered the forest, somehow the darkness around him brought gloom to his heart. He had always been a wanderer, but never before had he faced loneliness. Now it came to him like a great stirring from within. He sat under a tree wondering at this strange, despairing emotion. He opened his eyes a long time later on hearing sounds nearby. The forest, he knew, had no large beasts, only deer, gazelles, foxes, wolves and lynx, and their proximity did not bother him. Nor was he afraid of bandits, who never harmed an ascetic. But what he saw was people from the settlement searching for the little girl he had left with them. The girl, it seemed, had fled to follow the ascetic into the forest.

The ascetic was now frantic with worry. All his life's indifference to human companionship was washed away in a single moment. Passionately, desperately, he wanted to find the child and keep her with him. For two days, the girl could not be found. The people from the settlement went back. The ascetic searched desperately, the agony was like a physical pain in his heart.

It was on the third night that he found the girl, sleeping under a tree. She opened her eyes, unsurprised, as if she was expecting him to come, and asked, 'Did you miss me?' Silently, the ascetic gathered her in his arms and turned towards the settlement, but the child pointed in the opposite direction. He understood and promised, 'I shall never leave you again.' She had fever and he wanted her to rest. Later, after she was rested and well, they both left through the forest.

The ascetic's passion for wandering had ended. It was more from habit that he kept moving. At last, he settled down in a forest with his 'daughter', in Iran. The girl was fifteen years old when the Aryan groups arrived. People told the newcomers about the girl, saying, 'She never walks the earth, and is always swinging from one tree to another, afraid of neither man nor beast.'

It was two years after Purus came to Iran, that he saw her or perhaps it was she who saw him first. Purus, along with six companions, had been ambushed by a large group of bandits intent on revenge. An arrow was embedded deep in his leg, and several others had struck his horse. In a frenzy of pain the horse, with Purus still in the saddle, bolted headlong into the forest until it got caught in a maze of thorny, prickly shrubs. Without warning, the horse suddenly reared up, its forelegs high in the air. Purus fell on the ground, striking his head against a tree.

It was the girl who saw him, unconscious. Swinging from tree to tree, she gathered some fruit and sprinkled their juice over his face. From the broad-leafed evergreens, she selected leaves to press on his bleeding head. With the threadlike tree vines, she tied up his leg at two places and carefully took out the arrow. She applied pressure to the wound to stop the flow of blood and then bandaged the wound. She summoned her father, and together they carried Purus to their shelter. Soon they found the injured horse, and tended to it as well. The horse recovered before Purus did.

Later, some Aryans said that the wound on Purus's head must have been severe, for he asked the ascetic for his daughter's hand without asking the marriage-customs of her family. They knew that marriage-customs varied wildly, even widely, with sometimes a wife married to more than one husband. For instance, five or six brothers, or even friends, would pool together to get a single wife to serve them all. Nor was there a bar to someone buying a wife or husband. But Purus asked no questions. He was determined to marry her. All he asked was her name. 'She has no name,' the ascetic said. 'I have always called her "my princess" and she will be your queen for life.'

The wild girl was now shy, fully dressed, her face scrubbed, her hair groomed, no longer wishing to swing from trees. They were married with the ascetic's simple words, 'You are now husband to my daughter, unborn to me, but my child always, and she is now your wife and queen for ever.'

Even so, the Aryans lit the sacred fire and Purus and his 'queen' went round it, with offerings of grain and flowers. Many animals watched from a distance and would have come nearer, but for the sacred fire that was burning brightly. The Aryans came to love this once-wild girl. It did not take her too long to learn the language of Bharat Varsha. For the older women, she brought, from the forest, wild fruits, flowers and scents unlike any others—roses from which she made an enticing perfume. For the young, she made a delicate, subtle perfume from a combination of many flowers, mixed largely with berberis—a prickly stemmed shrub with yellow flowers. Women, young and old, clustered round her. The men were impressed with her ability to ride and throw javelins accurately, but rarely did she show off. She reserved her skill for moments of peril. And when those moments passed, she spoke of the bravery of others. For her, it was enough that her husband loved her. She sought no more.

Yet, praise her they did and so she said to Purus, 'They love you so much that they praise even your wife!'

He laughed, and said, 'I love them too but I don't go about praising their wives.'

And with mock-jealousy she retorted, 'Don't you ever dare praise their wives!'

She was even more popular with Aryan vaids, for she found for them almost all the herbal remedies they were seeking and many more they knew nothing about.

She still had no name. The Aryans simply called her 'Purus's queen', or sometimes just 'Queen', as Purus himself called her. Centuries later, this title of 'Queen', given to her out of love, would mystify many.

Purus died, tragically, twelve years after his marriage. After his death, his wife took on many of his duties, including leading the Aryans in Iran and even supervising their movements to other lands. She did not remarry. She and her son and two daughters from Purus remained in Iran, though most of the Aryans and many locals—tied by bonds of marriage, love or friendship, or inspired by curiosity and the spirit of adventure—went to Bharat Varsha.

Centuries later, someone supposed to be either the forty-eighth or eighty-fourth or even a later descendant of this

'Queen' and Purus, is believed to have said: 'My ancestress was the first Queen of Persia, whose cradle-land was the plain of Oxus and Jaxartes. A sage, who foresaw her great and glorious destiny, travelled far to bring her to Persia when she was just three years old, and trained her in all the arts. When the sage was old and could teach no more, he got her married to a valiant commander of the Aryan armies from the east, who was fated to live for twelve years more. Later, she herself trained armies of her own, permitting the eastern armies to go back home, but many of them remained to witness the glory of the first and foremost Queen of Persia, whose reign was magnificent. And her glory and greatness is ever revealed in the traditional memory of the people and in the Sacred Leaves.'

No one knows how reliable this statement is of the descendant of the little girl who came from the vast plains of Oxus and Jaxartes, and who later married the Aryan commander Purus. Particularly curious is the reference to the Sacred Leaves. There is no such record in any sacred book of Bharat Varsha. Nor could the reference be to Avesta, the pre-Islamic, Zoroastrian holy book of Iran (and of Parsis in India). The Avesta was composed long centuries after the 'Queen of Persia' purportedly existed, and even this particular descendant may not have been around at the time of its composition. In any case, there is no reference in the Avesta to this 'Queen of Persia'. However, only the fourth part of the original Avesta was saved after the Arab conquest of Iran in the seventh century; the rest of it was burnt by the conquerors in a frenzy to destroy books relating to the religion of the conquered race. So, it is not possible to check if this 'traditional memory' is documented in lost tracts of the Avesta. Certainly, there is no record of it in the Gathas—the hymns of Zoroaster—that survive.

Purus had become a man of caution in the years after his marriage. Gone were the days when he willingly courted danger. He concerned himself more and more with protecting Aryan groups, rather than rushing headlong into attacks to free slaves from bandits. Some said that he had assumed imperial airs after his marriage, for he travelled in a chariot or was carried on a chair. But this was because he was unable to run or ride until his leg healed completely, and yet he had to rush from place to place to inspect, defend his people and organize counterattacks against the bandits. Rarely did Purus make frontal assaults on them, simply frightening them into fleeing by a show of strength.

With the arrival of more Aryans and many locals joining Purus, the Aryan settlements outside the mountain ring grew. The largest Aryan camp was set up at Bhakti Gaon—modern-day Bakhtegan—at Daryanchen-je Lake. Another large camp was established at Hari—south of modern Tehran. The largest number of camps, however, was established in the Hara region. After Purus's death, it came to be known as the Purus region, or as later Assyrian records show, Parsumash or Purusmath. Presently it is known as the Parsa or Fars province of Iran. The ruling dynasty of Persians settled here after the Medes were overthrown in 550 BCE.

Purus had also insisted on drill, discipline and even showmanship. His Aryan groups would move with banners, as though always on the march, fearing no opposition and assured of victory should anyone attack. He chose four banners for his people: a white flag for men of the mouth—singers, marching ahead with their songs to keep everyone's spirits up, route-finders, and scouts; a green flag for men of arms—fighters and warriors; a red flag for the people of the breast—women not trained for fighting, children, the old and infirm; and a blue flag for people of hands and feet—artisans, peasants, workers, artists, food-gatherers, untrained for war, but expected to protect those bearing the red flag if the need arose.

The banners and flags were, somewhat, for show, but their movements were also to signal danger and summon help, when the columns were at a distance. Normally though, bearers of the white flags would march ahead while those of the green flags formed an outer ring with the red and blue flag bearers inside the protected ring. However, in case of danger, the white flags, too, could seek refuge within the protective ring.

There are those who have tried to see a common link between this fourfold colour classification of Purus and the caste system which came to distort Hindu society, some thousands of years later, in the post-Vedic modern era. But there is no connection at all. This foolish misunderstanding arose as there is no word or phrase in the ancient Indian Sanskrit language for caste. But that is so, because the caste system is not at all a basic tenet of Hinduism and was devised later, and made all the more rigid, with the emergence of foreigners in India.

Purus's classification of people and his identification of them with different flag colours was simply for the purpose of attack, defence, protection and to ensure that those joining the march, on the way, would know which formation to join and thus avoid a disorderly scramble for a place in the 'army'. Besides, the man leading people from one settlement to another, or to chart a new area, had to know at a glance how many fighters he had and how many he had to protect, which in turn determined his movements and route. But there never was a question of who was lower or higher than another.

～

Purus had been ambushed by bandits. He had foolishly rushed off with only three others when a local complained that his wife had been molested by an outsider. All four men were killed. While the bodies of the three men were left as they were, Purus's body was butchered and the parts thrown along the wayside for the vultures.

Enraged, Purus's wife moved swiftly with armies of locals to hunt down the killers, wreaking brutal vengeance on those responsible for the death of her husband. To the Aryans of Bharat Varsha she said, 'This vengeance is ours.' But they said, 'Purus was ours before he was yours and for ever now, yours and ours,' and they, too, moved against the bandits under her banner. Purus's wife caught the murderers, but her attack did not end there. She hunted even those bandits who posed no threat to Aryan settlements. Summarily, they were hanged, along with their followers and families, and their bodies thrown to vultures.

Her ascetic father, old and emaciated, came to accuse her, 'This was not your husband's way! He taught love, mercy and understanding! Vultures devoured his flesh, but by your actions you deny him his soul everlasting! And you defile his memory!' She wept and stopped her tempestuous reprisals.

She would shed more tears later at her father's deathbed, for he had declared it his wish that his dead body be left, unburied, for vultures and animals to devour, as the dead body of Purus was. 'Let it be my salute to him, to go the same way, and be it also a symbol of my offerings to birds and animals, from whom so much mankind takes!'

When he died, the Aryans built a fire for cremation, and the locals dug a grave, but the ascetic's will was carried out. The fire remained burning, the grave remained empty. But even after a day, the body was untouched, for the ascetic's old dog kept the vultures away. The dog was bleeding, half-blinded from its skirmishes with the vultures, and had to be forcibly taken away. Later, locals buried the remains of the ascetic's bones. The dog died a few days after his master. He refused food; even the ascetic's daughter whom the animal loved could not coax him to eat for he kept growling at her. In the end, he dragged himself to her, licked her hand and died.

Purus's wife declared that, on her death, her body too must be left to animals and vultures. Inspired by the ascetic, and 'in memory of Purus', even before her death, this custom caught on in Iran among the locals. To an extent, it inspires the customs of the Parsi community in India.

∾

Purus's wife remained in overall command of the Aryans. Her later history is surrounded by mystery, particularly after most Aryans returned to their land. Many do believe that she led the contingents of locals who called themselves Aryans and a few of the original groups who chose to remain behind in Iran. With their help, she eventually became the queen of Iran, which eventually came to be known as Persia, thus maintaining its link with Purus. Though, in modern times, it has reverted to its earlier name—Iran—to mark its link with Aryans.

Although the Aryans did not remain in Iran for long, their influence was considerable. This is especially noticeable in the Iranian language—Persian art and culture. However, the Aryans' influence on the spiritual philosophy of Iran was limited. Clearly, the sages of the Ganga, Sindhu, and Dravidham held that the scheme of salvation was not restricted to those who held a particular view of God's nature and worship. To them such absolutism would be inconsistent with an all-loving, universal God. 'There are none that are chosen of God and God is denied to no one, for what counts is conduct, not creed.' How was it then that the Aryans from Bharat Varsha failed to leave the foundation for their belief that God's gracious purpose included all aspirants irrespective of their creed, and even non-aspirants without a creed? The fact was that these simple Aryans had no sages, philosophers or even poets among them. They had travelled across great distances, some in fear of persecution, others fired by faith in their personal god, to lead them to the land of the pure. What spiritual legacy could they leave behind! Even Purus, who led the Aryan groups to Iran, was stirred by a sudden bond of sympathy with Aryans and not by the belief in any god or any spiritual philosophy.

In fact, sometimes the Aryans were actually responsible for creating false impressions that stayed with the people of Iran. The Aryan groups from Sumer narrated to Purus their sad tales of shipwrecks that had killed many on the way. According to them, they had prayed 'day and night to the god Indra, but the god did not listen, and the cruel sea swallowed them . . . ' Someone later asked Purus, 'Is the god Indra so unkind?' And Purus replied, 'Gods are capricious, maybe Indra is more capricious than others.'

These lighthearted words became etched in the memories of the people in Iran. Purus had reached such a commanding position that people spoke of him as they did of legendary heroes, and every word he uttered was remembered, repeated and retold. No wonder then that though the Iranians honoured many gods of Bharat Varsha, Indra was never highly rated. The Avesta of Zoroastrians, for instance, honours the god Mitra, but depicts Indra with some demonic qualities, perhaps as a result of Purus's lighthearted comment that remained in traditional Iranian memory for centuries before the Avesta was composed.

Nevertheless, the Aryans did not go out to impose their gods on others, or to leave behind a legacy of their spiritual belief, since their own tradition itself taught them respect for the beliefs and gods of others. They believed that whatever God one chose, he is that God and Dharma was His Will. As it is, Hinduism shunned dogma, encouraging intelligent thought, and was opposed to any persecution of heretics or any hostility whatsoever towards unbelievers or atheists.

THIRTY-SIX

ARYANS OF BHARAT VARSHA IN IRAQ

5005 BCE

Several Aryan contingents reached the coastline of the Persian Gulf by boat and thence went to Sumer, flanked by the Euphrates and Tigris rivers. Others travelled from Iran, along the Zagros range through the rugged, forbidding ridges and narrow gorges into the plains of Sumer.

Here, the Aryans did not face the kind of problems they had in Iran. The land had no organized bandits or robbers. But they had something worse—priests who ruled the land and people. The priest's authority was total in each area. People could not leave their area to reside elsewhere, unless the priests of both areas agreed and appropriate payments were made. The priest had no army to enforce his will. He did not need it; his word was law. At his bidding, everyone would obey and the offender would be stripped, strangled or hanged, whatever the priest willed. While the priests prospered, for the rest, there was widespread poverty, over-reliance on hunting, and death—often by starvation and animal attacks. The priest was entitled to a portion of the hunt, produce and goods made by artisans and it was for him to determine his portion. On the death of an individual, all his worldly possessions were supposed to belong to the gods and thus went to the priest, who would determine if a part of those goods be given to the deceased's family. Priesthood was hereditary. On the priest's death, his eldest son succeeded him, though occasionally a priest would divide the area so as to favour his other sons as well.

Before the Aryans reached a village in Sumer, they met a few individuals who had fled from their priests' tyranny. These unfortunate people were outside the pale of law. Everyone was encouraged to hunt down such renegades, and no one could have social contact with them.

From these outcasts, the Aryans understood the power of the priests, though the language barrier often led to exaggerated gestures and signs.

Yet, when the Aryans reached the first village, they thought that their fears had been baseless. The priest welcomed them with delight. The land was vast, but people were few, and the power and prestige of the priest depended on the number of people under him. From a gestured conversation with the Aryans, the priest realized that many of them were hardworking and skilled and he pointed to his vast land as if to say, 'All this land is yours, make of it what you will.' Some Aryans he sent back, with instructions to guide any more arriving Aryans to his own area.

The task assigned to the first Aryan group was to raise an artificial mountain—a ziggurat. The ziggurat was a pile of towers, each a little smaller than the one on which it rested, and the effect from a distance was that of a stepped pyramid. The topmost tower had a small room with a large comfortable bed, perfumed incense and a platform outside the room.

Each priest wanted his ziggurat to be the largest and highest.

To the Aryans, it seemed like a miniature temple built along the lines of Mount Meru, which in the Hindu mind was conceived as the mythical seat of the gods. They went about the task of building the ziggurat with enthusiasm. It was to be their pride and delight. The gratified priest gave the Aryans every encouragement and saw to it that everyone in the area brought food for them.

The Aryans saw poverty, even starvation, among the people around them. Though at first glance they often found unhappiness, people laughed, joked and even made merry, certain that their time for 'great happiness in the great beyond' was to come. They believed it was simply their fate to suffer in their life on earth, and at death they would rise to their starlit heaven. They were the fallen angels who had sinned and been sent to earth to suffer and as long as they obeyed God's commands on earth, conveyed to them by the priest, they would, in the end, return to their heavenly homeland. Meanwhile on earth, God's commands were stern, pitiless, demanding and dire, and yet they had to be obeyed without question or qualm, irrespective of personal or family feeling, for such commands were made only to test if they should go back as a bright or a dull star, or a star that is shot with deadly lightning that sends them back not to land, but into the bowels of the earth where there were no priests and therefore no way to reach heaven. To them heaven was filled with human beings who had turned into stars, with six thousand gods above them all, who appeared on earth in the garb of priests.

The multiplicity of gods never bothered the Aryans. They, too, believed that gods could appear in human shape though those gods, in the Aryan mind, were simply markers to show the way to the One-Supreme. What they found peculiar, however, was the belief that sorrows and sufferings were the result of fate and that there was nothing that men could do to alter their destiny. The locals had no room for human will in their principles, and felt that by total surrender to fate and the commands of the priests, their lives would be freed of impurities. The Aryan belief in karma, on the other hand, was different. One's karma in a previous life determined one's social standing, fortune, happiness or misery at the beginning of this life, but karma certainly excluded fatalism and man could exercise free will and rise above his condition to 'raise self by self', and not be a pawn of fate. By his own effort, it was open to man to transform his weakness into strength and his ignorance into illumination. The Aryans could not believe that life simply provided an unfolding of a passive, prearranged plan and total slavery to the whims of a priest! Surely, each individual had opportunities to strive until he realized the divine destiny of salvation for which he was intended! It was after all their belief in karma that had tempted the Aryans to take destiny into their own hands and go in search of a better land. Besides, they believed that God was not only a Universal Spirit but also a personal being, full of love for his creations, and such a loving, just God would not make the kinds of demands that the priests made on their helpless people, nor consign His creations to the torments of hell eternal.

However, despising another's faith was to despise the people themselves, and the Aryans had come to love these simple people who shared everything they had and were cheerful despite their adversity. Yet, slowly, sullenness entered the Aryan soul as they saw the pitiable conditions that people lived in. Their first sense of horror came when the priest's wife gave birth to a son. It was a day of celebration. But a baby born at the same time to another woman in the village was crushed to death, lest its destiny should rob the priest's son of his. Messages were also sent to priests of other areas to kill babies born at the same time. All priests were honour-bound to comply.

What happens if a priest's wife had twins? Would not one rob the other of his destiny? asked the Aryans. 'Of course,' was the answer. 'If the twins are a boy and a girl, the girl will be killed. If both are boys, the one who appears weaker will be killed. In any case one of the two has to be killed.'

The second shock to the Aryans came when they learnt that the ziggurat on which they were working was a different kind of temple. At death, the body of a person was to be taken to the platform of the topmost tower and kept there for two days, so that the gods may view it from heaven and assign the right kind of star. The priest would also ascend the ziggurat while the dead body was there, with a virgin chosen from amongst the people. But the 'virgin' could also be the wife of another, for apparently being chosen by the priest cleansed her of all prior sex and she came forth chaste, undefiled, shining, like a child of God, and ready for deflowering by a god. Below, another 'virgin-in-waiting' selected by the priest would be ready, just in case he needed another. After two days, the priest would send the dead body down, as by then its soul was supposed to have ascended the right star. The body would then be used as bait to trap animals.

All this, the Aryans heard second-hand. It was happening at another ziggurat far away from the one they were building.

More Aryans arrived, many of whom were from Iran and they reported that Iran was infested by bandits. And the cheerless thought in the minds of those who had been in Sumer for a while was that this land was corrupted as well. The only difference was that a bandit robbed people at sword-point, while the priests were robbing their people by instilling terror in their souls.

And the Aryans wondered: where was the Land of the Pure then? Where had all their wandering led them! To what useless, senseless inconsequence!

But the greatest shock was yet to come. News came to the priest that someone had died. He gave instructions for the body to be bathed before being taken to the ziggurat. He immediately selected a woman from his people as the 'virgin' to follow him. She was married and even had two children but the benediction 'cleansed' her. The priest was about to leave when, suddenly, the desire to taste fresh flesh came over him. He pointed to an Aryan girl, thirteen years old.

She understood nothing when the priest pointed at her and simply smiled in response. But an older Aryan understood and shouted, 'No!' He shielded the girl behind him. Other Aryans came forward and stood beside him, frozen with fear. Their numbers were large and if they were to put up a fight, there was little the priest could do, yet fear of the priest held them back.

The priest regarded himself as a kind, benevolent man, who had always been gracious to these newcomers. He was ready to forgive the foreign fool who had shouted at him. He even regretted his hasty decision to pick an Aryan 'virgin in waiting'. The girl was thin and hardly had breasts. But the decision was now unalterable, to change it would mean losing face, and doing so would cast its shadow on future relations with these newcomers who had to learn unquestioning obedience.

Quietly, the priest told his people to take the girl, but leave alone the foolish Aryan who had shielded her. This was well within their tradition—not to harm a madman.

The priest's men started walking towards the girl. They would have obeyed even if such an order was about one of their own children. Dhrav, one of the Aryans who had come from Iran after a brush with bandits, hastily took out his dagger. But old Sumaran, who had led the Aryans by the sea route and was regarded as leader of all the Aryans in this land, put up his hands in a placatory gesture.

Respectfully, he called out, 'Gracious lord priest! A moment please, for a word in your kind ear, if your lordship permits.'

'What is it?' the priest asked. Everyone stopped.

Sumaran walked up to the priest and bowed low, 'For your ears alone, gracious lord priest.'

The priest glared at his men and they moved far back, out of earshot. Sumaran spoke quietly, his attitude clearly humble, his face wearing the smile of a slave speaking to a great lord, 'Listen lord priest, and listen well. If anyone dares take our girl, I shall personally cut out your testicles with the chisel with which I carve figures on your ziggurat. And that goes for each member of your family. I swear it on your gods and mine.'

Never, even in his nightmares, had the priest heard anything resembling a threat—neither from gods nor from man. Fear gripped him. His eyes went to the chisel in Sumaran's hand. Yet how could he recall the order! He stammered, 'But I have already spoken!'

'So be it, lord priest,' Sumaran said. 'Let our girl be considered a virgin-in-waiting. We shall be the ones to bathe and dress her. You may make the announcement. But if you really send for her, I suggest you cut out your own testicles, as my method may not be as painless.'

At last the priest nodded. To his people, he announced, 'They beg to bathe and dress the virgin-in-waiting with holy water of their own gods brought by them to do greater honour to our gods. So be it.' If his voice trembled, obviously his men thought that it was in joy that Aryans should wish to honour the priest's gods.

Sumaran bowed to the priest and walked back. Dhrav, the Aryan from Iran, was waiting to stab Sumaran, for all he understood was that the girl was to be handed over to the priest. Instead of arguing with the hot-headed man brandishing a dagger, old Sumaran deftly twisted Dhrav's hand, hit his legs with his own and lifted him on his back. Dhrav's dagger fell to the ground, as did he. Quietly then Sumaran explained.

From a distance, the locals watched in dismay. Violence was alien to these gentle people. If they killed a man, it was only at the command of the priest, and they did it swiftly, with mercy and without anger. An animal, ready for the kill, was treated with gentleness; only a powerful man was permitted to kill a trapped animal and he was expected to slay it with one blow, so that the animal, unaware, would suffer neither fear nor pain. Large, trapped animals were often fed herbs mixed in their food, so as to dull the pain from the death blow. After the animal's death, the killer and others would bow and pray to the spirit of the departed animal. They were shocked to see Sumaran being threatened with a dagger and Dhrav lying on the ground, injured, while the rest of the Aryans shouted. But the priest explained, 'That young lunatic was against treating their own gods lower than our gods by bathing my virgin-in-waiting with holy water.'

The priest's explanation, they saw, was correct, for Dhrav was kneeling before Sumaran in obvious apology, and then being embraced by the older man. The fact that Sumaran would treat a madman with such affection raised him in their estimation. In their own belief too, a mad person was supposed to float in the higher reaches of god's angels. Moreover, the thought that their own gods were rated higher by the Aryans was heartwarming, though they were surprised, too. How could one god be lower or higher than another? Someone voiced the question timidly. 'Their gods are false gods,' their priest answered. 'They are devils!' This opened the floodgates of astonishment and against his better judgment, a local asked, 'But, my lord, they are working on our ziggurat!'

Contemptuously, the priest answered, 'You understand nothing! They are performing a penance. It is God's will!' Upon hearing that, the people's hearts went out to the Aryans. A sinner who repented was surely to be admired; how much these poor Aryans must have suffered under their false gods!

The priest went up his ziggurat. The local 'virgin' he had selected followed. The Aryan girl, perfumed and decked in flowers, waited below with the Aryans, but she was not summoned. Ignoring the virgin-in-waiting was common, for often the priest needed no one else to 'satisfy the gods'. But some locals began to speculate: perhaps, the priest did not want a girl who had once belonged to false gods until the penance by her people was complete. Their respect for their priest and their sympathy for the Aryans increased.

Two days later, when the priest descended from the ziggurat, Sumaran approached him, 'Gracious lord, we seek permission to leave.' True, the Aryans could leave without permission, for their numbers were large and the priest was powerless to stop them. But they might then be considered outside the pale of law. No priest anywhere in the land would give them passage, and none of the locals would speak to them. They would be hunted down wherever they went. So why go into an uncertain future, in an alien land, and invite an era of bloodshed!

The priest did not want these people in his village any more either. Clearly, he foresaw trouble and treason from such crude, coarse people who would dare to threaten his sacred, inviolable person. If they raised such a fuss over a plain girl with stunted breasts, how much would they fight if their property was threatened! And they would corrupt the attitude of his own people!

But there was something that the priest wanted more than his self-esteem, and he said, 'You behave as if you are a law unto yourself. Why don't you, then, go on your own without my permission?'

'We shall leave, with or without permission,' Sumaran said, 'though we prefer to go with your blessing.'

'My blessing has to be earned.'

'Ask what you will.'

'First, none of you shall speak of what we disussed the other day.'

'I promise,' Sumaran said.

'Second, you shall not serve any other priest.' Obviously the priest did not want these useful workers serving another area. Sumaran agreed. 'Third, you will not entice anyone from the area to follow you. Fourth, while you prepare to leave, you will speak to none of my people here, even if they address you.' Clearly, the priest did not want these foreigners corrupting his people. Sumaran nodded in agreement. Now the priest came to what was nearest to his heart. 'Finally, you will leave after the ziggurat is ready.'

Sumaran hesitated, 'That will take time.'

'I have time,' said the priest, ending the discussion.

The Aryans debated furiously. Dhrav said nothing, but others who had come from Iran favoured leaving immediately. 'We did not join the bandits there. Why do we need the blessing of this priest?'

Sumaran explained that the bandits in Iran terrorized people, but here the people were behind their priest. But the others argued, 'What can they do to us? They are not fighters!'

And Sumaran asked, 'Are we fighters? Is it to fight that we left our land?'

It was then that Dhrav spoke, 'If fight we must, fight we shall. One lives with the conditions that life offers.'

'Really! Then why did we not remain in Bharat Varsha to live within the conditions that life offered there?' Sumaran asked.

'We left to escape the unjust, and here you ask that we associate with the unjust! I say, we go!'

'Go where? From nowhere to nowhere! And leave a trail of blood wherever they find us!'

'It won't be our blood!'

'And their blood is cheap?'

Back and forth went the argument. At last no one had anything to say. In silence, they waited for Sumaran to give the decision. They knew he hated to decide when views were divided. Still, that was his task. Suddenly, with a flourish, Dhrav took out his dagger and said, 'Brother Sumaran, I may not be a great fighter against you, but I daresay I am a better builder. Will someone please accept my excellent dagger in exchange for a good hammer to work on the ziggurat?'

There was laughter; now the only question was whether work on the ziggurat would begin immediately or the next morning. They began that evening itself.

Fires were lit every night for work to press on. The priest assigned more locals to assist the Aryans. True to Sumaran's promise, the Aryans did not speak to the locals, who were dismayed by their silence. The priest explained, 'The Aryans are in the final phase of penance to complete the ziggurat during which they cannot speak to people of the true gods.'

Again, the people's hearts went out to the Aryans. How much more would these poor unfortunates have to endure to get away from their false gods!

The locals even prayed to their priest to ease the penance of the Aryans, but he was stern and said, 'The flaming wrath of our righteous gods is roused against their false gods who abominate the earth. Ask for no mercy, no charity for those who once served false gods, lest you too be defiled!'

The Aryans moved out after eleven months of back-breaking labour. The ziggurat, when complete, was the tallest pyramidal tower of Sumer. But there was no pride of achievement, no thrill of accomplishment.

Sumaran spoke for them all, 'I wish I could smash this ziggurat to bits. It is the tower of evil.' To Dhrav he said, 'You were right, sometimes, one lives within the conditions that life offers. We leave behind this monument of evil that will outlast you and me.'

Dhrav understood Sumaran's anguish, 'Evil would have remained, neither more nor less, whether we built this monument or not.'

'Yet, we left our land to be away from evil and here we participated in it!'

Dhrav did not respond but said, as if speaking to himself, 'Purus said to us in Iran—no one can flee evil by fleeing his land.'

They were silent. Each had a question in his heart. Each dreaded the answer.

The priest had told Sumaran about the lay of the land, and how to reach areas outside the control of any priest. Apparently there were many such areas—wild and barren. Nothing prevented a priest from extending his area, so long as it was unoccupied by another priest, but with a limited population and vast area, priests rarely ventured into lands that offered nothing but required great effort.

Some believed that the priest gave such information so that the Aryans would not serve another priest and make him great and strong. Others said it was to protect other priests from the corrupting Aryan influence.

The Aryans moved on and in the areas they crossed, they came to be known as 'Aryans of the Clay Tablet', for they carried a tablet of clay from the priest whom they left. First, the tablet permitted them to leave the priest's area and go elsewhere; second, it obliged all other priests to permit them to cross their land, unless the Aryans agreed to serve another priest, in which case the original priest would decide on the payment he was to receive; third, the Aryans could settle in areas unoccupied by a priest, though a priest could enter that land at any time, in which case the Aryans would either have to leave or serve the new priest, with a payment being made to the original priest; fourth, upon their death they would not be honoured with exposure on a ziggurat since that would abominate the true gods, but their bodies could serve as bait to trap animals, though those animals would be sacrificed to the gods; fifth, the Aryans would have to send to the original priest a share of their hunt, produce, and goods as decided by the priest; sixth . . .

The list went on. And so, the idea of this plain clay tablet, with a single graven image, was that the sovereignty of the original priest continued, and there was no place the Aryans could run to and hide forever.

Dhrav commented, 'Priests here are masterly in making laws. Do they know as much about their gods?'

'How can you know such laws and gods at the same time?' Sumaran countered. 'Laws were intended to subvert the gods and exploit the exploited.'

'Surely, there are God's laws too!'

'God is not a law giver. He wills a rich harmony, not a colourless uniformity. God does not decree one, single common creed. He demands no worship in any fixed form and excludes no one from His scheme of salvation. He is an all-loving, universal God, for Him every individual is worthy of reverence . . . '

'Brother Sumaran, you should have been a priest.'

'I was.'

Dhrav laughed, 'No wonder you could fool the priest here into giving the clay tablet. Truly, a priest alone can outwit another priest!' But then seriously, he asked, 'What made you leave Bharat Varsha?'

'My son and my wife.'

'Where are they?' Dhrav asked.

'My son died years before we left. He had joined Chief Jalta's command to free the slaves. He died the next day. My wife died when our ship was wrecked on our way to this land.'

Dhrav was silent. Yet there was a question in his eyes. Sumaran answered it, 'No we are not descended from slaves. I was a landowner and wanted to be a hermit, but my wife's brother, who was a council member, built a temple in my son's memory and I agreed to be its priest. When the cry came from some rya to be arya, my wife knew, and I knew, that our son wanted not a temple, but to protect the exploited. My wife demanded that we leave . . . I am still following her . . . '

~

In their long, tedious journey, the Aryans found some areas, though wild and barren, inhabited by people outside priestly control. These people had, among them, artists, singers and even hermits. Their day-to-day activity was to hunt and gather food that sustained everyone, including the weak, infirm and orphaned.

'Why do you not improve this land?' asked the Aryans.

'Because then the priests will come and take it over from us!' they countered. 'It is open to a priest to take over any non-priestly land. What do we do then? Serve the priest? Run elsewhere? No, let the land remain unattractive and unappealing to the priests.'

'Why do you not unite against the priests?'

'How do a few trees unite against a million locusts!'

Some hermits, the Aryans noticed, were immersed in calculating time and angles, while others focused on astronomy, the zodiac and its signs. A few were trying to evolve a method of writing through pictographs—an achievement that was just a step below the writing that had been developed in Bharat Varsha. Only a few Aryans, like Sumaran and Dhrav, were fully familiar with the art of writing. How artistic these Sumerians were, with their music, painting and sculpture! They made no idols, but figures of animals, birds, men and women with beautiful slender bodies and women suckling children. Local artists saw the seals that the Aryans carried and they made almost exact copies in clay, with every detail of the engraving clearly visible.

'Why don't we all go together,' the Aryans asked these locals, 'and settle where the land will hold us all?'

'Send for us when you find such a land,' they replied. 'But if you don't find it, come back and be with us.'

The Aryans went on.

Later, these locals would find asylum in areas where Aryans had settled.

Hindiya—modern-day Al Hindiya, south of Baghdad—

was the first place where the Aryans established their largest camp. The second largest Aryan camp was at Hari Nath—modern-day Hadithah. There were many other Aryan camps spread all over Mesopotamia, between Rama and Ramji on the Euphrates and the bend of the Tigris below Sumaran.

In these camps, the Aryans encouraged the locals to dyke rivers. In the south—dry and barren—they began artificial irrigation, bringing water to large stretches through a widely branching network of canals. The soil was fertile and with irrigation and proper drainage, it would soon become a land of plenty. Thus began concentration on agriculture rather than hunting, with tree-farming, cattle breeding, weaving, date-palm cultivation, reed utilization, and later even quarrying of limestone and marble.

With local help, Aryans built a huge granary with six chambers, each holding a different kind of grain and lentil. They even built a huge ziggurat, not as a house of evil for misuse by a priest, but as a real temple where people could pray. There was no platform for dead bodies and no priest at all. Strangely, many of the locals, through earlier persecution, had become atheists, whereas the Aryans who had fled their land after witnessing persecution had achieved greater faith. Yet the locals and Aryans delighted in this difference and it did not divide them. In art and aesthetics, in culture and philosophy, the Aryans had as much to teach as to learn from the locals. In fact, over time, they all came to call themselves Aryans.

Many stories would be told of how Sumaran—the Aryan leader—obtained more and more land for Aryans from the priests. Some praised what they considered his negotiating skills; others simply called it bribery. But the fact was that the priests were promised—and given—untold wealth from time to time if they left the Aryan areas undisturbed.

Though more and more locals joined the Aryans, it hardly bothered the priests, for their compensating revenue rose.

That they pocketed such payments, blatantly disregarding
the established practice of compensating the original priest,
was understandable when seen in terms of Sumaran's
explanation: 'There is no honour among priests.'

Sumaran would know. He had once been a priest himself.

BHAGWAN S. GIDWANI

THIRTY-SEVEN

ARYANS AND KINGS OF ASSYRIA

5005 BCE

The Aryans were still in Iran and Sumer. Many stayed back there, but more would leave for other regions.

And for every Aryan from Bharat Varsha who moved to new lands, there were at least five locals from Sumer and Iran who joined them. Perhaps the locals, too, came to accept the strange belief of these Aryans that, somehow, somewhere, there was a land that was good and pure. It seemed inconceivable that every land on God's earth should be full of fear, hate, turmoil and injustice—'God hides his land of glory. But why?'

Why! So that we accept the challenge of faith, to go out in search.

And locals from Iran and Sumer, who far outnumbered the Aryans of Bharat Varsha, marched to the tune of the same song,

'Onward, Noble Aryan, onward in joy,
Onward to the land where waits He;
Onward to the land, pure and free.'

There were many such songs, and each one proclaimed the noble aim of Aryans, their noble quest and pursuit, to seek a land that was pure and free. It was not just faith and fervour that these songs voiced. They led to new horizons and in turn, these horizons would lead to a new identity.

Soon, the word 'Aryan' lost its original meaning and acquired a new shine. At its origin, no doubt, Aryan meant non-people or exiles. But no more. The title Aryan itself became a badge of honour, a sign of quality—for to be an Aryan meant to be noble, for such was their quest. No longer did it indicate the degradation of the uprooted and dispossessed. Instead, it became a mark of nobility for these valiant men, who were ready to face howling winds and the heat of deserts and the numbing cold and deep snows of the mountains, in their search.

It did not, then, take too long for the word Aryan to be considered synonymous with the word 'noble'. Yet its limitations were also explained by Sumaran at Sumer, when an Aryan group was parting from him. 'Maybe it is best that you call yourself noble Aryan, for sometimes men will try to live up to their name and title. But remember! To be called Aryan or noble is not a personal honour . . . It demands that we act nobly. It imposes a duty, an obligation . . . it is a title not of arrogance but of humility, for we ventured out to seek God's glory not our own . . . '

From Iran, some Aryans moved along the Zagros range into Armenia. Others from Sumer and Iran travelled to many lands, including those which are now known as Egypt, Syria, Palestine, Israel and parts of Africa.

༄

It was Nilakantha of Bharat Varsha who led groups of Aryans, and large numbers of locals from Iran and Sumer, to Egypt.

Nilakantha had a powerful singing voice and a powerful physique, but he was as gentle as a lamb. Though he was popular, the most respected member in the entire group was the hermit-king, Lugal of Assyria.

Lugal was originally from Sumer. His father was a builder, but Lugal himself aspired to be a great architect and as a young man he had built the first ziggurat in Sumer which was sixty feet tall. Earlier ziggurats had been no more than twenty-four feet tall, with a single room on a stepped flat platform. But young Lugal was ambitious and careless, which almost proved to be his undoing. He had built his ziggurat with mud, mixed with straw and wood rafters. During a heavy rainstorm, the ziggurat fell while the priest and his virgin were there. Two bodies were found under the debris—the priest and the dead man whose body had been taken up on the ziggurat. Miraculously, the virgin was unhurt. The penalty for causing a priest's death—intentionally or otherwise—was terrible; the culprit had to die a slow death and was finally tied up as a live meal for rats, whose numbers were kept small so that the ordeal lasted longer.

Lugal fled to the forest. As he went deeper, he found he was not the only human there. A recluse was living under a crumbling mud shelter which no doubt had seen better days. Lugal kept his distance. He feared that his death penalty would apply equally to anyone who harboured him. Also, if the recluse ever had visitors, Lugal's own whereabouts would become known to the priests. He built a shelter for himself far away from the recluse, but his desire for human company remained. Often, he followed the recluse, who regularly visited the barren, rocky terrain, which rose beyond the forest. But the man did nothing there except watch the sky and shift the position of stones on the ground. When the rainy season came and the recluse did not emerge for days, Lugal began to fear that the man was sick and went to his shelter.

'Why did you take so long to come?' the recluse asked, much to Lugal's surprise.

Although the recluse did not show any curiosity, Lugal told him that he was under death penalty for killing a priest.

The old man simply said, 'It is not good to kill anyone, but if one is fated to kill, it is better to kill a priest than anyone else.'

There were strange words indeed from someone who was the only son of a priest and would have become one himself upon the death of his father! For that was who the recluse was. Yet, not so strange from a man whose priest–father had selected his loving son's wife as the virgin to take up to the ziggurat. In disgust, the son had abandoned his home and disappeared before his father and his wife descended from the ziggurat. He had been a raving lunatic for some time until he found peace in the forest as a recluse, watching the sun by day and the stars by night.

A close friendship developed between the recluse and Lugal, who wanted the older man to move to his own shelter, which kept the rains away. The recluse showed him openings, holes, cavities and cuts in his shelter, made so that he could watch the stars at night from various angles, and enjoy the play of sunlight during the day. Lugal studied them all. Four months later, he took the recluse to his shelter where he had duplicated every opening in the old man's shelter and had added many more, with shutters to close them fully or partly. From then on, the recluse stayed in Lugal's shelter and soon Lugal, too, got caught up in the fervour of watching the skies, day and night.

With age, the recluse got weaker and began to lose his sight. Lugal acted as his eyes and described the sky to him. But often the recluse knew without being told and would even correct Lugal's inaccurate observations.

The recluse started sinking into a depression. Forty years in the forest were taking their toll. He thought of his father and his wife, but it was no longer with bitterness. He thought of his people and wanted to die in their midst. He loved Lugal like a son, but that did not fill the recluse's loneliness.

But then many refugees, escaping from various priests, found sanctuary in the forest. Lugal assisted them in building shelters and they, in turn, gathered food for the recluse and Lugal. The recluse forgot about the sky, except to tell its stories to the children of refugees around him. Lugal continued watching the sky.

A nearby priest entered the forest to claim it as his own, and all its residents his subjects. None of them could have stopped the priest, but the recluse claimed that he, as a priest, had already occupied the forest.

He, a priest! Impossible! More probably a madman! Yet the newcomer wavered and detailed inquiries began.

Indeed the recluse had the claim to priesthood. Being the only son of a priest, he was entitled to that office on the day his father died. That entitlement could not be denied. In his absence, it was the son of the recluse who had been officiating as the priest. And it was he who came, bringing with him the 'seal of the priest' to surrender to his father. They embraced joyfully and in tears. Was the recluse really the father of the young priest? They had never seen each other. The young priest was born eight months after the recluse's wife had ascended the ziggurat with his father; and he would never know if they were brothers or father-and-son. But it no longer mattered. The recluse was happy to see his 'son' and his son's family, and even said a soulful prayer for his wife who, he learnt, had died in childbirth.

Though his son insisted, the recluse declined to accept his priesthood. The only request he made was that, as priest, his son assume jurisdiction over the forest so that no other priest could claim it. 'Let the forest be free under my other son, Lugal,' he said.

The son agreed but begged his father to return with him immediately.

'Give me a few more days and be with me till then,' the recluse requested. He died on the third day with a smile, 'I made the gods wait! How beautiful is the end!' Many heard him but no one understood his words. Perhaps he had been referring to his wish to die among his people.

The son kept his promise, and more. Lugal was now in

command of the forest, with no interference from any priest. He was even given the right to extend his area, as long as such new lands were unoccupied by a priest. The son gave many 'indemnities' to several priests to have this impossible situation accepted. From this arose the myth that Lugal of Sumer had valiantly vanquished priests of Sumeria to establish his undisputed reign in Assyria.

There were quite a few refugees around Lugal. They were under his protection and affectionately called him 'King Lugal.' But he joked, 'I can only be king of kings here, as all of you here are kings.'

Despite the people around him, Lugal felt terribly lonely without the recluse.

One day, a messenger came from the priest. 'Brother mine, it was my father's wish that you be married. With care I have chosen three wives for you. Should they not suit you, use them as you will and I will send you more.'

With the messenger were three girls who were sisters.

Lugal remembered the recluse's words in his dying days, 'Nothing on earth, nothing in the sky, nothing in the great beyond, nothing now or ever, nothing here or hereafter, can compensate for man's loneliness in life. Find a wife for yourself, Lugal!'

Lugal had humoured the recluse and said, 'How do I find a wife in this wilderness!'

After deep thought, the recluse had said, 'Then I will ask the gods to find a wife for you.'

Clearly, the recluse had spoken to a god, his own son— for a priest was no less—who had sent these three women, eager to share Lugal's lonely bed. His first reaction was to protest, but the messenger said, 'The lord priest has performed the marriage ceremony. But you have freedom.'

Lugal knew what that 'freedom' meant. They were his wives. There was no system of divorce, as such. He could put them to work as his slaves or sell them. If he kept them, they could remarry six hundred and sixty-six days after his death. If he sold them, he could buy them back at any time by paying double the price he had received. A man could marry any number of women, but a woman could have only one husband, though she could have sex with other men with her husband's permission, provided no one received payment for such sex.

Lugal remembered what his mother had once said, 'God is a kind soul. He allows the devil to make laws!'

Lugal saw the silent appeal in the eyes of his three 'brides' and the eldest said, 'Do not deny us.'

Lugal kept the three wives though he made a feeble protest, 'Be with me, but you are like sisters to me.'

Happily, they responded, 'Yes, sisters and wives.'

Within a year, Lugal was the proud father of three infants.

Later, Aryans from Bharat Varsha congregated in the forest to set up a major camp. From there, acting on Lugal's advice, they branched out to other areas in Assyria unoccupied by priests. In each such area, new settlements arose, attracting locals.

For himself, Lugal wanted nothing. He had almost given up sky-watching. His three wives and three children were his pride and joy. If he sometimes looked up at the sky, it was as if he expected his mother and the recluse to be there, smiling at his children. How his mother had wanted him to marry when he was young! But no, everything else had had to wait till he had achieved his single-minded ambition to be the greatest architect in the land!

Now, three wives and three children later, he was again an architect and a builder, supervising a vast variety of activities, including the building of houses, cattle sheds, granaries and reservoirs. Though some of the ideas came from the Aryans of Bharat Varsha, even they had to acknowledge that he was a superior builder and organizer.

But he did request a part of the produce from these

settlements, though only to 'gift' them to nearby priests. Even though the newcomers were settling in virgin areas, unoccupied by priests, the hostility of the priests was on the rise, and Lugal tried to placate them with gifts.

But how long can one 'buy' friends, he wondered! How long will this friendship last! Lugal prayed for the long life of the recluse's son, who was his protection. What about those who would succeed him! He was not worried about his own future. But what of his children and their children? His mind dismissed the wishful hope expressed by some that a day would soon dawn when priests would be powerless against their settlements. What a foolish hope, he thought, despite their effort to learn all the new ways of self-defence taught by the Aryans of India.

The Aryans themselves were constantly on the move, but even if they were to remain, the priests controlled vast territories and massive numbers of men; not many would dare oppose a priest's direct order! Old beliefs died slowly and priests, after all, were regarded as gods in human garb.

Maybe the Aryan hope that somewhere there is a land that is pure and free is also a foolish delusion, but if there is such a land, God, lead me to it, Lugal prayed.

Lugal had not met Purus, the Aryan leader in Iran. But the Aryans recalled his words: 'There is no land that is pure, unless we make it so, by our own will and effort.' Purus was right, thought Lugal. But these lands of Sumer and Assyria were far too corrupt and it would require a superhuman effort to release them from the vicious stranglehold of the priests. But surely then, their aim should be to find a land that is relatively free from the control of men of evil.

It was then that Lugal felt that for the sake of the future, and his children, he should join the Aryan quest for land elsewhere. Yet his heart was heavy. The locals in these settlements admired the Aryans, but Lugal was the one to whom they looked up as their leader—emotionally and even materially. He was the one to whom they came with their problems, concerns and hopes.

Lugal remained silent, but not for long; he spoke to the locals and was amazed to find them receptive to the idea of his leaving. 'As long as you take us along with you,' they added. In the end, many had to be persuaded to remain and Lugal said, 'If we fail, we return here; if we succeed, you come there. Both ways, we lose nothing.'

Thus left King Lugal, though not a king really, except in the hearts and imagination of the Assyrian settlers, on his quest for new lands with the Aryans.

For every Aryan from Bharat Varsha, there were twenty-four locals, and they, too, called themselves Aryan, the noble.

'Hermit-king Lugal, take command!' begged Nilakantha, the Aryan leader from Bharat Varsha.

'No,' said Lugal. 'Your faith is greater. You lead.'

THIRTY-EIGHT

KINGS OF EGYPT AND THE LANGUAGE OF THE GODS

5005 BCE

After what seemed an eternity, the Aryans of Bharat Varsha and locals from many areas, entered Egypt under the command of Nilakantha, along with Hermit-king Lugal. On the way, some Aryan groups, and many locals from Iran, parted to go to other areas, now known as Syria, Palestine, Saudi Arabia, Jordan and Israel. But the locals from Sumer and Assyria would not leave King Lugal and followed him all the way.

The journey was long and tedious and before they reached Egypt, many Aryans were overcome with melancholy: where are we going and why? They would sing loudly to keep their spirits up, but often the songs did not allay their restless grief. Where was the land in which God ruled in his splendour? Was it all an illusion? But they remained silent, unwilling to share their forebodings with others. There were those who understood each other without words and they thought, how powerful and alive we were with faith when we left Bharat Varsha!

On their way to Egypt, they met many whose eyes had been put out, or who had had their limbs cut off and tongues torn out because they had not completed their allotted work on time, or sometimes to set a stern example to other workers, and often, for sport or simply to terrorize. Such unfortunates lived and died miserably, in poor settlements. There were also youngsters who were on the run to avoid being taken to the land beyond—army service for men and slavery or prostitution for women, though prostitution among men was equally common.

The land beyond was called by many names—'Valley of Kings', 'Land of the Sun', 'Land of Glory'—but the glory belonged to the king and the sun was simply a reflection in the sky of the king's glory.

At first, the Aryans believed that the land had a single king. But later, when they understood the language of these people better, they learnt that there were thirteen kings. Each king viewed the others with hate and spite, and they all were at war with each other. Borders were undefined, raids common and loyalties shifting. In one settlement, mostly barren, where the Aryans became friendly with the locals as a result of looking after their sick, a local brought out from hiding two gold cups to offer water to Nilakantha and Lugal.

Eventually, the Aryans learnt that in the hills beyond was a hide-out of robbers, who supported the settlement. In turn, the locals would warn the robbers of any strangers around looking to apprehend them. Yet these robbers rarely robbed the living. They were grave robbers.

In all these kingdoms, each man, upon his death, was buried along with all his living wives clad in their best clothes and whatever jewellery they had, and items of daily necessity, such as pots and pans, for use on their journey to heaven through the bowels of earth. In addition to his wives, a man of status would have at least one slave buried with him and a variety of luxury items, including wine and goblets to make the journey pleasant. Such a journey was supposed to take twenty-seven days, but for those who had a live donkey, horse or camel buried with them, it would take less time, depending on the speed of the animal.

Grave robbers were cursed beings for they would never ascend to heaven, and if caught they were crucified and their bodies smeared with a honey-like substance to attract flies and ants. The family of a grave robber was gifted as 'bounty' to the person or group arresting a grave robber, and they could sell them as slaves or as prostitutes.

The Aryans gained much of the information on the land beyond from the grave robbers—how to cross safely, how to evade the clutches of the kings, how to outsmart their little armies and where to hide. They even gave information on the huge catacombs where the Aryans could hide, if the need arose. 'If soldiers ever enter there, they never come out alive and thieves are too honourable to steal from anyone hiding there.'

Indeed, the grave robbers had a high opinion of the men of their profession. When they stole from the living, they were convinced that the man must have exploited the poor to amass so much, 'for how else is a fortune made except by robbing another's share'! As for grave-robbing, they never approached a grave during the first twenty-seven days that it supposedly took the deceased to ascend to heaven, and just in case a heavenly traveller turned lame or lost his way, they waited an additional twenty-seven days. 'For by then, his heavenly ascent is surely accomplished and he needs nothing in the grave any more for the journey. So why burden the earth with what it needs not, but we do!'

The grave robbers were friendly and informative, but they knew little of the lands beyond. They felt that the Aryans could at first avoid the river where it was populated and then follow its course to the south where the desert began. 'Maybe the river and desert will lead somewhere or maybe nowhere but the north holds no prospect, for the river itself drowns into a huge body of salt-water.'

The river was called Kemi, meaning 'black', a reference

to the sediment. Later, after the Aryans entered Egypt, the river came to be known as Ar, Ary or Aur. Much later it came to be known as Nil or Nile from Nila, and many believed it was to honour Nilakantha, the Aryan leader. Others claimed that the name Nile could have come from the Greek *neilos* which is derived from the Semitic root *nahal*, meaning a valley or a river valley and hence by extension, a river. This seems too farfetched.

The Aryan contingent moved on, leaving behind thirty-six men, women and children, too sick to travel farther. Ajitab, an Aryan from Bharat Varsha, was put in charge. Such farewells had taken place often before, but they were always heart-wrenching. The grave robbers consoled Nilakantha, 'Maybe, we will teach them our arts if they cannot rejoin you.'

Nilakantha smiled, 'No, you have taught us much of your language. That is enough. Teach us not your arts. But I hope our people will teach you our arts of sowing, planting, and building to live differently and well. Meanwhile, protect them.'

'With our life and honour,' the grave robbers promised.

Nilakantha also gave them a 'way to die well'. With Lugal guiding him, Nilakantha had searched far beyond the area for a particular wild plant. They found many. Its leaves, once dried in the sun and pounded, yielded a bitter powder that dulled pain and even caused deep sleep when taken in large quantities. This was his gift to the grave robbers to use if ever they were caught and were to be crucified. It would not save their lives, but would save them from the torture of a painful, lingering death.

'Be as silent as the graves we rob,' the robbers had warned the Aryans as they moved out. They sang no more and marched with quieter tread.

Unbidden, dark and gloomy thoughts assailed them and Nilakantha asked Lugal, 'Should we not go back?' But it was too late.

Their mistake lay in assuming that like the robbers they could steal their way through unknown, uninhabited paths. But where the robbers went in groups of three or four, theirs was a huge 'army'. The Egyptian kings had spies everywhere and this large movement did not pass undetected. Also, the Aryans were wary of getting lost on unknown tracks, so they went slowly. Superstition had compelled them to decline when a grave robber had graciously offered to guide them. Their slow, unsure movement gave the local king enough time to mobilize his men and face what he thought was a challenge.

Suddenly, the Aryans stopped. Just ahead stood the local king's men, massed like an ocean. The commander of the troops shouted from afar, 'Animals! Get down from your animals! Throw down all you carry!' The Aryans complied as Nilakantha repeated the order. He had learnt enough of their language on the way to understand what the commander desired. The commander was surprised. He expected the 'enemy' to offer resistance or try to run away. With ten slaves shielding him, he came forward slowly, afraid to be within the range of their arrows. But what he saw surprised him. These men and women looked different from his people. Even their clothes! And they had children too!

As a victorious commander, he was entitled to a hundredth part of the captured booty in slaves, women and goods. Already, he was eyeing the women, men and their goods, as if relishing his own share. Then the commander remembered the condition that some blood must be shed on his side for him to be entitled to booty. This condition, perhaps devised originally to reward great warriors, had degenerated into a senseless token formality, yet it was unavoidable, or else the booty was lost. The commander quickly gave his order. His slaves held down the oldest among them, and another slave ran a sword through him, killing him.

The Aryans understood nothing of this bloodthirsty rite. But fear gripped them; they thought this was the start of a merciless massacre. Nilakantha moved towards the commander with a hand on his dagger. Lugal came forward too. Without being given an order, the Aryans picked up their weapons and mounted their animals, determined to die fighting rather than be slaughtered.

The commander raised his hand and shouted, 'There is naught to fear. None of you shall be harmed.' But he was afraid, too. These newcomers, he knew, could not stand against his superior force. But he feared he would be the first to fall, given his proximity to them. He took a few steps back. The Aryans inched forward. He halted and barked, 'Remain where you are! The sun-god shall arrive soon.' Meanwhile, he explained to Lugal and Nilakantha that killing the slave was no more than a necessary rite and meant no threat to them. He was simply ensuring that he got a part of the booty due to him. His explanation, instead of reassuring Nilakantha and Lugal, actually terrified them. They turned back to the Aryans as if to translate his words, but said, 'Whatever happens, keep your arms ready, and be prepared to surround the king and the commander.'

At the commander's order, a slave rushed off to advise the priest, so that their king was informed of total victory.

Face to face, the two armies stood.

At last, the king came. But he was not like his foolish commander, overpowered by greed. He was hardly visible through the outer ring of priests and inner ring of soldiers that surrounded him. He stopped at a distance from the two groups. Six priests came forward to inspect the Aryan 'army' and reported back to him. The king demanded to meet their commander. Nilakantha insisted on taking Lugal.

'No one approaches the sun-god with weapons,' the priest said, so Nilakantha and Lugal went unarmed.

'Kneel, dogs, kneel, before the sun-god,' the priest barked when they reached the king's group. Nilakantha and Lugal knelt.

The king would have to shout to speak directly to them. But he spoke through the six priests he had lined up.

'Why do you have two commanders? I asked for one,' was the king's first question.

Nilakantha answered, 'Sun-god, I am in command, but we all respect Hermit-king Lugal, so I brought him.'

'The only kings that enter my land are dead kings,' the king responded.

Nilakantha regretted his foolish response, but Lugal spoke, 'Sun-god, I am not a king in the royal sense. I am known as king of architects and builders.'

'So what do you come to build here?' asked the king.

'To build a dream,' said Lugal, but before he conveyed the reply to the king, the priest muttered, 'Explain, dog, explain!'

Lugal explained, 'A dream came to me, Sun-god, that I build a glorious temple in your land to honour you.'

'What need have I of a temple to honour me when, wherever I am, a temple lies unseen beneath my feet!'

'True, Sun-god, but just as the sun shines in the sky to reflect your glory and is seen by all, there has to be a temple on earth, seen by all, to reflect your glory here.'

'How will a temple reflect my glory? Will you build a sun on earth?'

'Yes, Sun-god. Something like the sun—to reflect its glory and yours.'

The man must be mad, the king thought, but Lugal had piqued his interest. 'Explain!' the king shouted for the first time.

As Nilakantha watched uncomprehendingly, Lugal said, 'Sun-god, like all great architecture, the idea in my dream is profoundly simple. The movement of the sun that revolves around you throws its light differently in various phases. Your temple shall have a number of obelisks in pyramidal and tapering squares. The rising or setting sun will, at different times, gild with a bright gold glow the tip of each obelisk.

And in those golden glimpses, everyone shall observe with awe and reverence your glory that is reflected in the sky as it shall be reflected on earth.'

'But surely,' said the king doubtfully, 'sunlight shall fall equally on every obelisk.'

Lugal explained the technical aspects of the plan to the king, but it was beyond his comprehension. 'Bring Hutantat,' the king ordered.

Hutantat was a celebrated astronomer in his land.

Well before Hutantat arrived, Lugal started drawing all kinds of figures on the ground. With the king's permission, he called one of his men—Himatap, an Aryan from Bharat Varsha. During the journey, Lugal and Himatap had discussed and observed the movements of heavenly bodies including the sun. Now, under Lugal's instruction, Himatap began drawing many figures on the ground with an arrow-tip— lines, squares, angles, triangles. Even the king came closer, with his entourage, to watch while they waited for Hutantat.

Nine soldiers, carrying Hutantat's litter, arrived. Hutantat had no priestly or secular titles. But his claims to fame were many. He often predicted, accurately, when the river would rise in flood and when it would recede, and when there would be an eclipse. But more than that, when six kings had joined together to attack the kingdom when the present king's grandfather had ruled, he had predicted the defeat of the six kings, even though no more than eighty soldiers were left to fight against them. At his bidding, it was said, 'the rivers rose, drowning all that came before it and the six kings fled and one of the kings even died before reaching his land.'

Since then Hutantat was known as the 'oracle who could alter events'.

Perfunctorily, Hutantat bowed to the king. Anyone else making such a careless bow would have been beheaded on the spot, but Hutantat was not 'anyone else'. It was the king who returned the bow. At the king's order, the chief priest began explaining Lugal's impossible dream.

Without waiting for the priest to finish his explanation, Hutantat walked over to Lugal and Himatap who were still drawing figures on the ground. Impatiently, and a little angrily, Hutantat rubbed out with his foot a figure drawn by Himatap. He snatched Himatap's arrow and redrew the figure differently and at a greater distance. Lugal nodded in agreement with the correction.

Then Hutantat scrutinized the figures that Lugal had drawn. He rubbed off no figures but drew and redrew, and Lugal too drew and redrew. It was as if both were discussing, by means of figures, the best way to achieve the objective.

Hutantat ignored two interruptions from the impatient king who wanted to know his views immediately. When the king sent a priest to call Hutantat, the astronomer shouted at him to remain away, lest he disturb the figures drawn on the ground.

Lugal and Hutantat were both tired. They stopped and looked at each other in silent appreciation. Lugal felt that Hutantat had the eyes of his mentor, the recluse, who had taught him all he knew about the sun's movements.

But Hutantat's words were pitiless as he responded to the king's inquiry, 'Only a fool would begin such a project.'

The terrible words were spoken. Lugal felt no anger—only a sad weariness.

The priests, who had known all along that it was an impossible idea, and had said so to the king, were pleased.

The king was already discussing with his commanders how the Aryans could be surrounded to avoid undue bloodshed. The idea of having so many different-looking men and women as slaves pleased him.

Lugal hardly heard Hutantat who was speaking to him. 'How can you think of wasting so much time and effort over a useless temple to satisfy the ego of an arrogant king when most people here are hungry, naked and without shelter? Do you know how much it would cost? And the poor here will groan and suffer! Are you without pity?'

'Pity! Yes, I have pity. But for my people too. From what the king's commander said, clearly we are to be enslaved here. It was pity, then, that moved me to offer to build a temple. Do you think it is wrong to have pity for one's own people?'

'Then it was not a dream that brought you here?'

Ruefully Lugal laughed, 'I have many dreams, but this is not one of them. It suddenly occurred to me when we were threatened with slavery or death and I thought it was worth a try.'

'Yet, it is a glorious idea,' Hutantat said almost to himself and fell into a reverie. Suddenly, he shouted across to the king's entourage, 'And I must see the site where this temple is to be built.'

'What!' the chief priest shouted back. 'I thought the proposal was dead.'

Hotly, Hutantat replied, 'You may be dead yourself. Why don't you ask the king?'

It was the king who spoke, 'But Hutantat, did you not say that only a fool would start such a project!'

'Of course,' Hutantat replied and he pointed his hand at Lugal, 'is he not a fool, who comes from afar, pursuing a dream, not for his glory but yours! And he stands in the sun, his people without food and water, while even your eunuchs are having refreshments with umbrellas over their heads. Certainly he is a fool to start this splendorous project. But only a great king would embark on such a project. Are you a great king?'

The priests winced. Hutantat never called the king by his true title of 'sun-god'. But to invite the king's wrath with such impertinence!

The king ignored the question and asked, 'You think the project has merit! You really think so?'

'I don't think so. I know so.'

'It cannot fail?' the king pressed.

'Certainly, it can fail if the sun moves away, elsewhere, for ever, or if the earth under our feet disappears. But otherwise, how can it fail? This dreamer here may be a fool to pursue his dream for your glory, but his dream is solid and splendid, based on the movements of the sky and earth and the manner in which the sun's rays invariably fall. No, it cannot fail.'

There was silence all over. But the king soon ordered four umbrellas to shade Hutantat, Lugal, Nilakantha and Himatap. A refreshment cart was also brought and left for them. Hutantat took a little, Lugal took nothing. He was thinking of all the Aryans—his wives and children among them—sweating in the hot sun, unaware of all that was happening here.

But Hutantat told Lugal, 'Take a little. My insolence they expect and appreciate; yours, they may not.' They drank and ate and it occurred to Lugal that Hutantat possibly used his impertinence as a screen.

At last the king spoke, 'Sage Hutantat! Will you help these men select a site for the temple?'

'That I shall,' Hutantat replied. 'But first let a site be found to house them and all their people.'

The chief priest spoke, 'Our men will assist too. Surely, not all the people brought by them are needed to work.' The chief priest was simply translating the king's desire to have some of these different-looking men and women in his household.

'Are you mad, eunuch?' Hutantat shouted. 'Do you think these people came from so far off to rest here? They, too, come chasing this fool's dream for the greater glory of our king. Do you realize that if a single one of them does not work or is hurt or harmed, this project of glory will suffer? Or is our king's glory of no consequence to you? So see to it, then, that they are all able to work and he who disturbs or harms them is punished with the highest penalty. You are personally responsible for that.'

Sadly, the chief priest looked at the king. They spoke. How could these people all be workers! Some were old and quite a few women had children. The king spoke, 'But Sage Hutantat, some of their women have children . . . !'

'Exactly, king, exactly!' Hutantat interrupted ecstatically, as though agreeing with him. 'That is what your priest does not understand and never will. They even brought children for the promise of this glory. You are absolutely right, king, and wise too!'

No one understood what he meant. Perhaps Hutantat did not either, but how could the king disagree with a sage who not only agreed with him but even called him wise. The king could not recall a single other occasion on which Hutantat had so complimented him.

The king's orders were now clear. All these people were to be treated well and housed in comfort and anyone trying to harm them would meet a terrible fate.

Finally, the king said, 'Sage Hutantat, when you select a site, come to me and bring this . . . this . . . ' He pointed to Lugal; maybe he disliked addressing him as 'King Lugal' or perhaps he had simply forgotten his name.

But Hutantat immediately said, 'Certainly, my king, and I shall also bring the king's architect Lugal.'

'King's Architect! Good title! Yes, let that be his,' said the king.

The chief priest and the king came forward. The priest shouted at Lugal, 'Kneel dog, kneel!' Lugal knelt, bewildered.

The king gently touched Lugal's head with his whip. The priest shouted, 'The sun-god has spoken. And all shall honour you as such. Rise! Honourable king's architect, rise with honour!'

Obviously, it was a great honour. But the day had been

crowded with so many startling events that Lugal did not know whether to laugh or cry.

The king and his entourage left. The commander and his soldiers remained to carry out the king's order to arrange for food and housing for the king's architect and his people. The commander discussed arrangements with Hutantat and Lugal.

Nilakantha ran back to the Aryans, breathless, laughing, crying, unable to utter a word. And they thought he had brought news of the calamity awaiting them. At last he said, 'We are saved! Sing, sing, sing!' And many sang, though others shouted questions at him and at each other, while still others exclaimed, 'Sing! He says we are saved!'

The king's commander heard the off-key song, mixed with chatter; to him it sounded like a disorderly lament. 'Why are they bleating like goats and sheep?' he asked Lugal who himself was surprised by the tuneless song.

But Hutantat said, 'They sing in a language that God understands better—the language of goats and sheep.'

'God understands the language of sheep and goats better!' the commander asked. 'How is it then that our king, the sun-god, does not speak the language of goats and sheep?'

Hutantat wondered if the commander's question was a trap to entice him into saying something indiscreet about the king. He said, 'The king knows all he needs to know. It is for you to know better—perhaps the cry of slaughtered slaves, and the lament of those that you call sheep and goats.'

Many heard what Sage Hutantat said, and the story would be told and retold that these outsiders spoke the language of sheep, goats and even gods! The language of the gods! Who says so? Why, Hutantat himself! And Hutantat, they knew, was never wrong and never spoke lightly.

The locals, obsessed with the idea of the afterlife that awaited them after a brief journey of twenty-seven days, regarded the coming of the Aryans as auspicious. True, the locals took their wives, pots and pans, even their slaves, mules, donkeys, horses and camels, to the grave for their journey to heaven. But these foreigners went armed with the language of the gods! Many aspired to crowd around these newcomers to learn their heavenly language.

Some thousands of year later, far into the modern post-Vedic era, possibly around 1200 AD, the poetess Satyali of Sindh would sing an echo of Sage Hutantat's words and say, 'The Aryans took our language out to lands distant and near—oh, where did they not go and so few came back!—But they left their words on the lips and hearts of many in those strange lands, the strangers were strangers no more and those that returned, rich they came with much they learnt of what was on the lips and in the hearts of them that they left.'

The Aryans were now about to leave to follow the commander. Suddenly, a shrill voice rose, 'But where is brother Himatap?' They all looked. Far away, alone, Himatap was still drawing figures on the ground, untouched by the bewilderment that had affected everyone that day.

'What is he doing?' asked Nilakantha.

'He is trying to discover God's law,' Lugal said.

'Yes,' Hutantat rejoined grimly, 'so that the devil may be served better.'

Nilakantha misunderstood and said, 'Himatap is a good lad.'

Lugal and others shouted to Himatap to return. Himatap seemed surprised to find himself alone. He had been much too absorbed in refining the figures to notice that Lugal and Nilakantha had gone to join the others.

❧

The king approved of the site for the temple. Hutantat said to Nilakantha, 'Many untruths were spoken to the king. Yet, I am bound by the promise that you shall build the temple.'

Nilakantha felt sad that Hutantat doubted Aryan sincerity and said, 'Each of us is honour-bound and I swear by the light of the sun . . . '

Hutantat smiled, 'Enough! But learn a few rules before you break them. Never swear by the sun. The sun may not object, but as all here will tell you, the sun is only a reflection of the king, and never annoy him if you hope to die of old age.'

Nilakantha was still hurt, 'But you doubted our sincerity, did you not?'

'Sometimes I doubt the sincerity of God, the Creator, too.'

'Doubt the sincerity of God!'

'But then, perhaps, god does not exist, so why question his sincerity?'

Nilakantha looked at him with sadness. Hutantat asked playfully, 'Why! Does everyone in your land believe that God exists?'

'Oh no! There are some who disbelieve in God.'

'And they are evil men?' asked Hutantat.

'No, not at all. Many are good, though I think they are . . . inside them . . . ' he groped for a word.

'Lonely?' Hutantat prompted.

'Yes, there is loneliness, emptiness inside them.'

'And you try to bring to them your belief in God?'

'Me! How? Each person reaches his belief himself, within himself.'

'Nothing outside of him influences him?'

'Of course! Parents, teachers, neighbours will influence one, but the greatest influence is what one's soul tells one.'

'Oh! So you, too, have a talkative soul!' Hutantat said. 'But tell me, in your land, does a man who disbelieves in God go to heaven?'

Nilakantha, too, now had the urge to be playful and said, 'No one in our land is expected, ever, to go to heaven.'

'What! You live a life and die. That's all?'

Nilakantha then told him of his belief—there was no heaven, no hell, but only moksha, when the human soul united with the soul of God if the individual had lived with righteous karma during his earthly journey, or alternatively a chain of rebirths till he achieved righteousness, though no one was ever denied either the opportunity or the hope to achieve salvation.

'And surely this moksha will be denied to those that disbelieve in God?' Hutantat asked.

'Why would it be denied if the man's karma was righteous?'

'Surely, God decides!'

'How can God be unjust?'

'You mean that your God is neither angered by neglect, nor placated by praise! But then what is the point in believing or disbelieving in God, or loving or hating him, if moksha is unrelated to it?'

'Sometimes, the love for God in a man's heart will overflow. If a man can love his father and wife and even an unborn son, grandchild or friend, why is it inconceivable that he can love and believe in God? That love and belief itself will incline an individual towards right conduct. But whether he believes in God or not, if his karma is righteous, how can God deny him moksha! How can a just God ever refuse to a man what he has earned?'

Hutantat asked many questions in order to clarify things. But in the end he said, 'Interesting. But I believe none of it.'

Nilakantha smiled, 'That is your privilege, sage. Many in my land too do not believe it. That is their privilege.'

Hutantat asked heatedly, 'You mean there is nobody in your land to tell disbelievers to believe?'

Nilakantha had difficulty in replying. He was wondering how the wise sage could ask such a preposterous question. At last he said, 'But how, by what right . . . '

'If you believe, why don't you make others believe?'

'Why? How? If I, a believer, force myself upon another,

does the non-believer not have the right to force his disbelief on me?'

'Exactly! And in the end, force will decide whose belief succeeds.'

'But faith achieved through force and assault! What kind of faith would that be? A faith conceived in sin! And he who tries to impose such a faith on another, what kind of a person must he be? Truly, an enemy of God, or one who believes himself above God, for God never demanded what a man should or should not believe . . . '

Nilakantha stopped abruptly, realizing that he had been lecturing an honoured sage and said, 'Forgive me, master, I know so little and I have no way with words. But you know we all love and honour you . . . '

'Even if I don't believe in God?' Hutantat challenged with a smile.

'That, master, is between God and you. But I simply wanted to respond to your first question, to promise that each of us will work sincerely to see that the temple you have promised the king shall be built.'

Hutantat was serious now. 'Good. The king has released 1500 slaves to work on the temple despite the chief priest's protests. These slaves will be freed into my custody when the temple is completed, and the king will give me six villages where they can remain in freedom. Already hundreds of others work in freedom in villages which the king gave me three years ago. I care not at all for the temple. But if my promise for the temple fails, no harm may come to me, but the axe will surely fall on the slaves.'

Nilakantha was looking at him with a fixed stare. Hutantat thought he had spoken too fast in a language that was unfamiliar to these people. He was about to explain but Nilakantha spoke, 'You saved us! You save the slaves! Can God have greater love than that a man should love his creatures so much! I wish I could trade my faith with your karma.'

'Do not give away so much for so little!' Hutantat rejoined.

∽

As he saw hundreds of slaves being driven to the construction site by the whip and the lash, with wounds and sores on their bodies and terror in their eyes, Lugal thought of karma and free will of which the Aryans spoke, of the idea that the soul was a source of liberty, that a human being had the capacity to go beyond his heritage, that no one was denied the hope and opportunity to advance!

But where was man's free will, Lugal wondered. And where did it lead? Nowhere. It was simply an illusion—an escape from one tyranny into another. Did these slaves have free will? Did he have free will? In his land of Sumer, priests were the tyrants and here the king terrorized his people with the aid of the priests, commanders and soldiers under him. The only difference was that here the tyranny was more visible, more naked, more brutal. And now, they were building a temple to the glory and vanity of a king who ruled with indescribable horror! Where had his free will led his people? From one horror to another! No, there was no free will, no mysterious, benign presence that governed the universe! Man was simply a pawn of fate, a slave of necessity.

Lugal's gloom actually arose from being rebuffed by the commander in charge of the slaves, who had tersely told him, 'Lord architect! Just tell me what you want these slaves to do and my soldiers shall get it done. Don't tell me *how*!'

Later, Hutantat told Lugal and Nilakantha, 'The king's architect cannot interfere with the king's commanders. Only a priest can.'

'Then get Nilakantha appointed a priest,' Lugal urged. 'He sings, he prays, sometimes he even thinks deeply, and his thoughts are always auspicious.'

'Although Nilakantha will gain much by being a priest, he

will lose a little too,' Hutantat said. He went on to explain that the king appointed ninety-nine priests, no more, no less, and he bowed to them every morning. He could not dismiss them once they had been appointed. If he disliked a priest and wished to appoint another in his place, the priest had to die. And even those who killed the priest at the king's command had to die, for it was a sin to strike a priest.

Hutantat continued, 'Maybe no one sheds tears over a priest's death, as it means one vicious person less, but imagine Nilakantha in that role! Besides, after two years, he must lose his manhood and become a eunuch.'

'What!' Lugal and Nilakantha shouted in surprise.

'Yes. For the first 730 days, a priest has the freedom to pick any man's wife, sister, daughter, mother, except the king's wives or family, and take her to bed. No one can protest. But on the seven-hundred-and-thirty-first day, the priest undergoes an operation and becomes a eunuch for life.'

'Why this madness?'

'Simple. When the king dies, his queens and his ninety-nine priests are buried with him, alive. Queens are mostly of royal blood, for the king must marry all his sisters, whatever their age, though he can marry other women too. In that cramped grave, where so many are entombed, only eunuch males are allowed lest they corrupt the queens on their celestial journey. But of course, the belief is that when they reach heaven, there is an abundance of everything, including human spare parts, so their manhood is promptly restored and they can once again claim any woman that their hearts desire.'

Nilakantha was speechless, but Lugal asked, 'Are the priests and queens the only ones buried alive?'

'No, many slaves are, too. They are castrated as well, as are the horses and asses before being buried alive with the king, lest his queens begin to suffer from unholy desires during that brief journey to paradise. The only difference is that the slaves and animals do not get their spare parts back.'

'Why?'

'Don't ask me! I don't rule heaven,' Hutantat said. 'If I did, the first thing I would do is to banish the God who rules over earth and heaven and permits such revolting cruelties.' He paused to ask, 'Brother Nilakantha, would you like to be a lord priest?'

Later, they were told why a priest was castrated during his lifetime. A priest was always with the king. He escorted the queens to the king, served as their teacher and physician. Nobody could see a queen except the priest.

But why not assign such duties to women, they wanted to know. Hutantat said the women here were considered fit only to work in the fields or satisfy a man's hunger and produce children.

'But Aryan women work! They are even teachers, singers and doctors!'

'Well, maybe here they will say Aryan men are not manly enough and their women not feminine enough.'

'Does anyone then wish to be a priest?'

'Why not!' Hutantat exclaimed. 'Two years of riotous living to compensate for castration, then living in the lap of luxury. Sex? But even a eunuch does have some inlets and outlets to satisfy his desires. And remember! He has the absolute certainty of reaching heaven with his manhood restored and bliss everlasting!'

'Does anyone believe it?' Nilakantha asked.

'You believe what you believe; they believe what they believe.'

'What do you believe?' Nilakantha pressed.

'I believe everything and nothing,' said Hutantat. 'One day I may know what I should have believed, but by then it may not matter!'

~

It was Hutantat who secured better treatment for the slaves working on the temple. Most of their heavy work was outdoors, like bringing huge stone blocks, baking bricks, and levelling the vast hilly terrain of the construction site.

Nilakantha asked Hutantat, 'The commander is unduly brutal with the the slaves. Is there no way that you can get another commander?'

'Another commander will be equally brutal,' Hutantat said, but added after a pause, 'Good idea, Brother Nilakantha! You cannot be a priest, but you could be appointed to serve as a commander.'

'You mean you can appoint me as commander?'

'No, only the king can. But it is a brilliant idea. You replace the commander and your men replace his soldiers, who are even more brutish than their commander! And certainly, the slaves will respond to your gentleness. They know the king's promise that they will be freed once the temple is complete.'

'I hope the king will remember his promise to free the slaves when the temple is completed.'

'He forgets no promises. He just won't keep them. If I count all his promises to me, I should have had eighty-five more villages with thousands of slaves freed. But sometimes, he keeps a promise. For now we must focus on your ambition to become the king's commander, or are you to remain a commander only of your Aryans?'

'Ambition!' Nilakantha scoffed. 'But please don't call me commander of the Aryans. It is Hermit-king Lugal who leads us all. He commands that I march ahead, as I am simply a singer of songs.'

'Yes, Lugal knows that in a better world it is a singer of songs and a dreamer of dreams who must lead mankind.'

Hutantat influenced the commander, not by moral force which would only meet with indifference, but by threatening him. 'You are maltreating and starving the slaves, which does not bother me at all, except that it disrupts work on the king's temple. Beware, the king may make you not a priest but simply priestly!'

The commander would have struck down anyone else, but not Sage Hutantat. Often, the king came to the construction site, demanding Hutantat's presence. Gratefully, the commander would hear Hutantat praising him to the king for his work. The king had even said to the chief priest, 'Remind me to promote the commander when the temple is complete.'

Hutantat also lined up a few Aryans, visibly, to keep an eye on the treatment of the slaves by the commander and his soldiers. It had its effect and soldiers no longer interfered with Aryans offering food and water to the slaves, or tending to their wounds. In fact, they became less harsh with the slaves, and even upon occasion, considerate.

'Work goes slowly,' Hutantat said to Nilakantha, in mock complaint against the good treatment of the slaves.

'But auspiciously,' said Nilakantha, happily. 'And I thank you, master.'

～

Among the Aryans, Himatap was perhaps the only one unconcerned with the slaves or any other matter. All his dreams and waking thoughts were centred on the temple.

The king often came, each time to demand that the temple be made bigger and grander than Lugal's conception. Hutantat would agree readily, only to demand more slaves who would be freed when work was complete, and more villages to house them in.

'Do not promise lightly, my king,' Hutantat said, 'for you know the curse on him that vainly promises in the temple's name, and keeps not his promise.'

The king did not know the curse and asked him to explain. But Hutantat only said, 'Too much I honour you, king, to utter such a curse in your presence.'

Thoughtfully, the king promised more slaves, but Hutantat never demanded too many, knowing that each superstition had a limit.

In the centre of the temple, the king demanded a palace surrounded by tapering obelisks, monolithic shafts with a pyramidal apex, on which the sun's rays gleamed with a golden glow. Yet, he also wanted a place where he would be buried with his entourage.

'Why not a ziggurat for the king to ascend to the heavens directly from the sky,' said Lugal, with his Sumerian experience. But he silently realized his mistake—bodies decompose and surely on that open platform, everyone would see the condition of the king's body with horror. Besides, the king's body was not a bait to trap animals, as in Sumeria.

The king's objection was different. 'Grave robbers steal even from closed pits; an open ziggurat won't do. Instead, think of how to keep robbers away from our graves.'

Himatap had a suggestion, 'Let it be a closed pyramid then, sealed forever.'

'How will bodies be placed in an enclosed pyramid?'

'There will be an opening,' explained Hutantat, 'which will be sealed with bricks after the bodies are kept inside.'

'Is heavenly ascent possible from an enclosed pyramid?' the king asked.

'Yes, the king's spirit is mighty.'

'But what of those that must accompany me?'

'The king's might will guide them too, but holes shall be provided at the top of the pyramid for the weaker ones.'

'But so far, heavenly ascents have been made from earth. What if the sky route is impossible?'

'No problem. The earth will be under your feet.'

Except cost and effort, every problem was considered.

'Build the pyramid, Hutantat,' the king said at last. 'You will get 900 more slaves, to be freed at the conclusion of construction, with two more villages. No more, but no less.

That is a promise.'

Each visit by the king resulted in intense discussions, especially between Hutantat, Lugal and Himatap, with all three drawing and redrawing figures, diagrams and lines, sometimes disagreeing, often pondering, and even striking their foreheads in frustration.

Later Western and Indian historians would write about the theorem of Pythagoras of Samos, a Greek philosopher and mathematician. Some could argue that somehow Hutantat, Lugal and Himatap learnt it from Pythagoras, except that the Greek lived in the sixth century BCE while Hutantat, Lugal and Himatap worked on the first pyramid in Egypt some thousand years before Pythagoras. But that apart, there are well preserved pyramids and funerary monuments in Egypt, built long centuries before Pythagoras, and it may be worthwhile for Indian historians to take a trip to Egypt to see how this simple theorem was well within the grasp of those people.

It is difficult to say who came upon the theorem first—Hutantat the Egyptian, or Lugal the Sumerian and Assyrian, or Himatap the youngster from Bharat Varsha with the Tibetan mother. In any case, a later poet's claim, 'surely this knowledge flowed from my land (India)', may have some basis as the Indus Valley finds clearly show that pre-ancient India was well aware of the application of this theorem. Many poets from Bharat Varsha credited Nilakantha, deservedly, with much that Aryans did in Egypt, for after all he was the leader, though he distinguished himself largely through self-effacement.

Hutantat was their spokesman with the king and the commander. All work was organized by Hutantat and Lugal. Nilakantha was supposed to supervise everyone. But he was so sure that they were all working excellently that he hardly supervised, except to appreciate their work. And since he realized that he achieved nothing by supervision, he did what pleased him most—going to the slaves and often serving them food. Sometimes, he detached Aryans from work to prepare some delicacies for the slaves, always making sure to offer them to the commander and soldiers first, then to the slaves. He would talk to the slaves, addressing them as 'brother' although many did not understand him, for they had been caught from lands to the south of the Nile. Nilakantha would wonder about the darker colour of the slaves' skin. He sometimes sang for them and encouraged them to sing, for he understood the sadness in their songs, if not the words.

The commander did not interfere with Nilakantha's interaction with the slaves. After all, everyone, even Hutantat, respected Nilakantha as a leader. He was a fool but a delightful fool, thought the commander. The soldiers considered him funny, but pleasantly so. Only the slaves regarded him as lovable, without reservation.

Nilakantha was the son of a celebrated singer and the grandson of a poet. Why did he leave with the Aryans? To seek a better life for himself? Maybe, to seek a better life for others.

Lugal saw Nilakantha often speaking or singing to the the slaves and said what Hutantat had once said, 'Work goes slowly.' And Hutantat replied, repeating what Nilakantha had said, 'But auspiciously, master.' Both laughed. Nilakantha saw them from a distance. Somehow he knew they were laughing at him. But even so, he was happy, for so overwrought were these two with work and worry, that it delighted him to see them laugh—even if it was at him.

But this is a simplistic view of all that Nilakantha did. He was perhaps the ablest listener. Everyone came to him with their troubles. He listened, rarely saying much. But, often, the mere recitation of woes softens distress.

One wound remained in every heart. Where was the object of their long quest? Why were they caught in this land? Was it for this that they had left their homeland? Nilakantha had these doubts too and his voice trembled as he sang, 'So onward Arya, onward all . . . '

What more was needed from a leader who kept his hurt to himself and cheered his troops and raised their morale and sanity when there was no way of going forward or back!

Poets from Bharat Varsha wrapped many fables and legends around Nilakantha as if he were the inspiration behind all the monuments and mathematics of Egypt. Even his narration of the story of the Egyptian calendar was misunderstood. Nobody paid attention to the story as a whole. Everyone merely heard the title of the story and assumed that Nilakantha had established the Egyptian calendar.

Hutantat, who often praised Lugal, once said to Nilakantha, 'Every day, Lugal gives me a lesson in humility, and teaches me something new.' Actually, all that Lugal had done was to prove to Hutantat that a year consisted not of 365 days but 365 ¼ days. 'And I was the foolish one,' said Hutantat, 'to declare to the king's grandfather that the year begins when the brightest star is seen in the morning sky in direct line with the rising sun. All my observations showed the year to have 365 days.'

Nilakantha knew that in Bharat Varsha and in Sumer, a year was known to have three-hundred-and-sixty-five and a quarter days, but he did not know how or why. But he was sure that so insignificant an error of a mere quarter-day hardly mattered and he said so. But Hutantat gravely said, 'It makes a difference of a year in 1,460 years.' Apparently, Hutantat did not take this lightly.

However, in calendars in Bharat Varsha, a day was divided into twenty hours, an hour into hundred minutes, a minute into hundred seconds, and a second into ten subdivisions. In Sumeria, a day had twenty-four hours, each hour sixty minutes, and a minute had sixty seconds, with no subdivisions for seconds. But then, the Sumerians always had six as their sacred number. Everything had to be a multiple of six, whether it be their gods, immortal angels, the number of lashes to punish a culprit, or division of days and minutes. Even the manmade cycle of a 'week'—an artificial cluster of seven days—owed its inspiration to the Sumerians. 'Six days of the priest and one day of sin', they believed, which simply meant that each person owed his six days, out of seven, to labour for his priest, while the one remaining day was, inauspiciously, for a person's own individual, private pursuits. Whereas the people in Bharat Varsha had a ten-day week, the eleventh day was a day of rest and to entertain friends, and the twelfth day was for public festivities and entertainment, after which the ten-day week began once again.

It was actually from Sumeria that the system of twenty-four hours for a day, sixty minutes for an hour and sixty seconds for a minute, and even the concept of a week as a bouquet of seven days, reached the Romans, Christians, and others. And while the origins and routes of borrowings are obscure, it may be that the Sumerian system came to Bharat Varsha not through returning Aryans, but later, indirectly from Europe.

On the Sumerian use of multiples of six and Bharat Varsha's preference for multiples of ten, Hutantat asked, 'Is ten a sacred number in your Bharat Varsha?'

'Not at all,' Himatap said, 'but ten is a convenient number for decimal placement. Many say that in its pre-ancient origin, the popularity of the number ten arose simply for its convenience, as man had ten fingers and counting up to ten was easy.'

Lugal laughed, 'Maybe the first Sumerian who began counting had six fingers in his hand, or maybe he had six children and no more and stopped counting after six. Who knows! But the fact is that six has always been a sacred number for us.'

Nilakantha pleaded, so Hutantat took him, along with many others, to bring back Ajitab and the thirty-six sick and injured Aryans they had left behind at the settlement under the protection of the grave robbers.

When they reached, they found no settlement, only skeletons of the dead, fleshless bodies left there to rot. There was no one in the hills where the grave robbers had had their hide-out either.

Although they did not know it at the time, this tragedy was related to the temple that the Aryans were building. The king's soldiers had fanned out everywhere to hunt for new slaves to work on the temple, and had reached the hide-out of the grave robbers. Apparently, everyone too young or too old to serve as a slave was killed and the rest were dragged away as slaves.

Hutantat sent out his men everywhere to look for any of the slaves taken from there, but none could be located. He tried to console Nilakantha, 'Maybe, your Aryans joined the grave robbers to escape.'

'Don't worry,' Lugal told an anguished Nilakantha. 'If they are robbing graves, they are working less than we are and living better.' Nilakantha shook his head.

Both Lugal and Hutantat knew what Nilakantha was thinking: would the Aryans burdened with the karma of their last life soil their karma for the next life by committing the evil of robbing a grave? They did not want to intrude on Nilakantha's anguish. Yet they were both thinking that each man had his destiny and neither tears nor hopes could wipe it away!

There was silence in Nilakantha's heart. Laughter did not come to him as easily as before. Around him, he saw the graveyard of hopes—his own and those of the Aryans who relied on him. How comforting it would be to adopt the philosophy of Hutantat, that our hopes and dreams, our effort and will did not matter, everything was ruled by destiny.

THIRTY-NINE

EGYPT AND THE KINGDOM OF AJITAB

5005 BCE

Ajitab and his thirty-six Aryans had fled from their hideout at the settlement of the grave robbers, when the soldiers had come to hunt for more slaves.

After many adventures, they moved into another Egyptian kingdom. They were caught, enslaved and made to work in a quarry. Only five Aryans, including Ajitab, and sixteen grave robbers survived after two years of dehumanizing brutality; the rest died, collapsing where they worked.

Ajitab organized a mass escape. Twelve guards and eighty slaves died. But Ajitab escaped with four Aryans, thirteen grave robbers and more than 400 other slaves. On the way, they attacked numerous places, freeing the slaves who worked there. There were many minor skirmishes and their initial success was spectacular. Their ranks swelled but their days seemed numbered as the soldiers of the kingdom closed in on them.

Eventually, the slaves revolted against Ajitab. He wanted to press on, to be ahead of the soldiers hunting them, but many slaves felt invulnerable with their increased numbers and wanted to stay back to loot, steal and fight. Ajitab allowed defections, while he pressed on. Perhaps that saved him and his group, as battles raged against the slaves who had stayed back. He returned to the hills from where they had originally fled, but the area was no longer safe.

Taking circuitous paths, Ajitab and his troop of four Aryans, eleven grave robbers and ninety-nine slaves reached the catacombs. The catacombs, with their many hiding places, trenches and tunnels were safe, but only for thieves, robbers and cut-throats. For soldiers, it was a deadly place, not only because of the dangerous men who hid there, but also because they were terrified of contagion from the many lepers who lived there too.

Early on, Ajitab became involved in a deadly tussle with Dahzur, who had become chief of the catacombs by strangling the previous chief. He had then turned his ferocity against the lepers and had them burnt alive. Thereafter, he cleansed the catacombs of many old robbers who in their youth had stolen much from outside, but now depended on charity. Finally he began a reign of terror against many whose personal loyalty he suspected. In a short while, Dahzur's command was absolute. He demanded a share of loot from all in the catacombs and enforced his demand ruthlessly. Those who objected disappeared mysteriously. Though he never ventured out himself, he paid close attention to the teams he sent out to loot. His planning was faultless, but if some teams were caught, he showed no remorse for there were others who would take their place.

Dahzur had welcomed Ajitab's group. He recognized the grave robbers with Ajitab and was pleased at this addition to his strength. Soon after, a team was to be sent out to loot, but one of them was sick so Dahzur asked an Aryan to go instead. The Aryan declined. Dahzur insisted good-humouredly, ready to be gracious to the newcomer who was unaware of his power. But Ajitab intervened, 'Enough! Did you not hear him say that he would not go?'

Dahzur exploded with rage. He saw it as a challenge and decided to set an example; he motioned to three henchmen. They moved towards Ajitab, with daggers unsheathed. With his instincts sharpened by years of danger and adversity, Ajitab lunged at Dahzur's throat. The powerful chief collapsed at this unexpected, ferocious attack and Ajitab fell on top of him with a vicious grip on his throat. One of Dahzur's men misjudged his blow and stabbed Ajitab in the fleshy part of his thigh, but the searing pain only tightened Ajitab's grip over Dahzur's throat. He heard a gurgle. Suddenly, with a jerk, he got up, and the three who were trying to pull him away, fell.

Someone said, 'Dahzur is dead.'

Ajitab nodded as though he knew. No one stopped Ajitab as he walked away slowly, bleeding but unsupported. In his shelter, four Aryans washed and bandaged his wound. Then he collapsed.

Later, the three who had tried to attack Ajitab were brought to him to be disciplined. But Ajitab said, 'Let them go. They were under orders.'

From that day, gradually, the men in the catacombs began treating Ajitab as their chief. He demanded that lepers who entered should not be killed. Separate areas were reserved for them. Nor were the old and infirm to be eliminated. He did not demand a share of the loot, but a share was kept aside for the lepers, the old and infirm. Dirt and garbage in the catacombs was burnt; medicines and herbal remedies were stocked. He asked them to locate and smuggle into the catacombs a slave who knew more about medicines. He insisted on building more trenches and tunnels to hide in and fight against attacks; a reservoir to store water; shelters, amenities. 'Let us live like humans even if we must die as beasts.'

Ajitab even put the oldest to light work, sending them to follow raiding parties, so that if the raiders were arrested, he would know where they were taken and rescue them. His men also located two slaves with physicians' knowledge in a slave camp of forty-eight. Ajitab himself led the attack, freeing all the slaves in the camp and smuggling them into the catacombs.

But Ajitab was astounded to discover that the freed slaves were being treated as slaves in the catacombs. He tried to stop it, but failed. That was when he realized, as Dahzur did, that the way to reach the hearts of these ruthless cut-throats was not always through gentleness. With a ferocity and savagery that Dahzur would have envied, he enforced his will and declared, 'He who enslaves another shall be chained and left outside the catacombs as a soldier's reward.'

After the ensuing bloodbath was over, no one dared challenge Ajitab. He was the king of the catacombs and his word was law.

Much remained unsaid between Ajitab and the four Aryans with him. But each knew the other's anguish! They thought of the time, seemingly centuries ago, when they had left home, singing, 'Noble Arya, onward, on . . . ' And now they lived to loot, kill and crush, with countless unseen daggers aimed at their hearts!

God! Where have you guided our footsteps? And why? Is this your karma or ours?

Suddenly, astounding news filtered to the catacombs—about a hundred miles away, Aryans were building a temple!

A hundred miles! What could a hundred miles matter to men who had traversed thousands? Yet, the route would have danger at every twist and turn. An old robber volunteered to carry Ajitab's message to the construction site, and many others offered to help. It was decided that the old man would go with six former slaves carrying a coffin, as if headed for a burial. No one would attack coffins or even graves for the first twenty-seven days. Even so, the slaves would go visibly armed, so that no one was tempted to attack.

At the last moment, one of the four Aryans insisted on going with them. Ajitab pleaded, 'Only four of us are left.'

'Would it matter if none were left!'

Ajitab understood the anguish, but insisted, 'I don't know what our Aryans are doing there . . . If they are captives, we must organize a massive attack to free them. Please!'

'No, let me die! Let me even become a slave for I cannot live here in this . . . this kingdom of yours.' Suddenly tears came to his eyes, 'Forgive me, brother Ajitab, but let me go. Last night I swore I would not remain here, neither to kill, nor to hurt anyone. If I'm forced to remain here, you will grieve over my body soon.'

'Go with God,' Ajitab said. He embraced the Aryan with tears as he left. The Aryan went as the father of the child in the coffin carried by the six slaves, and the old robber joined them as the grandfather.

No one felt tempted to attack them all along the route, but as they neared the construction site, a soldier stopped them. He had seen such a ploy by thieves before. He summoned some more soldiers and demanded that the slaves put the coffin down for inspection.

The Aryan knew his moment had come; he was only sorry that the others too would die with him. He claimed sole responsibility, saying none of the others knew anything. A soldier shoved him aside, but the officer looked hard at him, and wondered: he looks different, speaks with an accent, certainly not a local!.

'Are you Aryan?' he asked.

'Yes, yes, I am Aryan!'

Still suspicious, the officer ordered, 'Sing the Aryan song!'

'Noble Arya . . . onward . . . on—'

'Enough, stop! With that kind of voice, you should never sing. Now give me some Aryan names,' the officer commanded.

'Nilakantha, Lugal, Himatap—' he recited.

'What about Hutantat?' the officer asked. The Aryan said nothing, not sure if it was a trap or not, for he knew no Hutantat. But the officer was already convinced that he had an Aryan before him. Still, he demanded to know what was in the coffin. The old man simply pointed to the Aryan, then to the sky and the construction site. He pretended to be dumb so that he told no lies. The officer understood nothing, but he remembered the king's warning that anyone who harmed the Aryans at the construction site would be severely punished. He asked the Aryan's name and at his order, a soldier rushed back to the site.

Four hours they waited, guarded, but unharmed. And then Nilakantha, Lugal, Hutantat and many of the Aryans from the site arrived. None of the Aryans at the construction site slept that night. At dawn Hutantat, Nilakantha and some others left with the Aryan and the old robber. On the way, both the Aryan and the old robber thanked the officer and soldiers so volubly that they wondered how it was that the old man who was mute the day before could now speak. The old man simply pointed to Hutantat as if to say he had wrought the miracle. Everyone knew Hutantat's power of prophecy, but now some would regard him as a man of miracles too.

They all waited at a distance from the catacombs while the old robber went in and brought out Ajitab and the three Aryans.

Together, they travelled back to the construction site. Nilakantha had no words, no songs; his heart was too full with the joy of having Ajitab and four others restored to them. He had often shed tears for the many Aryans that they had lost, and though he thought of them now, this was not the moment for tears.

Yet Nilakantha's joy was short-lived. Ajitab had passed only two nights at the site when he flared up in a violent temper. 'You make slaves work for you here!'

Nilakantha explained, but Ajitab's contempt increased. Nilakantha did not point out that Ajitab had stolen, lied, even killed, to save himself, for in his heart he realized that to hold an innocent in captivity was a sin more heinous than any of Ajitab's sins in self-defence. He knew also that not all Ajitab's offences had been to protect himself alone.

Ajitab asked, 'Is this why you led us here?'

Nilakantha pleaded to no avail. Ajitab was firm. 'So long as I am here, I shall try to free these slaves.'

'We are under oath to Sage Hutantat to complete the temple,' Nilakantha said.

'I am under no such oath,' Ajitab said.

'The oath binds us all.'

'Not me.'

Nilakantha was silent. Ajitab's father and mother had been held as slaves in Bharat Varsha, although slavery had been declared unlawful. Some time after his father's death, when Ajitab was six years old, his mother had been molested by the slave owner. While Ajitab had stood, stricken with fear, his three-year-old sister ran to their mother. The slave owner had picked up the child and thrown her forcefully against a rock, killing her instantly. Though a voice in him had urged him to pick up the stones lying on the ground and hurl them at the man who had killed his sister and was ravishing his unconscious mother, Ajitab was much too frightened, and ran away instead. When his mother regained consciousness, she saw her daughter's dead body, and when she could not find Ajitab anywhere, assumed that he too had died. Overwhelmed by grief, she had jumped into a well. When Ajitab finally came back he saw his sister and mother being cremated, and ran away again. Over the next few years, in every nightmare, he saw the stones he had not picked up and hurled at the slave owner, he saw his sister's dead body, and the flames from their funeral pyres that mocked him.

A sadhu gave him shelter and taught him yoga, but after a while Ajitab lost interest in it. He wanted to learn to fight, shoot an arrow, throw a dagger, and wield a sword. 'Why?' asked the sadhu.

'Because I am a coward.'

The sadhu did not want Ajitab to grow up thinking he

was a coward, so he taught him as much as he could and then left him in charge of an old pupil who trained athletes, wrestlers and fighters.

At sixteen, Ajitab went to his old village to kill the slave owner, but he learnt that the man had died after being stung by a scorpion. When he returned the sadhu asked him, 'You did not wish to kill the slave owner's children?'

'No,' Ajitab said. 'Only cowards kill children.' The sadhu embraced him.

Ajitab's life became purposeless. He assisted his teacher in training others to fight and proved to be a better fighter than his teacher. When the Aryans were leaving Bharat Varsha, he joined them, hoping for a better, purer land, elsewhere.

It was while Ajitab was being brutalized as a slave in Egypt's adjoining kingdom that he decided he would devote his life to free the slaves. That determination stirred to life when his men tried to enslave the forty-eight slaves who had been smuggled into the catacombs. He was merciless with those who did not listen to him to treat the slaves as free men. And now, as he saw hordes of slaves at the construction site, he was more determined than ever to free slaves, anywhere and everywhere.

Nilakantha and Ajitab sat facing each other, without speaking. In those silent moments, each understood the anguish of the other. Both knew that their faith in finding the Land of the Pure had dwindled and this long journey had been in vain.

Nilakantha pleaded, 'Our hearts are the same, our goals no different—freedom for these slaves and the safety of our people. That is why we have to complete the temple.'

Ajitab's fury was spent. 'Don't worry, I shall not interfere.'

Nilakantha's happiness died as Ajitab continued, 'By your will, I shall leave as an Aryan.' Clearly, he was suggesting that it was Nilakantha's tolerance of slavery at the temple site that was forcing him to leave as an exile.

'I would rather run a sword through myself than dream of exiling you,' Nilakantha said.

Ajitab apologized. He realized it was his inner frustration that had made him blame the gracious Nilakantha. He added, 'No, I leave by my will. You have to look after your temple and slaves here. I shall look for slaves elsewhere.'

Perhaps only Hutantat understood Ajitab's resolve and said, 'Each man comes to his decision himself. Yet a man who lives in the desert must know the source of water, a man in high mountains must learn to protect himself against falling rocks, a man in the river must know how to avoid crocodiles.'

Nobody understood. But he explained, 'Your heart tells you to free slaves. So be it. But your head must come to terms with that decision. What will you do when the slaves are free? Leave them to be hunted again? Where will they run and hide? In your catacombs! Today, the soldiers ignore the catacombs. But when you shelter numerous slaves there, will the king stay his hand? Everyone there will die in unspeakable horror. You will die happy, perhaps in the vain belief that you died to fulfil a mission, but you are the one to doom your own mission from the very start.'

Ajitab glared, while Hutantat continued, 'And what karma will you teach slaves while they hide in the catacombs? To steal, loot, and kill! Do you know anything other than violence? You will simply raise legions of robbers and murderers out of slaves, so that they rob others of life and liberty, before they, too, vanish into nothingness! Is that why you left your land, Arya?'

Hutantat was pitiless: 'I suppose you will also unfurl the Aryan flag over your thieving, murdering slaves, so that the Aryan name and mission is forever cloaked in dishonour in the history of this country, if not in yours and everywhere else!'

Ajitab shook his head, but Hutantat added, 'And finally, your achievement will be that Aryans here too shall be wiped out for the dishonour of associating with you . . . you, who wish to be known as a great freedom fighter, ready to lay down his life for his cause, regardless of the doom of slaves and eternal dishonour to Aryans!'

'You know that is not my purpose,' Ajitab said.

'No, it is only the inevitable consequence of what is in your immature mind.'

'And you think I should happily live here like Nilakantha?'

'No, each man must heed the call in his heart. It is beyond you to even understand the extent of Nilakantha's silent, living sacrifice. One day, when you and Aryans like you understand, you will turn to him with tenderness, affection and gratitude.'

'I am ready to touch Nilakantha's feet now,' Ajitab joked.

'It will be an empty gesture, like the glorious death you foresee for yourself. But remember, dying is easy. It is life that presents difficult choices and sometimes a man must condemn himself to live, when there are promises to keep and when duty beckons. What kind of a dream is it that not only the dreamer must die, but along with him the dream itself be cursed and dishonoured by all?'

'Sage, I do not understand much of what you say.'

'I feared as much. Nilakantha understands as does Lugal. Many others will. But it is beyond you. To understand it, you need courage in your heart and not rashness.'

Nilakantha feared that Ajitab would explode with anger. He did not. He was humble and contrite and said, 'You are right, sage. All I hear is the voice in my heart that tells me what I should go after. That voice echoes within me and I know I do not hear it in vain. I shall not shut it out. But for the rest, you are right. I do not know how I should respond to its call. Perhaps, your words shall show me the way.'

Later, quietly, Hutantat clarified to Ajitab, 'First, you will have to leave here as a renegade Aryan, hated and despised by the Aryans here. Nor must you proclaim yourself as an Aryan. Second, the catacombs must not shelter slaves, for that will invite massive attacks by the king's forces. Third, there are larger areas, barren and deserted, where only lizards live, which are reachable through mountains by paths difficult for soldiers to cross, and slaves may live there while you teach them the only art you know. Fourth, a thief never robs from just one house; it will be folly to restrict your activities to this kingdom alone, unless you want undivided attention from the king here. You must diversify.'

'But other kingdoms are far away!' Ajitab said.

'For a man who has travelled this far, you are really modest! And where do you think your hide-outs will be? Next to the catacombs? No, you will have to go much farther.'

'But how are the slaves to live in those barren areas?'

'Perhaps you are beginning to understand after all,' Hutantat said, 'that it is easy to die but difficult to live. Yes, the slaves must learn to make those areas fertile. You too must learn in order to teach!'

'But that will take time!' Ajitab replied.

'What else does life have except time! From birth to death, there is only time. A fool fritters it away, the wise guard it.'

For days, Ajitab remained at the construction site. Hutantat took him to his villages that once were barren, but were now lush and green, with freed slaves working under his protection.

'I have a few freed slaves who have the same dream as you,' Hutantat said. 'If they are ungrateful and run away from here to join you, there is nothing I can do.'

Hutantat and Ajitab then spoke of the faraway barren areas, the routes to reach them, the methods to tap water, the routes to neighbouring kingdoms and the locations of possible hide-outs.

Finally, Hutantat advised, 'See my hut there! It has a great deal a thief can want. When you are ready, ransack the hut and take everything.'

'Steal from you?' Ajitab asked, shocked.

'Why not! What else will a renegade do! You will "steal"

also from the Aryans at the construction site! They must distance themselves from you.'

'So I appear a dishonourable thief and a common scoundrel, condemned and scorned by all those I love!'

'It is your choice, remember? The only question is: do you fight for yourself and your name or for your dream?'

Irrelevantly, Ajitab said, 'My little sister died with her head smashed, and my mother jumped into a well.'

'I know,' Hutantat said, for Nilakantha had told him.

'They died in vain and I shall die in dishonour.'

'Your sister and your mother died not in vain. Their death inspires you and your cause. Nor shall you die in dishonour. You shall die for a cause that is larger than your life, far above the empty pretence of honour and virtue, and you shall die only in your body, for your spirit will live, inspiring others to reach out for the day that is to come.'

'Am I doing the right thing, Sage?'

'That judgement must be yours. All I know is that whether you live or die, I shall pray for you, day and night, far more than I pray for myself and my soul.'

Hutantat and Ajitab were together often after that. Escorted by soldiers and Hutantat's freed slaves, they travelled to distant lands, ostensibly to look for materials for the temple. But their real purpose was for Ajitab to see the areas, chart out routes, and find hide-outs and sanctuaries. Surreptitiously, a few freed slaves left Hutantat's lands, and Hutantat pretended to make anxious inquiries everywhere but shrugged his shoulders—'They had a right to leave. But to depart without a word of farewell!' Many sympathized, 'What ingratitude!' But some said, 'This comes from giving freedom to the undeserving!'

For some time, Ajitab's plans were known only to Hutantat, Lugal, Nilakantha and the Aryans who were with him in the catacombs.

Larali was a young Aryan woman who had once been chosen as the 'virgin in waiting' by a priest in Sumeria but had been saved by the timely intervention of Sumaran. Since then, she had moved with the Aryans to Lugal's domain in Assyria and thence to Egypt.

It was when the Aryans rested at the grave robbers' settlement on the outskirts of Egypt, that Ajitab and Larali spoke words of love to each other. Both felt in their hearts that at their next meeting they would speak of an abiding relationship.

Larali and Ajitab were both supposed to be in the first batch of Aryans to move out from the settlement. But at the last minute, Nilakantha had asked Ajitab to wait. The Aryan who was expected to remain with the thirty-five sick and injured had been showing off, jumping from hill to hill. Unfortunately, he lost his footing and injured himself. Since Nilakantha could not leave an injured man in charge, he had told Ajitab, 'This high jumper was to look after thirty-five. Now you look after thirty-six.' Larali had left with the first batch, hoping Nilakantha and Ajitab would join them soon.

When the chilling news had come that there was no trace of Ajitab and the thirty-six others and that the settlement itself had been wiped out, Larali said to herself, 'Always, it is my destiny to wait.'

Thereafter, many sought to marry her but she declined, saying, 'I wait.'

Months followed, and then suddenly came a lone Aryan from the catacombs, bringing joyous tidings that Ajitab and three Aryans were still alive, free and safe. Yet, she feared to ask the question wrenching her heart. Instead, she asked, 'How is your leg?' for he was the one whose leg had been injured in the bravado of leaping from hill to hill, forcing Ajitab to stay back to look after the sick. 'My leg is fine, so also is he who looked after me and my leg, and he loves you, always, every moment, waking, dreaming, sleeping!'

They smiled, and Larali thought—at last, my waiting is over.

But that was not to be. When Ajitab came, he looked into Larali's eyes, held her hand, but the question he was to ask, to bind them forever, remained unasked. Was it possible for a man to contemplate marriage while he charted such a perilous path for himself? Was there any hope of his survival as long as he made it his mission to defy kingdoms and free their slaves? He was ready to die, certain that his death would not be in vain, that someone would pick up the fallen torch. But marriage! It was out of the question.

Once only did Ajitab pour his heart out to her, to speak not of love but of what lay ahead of him, and she was silent. In the weeks that followed, he went away for long stretches of time with Hutantat. When he returned, he was surrounded by people. She finally confronted him, and in a voice that did not falter, said, 'There was one question I forgot to ask you that day. Do you or do you not love me?' Quietly, unmindful of the others, he replied, 'Yes. Always.'

Her voice rose, 'Brother Nilakantha, I shall marry Ajitab. Please perform the ceremony.' Since they had no regular priest, performing the marriage ceremony and other rites fell on Nilakantha.

But Nilakantha, surprised, said, 'But Ajitab has not spoken.' The husband-to-be was always the first to declare his desire to marry and to take a five-fold marriage-vow promising his wife, 'piety, permanence, pleasure, property and progeny'.

Larali replied, 'My husband-to-be is too tongue-tied, too timid, and too afraid to speak.'

Timid and afraid! Ajitab! Impossible.

But Ajitab spoke now, 'Yes, Brother Nilakantha, please, I wish to marry Larali.'

Nilakantha pleaded, 'Wait . . . ' But that was the wrong thing to say.

'Wait!' Larali stormed. 'Always, I wait. And all because of you! But this time, I have waited enough!'

But Nilakantha pleaded, 'I never perform the ceremony without taking a bath.'

At that even Larali laughed, 'That much I shall wait.'

And Ajitab said, 'Hurry, brother, hurry!'

Hutantat put his arm around Larali and drew her aside to ask, 'Daughter, do you know what Ajitab is to do and why and where?'

And she answered, 'I know *what* and *why*. But as to *where*, surely, I shall know soon as I shall always be with him.'

Gravely, Hutantat said, 'It may be a place of no return.'

In her heart Larali had no fear of the future. But she was afraid of the sage who might influence Ajitab, even now, not to marry, for the sake of the task he was to undertake.

But she said, 'I have no mother, no father. Bless me, sage, and give me away as the bride.'

He held her to his bosom, 'So be it, child, if that is your destiny. My blessing to you. May your union be fruitful. But accept, in good grace, destiny's triumphs and wounds.'

Her reply in her heart remained unspoken, 'I make my own destiny to meet my destiny.'

They were married.

Ajitab and Larali shared only a few nights of love. For weeks, he would be away with Hutantat or on his own. Many said, 'He was a secret lover, and now a secret husband.' Some sorrowed for Larali, 'What has she done to deserve such neglect?'

Many now saw a more terrible aspect of Ajitab, for he was preparing himself for the role of the renegade who would desert the Aryans. He openly quarrelled with Hutantat, Lugal and Nilakantha. Some, including the commander, soldiers and slaves, wondered: 'Why do they tolerate him?' But Ajitab was considered a master in locating the right building materials for the temple, and it was well known that Hutantat and the Aryans would go to any lengths, in the king's cause, to build the best temple.

Meanwhile, Ajitab quietly visited the catacombs. Of the forty-eight freed slaves there, he sent many to a distant area to work on the land. The freed slaves from Hutantat's land were already there with the necessary implements.

Four months after his marriage, Ajitab's arrangements to move were nearly complete. 'A few days more and we leave,' he told Larali.

'You must go alone,' she replied. 'I can wait. Your child cannot.' He was delighted that he was to be a father. But he teased her too, 'You said you would be careful.'

She laughed, 'Destiny! After all, Sage Hutantat blessed our union to be fruitful.'

Anxiously, he asked, 'Do you want me to delay my departure?'

'No,' she said. 'Your task remains. Let no one accuse my unborn child of delaying you.'

'*Our* unborn child,' he corrected her happily.

'Yet I must speak for him, if you will not.'

❧

Suddenly, some five months after his marriage, Ajitab disappeared from the construction site, along with the four Aryans who had been with him in the catacombs.

Every Aryan at the site felt desolate at Ajitab's desertion. They had seen him in moments of joy, interrupted by quarrels with Hutantat, Lugal and Nilakantha. But how could they know that he was *acting* the part of one about to desert! They were shocked when they learnt that he had even robbed a hut containing Hutantat's valuables stores.

The king, who heard of it from his gleeful chief priest,

sympathized with Hutantat and learnt that the fugitive Aryan had robbed his Aryan brethren too. 'I thought all these Aryans were honourable,' said the king.

'The best fruit tree can be attacked by worms,' Hutantat said.

'True. If out of my nine sister-wives, two are rotten, surely these many Aryans are entitled to have a few scoundrels.'

'Well said, king. You are truly profound,' Hutantat responded.

Pleased, the king added, 'But I shall ask everyone to hunt for the renegade.'

'No, king. Your words of wisdom were spoken when you had said that anyone harming an Aryan will receive the highest penalty. So let him alone, if by chance he is seen.'

'But he may steal elsewhere!' the king objected.

'Yes, but if he is caught he must be brought to the Aryans, unharmed. He has hurt them terribly. They must be the ones to punish him. How grateful they will be and how mightily they will work for you!'

'You speak wisely,' said the king.

Hutantat responded, 'When I am in the presence of my king who is the fount of wisdom, what else can flow from my lips!' The king was delighted.

No one saw the relation between the events for they were separated by time and distance, but four months after Ajitab left the construction site, attacks started on various posts to free slaves.

Meanwhile, work on the temple continued. The entire surface of the hill and its sides were flattened and smoothed. Bricks to cover the hilltop were being baked and glazed. Steps ran along the four sides, so that the hill itself had the appearance of a 'stepped square'. There were makeshift ladders to go up the 'squared' hilltop. Surrounding the hill, below, was to be an ornamental garden; already large tracts had been cleared, streams diverted, trees planted and areas

BHAGWAN S. GIDWANI

earmarked to house soldiers and slaves in artificial valleys with wide trenches that would hide the huts, maintaining the aesthetic appearance of the garden. On the hill, the temple's outer structure was ready and two out of twenty-five obelisks had been erected.

Lugal was considered the creator of the temple complex. But it was Himatap who was everywhere, supervising digging, erecting, clearing and experimenting. Often, Himatap would run to Lugal for ideas, advice, calculations and even help and inspiration, but then he would improve on those ideas and try to create something far more ambitious. Sometimes he would have a structure demolished only to rebuild it differently, because a better idea came to him. Lugal would try to stop him: 'Brother Himatap, we build all this not for the glory of God, but to satisfy the vanity of a tyrant who cannot distinguish between what is perfect and what is flawed. Build well, but do not seek perfection. The sooner we finish, the sooner we may be free.' Himatap would agree for the moment, but in the joy of building, everything was erased from his mind except to seek perfection in whatever he built. Nothing else mattered.

Lugal insisted that the obelisks should be erected at the end. He was the one who had boasted to the king of his ability to erect obelisks whose tips would attract the golden glow of the rising and setting sun at different times. The conception was clear in his mind, but theory and actual construction were not the same. Lugal remembered the first ziggurat—thoughtfully conceived and elegantly built—he had erected in Sumer that had fallen in the first rainstorm.

It was with this fear that Lugal had urged that the obelisks be erected last, hoping that, on seeing the grandeur of the other structures, the king would forget about the obelisks. But Hutantat told him, 'The king never forgets a pledge made to him.' Himatap was delighted to be allowed to erect the obelisks. The idea that Lugal's conception might not work never even occurred to him. He would work on it and if it failed, he would re-calculate and begin anew. Time and effort meant nothing to him.

But fortune smiled on them. Lugal's calculations, which Hutantat and Himatap had also worked on tirelessly, were flawless. When the first obelisk was ready, the sun's glow shone on its tip every day at the same time. They did not have to look at the obelisk. Looking simply at the sky, with the obelisk behind, Himatap would raise his hand to signal when the sun's glow would hit the obelisk and indeed, it was so!

A miracle—many said. Lugal and Hutantat agreed that Himatap was the miracle-maker. The human mind can conceive anything, they said, but to bring it alive requires genius.

∽

Himatap's grandfather had been one of the 140 explorers who, in Karkarta Bharat's time, had crossed the Himalayas into Tibet to find the source of the Sindhu river. He was one of the few who had survived, but he had lost his eyesight from the sun's reflection leaping back from ice in the mountains. Rather than return to Sindhu, he chose to remain in Tibet and married a local Tibetan girl. His only daughter also married a local Tibetan. Their son was named Himatap, in loving memory of his grandfather (Himatap means the heat of snow).

Later, even after most Aryans left Egypt to return to Bharat Varsha, Himatap remained in Egypt and married a local girl. A hundred girls from Egypt wanted to marry him, as he had announced that his wife would not be buried with him when he died, for who would pray for him when he was no more! To a Tibetan, it was unthinkable that a person should die with no one to pray for him, for it was not just a person's

BHAGWAN S. GIDWANI

own karma and prayers that mattered in the afterlife, but also the prayers of others on his behalf. To the Egyptians who argued against his stand, he said that his wife could not be buried with him, as he, like all Hindus, would be cremated. But still they asked, 'Why then can the wife not be cremated with the husband?' Himatap said that he could not conceive of a more heinous sin and asked, 'Would not such a sin damage my soul and the souls of all my children and grandchildren?' A Hindu he was, but he also held the Tibetan belief that one's sins jeopardized the souls of one's children. In disgust, the Egyptians asked Himatap, 'You will leave your wife to be claimed by some other man?' But he said, 'God will claim her in His own time.' He rejected the hundreds of marriage proposals that came his way, for as a Hindu, he explained, he would be married only to one wife, lifelong, and he had already selected his bride. It so happened that Himatap's wife was neither buried nor burnt on his funeral pyre with him. She died after sixteen years of marriage, having given birth to four children. He outlived her by many years, but never remarried.

～

The king was delighted with the obelisk that captured the sun's glow. So visibly impressed was he that Hutantat promptly asked for more villages and more slaves to be freed.

'Villages I shall give,' the king said, 'but for slaves, wait until all the obelisks are ready. I have difficulties at the moment.'

'How can you, king of all, have difficulties?' Hutantat asked.

The king spoke of attacks on slave posts. 'But soon, the perpetrators will be found, and then you will have what you seek.'

Obviously, Ajitab had begun his attacks to free the slaves in Egypt.

The attacks on the slave posts seemed senseless; there was no effort to steal anything, only to free slaves. Besides, the runaway slaves could not hide for long; detection was inevitable, for each slave was branded on their left and right upper-arms. A slave would have to cut off both his arms to plead that he was never a slave. Punishment for escape was terrible. No wonder, the guards were often so careless and lax. Still, the attacks on slave posts continued. They came in a series and then stopped, only to start and stop in the next kingdom, then to begin and end in another, and so on. Initially, the kings were not overly concerned. The loss of slaves simply meant that they had to pick others to fill their place. With the exception of those who held priestly or official titles sanctioned by the king, everyone was regarded as a slave. The only difference was that branded slaves were kept for manual labour at particular places under the supervision of soldiers, with no freedom of movement, while others— peasants and artisans—had considerable freedom, though much of what they produced was for the king. It was the privilege of the king to have any of those peasants and artisans branded as slaves though this was not done often. However, with attacks to free branded slaves becoming more frequent, peasants and artisans were being branded as well.

When the second obelisk had been erected and the king expressed his delight, Hutantat asked only for a title for all Aryans so that they were immune from slavery. Having already given the title of 'king's architect' to Lugal, the king now asked, 'What title do you seek for them?'

Hutantat suggested, 'Soldiers of the king's architect.'

'Only the king has soldiers,' the chief priest intervened.

Hutantat really did not care what title was given; any title sanctioned by the king would prevent all future designs to brand Aryans as slaves. He knew that some people had even been given titles like 'king's donkey', 'king's fool' and 'carrier of king's shit-pot', and they too were immune from

BHAGWAN S. GIDWANI

slavery. Pleasantly, Hutantat said, 'Very well, give them the title of Aryan.'

But the king asked 'Aryan! What does that mean?' The king thought that Aryan simply indicated the lands from which these strangers came.

Hutantat said, 'Aryan means noblemen who work for a noble cause.'

But the chief priest interrupted again, 'Noble! Only priests, commanders and the king's architects are noble!'

Hutantat shouted back, 'So I suppose your king is not noble, nor are the men who work on his noble temple. Do you want me to tell these people that they work for a king who is not noble?'

The chief priest wilted. Anyone else would be cut down for saying so much, but not Hutantat.

Generously, the king said, 'Yes, I shall give them all the title of Aryan, except one.' And while Hutantat worried, the king pointed to Himatap, 'He shall be given the title of master builder.'

'Oh king! To be in your shadow is to learn wisdom!' Hutantat said with great feeling. 'And I wish it could flow to your priests as well!' But he added, 'Yet, it may degrade your master builder in the eyes of all, if his commander Nilakantha is not honoured.'

Quickly, the king asked, 'And what prevents me from making him a commander?'

'Nothing, my king! Nothing is beyond you and your power and your majesty!' and before the chief priest could interfere, Hutantat shouted to Nilakantha, 'Kneel, dog, kneel!'

Nilakantha knew the ritual for receiving titles. He knelt and the king's whip touched him.

Grudgingly, the chief priest intoned, 'The sun god has spoken. And all shall honour you as such. Rise, honourable king's commander.'

Himatap too knelt, and rose honoured as the king's master

builder. Then came the turn of the other Aryans. But they were too many, and the king's hand was tiring. The chief priest said, 'Enough for the day . . . '

Hutantat interrupted, 'Yes, enough, my king, you make the ritual and you unmake it. Enough, if you flick the whip in the air while they all kneel, and I shall leave their names with the king's clerk.' He shouted to all the Aryans, 'Kneel, dogs, kneel. All of you!' They all knelt. Gratefully, the king flicked his whip in the air and the chief priest again intoned, 'Rise, honourable king's Aryans.'

The next day, Hutantat met the king's clerk with the names of all the Aryans at the site who were deemed to be honoured with king's title and he even added five more names—of the missing Ajitab and his four Aryan companions—to the list.

The Aryans were not fully aware of all that came to them with the king's titles, apart from the red bands they wore. Hutantat said, 'All it means is that no one can ever enslave you, but then is not the promise of liberty superior even to the guarantee of life?' No one disagreed and he added, 'But Himatap, as the king's master builder, has many rights, and as the king's commander, Nilakantha has many more, including the authority to free slaves and make them soldiers under his command.

Nilakantha pleaded, 'Oh brother, let us free all slaves here and make them soldiers!'

Hutantat said, 'The authority is limited. You can free only unbranded slaves.'

'But practically all of them are branded,' Nilakantha wailed.

'Thirty-six are not,' Hutantat said. Those thirty-six had come later, but as they were about to be branded Hutantat had pleaded with the commander, saying the slaves would be unable to work for days with the pain and blisters from the branding. 'Why delay the king's work? Wait for a lull in the work,' he had suggested. The commander had agreed, but a

BHAGWAN S. GIDWANI

lull there never was and so they had remained unbranded. Now it was open to Nilakantha to free them as soldiers.

'But the commander may object,' Nilakantha feared.

'Don't worry,' Hutantat said. 'You have rights as the king's commander. But even so, tell him you need about fifty soldiers. Surely, as king's commander, you can demand that pitiful number. He will hate to lose a single soldier. Then tell him that you will accept unbranded slaves instead. He will be delighted; he may even kiss you.'

The commander did not kiss Nilakantha, but heartily agreed that unbranded slaves be made soldiers. He wanted to lose not a single soldier of his.

Nilakantha was proud commander of thirty-six soldiers who once were slaves. Hutantat said, 'Brother, these are your thirty-six noble deeds to count towards your karma!'

'No, master, this is your karma!' Nilakantha said.

'What will I do with karma, friend, when the goddess who rules me is unconcerned with deeds, unmoved by intention and untouched by pleas?'

'Which goddess is that?' Nilakantha asked.

'That one and only goddess—the Goddess of Destiny.'

'But surely she too follows the laws?' Nilakantha said.

'Oh yes, hers is the inexorable, relentless law—the law of dice—and by a throw of dice, she determines the future of us all.'

'But that is no law,' Nilakantha objected.

Hutantat shook his head and softly chanted:

'Why not!
It all depends, as before
On the roll of dice—no more,
Not on the thrower's will or tears
Not our prayers, hopes or fears.
But the unthinking dice unfolds
All that Creation's future holds.'

'You mean the goddess herself is not in control?' Nilakantha asked.

'Who can control a roll of dice?' Hutantat said.

'Brother, is life then nothing but a meaningless play of chance forces? That we rise from nothing to end in nothing!'

'I don't know what we rise from. But I am content, if it all ends in nothingness . . . Yes, eternal forgetfulness.'

Nilakantha was silent. It was not in him to quarrel with another's faith. But suddenly he spoke with emotion, 'Brother Hutantat, you are far greater than all of us Aryans.'

'And how did you reach this profound conclusion?' Hutantat mocked.

'We seek salvation through good karma. You seek nothing—neither salvation nor bliss. And yet, seeking no reward or return, your karma is pure. Your soul reflects the sufferings of others. The pain of another brings tears to your eyes . . .'

Hutantat interrupted, 'I suppose, next you will say that the sun rises and sets over my head! But brother, think! If man had control over his thoughts and deeds, why would he ever contemplate evil? Why should he build on the shaky foundation of the anguish, despair and terror of others? If the road to salvation is as clear and unambiguous as you say, would not people perform great deeds of mercy and charity?'

'But you do!' Nilakantha interrupted.

'The evil I do, the good I do, the evil and good we all do, every step we take, every word we utter—they are all facets of the roles assigned to each one by destiny,' Hutantat said.

'And God, who created us all, is without a role!'

'You who will create this temple and depart . . . what influence will you have over the lives of those that come to occupy it? None. Perhaps God made the world and departed.'

That night Nilakantha begged, 'God, I pray for a soul nobler than us all. I know not what to ask, but I simply pray.'

BHAGWAN S. GIDWANI

~

Ajitab's attacks continued in swift succession. Each assault brought with it a harvest of freed slaves. But Ajitab learnt bitter lessons too. He had hoped to convert slaves into a cohesive force to free others and, initially, they cooperated. But, later, they became undisciplined. Defying orders, they would pursue and attack fleeing guards even after they had successfully freed the slaves. They would even loot and burn the slave posts, and while returning they would attack innocent targets on the way. The worst was that all semblance of discipline broke down when they remained too long in one place. Then there were violent fights for no reason at all except to show superiority against weaker slaves. Ajitab's terrible tongue-lashings were effective, but not for long. His entire plan was going awry. What he had hoped was to create a disciplined force of freed slaves who would not only free others, but also learn live peacefully, till the land and be self-sufficient. But he failed to make them tend to the land and cattle. To them freedom was freedom; we have not exchanged the king's slavery for this new slavery, they cried. Instead, these freed slaves, dehumanized and brutalized by past terrors, burned with the desire to hurt others, even those who had never harmed them before.

Sometimes Ajitab even saw their smouldering rage against himself when he tried to curb their violence. But he had learnt much in the catacombs and could be as brutal. Once, he ordered that four of them be hanged for beating an old man to death. Again, for a woman's rape he had two hanged and sixteen flogged for not stopping it. Ajitab felt unclean and soiled but he saw no way out, except a reign of terror against any crime by his men. He felt that no one would understand what he was doing. But Hutantat would have said, 'Destiny.'

Ajitab learnt that he had to keep his men on the move and attack more often, if discipline was to be maintained. His attacks on the slave posts became more frequent than he had originally intended, but they were not limited to the posts. He had to attack even the king's granaries, as their own land was hardly productive. Gradually, the freed slaves learnt the advantages of being disciplined during the skirmishes; they found that those who tarried behind to loot on their own were often caught by the king's soldiers and mercilessly tortured.

It did not take them long to turn into a real fighting force, for disobedience led to capture, and death was certainly preferable to being caught alive. Many lost their lives, but even so Ajitab had far more men under his command than he had planned.

The attacks on the king's granaries and food stores also multiplied. The king's men went round in all directions to probe. Some commanders even suspected the location of their hide-outs, but chose not to enter inhospitable, possibly fortified, terrain. However, having come that far, they vandalized the lands of adjoining kingdoms. These kingdoms had already suffered much from Ajitab's assaults and with this new spate of attacks they began to suspect that these onslaughts were all inspired by the same source—the vile king who was having a magnificent temple built in his honour.

The fact was that the king was boasting too much. When he saw the first obelisk with the sun's golden glow at the predetermined time, his enthusiasm knew no bounds and he declared, 'From one end of the earth to another, there will be no such magnificent temple.'

True, the king's idea of the size of the earth was limited, and did not extend beyond the few kingdoms around him. Certainly, for him and for his people the world ended where the Nile met the great waters of the Mediterranean. In the Egyptian mind, their land of thirteen kingdoms was regarded as a planet on its own, unrelated to any other land, cut off as it was by a cruel sea in the north and vast, barren deserts in all other directions. To them, the rhythm of the river was the rhythm of life. If the sea could drown their auspicious river, what would it not do to humans! No boat would ply in the sea. Even to look at it may bring evil.

Spies and informers of other kingdoms had many tales to tell their own kings they spoke of the visions of glory that this temple-building king suffered from. The kings of the adjoining lands gritted their teeth and made their arrangements to attack.

Ajitab's slave army moved into an elaborate ambush in the adjoining kingdom. Ajitab barely saved himself. Thirty-one of his men, including an Aryan, were killed outright. Many were wounded and had to be left behind. The bulk of Ajitab's men managed to escape not just because of their fighting skills, but also the enemy's failure to pursue. The carnage on the enemy's side was frightful, too, despite their superior forces.

The dead Aryan and the dead and wounded slaves left no doubt in the minds of the other kings as to who was behind these attacks. So the enemy king had imported men from beyond the deserts and stolen their own slaves to fight against them, keeping his soldiers in reserve for future strikes!

Ajitab counted his losses. They were many. He did not know that a large number of his men had fled in the opposite direction, deeper into the adjoining kingdom. But even if he had known, there was no way he could go to their rescue. A scream of anguish rose in the adjoining kingdom where his leaderless men, terrified of capture, went on a rampage. When they came across a soldier with four slaves, they killed not only the soldier, but also the slaves who refused to join them. For no reason at all, they killed bystanders. They ransacked huts for food and then burnt them. News of their violence and viciousness reached the commanders and the king of that land, but only much later, and by then the number of these fugitives was so exaggerated that the commanders paused to muster larger forces before pursuing them. Some commanders even rushed in the wrong direction to give the impression of pursuit while ensuring their own safety.

Eventually these leaderless fugitives realized that since they had not been caught for so long, perhaps there was hope! They fled without wasting time in senseless murder and mayhem, stopping only to snatch essential food and attacking slave posts to increase their numbers. They also decided that the first among them to kill the guard at the slave post would be their leader, though when the attack was over, they could not agree which of the three contenders had killed first. In sheer disgust, they chose the fourth as their new leader, whose first order upon assuming charge was to change their route. He feared that they would be caught easily if they kept going in the same direction. He avoided habitations and led them through deserted areas and forests. Their numbers had swollen with newly freed slaves, though they did not have enough weapons to go around. Suddenly, they came upon two unsuspecting soldiers. They killed the soldiers. The leader and another then put on the soldier's clothes along with their armbands to give the impression that they were leading the slaves on some official errand, and the group continued on its way unmolested.

Some five days later, the two dead, half-naked soldiers were found with their armbands missing on a route that led to two neighbouring kingdoms. Suspicion immediately fell on the slave army. Messages were rushed to both kingdoms, to watch out for villainous attacks from the murderous forces of the king who was building a temple to himself. The slaves walked into a formidable trap. Although their leader was not fatally wounded, he killed himself for he did not want to be taken alive and had promised himself he would die laughing for the few months of liberty that destiny had granted him.

Meanwhile, Ajitab returned to his headquarters only to find some outsiders watching from a distance. He did not know whose spies they were, but quickly decided to evacuate to another area with his men. He had three such areas, each at a distance from the other, and reached one of them through circuitous routes. However, informers from other kingdoms had become more vigilant and the news of the slave army's movements had reached various kings. To what end was the slave army on the move, the kings wondered, if not to launch another, more vicious attack against them!

Ajitab would have been shocked to know that the other kings considered his men tools of the temple-builder king. That king too would have called on the sun itself to bear witness that he had nothing to do with Ajitab and his men. But the king hardly had a chance to explain. Four kings from adjoining kingdoms conferred and conspired and launched an attack from different directions. Two more kings joined them. This was the first time that the kings had attacked the land of another without warning, but they felt that they had been provoked beyond reason.

The temple-builder king was at a resort with two of his sister-queens and all his priests. A commander was there with many soldiers, but hardly enough to halt a sudden, unexpected attack. The dazed king was instantly beheaded and his eyes gouged out, so he would not be able to see his way to heaven. His head was mounted on a tall spear to be immersed with his body into the monstrous sea from which no one could ever ascend to heaven. He would never be buried and so the question of burying his wives, priests or slaves alive along with him never arose. His sister-wives and priests were spared, for no one would dishonour women from a royal household or harm a priest.

The king's chief priest killed himself by running his sword through his body, and declaring with his dying breath that he be thrown into the sea along with his dead royal master. He knew that his soul in the sea would wander in hell, never achieving paradise, never meeting his royal master, for each one suffers alone in hell. Let me suffer the same fate, he said, and perhaps a lonely cry will reach out to let my master know that he wanders not alone.

After their first flush of victory, so easily achieved, the victorious kings foresaw no future obstacles to taking over the kingdom. Their armies moved leisurely so that the people would see the lifeless head of their dead king and submit to their new rulers. One army moved to seize the king's sons so that there would be no claimants to dispute their mastery, and another army moved to the temple. The conquering kings decided not to destroy the temple since it would now belong to them, but only to wipe out the aliens working on it.

While the victorious kings marched in triumph, news of the king's death reached Hutantat. He grieved, 'He had the brain of a flea but he was good man, far better than the scoundrels who now come.' Even of the chief priest who killed himself in grief over his king's death, Hutantat said, 'I called him a eunuch, but he was not a eunuch at heart. He was a man.'

But grief could wait. What worried Hutantat was the widespread rumour of the kings' intention to destroy the temple and kill all the Aryans building it. Why, he wondered. He had no idea that Ajitab was seen as the dead king's puppet and all Aryans as his partners in crime.

It was time to act, not think! Hutantat went to the commander, who had heard everything, and would have to either submit to the new masters or die.

'Of what use is your submission to them when their anger is against the temple and those that built it?' Hutantat asked. 'Why would they spare you when you, too, have assisted at the temple?'

'But I had my orders,' the commander replied.

'So had these Aryans. Yet they are unprotected.' Hutantat suggested that he flee with his soldiers: 'Hide and resurface when things are quiet.'

'But what will I do with the slaves here?'

'Leave them here. Nilakantha is also the king's commander.'

The commander thought, yes, it was a way out. He said, 'Sage, you are good to me.'

'I will do even better. If the new kings listen to me, I shall say that you hated the temple and all the Aryans, so that none of them seek to harm you.'

The commander was almost certain that the conquering king would listen to the sage who was honoured and respected everywhere. 'I am grateful,' he said.

But Hutantat said, 'I, too, need something. You and your soldiers must leave most of your weapons behind.'

The commander nodded and said, 'I shall do so gladly. But the Aryans have no chance. Weapons will avail nothing against those formidable armies. They will all be slaughtered.'

'I fear so too. But to some what matters is not whether they live or die, but *how* they live and die.'

The commander nodded. He did more than leave weapons behind. He went to the arsenal with Hutantat. The guards there were already panicking, having heard the terrible rumours that were afloat. He dismissed them saying that his soldiers would take charge of the arsenal and granary next door, lest there be looting in these disordered times. The guards were delighted to be relieved of a duty that would probably bring disaster to them, and left quickly.

'It is all yours,' the commander said to Hutantat.

'Thank you, you are really good to me,' Hutantat said gratefully.

The commander and his soldiers departed. All construction stopped. Everyone was busy removing weapons and food from the arsenal and granary to store at the site.

Hutantat turned to the slaves, 'The soldiers have left. You are free to leave.'

'Where do we go, master? All of us will be hunted as slaves everywhere. Let us remain as slaves here.'

'You know the Aryan way! There will be no slaves here! They will set you free.'

But really he was going too fast for them. To them it was unthinkable that a branded slave could be freed. It was as if the brand on their arms was a heavenly decree that no earthly power could erase. Why, even after death they would be recognized in the sky as branded slaves and set apart in a horrible hell. It was not only in the eyes of others that they felt degraded, but in their own too.

Hutantat explained, 'The freedom to depart is yours. Outside, you may have a chance. But if you remain here, your freedom is illusory, for you shall surely die with the Aryans.'

'But we are branded slaves!'

'The brand is neither in your soul nor in your heart. Destiny willed that someone would degrade you and you felt degraded. Now destiny has turned; you can escape or be free and die here!'

'We will die here as free men, master!'

Grimly, Hutantat explained, 'You have time to decide and each must take his own decision. But when the armies arrive, the moment will be gone. Then you shall be treated as soldiers, awaiting crucifixion. The Aryans will fight, but what chance do they have against mighty armies! Be under no illusion. As long as you are here, death is inescapable.'

'But we will die free, master!' repeated a slave.

'You can also escape and live free,' Hutantat said. He went and spoke to Nilakantha.

It was Nilakantha who now addressed the slaves: 'I, Nilakantha, the king's commander, in the absence of the departed king, hereby assume control of this site, and declare you all free. I order that you are free to leave any moment until the armies can be seen by the sharpest eye from this distance. Further, I grant to those who remain with us the title of Aryan, and those who leave shall be known as friends of the Aryans, so that no one shall ever dare enslave them, anywhere, anytime.'

A slave asked, 'Sage! Does he have this authority?'

Hutantat glared, 'He thinks he has the authority. You think you are a slave. I think we are all doomed. We all think so. But does thinking alone make it so! How easy would it be then to think, rethink, to make, unmake and remake. Go, think for yourselves!'

Nilakantha did not even hold up a branch in lieu of the king's whip while conferring the titles on the slaves. Everything he said to them was prompted by Hutantat. But his eyes were now closed and a vision passed through his mind of a day long past, in his childhood, when his older sister had held him in her arms as Sindhu Putra was about to leave with Jalta and his men and the men of the silent tribe, who had just been released from slavery. He had been the first to hear and be blessed by Sindhu Putra with the chant of 'Tat tvam asi.'

Nilakantha's lips were now moving, as though in silent communion with someone unseen. Then slowly, he said with a tremor in his voice, 'I spoke to you in the name of the king. That was wrong. I speak to you in God's name. You are free, my brothers and sisters, always. You are free, Tat tvam asi.'

Hutantat was standing by, ready to shout the words of the king's ritual—'Kneel, dogs, kneel'—so that the ceremony could be completed, but he remained silent. Strange, he thought, every slave had had disbelief on his face when he spoke in the king's name. But now, they seemed to believe his every word even though they knew that only the king could speak in God's name, not even the chief priest.

Lugal said to Hutantat, 'When Nila thinks, he thinks powerfully.'

'His faith is powerful,' Hutantat replied.

Farewells, laughter, tears! Of the thirty-six slaves who were made soldiers after Nilakantha became the king's commander, twenty-five left. They were unbranded, with the best chance of being able to merge with the population, unrecognizable as former slaves. But four returned the next day, even though no danger threatened them outside. Of the branded slaves, many left with food and arms for the journey, but one of every ten that left, returned the next day, followed by more.

Many freed slaves, too, moved from Hutantat's villages to the construction site. The temple was now a granary and an arsenal. The walls were improvised, with openings from which defenders could watch, shoot arrows, or hurl stones. Except Himatap, whose mind was still on the temple, everyone was busy collecting stones for defence.

Lugal said, 'Don't let Himatap go out. He will drop everything he picks up and probably lose his way.' He knew how Himatap almost 'sleep-walked' when his mind was focused on problems of temple construction. But later Himatap, too, was given a job—break each brick inside the temple to give it a jagged edge.

The area around was deserted. The rumour that the kings were coming to destroy the temple, and its builders, had spread. No one wished to remain where soon arrows were to fly. The Aryans were frustrated; they had never wanted to build the temple! They had to do so or become slaves. All they had ever wanted was to leave this land, but they were not being allowed to go.

Grimly Hutantat said, 'They will not let you go alive.'

'But why?'

'There is no reason in unreason!'

'But we want no fight,' Nilakantha said.

'It is not a question of what you want. It is what you get; the alternative to self-defence is death by torture or the brand of a slave.'

Lugal and others collected thorny bushes and scattered them all over the hillside to obstruct climbing. Day and night they worked and Lugal said, 'Maybe we will be asleep when the enemy comes charging in.'

Lugal's next order saddened many: the plants and trees on the approaches to the temple were cut down. He said, 'Let them have no cover to hide in and aim their arrows.'

An anguished cry rose in Nilakantha's heart: 'Was it for this that we left our land?'

Their most tedious, back-breaking job was to store water. The stream that had been diverted reached the bottom of the hill, but would be unreachable if the temple was surrounded. Every hut around was scoured for pots and pans; from Hutantat's villages, too, came every vessel there was to hold water. His men went around, buying, begging, and stealing pots. They were kept filled to the brim. Ditches were dug in the palace floor and lined with bricks to hold water.

Lugal commented, 'We are destroying this place before the kings reach to demolish it. But why not!'

When Himatap wondered what a man was doing on the top of an obelisk, Lugal said, 'See! He is bald, and he thinks the sun will glow more brightly on his head than on the obelisk!' But the man was there to watch out for the army's approach.

Everything Hutantat wanted was completed in time. The kings were slow in coming. Receiving homage on the way meant much to them.

At last, the man perched on top of the obelisk shouted that the army was on its way, and would be at the site in a few hours.

Everyone collected around Hutantat and he said: 'There are tears in my heart, but I shall not bring them to my eyes, for I must see you all clearly as it may be the last time we are together. So let us part smiling.' But there were tears all round. Everyone had hoped that Hutantat would remain. But Lugal had insisted, 'Who then will speak for us outside, while we remain holed up like rats in here!'

Hutantat embraced Lugal and whispered much in his ear. His last words were to Nilakantha: 'I have little hope from these six jackals who call themselves kings. But they cannot harm you if you remain firm here. Beware of treachery. Refuse to leave without weapons, or at a time of their choosing. Refuse, unless they withdraw. They cannot be here forever. I may not come but someone will come to tell you if they withdraw to their lands, or if an ambush awaits you.'

They embraced.

Hutantat paused to kiss Larali's baby daughter, the youngest Aryan there. Then slowly he went down the heavy makeshift steps. He was the last to use them. The Aryans descended shortly after, using rope-ladders to break the steps, section by section.

Hutantat knew only two of the kings, but the other kings knew him by reputation. One of them kindly said, 'You seek mercy for these Aryans in vain. My own kingdom was ravaged by their attacks. They even stole our slaves to raise the slave army that attacked us.'

Hutantat at last understood. 'But that was done by a renegade Aryan who deserted them to battle on his own. The Aryans are not guilty, and the king you killed knew nothing.'

'Be not so foolish as to make me out to be a liar,' the king commanded. 'We attacked this kingdom for the vileness of its king and complicity of these alien temple builders. Did I lie?'

'But . . . ' Hutantat began.

'Take no risks with your life and liberty,' the king warned him. 'Leave before I change my mind.' He then shouted to those around him. 'If this Sage ever approaches me or any other king, cut out his tongue and throw him out.'

Even the other kings were surprised at such treatment of such a famous sage. But there was much on their minds. Four sons of the dead king had been caught and beheaded, but the youngest—a six-month-old infant—had been smuggled out by his maid. They could not be found. The woman's husband was blinded and her father killed, but still there was no sign of her.

The defenders in the temple had two days of respite. They went down the rope ladders to bathe in the stream, replenish their water supply, and collect bushes and firewood.

The kings were in a bad mood, quarrelling over division of territory and their failure to locate the missing infant. They retired to a pavilion which was prepared for them on the river bank and more troops were sent out to hunt for the dead king's son.

A small battalion left for the temple site to arrest everyone there.

Meanwhile, an old man and a woman with a bundle approached the temple. The man spoke the code word to prove that he came from Hutantat. A rope ladder was sent down. He climbed up with the woman and the bundle, which concealed an infant. The message from Hutantat was:

'Guard this infant as you would my one and only son. The kings have rejected my plea. Expect no mercy from them.'

The old man left. The woman and infant remained. Obviously, she was the mother, as she was breastfeeding the baby. A sympathetic question about the baby's father frightened her. Maybe an unwed mother, the Aryans thought, and asked no more.

Perched on a high hill, the temple stood like a fort. There was no way that the small force sent against it could succeed. But it marched with supreme confidence, expecting instantly to seize everyone inside and slaughter them.

'Brother Nila,' Lugal said, 'let yours be the first arrow.'

Nilakantha's arrow sped. The attackers were far away, but the arrow was aimed to warn them of the limit of their advance. Only one arrow! The attackers laughed and unleashed a flurry of their own arrows. But the temple was beyond their range and the arrows fell far away from the hill. Yet the barrage continued for it gave them a feeling of power. And they advanced beyond the spot where Nilakantha's arrow had fallen.

Lugal shouted. The invaders did not hear. The defenders did. And arrows sped from the temple. Four of the invaders were hit. Their leader shouted commands and now their arrows flew without pause.

A few advanced to form a semicircle. More were hit. Another angry command from their leader, and they halted and watched their men in the front being pelted with arrows and stones.

Quickly, they retreated behind Nilakantha's first arrow. The wounded were trying to return to their troops. Nilakantha ordered his people to stop. Many stopped, but the newly freed slaves kept aiming at the wounded. By shouts and force, Nilakantha stopped them. Some of the injured outside died from the continued assault. Then came the lull. Nilakantha complained bitterly against aiming at the injured.

Lugal said, 'As commander, feel free to behead those who disobeyed you. But be happy that the point has been made successfully: expect no mercy from the attackers and show no mercy to them, so that they fear to advance.'

Not a single enemy arrow had fallen near the temple. An Aryan said, 'God was on our side.'

Lugal was angry, 'God is on everyone's side. Theirs and ours; the killers and the killed!' Actually, Lugal was annoyed, not with those who had shot at the wounded, but with the six Aryans who were late at their posts because they had not finished praying. He continued, 'If God is what I believe Him to be, I am sure He gets annoyed with prayers when some duty remains neglected.'

'Brother, you put it differently,' said Nila. 'But what you say is near to our heart, too: karma is *above* prayer and piety.'

'Yet there were those who forgot that and came late!'

Nilakantha nodded and looked sadly at the culprits.

Suddenly, shouts came from the watchers at the walls and the obelisks. Everyone rushed to their posts. The attackers were moving within range, away from each other, obviously to avoid being easy targets. Some of them ran forward, some straight, others circuitously, hoping to reach spots from where their arrows would be effective. They failed. The arrows from the temple came in rapid succession at Lugal's command.

And the attackers ran back even faster. Those among the wounded who could were limping back painfully. Others just lay there, unable to move.

The sky was filled with vultures circling overhead. The Aryans shuddered.

Again, the watchers in the temple shouted and they all rushed to their posts.

The enemy commander and two men were approaching, their arms raised. Lugal shouted, 'Let them come, unharmed.' The men simply picked up their wounded, and went back slowly. The attackers now passively waited at a distance, possibly to postpone reporting their failure. At last they left, before sunset.

A grateful cry rang out in the temple. But Lugal warned, 'They will come back, stronger, with greater numbers, better armed and ably led.'

Even though they were not expecting to be attacked at night, a strict watch was kept.

Nilakantha saw enemy arrows stuck in the thorny bushes along the hillsides. He ordered the six Aryans who were late arriving at their posts to go and collect them, 'with feet, hands and legs bandaged, lest the thorns prick you'. They had plenty of arrows and Lugal wondered if he was merely punishing the six. But then Nilakantha went with them. After they had recovered the arrows, the six were given the task of filling buckets from the stream, to be pulled up by a rope from the temple by others, to replenish water used during the day.

Exhausted, they returned using the rope ladders. Lugal was still up and Nilakantha said, 'We are back from our prayers.' Lugal laughed, 'If such are our prayers, the enemy has no chance, brother.'

They had five days of respite. More pits were dug in the temple to store more water.

The kings were livid. The entire kingdom should be grovelling at their feet. How was it possible that these miserable aliens dared to stand up to them! But since the defeated commander spoke of terrible losses, they decided to wait for their large armies to regroup. On the sixth day at sunrise, a formidable force marched towards the temple. Its commander was certain of an easy path to the hilltop. His horsemen led and foot soldiers followed. But then he made the same mistake as the first commander. Horses presented easier targets; they got caught in the thorny bushes, while arrows, stones and jagged bricks rained on the riders and foot soldiers.

The commander had the drum sounded, signalling retreat, but the Aryans thought it heralded another attack. Their arrows flew, unable to distinguish between retreating, wounded and arriving soldiers. Even the drummer, a young boy, was hit and lay dead, his drum by his side.

The commander viewed the situation grimly. He sent for burning torches and threw them on the dry bushes. Other soldiers mimicked his actions and soon the bushes began burning.

'There is water in my head, but no brains,' Lugal said. 'Why did I not drench the bushes with water to avoid fire?'

Nilakantha promised, 'Let the day pass; tonight we will spread more bushes and douse them with water.'

But it was not to be. Sunset came. The enemy remained. They erected tents for the commander and officers, the soldiers remained in the open. Obviously, they were preparing a siege; the assault would follow.

The commander kept sending out his men who would rush back as soon as there was a volley of arrows from the temple. He was neither teasing nor courting danger, but simply testing the range of the arrows being shot from the temple. He sent many men to the sides and back who tried the same ploy.

Lugal ordered, 'Aim your arrows short.' Only the soldiers at the back were foolishly near. The rest, prudently, remained far away. But far or near, the stream below was surrounded, no longer within the reach of the Aryans.

All night, the enemy kept up a battle of nerves. Some galloped close, inviting arrows, maybe to see if the defenders were watching. They were, but their arrows found their mark only if they were lucky. And what would a few casualties matter to such a huge army!

By morning the enemy's plan became clear. They were building long ladders while some soldiers were practising with shields.

Lugal said, 'They are going to use ladders to breach our walls and shields to deflect our arrows. We must fight not from behind our walls but from the top.'

They saw the dead body of an old man being strung up on a ladder. It was the man who had earlier brought the woman and the infant to the Aryans. Apparently, he had been trying to sneak into the temple again with another message from Hutantat when he was caught.

Later, they saw with horror Hutantat's dead body mounted on another ladder.

Something died within them all.

Lugal spoke to them calmly. 'We weep together, we pray together, but more remains to be done.' They understood and Nilakantha said, 'Yes, they killed the best and noblest Aryan amongst us all. But he lives, always, in our hearts.'

The Aryans saw a cavalcade with decorated umbrellas— a sign that the six kings were approaching.

Soon, the commander walked up to the temple, his arms

raised. He gestured for permission to ascend. A rope ladder was thrown out to him. The commander greeted Nilakantha coldly. Lugal sent everyone away. He did not want anyone to be recognized if they ever were to escape. He sat nearby, his head bent as if in prayer.

The commander said, 'The kings desire to forgive you all if the infant is given to us.'

'What infant?' Nilakantha asked.

'The infant that Hutantat brought here.'

'Sage Hutantat brought no infant here,' Nilakantha said truthfully.

'Then give me all the infants here,' the commander said.

Nilakantha shook his head. The commander said, 'Your life, your freedom depends on it.'

'Of what use is life or freedom without honour!'

'You come from the deserts beyond. Of what use is this infant to you?' the commander asked.

'Which infant?' Nilakantha asked.

The commander looked at him with respect and said, 'You will all die; I shall regret it.'

He left.

The Aryans rushed to Nilakantha, 'What did he say?'

Nilakantha replied shortly, 'He demanded the impossible.'

Lugal nodded and silenced their questions: 'Ask no more!'

They silently wondered what terrible demands had been made that Nilakantha and Lugal would not even speak about them. Left alone, Nilakantha and Lugal wondered too. Why were the kings seeking the infant that Hutantat had sent to them, asking them to protect him? Was he really Hutantat's son from the woman who brought him to the temple? True, she had shed tears when she saw Hutantat's dead body. But hadn't they all? Why would the kings want the dead Hutantat's infant son! It made no sense.

For the next two nights, the enemies continued their shrieking and galloping unmindful of casualties, maybe to frighten the Aryans or keep them sleepless, tired and nervous. On the third night, well before dawn, Lugal took his little revenge and arrows rained on those who had imprudently slept within range behind the temple. Their casualties were many, the commotion even greater. Even the commander rushed out of his tent, thinking the Aryans had come out to attack.

The next morning Nilakantha again saw the distant cavalcade of the kings. He sadly thought of the enemy dead below. 'Those soldiers are innocent. The kings are responsible,' he said.

Lugal nodded, 'Criminals always go free. Only innocents lose their lives as soldiers and servants, in the vain belief that they serve a worthy cause.'

Lugal concluded, 'The assault shall soon begin. Maybe the kings are pressing the commander.'

Lugal was right. The commander wanted ten days. The kings gave him till the next morning.

At sunrise, the assault began. Wave upon wave of enemy soldiers, protected by shields, rushed up the tall ladders. The cavalry galloped ahead of them to take the brunt of arrows, as if casualties did not matter as long as the foot soldiers reached the temple.

The Aryans were ready. Led by Lugal, more than 200 waited on top of the wall to pounce on the ladders that rested against the hill. The cavities in the temple wall were being used to fling burning torches and shoot arrows at the soldiers. The enemy attack was ill conceived, with too many men trying to do too little; only sixty ladders stood against the temple wall, to be toppled by the Aryans. The enemy cavalry itself blocked its own men from running back to safety, away from the burning torches.

Even so, the Aryans lost twelve men, due to their own foolish enthusiasm to rush too quickly at the ladders and go down with them, and even more foolishly, to stand on the edge to strike down the enemy soldiers. On the ground below, there was chaos, confusion and the cries of the dying and the wounded in the enemy ranks.

From a safe distance, the kings saw the ladders toppled and the carnage in their ranks, and left. Only then did the commander dare to sound the retreat.

Much was said by poets on the Aryans' glowing victory over a commander who was one of the best in the land. Actually, it was due to the temple's commanding position on the hilltop, and to a greater extent, because of the folly of the six kings, who ignored the commander's plea for time to prepare for the difficult assault.

The kings were stern and unforgiving to the commander. He had failed to get the infant, believed to be the king's son hidden by Hutantat in the temple. He had failed in his attack, and was summarily replaced.

The kings paused before ordering a new assault. Two slaves, caught as they were leaving the temple, had divulged details about the Aryan defence under torture. They said that the Aryan commander, appointed by the previous king, had no soldiers, only untrained slaves and his own Aryans, who were builders and worshippers, not fighters.

But if they had no real fighters, the kings wondered, how did they cause such havoc among the troops? Obviously, it was their commander who had planned it all, and his must be the skill and inspiration that had frightened away the troops. If they enticed away the commander, would not the Aryans' entire resistance collapse?

One king's chief priest walked towards the temple, arms raised. 'Refuse him entry,' some said. Their hearts were anguished over the twelve whose bodies were scattered below. But Nilakantha said, 'There are others to save. Maybe he offers a way out.'

Lugal nodded. A rope ladder was thrown down for the chief priest. The priest graciously bowed, 'It is by command of the six kings that I request you to meet them.'

'Why? What do they want?' Nilakantha asked.

'What can kings want? Nothing. They desire that you leave the temple to them and be in peace, free to remain to work for them or free to leave with honour, as you wish.'

'But that is all we want—to leave.'

'So be it. The kings will even pay handsomely for the work you did on the temple.'

'There is no demand for an infant?'

The priest laughed, 'That was a foolish mistake. No, all your people—infants, men and women—go with you.'

'Good. What guarantees of our safety have we?'

'The kings will themselves give you their oath.'

'Then why did so many have to die?'

The priest smiled, 'The kings fully believe what they suspected before—that this temple holds the power of the sun god and its builders are blessed. If they needed proof positive, it was the victory of so few of you against so many. Never will the kings dream of attacking you, in the temple or anywhere, for they believe that any harm to you diminishes them all.'

'Yet your troops are amassed there!' Nilakantha protested.

'Any moment, orders will reach them to depart.'

Lugal spoke, 'Why must our commander go to the kings? You can tell us of the arrangements for our safe departure.'

The priest was annoyed. 'Who is he?' he asked, unable to see Lugal's face, who sat as if absorbed in prayers.

'He is King Lugal . . . ' Nilakantha began but Lugal interrupted, 'I am a priest here.'

They have a king who calls himself a priest, the chief priest wondered, but truly that is how it should be—only priests should be kings! Respectfully he said, 'In that case, lord priest, you may join your commander to meet the kings. But I cannot take oaths for your security on behalf of the kings; these oaths must come from the kings themselves.'

Impulsively Nilakantha said, 'I am ready . . . ' but Lugal interrupted again, 'Yes, the commander will be ready to give you his answer in two days. He has to consult all.'

The chief priest smiled, 'It is for the commander to speak.'

Lugal glared at Nilakantha who said, 'Yes, I must consult the rest . . . two days.'

'So be it,' the chief priest said. 'I shall come again.'

Lugal suggested, 'Meanwhile, your troops will move back? Twenty or thirty miles away?'

The chief priest nodded, 'Of course, instantly.'

And Lugal added, 'We will keep your ladders, tents, everything in the temple for safety.'

'Yes, please do that. And if you need food or anything else, I shall have it sent to you.'

'No, we have everything,' Lugal replied.

The rope ladder was dropped once again. But before leaving, the chief priest spoke to Lugal, 'Lord priest, I honour and respect a priest like you who questions and checks everything. Do join your commander to meet the kings. And you will realize that they will be generous beyond your dreams for the great temple you leave behind.'

Still, Lugal asked, 'Why can I not go instead of the commander?'

But the chief priest said, 'Why make the kings feel small when they ask for your commander? But certainly, you and even others may join him. It is always nice and proper for a commander to go well-attended.'

Nilakantha later apologized to Lugal, 'Forgive me for wishing to rush to the kings without waiting to consult you.'

'We have been brothers too long to apologize to each other,' Lugal said. 'But I fear the kings are up to no good. There is treachery in their hearts.'

They all discussed the matter but were unsure of what this new development meant. Suddenly, a cry came from the obelisk: 'The army is on the move!' The chief priest had obviously kept his word.

The discussion was halted. The bodies of the twelve Aryans had to be brought up for the last rites. The three who were from Bharat Varsha were cremated and the nine locals were buried in a grove near the temple.

Lugal said, 'They will have died in vain, if we sit back to mourn.'

Groups were sent out to replenish water from the stream, bring in the stores and ladders left by the enemy, drag the dead of the enemy away from the temple approaches, collect thorny bushes to spread on the hillside and flood them with water, so the bushes would remain wet.

'No sleep, no rest, only work and more work for two days.' Lugal said to them.

Nilakantha asked him, 'What is your suspicion?'

'That they will kill you.'

'How will my death serve them?'

'You command the Aryans here.'

'Brother Lugal, you are in command! I serve only to voice your orders.'

'And what will happen to us if you die?'

'The torch is safe in your hands.'

'And what of their hearts, their morale!' Lugal said indicating the other occupants of the temple.

'It will hurt them, yes,' Nilakantha replied. 'As it hurt us terribly when we saw Sage Hutantat's body. But that only increased our resolve to fight.'

'Yes. But another blow will shatter them. I know it will shatter me.'

Nilakantha put his arm around Lugal's shoulder. 'Brother, have we a choice? The kings promise safety. But if we spurn their offer, we stay and fight for what? And how long? Can time and events wait? Can we win? Never! Eventually, we will try to escape and be simply cut down. Why not get their oath to leave us alone to go our way!'

'Only, I have a ghastly, nightmarish feeling that they mean treachery.'

'Treachery! You fear they intend to kill me. A single life! What will it avail them? Even if they do, so what? I stake my life to gain freedom for us all. And if I don't stake it, we all die in any case. If they kill me, I will simply die a little earlier.'

Lugal was silent, but Nilakantha again asked, 'What can they hope to gain by killing me? Do they expect that you will then kiss their hands to be ready for slaughter?'

Though all the others were busy working at the temple, they were aware of Nilakantha's hopes and Lugal's fears. No one wanted Nilakantha to go, but was there an alternative? What did the kings hope to gain by enticing Nilakantha? Were they really sincere? These butchers who had killed Hutantat! Perhaps, the kings wanted to avoid more bloodshed. Maybe they wanted to rush back to their kingdoms and wished to resolve all this peacefully. Lugal's concern was etched clearly on his face, but then everyone knew of his compassion and tenderness, and they also knew he loved Nilakantha like a brother.

'All will be well. I slept only for an hour, but I had a beautiful dream,' Nilakantha said.

'Do your beautiful dreams always come true?' Lugal asked.

'This one will. I dreamt we were all back in Bharat Varsha and you were with us too.'

'Then your endless journeying is over?'

'Yes, Purus was right. Our land is beautiful. It is we who fail if we do not keep it pure.'

Many gathered to hear what Nilakantha was saying. 'I am telling Lugal of my dream about returning to Bharat Varsha.'

They nodded. Once their dream, too, had been to find the Land of the Pure, but no longer.

Two days later, the chief priest arrived. Graciously, he

smiled at them all, 'I see you have watered the approaches to your temple.'

Lugal replied, 'Yes, there was too much blood, carnage and death! We had to wash it away.'

The priest nodded appreciatively, 'Very auspicious.'

Nilakantha was bidding farewell to the Aryans. He kissed Larali's child. The chief priest came forward to look, 'Beautiful child. Your son?'

Larali replied, 'My daughter.'

Lovingly, the priest picked up the child, fondling it. He checked what he wanted to check and looked around. He saw no other infants—the one he searched for was hidden in the granary. But the smile did not leave the chief priest's face. He turned to Nilakantha and asked, 'Ready?'

Nilakantha nodded. Casually, the priest said, 'It would be nice if you came attended. Commanders always have attendants.'

A freed slave pleaded, 'Master, let me come!' Nilakantha saw Lugal nod.

Nilakantha and the slave went with the chief priest.

'Kneel, dog, kneel,' Nilakantha was ordered as he approached the kings. But it did not worry him. This was the ritual in the kings' presence.

'Welcome, commander,' a king said pleasantly. 'Now, return to the temple with our men and ask all your people to come out with their hands up in the air and bring out the infant.'

Nlakantha stared, 'Is this a joke, your exalted majesty?'

But the king said, 'We do not joke. You had better obey.'

Hoarsely, Nilakantha said, 'I would rather die.'

'Honourable choice. Foolish, but honourable. Oblige him,' the king looked at his men.

The men held Nilakantha down. An axe was poised to strike, but the king said, 'No blood here! There!' They dragged him to the river. Nilakantha's neck was severed from his body. His head fell into the river. The soldiers threw his body in as well.

The kings looked and then turned their attention back to the food before them and began eating.

The freed slave who had accompanied Nilakantha was held tightly by the captors. The chief priest hit his face with a stick. 'Listen, dog! Go to the temple. Tell them to throw the infant down instantly. Only then will we show mercy to the rest of you. Understood?' The man nodded. The soldiers escorted him back to the temple.

Meanwhile, Lugal and the others waited. Weary, tired, dazed after days of ceaseless work and worry, they still could not sleep in their uncertainty over Nilakantha's fate. Suddenly they noticed Nilakantha's companion returning with several soldiers. Surely, Nilakantha was following! A rope ladder was lowered. The man came up alone. He was besieged: 'Where is Nilakantha?' They saw his tears. There was silence. At last he spoke, 'River Kemi is red with Master Nila's blood . . . red river . . . Master Nila . . . Nila . . . river.' He sobbed.

'What do they want?' Lugal asked, pointing to the soldiers who waited below.

'They wait for the infant,' and the man repeated the chief priest's message.

Lugal collected a bundle as if holding a baby. He gestured from the wall. One of the soldiers came forward and motioned to Lugal to throw down the infant. Lugal simply pointed to the rope ladder. The soldier ascended. 'Give me the infant,' he demanded.

Lugal grovelled, 'Master, we will give you the child. But will you then be merciful to us?'

'Yes, the kings are merciful.'

'But master, we beg. Promise us mercy.'

'Yes, I shall speak to the commander.'

'Master, where is the commander?' Impatiently, the soldier pointed beyond the wall and Lugal wailed, 'But master, that is not the commander. We know the commander. He was here before.'

'You fool, it is the new commander! The old commander is no more!'

'Master, no offence, but then please ask the chief priest to come here; we know him. He is gracious.'

The soldier stormed. Cravenly, Lugal heard him, head bowed. The soldier left in anger.

A debate was on in the pavilion of the six kings. The report was clear. The men and women in the temple were dispirited, frightened; the children were crying; their spokesman was grovelling like a dog with his tail between his legs, begging for a personal promise of mercy from the chief priest.

'Send the commander,' the chief priest advised, with no wish to risk his precious life.

But the commander argued, 'They say they don't know me and will only deal with someone they know.'

The chief priest said, 'Then send the old commander.'

'But they were told he was no more.'

'Why did we give that information?'

One of the kings spoke to the chief priest, 'That question can wait. What is important is that you go and bring the infant.'

The chief priest looked at his own king. 'I know their spokesman. He is a sly fox. It is a trap.'

'Trap for what? To kill you! No one ever kills a priest.'

'They are aliens, bound by no scruples.'

'And they will sacrifice all hope only to kill you?'

'They have no hope,' the chief priest said miserably.

'He who lives, hopes. He dies hoping,' the king said. 'And you worry over your life when we must have the infant!'

The chief priest made one last appeal, 'Consider the insult to your majesty if they lay hands on your chief priest!'

'It is a sorrow I shall bear,' the king replied brutally. 'What I cannot bear is your cowardice.'

The chief priest went to the temple. He felt like a lamb

going to slaughter. But sadly, he thought, God blessed lambs with no such foreknowledge. Only man knows when he is headed to his doom. A rope ladder waited for him at the temple.

If the chief priest had any hope, it left him as soon as he saw Lugal's cold expression. 'Speak the truth for once in your life, before you die. Who is the infant?' Lugal asked.

'Surely you know!' the priest answered. 'He is the king. The last son of the last king.'

'But they have conquered the kingdom. Why kill him?'

'They cannot be kings while he lives. It is the law!'

Everyone has a law and all laws are mad, Lugal thought. He asked, 'But the child's mother . . . she does not look like a queen!'

'She is no mother,' replied the priest. 'She is the wet nurse who breastfeeds the baby. She smuggled the child out.'

'But why this mad rush to kill the infant?' Lugal asked.

'The kings always fear being absent from their kingdoms for too long. They must return.'

Both were silent. Sombrely, Lugal asked, 'You know why we sent for you.'

The priest nodded. Lugal continued, 'You may pray before you die.'

'I prayed before I came,' the priest said.

They looked at each other. The priest saw the rope in Lugal's hand. Quietly, he asked, 'If possible, could you kill me by the sword? You can hang me, thereafter.'

Lugal nodded and picked up the sword.

'Thank y—'

Lugal's sword caught the priest's unprotected throat before he completed his thanks. Blood gushed forth. The chief priest was dead.

Lugal announced, 'I killed not in anger or for revenge, but to let them know that they can expect no mercy from us. And so you will learn not to expect mercy from them, ever!

Remember that, whether we die together or one by one! But we must try to live, for Hutantat had a dream to save this infant, and Nilakantha dreamt that we all go to his land. Anyone dying needlessly hurts that dream. The kings must return to their kingdoms. They have no time. We do. Remember, those from the enemy who come to speak to us mean more harm than those who shoot arrows at us.'

The chief priest's body was hanging from the temple wall.

'To kill a chief priest!' the commander reported to the kings. 'They are inhuman!'

'Be inhuman with them!' the kings commanded.

The enemy army did not appear for days. But when it came, Lugal knew why there had been a delay. Thousands of slaves came carrying huge wooden ramps, heavy ladders with steps, long poles with torches at the end. Long lines of the enemy's troops followed.

The huge ramps were being assembled right there to make them even bigger. Hundreds were carrying them, sheltered under them from arrows, and placing them against the temple walls. Perhaps soldiers, even those on horses, would rush on to those ramps, while innumerable heavy ladders were raised everywhere.

Multitudes of slaves were driven there, hour by hour, to work on the ramps and ladders. The enemy was even planning war with itself. Fences were being erected so that their soldiers could not retreat or rush back; they would have no choice but to march forward and kill or be killed.

Lugal said to everyone in the temple, 'Join me to pray that we die like warriors. That is what we all are, Aryan warriors, each one of us, no matter where this journey began.' He spoke of the fate of those who might be caught alive: 'It shall be far more terrible than death.'

It was the first time Lugal had called for prayers, a task that Nilakantha had always performed. They prayed with tears, and embraced each other. Former Egyptian slaves, branded slaves, Hutantat's soldiers, men from Bharat Varsha, Iranians, Sumerians, Assyrians—Aryans all.

The wet nurse came forward with the infant. She asked Lugal, 'Bless me as Aryan and this infant who shall be Aryan.'

Lugal embraced her and kissed the infant, 'You are Aryan and so is the child.'

Somehow, they did not seem dejected any more. Only Larali. Hers was a difficult task.

'You must live,' Lugal had told Larali. 'In the confusion of battle, you must take the king's son, his nurse, your own daughter, and the other children to safety if you can.' Lugal pointed to spots from which rope ladders would run and the bundles in which children would be wrapped and lowered safely. 'Even if one child is saved, it will not be in vain,' he said.

And then, unexpectedly, Lugal added, 'I choose you, not because you have your own infant, nor because you must meet your husband Ajitab, but because of my faith.'

'What faith?' she asked.

'My faith says that everything repeats itself in time, out of time, in life, out of life. And I know, my dear virgin-in-waiting, whenever someone forces you to wait, something good always happens.'

She smiled through her tears. 'You really believe it?'

'Yes, I believe you will meet your husband, that he will kiss his daughter, and your life will be complete, fulfilled.'

Her eyes filled up with tears, 'My life will not be complete, Father Lugal, if you are not with us.' He took her in his arms and she wept.

Lugal gazed at the moon, 'Farewell, moon of tonight! Look for us elsewhere tomorrow!' He turned to address everyone else, 'Let us sleep early, sleep well and rise early. The attack comes at sunrise, I am sure.'

Lugal did not sleep immediately. He went around, checking on his people. It pleased him that his watchers were alert and the rest were sleeping peacefully. We have all come to terms with destiny, he thought.

He lay down to sleep. Three hours before sunrise, something woke him up. He peered out into the dim light. No movement. He called out to those on watch. 'Nothing,' they replied. Sheer nervousness, he thought.

But then it came, like a distant thunderstorm. The watch called out. The noise increased in volume. Lugal stood on the top of the wall. He saw nothing. The watchers on the obelisk saw some burning torches in the far distance. 'Why do they need more army units?' Lugal wondered aloud. Everyone was up by now.

'Our moment arrives,' Lugal said. Still, he was sure that the attack would not begin before sunrise. He saw the torches burning in front of the ramps and ladders. They remained unmoved. Obviously, the slaves would need hours to bring the ramps against the temple wall, and judging by the noise in the distance the enemy was waiting for reinforcements to arrive.

He cried, 'Larali! Live to tell how many they needed to fight against us!'

Suddenly, the noise ceased and the torches disappeared from view. Maybe some large movement of soldiers headed elsewhere, thought Lugal.

Nobody in the temple slept any more. Their task was simple. To fight with arrows and swords when needed, but mostly to throw burning torches on the men carrying the ramps and, inside the temple, on any enemy soldiers who tried to stop Larali and the children.

Fortunately, they had many torches to burn. Their own arsenal was full, and when the enemy had evacuated after the chief priest's first visit, they had left behind endless supply.

An hour before sunrise, drums sounded in the enemy camp. Lugal looked around. Everyone nodded, a prayer in each heart. Slaves were rushing up with ramps and ladders. Arrows would be ineffective against them. They stopped at the thorny bushes, but sheltered under the ramps were also those who had long pointed poles. With those they swept aside the bushes to make way for the slaves to go through.

The burning torches the Aryans flung on the ramps were ineffective, as were the torches hurled on the ground; they slowed the enemy down, but were eventually swept away with the long poles.

Slowly, inexorably, the ramps moved forward.

Lugal looked around at the Aryans, as if to see them for the last time. All his arrangements had failed so far and he wished he had been a better leader to his people. He considered going down by a rope ladder to throw burning torches directly at the slaves carrying the ramps. But there were soldiers under the ramps too, and they would cut down his group to pieces before they could do any significant damage.

The enemy soldiers were forming lines with shields and spears. Their horsemen led the way. And then came a deafening roar, as if a thousand demons were shrieking. It rose. Lugal saw little in the dim light. There was confusion everywhere. The enemy lines had become disorderly. The movement of the ramps stopped; a few of them fell, possibly crushing those who carried them. Everyone was running helter-skelter. Slaves and soldiers who extricated themselves from under the ramps were running too, but towards the temple, within range of the Aryans' arrows.

Who was chasing whom? In his bafflement, all that Lugal did was to order everyone to stop their assault.

The tumult increased. Everyone watched from the temple, witnesses to a drama that they could not comprehend. Their hearts were pounding with each roar from outside. Suddenly, an Aryan cried out, 'I always knew God would come to save us!'

It was Ajitab! He had come with his legions of slaves and

cut-throats from the catacombs.

Long before Hutantat was killed, he had sent six messengers to Ajitab of whom two had reached the Aryan. As soon as Ajitab realized the danger Lugal and Nilakantha and the others were in, he began marching, stopping only to attack slave posts and increase his numbers. His last stop was at the catacombs. With the armies diverted to attack Aryans at the temple, he faced few hurdles. Just before he neared the temple, his numbers grew even more with all the slaves who until recently had worked for the enemy army under the lash.

There was slaughter all around the temple. It took Ajitab six hours to reach the temple hill. The Aryans shouted joyfully upon seeing him. Lugal asked Larali to throw down the ladder, and within moments she was in Ajitab's arms. An Aryan shouted, 'Ajitab, the saviour!'

But Ajitab's cry was more astonished as he looked at his infant, 'I am a father! A father!'

He asked where Nilakantha was. When he heard what had happened, he stormed, 'That river shall flow with blood!'

But Lugal said, 'Let them die who deserve to die, but let not their blood pollute Nila's river!'

Everyone was talking to Ajitab at once. Outside, confusion reigned. But the loudest cry—resonant and booming—was, 'King Ajitab! Ajitab! King Ajitab!'

Some of the Aryans remarked in surprise, 'They call you king!'

Ajitab dismissed it, 'I was called the king of the catacombs when I led thieves and robbers for a time. The title still unites freed slaves around me and adds to their morale.'

'Who but a king could save us!' an Aryan said.

'I am no king,' Ajitab retorted. 'Lugal is the one whom we call king.' And he picked up the dead king's son in his arms and said, 'And we have a real king too.'

'And outside, six more kings wait to kill him,' Lugal said.

'They will die,' Ajitab said evenly.

Ajitab was in the temple less than three hours, then he left, saying his army of former slaves would go wild with bestiality and brutality unless he was out there to control them. 'My men will guard the temple outside. Let them not come up. They are not a well-ordered lot.'

Ajitab returned after nine days. All six kings had been caught. They were stabbed in the heart and left to rot beside the river. 'Let them watch the river where Nila's blood flowed,' Ajitab said.

But the next day, five of the bodies were missing from the riverbank. It was later learnt that the chief priests of five kings had taken away the bodies to bury them. Only the body of the king whose chief priest had been killed at the temple remained rotting by the riverbank. Why would the other chief priests help a king who had sent his own chief priest to his death! And for him, came the vultures.

After the battle, Ajitab's visits to the temple were brief.

In the temple, every heart had only one question: How long shall we be here in this land? How long! Himatap said, 'Long, very long,' but he was thinking of the damage to the temple, with water ditches, battered walls, broken bricks and burning torches, that had to be repaired.

Peace came slowly to the six neighbouring kingdoms and then in all the thirteen kingdoms. It was a peace imposed by Ajitab's contingents. Soon all the kingdoms would be called the kingdom of Ajitab and eventually come to be known as the kingdom of Egypt.

But then Ajitab was no longer called king. Nor was Lugal. Ajitab's new title was king's commander-in-chief. And Lugal was known as the king's keeper or the regent. The title of king belonged solely and exclusively to the infant, the last son of the previous king who was killed by the six attacking kings. The infant's nurse who had protected him was honoured as the king's 'mother'.

Many months later, the Aryans left the kingdom. Their quest was over and now they were homeward bound, with no desire to go elsewhere or resume their search for the Land of the Pure. They were escorted by a large contingent of Ajitab's well-trained, disciplined troops. Everyone who was at the temple left with them except Himatap, Lugal, Ajitab, Larali and their daughter.

'Come with us,' the Aryans pleaded with Lugal. 'The best of Aryans must not remain behind.' But Lugal had promises to keep. He thought of Hutantat's message: 'Protect him as you would my one and only son.' It was a promise he had to keep. When the infant was older and safe in his own kingdom, Lugal decided, he would go back to Assyria and Sumeria. There was a dream in Lugal's heart about his homeland, a dream that was vague and formless, but sometimes it was like the lament of a bird that has lost its mate.

Lugal would leave the kingdom sixteen years later, when the king was old enough to take command. The king called himself Aryan, bound by his oath to govern righteously by the noble Arya code of conduct.

Meanwhile, Lugal abolished slavery in the kingdom. Anyone who disobeyed and kept a slave had his upper arms branded and his wealth confiscated. There were no eunuch priests in the kingdom any more. Marrying one's sister was considered incestuous.

Ajitab, Larali and their two sons—fourteen and twelve years old—left with Lugal. Their daughter married the king, and stayed behind. Poets say that she and the king fell in love when they were infants together in the temple.

For three years, Lugal and Ajitab would be in the thick of fighting in Assyria and Sumeria. They had brought troops from the kingdom of Ajitab. But their larger support came from the Aryans there and the locals who had joined them.

Lugal eventually became the undisputed ruler of Assyria and Sumeria. He had no imperial ambitions, but if the priests' exploitative practices were to be ended and the noble Arya Code introduced, he had to assume the mantle of ruler. Always at the core of his heart was the sadness that despite extensive searches by him and his teams, Lugal could not find his three wives and three children who were left behind when he had ventured out with the Aryans on their journey towards Egypt.

Ajitab remained with Lugal as his commander for another two years. Then he left with Larali and their four sons. Lugal kept back Ajitab's nineteen-year-old son. He told Larali, 'You have many sons, I have no one.'

Lugal promised to leave Sumeria after three years to visit Bharat Varsha. He did. He nominated his adopted son, born to Ajitab and Larali, as his successor.

The Aryans who had returned to Bharat Varsha long ago, thronged to meet this Sumerian Lugal of whom it was said that he was the highest and noblest of all Aryans.

Lugal never went back to his homeland. He passed his last days on the banks of the Ganga, and when someone asked him if he had understood the mystery of the universe, he said he had not even grasped the mystery of the Aryans of Bharat Varsha who had left their land of promise, purity and glory for an elusive quest into the unknown.

FORTY

ARYANS IN EUROPE

5005 BCE

To the Aryans in Iran, Sumeria and Assyria, the realization came that those lands were not the sacred destination they had sought. Their minds were assaulted by images of cruelty all around them.

Purus, who led the Aryans in Iran, had already recovered from his initial shock, and he was certain: there was no land of purity anywhere except when man made it so by his own effort. Many Aryans would come to agree with Purus and realize that their wandering days were over. Their only dream was to return to their homes in the heritage of Bharat Varsha. But it was only a dream. They feared that the journey back would be as perilous as their journey here had been.

But not everyone heard the voice of Purus. True, the Aryans from Iran, Sumeria and Assyria met and mingled, but not often. Different events as they occurred in one area rarely came to be known in another. Besides, Purus did not lay down the law. He was determined to remain in Iran or return to Bharat Varsha if the opportunity arose, but that was a personal decision. To pilgrim Aryans who wished to go forward in faith, he said, 'I hope I am wrong, though for myself, my journey is over. But I honour your footsteps that go out to seek the land of the pure.'

Thus it was that even those who shared Purus's view, assisted contingents that left for the land that came to be known as the kingdom of Ajitab and, later, as Egypt.

A request was invariably made to those that left: 'Somehow, send us word of where and how you reach.' But it was an impossible request. Certainly, no news came from Egypt while the entire Aryan contingent was forced to labour on the king's temple. But the absence of information did not shake the faith of many. Surely all is well, they believed, since no one has rushed back or sent a message of distress to seek help.

Meanwhile more Aryans arrived in Sumeria from Sindhu, and streams of Aryan pilgrims from Bharat Varsha through Avagana to Iran continued. Right until his death, Purus and his men assisted these men and women in reaching areas of safety throughout Iran, Sumeria and Assyria. After his death, his wife took over this task even more zealously. Her view was similar to her husband's: 'Be proud, noble Aryans! With God's help and yours, we shall make Hari Haran Aryan the Land of the Pure! Be with us, though honoured be your footsteps, wherever you go, and whatever your decision, I shall always be proud to assist you.'

But many who came to Iran from Bharat Varsha were prisoners of their own dream. What Purus and his wife said meant little. To them, even the whisper of their dream was louder than any warnings. Knowing that there was grim brutality and bestiality in Iran and Sumeria actually strengthened them. One must walk through total darkness to find total light, they said. No, we shall not stop in our quest for the land of the pure, the dream shall not die.

Some even had contempt for those who held Purus's view: 'All they have is the triumph of being alive, but what is life if the dream dies!'

Yet those who wished to leave were not without apprehensions about the dangers that lay ahead. Their dream was large, but they felt small, afraid and ignorant. Land routes, they knew, were littered with savages who robbed, murdered and enslaved. Besides, Nilakantha had already led a large caravan by land, so why duplicate the effort. Later, hopefully, there would be continuous mutual enrichment, as each group was able to send out information to the other.

Thus it was that several groups decided to leave Iran by sea. Among those supporting this decision were the seamen of the Sindhu, who had reached Sumer, the Persian Gulf and Iran, initially, by sea. The sea routes did not hold terror for these sailors, blessed as they were with familiarity with long, navigable rivers and deep harbours opening to the Sindhu Sammundar. There were shipwrecks, but those were due to faulty planning and haste. This time they would plan and build better ships, and all the vessels would leave together so that a ship in trouble had instant help.

The river entrance to the Caspian Sea in Iran became the centre of the boat-building activity. The locals watched the Aryan fleet of boats in wonder. It was not the number of vessels, but their sheer size that awed them. Hundreds of Aryans, with no intention of going themselves, had assisted the seafarers in building those ships. Their massive size only increased the fear that they might sink rather than sail. But sail these ships did, beautifully and majestically, at initial trials. Many more Aryans then, including locals, conquered their fear and joined the convoy.

Each boat had a commander. The entire fleet, however, was under the joint command of two brothers, Atul and Atal, grandsons of Dhrupatta, the twentieth karkarta of the Sindhu clan. Together the ships set sail on the Caspian Sea where no one had gone before. Perhaps the first mistake arose from the command ship itself. Atul and Atal, in their enthusiasm, wanted their ship to go faster; the broad, open sea fascinated them and they were not content to hug the coastline as originally planned. The other ships tried to keep pace, but soon because of the vagaries of wind and the waywardness of the command ship, the fleet split into groups.

A ship, looking in vain for those that went ahead, ran

aground along the coastline. Four of the ships slowed down in order to assist it. The rest of the fleet continued through fog, thunder and lightning. The winds were more in command than the crew. But they were committed to the unknown; besides, even if they wished to return, they could not. But their faith—that God would lead them to their goal—remained unshaken.

Meanwhile, of the four ships that had rallied to assist the vessel floundering along the coastline, one was battered by a sudden storm, and it hit some rocks and sank. And although it was near the coastline, more than half the people on the ship were cast into the abyss of the sea, never to be recovered. Nor was there any hope of saving the ship which had run aground earlier. Unseen rocks had damaged its bottom. The crew and passengers swam towards the coast, several of them making multiple trips to bring food and supplies. Thereafter, all energies were diverted to carefully towing the three remaining ships to the shore.

Far in the distance, two more ships were seen approaching, but there was no way to warn them of the treacherous coastline. One of them hit the hidden rocks and capsized. Fortunately, no one was hurt and everyone made it ashore safely. Seeing the fate of its sister vessel, the second ship veered away from the coastline and slowed down. Its commander, Sakaru, jumped into the sea and swam to assess the assistance needed by the stranded Aryans. But with dismay he saw that his own ship could not wait for him to return. Strong winds sent it forward. 'My own son exiles me,' he said ruefully.

His son Rohrila was second-in-command on the ship and was an excellent seaman. Only that morning Sakaru had complimented his son, 'You are a better seaman than I am,' and Rohrila had cheekily replied, 'But I always knew that!'

Sakaru was certain that Rohrila would bring the ship back to pick him up as soon as possible. He waited along with the other Aryans at the mountainous coastline for days on end.

But no ship passed by. Even Sakaru's hope for his son's return dimmed. They had food and other essentials which had been brought over from their ships. For fresh water, there was rain and depressions in the mountains that served as natural reservoirs. Weeks went by. Finally they anchored and secured their ships, and carrying all their supplies, they travelled inward on foot. Somewhere, they hoped, the mountainous region would end and perhaps then there would be trees with suitable wood which could be used to repair their ships and even build boats.

At last, on a day that was bright with sun, the high cliffs were behind them and they moved to the grasslands. They were shocked to hear a thunderous roar like that of a fast-approaching hurricane. But it was simply a large herd of wild horses stampeding. The Aryans, now, had no doubt; if there were horses here, people could not be far away! They went on, carefully though, for their experience in Iran had taught them that people could be hostile.

The area they had reached was below what is now known as Stavropol, beyond the northern boundary of the Russian Caucasus, between two rivers, Kuma and Kuban, though those rivers have changed their course somewhat since then.

They had their first casualty there. The Aryan Dharmavir died from no apparent cause, though they spoke of his age, exhaustion and the grief of his daughter's death; she was on board the ship that had capsized. The area in which Dharmavir died is now known as Armavir, in Russia.

After trudging along, the Aryans reached a settlement which was friendly and curious. Its entire population lived under one roof that went on and on, in undivided sections, made up of dry grass, supported by poles. The locals hardly had any utensils or articles of day-to-day use, apart from the horseskins they wore and the patches of dry grass on the mud floor on which they slept. It looked more like a camp than a settlement or a village, but that is how they lived.

They generously made place for the Aryans. Many gave up their own places for their visitors' comfort, and rushed to add extensions to the roof and the mud floor for themselves.

Sakaru had a friendly quarrel with the local chief—conducted in gestures. The chief wanted to give up his own place to Sakaru. He was the only one to have a canopy overhead, made of horseskins and supported on poles.

Initially, the language barrier prevented the Aryans from learning much about these people. They wondered why the locals were all cramped together when there was so much land around. Wild animals, the locals explained, did not attack when they were all together, and if they did, it was easier to defend themselves. They pointed to mounds of stones around their sleeping areas. Those were their only weapons.

Over time, the Aryans discovered that it was not a village as such, but an extended 'family' that kept growing. Their customs, the Aryans realized, were vastly different from their own. There were no marriages at all. Each person was free to have sex with the other; there was no bar on a man sleeping even with his daughter, for no one knew who was whose daughter. There was however a customary prohibition against sleeping with the mother, though there was nothing against having sex with a sister. A man could cohabit with the same woman for an extended period of time, but such exclusivity was frowned upon if it extended beyond four moon months. Any woman could seek sex from any man or vice versa, but there was no obligation to comply with the request. However, asking someone for sex was regarded as a compliment. Sex was a ritualized affair; a bath before and a bath after, a perfumed paste of flowers to be applied on the body, and except on a full-moon day, partners had to be chosen a day in advance and the act itself could begin only after the couple slept side by side in love for an eighth part of the night. Nobody was really counting, but all these guidelines meant that one did not simply give in to sudden, momentary urges.

BHAGWAN S. GIDWANI

Exclusiveness in sex was frowned upon; group sex was favoured, in order to give the entire village the feeling of togetherness. To them, the idea of a man and woman, committed to one another, and having children identifiable as their very own, was too ridiculous even to think about. Besides, there was the fear that it could lead to the formation of separate families, hostile to each other.

They had a complicated calendar whereby nobody could have sex on certain days depending on the size of the moon, unless it rained and the moon was covered by clouds in which case the prohibition was off. Practically, it meant that sex was available for about eight days out of every twenty-eight.

Everyone in the settlement loved children, and never raised their voices to them and were rarely angry. They had no art other than making crude toys for children. They made lovely floral arrangements in intricate patterns and often decked their body and hair with flowers. For sport, they loved using round stones which would be covered by layers of horse skin. Young and old played games with this 'ball'. Every victory was punctuated by dances—vigorous rather than artistic.

Their season of youth was short. They were not a healthy lot. To the Aryans it seemed that this was largely due to their sole reliance on horse meat.

There were wild horses all over, but the horse was never domesticated. Villagers would hurl stones at selected horses. When the horse was disabled, more stones would be pelted, until it was helpless and unmoving and finally a rock would be used to smash it to death. The animal provided flesh to eat, skin for clothing and manure for fuel. But horses were killed not for survival alone. Over the pit in which a dead person was buried, the head of a pure white horse would be kept, to be replaced from time to time. If a child died, there would be the heads of five horses and, if the chief died, ten horses, all of which were replaced regularly. The flesh of these horses would not be eaten nor their skin used.

The customs of the locals shocked the Aryans although they realized that sex, marriage and family were personal or social affairs and maybe there was no one true way of dealing with them. But even so, there was much that was, in their view, fundamentally wrong in these local customs, particularly group sex, sex with sisters, indiscriminate sex that meant no one knew who their biological father was. Nevertheless, Sakaru's instructions to the Aryans were clear, 'You may tell them what your own customs are when you learn the use of their language better, but at no time, now or hereafter, try to criticize them or their customs in any manner.'

Their brutality to horses revolted the Aryans. When the locals met again to stone a horse, Sakaru, with a heavy heart, aimed arrows at the horse and killed it. Better to kill it outright than stone it to death, he thought. The locals were fascinated with the Aryan bows and arrows and surprised that only a few arrows were sufficient to kill a horse. Yet they left the dead animal alone and targeted another because they thought it was unsporting to kill a horse with distant arrows. What chance did the horse have against the unseen, distant arrow! To the question what chance did the horse have against stones, they said, why, the horse could bolt, leaving other horses as victims. 'Sometimes, we even come away without killing a single horse, as they all flee faster than our stones.'

Sakaru remained with the sorrow of having needlessly killed a noble animal.

The locals did not domesticate cattle. They did not drink milk, other than as infants suckling at their mother's breast. They killed no animals other than the horse for food. If wild animals ever came near, they were stoned, but never eaten.

As it is, the wild animals also kept away from the locals. There were enough horses to go around and horseflesh was certainly tastier than human flesh. Besides, men made the task of wild animals much easier—horses, wounded and fleeing from the stones hurled at them, were easy prey for wild animals. In fact it so came to pass that whenever the locals began throwing stones at horses, wild animals collected in expectation of a meal.

Why did they kill and eat only horses, the Aryans wondered. When the goddess gave birth to human children, the locals explained, all the animals gathered to admire them. The largest among the female animals quickly ate two human children. The goddess cursed the animal and the animal crashed to the earth from heaven, but it took forty million sunsets for its crashing body to reach the earth from heaven. Meanwhile, the animal, being pregnant, gave birth to two offspring on the way. These fell to the ground as well, landing on their mother's soft belly that later hardened to become the mountains behind. Having been unable to feed on the long way to earth, the offspring had become smaller, and came to be the ancestors of the horses they saw before them. So when human beings came to earth, they were allowed to eat horses, which were descended from the dreaded animal who had eaten the first two human children.

Wistfully, Sakaru said to his Aryans, 'I would give up my quest, if only I could show them the way to understand and love a horse.'

They agreed, though their pressing concern was to locate areas where they would find trees with which to rebuild their ships. They had very little food left from the ship. But the vegetation nearby had roots, wild fruits and mushrooms to offer. Why did locals not eat them? 'That food is for horses. We eat as man should,' they said. The Aryans had no idea of the lifespan of these people but it seemed to be around thirty-five years though they boasted about living longer than any animal and certainly longer than horses.

In their search for the right trees for building boats, the Aryans came across another settlement with similar customs and rituals as the first one. They found suitable trees not too far away. They would be right for building small boats or repairing ships, but that is all they had hoped for. They returned with wood to the first settlement, and were shocked to see that the locals had killed several more horses to provide skins for the roof under which the Aryans slept and a special canopy for the Aryan leader, Sakaru. In the days that followed, the locals assisted the Aryans in carrying wood and building boats. They had never seen boats before, but were able to help in many ways.

Sakaru, meanwhile, was determined to show the locals that the horse was a noble beast, a wonderful friend who could carry man above others, give him power and speed, haul goods, and was great for sporting activities. To that end he even created a myth of his own, claiming that the horse, sad at the First Mother's original sin of eating human children, was keen to do penance and support man in every way. But old myths die hard.

Sakaru had trouble capturing the horses initially, for, for many centuries, the horses had had no enemy greater than man. Yet with patience and gentleness, he trained the horses that he caught, earning their respect and affection. He would eventually need them to haul boats to the coastline, but meanwhile he was more keen on developing an understanding between horses and the locals.

The Aryans were gathering and planting food too. They could not offer it as food to the locals, but they did serve it as 'medicine' for those who were in bad health—and many were. To others, they served it to preserve their good health. Often, the locals found the Aryan medicines to be tastier than the monotony of horse flesh. But what was more dramatic was improvement in their health. Soon the Aryans rounded up cattle and fowl, not to eat but for milk and eggs. Farming of fruit and vegetables began resulting in improvements in health.

It took the Aryans over two years to return to the Caspian coastline, during which time they patiently worked on building boats. With the new vessels and the ships which they had left anchored on the coast, they hoped to continue on their journey.

Sakaru had mixed feelings about leaving; he felt needed here. But he was the best seaman among the Aryans. They admired his leadership qualities. He saw the appeal in their eyes, and decided to leave too; the Aryans were his first responsibility.

Their goal? Back to Hari Haran Aryan, and then, God willing, to return to Bharat Varsha. Perhaps Purus was right, after all: maybe the Land of the Pure was only high up in heaven!

A cry of despair rose in the Aryan hearts as they inspected their ships along the coast. Wind and weather had not harmed them much, but worms had destroyed the wood. They were no longer seaworthy and quite beyond repair.

They went back to the settlement. The locals were jubilant.

∽

Meanwhile Sakaru's son, Rohrila, had taken over command of the ship after his father had jumped out to assist the stranded Aryans. But the wind was merciless. His ship lurched forward, unstoppable, buffeted by storms. All he hoped for was to steer clear of the coastline and avoid any rocks. Then came the time when he could neither go forward nor back, but had to keep circling around.

When the winds cleared, there was a roar of joy, as Rohrila and his companions saw another ship ahead, and the feeling of loneliness in the vast expanse was gone. But tragically, the ship ahead was breaking up on the coastline, bit by bit. Rohrila would not stop to assist it and was called hard-hearted for abandoning the floundering vessel. He was sad, but his first responsibility was his own ship.

Later, when he returned, the ship was nowhere to be seen. His crew suggested that he should go where Sakaru had left the ship. There, they saw the abandoned ships lined up on the coast, but no sign of life. He dared not take his ship farther towards the rocky coast. Nor could he leave his ship to less experienced men and investigate himself. For days, he sailed along the coast but had no luck.

Everyone on board the ship wanted to go back to Hari Haran Aryan and then return to their own homeland. If they could not reach the Land of the Pure, maybe God would bring it to them. Was it any different from what Purus had said—that man makes his own land pure with his effort?

They had chosen to travel by sea to avoid robbers and thieves. But nature was no less cruel. They had seen ships broken up on the way, with their men drowning and their commander even unable to rescue his own father!

Rohrila safely guided his ship back to Hari Haran Aryan. He was single-minded in his purpose. He must take ships, he insisted, with Aryan warriors, to the area where his father and so many other Ayrans were stranded. But, he was told, the ships that were being built were for the journey back to Bharat Varsha. He protested, 'By all means, give up your quest for the Land of the Pure, but surely you cannot go with the impurity of deserting your own Aryans in distress! Are you not Noble Aryans?'

When someone slyly remarked that Rohrila was not thinking of saving stranded Aryans but rescuing his own father, he simply said, 'Very well, I shall not bring my father back even when I find him.'

Rohrila's words proved prophetic. He led a fleet of seven ships to find Sakaru and the others. They were found. A touching reunion between father and son took place. All the Aryans left with Rohrila, except for Sakaru and sixteen others.

Rohrila was desolate that his father would not join him. He begged and pleaded.

An Aryan reminded Rohrila, 'Did you not say you would bring back all, except your father?'

Rohrila replied, 'I lied, for a good cause.'

But how could Sakaru leave! He was in the middle of his programme of domesticating horses, cattle, fowl, and even wild dogs for companionship. How strange, he had once told the local chief that in his own land it was the dog, then the cattle, fowl and later the horses that were domesticated.

The chief had laughed, 'No, brother. You were the first to be domesticated by us, thereafter you domesticated us all. Everything good then has followed.'

The chief was nearly forty years old and he had suddenly called everyone to declare his last Will. He said, after him, Sakaru would be the chief. Sakaru had laughed and in bravado he said that if they agreed to eat what he prescribed and never stone horses, or put the heads of the animals over their graves, he would accept to be their chief. The chief had quickly responded, 'I knew you would so ask. I come ready to say, yes, yes, yes to all you ask.' They all stared at the chief—how could he give up the honour of having horses' heads placed over his burial site!

The chief had died three days before Rohrila arrived to pick up his father. Sakaru was now the new chief.

How could a chief desert his people?

Sakaru remained.

With his encouragement, many nearby settlements merged to form a tribe. Horse and man became the best of friends. The horse ploughed fields, brought in harvest and tracked cattle. Above all, it proudly carried the men above those who trudged on foot. The people of the tribe became accomplished archers, shooting arrows from horses for sport. Later they would become talented artists, too, but only after Rohrila returned six years later, bringing his wife Rausini and daughter Pamira and a group of twenty-two artists to settle down there.

Sakaru's introduction of a system of 'marriage' had limited success even though he created what locals called a 'myth' that the children they all loved would live longer and healthier with such a system. Sakaru knew the problems arising from inbreeding and he spoke to them of the Hindu custom of avoiding marriage among near relations. He then spoke to them of birth defects among children of various tribes outside the Hindu fold which permitted indiscriminate sex. The system was upheld by Rohrila after him, and eventually by Pamira who achieved greater success with the implementation than her father and grandfather.

Thus it was that a new tribe composed of hundreds of settlements was formed under Sakaru. He wanted to call it the Tribe of the Horse, but the tribe came to call itself Sakaru's tribe or the Saka tribe. In later centuries, archaeologists would call them Scythians or Seythians. However, in Bharat Varsha their name would always be what they called themselves— Sakaru or Sake.

FORTY-ONE

ARYANS IN FINLAND, SWEDEN AND NORWAY

5005 BCE

The fleet of ships carrying the Aryan contingent led by Dhrupatta's grandsons, Atul and Atal, sailed over the Caspian Sea to reach Europe's largest river that the Aryans called Ra Ra—the present Volga.

Sailing up the river, the Aryan fleet reached the confluence of the Volga and the Kama rivers. It was near the source of the Ra Ra that they finally left their boats and went trudging on foot, until they reached the southern part of the country— Finland.

The initial enthusiasm of the Aryans was fast disappearing. Their experience at each stopping place had given them the frightful feeling that the Land of the Pure, which they sought, was nowhere.

They had seen their ships scatter and their men drown. The song 'Noble Aryans, onward, on . . . ' which had always inspired them before, was now an empty, ritual murmur that no longer came from the heart.

It had taken them four years to reach Finland and there were only 1,220 left out of the 6,080 that had left Iran. Their hope was that at least a few of the people on the other ships they had separated from at sea were unharmed and had found a safe haven somewhere.

The Aryans set up their camp in Finland. Harsh reality

had taught them that their first imperative was to defend themselves. They built protective fences around the land they farmed and tried to live in seclusion from others. But the locals came, one after another, and then in batches—always old men and women, often hungry, starving, ill, distressed and dying. There was a language barrier and so the Aryans could only wonder if these old people were hermits uprooted by sudden storms or animal attacks. Or whether they were simply exiles.

The system, they later found out, was simple. Every old person who was unable to work had to leave the group and fend for himself. But how can you have such a heartless system, asked the Aryans. 'It is not heartless,' they were told. 'We did it to our fathers, and they to theirs. How can the tribe flourish or even survive, unless it casts off the burden of the old? We can neither march nor hunt; we will only tie down the younger, productive members. There were tribes in the past which treated young and old alike, carrying fully the burden of the aging, but those tribes withered away.'

'And the helpless ones must leave, exiled?' the Aryans asked.

'Children are the really helpless ones,' they said. 'They are loved, cherished, protected; they are the future promise. What promise does old age hold? Do your people not retire?'

'We do,' the Aryans replied. 'Then we become hermits and pray and meditate.'

'We can do that too, if we want to.'

The Aryans explained that it was everyone's duty to help, if a hermit could not fend for himself.

'Even if he is not of your tribe?' they asked.

'A hermit belongs to all tribes.'

'Do animals, fish and birds rush over to you to be eaten?'

'No, our land gives us what we eat.'

'Your land, then, must be rich?' the old people said.

'Land is always rich. Everywhere.'

BHAGWAN S. GIDWANI

Clearly, these castaways saw, it was so in the sprawling Aryan camp. There were neat rows of plants, even cattle and fowl used not for slaughter, but for milk, eggs and breeding.

They wanted to leave after their immediate distress was over; they were proud people and sought no extended hospitality or charity from the Aryans. They had left their tribes on their own when they realized that their usefulness was over; nobody had had to tell them to leave.

But the Aryans insisted that the castaways remain. 'You can help us,' they said, 'to learn your language, farm more land, milk cattle, and domesticate fowl.'

These were tasks the old could do as well as the young and so they stayed. The youngsters in their tribes were proficient in throwing stones to kill animals or marching endlessly to hunt, but in this job that required tender, patient care of land, cattle and fowl, perhaps age was an advantage. These men and women discovered new vitality in doing useful jobs. The Aryans also had the same feeling as Sakaru did about his Saka tribe, that it was the all-meat diet of these people which made them prematurely old and unhealthy.

Word went round that the old were welcome at the camp of these strange Aryans. The aged arrived in droves, but they were a proud people. They wanted work, not handouts, and they all worked to the best of their ability. Often, food would be in short supply when too many came. But they never stole or took anything that did not belong to them. If they found eggs, they would bring them to the camp; if they caught a fowl, it, too, was brought to the camp. This was now their very own tribe. They belonged.

The Aryans did not know it, but these old people were their best protection. Word had travelled that these strangers offered refuge to the old and infirm. Sometimes, a group brought their old and left them at the Aryan camp. The system itself may have decreed that the old be abandoned as useless, but it is not as if every bond of affection was snapped at parting. When tribes learnt that there was a group that gave shelter, food, comfort and even good health to their old fathers, mothers and grandmothers, their hearts went out to the Aryans.

Initially, the locals suspected the motives of the Aryans and came to check on them. But they found in their old, not a sense of isolation, but of respect, dignity and even affection.

Who could then attack the the Aryans! Word even went forth that an attack against the Aryans would be treated as an attack against themselves. The old people, sheltering with the Aryans, said they would die rather than allow the Aryans to be harmed.

Tribal warfare was common in the land. But never would their sense of honour permit the locals to steal. They had to kill or enslave the other tribe before they took their goods by right of conquest. Thus the Aryan tools and implements which the locals envied, and even their surplus food stores spread across the extensive Aryans lands, remained untouched.

But something more dramatic happened. Slowly, the locals realized what the Aryans were doing. They, too, began to progress from their existence as hunters and fishermen to a more settled life as agriculturists.

Some old refugees, sheltered by the Aryans, felt refreshed and renewed. They even wanted to visit their tribes to show them how to make implements and tools and how to make their land productive. Atul said to them, 'But come back! We shall be lonely without you.' And the hearts of these old men warmed all the more with a sense of belonging.

When these old refugees reached their tribes, their own people wondered, 'They left us old but they return young!' For there was a new tone of authority in these old people.

And the old came back to the Aryans, bringing their youngsters to learn how to set up fields and farms. One old man brought his entire tribe along with the tribal priest Ugera

BHAGWAN S. GIDWANI

to the Aryans to learn farming.

While they sat by the side of a stream, Atul told Ugera of their adventures on the way from Bharat Varsha and Iran. The priest said, 'Our people should have learnt these arts of farming much earlier, but the devil kept your people away from us.'

Atul, who was an artist, stood on the pedestal of the statue he was working on and, looking at his reflection in the water, said, 'The devil exists as much as my reflection in water.'

This observation of Atul remains in the traditional memory of Finland even today, but with a different meaning. The priest Ugera himself inspired the myth that God stood up on top of a statue and 'ordered his reflection in the water to rise, and this became the devil!'

But Ugera was not at fault since that was how, initially, he had understood Atul's observation. From the other Aryans he had learnt of dualism—of good against evil. Was it any different from God and the devil? And when the Aryans spoke of God giving man the ability to scatter seed and make the earth fruitful and smiling, was it not the devil's defeat and the unmasking of his deceit! But why did God bring forth the devil? Was it because growth was not possible without challenge?

To begin with, it confused Ugera that every Aryan he talked to gave him a different conception of God. But then that was the Hindu way. Each was entitled to his own view of the Ultimate Reality without disrespecting the views of others. But later Ugera understood that all these stories were the many stories of God and it was folly to attach oneself to a single view or dogma.

He was fascinated by the Aryan stories of the Shiva Lingam, and for his people, he evolved a conception of the god of the sky—Skaj, the creator and birth-giver, and also Niskepas, the great inseminating god who is all-knowing and all-seeing and can grant great and gracious boons, but approach him not lightly for what is trivial.

The priest had a tall mud pillar built, representing it as a symbol of the Shiva Lingam and the world order. The Aryans smiled, for in their own land they had not seen such a tall representation of the Shiva Lingam. Soon after, when the topmost mud portion fell off much to Ugera's disappointment, they all pitched in to make baked bricks to rebuild the lingam and the priest's joy knew no bounds as the tall pillar once again rose to a commanding height.

Ugera's affection for the Aryans grew, but not because of their success in tapping wealth from the earth. He was fascinated by their myths and moral values, and he even wondered if their success was a result of the Aryans' spiritual outlook. But Atal laughed, 'A plant will grow whether it be a saint like you or a sinner like my brother Atul who plants the seed.' Atal always lovingly called his brother a sinner as he devoted all his time to his painting and sculpting, instead of tending to the land.

Ugera wanted his people to learn from the spiritual values of the Aryans. But initially the impact on his people was more social than spiritual. When the tribes that had settled in the vicinity of the Aryans' lands wanted to call themselves Aryans, Ugera emphatically said, 'No. You have not earned that privilege.' They protested, 'The Aryans honour our gods and they do not ask that we must honour their gods.'

But Ugera replied, 'They care not what gods we believe in. But goodness they believe in. And do not call yourself Aryan until you learn to treat your old and infirm the Aryan way.' The priest's words were heeded even in the lands beyond, now known as Scandinavia. He was their most renowned priest and poet. For him, as a priest, there was no threat of exile in old age, yet he spoke with fire and sang with passion. His words went to the heart of his people. 'God gave some of our people long lives, but you condemn your old to isolation and slow death. Are we to learn nothing from these noble Aryan messengers whom God sent over mountains, seas and rivers to speak to us of their traditions of honour?'

Even the Aryans protested. 'Do not impose this arrogance on us. No man has the right to call himself a messenger of God.'*

But Ugera said, 'God sends a message, though the messenger himself may be unaware that he carries God's message. Did you not tell me that the song of the Jatayu birds guided the Hindu tribes to your Sindhu river? I am sure God sent the birds, but did the Jatayu birds know why they were sent? Or even, who sent them?'

Opinion may have been divided about the extent of the birds' knowledge of the message, but among Ugera's people, slowly and surely, the system moved to respect old age and later, it became a point of honour with the tribes to keep their old and infirm until their dying day with respect and dignity.

Ugera called the Aryans and locals, who clustered round them, the Moksa—moksha—people. He explained the Aryan belief in moksha to say that they all would be gods, as their right karma would free them from the bonds of birth and rebirth and their souls would merge with the soul of God.

---

* A Hindu always considered it an act of arrogance to be regarded as a messenger of God. They knew that many nearby tribes not affiliated with the Hindu way of life had different beliefs and suffered from no such modesty. In tales of their tribal priests, their gods came forth in a shining blaze of glory, roaring with claims that all must take refuge in them and none else, or else they would be punished with everlasting destruction and forever be denied the glory of His power; and only those that believed in them would be saved, and the rest would remain roasting in hell-fire eternal. If a trace of modesty ever did creep into their exhortations, it was only that those gods chose to call themselves *not* the All-mighty god who created the universe, but simply His Viceroy on earth, or His Son, or His Prophet, or His Messenger, or His First Chosen Deputy to speak to His chosen people . . .

Even today, this pre-ancient Aryan belief continues to influence the traditions of the Finno-Ugric people who inhabit certain regions of Scandinavia, Siberia, the Baltic and Central Europe.

Despite their obvious prosperity in this new land, the emptiness at the core of the Aryan heart remained. The realization grew that the whisper of their dream, to seek out the Land of the Pure, was based on fantasy. There was slavery, injustice, misery and tears all around, and if they were able to reach out and touch a few hearts, it was simply a drop in the vast ocean. Many Aryans, led by Ugera, spent two years in the neighbouring countries—present-day Sweden and Norway—and realized the situation there was no different. Their desolation was all the greater as there was no possibility of going back the same way. Their boats, in a terrible state, were abandoned near the source of the Ra Ra river. Nor did time erase their memory of the terrors of the Caspian Sea.

Yet they had no intention of remaining in the Land of Ugera—present-day Finland. A new dream had formed in their mind—to search no more, but go back to their homeland of Bharat Varsha.

FORTY-TWO

ARYANS IN LITHUANIA AND THE BALTIC STATES

5005 BCE

The Aryans from the Land of Ugera built small boats to cross over the narrow strip of water now known as the Gulf of Finland. Thereafter, they hoped to travel by land to find the route that led to Bharat Varsha. But what if they couldn't find it? It was a chilling thought that they wanted to shut out. Ugera told them, 'Return here, if God wills it; this is my home and yours.'

Only Atul, the artist, and twenty-six Aryans stayed behind. Ugera's son and nearly 300 locals went with the Aryans bound for Bharat Varsha. Many more went but only for a short while, to bring back the boats once the Aryans reached the other shore. These boats were the Aryans' parting gifts to the people of Ugera who had earlier seen only basket boats—dangerous and unable to hold more than one person.

As soon as the Aryans crossed over to the other side of the Gulf, they received hostile glares from many of the locals there. But as they wearily trudged inland, they were astounded to see people greeting them. Some even stopped, smiled and called them 'Aryans'. It dawned on them, then, that other Aryans had already reached this land. Breathlessly, they asked for more information with words, gestures, and signs. The locals pointed southwards.

They continued forward with great joy in their hearts.

What had actually happened was that several smaller ships that had followed the ship at the head of the fleet into the Caspian Sea and the Ra Ra river had got left behind because the larger vessel travelled much faster. But then, while Atul and Atal's contingent had gone to the Land of Ugera, these Aryans had taken a different route and reached what is now known as Lithuania.

The locals in Lithuania gathered around these new Aryans who came from Ugera. There were greetings and good cheer all round. They even greeted them with 'Namaste' and 'Om'. There was now no doubt in the minds of the newcomers that other groups of Aryans had already arrived in that land, in large numbers.

There was also terrible poverty all round. Yet, when the the Aryans offered them the food they had brought, the locals took the tiniest portion, out of courtesy.

The locals ran in relays, day and night, from one village to the next, to inform the Aryans settled in Lithuania about the newcomers who had arrived. After long, weary marches, the two groups of Aryans—from Ugera and Lithuania—met face to face. There was a roar of delight and then silence as each ran to embrace the other.

The Aryans from Lithuania brought wine. 'To old dreams, to new dreams,' said their Aryan leader, Bala, as he raised his wine cup.

Everyone drank. It was a long time since the Aryans from Ugera had tasted wine! It tasted like nectar.

Bala, who led the Aryans in Lithuania, had a dream that was different from the yearning of those that had arrived from Ugera. He had been a farmer when he left Bharat Varsha. The parents of the girl he was expected to marry had risen in the social hierarchy and acquired greater ambitions for their daughter. Bala was happy to release her from the marriage vow. For himself, he desired nothing, coveted nothing; his parents were dead. But somehow he heard the oft-repeated Aryan cry to seek out the Land of the Pure. Almost on an impulse, he joined them, fired by the dream shared by thousands. But that dream was no more. Still, he did not wish to return to Bharat Varsha. He saw abject misery and poverty in the land of Lithuania, and though his affection for his homeland had grown over the years, so had his determination to remain among these unfortunate people.

The entire coastline of the Baltic Sea and the river was controlled by eighty-nine families, each with over one hundred members. They alone had the right to fish. Anyone else seeking to fish in those waters had to share the major part of their catch with these families and perform other services for them.

These families developed as a race apart, with contact only among themselves, never with the locals except those who were their servants and serfs. Occasionally, a man or a woman would be taken from among the locals for pleasure and sent back, rewarded with supplies of fish.

The families had viewed the arrival of the 800 Aryans under Bala with indifference. Nobody had questioned their authority before and nobody—they were sure—would, in future.

The landscape was bleak. Nothing edible for man seemed to grow there, but there were wild plants and trees to provide food for migratory birds and small animals. Bigger animals were highly prized, and when caught or killed, fetched a handsome reward in fish from the families that controlled the coastline. But large animals were difficult to catch or kill, in the absence of hunting implements other than sticks and stones. Everything that moved or flew was eaten, including ants, frogs, insects, reptiles, mongoose, bats, cats, dogs, roaches and rats.

No attempt had been made towards agriculture or domestication of livestock. If many starved or suffered from malnutrition, they had no complaints; it was their fate, determined by Laima, the goddess of destiny.

Bala had a simple mind; he acknowledged destiny's role, but as a farmer he knew that the earth responded to effort. The soil in Lithuania was mostly sandy and, at places, marshy, but Bala put his Aryans to work, not only to plough the land, but to raise livestock. Initially, he was afraid of the locals, but his fear was unfounded, for they neither stole nor battled to possess anyone's goods.

The Aryans were fortunate enough to capture four wild horses and when they had been domesticated, it was not difficult to go farther to capture cattle for breeding and milk and wild fowl for eggs.

To Bala, belongs the credit for introducing butter and eggnog in the Baltic States. That is what his mother used to serve him, sometimes, as a child. But Bala's masterstroke was the making of wine. He had seen his father making wine from fruits, but there were no such fruits here in Lithuania. So he tried, unsuccessfully, to make wine from mushrooms and vegetables. But, on one of their long forays away from the settlement, the Aryans saw a few plants with edible berries. Bala succeeded in making wine from them, though it was more bitter than sweet. He then had these berry plants transplanted to the Aryans' lands. But their growth was slow and he relied on collecting berries from marshy lands, until his plants and fruit trees came up.

Bala had encouraged the locals to work on the Aryans' lands. The locals expected it to be no different from working for the eighty-nine families, where they received a tiny part of their produce. Instead, here, they got it all. But Bala never gave wine to the locals. Instead, he sent it as a gift to the families, who wanted to buy it. It took days to negotiate the price.

In exchange for the wine, the families allowed Bala to send a hundred people for two days to fish as much as they wished. Bala was ready. The Aryans had already prepared nets, and three of them had practised much with the locals. Three

Aryans and ninety-seven locals went fishing, and their catch was so phenomenal that hundreds of villagers were invited to feast on it.

To Bala, then, belongs the dubious, unsporting honour of starting net-fishing in these waters and all that can be said in his favour is that he was a vegetarian and never ate meat or fish.

These momentary thrills apart, there was growing melancholy in the Aryan camp in Lithuania. The dream, with which they had left their homeland, had promised so much. But it was over. They too had woken up to the reality that the Land of the Pure did not exist. Yet this truth did not liberate their hearts. Their affection for their homeland grew, but with it came a silent, profound grief and tormenting questions. What folly tempted us to leave our homes? How do we return to our gracious rivers and sacred soil? Are we to die in this wilderness like tired, old animals unloved, alone and empty?

Bala remained untouched by the storm in the hearts of the Aryans around him. He remembered his father who had not been very prosperous, but had always given much to his neighbours. 'Their need is greater,' he would say. When his father had died, there were tears in the eyes of every villager. As he now viewed this wilderness, Bala thought of his father's words—'their need is greater'—and he decided he would stay back, even if there was a prospect of return.

Bala worked like a slave but was also a slave driver, except that he did not command with a whip and lash, but begged and pleaded with the other workers. The Aryans had enough for themselves and even for the locals who worked with them. But Bala encouraged the locals to bring in more people to till more land and until lands became productive, the locals were given food and other necessities as an 'advance'. And though some feared that the locals would run off with the advance and the tools given to them, it never occurred to the locals to flee when a debt was unpaid. Later, the Aryans learnt that many locals were working with the eighty-nine families to clear debts that their fathers and grandfathers had incurred.

Eventually, the families found out that the exquisite wine Bala sold came from the berry plant. They sent hundreds of serfs and servants to collect the plants, but since they were unaware of the process, the families failed to make wine out of them. But so many plants were uprooted that it became difficult for Bala's men to locate more. However, this actually helped Bala in the long run. He experimented more with the few berry plants his men found, by mixing them with wild herbs and flowers. The concoction he produced was no longer light; it was bitter, intoxicating, but somehow its taste lingered, with a continuing desire to have a little more. Bala's price for this wine went up ten times, but the families did not care. The waters were teeming with fish, so it did not matter if the aliens fished for a few additional days, in return for the cherished wine.

Yet, the principle itself bothered the 'wise' among the families. Their wealth, power and eminence were based on the poverty, misery and hunger of the people inland. That barrier must never be broken. And so the families reached an instant decision—to separate the Aryan chief who made such great wine from the locals.

Ceremoniously, a procession of nearly 900 servants and serfs left the living quarters of the families. Each carried a tray made of bone on which every kind of fish and seafood was decoratively placed. The Aryans understood nothing, but the locals did. It was a marriage proposal from the families for Bala. This was the first time that the families had sought a husband or wife from outside. All their marriages otherwise were among themselves.

But to the horror of everyone, Bala refused. Instead of gratitude at this extraordinary honour, his mind went to the family of the girl in Bharat Varsha who was to marry him— 'They wanted me not to be *me* but *them*.' He had released that girl from the marriage-vow and wished her well, but he still remembered that ineffable feeling of freedom when the relationship had come to an end.

But maybe there was a stronger reason for Bala to turn his back on this golden door of opportunity. A year earlier in Lithuania, a local girl had come to work in place of her father who had died. The father had received an 'advance' and she felt responsible for the unpaid debt. Bala had never subscribed to this heartless system of 'unpaid' debt from father to children and discouraged her, and when she insisted, he had asked, 'But how are you responsible! He is dead.' He saw her tears, but did not realize that he had said something cruel. His poor knowledge of their language was at fault. In their language, animals died, humans did not. Bala looked at her slender, delicate figure and instead of hard labour on the land, asked her to milk cattle. But she had no experience of milking, and cattle can sense the nervousness and fear of those trying to milk them. She was kicked on the head by a cow. Bala, already sad that he had hurt her feelings by calling her father 'dead', blamed himself for her injury, for sending her out to milk cattle without first showing her how. But was that a foundation for love? Bala himself did not know what it was. As far as he knew, love came after marriage and not before— that was the system of the times he lived in, when marriage-vows were exchanged in childhood and people married early. All he knew dimly was that he liked this girl near him, and he kept her to work on the flowers and herbs that he used for making wines.

Earlier, Bala had been much too preoccupied to think of marriage. Now, the marriage proposal from the families turned his thoughts, fast, in that direction. And in his mind came the vision of this local girl who mixed herbs and flowers for his wine. There was a yearning in his heart that he did not understand.

He spoke to Mathuran, the oldest of the Aryans, who said, 'Brother, marry her. You will be very happy.'

Bala married the girl.

In time, the eighty-nine families might have forgiven the insult of having their marriage proposal rejected, but to marry a local girl immediately thereafter and have a public display with wine flowing freely among the Aryans and the locals alike was an affront past bearing. A cold war ensued between the families and the Aryans. Its first salvos were tame. The families refused to buy wine from the Aryans. Fishing requests made by the locals were totally denied. Immediate payment of all debts owed by the locals was demanded. None of this hurt the Aryans. Yet there was concern. Would this cold war lead to something worse?

But then came the joyous, fantastic news that a huge contingent of Aryans was coming from the north towards them. All else was forgotten. It was Mathuran who said, 'Brother Bala, I told you, your marriage with her will bring bliss. Truly, she is what they call Laima, the lady of luck and happiness!'

Actually, Laima was the goddess of destiny, but the word 'Laima' also meant luck or happiness. The locals had cried out with joy at her wedding that she was 'lucky' and 'happy' to be marrying the Aryan chief, and hearing them, Mathuran and most of the Aryans began referring to Bala's wife as Laima. The locals were intrigued initially but later they too began calling her Laima and, a few centuries later, the myth that Bala's wife was the first Laima, the first goddess of destiny, emerged. She was credited to have enticed, with her magical powers, men from another planet so that they would bring joy and prosperity to her 'chosen land'.

The Aryans from Ugera were now with them. After a joyous reunion and a thousand questions, their minds turned to their most heartfelt wish—to return to Bharat Varsha.

Atal said, 'We came by sea and river, but we will go back by land in the same general direction, if we find it. The rest we leave to the gods.'

Bala remained silent but many of the Aryans from Lithuania agreed, 'There is danger certainly, but no ships to lead us astray and away from each other.'

Others spoke of the dangers of remaining in Lithuania now that the families were angry. The locals had reported that the families were sharpening their weapons. However, whatever the eighty-nine families were planning had been put on hold. They wanted to teach the Aryans a lesson, but they had seen the Aryan contingent crossing over from the sea and had wondered if the Aryans had summoned others to assist them. How had they found out what was being planned? How did they send word over the sea? How had their men come so quickly? Were more contingents arriving?

Meanwhile, unaware of the families' turmoil, the Aryans spoke of their fervent wish to return. Mathuran said, 'I want to go back to my land and I want to remain here too. My heart belongs to both places.'

Someone rejoined, 'There is a myth that Dhumarta was loved so much by two maidens that they cut him in two and each took a piece away, saying that half of Dhumarta was better than none, and both maidens lived unhappily ever after. Shall we cut you into two pieces, Mathuran?'

No one laughed. The echo of what Mathuran had said was in many hearts.

Atal turned to Bala, 'You have been silent!'

'For me, there is no going back,' Bala said.

Many asked, 'Why?' Bala remained silent. He did not want to say that this land needed him. His father had been ridiculed when he had treated another's need as important, and yet his father's example had influenced many. But Bala had no wish to be ridiculed or to influence.

Someone said, 'Bala is staying on because his wife is from here.'

But Atal said, 'Nothing prevents his wife from coming with him!'

And quietly added, 'My brother Atul stayed behind in Ugera. I knew the reason. Yet he himself spoke of it only when we were parting from him.'

'What was the reason?' asked some.

'Who am I to speak the heart of another?' Atal said. 'Bala will no doubt tell you when we part from him.'

But the irrepressible Mathuran shouted, 'I know, I know why Bala will not leave! They need him here! This land needs him. I will remain too. I won't go!'

Later, a few came to Bala with the inevitable question: 'Should we stay back?'

Bala replied, 'Your feelings must guide you.'

When they insisted, he said, 'Since you ask this question, obviously there are two voices in your heart. You must not stay here with your mind clouded and convictions unsettled. For you will not be able to leave later.'

About sixty Aryans including twenty women decided to stay back while the others prepared to depart. But Atal was in no hurry to leave. He was concerned about the sixty remaining behind.

With Mathuran and Laima as interpreters, Atal questioned the locals. The families are angry, the locals told him. They have 9000 adult members and many more serfs willing to fight for them. The families had sticks with large sharp fish bones that hurt terribly. Their short sticks with pointed fish bones could hurt even more. They hurled those over long distances at the local children who entered their area without permission. They had 8000 horses, maybe more, and were excellent riders.

Have they ever battled before?—No, not in living memory.

Do they have bows and arrows?—No, the locals replied when Atal showed bows and arrows. This was the only bit of information that pleased Atal.

The next day, Atal demanded that ditches be dug around the Aryans' camp, so deep and wide that horses would not be able to jump across them. The ostensible purpose was to grow special plants for wine. All the Aryans worked on the ditches, except the sixty who were to remain behind. These sixty went to a secluded spot with Atal.

'You are unfit to stay back,' Atal thundered when he found that only fourteen of them had good aim. As it is, in Lithuania, the Aryans had never practised with bows and arrows, lest the locals learn and start hunting animals, instead of planting crops.

Atal assigned his best marksmen to teach them. He gave his ultimatum: 'Either you all learn to shoot or I cannot leave you behind.'

Atal then wanted a wall built around the Aryan camp. Bala objected, 'The families will see it as provocation.'

Atal said, 'That is less harmful than your being vulnerable to them.' But he advised, 'Let the locals know that walls are being built for climbing creepers and vines to make liquor.'

Though work began on the walls, Bala often diverted the builders to work on the land.

Atal warned him, 'You left Hari Har Aryan under my command. My command does not cease because we separated.'

'But how can we neglect the land? Food is necessary to live,' Bala protested.

'Life is necessary to live,' Atal rejoined.

'Do you think sixty can defeat thousands?'

'That we must determine later,' Atal said. 'If I fear you cannot survive against them, I will not leave you behind.'

'No, I must stay back,' Bala pleaded.

'Of course, you must. I shall not interfere with your decision to remain. But I must determine whether we leave or remain here to protect you.'

'You mean you will give up leaving for Bharat Varsha for my sake?' Bala asked.

'Your sake! My sake! Bala, how did these differences

emerge in your mind?'

Now Bala was frantic to help with the defensive measures. He did not want it on his conscience for the Aryans to stay back because of him and give up their chance of returning to Bharat Varsha.

Their daily archery exercises continued. Bala swore that he would shoot at a target successfully with his eyes closed by the time he was through. But Atal remained dissatisfied with their progress.

Bala tried to assure him, 'The families mean no mischief. They have never battled before.'

Atal replied, 'Good, but if they do, you may have to teach them never to battle again.

Bala was certain that he was delaying Atal's departure and was desperate to do everything, possible and impossible, to improve the defences so that they met Atal's exacting standards.

But Atal had other plans. He wanted to capture horses.

A hundred Aryans and many of the locals went in search of wild horses. Strangely, it was a serf of the families who told them of a faraway valley where herds of wild horses roamed. The families, it seemed, went to that valley, sometimes to hurl short sticks with sharp fish bones at the horses to kill them for their meat. They never captured the wild beasts to domesticate them since they had kept domestic horses for generations. They never killed these horses for meat. The old and infirm ones, like their old and sick serfs, were treated kindly, well cared for, well fed, until their death, and then they were buried ceremoniously.

Atal set up a camp in the valley with the other Aryans. For seven months they remained there, uprooting trees, making fences, enclosures and corrals to capture wild horses. Their success, though slow at first, was phenomenal. They captured 1100 horses. But Atal wanted over 2000, one hundred of which he would leave with Bala and the rest for them to ride on their journey homewards.

The families watched these preparations in anger. They were concerned about the ditches and walls in the Aryan camps. Although they had heard those were for plants to make liquor, there was much more that troubled them. The families had never intended to go into battle. All they had wanted was to demonstrate their superiority, as their fabled ancestors had done before them—to ride out, strike some with sharp sticks, burn a few huts, take a few men and women as prisoners and release them after a while. Surely, the lesson then would be clear.

They thought of their first family, which had risen to command the sea and waters in the land and subjugated the locals with valour and glory and bloodshed. Out of that first family had grown these eighty-nine families, the proud successors of that illustrious line. And though at times, in the distant past, the locals had misbehaved, the last three generations had been so docile that the question of teaching them a lesson had never risen.

However, with the coming of the Aryans, something had gone wrong with the locals. It was as though their aura of reverence for the families was not the same.

The families halted their plans, and waited for the imminent departure of the Aryans. But months passed and the Aryans stayed on.

Atal and his men, while looking for horses, captured cattle too. He freely gave the cattle to the locals in return for their help in capturing horses, which he kept for the Aryans exclusively.

The families now watched with growing anger. They saw the locals with cattle. They saw hundreds of horses in the Aryans' camp. No doubt, the Aryans would soon be asking the local beggars to mount horses and ride like lords.

The serfs of the families reported to their masters about the indifference with which the locals spoke to them. No longer did hordes of locals collect to offer their services in return for permission to fish. None of this affected the families' lifestyle, but they saw the change in the locals' attitude and fumed.

Strangely, Atal was far more popular with the locals than Bala was. Atal made them laugh. Bala was more intent on work. Atal put them through the high adventure of capturing horses. He even gave them cattle, without demanding a promise that they not kill the animals. Bala was quiet, serious-minded and would insist that cattle were for breeding and milking, never to be killed for food.

Atal suspected that after he left, Bala and the sixty Aryans would be wiped out by the families. He was keen for the war with the families to begin while he was there with his full contingent. Under Atal's order, every Aryan practised horse riding. One day, Mathuran and Isran were out riding. They stopped to chat with some locals, among whom was a ten-year-old boy who often rode with Isran. While Mathuran and Isran chatted with the locals, the boy got on the horse and started goading and prodding it. The horse, sensing the young rider's uncertainty, bolted, even as the frightened boy hung on to the horse for dear life. Mathuran leapt on to his horse to overtake the errant boy and horse.

The fleeing horse entered a colony of shacks that belonged to the families, who rested in these makeshift dwellings when travelling. Here, the horse suddenly stopped, finding no exit. A serf, angry at this invasion of the colony, kicked the fallen boy and hit the horse with a sharp fishbone stick. The horse bolted back to the Aryan camp.

But then Mathuran came charging in, on his horse, and whether out of viciousness or fear, the serf threw the stick at Mathuran. It hit Mathuran in the face. Bleeding profusely, Mathuran picked up the fallen boy, put him on his horse and left. The boy was unconscious. Mathuran fainted as soon as he reached the boy's home.

It was clear that Mathuran had lost an eye. Although he

did not know who had hit him, he was certain it was not someone from the families, so it had to be a servant or a serf.

Atal sent the Aryans to the colony to demand that the families surrender the person responsible for the injury within a day. It may be that the serfs did not inform the families of the message or that no one knew who the guilty serf was. When no response from the families was forthcoming, Atal went with several Aryans to the living quarters of the families. In front of everyone, he grabbed and abducted a family member, announcing, as he left, that the man would be released only when the guilty person was delivered.

Atal's action sent shockwaves through the local population and even the Aryan camp. To abduct and imprison a member of the families! Did he not know that their person was inviolate? That the families were above the law? That no one may even approach them except at their command?

Even Bala begged, 'Brother Atal, there are better ways to . . . '

But Atal cut him short, 'I shall think of those ways later, brother.'

The Aryan camp remained on alert. All the locals left the Aryan camp lest the families considered them guilty by association. In their view, what Atal had done was terrible and something far worse was bound to follow. Accusingly they looked at Atal, the man they had admired so much, for now he was about to shatter their peaceful way of life.

Atal seemed unperturbed and simply cried, 'Laima! Laima!', invoking the goddess of destiny.

In a few hours, the serfs from the families came, and threw a man, bound and gagged, on the ground. Atal released his hostage. The man had been treated well, but there was blazing anger in his eyes as he left.

The serf delivered by the families was still where they had left him. Bala was frantic and asked Atal, 'What will you do with him? Blind his eye? Will it bring back Mathuran's eye?' And when Atal did not respond, Bala shouted, 'What makes you think it is the same man who hurt Mathuran?'

There was no certainty. It was an old serf, deaf and dumb. Mathuran could not identify him with his half-blinded vision. The young boy would never agree to identify him or anyone else; afraid of the families' reprisal, his parents had ordered him to refuse.

Quietly, Atal said, 'I never intended to hurt the serf. Our quarrel is with the families.'

There was silence in the Aryan camp. The locals remained away. All work stopped. They expected an attack that day itself. Nothing happened.

That night the Aryans said to Kataria, who often led their prayers, 'Brother Kataria, pray that God may protect us.'

Atal said, 'No, brother, let us pray that we protect ourselves. That is our duty, not God's. Let us not ask God to take sides, nor ask Him to do what we must do ourselves.'

Perhaps for the first time, Bala, rebelliously, raised his voice, 'Do you, Brother Atal, assume for yourself the right to tell us how we pray and what we seek from God?'

Humbly, Atal replied, 'No, brother, I spoke for myself, of my own grief, and of the anguish of many—that we did not fight for what was our right in Bharat Varsha itself, that in our reliance on God we abandoned our homeland, that we devoted our energies not to protecting righteousness in our land, but fled to knock at other doors to find ourselves.' He paused and softly added, 'The dream was within our grasp, but we left to chase it elsewhere. That was not God's doing. And what we do now shall not be God's doing, but ours.'

The attack came on the third day. But strangely, not on the Aryans.

Hundreds of serfs came, many on horses, to attack the locals. Clearly they knew which of the locals had been working for the Aryans. Those were the first to be taught a lesson. The attackers' intention was not to kill, but just to burn a few huts and leave the mark of fishbone sticks on a few faces. But violence sometimes assumes a life of its own. Six locals died, possibly when they sought to save others. The young boy who had inadvertently found himself in the colony and his father were killed as well. The boy's mother was let off with the tell-tale marks of fish-bone on her face.

The attack on the Aryans came two days later. Grim-faced, determined to teach an unforgettable lesson, 5000 horsemen left the families' quarters. They halted at a distance from the Aryan camp. Their serfs, mostly on foot, lit up torches and passed them to the riders to burn the camp. The horsemen charged. Suddenly, arrows rained on them, from the 2000 marksmen in the Aryan camp. Horses and riders fell on each other. The cries of the wounded and dying rent the air as their bodies crashed into the mud. Some were burnt by their own torches. Dazed and demoralized, many of them fled while others staggered off. And even when they escaped beyond the range of arrows, they rode or ran wildly.

Somewhere along the way they stopped and did what men crazed with rage and humiliation do. Instead of returning home to lick their wounds or to renew their attacks on the Aryans, they went into the village, hitting, hacking, crushing every man, woman and child they came across. It was an unplanned, cowardly assault and later even the attackers did not understand what had brought it on, but at that moment their impotent fury over their debacle against the Aryans was desperate for an outlet.

Some of the attackers retreated, not to strike the locals, but to rally the huge throng of serfs. They realized that the Aryans had these mysterious flying weapons against which they were powerless and their own horses provided an easy target. The serfs were now dispatched with burning torches and sticks to bring their wounded back and to hurt the enemy. The serfs marched forth, but scattered even faster than their masters. They too rushed to the village for easy pickings.

A lull ensued. The villagers were now rushing to the Aryan

camp to seek sanctuary. It was difficult to distinguish a friend from a foe.

'They are without pity,' the villagers wept, as they told their tale of horror.

'So shall we be,' Atal promised.

The sun was about to set, but a bright, flame-coloured light was still there. Atal rode with 850 Aryans far into the families' compound. They were not expected. A scream rose.

Perhaps Atal had simply intended to warn the families that there was no safety from the Aryans if their hostilities continued. The Aryans, however, were amateurs at this deadly game and, like all amateurs, they caused more harm than necessary. Their own fear made them hit harder.

At the point of his spear, Atal made the serfs release the horses in their stables. There were only 400 horses in that compound. But Atal saw the carnage by his men and had no desire to raid other compounds, and retreated with his men.

The dead and dying were everywhere. An Aryan returning with Atal tried to assist some of the enemy's wounded. They seemed grateful, but one of them rained blows on him with his fish-bone stick. His head split. He died that night. He was the only Aryan casualty on that day on which so many others died.

That night, the patriarch of the families came, borne on a litter, with serfs carrying torches. Atal readily gave them permission to carry away the bodies of their dead and the wounded.

The next day, the patriarch came again and Atal responded to his question to say, 'Peace is all we want.'

'But peace there was, until you came!' the patriarch replied.

'Peace there was, only for the families,' Atal said.

'But there have to be masters and servants.'

'Then let the families assume the role of servants; they have been masters for too long.'

Peace was reached. According to their agreement, the property and person of the families would not be violated. No one would interfere with their serfs. Everything taken from the families' compounds—including horses—would be restored. In turn, the families would not attack the Aryans or the locals. There would be no reprisals or vengeance for the lives already lost. The locals would not be taught to use, nor given, arrows, nor would the Aryans use them against anyone or even for practice, in the presence of any locals, lest the the locals learn the art. And, the Aryans would show the families the method of making wine and liquor.

The sticking point was the right to fish. Atal demanded that the seas and waters should belong to all. The patriarch held that they had always belonged to the families. Then it was high time the roles were reversed, Atal countered. Finally, it was decided that wherever on the waterfront there was a house, shack, structure or compound already built by the families, no local would fish there or within 10,000 footsteps on either side of the structure. The families could build more structures on the waterfront, to which a restriction of 4,000 steps would apply. The families could fish anywhere even if the locals had structures on the waterfront.

Later, some criticized Atal. They said he should have demanded freedom for the serfs and refused privileges to the families. They argued that he had had the upper hand and could have wiped out the families; had that young boy, hundreds of locals and one Aryan died in vain?

Others contended that Atal knew the situation. His force was small; a single conquest did not guarantee future victories. Had he persisted, many more Aryans could have died, delaying everyone's return to Bharat Varsha. And were these steps not enough to lead the locals to eventual equality?

Atal was now ready to return. He had remained there for eighteen months. Even the family patriarch, who had become friendly with him, asked, 'Was it to war with us that you waited this long?'

Atal confessed that it was his need of horses. As it is, he had only 1400 horses for his contingent of over 2000.

'Then, why did you agree to return our horses?' the patriarch asked.

'You asked for them,' Atal replied.

'Let me then loan you 800 horses,' the patriarch offered.

'Loan? How can I return the loan?'

'Your men know how to capture horses. Let their first 800 be mine.'

'But if they cannot catch so many horses?' Atal asked.

'Let it be a gift then.'

Atal accepted the horses. Some warned Atal, 'The patriarch wants you to leave so that the Aryans here will be unprotected. Hence this gift to hasten your departure.'

They were wrong. As it is, the families had lost their aura of invincibility after their defeat by the Aryans. Respect for the families among the locals diminished for no one could erase the memory of the severed head of a ten-year-old boy being held aloft and paraded through the village. Many mourned their dead and carried marks of the families' brutality on their bodies. No longer were the families regarded as benevolent nobility.

Atal was certain that if ever a conflict erupted, it would be the families that would need protection from the locals. He was told that the locals did not fight. 'Now they will, they have their fishing rights to protect,' he said. 'Make a man rich and he will fight for his land.'

Meanwhile, the Aryan camp was turned into a hospital to look after the wounded and to console the locals who had lost their near and dear ones. The Aryans looked at them with compassion, tended to their wounds and treated them with tenderness. Bala and his men also went round to assist the locals in rebuilding their destroyed huts. The locals were touched, their panic disappeared, replaced by calm strength, and they were all certain that they would rather die than allow an Aryan to be harmed.

Yes, Atal was convinced that Bala's group would be able to protect itself.

In a secluded area, Atal's men were working on making a boat. Thirty men carried it, as a gift from Atal, to the family patriarch. It was his way of thanking him for his 'loan' or 'gift'—and perhaps some form of insurance for the future. Atal had intended the boat for Bala's group, in case they ever had to flee. He had told them of the land of Ugera and how to cross over there from the Gulf. But since Bala and the other Aryans had learnt to make boats on their own, Atal could gift this vessel to the patriarch.

The patriarch was fascinated with the boat. The families were delighted. The locals were awed. How different was this magnificent boat from their basket-boats! There was no limit to the wonders of these Aryans—their exquisite wines, boats bigger than huts, milk and butter, clothes out of thread made from tree offerings, clothes from cattle hair, musical strings from horse hair, nets for fish and fowl, corrals for horses, and arrows that flew . . .

It was better to have these Aryans as friends and partners, rather than strangers and enemies.

Many locals begged Atal that they be allowed to go with him. 'No,' said Atal, 'he who abandons his home belongs nowhere.' Later, he relented, and sixty-six locals who had captured their own horses were allowed to go with him.

The time came for Atal to depart. Affectionately, Bala's wife said, 'You waited all this time for my husband's sake, is it not?'

'No, I waited here for my sake,' Atal replied. Laima smiled as if disbelieving him and he added, 'Maybe I thought of my father, my grandfather, maybe of your husband Bala, your children, yours, all.'

'My children shall go to Bharat Varsha,' Laima said.

'Yes, they must,' Atal earnestly replied.

There were tears in many eyes as they parted. Atal begged Bala, 'Please don't touch my feet.'

'Why not? You are an elder . . . and . . . and your footsteps shall reach Bharat Varsha earlier than mine.'

Atal embraced Bala. He embraced Laima, but through tears she asked that he should embrace her not once but twice, 'One for me and one for the Aryan I carry inside me.'

Joyfully, Atal shouted out the happy news to all. Smiling, with their eyes still moist with tears, they left.

Bala and his group continued to live in Lithuania in peace.

Six months later, the entire area erupted in joy as Laima gave birth to a son. It should have passed off as an ordinary event, but the locals said, 'There is reason to celebrate, it is the first Aryan born here!' He was their first, their very own Aryan! Was he not born to their Laima, their own local girl! How could they not celebrate!

Bala and Laima's son was named Atalvia, in honour of Atal.

Later, Bala tried to give 800 recently captured horses to the family patriarch but the latter declined, saying that he had gifted, not loaned his horses.

Slowly, but surely, distinctions between the families and the locals started disappearing. Much of that arose due to the rising affluence of the locals from fishing privileges, boat-building, housing, agriculture and breeding cattle. However, it would take a century or two before the notion of the nobility of the families was laid to rest.

Fourteen years later, Atalvia, eldest son of Bala and Liama, left Lithuania with Mathuran and over 200 locals who called themselves Aryans. It took them many years to reach Bharat Varsha. Mathuran died soon after reaching his homeland.

Atalvia met Atal in Bharat Varsha. Atal said, 'I adopted you as my own son in my heart when your mother said you were inside her. But I renounce that adoption if you will be my son-in-law.' Atal was a bachelor, but he had adopted his twin brother Atul's daughter who had arrived from Ugera, accompanied by hundreds. Atalvia and Atul's daughter were married, and remained in Bharat Varsha.

Thirty years later, Laima arrived in Bharat Varsha with many others bringing Bala's ashes for immersion at Varanasi. She stayed back with her son Atalvia, his wife and four children.

～

The close links between the languages of Lithuania and the Baltic States with pre-ancient Sanskrit are there for everyone to see. Many of their words are adapted from Sanskrit. The relationship between pre-ancient Sanskrit and the language of the Baltic was even closer at one time, before learned grammarians in Bharat Varsha intervened, with their rules and codes, to transform Sanskrit into an unnaturally rigid language resulting in the near-death of this most elegant and expressive of all languages.

Apart from the affinity of the languages, one can see evidence of the similarities between the two traditions in the extensive folklore of the Baltic States and Bharat Varsha. Baltic folk songs and folktales, perhaps the most extensive of all the European peoples, show a definite influence of the folklore of Bharat Varsha. That Bharat Varsha's contact continued with the Baltic States long after Bala is also clear from the similarity between the material structure of *dainas* (the four-line folk songs of the Baltics) and the short verses of the *Rig Veda*. Baltic *dainas* reveal a high level of artistic expression and their subject matter often followed the *Rig Veda* in its conception of the totality of human life, strong individualism, high ethical standards and love of nature.

The religion of the Baltics also came to be centred around gods called deva and devas (dievas)—friendly and benevolent gods assisted by a number of lesser gods patterned largely on the conception of the Aryans from Bharat Varsha. Their god Saule—the sun—is so similar, in specific functions and attributes, to the Hindu god Surya that no one can doubt close and continuing contact between the two people.

The same goes for the treatment of practically all those who occupy a central place in the pantheon of the Baltic gods. The old Baltic conception of Laima, the goddess of destiny, did undergo a change under the Aryan influence. Laima was no longer regarded as inexorable and inflexible, and though she was still believed to control human destiny at birth, the individual now had the opportunity to lead his life well or badly. However, she still determined the moment of a person's death, arguing sometimes about it with the friendly, benevolent god, Deva (Dievas).

New religions that have entered the Baltic region have had their share of influence on the region. These new religions try to curb the tendency to intellectualize the Ultimate Reality, frowning upon any philosophy, fancy or romance or even the spirit of tolerance, if it deviates from their rigid dogma.

Even so, till today, in the Baltic mind, pre-ancient Hindu folklore and the traditional memory of the Aryans remain.

FORTY-THREE

THE ARYANS IN GERMANY

5005 BCE

Through the Black Sea and the Danube river, a large Aryan contingent eventually reached the land presently known as Germany. The contingent was led by the three sons of Manu of Tungeri.

The influence that these men left in Germany is both profound and lasting. Even thousands of years later, in his historical work, the *Germanica (De Origine et situ Gennanorum)*, Cornelius Tacitus relates that according to their ancient songs, Germans were descended from the three sons of Manu and that the people of that area came to be known as Tungeri. Tacitus was, of course, a renowned historian of the first century AD; he was a great public orator and high official in the Roman Empire. Some of his information about Germany also came from his father-in-law, Gnaeus Julius Agricola, Roman Consul, and later Roman Governor of Britain.

Actually though, Tacitus was wrong in suggesting that German people were descended from the sons of Manu of Tungeri. The fact is that Germans existed long before the three sons of Manu of Tungeri led the Aryan contingent to Germany around 5000 BCE. For the rest, Tacitus is right; there certainly were innumerable songs about the three sons of Manu throughout the German lands, and the name Tungeri came to be adopted by the people there.

As it is, in Germany and even in the Bharat Varsha of

today, there is a great deal of mystery about the origins of Manu of Tungeri. Some say that Manu's father was a dacoit who may have come to Avagana either from the north or from the west. He joined a gang of robbers and raiders camped at Sindhan in Avagana. Eventually the camp was attacked by Sadhu Gandhara in an attempt to free the region from the brutality of raiders. Everyone at Sindhan was overpowered and captured, but Manu's father was treated kindly for he held an infant in his arms and Gandhara's men assumed that he was a victim of robbers, not one of them. When they asked him about his wife and the mother of the child, he had tears in his eyes. The men concluded that the raiders must have killed or sold his wife as a slave, and were deeply sympathetic. Soon, Sadhu Gandhara converted the Sindhan camp into an ashram. The child, the youngest there, was loved and his 'father' was treated kindly. But some refugees who came to the ashram recognized the child's 'father' as a robber. Sadhu Gandhara dismissed their claims, assuming they had made a mistake in their eagerness to catch a criminal. However, the next day, the child's 'father' fled, stealing a horse, a sword and a few belongings of others. The child was left behind.

The sadhu saw everyone's love for the child turn into contempt, and was surprised that people would punish the infant for his father's crimes. He promptly announced that this was not the child of that man, but simply an infant who had been cruelly snatched from the loving embrace of his parents who were murdered by the dacoits. When the sadhu was asked about the identity of the child's parents, he said the child belonged to Manu, a learned sage.

The child regained everyone's affection with the sadhu's announcement that he was the son of a learned sage, though some people had lingering doubts, for after all, Manu was at an advanced age and it was odd that he should have a one-year-old child. But they realized that for a child to be born, a man's age did not matter, only a woman had to be young, as nature, in its infinite wisdom, ordained that in each child's life there be many years of a mother's love and care, while a father was, at best, only an asset.

But their doubts resurfaced when, six years later, the dacoit who was briefly known as the child's father was mortally wounded in an encounter. He asked about the child at the ashram. Quickly, the child came, but the dacoit had died by then. The child wept. The people at the ashram told him, 'He was not your father. He is nothing to you.' But the boy replied, 'He called me his son!'

The elders, apparently, did not understand the orphan's world, that he wanted to belong.

Before he died, the dacoit was asked if he was really the child's father and he replied, 'I saved him once, he saved me once. And the bond lives. He will save me after I die.' Many regarded the dacoit's words as ramblings of a dying man. But others maintained that when the real parents of the child were killed by raiders, the child had wrapped his tiny arms around the leg of the dacoit. He had felt sorry for the child and decided to save him. Later, when Sadhu Gandhara attacked the robbers' camp, it was the child in his lap that saved the dacoit. Maybe, the dacoit even hoped that the child would pray for him, to bend God's will to grant him mercy.

The seven-year-old child now was disenchanted with the sadhu's ashram at Sindhan. He had begged that they dig a grave for the dacoit whom he regarded as his father, but he was refused. The bosom of the earth, he was told, was too sacred for robbers.

The child left the ashram. After years—and no one knows how and when—he reached the heartland of Bharat Varsha. There, too, he was a wanderer. Finally, at the age of twenty-two, he settled on the banks of the Tungabhadra river. He had no name as such, except that Sadhu Gandhara had called him Manu's son at Sindhan.

At Tungeri, he experimented with herbs and became renowned for his healing powers, both with humans and animals. He taught his healing art to many. No longer was he known as Manu's son, but as a Manu himself: Manu of Tungeri.

While Sindhu Putra was in Dravidham, Sage Yadodhra went to meet Manu of Tungeri. But Manu died just before Yadodhra reached, leaving behind three children, no more than five years old, who were known to be his sons. Manu of Tungeri was old when he died, with no women nearby, and it was difficult to believe that these three dark-skinned children were the sons of the fair Manu.

The three children went with Yadodhra to Sindhu Putra who adopted them as his own, but they would always be known as the sons of Manu of Tungeri.

৵

For the three sons of Manu of Tungeri, who commanded an Aryan fleet from Bharat Varsha, it was an enchanted voyage over the Sindhu Sammundar up to Hari Haran Aryan. They suffered no shipwrecks or mishaps. But there was much there that they found disheartening. Purus, the Aryan leader in Hari Haran Aryan, had no cheering information. He spoke of Aryan disappointment everywhere in Iran and in nearby Sumeria and Assyria.

Why not give up this journeying, Purus asked. But those who were with the sons of Manu of Tungeri asked, why not try elsewhere!

Many Aryans, disenchanted with Iran, Sumeria and Assyria, joined them and their numbers grew. They knew that two huge Aryan contingents had left before them—one by land, which eventually reached Egypt, and the other by the Caspian Sea, which reached Russian Scythia, Scandinavia and the Baltic States.

The Tungeri brothers' group moved towards the land presently known as Turkey. Their experience was discouraging. Their numbers were large, their weapons many, but they had to remain on guard against sneak attacks and robbery. This certainly was not the land of their seeking. When the Tungeri brothers tried to be friendly, even to give away gifts, the locals saw it as a sign of weakness and their demands and attacks grew. Their difficulties multiplied as they went deeper inland. The thought of returning to Iran and thence to Bharat Varsha began to seem more and more attractive. But the inviting spectacle of a vast body of water—the Black Sea—reminded them of their smooth passage across the Sindhu Sammundar, and the hope that beyond those waters lay the land of their quest was rekindled in their hearts.

They camped near the coast for over a year and built boats. Their voyage across the Black Sea was smooth for the most part. They saw in the calm sea a portent of things to come—a fulfilment of their dreams at their journey's end. But suddenly, they were beset by angry storms that whipped up the waters. A boat got separated and was lost, never to be seen again. Two other vessels capsized, though except for one woman, everyone was rescued.

Ahead and around, more terrible storms were brewing. The sky was overcast and the sea assumed a savage aspect, its currents gave up their sense of direction, intent on forming whirlpools to suck in the Aryan boats. Was this, then, the end of all their hopes and dreams?

And then the Aryans did what they knew best—they prayed. And the believers were certain that it was their prayers that dispersed the threatening clouds, dissipated the storm and brought calm to the turbulent waters. And suddenly, to their left, the Aryans saw a river, calm and tranquil. They called it the river Dana, for surely this was a bounteous gift from the gods. Thus, the name of the Danube in every country bears the closest relationship to its original name Dana which the Aryans gave to it.

Slowly, the Aryans proceeded up the river, stopping often, but only when the banks were deserted. Somehow, for reasons they never understood, they faced hostility from the natives, who threw stones at their boats and ran when the Aryans tried to come closer to the bank. Perhaps the locals feared that these strangers were some kind of sea-monsters, intent on mischief against them. Fortunately, there were many deserted areas along the river where they could dock the boats to repair them and rest. Months passed, their voyage continued. At times, they forced their way to the banks, despite the locals' resistance and remained there for months, waiting for the weather to turn merciful.

Doubts, even despair, assailed them on this endless voyage. Shadows on the river, even when it was calm and serene, began to seem like the spirits of demons. The dream that had once inspired them lay dormant and the agonized question in their minds now was: where are we going and why?

The land around the banks was generally inhospitable, though once inland, they could gather fruits and herbs. It took them more than two years to sail the 1,700 miles of the Dana. Now there was nowhere for them to go, for they had reached the end of the river, where it rose in the mountains of West Germany.

The locals saw the Aryans disembark, but instead of fleeing, they kept their distance. The Aryans were in a quandary. Should they remain, or return? Their boats were no longer sea-worthy and needed extensive repairs. Their own need for rest was urgent. The locals did not respond to their friendly gestures, appearing to be more hostile than curious. The next day, the crowd of locals grew larger and their excitement rose as an old man arrived. He was Odin—their most renowned and most respected priest.

Slowly, Priest Odin approached the Aryans. He was shivering as he asked his question, which the Tungeri brothers did not understand. At last, he pointed to the sky, and then to the earth, as if to ask where they came from. One of the Tungeri brothers pointed to the earth, denying that they came from heaven.

The answering gesture terrified Odin. He had asked if the Aryans came from the sky, where heaven was located, or from the nether world beneath the ground, where hell was located. The idea that these Aryans belonged to the mortal world of earth itself did not readily come to Odin's superstitious mind, nor had it occurred to the locals watching the scene unfold. They had never seen boats as large as the Aryan vessels, or such strange bows and arrows. The strangers dressed differently, and the speed with which they had put up their huge tents was something remarkable. But what astounded the locals most were the dark skins, black hair and brown eyes of these newcomers, which led them to conclude that these strangers came, not from the earth, but from a different realm altogether. Their own world, they knew, was peopled by men with blond hair, blue eyes and fair skins, and though in their own festivals the actors appearing as devils or angels would colour their skins and hair black, the locals could not believe there was a place on earth where people could be so different.

Even so, a visit from the denizens of either world would not have been so frightening except for the age-old prophecy that either angels would arrive to transport mankind to the moon or devils would come to take them to hell, where wolf-headed women, flying serpents and malignant spirits would laugh at them while they burnt in slow fires during the day, and were thrown in deep, dark wells and stung by scorpions and wasps each night.

The tragedy about this prophecy was that it affected the entire tribe. The fault of any one tribe member would result in the tribe being damned. Their greatest sin was the failure to maintain the purity of the tribe, by either marrying a member of another tribe or allowing a deformed child to live. Even Odin, who now appeared before the Aryans, was responsible for allowing his own child, born with a birth defect, to live. Thus, unknown to others, he himself had contributed to the impurity of his race. Each member of the tribe had to be pure and without deformity. And if even a single member strayed from this path of purity, the entire tribe would be sent to the nether world. There was no individual salvation. They all rose or fell together.

The Tungeri brothers were unaware of the devastating effect their reply had on the old man. They were busy ordering a cask of wine they had brought from the Sindhu–Saraswati region to be opened in order to serve the guest, to earn his friendship and goodwill.

But Odin shivered all the more. Deep in the throes of his superstition, he was sure he was being offered the draught of the devil that would end his life, condemning him to eternity in hell. He pleaded, begged, to be given five days to put his affairs in order.

The Tungeri brothers did not understand; they saw the old man's emphasis on his five fingers and thought that the old man was simply pleading that he had given up drinking five years earlier. But what a kind, courteous man he was, they thought, to have tears in his eyes for resisting a drink from his hosts! With gestures they assured him that they understood. The Tungeri brothers themselves never touched wine, and told him so. Odin saw that they were not insisting that he drink and was relieved and grateful. Touched by Odin's courtesy, one of the Tungeri brothers brought out a svastika seal and gave it to the old man as a gift. With words and gestures, he explained that it was the svastika seal of Sindhu Putra, his adoptive father, who was now in heaven; and his finger was raised to the sky to indicate heaven.

A thrill went through Odin. Reverently he placed the svastika seal against his breast. Surely these celestial beings were not the emissaries of the devil, but of God in heaven. If they now came from the nether world, it was undoubtedly God who had sent them there for His own divine purpose. They had offered him His seal! And they were leaving it to him to take the last draught of the devil, or choose this seal of God! Humbly, he bowed to the Tungeri brothers and was about to place his hands near their feet, but one of them quickly raised him and instantly they were locked in an embrace.

Limply, Odin lay in his embrace, unable to move, even to think. He knew, as everyone in his race did, that to be in the embrace of a devil's emissary meant immediate death and eternity in the nether world, and to be clasped to an angel's bosom also meant the end of life, but an afterlife in heaven. The old man's life flashed before his eyes—he did not want to die, even if it meant going to heaven. There was something terribly urgent he wanted to do, before he died, for his unfortunate son. Heaven and hell could wait. But that, as even a child would tell him, was impossible.

Odin came out of the embrace numb and dazed, his eyes closed, for he wanted to shut out the sight of whatever awaited him in the land of the dead. But nothing seemed to have changed. The earth was firm under his feet. The familiar sounds of the living were all around him. Am I not dead? Or have I died yet do not realize it? Is there no difference, then, between the dead and the living?

Then like the passing shadow of a fast-flying bird, his own superstition, formed by his ancestors of centuries past, vanished into nothingness. Still, he lacked the strength to speak. Everything was drained from him. Silently, he pointed to the cask of wine. Gladly, they poured soma wine for him. Odin felt ecstatic joy as he sipped the soma. His mind began to clear and he looked at the strangers closely, noticing the dark-skinned Tungeri brothers as well as others of lighter complexions. He saw differences in the colours of the hair and eyes of many. Yet they were together as a single tribe!

He had many questions but did not know how to ask them. The Tungeri brothers sketched lines to show how they had come from beyond the river. But that was impossible, Odin gestured. Surely the river went into the forbidden realm of the gods? No, he was told, it merges into bigger waters which led to many lands and thence to another sea—the Sindhu Sammundar—and, finally, through many lands and rivers, to the land of Bharat Varsha.

Odin had a sobering thought: there was a vast world beyond their river, and many tribes lived in the land of these strangers. Yet they did not kill each other, even though the complexion and physiognomy of some was different from others. But why had this tribe of dark people come here? With all their gestures, the Tungeri brothers could not explain that they had set out to seek the Land of the Pure. All that Odin understood was that they were wandering everywhere.

But why wander around, far from home, without lust, hunger, hatred or greed, Odin wondered. Clearly their gestures implied that they left, not for want of food, floods or the ill-will of gods. Why then? Were they going to enslave people and select sacrificial victims for the altar of their gods? But, if that was their intention, why would they not say so? Odin's own tribe never fought deceitfully. Openly and boldly, they informed other tribes of their intention to attack. Other tribes, too, never marched stealthily. Their tradition of honour and gallantry would never allow such treachery. And if some unforeseen tragedy—such as floods or the death of a priest— affected the enemy tribe, the onslaught was postponed. Only robbers and thieves attacked without warning. Battles were fought honourably.

Odin was a priest—one of the twelve—of his tribe. He had to ask the strangers about their intentions, even though it was undignified, for to ask was to be suspicious, even insulting. Yet, he felt, he had no choice. He pointed to the swords, daggers and arrows which they had shown in response to his curiosity, and he asked, with gestures that were eloquent and expressive, whether all these weapons were intended to cut the throats and pierce the breasts of his own tribe.

The question saddened the Aryans, but knowing what they did of the bloodshed in Iran, Turkey, Sumeria and Assyria, they concluded that these people had good reason to ask. With every possible gesture, they reassured the old man that they came in peace, that they sought nothing, wanted nothing, and coveted nothing but harmony. The Aryans even started embracing each other and then pointed at the locals standing at a distance to show the affection they felt for them.

Odin looked into their friendly eyes, into their open, honest countenances. They were people of honour, he was certain, and the path they would take would never be one of treachery. His parting from the Aryans was friendly. With gestures he welcomed them to the forest. The Aryans, though, wondered if he was suggesting that they not venture too far out of the forest. But then the forest was so vast. It had everything. They had no intention of moving out.

Till today, the forest that was occupied by the Aryans is known as the Black Forest—named after the dark-skinned people from Bharat Varsha.

Similarly, the Tungeris' hut was later erected at a place now known in Germany as Karlsruhe. When the Aryans set up camp there, it was called Kararuhe—which meant 'appearance of black people' or 'place of rest or leisure of black people'. Subsequently, it was named Karlsruhe, after King Karl established his lodge there.

Odin was certain that the other priests would agree to a peaceful attitude towards this new, wandering tribe of dark-skinned people. All twelve priests and the chief priest gathered two days later; the meeting was fiery. The priests were wrathful towards this new tribe that they considered a symbol of evil, because it was so different. A fair amount of anger was directed at Odin as well. He had not realized before how unpopular he was with his colleagues, and the more he supported the Aryans, the greater was their venom.

A priest enjoyed a position of wealth, prestige and honour. Wealth came to priests from offerings made to them on the days of sacrifice, which were thirteen in a year of 339 days. Before each sacrifice, the priests had publicly to immerse themselves in ritual prayers for thirteen days. The offerings made to priests participating in sacrificial prayers were so lavish that even if gravely ill, a priest would have himself carried there so as not to lose those gifts. Thus, the priests spent the days of public prayers on the thirteen annual sacrifices. The number increased when a battle against another tribe was won and enemy prisoners were taken for human sacrifice. The formal meetings of priests took only a few days. For the rest of the year, it was believed that the priests were engaged in private prayers, though everyone knew that such free time was devoted to entertainment.

Two years ago, Odin had annoyed his brethren when he stopped attending sacrificial prayers. Initially, it was understandable, as he had a newborn son. But his absence continued, and later he said he would pass all his time in private prayers. He left his priestly cottage and went to live with his wife and infant son and a nurse in a hut deep in the forest. Out of curiosity, the priests visited him at his hut, but Odin did not receive them. He discouraged their visits and would not speak, remaining engrossed in prayers when visitors came. The institution of hermits was, at that time, unknown in that land. No one was reputed to have retired to silence and solitude, and certainly not priests who led a charmed life with the best liquor, music, entertainment and rights of intimacy with virgins selected for sacrifice. The priests laughed at Odin, but there were others who did not share that laughter. As news of his seclusion spread, people came in large numbers to seek his blessings. Odin begged for silence lest his communion with the gods be disturbed. In response, people built fences for him so that visitors to his hut would remain at a distance. But there was no way to prevent throngs of people collecting beyond those barriers.

Something strange always occurs whenever crowds collect for blessings. Some are healed by miracles of their own faith and credit the healing to the blessing. Others spread the word of those miracles, if only to prove that they had witnessed something that many had not. Whatever the reason, faith in Odin's blessings grew, as did the crowd seeking them. Many left gifts, proof that their wishes had come true. Odin sometimes mingled with the crowds to distribute the gifts left by so many. That only sent Odin's popularity soaring.

The chief of the tribe was old and unlikely to live much longer. Upon the chief's demise, the successor, appointed from among the priests, was chosen by a council of thirty-nine. The position usually went to the chief priest, but not always. As Odin's fame grew, the priests began to fear that the council might select him, bypassing all the other priests, including the chief priest. Already there were rumours that some council members were enchanted with Odin.

As for Odin himself, he had been living a lie for the last two years. Before that he had hunted, drunk and sung with the other priests, and even delighted them with his poetry and painting. If he had one sorrow, it was that he had married late and nine years of marriage had not given him a child. At last a son was born to him; Odin was ecstatic. But there was no joy in the eyes of his wife and the nurse. The child was born with a twisted foot. The law was clear and inexorable—any infant born with a birth defect had to die. How else could the purity and strength of the race be ensured! Even a child born to the chief of the tribe had been killed to appease the law. For Odin, there was no way out. He knew it. His wife knew it. The nurse knew it. But Odin shut out that knowledge.

Iron entered his soul. I shall keep my son, he vowed. Swearing his wife and the nurse to secrecy, he swathed the child in blankets and carried it out to accept everyone's congratulations.

Odin thought that if he could keep his child invisible for two or three years, he could then fake an accident to show that the foot was not deformed at birth, but injured in the accident. Many had tried this trick before, but too soon after birth, leading to suspicion and arrest. He would wait.

But a priest and his family were highly visible and it would not be easy to sustain the charade! Finally, he reached his decision. He would remain in isolation on the pretext of devoting his time to personal prayers to commune with the gods. With his wife, nurse and baby, he went with his 360 slaves to a remote area, next to a stream. The slaves built a hut and sheds to store his supplies. Thereafter, they hauled rocks, felled trees and dug ditches to make the approach to the hut difficult. Once the work was complete, Odin freed the slaves and sent them away.

The nurse had 'bought' a healthy baby from a mother willing to part with her son for a large sum. There were now two children in Odin's hut—one of them hidden. Distant watchers saw the baby playing and frolicking. At times, Odin even took the child with him to meet the crowds that gathered outside the hut. The baby, people saw, was healthy and whole.

At last the day came for the child to 'fall' from a tree and hurt his foot. Just as they were about to begin the charade, messengers came rushing to Odin to announce the arrival of a strange new tribe. Other priests had also been sent for, but Odin was the closest, and as a priest it was his duty to check on behalf of everyone if there was any danger.

His meeting with the Aryans convinced Odin that they had no hostile intent and would soon return after they repaired their boats and built new ones. Odin even hoped that his own people might learn about building boats from the Aryans in the process.

Now, as Odin met with the other priests, his every thought was dismissed with contempt. The priests were determined— this Aryan tribe was evil and had to be wiped out. Odin felt the heat of their personal anger against him, but he remained unperturbed. Priests rarely recommended war with tribes. A defeated tribe had to surrender six priests to the victors for human sacrifice. No wonder then that the priests never chose war and only the council or the chief of the tribe took such decisions.

Odin shrugged his shoulders and said, 'Very well! Consult the council and the chief and if war it is to be, tell the strangers, as custom dictates.'

'War!' thundered Loki, the chief priest, 'who spoke of war? They are not a tribe. They are thieves, robbers. We don't declare war on robbers!'

Odin protested, 'Lord priest, they are not robbers. But have it your own way. They can be told to leave.'

'Are you mad? Let them leave, taking their boats and all they have? I hear they even have gold.'

'I saw no gold with them,' Odin said.

'How could you? You were too busy drinking their liquor and embracing them!'

Odin realized that the bystanders had obviously been questioned. Simply, he said, 'That was necessary to assess their intentions.'

'Really! And did they not give you a gift of gold?' Odin showed his svastika seal. Loki laughed. 'Is that all they gave you? These robbers are not generous. We should make them part with all they have.'

'I wonder,' asked Odin, 'who the robber is. They that came with gold or they that wish to take it away from them!'

'Look at this seal, Odin! See the rods pointing in all directions. They rob everywhere. What is our duty, then?'

'To tell them to leave, since I promised them they could

stay in the forest,' said Odin.

'That right you did not have.'

'Certainly, I had the right. A priest speaks for all priests in their absence. All I must now do is to tell them to leave.'

'You will do nothing of the sort,' Loki ordered. 'You will have no contact with them. I don't want them warned. Do you understand?'

'Perfectly. They are to be killed while they sleep! But my lord priest, is this your decision or everyone's?' He continued, as all the priests nodded, 'I see. Who am I then to question or disobey?'

Loki said, 'I want a priestly promise from everyone present that no one will speak of today's discussions lest it reach the ears of the intruders.'

When Odin made the oath, Loki asked him, 'Your word to the Aryans to stay, troubles you no more?'

'If it does not trouble you, why should it trouble me?' Odin replied. 'I spoke then on behalf of all the priests. But now my solemn priestly promise overrides all.'

Loki smiled, 'Do not grieve, Odin. Too long have you lived in seclusion to understand present realities. Go enjoy your two huts, two women and two children.'

Odin's heart raced. Two children! Loki had said. Did he know something? He left, his mind in a quandary. How did he know? Had the nurse been indiscreet? Did the slaves who had escorted the nurse when she went to buy the other baby suspect something? Had someone seen his child's defect before he moved out? Did Loki know of his son's deformed leg? If he did, why had he not unmasked Odin? Was he waiting for the opportune moment? Perhaps he intended to denounce Odin when the chief of the tribe died, and be nominated chief himself.

Odin's thoughts became more confused. Was it simply a slip of the tongue—*two* women, *two* huts, *two* children? But then why that silky smile? Loki was too crafty to speak carelessly. Why had he spoken at all, if not to frighten Odin? Over the next few days, Odin became certain that Loki would expose his secret, condemning his son, his wife, the nurse, and the other baby to death.

He asked the nurse if anyone could have seen the child's impairment, but she was positive that it was not possible for the child had always been well-covered. But she did give him some terribly disquieting information. She had seen the village woman from whom she had bought the other child among the crowd outside the hut twice. The nurse had not told the woman who she was when buying the child from her and, later, had pretended not to recognize her when she came to speak to her outside the hut, and asked how her child was doing. The woman had gone back, disappointed. The nurse had been able to learn that the woman had moved from her native village and was now married to the man who looked after the upkeep of the house of the chief priest. The second time the nurse saw the woman, she had come with a number of people, among them two servants of the chief priest. But the nurse had not considered that strange as many gathered outside the hut to seek Odin's blessings.

Odin was certain: Loki knew the truth. He made his decision, and later that night, along with his wife, nurse and two bundled-up children, he left for the Aryan camp. Surprisingly, the route was active and busy, with so many locals having pitched camps nearby. He was stopped six times by his own people, but no one questioned him. It was Odin who asked why so many sentries had been posted in these deserted areas. The men knew nothing except that they were so ordered. Odin was amazed at how quickly the chief of the tribe had approved the attack on the Aryans!

He reached the Aryan camp long after midnight, to find everyone asleep, unaware of the impending danger. Leave, Odin warned them. Leave tonight, when nobody is watching. His gestures were clear. There was danger, terrible danger.

But where could they go at night, the Aryans wondered. By land, they would be chased and hounded. By river? The condition of their boats was poor; the journey had taken its toll, and repairs would take days and months. Assured of their safety after meeting Odin earlier, they had taken apart the rafters from many of their boats to repair and refashion them. There was no question of some Aryans leaving and others remaining behind. They would all live or die together.

Odin was in a daze. He wanted no battle. In his confused mind, he had thought that, once warned, the Aryans would flee and he would leave with them. But he had no idea of the distances involved or of the danger and hostility that the Aryans had met everywhere on the route. For Odin, there was no going back; he had been seen on the way and his people would know where he was. But how could he remain with these Aryans who would have to fight his own people! 'Oh, for one crime, how many crimes have I to commit!'

Among his own people, the chief of the tribe and priests were considered strong; the rest were frail and fallible creatures who needed strong leaders to guide and discipline them. It was for the priests to establish a lofty moral order that each person in the tribe would adhere to, otherwise the impurity of one would contaminate the many and the entire tribe would perish. He recalled how Thor, the illustrious founder of their race, had ordered that anyone impure be purged from the tribe, and how hundreds had been caught and wiped out in a single day, not in hatred or anger, but with compassion, only to ensure that the tribe was not corroded with those who were born mentally deficient, handicapped, ill-formed or limbless. 'The weeds must be pulled out,' Thor had said, 'or else they will crowd out the flowers.'

But now, Odin did not feel strong and powerful. He decided to leave his wife, the nurse and the two children with the Aryans, and go out to die by his own hand. That is what the gods would demand for the crime of threatening the purity of his race. Yet, in his mind, he bargained with the gods: 'I leave my child to these Aryans. His impurity shall be theirs and shall not soil my tribe. And for my crime of sheltering my child and violating my priestly vows by warning the Aryans, I shall give up my life. Is that not enough? Surely a priest's life is worth the lives of a thousand men, if not more! In return, protect my child, my wife, the nurse and the other child. They are innocent; I am the one who forced my crime on them.'

Odin stepped outside the hut assigned to him and looked around. The Tungeri brothers had left to warn the other Aryans to be prepared for battle. Frigga, his wife, came out, tears in her eyes. She understood Odin's anguish. 'I want to come with you,' she said to Odin. Miserably, he looked towards the hut where the nurse slept, unconcerned, with the two children. She understood, but said, 'Your gods are wrong. . .'

He covered her mouth with his hand to stop her blasphemy. This was not the time to annoy the gods. By surrendering his life to the gods, to protect his family, he felt free and purified of all sins.

He looked at his wife's anxious face, 'Frigga, dearest, do not try to shake my resolve. There is no way out, except that I die.'

'What will your death avail?' she asked. 'You think Loki will spare your child after . . . '

Odin replied sombrely, 'No, Frigga. Loki hates me. But what has he against you? With my death, his hatred shall be no more. And you will be sheltered by these Aryans.'

'For how long?' Frigga cried. 'This forest is going to be attacked soon, and these Aryans . . . those who do not die in the battle will be sacrificed to the gods. And my son . . .' Frigga wept.

Odin pleaded, 'Frigga, try and understand. Loki is your cousin. The ties of blood will prevent him . . . '

She laughed bitterly, 'Those ties did not stop him from plotting against my father.'

'But that was only so that Loki himself could become the chief priest,' Odin replied. 'Remember how gracious he was to your brothers, sisters and to you after that. He even helped your brother . . . '

'Yet he always hated you!'

'Yes, but with my death that hatred shall cease. What can he gain by pursuing you?'

'Gain? He will show the tribe that for their sake he is ready to persecute his own. Your illustrious founder, Thor, did that,' Frigga cried. Thor had had his own brother-in-law, a cripple from birth, killed.

'You grieve unduly,' Odin said. 'Loki may hate me, but there are those who love me. They will protect you. If these Aryans can flee, go with them. If they cannot, rejoin your people and claim that the Aryans forced you to stay away. As for our son, say what we had decided—he injured his leg in a fall from a tree . . . an accident.' Odin embraced Frigga and said, 'There is no other way, let me leave.'

'I cannot part from you, my husband. I part from a priest. Bless me as a priest when you leave.'

She knew she had hurt him with those words. She wept. And quietly, he said, 'So long as I live, I am unforgiven by men and gods. I need their forgiveness, not in life, but in death. But from you . . . '

She embraced him, and words tumbled out of her, 'There is nothing I can deny you! But you are wrong, your gods are wrong. Gods that do not love, have no right to live, they are the ones that are deficient, they are the ones who must be sacrificed. Not an innocent child. The gods must learn to forgive, to love. Whatever you did for your son was out of love. You are a better god than those unfeeling, unseeing, sightless gods. You are better, more noble . . . your gods are not . . . you are merciful, kind . . . your gods are not . . . '

BHAGWAN S. GIDWANI

A chill entered Odin's superstitious heart at his wife's words. He knew that the gods never forgave an insult. He prayed, 'Forgive her! It is a momentary madness.'

He kissed his wife. He kissed the sleeping nurse on her forehead. He kissed the other child and turned to his son. With a rush of feeling, he kissed the boy on his lips, eyes and forehead. Surprisingly, the child was smiling in his sleep. Softly, Odin said, 'My son! I have nothing to give you except my love, but that will remain till the end.' He kissed the child again. The boy opened his eyes, looked around and went into his father's embrace.

'Why is mother crying?' he asked. Odin did not reply.

'Why is nurse sleeping?' he asked.

'Because she is tired,' Odin answered.

'But she never sleeps when I am awake.'

Odin smiled and said, 'Goodbye, I must go.'

'Where?'

'To meet God.'

The child closed his eyes. Odin waited a moment, clasped his wife's hands once more and left the hut. He paused outside to look at the star-studded sky. As he began to walk away, he heard the child's shrill cry, and rushed back in.

Excitedly, the child was saying, 'Don't go, father! God is here. You will not find him outside. He is here! Here! With me! Here!'

Odin was staring at his son. Frigga said, 'Listen to your child! He speaks with the voice of God!'

Odin's gaze was glued to his child's eyes, awake, bright, with no sleep in them. They are the eyes of a god, he thought.

The child said, 'Yes, father! God is here,' and went back to sleep.

Legend has it that the child had seen a vision of God that exists within all beings, but there were others who believed that the child saw nothing of the sort. They claim that Odin had given the svastika seal presented to him by the Tungeri brothers to his son. When the child had asked what it was, Odin had said that it was the seal that belonged to the God of the people who had come from a land far away. When Odin told him he was going to meet God, the child wondered why his father would look elsewhere when God was there with him. Worried that his father thought he had lost God's seal, the child had clutched the seal and cried out, 'Don't go! Don't go! God is here, with me, with me!'

Nevertheless, Odin and Frigga's aching hearts wanted to believe what the child said and treated the boy's cry as the words of an oracle.

Quietly, Odin said, 'I shall not go.'

Frigga nodded, 'You must not go.'

'If God wills me to die, so be it, but He is the one who will send for me,' Odin said.

'God wants you to live,' Frigga told him.

'But I broke my priestly promise.'

'You broke a promise made to that devil, Loki. God will be pleased,' Frigga replied.

'I broke the commandment of Thor.'

'Thor wanted to commit incest with his sister and to have his brother-in-law killed. His was not the commandment of God.'

'Then what is God's commandment?' Odin asked.

'To love.'

'I love my people. Do I desert them and stay here among these enemies with whom my people will fight on the morrow?'

'Who made them enemies?' asked Frigga. 'Did you not say they were simple wanderers on God's earth?'

'That they are.'

'Then Loki made them enemies. Loki is the devil. Would you side with the devil?'

'No, but I will not fight against my people,' Odin said.

'No, that you shall not. God wills us to love, not to battle.'

Odin nodded.

BHAGWAN S. GIDWANI

'But if someone seeks to harm my child,' Frigga added fiercely, 'he must burn here, as he will burn later in hell.'

The Tungeri brothers returned to their hut. They knew nothing of the upheaval that had taken place in the superstitious hearts of Odin and his wife, where one superstition had replaced another. When Odin had suddenly arrived in their camp, they had thought that they understood something of his anguish. Obviously, out of the goodness of his heart, he had come to warn them to flee. They also realized that he wanted to leave with them because his tribe would be angry with him for revealing their plan to the Aryans. And yet he seemed to be anguished, not about himself, but only about the son with the twisted foot. It seemed as if he was asking the Aryans to look after the child. The language barrier made it impossible for the Aryans to understand Odin. One of the Tungeri brothers had simply petted the child and lifted his finger to the sky to indicate that God would look after the child.

Under other circumstances, Odin would not have seen anything extraordinary in that gesture, save a mere assurance of God's mercy and grace. But now he interpreted the Aryans' gesture to mean that his son had communion with God. His heart was bursting to tell them that he had understood at last. With rapture he pointed to his son and then to the sky. The brothers nodded in response, though they had no way of realizing what it was that had brought that look of faith, wonder and rapture on Odin and Frigga's faces.

But they did understand from Odin's gestures that he would remain aloof from their fight with his people, and they respected his decision.

∼

The attack began. Initially, arrows flew. But in the thickly wooded forest, they were ineffective. A tree would halt an arrow before it hit the intended target. It became apparent that it would have to be a hand-to-hand fight.

The attackers mainly used burning torches and long lances with pointed ends hardened by fire. Many also carried wooden shields strengthened with animal skins. Their plan was simply to surround the Aryans and then attack them from all directions, using the woods as cover. They strode forward confidently; there was naught to fear, they had been told. They would be facing a gang of robbers and thieves, not a fighting tribe. Even the rules of warfare did not apply— only the uninjured enemy would be taken as prisoners and sacrificed to the gods. Those who sustained injuries were to be executed on the battlefield itself.

On an impulse, Odin left his hut where he was to remain sheltered with his family, and walked towards the attackers. The Aryans tried to stop him, but he continued with resolute strides.

From a distance, the attackers did not recognize Odin. They laughed, assuming the strangers had sent someone to plead for mercy. Well, they would cut off his legs. But their leader said, 'No, let him come and have his say. Then we will cut his tongue out and send him back.'

But then they saw that it was Odin. They gasped and bowed as one, for the men belonged to the area nearest to the Black Forest, which was where Odin resided, and was greatly revered.

'Go back,' said Odin. 'They are good people. Do not seek to harm them.'

'But they are robbers, lord priest!' the commander said.

'No, they are God's people,' Odin replied. 'We are the ones who seek to rob them.'

'Our orders come from the chief of the tribe and the chief priest,' the commander pleaded.

'My orders come from He who is greater than them.'

'From Thor?' asked the startled commander.

'No, greater even than Thor.'

The commander wilted, 'But what shall I say to the honourable Loki?'

'Tell him that if he hears not the higher voice, he shall be smitten. And for his crime, all of us will perish. The tribe shall crumble and be humbled into the pit of the nether world.'

'I dare not say that to the lord chief priest, master,' the commander pleaded.

'Good! Better it is not to consort with evil.'

The commander still continued his weak protest, 'My lord priest, you still wear the priest's sacred ring blessed by the chief priest!'

'You are right, son,' Odin said, looking at the offending finger that bore the priestly ring blessed by Loki. 'Marks of evil do not leave us easily.' He took off the ring and threw it on the ground. Taking a burning torch from a soldier, he put its flame on the ring, and said, 'Bring your torches nearer— let this evil burn, so that your hearts are cleansed. Then you shall hear God's voice and not the voice of the evil Loki.'

Hesitantly, as though against their will, some brought torches to burn the ring, and they felt as if they were purging evil from their hearts. Still, the men were bewildered. They no longer had the heart to attack the strangers, but what could they do? How would they go back? With what face? What were they to say? Never before had a soldier ignored the call of his tribe. They had always been ready to lay down their lives, even when defeat and death were certain. The honour of the individual and the honour of the tribe called for supreme sacrifice. But now this! Was it not desertion? Was it not cowardice?

'What are we to do, lord priest?' they asked Odin in agony.

'Do?' Odin asked. 'Do what your honour demands. You must protect these Aryans.'

'And forsake our own tribe?'

'Only to save it. To help it keep its covenant with God.'

'But what of our covenant with our tribe? Our tribe will forsake us.'

'A greater destiny awaits you. You shall belong to the tribe of Aryans, the people of God.'

Thus the first attack failed, even before it really began. Many hesitated, unsure of which path to choose. Many more left, not knowing what to believe. But some remained, following Odin's example, determined to prevent future onslaughts against the Aryans.

As the commander walked away, the effect of Odin's words withered. 'I am a fool to have allowed him to speak,' he berated himself. But he realized that it was too late now to rally his men to attack; most had scattered, and the rest were under Odin's spell. Dejected, the commander wondered how he would explain their failure to his superiors. But what is there to explain? It was Priest Odin who stopped us. How can I ignore a direct command from a priest? But surely you knew the priest was a deserter, the voice in his head persisted. No, not until he spoke, and then it was too late, the commander protested. Really! Did he not say the chief priest was evil! Did he not arrogate to himself the right to speak on behalf of the gods above Thor? Did he not burn his priestly ring—the one blessed by the chief priest? Even then, you did not suspect that he was a deserter? What would you have done had it been someone else preventing your men from attacking? I would have cut them down, but not a priest. Priests are inviolable. Yes, priests are inviolable, but not the Aryans. Why did you call off the attack? I did not call it off. My men deserted me. But not all, some were still with you!

The commander's thoughts were conflicted. He feared that it was his fault entirely. To his regret, he had allowed himself to be charmed by Odin's words and failed in his resolve at the decisive moment. All he knew now was that somehow he had to save his face against the Aryans. But the men with him were few. He led them with him inside the forest simply

BHAGWAN S. GIDWANI

to make a show of force, enough to satisfy his superiors that he did everything he could despite the desertions enticed by a renegade priest.

Through a gap in the trees, the commander saw the Aryan huts. We could throw torches and burn them, he thought.

He deployed his men along the line and gave orders, 'On my command, aim torches at the huts and then we all run to the village.'

His second-in-command pleaded, 'Don't do that. Order the men off.'

The commander flared up, 'Why didn't you go with that priest then?'

'My duty is to follow you. But there was goodness in Priest Odin's words—and wisdom.'

'And there is treachery in yours,' the commander shot back. 'Now light your torch and throw it.'

'No!'

All the frustration in the commander's soul exploded. He waved the burning torch in his deputy's face as if to hit him with it. A fight ensued, and somehow, the torch struck the commander's face. The commander roared in pain. That, thought his men, far along the line, was the command to hurl their torches. They threw them and ran, stopping only when they reached the village.

'Where is the commander?' they asked, as did the second-in-command.

Meanwhile, the few local soldiers who had joined Odin had reached the Aryans who welcomed them gratefully. Frigga, too, came out of her hut.

Suddenly torches began to rain on their huts. Odin's hut caught fire, and the nurse, who had been sleeping, rushed out, carrying the children, shielding them with her body. She was on fire herself. Outside, she collapsed, falling over the children. The Aryans rushed to roll her on the ground to smother the flames. But the nurse was dead.

Frigga's voice rose, 'Let him who ordered this burning, burn on earth as he will burn in hell.'

Maybe, Frigga was cursing Loki. But it was the commander who was found later, burnt to a cinder. Since nobody knew that it was his deputy who had hit him with the torch and run away, thus causing his death, they agreed that Frigga had a powerful curse.

Odin and Frigga's son had also sustained injuries in the fire. The blazing fire in the hut had burnt his foot and part of his leg was also singed. The child was in agony, and some feared for his life. The other child was unhurt. In the presence of all the locals and Aryans, Odin and Frigga adopted him as their own son. In the days that followed, one of the Tungeri brothers was always by the bedside of Odin's injured son, sometimes praying, but often applying herbal extracts and compresses to the child's blistered foot and leg. The Aryans owed a vast debt of gratitude to Odin who had come to warn them and protect them, bringing locals to aid them, and they felt it their duty to look after his child.

To Odin and Frigga's anxious inquiries about their son, the Tungeri brothers simply pointed heavenwards to say, 'God's Will shall be done.'

But suddenly, after days of vigil, in the midst of his prayers, one of the Tungeri brothers saw a half smile forming on the lips of the child. In joy, he cried out, 'Bal Deva, Bal Deva.'

Odin and Frigga heard his cries and rushed to his side, terrified that their son had succumbed to his injuries. But the child opened his eyes and smiled at them.

The Aryans collected and echoed the cry, 'Bal Deva! Bal Deva!'

Each day of the child's agony had gnawed at the hearts of the Aryans. The innocent boy had suffered because his family had come to protect them! Now that fearful tension was over. The child would live. They were ecstatic, each feeling as though his own child had been spared.

Odin, Frigga and the locals would repeat the cry of 'Bal Deva!' without comprehending it. Later, they would find out that it meant the power and will of the gods. But while they thought it meant that the child was saved by the will and power of the gods, the Aryans felt that the child had, within himself, the will and power of the gods. That is how the child would come to be known as Bal Deva, and later epics, myths, stories and fables would be woven around this child, who came to be known in the mythology of Germany and Europe as God Bal Deva—Balder or Baldr—son of God Odin and Goddess Frigga, at whose feet bowed all, for with one foot he put all the dwarfs of hell to flight and took on the sorrows of the Aryans whom his father and mother had vowed to protect.

Many locals left the Aryans thereafter—a few never to return, but others came back with their belongings and their families, and even their neighbours. Odin's words of brotherhood with the Aryans—people of God—were being repeated all over. Already, Odin had left his mark on many during his two years as a hermit. And now they came, in hope, in faith and to be healed.

Loki was irritated beyond endurance. There was little that he understood. Nobody could give him a coherent account of the battle. All he understood was that Odin had broken the priestly vow and was being sheltered in the Aryan camp. A priest turning traitor was unheard of! Nor had their soldiers ever deserted a battlefield! Even the commander was dead. All because of that odious Odin. And how had the Aryans suffered? A few burnt huts. Not a single Aryan had died!

Yet Loki was glad that Odin and Frigga had not died. He looked forward to the moment when he would finally unmask the traitor. The nurse's death had been a blow to Loki's plans; he would have loved to hear her confess, under torture, how Odin and Frigga had conspired with her to hide their son's birth defect. True, the woman who had sold her son to the nurse was under his thumb, but it would have been nice, he thought, to make the nurse confess, too. But perhaps some of the slaves freed by Odin would know the truth. And then Odin would be unmasked by his own men—the final blow to his humiliation.

Loki issued orders, 'Let all those who were Odin's slaves be arrested and brought here.'

As for attacking the Aryans, Loki was not worried. He had sent an inexperienced commander with a small number of men who had been overawed by Odin the first time. Now, he would send a formidable force and make sure that none of them was from Odin's area.

There was only one cloud on Loki's horizon: neither he nor the chief of the tribe could order the death of Odin. A priest could not be harmed. Even though Odin had thrown away his priestly ring and burnt it in the fire, once anointed, a priest's person was sacred. Which was just as well, Loki decided, for he wanted Odin to live in shame and humiliation, unmasked and scorned! Frigga! Frigga would die instead, Loki thought. And her son. It would be a living death for Odin, to be deprived of wife and child at once.

Loki was not the only one shocked by Odin's conduct. There was consternation among all the priests, the council, and the chief of the tribe. The Aryans had to be wiped out. They were the emissaries of the devil to so tempt a priest. Loki took advantage of their anger and demanded a large army, under his direct orders. So be it, said everyone.

But something happened to bring everything to a standstill. The chief of the tribe died. Many agreed that he was old and ailing, that it was his time. But there were some who said it was Frigga's curse that did it.

The council met. There was no time to waste, with one priest who had turned traitor, an alien Aryan gang of robbers at their doorstep, and desertions in their midst. Quickly, in keeping with tradition, the decision was taken to appoint the chief priest as the chief of the tribe.

The ceremonies began in earnest. Those were more important to Loki than any attack against the Aryans. Retribution against Odin could wait. Strictly, it wasn't even necessary any more; Loki had intended to expose Odin's secret only if anyone opposed his appointment as chief of the tribe. But even though this high honour and position was now his, he still had the burning desire to make Odin suffer.

When Odin's former slaves heard that Loki had issued orders for their capture, most of them fled to the Aryan camp. Those who were caught would not admit, even under harsh questioning, that they had seen Odin's child with a birth defect. Quite apart from their sense of loyalty to their former master Odin, who had freed them with generous gifts and respect, the fact is that they knew nothing about the child's deformity.

The slaves were paraded before the woman from whom the nurse had bought the other baby. Loki hoped that she would recognize the two men who were with the nurse at the time. She could not.

The thirty-nine days of ceremonies to mark the anointment of Loki as the new chief of the tribe were over. A formidable army was being assembled to attack the Aryans. At the same time, locals loyal to Odin were trickling into the Aryan camp to be with their mentor. Loki was not bothered: let all the traitors congregate at a single place so they could be annihilated at one stroke.

But before a victory by arms, Loki wanted a moral victory, to raise the righteous indignation of his tribe against the criminal conduct of Odin. Frigga was his cousin, which made Odin a sort of brother-in-law, but Loki wanted to let the tribe know that he was of the incorruptible mould of Thor who had denounced his kin for the good of the tribe. In front of a shocked audience of priests, council members and others, he accused Odin of hiding the birth defect of his son. Since Loki could not admit to having known about the deceit all along, without implicating himself, he claimed he had obtained the evidence only recently.

Messengers went through all the tribe's lands, their drums beating, as they repeated Loki's speech, cataloguing the charges against Odin. Unsurprisingly, in the area near the Black Forest where Odin had many loyal followers, two of the messengers were beaten with their drums tied to their backs, 'So that you will always know that your god is in front of you and your backside is behind you.'

After his masterly speech denouncing Odin, Loki ceremoniously ordered Odin's effigy to be hanged, following the example which Thor had set. A priest was inviolable, but not his effigy. It was supposed to warn the priest of public scorn and to suggest to him to do to himself what was done to his effigy.

But it all backfired, terribly. Thor, the illustrious founder of their race, may have done that, but Loki was not Thor. Nor was he regarded as illustrious, yet. The priests were hurt. True, many were angry with Odin, but they had all pleaded that he should not be harmed. Yet Loki had taken matters into his own hands. The council, too, was annoyed. None of them really liked or admired Loki. They knew he was power-hungry; they all remembered how he had plotted against his own uncle—Frigga's father—to become the chief priest. Even as a priest, he had not been faithful to his vows. If only Odin had not taken the awesome step of deserting the tribe for strangers, he would have been considered for the position of the chief of the tribe. Not that what Odin had done was right, but the council was upset about the division and dissension within the tribe. There were six in the council who felt personally affected. They distanced themselves from Odin's association with the Aryans, but they were also perturbed by the chief's announcement: 'I shall not violate a priest's person, but those that consorted with Odin, at any time, shall meet a cruel fate.' Actually, Loki had meant Frigga, her son, the other child, and the locals who were now in the Aryan camp. But these six council members were known to have nominated Odin as chief of the tribe, prior to his desertion, and there were two others, whose daughters had been cured by Odin's blessing while he was a hermit. 'Are we the targets too?' they asked themselves, for the inviolability of priests did not apply to the members of the council.

But there were objective voices too in the council. And openly, they demanded of Loki: 'What proof do you have?'

'Proof!' Loki sneered. He asked that the mother of the child the nurse had bought be brought before the council.

But the mother could not be found. He was told that she had gone to a distant village a few days ago and had not returned. 'No problem,' he said. 'She will be back soon. And then you will know all.'

The woman and her husband had gone to a distant settlement, for one of Odin's former slaves had admitted while being questioned that the nurse was never accompanied by the slaves, but by her foster brothers, cousins and uncles who resided in a distant settlement. If she had indeed gone to buy a baby, she would not have taken slaves with her but her own brothers or near relations. The woman and her husband went quickly with the slave to that settlement, to see if she could identify anyone. But the husband and wife never returned. No one knows what happened to them. Some people said they met with an accident, for the slave was a pious man and would never take a human life to benefit himself. But others believed that the couple pined not for the child they had sold, but simply wanted to serve Loki and his evil design, and so deserved whatever had befallen them.

Meanwhile, Loki regaled the council with the story of how Odin's child had been born with a birth defect, and how he had hidden that fact while pretending to be a hermit. He told the council that the nurse had bought a baby that had been shown to everyone while the deformed infant was hidden. Finally, Loki said, when Odin realized his deceit was about to be exposed, he had rushed off to hide with the gang of robbers and thieves who called themselves Aryans.

'Yes, you will have the proof. The woman from whom the nurse bought the baby will come to tell you the truth.'

And so they all waited, some agog with excitement, others in sorrow.

The news reached almost everyone in the tribe. People came in droves to hear the testimony of the woman. But days passed, yet the witness was nowhere to be found. Some said that she was dead, others said that she was hiding in the Aryan camp. But many laughed: 'She never existed, except in the small brain of the great Loki. Or if she did, she knew the truth, and so Loki made her disappear for he hates truth.'

Loki's actions were severely criticized by the people, especially the poets, one of whom declared that Loki's story originated from 'maggots in the flesh of Loki's brain'. This was the first time that a chief of the tribe had been so dishonoured in a poem. Thus was born a new aspect of German poetry—ridicule and criticism of the master of the tribe—unknown and unheard of before.

There was much that angered people. Loki's reliance on dead witnesses like the nurse, and missing witnesses like the woman and her husband may have been forgiven. But no one could forgive his crude and obviously false charge against a poor child, whose foot was burnt in a blazing fire and who was even now hovering between life and death. How dare he call the injury a birth defect? One may as well castigate a soldier who loses a leg in battle and call it a birth defect! It was outrageous. And to accuse Odin, a saintly, godly man who loved and blessed all and healed so many, of going into exile to hide the child's defect. And Frigga! How could Loki accuse Frigga! She, who shed tears whenever anyone was troubled, hurt or dead, who brought gifts and aid to the needy!

Did any other priest's wife ever do that? No, the priests only took, they never gave.

If Loki could fabricate such crude and wild charges against Odin, Frigga and the child, could it be that somehow Loki had also conspired to force Odin to join the alien tribe of Aryans! What could he have done to achieve that? Were there any limits to Loki's duplicity and subterfuge?

Perhaps these new people were really and truly a tribe of God! Maybe, that was why Odin was drawn to them.

In this environment of doubt and suspicion, came the news that Odin's child lived . . . and had the power and will of God—Bal Deva! But who says, the child is thus blessed—asked some. Has the oracle of Thor spoken? No, it is the voice of gods above Thor!

More and more people began trickling into the Aryan camp.

Those whose newborns had been strangled because of birth defects wept anew in memory of those they had lost. Whether they believed that Odin's son had been born with a deformity no longer mattered. The fact was that Loki had accused Odin without any proof and threatened the life of the child. Their hearts went out to Odin. And they cried, 'He who fights against Odin aims his dagger at us.'

Many of Odin's former slaves had fled to the Aryan camp for sanctuary. They were ready to become Odin's slaves again to escape persecution. But, by now Odin had learnt enough of the Aryans to understand that one could not be an Aryan and still be a slave owner. And so he asked them, 'If you were ready to live with me as my slaves, will you not live with me as my brothers?' News quickly spread that the slaves lived there as the brothers of Priest Odin and all the Aryans! Equality with a priest! With the Aryans! And they called these good people robbers and thieves! Who could blame slaves everywhere in the tribe if they escaped to hide with the Aryans?

Even those whose slaves ran away wondered what kind of a new chief the tribe had! There had never been such disorder within their tribe; what ill-wind had this new chief brought?

Suddenly, the poets started singing of Priest Odin—the godly, with blessings for all, of Frigga—the goddess who grieved for all, and of Bal Deva—who possessed the power of the gods that soared above Thor. There was a breathless wonder among the people as they listened to the songs, mesmerized.

Loki, however, was not impressed. He had sense enough to realize that somehow his arrows against Odin had missed their mark. And nothing is so galling to a chief as being ridiculed by poets. He deeply regretted the loss of age-old values. Thor would promptly have roasted such criminal poets alive. The law was clear. He who offended against the dignity of the chief of the tribe offended the entire tribe and it was the duty of everyone to report such criminals.

The time for reckoning would come, Loki was certain. Meanwhile, the Aryan camp had to be attacked. Once the Aryans were wiped out the tribe would thank him, give him the respect that was his due. The Aryan boats, their gold, even their women would belong to him. And he would keep nothing. He would give it all to the tribe. They would then wallow in the memory of their ingratitude to him and repent. Even so, he would be gracious. He would distribute the Aryans as slaves to his people, keeping only a few to be sacrificed.

Loki's mind was made up. He gave his orders. A formidable force was ready to march against the Aryans. As he addressed the soldiers and the commander, there was a touch of piety in his voice. He said, 'See that no harm comes to Priest Odin or his family. In my view, he is simply misguided and I long to hold him in my embrace. Show no mercy to the men among the Aryans, but spare their women and their property. If any of our men are with Aryans, deal with them gently; be assured, they are prisoners of the Aryans. These Aryan robbers must be defeated and imprisoned. For the rest, mercy is our mission.'

The army moved. Some in the tribe accosted the commander and soldiers, 'There are some of our people too with the Aryans.'

But the commander was clear, 'No, we shall not harm our people. We go to destroy only the robbers and thieves . . . the Aryans.'

'But they are men of god!' said some.

The commander laughed. 'Everyone is a man of god— even thieves and robbers. We will kill them only to send them quickly to their god. And their god we leave to the Mighty Thor to destroy.'

'But their god is greater than Thor!'

'Really! Who is he?' asked the commander.

'Bal Deva.'

'Well, he may be greater than Thor, but here I stand, and my arrow can pierce a bird that flies higher.'

'You do not understand, commander. He is Bal Deva, the son of Odin!'

'Oh, Odin's son! You expect Thor to fear a two-year-old! Thor! He that destroyed the devils of the nether world with one wave of his hand! He that conquered giants, dwarfs and demons of chaos and brought order! At whose feet the gods bowed in wonder, awe and reverence!'

Yet, the soldiers felt there was something missing, something lost. Whenever in the past they had marched into battle, there had been applause, with men cheering, children waving and women blowing kisses. Why this sullenness now, they wondered, but in their hearts they knew the answer.

Their most cheerless time came when they passed through the area where Odin had resided as a hermit. A poet sang mournfully,

'Our bravest go out to kill the best,

Gods to kill, Gods to waste,
Oh make haste . . . make haste!'

The commander hit the poet. As bystanders helped him up, his eight-year-old daughter ran and asked a soldier on the march, 'Why did you hit my father?'

The soldier stopped in his tracks, halting the progress of those behind him. 'No, little one, I did not hit him. The commander hit him.'

But the girl asked, 'Why did you allow him to hit my father?'

The soldier smiled. 'We don't allow the commander. He is the one who orders us.'

The commander turned back, unhappy with the delay. 'You are a beast, a beast,' the girl shouted at him.

Enraged, the commander raised his hand as if to hit the girl. The soldier stepped between them, 'No! She is just a child.'

The commander sneered. 'I was not going to hit her. I was just trying to frighten her.'

'It is not good to frighten children,' the soldier replied.

The commander glared, but the soldier did not lower his eyes—perhaps he himself had an eight-year-old daughter or perhaps he understood the girl's anguish, or maybe he was not proud to be a part of the mission. The commander knew that this was a soldier who loved discipline and respected authority. 'Start marching!' he barked.

He waited for the soldiers to re-form their lines. The girl cried out to the passers-by, 'The commander hit my father.'

'Why?' asked some.

'Because he is a beast, a beast,' the girl shouted, unafraid.

Silently, the commander went to take his position in front.

They would hear those words—'Beast! Beast!'—again and again as they marched. The commander shrugged, unconcerned, but the soldiers were not so nonchalant. They had always marched with the support and love of the people;

BHAGWAN S. GIDWANI

their hearts had always been united. Why then this gulf, now? They marched, but no longer with pride.

The soldiers' destination was the Black Forest. The commander decided to set up camp in front of the forest. It was best to stay away from the areas inhabited by Odin's followers who had neither grace, nor sense, nor manners.

Meanwhile, the Aryans had devoted themselves to digging trenches, building walls, felling trees, strengthening their defences. This, thought Odin, was not the way to fight. In Odin's tribes, the opposing armies faced each other openly with lances, daggers, swords and shields, charge, counter-charge, regroup, charge. True, many hid behind the cover of trees to aim their arrows, but they never made much effort to conceal themselves as the Aryans were doing. It was only after a defeat that the soldiers hid themselves in pits, under boulders and elsewhere to avoid being captured.

But then, thought Odin, his own tribe was not fighting along traditional lines. The Aryans were being treated as robbers, and with so few of them compared to the inexhaustible resources of the tribe it was no wonder, then, that they were working on their defences. But could they really hide, he wondered. Odin knew that his tribe would attack suddenly, without notice or warning. His scouts were already in position. But the commander's decision to march right up to the Black Forest and rest his tired troops there made Odin's task easier.

Odin's army of locals, who were manning the frontlines, was hidden behind the trees at the fringe of the forest. Though their bows and arrows were ready, their hearts were not; should they fight their own tribe?

Loki's army moved towards the forest. Odin ordered his men to come out of cover; they massed behind him. The two armies gazed at each other across the distance—away from the range of arrows and lances. Odin ordered his men to stop where they were, adding that they were not to move or strike.

Was he waiting for Loki's army to make the first strike, his men wondered.

Odin went forward alone, with slow steps, towards the opposing army. The commander sneered. What was he hoping for? A repeat of his last performance when the miserable little contingent had simply fallen apart and its commander had died mysteriously? These were not troops from his own area, these were disciplined soldiers, picked up from remote parts where Odin's name was heard, even respected, but not worshipped.

Odin was well within the range of their arrows. Still he came towards them. When he was within the range of their lances, the commander shouted, 'Stop! Or else you will die like the dog that you are.'

The commander had no intention of letting Odin come too near. He knew what had happened last time—Odin had cast a seditious spell on the troops to make them desert their commander. Odin stopped.

The commander shouted, 'Tell the men of your tribe to throw down their arms and surrender. They will not be harmed. We are only after the Aryan robbers.'

'They are not robbers,' Odin replied. 'Your men will have to kill us all, your own people, your flesh and blood, before you reach the Aryans. I beg you . . .'

Odin could not finish. This was precisely the kind of talk that the commander wanted to avoid. He was the most accomplished lance-thrower in the tribe; he aimed at Odin's mouth, from which the seditious words were flowing and released his lance. Odin fell.

The soldiers were shocked. To kill a priest! That too during parleys! When he was unarmed! Even Loki had said, 'No harm must come to Odin, he is simply misguided and I long to hold him in my embrace . . .' And yet their commander had killed a priest, inviolable, innocent, unarmed! But the soldiers did not know what the commander had been told by the chief of the tribe in private.

A cry of anguish rose from the defenders of the forest. As one they rushed forward, not at the opposing army, but to the fallen Odin.

The tribe's arrows sped at them, for the soldiers thought they were being attacked. Some of the locals fell, but still they rushed forward. No one thought of hitting the enemy or protecting the Aryans or themselves. All that was erased from their minds when they discarded their weapons in their haste to reach Odin.

They ignored the soldiers, ignored the arrows and simply stood around their fallen leader, while a few of them lifted Odin's body reverently.

The soldiers finally understood, and guilt smote them. Their commander had killed an innocent, unarmed priest, and they had killed their own brethren who had rushed to mourn their leader. They were German soldiers, proud of their honour, gallantry and courage, and in the bodies of the innocents that lay on the ground they saw the loss of their own honour and gallantry.

Silently, mournfully, the locals started to move back towards the forest, carrying Odin's lifeless body. None of them even looked at the soldiers. But the commander had no intention of letting all these men go back into the forest. He ordered them to stop, allowing only the four who bore Odin's body to proceed to the forest. A few more tried to follow them, but the commander shot at them, watching them fall to the ground. He turned to the rest standing around like lost children, raised his hand and shouted, 'If any of you tries to leave, he will die like a dog.'

One of Odin's former slaves mumbled something—a prayer? a vow? a curse?

'What did you say?' asked the commander, ready to punish the man or praise him depending on his answer.

But the man's eyes were riveted on the commander's hand

that held another lance. All else had disappeared from his view, except the man who had felled his master. The slave jumped at the commander. The lance went through his shoulder, but undeterred he kept stabbing the commander.

With his dying breath, the commander ordered his men, 'Kill them, kill them . . . kill all. Kill.'

But his soldiers did not hear those words. Only Odin's men did. Most of them ran back towards the forest, fearing that the soldiers would let loose their arrows at them. But many stood by, dazed.

The German army was never without a commander. On the commander's death, his deputy took over command. At his order, some soldiers ceremoniously picked up the fallen commander's body while others moved towards the men standing by listlessly.

'Throw down your weapons,' the new commander ordered them. Most of them had no arms. A few had daggers in their belts. They threw them on the ground.

'Kill us, brother,' pleaded Hansa, one of the old men.

'Why would I kill you?'

'You killed our Odin, the best, the bravest, the noblest among us,' Hansa lamented.

'I did not kill him, but perhaps he had to die.'

The old man's eyes met the commander's and he said, as though pronouncing a judgment, 'You killed him,' and then he looked at the soldiers, and said, 'You all killed him, each one of you.'

'You would not speak so much if this lance went through your stupid mouth,' said the commander.

'I would not, but you will know, all the same, always, that you killed him . . . you all killed him.' He stood straight, 'Come, and let your lance strike!'

But the commander had no wish to strike the unarmed old man. Kindly, he said, 'Brother, we come not to kill our brothers. I am sorry about Odin.'

The old man was pitiless, 'Yet you killed him. All of you.'

Even the soldiers' eyes were downcast. They had a feeling now that they were all a party to the crime of their fallen commander.

The commander spoke, 'Please understand, we have nothing against you. You are our people. We are after the robber Aryans.'

'We are all Aryans. There are no robbers here. It is Loki, the robber, who sends you out to rob.'

The commander's hand gripped his lance. But he controlled himself. He ordered, 'All of you remain here. Do not try to go back into the forest.'

'Where will you go, brother?' the old man asked.

'We will go into the forest and bring those Aryans out,' the commander replied.

'Then you must kill us if you wish to pass.'

The man was mad, the commander was convinced. Gently, he said, 'Move, old man, move.'

But the old man stood there. With the back of his hand, the commander hit the old man in an attempt to move him aside. The old man fell. None of Odin's men helped him rise. They all stood, resolutely, blocking the commander's way.

'Do you all, really, truly want to die?' he asked as he extended his hand to help the old man to rise, but the old man cried, 'Do not, do not give me your hand, brother. It is red with my master's blood!'

The commander turned away, purple with rage. He looked at his soldiers. 'Move them aside; beat any that oppose.'

His soldiers stood silently, none of them moved. They had never disobeyed a superior's orders before, always willing to leap to their death and destruction, kill and be killed. Yet there they stood, their thoughts focused on a single question: had they killed Priest Odin?

The soldiers' gaze went to the forest. Bodies were strewn everywhere, men they had hit when they came towards the fallen Odin. Yes, the soldiers realized, we were responsible for their deaths.

They could, easily and effortlessly, have broken through Odin's men, unarmed as they were. Yet they stepped aside, some retreated. The new commander was in a quandary—where do I go from here? The target, he knew, was the forest. There lay the enemy who had to be wiped out.

But when he looked at his men, and even in his own heart, he realized his army had lost its spirit. That intangible, mysterious force that always in the past had inspired his men to give their last breath to achieve something without considering the cost to themselves, which made them feel that they were doing something bigger and nobler than themselves. But now he felt drained and he knew that his men were too.

He pointed to a spot at the back and quietly ordered, 'We camp here.'

Many said later that it was a mistake. He should have rushed into the forest. As it is, all the locals in the forest who had joined the Aryan cause were demoralized and distressed over Odin's death. The commander would have had no trouble trouncing the enemy.

The Aryans themselves were shaken. The Tungeri brothers clustered around Odin's prostrate body, tending to him. Fortunately, the commander's lance had not smashed his face. Odin had turned his face when the lance crashed into him. It had cut deep into the side of his face. He had lost one eye irretrievably. But would he lose his life? It seemed so. There was a wound in every Aryan's heart. The first attack had burnt Odin's son's leg, and killed his nurse. Now Odin lay at death's door. Over sixty of them had been killed by soldiers outside the forest—all of them locals, all those who had followed Odin. A heartbroken lament went up in the nearby village—Odin had fallen. Spectators had watched from Odin's nearby village. They could not tell that it was Odin who fell. When they saw the army camped, they came forward cautiously. They went back lamenting that Odin had fallen.

Soon, droves of men, women and children from the village headed towards the forest. But that was only the beginning. Hour by hour, others followed. They were all going there to pay respects to Odin and be with those whom Odin sought to protect.

The commander and his soldiers saw these endless processions. They could have prevented them. They could have demanded that everyone return, peacefully, to their villages. But would they have succeeded? Perhaps not, given they could not even withstand the resoluteness of one unarmed, frail old man.

'How many of our own people will we have to kill when we move into the forest? What glory will there be in that victory?' his deputy asked him, as they watched the villagers enter the forest.

'Glory! There never will be glory, never any honour . . . We lost that, when Priest Odin was struck. Why we did that I will never understand,' the commander replied.

'But that is what the chief of the tribe ordered!'

'Nonsense! I heard Chief Loki myself. He asked that the utmost consideration be shown to Odin.'

'Loki spoke to the commander separately. He said that Odin should be left neither here, nor in the forest, not in fact anywhere on earth.'

'Why was I not told?' asked the commander. 'I was to be next in command!'

'It was not for me to report to you what I heard the chief say to the commander. It was for the commander to tell you.'

'How is it that you were with the commander instead of me when the chief spoke to him?'

'Since you were on leave, you were not expected to join this contingent. In your absence I was to be the next in command.'

'Was there anyone else with you?'

'Only the chief's brother. But the commander did tell his orderly to convey these instructions to the next in command, if something happened to him in battle.'

'I have taken over command. But the orderly has said nothing about it to me.'

'Why should he? The deed has been done. Odin has fallen. But don't worry, he is bound to speak to you. He will even tell you how our own people who have joined these Aryan robbers are to be taught a terrible lesson.'

The commander went to speak to the orderly. It was an hour later that he addressed his troops. He said, 'I have to leave. Do not ask why . . . my reasons are compelling and personal. You will be led by an able commander . . . one who knows where he goes. Goodbye.'

Many wondered what had prompted the commander to leave in the middle of a campaign, but no one questioned him, save for the drummer boy. 'Lord commander, bad news from home?'

Kindly, the commander looked at the boy, 'Yes, son. News from somewhere we all come from.' He left alone, in the night, without his orderly.

The new commander spoke to them, 'Sleep early and well. At dawn, we must begin the attack.' He outlined for them the formation and method of attack and finally asked, 'Any questions?'

Only one question came, 'Why did the commander leave?'

'I am your commander and I have not left,' he replied shortly.

'No, we mean the last commander. Why . . . where did he go?'

'It was not the purpose of this meeting to discuss the reasons or the whereabouts of the last commander. As a commander, he exists no more. As a friend, he remains, and it would be unfriendly to pursue a question that he requested must remain unasked.'

Though the soldiers were silent, each wondered why the commander would have taken the awesome step of desertion, thereby courting dishonour. A nightmarish feeling stole over some. Next morning, sixty-two soldiers were missing.

The commander who had left did not join the Aryans. He went home and then, according to some, embraced a life of homelessness.

The new commander noted the absence of sixty-two soldiers with dismay. In no way did it really diminish the strength of his formidable force. Yet he waited, for no apparent reason, and decided to send a message to Chief Loki in the meantime. The message spoke of the fall of Odin, the death of the first commander, the departure of the second, and the desertion by sixty-two soldiers, as well as of the locals from surrounding areas who were flocking to the Aryans. He also mentioned the possibility of bloodshed, not only among the Aryans but also the people of the tribe who were congregated in the forest. And yet the message said not a word about what the commander proposed to do, nor did he ask for instructions. His message ended mysteriously—'I wait.'

Loki was far away. It took time for the messenger to reach him. He exploded, 'Wait for what? Wait to attack? Wait for my reply? Wait to be dismissed? For what?'

The messenger could not enlighten him. Loki asked, 'Is he attacking or is he not? Is he a fool?'

'He is the commander, lord chief,' replied the messenger with unmistakable reproach in his voice. Loki glared but the messenger asked, 'Is there a reply? Or do I return without a reply?'

'There is no reply,' said Loki grimly. 'And you do not go back. Consider yourself dismissed from the army.'

It annoyed Loki that the messenger was profuse in his thanks.

In spite of all his bluster, Loki suspected that the new commander wanted to hear openly what the chief wanted done to the German locals who had joined the Aryans. Loki sent his own brother. He was to congratulate and honour the commander if he had attacked and won, or to dismiss him if he had failed to attack, and assume command of the troops himself. Two priests and two members of the council were sent as well, so as to leave no doubt about the transfer of command and to keep up the morale of the troops. Loki's brother was not as senior as the man he might replace, and in fact he was junior to many of the deputies in the contingent. But in times of crisis, seniority did not matter much, and being kin to the chief of the tribe, surely, conferred something far more precious than mere seniority!

Meanwhile, strange events were occurring outside the Black Forest where the army was camped. Hansa, the old man who had stood resolutely, unarmed, ready to die, in front of the last commander, had been bringing food for the soldiers from the Aryan kitchen, despite opposition from the villagers and other locals who had refused to respond to this army's urgent request for food.

At his next visit to the camp, he cried out, loud and clear, 'Who can kill a god! Odin lives! Odin lives! He lives!'

This was the first time that the soldiers heard the news that Odin was not dead. At first, they did not believe him. Perhaps Hansa meant it in the spiritual sense; after all, gods could not die. But they still said, 'Impossible! Never did our commander's lance fail to kill.'

'It was not the failure of your commander. It was the success of your god,' said Hansa.

Within a few hours news of Odin's recovery spread like wildfire. He had lost an eye, though.

'How can a god lose his eye?' they asked.

'Gods make sacrifices too. Did not Odin's son Bal Deva lose his foot to save the Aryans?'

But the greatest surprise was not that Odin lived, but that the soldiers rejoiced in the news. A cloud lifted from their hearts; their own hands, they had felt, were red with Odin's blood, even though it was their commander who had let the lance fly. Even Hansa had blamed them for Odin's death, though he had apologized later, 'Brothers, forgive me, I spoke from want of faith in blaming you. No, your hands are pure, blameless, and auspicious. How can I even hate the late commander! He restored our faith in our god.'

Mad, this Hansa is—they thought. But may God give us this ineffable madness of infinite love! They loved him. They laughed at him. Yet they envied him.

But some of the soldiers asked him, 'One day, we will have to attack again. Will you love us then?'

But his answer perplexed them, 'If you will love me after I die, why will I not love you before I die! I know not how love starts, but I know now that it does not cease. Man dies. Love does not.'

But then Hansa had intrigued not just his own people. The Aryans were charmed by him, too. When he could converse with the Aryans, the Tungeri brothers asked, 'Why are you called Hansa?'

'Why not! My father gave me the name,' said Hansa. But then he explained that Hansa meant a person or a bird that joins many to form a league to do violence to the violent.

The Tungeri brothers laughed. They saw the connection between Hansa and their own word for violence—himsa. One of them said, 'Not Hansa. You should be called Ahansa.'

'What would that mean?' Hansa asked.

'It would mean that you are in league with many to do non-violence to the violent.'

'Oh, merely by adding *a* you give my name the opposite meaning?'

'Exactly.'

But Hansa said, 'No, I cannot change the name that my

father gave me. But you can call me Hansa that does Ahansa.'

When Loki's brother and his party reached the army camped outside the Black Forest, he viewed the commander and his troops with undisguised contempt. The priests and council members had rehearsed in their minds, and even discussed, the delicacy with which they would handle this transition. But Loki's brother ruined it all with his impatient bluntness in telling the commander, in the presence of the troops, that he had been sent to relieve him and to take over the command. Such messages were meant to be conveyed with finesse, away from the troops and eavesdroppers. One had to ensure that the exiting officer felt neither anger nor insult.

'It gives me great pleasure to renounce this command,' said the dismissed commander, and then he pointed to the priests and council members and included them in his insult to ask the new commander, 'Will they be your chief officers and advisers?'

'They are council members and priests,' said Loki's brother. 'Can you not see their rings?'

'Forgive me,' the dismissed commander said to the priests and council members. 'The glare of the dazzling glory of the new commander blinded me to all else. And you are so tongue-tied in his presence! How could I believe you to be respected priests and council members? Recently though I saw a priest of honour who wore no priestly ring!'

Contemptuously, he turned from them to speak to his soldiers, 'Men, I have just been relieved of command. I bid you goodbye. Your command now is in the hands of this . . . this . . . the brother of our chief. And he brings council members and priests, wearing priestly rings to see that you obey.'

It was an unfair insult to the priests and council members. But the commander felt insulted too—not so much by the dismissal but by the manner of his dismissal, and the fact that he was being replaced by a blustering, bullying junior. He had expected his own deputy to replace him. As it is, the German army always marched with a hierarchy of officers, so that if one fell, another was ready to take over. The commander himself was the third such officer to take charge. There were nine other officers after him, at least five of who were senior to Loki's brother in military service. Disgusted, the dismissed commander moved towards his tent to remove his belongings.

'Commander!' shouted someone, and the new commander, Loki's brother, responded, 'Yes!'

It was the dismissed commander's deputy who had spoken. Brutally, he told the new commander, 'I speak not to you, I speak to my commander.' Turning to the dismissed commander, he said, 'I do not wish to serve in the unit.'

The dismissed commander would possibly have said that he was no longer in command, but the new commander angrily said, 'Consider yourself dismissed.'

'What I consider or do not consider is my business,' replied the deputy. 'As to my dismissal, you do not have that right unless your brother is dead and you are a priest and have been nominated by the council to be chief of the tribe.'

Carefully now, the new commander spoke, 'I did not mean dismissal in the sense you choose to understand. I meant that your request to leave is acceptable. Report wherever you must for your new assignment.'

Without a word of thanks, the deputy left.

Four officers came out. Wearily, the new commander asked, 'You too wish to leave?'

They nodded. Nothing was said.

The commander nodded. The four officers left.

The priests wanted to address the soldiers and started to speak, but the soldiers moved away in disrespect. If they had been ordered to listen, they would have. But in the absence of an order, they felt that they did not have to listen to those that came as puppets and witnesses to insult their commander. Loki's brother thought, if they lack respect for me, how can they honour the priests and council members!

The dismissed commander left, as did the four officers.

Some time later, Hansa came, as usual, with food from the Aryan kitchen.

'Why are we taking food from the Aryans?' the new commander asked.

'There is no other place to get food for so many of us.'

'Good. Soon their kitchen will be ours,' the commander said, and then he asked, pointing to Hansa and his companions, 'Who are they?'

'They are Odin's men,' they said.

A priest intervened to say, 'But Odin is dead.'

The answering cry of 'Odin lives! Odin lives! Odin lives!' shocked the newcomers.

'He lives?' the commander asked, astounded.

'He lives! He lives!' was the reply.

'Then he must die! We were told a falsehood!' the commander said wrathfully. He clearly lacked the finesse of his brother, Loki.

'What falsehood?' an officer asked.

'The falsehood that Odin was dead!'

'That was no falsehood! He died. He now lives. He sacrificed his eye to save the Aryans,' the officer replied. Others nodded.

The commander stood aghast. I have an army of deserters and lunatics, he thought. Still he asked, 'But the chief of the tribe was told that Odin had died.'

'Priest Odin came to life after the last message was sent.'

Yes, the commander was convinced, they were all mad. 'Well, he will have to die again,' he said.

'Who will kill him?' some asked.

'You will. I will. We will. He must die!'

The answer was clear. The mist disappeared. They knew now that the commander who had died had not thrown the lance at Odin in a temper tantrum. The mission, obviously, right from the beginning, was to kill Odin. Still an officer asked, 'Commander, why is it necessary to kill Odin?'

'Because he violated Thor's law. He hid his son who was born with a birth defect and took shelter with the Aryans.'

'That is a lie,' one of the council members interrupted.

'I speak the words of the chief of the tribe,' the commander frostily said.

'A lie, be it spoken by anyone, still remains a lie,' the council member said. 'I do not say that the chief invented the lie. But he believed the lie of others.'

'You do not know all the facts,' the commander said.

'It is my business to know facts—and lies.'

One of the priests said, 'I would like to go and see Odin.'

The commander was quick to reply, 'We will invade the forest tomorrow. You will see him, dead or alive.'

So saying, he went with the officers for a tour of the area. Having arrived only that morning, he was tired, physically and emotionally, but he had to demonstrate that he took his duties seriously.

The priest asked the drummer boy, 'What can you do with that drum?'

'Everything! I can call on soldiers to attack, to retreat, to . . .'

'Can you call all the soldiers to assemble here, instantly?'

'Of course, if the commander orders,' the boy said.

'But, of course, I ask you in the commander's name.'

The boy began beating the drum, and within moments all the soldiers had gathered in the clearing. The priest said, 'You did not wish to hear me earlier. But give me only a moment. I speak to you of Priest Odin.'

He had their attention. He continued, 'It is not for me to judge. I do not know who threw the lance in Odin's face and who wanted him to die or why. But this I know. He is a priest, whether you honour him as such or not. Those among you who seek to harm him, commit a sin against God and a crime against Man.'

When he heard the drum, the commander rushed back to the camp where he was told what the priest had said. 'What idiots my brother has sent with me!' he muttered to himself, but he did not quarrel with the priest. He only said, to make the priest feel small, 'You did not speak the truth when you asked the drummer, in my name, to beat the drum!'

'There are truths and there are higher truths,' the priest said. The other priest nodded and so did the council members.

'Yes, commander,' the other priest said, 'we speak of higher truths and greater lies. We were told a different tale, but it seems those who command you always meant to kill Odin.'

The commander had no wish to argue further. Odin shall die by my hand, he said to himself. Tomorrow at dawn, I shall attack!

But the priest understood his unspoken thought. He spoke in a measured voice that carried across the camp, 'If you, directly or indirectly, cause Odin or his family any harm, I shall see to it that you are held personally responsible along with any officer or soldier who assists you.'

'I am in command here,' shouted the commander and left without waiting for a reply.

By dawn, much of the army had disappeared! A handful of officers and no more than 600 soldiers remained of the formidable army that had proudly marched to the Black Forest.

None of the twelve sentries had deserted. The chief sentry said, 'The task given to us was to watch for attack; no one asked that we guard against our men leaving, or hold them prisoners.'

'They were not our men,' the commander exploded. 'They were deserters!'

The sentry seemed unimpressed and said, 'Commander, none of our sentries left. They knew it was their duty to guard against attack.' The words were soft yet ominous. Did he mean that the sentries would have deserted too, if the duty to guard had not been imposed on them?

There was rage and hate in the commander's heart. He felt like strangling the priests. He was convinced that they, with their words of sedition, had caused this mass desertion. But he asked quietly, 'Which way did the deserters go? To the forest?'

'No, commander, it was mostly in the opposite direction that our soldiers went.'

Our soldiers! The commander looked murderously at the sentry. He turned to the drummer boy and said, 'Summon everyone.'

The remaining soldiers lined up. They knew why so many had left. The fear of God . . . their love for Odin and Hansa . . . the villainy of the chief . . . the cry of Bal Deva . . . the tears of Frigga! There were a hundred reasons—'We are soldiers, not killers!' The 600 who still remained did so for the soldier's code of honour, the code that overrode all fear, tears, curses and cries. Some secretly hoped that with so few left, the commander himself would abandon his plans to attack, and the men would not have to fight their brethren, while maintaining their code of honour as soldiers. But those were very few and they were wrong. The commander had no intention of deserting the battlefield. He had enough rage in his heart to war with all the gods in the firmament. Yet his words were quiet as he addressed his soldiers.

'Many have deserted us,' he said. 'Perhaps that is good. Those with the evil of desertion in their hearts, who violate the soldier's sacred code of honour, and seek to put this gallant tribe to shame . . . what could they have achieved for us, except to weaken our resolve and halt our advance! We now move and teach the Aryans what it is to face the soldiers of this great tribe. I know they shall not remember it for long, for they shall be dead and gone. Move!'

Brave words! And the commander died bravely, too. With him, died 160 soldiers and the drummer boy, and over 400 locals.

Hansa was among the locals who died in the forest. He had demanded a sword to face the army as it came marching in. Someone had said to him, 'But you are not a man of violence!' His reply was, 'That I am not. Nor am I a coward, I hope.' No one knew if he could wield a sword or if he hurt anyone or whose lance struck him in his chest. All they knew was that he died and they wept.

Of the Aryans of Bharat Varsha only two died. The Aryan defence line was deep inside the forest. The two who died were those carrying the news of how the battle was progressing.

Recalling how Bal Deva, the son of Odin, had lost his foot in the first battle, and how Odin had lost his eye in the second, the locals and Aryans alike wondered if the gods would demand yet another sacrifice from Odin's family in this third battle.

The gods had. Frigga wept, 'Two brothers I lost! One of blood, one of heart!'

They knew she wept for Hansa, the brother of her heart. But when they learnt that she also cried for the commander, Loki's brother, her cousin, some asked in surprise, 'You weep for him?'

'Who will, since none of you will?' Her heart was full of grief. She remembered this cousin who had been the playmate of her childhood days. She remembered the little boy with whom she had planned pranks. How they had laughed, giggled, played, frolicked and grown up together! How they had both laughed at Loki!

Later, when he heard she was to marry Odin he had kissed her on the mouth, passionately. She had blushed and stammered, 'That was not the kiss of a brother!'

'It was not meant to be a brotherly kiss,' he had said. 'Why do you marry an old man?'

'He is a man of honour,' she hotly replied.

'Honour! What has honour to do with loving, kissing, caressing . . .'

'My father says I must marry him,' Frigga interrupted.

'Does your father know that I am in love with you?'

'Maybe, that is why he wants me to marry him.'

He laughed, 'I thought you loved me, too.'

'I shall always love you. You always were and shall be my brother,' she had said and kissed him on the cheek.

Hansa was right: love never dies. Not hers, anyway. And so she wept.

Since then, she had been known as Frigga, the Mother, for she wept for every child on earth.

Later, in a jovial moment, an Aryan child had asked, 'Mother Frigga, you shed tears often and you laugh so little!'

It was Odin who replied, 'When she laughs, she sheds more tears and they never stop.'

It was true, for Frigga had laughed at Odin's reply and with that laughter came the never-ending stream of her tears.

But those were tears of joy. Her son had recovered. Her husband had recovered. And God, she felt, was right in her heart.

The Aryans felt that the hour of peril had passed. It was time, they thought, to rebuild their boats and return. They were wrong.

Along the river, Loki's men waited patiently, ready for the kill.

The attacks on the forest continued in a bid to frighten, harass and keep up the pressure, lest the tribe assumed that the war was lost. No one from the villages could go to the forest. The area where Odin had once resided became a cluster of ghost villages. Some said that Loki's men sacked it.

Others said that most of the villagers left to join the Aryans. Perhaps the truth lay somewhere in between.

Loki's men, who now attacked the people in the forest, came not to fight as soldiers, but as brutal prowlers, to maim and kill. Villagers, slaves, others seeking to go to the forest were, for them, the easiest prey. In the months that went by, fourteen Aryans from Bharat Varsha died in those attacks, as did a great many locals.

Those were difficult times in the forest. It had turned into a teeming city. Fighters were few, and those that needed protection far too many. The villagers came stealthily, crawling in the dark, from various routes. Those who were caught by Loki's men met with savagery.

Suddenly, however, all restrictions, it seemed, had been lifted. Everyone was free to enter the forest.

More villagers, more slaves escaping from all over, came in. Problems arose with so many men, women and children in the forest. But there was a sigh of relief too. No longer were Loki's men guarding the access.

It was then that the Aryans received more disquieting news. A slave from another tribe stole into the forest. He told them that Loki had sent word to every tribe asking them to participate in the attack against the bands of robbers and thieves congregated in the forest. Each tribe that participated was promised a share of the loot to be grabbed from the Aryans. Their share would depend on the number of fighters each tribe sent. For each person from another tribe who lost a limb, his share would be triple. For each that died, the tribe would receive six times the amount. Food, lodging and other amenities would be provided by Loki's tribe to other tribes, without affecting their share of the loot. All the Aryans would be enslaved and distributed among the other tribes in the same proportion as other loot. The locals, too, in the forest, irrespective of what tribe they belonged to, would be subject to slavery.

The slave had even more information. The other tribes had wondered why they were being pursued so much, with such generous offers. They wanted to know what would happen if the Aryans did not have as much gold or as many boats as Loki said they did. No problem, they had been told. If the loot was not what was promised, Loki's tribe would make up the difference. But would it be Loki's decision if a dispute arose over the distribution of loot and slaves? Not at all, Loki had told them and suggested that all the tribes elect a single team of judges whose decision would bind them all. Would Loki try to move away the locals hiding in the forest, to reduce their share of the slaves, the tribes asked. No, said Loki, no one would be allowed to leave the forest. Anyone who tried would be thrust back forcibly.

In those times, the chief's word was a bond, irrevocable and irreversible. No one doubted Loki's word. Nor did Loki contemplate breaking it.

The tribes moved to attack the forest. Not only their armies, but also their slaves, their ruffians and their cutthroats for the share of each tribe depended on the number of men it brought into the field. Their weapons varied but each 'soldier' carried a rope with which to tie the slaves.

The Aryans' boats were being prepared for departure. Odin said to the Tungeri brothers, 'You could make a dash for it when hostilities break out. We will keep them busy. No one will be watching for you in the excitement of battle.'

'Will you come with us?' they asked.

'There was a time when I would have given my life to come with you. But now . . . ' said Odin, and his hand pointed to the vast numbers of locals milling around. 'How can I leave them behind?'

'Exactly,' the brothers smiled. 'We find ourselves facing the same question—how can we leave you and them behind?'

'You owe us nothing,' said Odin. 'You do not belong to this land. You must leave when the battle begins or it will be too late.'

The Tungeri brothers laughed and one of them said, 'You are right. We owe you nothing, except our lives. We may not belong to this land, but you belong in our hearts. And we and all the Aryans believe these are good enough reasons for us to stay together and, if need be, die together.'

'It is a mistake for you to remain, a grave error,' Odin pleaded.

'Our error began when we left our homeland.'

'But naturally you must leave, and I am glad you all are rushing these last few days and nights to complete your boats?'

'Boats! But they have a purpose to serve.'

'What purpose? To make a gift of them to Loki?' Odin asked.

'Frigga has to take the children away.'

'What?' both Odin and Frigga shouted.

True, they had given up everything, the brothers explained, even the thought of defence and used every ounce of strength to complete the work on the boats with help from the locals. But the boats were not for their escape. He continued, 'As soon as the attack begins, all the children—Aryan and local —must rush into the boats. The only adults to go with the children will be the Aryan boatmen who must row the boats, and the mother of all these children—Frigga. Henceforth, all the children will be camped near the boats. As will the boatmen and Frigga. At a signal from us, the boats will leave. Our Aryans will run along the river and divert anyone watching. Hopefully, we will ensure that boats get beyond harm's reach. We will entrust the children to the care of God and Mother Frigga. Could we ask for a more powerful, more benevolent combination? Maybe they will all reach Bharat Varsha. If not, some other place of safety, God willing.'

Frigga said, 'You think I will leave my husband behind!'

One of the brothers said, 'No. You will be with your son Bal Deva. Wherever you are, wherever Bal Deva is, your husband is.'

Strangely, Frigga had no tears. Her eyes were hard. Firmly, she repeated, 'I shall not leave my husband.'

Calmly, the Tungeri brothers responded, 'That is your decision. It was not easy for us to persuade the boatmen to leave. They wanted to stay back and fight alongside us. But we insisted that they had a higher duty. We shall not try to persuade you. We just did not want all these children to be motherless. If you can persuade Odin to go with you, along with the children, we shall welcome it.'

Frigga looked at the brothers, their eyes both sad and resolute. She wept. 'I shall go, I shall go. My husband's place is here . . . Mine, I know is with the children.'

The sense of panic in the forest disappeared and was replaced by calm strength. They knew they were fated to die. Who could withstand the combined onslaught of all the tribes! But it seemed to matter less and less. Ever since the news had come that there was to be such a concerted attack, the Aryans had desperately been trying to complete building the boats. Clearly, the locals had thought that the Aryans were intending to flee—and why not, they had no hope of survival and this was not their land, so why should they not leave? Yet, somehow, the locals had felt forsaken, lonely, lost. But now they knew! The Aryans were staying back to fight with them, even die with them, if need be.

The Aryans had simply said, 'We are all brothers.'

Meanwhile, Loki was assuring his own people that this cooperation among the tribes would eventually lead to unity. They had been a single tribe once, under Thor; should they not be united again? It was during the time of Kvasir, grandson of Thor, that they had broken into two and then into three tribes, and finally, in succeeding generations, become twelve tribes. Old Kvasir had been tricked. He had sent his trusted advisers to sort out the differences in order to avoid a partition of land and tribes, but greedy for personal power, those men had contrived to outwit him and whip up such a frenzy of disunity that a split was unavoidable. Old Kvasir had retired in anguish from his position of chief. His sense of honour prevented him from blaming anyone but himself. Yet his dream remained that the tribes would one day reunite. Even in his retirement, Kvasir was loved. But he was assassinated by those who thought that he was still trying to influence his tribe to be too considerate to other tribes, possibly to rekindle in their hearts the dream of unity. Yet, clearly, his dream of unity died with him; and everyone realized that disunity, like all other evils, would only grow; and that it was impossible to undo the divisions and partitions among tribes when the personal ambitions of those that lead them lay in keeping them divided!

Many, now, were touched by Loki's words of unity—the trusting few who judged their leader mostly by his words and not by his actions. They did not realize that the honoured name of the old man, Kvasir, who had died chasing the dream of unity, was often on the lips of the most dishonourable men in the land, who had achieved positions of eminence, prestige and power—but never in their hearts.

Everyone in the forest waited for the attack as the tribes gathered. Loki's negotiations had taken a long time. Some tribes were yet to arrive and clearly the decision reached was that all the tribes should strike together.

The Aryans and locals in the Black Forest had one certainty —whatever happened, they would sell their lives dearly. There would be no bravado, no feats of heroism. They would not fight in the open, not even behind the cover of trees, but from pits, ditches, shelters and some of these would even be covered with domes. Only the tallest trees with thick foliage would be utilized, where a single fighter could wait in a

BHAGWAN S. GIDWANI

canopy of leaves and scaffolding to shelter him and his stones and arrows. Nor would many congregate at a single point, waiting for slaughter. Each fighter would be an 'army' unto himself. To reach him, the enemy would have to cross the obstacle of fallen trees, avoid arrows and stones, and navigate the sheltering walls.

What then? Extinction? Their only hope was that the children would be safe. Mother Frigga would be with them. Yes, through our children, our tribe shall live . . . Odin's tribe!

This was what many locals in the forest called themselves, initially, but Odin had disapproved. Then some of the women had said, 'We shall live through our children and Frigga is the one who leads them to safety. Should we not call ourselves Frigga's tribe?' It was Frigga who then said, 'No, the Tungeri brothers lead us. They send our children to safety. Maybe we shall be in their Bharat Varsha before they reach. Should we not call ourselves the Tungeri tribe?'

But the Tungeri brothers shook their heads. 'We are all God's tribe.'

It was strange that people waiting to die were concerning themselves with matters as trivial as a name for their tribe! Even stranger was that Odin had continued to compose poetry, claiming he was able to look within himself better, now that he had only one eye! The locals also continued to learn the language of the Aryans, and the Tungeri brothers discussed with the locals their ideas of life, the after-life, karma, moksha, dharma, bhakti, the roots of Sanatan Dharma and Sanathana and, even more, about the reality, personality and duality of the universal spirit, creation of the universe, evolution of man, conception of time and space and so many other abstract and philosophical concepts!

There were those who found this urge for more knowledge strange at a time when it would matter no more and life itself would end! Why seek wisdom when wisdom matters no more! Or was it their intention to confuse God with their superior knowledge when life has ended! Still more curious was the fact that they spoke, smiled, chatted, joked, laughed and sang as though the certainty of death did not matter any more. They were not like wild women and doomed men under a sentence of death. The women dressed well, cared for their appearance and even took time to part their hair properly, as usual, and apply the red dot on their foreheads, as the locals had learnt from the Aryans.

And the men! They never forgot to admire women. Several unmarried Aryan men even took wives from among the local girls. There were many moments of music and dance, frolic and festivity, laughter and mirth, love and longing in the forest. And the couples said that they would be true to each other all their lives—and never did they even ask themselves how short that life was to be!

But they knew that each day was a boon.

The Aryans and locals in the Black Forest did not even pray that their lives be spared. They prayed only for the safety of the children who were to be rushed out by boat. For themselves, they asked for nothing. Was it because they thought they could not be saved? Did they then lack faith? Did they believe that there were limits to God's miracles? Did they believe that God could not perform the impossible!

Yet the impossible became possible. Was it an act of God? No, it was an act of man.

Suddenly, came Atal and his 2000 horsemen from Lithuania!

Normally the might of 2000 men would not have mattered against the combined armies of twelve Germanic tribes trained in warfare. But 2000 horses! An animal that Germans had never seen before!

Oh Gods! Gods! They ride on wolves! These black devils!

The terror of the twelve local tribes poised to attack the forest was unimaginable. Their armies vanished, but their hatred was intense and directed towards Loki. So Loki knew!

they said to themselves. He had known that we would face not human beings but men riding on monstrous wolves! No wonder he had offered us so much, they said. Oh fools, we! To make us believe that Loki was giving away so much for a mere attack on robbers, when he was actually pitting us against monsters!

The armies of the twelve tribes collapsed and they fled, rushing back not to their homelands but deep inside Loki's lands for deadly vengeance. Loki's body was ripped apart and the pieces scattered everywhere in the hope that the monstrous wolves from the black world would halt to eat Loki's flesh and forget to pursue them! And in the process, the tribes vandalized each other. Promises to them had been violated, they were convinced, and so they violated and crushed everyone and everything in sight.

∼

Was it really a miracle that suddenly, out of the blue, Atal arrived to the rescue? The explanation was simple.

Atal had followed the Baltic coastline from Lithuania. Somewhere, he changed direction. On the way, Atal's men were learning the shifting, ever-changing language of the people they met. Sometimes, the language varied slightly and at other times, considerably, but always with shades and patterns that were faintly common and recognizable. Their horses frightened the people they met, but their friendly approach reassured the strangers. Somewhere along the route, they were advised by a friendly person to watch out, for men and women like them were being hunted for 'butchery and slavery' by all the Germanic tribes of the land, in a forest far away, that was now called the 'Black Forest'. 'Where?' asked Atal, and then he and his men rode to the Aryans' rescue.

∼

When the dust had settled, Atal was among the first to leave along with some men from his contingent and quite a few locals from Germany as also locals from Finland and Lithuania. They went by the boats which had been intended for the children and Frigga who were staying since there was no imminent danger. Horses were left behind under the Tungeri brothers' command. Many of Atal's men remained to teach horse-riding to the Tungeri brothers' and Odin's forces. They would leave later with the Tungeri brothers and the rest of the Aryans.

Much remained to be done. There was a desperate cry of agony from all the tribes as soldiers from the twelve armies went on their mindless rampage. These tribes had seen danger before but never like this. They were quivering under the heel of ruthless men who were senselessly killing, burning and looting. Families were torn apart, many were orphaned. They rushed out of their shattered villages. But there was no place to run and hide. A cry of pain was wrung from their souls by the terrible torment through which they passed. There was a broken prayer for mercy everywhere.

The looters laughed. Odin moved with the Aryan forces to tackle the renegades. Every tribe was God's tribe, he said, as Tungeri's sons had said earlier, and Frigga wept for them all.

Months passed. But, at last, in Germany there emerged one tribe as the tribes shed their separate identities and merged under Odin's leadership. They said it was the 'sword' that united them. But others said it was the sword that had divided them till Odin's mercy, the Aryans' love and Bharat Varsha's svastika united them.

What should they call this united tribe now?

'The tribe of Tungeri?' some suggested.

The Tungeri brothers objected, 'Call it Odin's tribe, if a name has to be given, for it is he who united you.'

'No,' said Odin. 'Let it be called the "Tribe of Aryans".'

Odin had the last word and so it was named the Tribe of Aryans. Frigga, though, called it the Aryan tribe of Svastika. She could not forget that her son had clutched the svastika seal in his tiny hand to prevent his father from going out to take his own life.

Led by the Tungeri brothers, many Aryans sailed down the river Dana towards the Black Sea to Turkey, and thence to Hari Haran Aryan and finally back to Bharat Varsha. With them went many locals from Germany, and many more would follow, year after year.

Of the mishaps, triumphs and adventures they faced on their journey, volumes can (and should) be written. But it is enough to say that one of the Tungeri brothers was killed in Turkey under tragic circumstances. The second brother died in a shipwreck, not too far from the Sindhu coast. The last surviving brother reached Bharat Varsha where he recited the names of all those who had died and prayed for them all, except his brothers. When asked why he had left them out of his prayers, he said, 'So long as I live, they live; so long as they die, I die.'

At the age of sixteen, Bal Deva suddenly disappeared from the Land of Tungeri. He arrived in Bharat Varsha ten years later. There, he married Nanna, the daughter of the surviving Tungeri brother. He had four sons and four daughters with her. For most of his life, he lived near the confluence of the Sindhu river with the Sindhu Sammundar. In his last years, however, he lived in Hari Hara Dwara—Hardwar. He was cremated on the banks of the Ganga at Varnash—Varanasi.

∽

Odin, Frigga and Bal Deva and indeed many others came to be regarded as gods in Germany and Europe. But later, in modern times, they could not withstand the onslaught of Christianity with its positive, monotheistic, forceful creed based on a dogma which demanded that all other gods be renounced and that redemption was possible only through Christianity and no other faith.

But somehow in Germany, the traditional memory of these gods endures.

∾

NOTES
The Aryan Influence in Europe
There were other regions, too, to which the Aryans of Bharat Varsha travelled. Unfortunately, the routes and the accounts of their travels are lost in the mists of time.

ITALY:
One source speaks of the Aryans of Bharat Varsha in Italy. But the account lacks a beginning and an end, and only a little of the rest survives. But then as a source points out, the ancient Italian culture is largely unconcerned with pre-Roman Italy and everything prior to the Roman Empire is stamped out. From the little that survives, one can say that the Aryans established camps in Italy in the area that came to be known as Hindurya or Indurya.

Later, after centuries, this Italian area of Hindurya or Indurya would come to be known as Eturia—parts of present-day Latium, Tuscany (Toscana), Umbria and possibly Campania.

The Aryans of Bharat Varsha in Italy came to be called the Aryansenna—army of the Aryans—or Ryasenna—people's army organized by the Aryans but composed largely of the locals to stop human sacrifice and prevent abduction of people for slavery. According to Herodotus, Rasenna—

Ryasenna of the Aryans—came from the east through Lydia or in general from the Aegean and probably through the Island of Lemnos.

But even with this information it is difficult to pinpoint their route or adventures and accomplishments.

Only a few fragments remain of the influence of the Aryans in Italy. They were the first to introduce the funeral rites of cremation. A theory was advanced by the Aryan leader there that contrary to the common belief that worms attacked a body upon decomposition, they enter the body the moment a person dies. Neither the name of this Aryan leader nor the scientific evidence for this theory was given. Instead, Dhanawantri's name has been mentioned. But there is no evidence to support the claim that she ever visited Italy. The Aryans also introduced agriculture and the domestication of animals and fowl in Italy. The Aryan leader's son—Gaipal—is known to have introduced the flute in Italy. The instrument came to be heard during Italian banquets and even the flogging of slaves and during lovemaking. For the rest, little is known of how far the Aryans influenced their moral, social, aesthetic and intellectual values.

GREECE:
Another source, which survives only in part, says, 'Eagerly, they went there and for long they could not leave but the imprint they left on that area, which centuries and centuries later would blossom forth as the fountainhead of European civilization, culture, literature and philosophy . . . and yet there was so much that they then found repulsive in that land where men remained married to men, and women were regarded only as producers of offspring, but entitled neither to love nor tenderness nor comfort—and that land had neither real rivers nor forests nor tall trees.' Some have assumed this to be a reference to Greece, but there is no reliable confirmation.

ENGLAND:
There is no evidence that Aryans from Bharat Varsha travelled to England. The English were a mongrel race, outside the periphery of any civilized knowledge or culture at the time the Aryans were in Europe. Even for long centuries thereafter, Britain remained under a vast shadow of darkness and ignorance. Much later, successive continental cultures came to exercise their civilizing influence on the land that was mired in superstition, filth, poverty, slavery, incest, homosexual activity, child abuse, brigandage, human sacrifice, cannibalism and parricide.

Later, it was the German civilizing influence that left its mark in Britain. The German Aryan gods came to be honoured in England—in particular Odin, Frigga, Bal Deva and Thor. In the beginning though, even the Germans ridiculed the English and said that Britain honoured only anti-god Loki— as one who was a 'changer of shape, from a vulture to a rat to a reptile'. This was intended to highlight the then well-known English trait of refusing to honour any word or vow, using all the deviousness and deception in their power to break it, for they lacked courage and relied largely on creating dissension among others. Loki was also known as a deceiver who cheated the gods and gave birth to many evils, and the Germans were therefore convinced that Loki, and the people of England, were ideally suited to each other.

GODS OF EUROPE (AND THE DAYS OF THE WEEK NAMED AFTER THEM):
Later, as the civilizing influence of Germany grew in England and throughout Europe, Odin, Frigga and Bal Deva began to shine in the eyes and minds of the entire western world. Soon they would come to be known as gods throughout Europe. However, to the Aryans of India, they certainly were not known or gods but simply as heroic human beings and friends alongside whom they had fought to eradicate slavery, blood

sacrifices and cruelty in Germany, and unite the warring German tribes. As a tribute, in Germany and throughout Europe including England, Odin—known as Woden in England—would have Wednesday named after him; Frigga would have Friday named after her; and Thor, whom Odin honoured as the founder of the German race, would have Thursday named after him. In praising Thor, Odin was trying to be politically correct as he recognized the fact that Thor was respected by many of his tribe though both he and Frigga were convinced that Thor had not always been honourable and had introduced the odious practice of 'race cleansing' by ordering the death of infants born with birth-defects. Bal Deva—Baldr—supposed to have the power and will of the gods, had no day named for him, for people believed it might render all other days inauspicious. His influence was thus regarded as all pervasive.

ODIN AS VIEWED BY LATER GENERATIONS:
In later centuries, Odin would come to be honoured more and more as a god in the mythology of Germany, Norway, Sweden, Iceland, Denmark and other European nations, particularly England. He is described variously in the later literature of Germany and Europe as the god of poetry, but also much more. He is known as the god of occult wisdom which he acquired as the result of his hanging. His hanging is presented as a symbolic act of 'sacrifice to himself'. He is believed to have said, 'A moment came when I desired my death, but Mother [Frigga] spoke to me. Oh foolish me, I heard her not! And then my son spoke and I was hearing him not! But then my Father [God] thundered in my heart to say, "Deny them not, for both mother and son speak with my voice!"—and clearly I heard them, then, and could I deny them any more? But Guardian Spirits had heard my vow that by hanging, I must go. And Loki came to my rescue, as they whispered in his ear and promptly he hanged a likeness

of me in straw and wood. And the Guardian Spirits smiled to say, "Your sacrifice by hanging is performed." Oh God! Multiply such Guardian Spirits in my land and in every land.'

Many more fables surround Odin, the god. His effigy was said to be hanging for 'nine endless nights' on the World Tree. Later, the effigy was pierced with a lance to show how the commander had stabbed Odin. But then what did the World Tree do? It turned into a horse, and the tree came to be known as Yggdrassil—Odin's horse—referring to the sudden appearance of horses in Germany (with Aryans) which enabled Odin to straddle Germany and pacify and unite the Germans into a single tribe known as the Tribe of Aryans or the Aryan Tribe of Svastika.

But all these fables and fantasies came later. Clearly, Odin led his united tribe with compassion, and he felt for the sorrows of all, trying to move heaven and earth to bring comfort and unity to his people—a task he succeeded in with enormous help from the Aryans of Bharat Varsha, and under whose influence he abolished the law of 'tribe cleansing', thus saving countless infants born with birth defects, and also abolished human and animal sacrifices.

EPILOGUE

The Aryans had left from many parts of Bharat Varsha, but not from Dravidham.

Many groups of Aryans came from the lands of Sindhu, Ganga and Saraswati to Dravidham, hoping to find routes which would lead them to distant destinations.

Dharmalila, the headman of Dravidham, was astounded. 'But why brother, why?' he asked. To him the idea of people leaving for the unknown in search of a new home seemed ridiculous, and he said so.

The groups of refugees, wishing to leave to search for the Land of the Pure, told their story. It was a familiar tale of deceit, greed and plunder by their lords.

'Help us,' they pleaded with Dharmalila. 'We must join the other Aryans. Many have already left.'

'I shall,' promised Dharmalila. 'But why don't you stay with us in this land that is yours and mine?'

'No master, others have departed long ago to find the land that is safe, blessed and pure.'

'Here walked Sindhu Putra, he who was purer than us all. Make this again then, with your effort, the land of the pure,' said Dharmalila. He did not know it, but his words echoed the thought of Purus, the Aryan leader in Iran.

Much more was said by many. Dharmalila silenced their doubts, 'Yes, stay with us for six months—a year. If you are still unhappy, I will help you to leave. I promise.'

Many stayed.

Several groups came thereafter, all intent on leaving. Again Dharmalila cried, 'Brothers, sisters, what madness is this! Here you have lands waiting to be made fertile, long valleys, coastal ranges, and spectacular sea shores. Do they not matter to you? Here you will enjoy the fruits of your labour and you will live with us as our own.'

Yet more stayed in Dravidham.

A series of strange messages also reached Dharmalila then. They came from the karkarta of Sindhu, Gangapati of Ganga and many other mighty lords and chiefs. None of them was aware that Dharmalila was dissuading groups from leaving. These messages simply requested Dharmalila to help various groups that might reach Dravidham to depart. The messages spoke of everlasting gratitude for providing such help and even promised to share with Dharmalila the information on the wealth and lands eventually found by these stragglers.

Dharmalila's response to these messages was polite, even enthusiastic, giving the impression that he would assist any Aryans who wanted to depart from his land. But this was not so. He simply welcomed groups that came and encouraged them to stay back. There was little that Dharmalila could do to discourage the exodus of Aryans from other parts of Bharat Varsha. He sent a few of his men out, to Ganga, Sindhu and elsewhere. His men came back to report that the Aryan movement and migration was widespread. 'Like a tidal wave,' said some, but they were exaggerating as messengers and envoys often do.

'But why,' asked Dharmalila, 'why were so many Aryans leaving?' The reasons, he was told, were many and varied, but mostly, it was a cry in their souls.

'Nonsense,' retorted Dharmalila. But some questioned his ability to understand such a reason! His was the deep-seated joy of wrestling with the soil rather than the soul. His heart was set on making the soil fertile and rich, to produce in abundance.

But Dharmalila did understand. He sent messages to many, including Rishi Newar in Nepal, Manu Sachal who led Yadodhra's ashram, Ekantra Baldana who was Sage Bharadwaj's spiritual successor, Sage Kundan and the poetess Chitra, asking them to stop the Aryan migration.

Dharmalila was a young man and his messages had the temper of a warm-hearted youth. He begged them, 'Declare that he who leaves for lands elsewhere betrays his land, and the waters he crosses to reach there are not auspicious . . . .'

Some laughed. But many understood Dharmalila's anger and anguish. Yet what could these philosophers, sages, rishis and poets do? Their congregations and disciples heard them, but they had never intended to leave with the Aryans in any case.

It was Rishi Newar who travelled to meet Dharmalila.

'How can you accuse those who flee of betrayal! You are calling the victims culprits. The crime is committed by the mighty lords of the land, and the corruption lies in the uncontrolled urges of the rulers.'

Dharmalila heard all this silently, and Newar challenged, 'Periyar! You, who are virtually the ruler of this land, will naturally find it difficult to accept that rulers are corrupt.'

'No,' Dharmalila said. 'The lords you speak of are a hundredfold more evil than they appear to be.'

'Why do you then blame the people?'

'Because the fault is with the people. The rulers do what they have to do. But the failure is not theirs, nor does it lie in the land, but in *us*. The fight should have begun here. You do not forsake your land for the evil of a few!'

'Few?' Rishi Newar interrupted.

'All right, many. You did not abandon Newar and they say only twelve of you were left, but your spirit kept them on, fighting, until the evil was rooted out.'

'You exaggerate my role, son. It was the spirit of my men that kept them fighting.'

'Exactly. I seek in Bharat Varsha the spirit of men who would fight against evil!'

It is said that Rishi Newar, always thoughtful, was even more thoughtful when he left Dravidham.

But it was too late. Most of the Aryans had already left from various parts of Bharat Varsha. Those that were still leaving were far beyond the reach of Dharmalila's words. Only the stragglers who found their way to Dravidham could be persuaded to remain.

Dharmalila even sent emissaries to Lord Kush of Avagana, Rishi Bonglada of Gangasagarsangam and Chandramukhi of the Land of Brahma requesting them to dissuade Aryans from departing for the 'pathless wild', and even to advise those that had already left to return.

But the Aryans had left long before the messengers reached. However, they would eventually return. Not because they heard Dharmalila's cry, but because of the cry that rose in their own hearts — in Germany, Finland, Norway, Denmark, Sweden, Scythia, the Russian land, Turkey, Spain, Assyria, Sumer, Egypt, Lithuania, Italy, Greece, Iran, Turkey— everywhere. The dream had vanished.

Thousands of these gentle, frightened souls had forced themselves, in joy and pain, to yield to the obscure urge to search for the land of the pure. Now they knew there was no land of the pure anywhere, except where they themselves made it so, by their own toil and effort. They wanted to go back to the healing power of their home, heritage and roots.

From all over Europe, the Aryans of Bharat Varsha travelled back. Most of them gathered in Iran. Many locals too joined them. And they all built boats, though some of them returned by land, too, from Avagana.

∾

'Did you bring the world back with yourselves?' asked Sage Durgan with heavy irony.

'No, sage, we brought ourselves back,' said Kamalpati, who had been the Aryan leader in Spain.

'But I am told you and your Aryans claim that you discovered many lands and people!'

'No, sage, it would be ludicrous for us, and insulting to them, to claim that we discovered them. They have been there for thousands of years before we reached.'

'Yet I am told they honoured you, respected you and bathed you all in their love and devotion.'

'We slaved and suffered, at least in the beginning. Eventually, they realized we meant no harm and that we were their friends, out to help them. That is how we parted, and a few of them have even come with us.'

'But then you could have had all the power, wealth, and attention from those people there. Who will bother about you here? Why return then?'

The sage's wife, Sitavati, herself a sage in her own right, interrupted, 'You can acquire all you want and still feel empty if you are uprooted from your home and land. That ache remains forever!'

'Why do you interrupt a conversation, Sitavati?' asked the sage.

'I learnt that from you,' she said with a smile and turned to Kamalpati. 'But then why did you leave your home in the first place?'

'As Sage Durgan often says, we all have to lose ourselves sometimes, to find ourselves.'

The sage asked, 'Did I say that? I must guard against such foolish utterances that are misconstrued by the ignorant.'

'What will you and the other Aryans do now?' Sitavati asked.

'Each of us has a dream,' Kamalpati said.

'*Each* of you?' Sitavati said. 'What each of you dreams remains a dream. Only when you dream together, does reality begin to be shaped by that dream.'

Sage Durgan said, 'Forget about your dreams. Learn all you can. Learn to read the seen language.'

'But sage, I began to learn that in your ashram before I left.'

'Yes, I remember; you were not one of my gifted pupils. Still, go out, learn to write about our land, the people, their music, poetry, culture, aesthetics, philosophy, hopes, aspirations—and even their courage to stay back to fight evil, rather than flee at the first whiff of smoke, as you did. Yes, write about their capacity to suffer and meet it with courage, instead of escaping.'

Kamalpati smiled at the sage's caustic words and asked, 'Am I the right person to write about the courage of these people?'

'Why not? It takes courage to live their life. Does it take courage to write about them? A brave man lives. Any coward can write. And, there is much to write. Bharat Varsha has progressed much in your absence—maybe because of the absence of people like . . . .'

Kamalpati's smile deepened. Nothing that the sage said, nothing that anyone said, would rob him of the happiness within. He was back home, back at last!

The Sindhu flowed on.

The Ganga flowed on.

The Saraswati flowed on.

The Kauveri flowed on.

Kamalpati gazed at the peaceful countryside and felt a glow of happiness and peace within. He was home—in Hindu Varsha. Bharat Varsha! Arya Varsha!

If there was a dark age to follow, Kamalapati did not know about it.

But then even today, who in this land—sieged within and without—knows of the dark age ahead!

Here, then, ends this novel, but not the saga of the Aryans.

ACKNOWLEDGEMENTS

My thanks, first, to my wife Leila, who organized the translation of over 4,600 songs and rearranged the vast research material. I cannot reward her enough for her cheerful and extraordinary help.

My elder son Manu, his wife Lori, and my younger son Sachal, his wife Anju, helped in a variety of ways. My brother Mangha, who is now no more, shared the same faith and helped me tremendously with research. My debt to him is endless. My brothers, Narain and Durgu, their wives Lachmi and Situ, helped too with advice and assistance. Help came also from my nephews and nieces, Sunder and Minal Gidwani, Neena (Muni) and Hiru Lalwani, Rajni Arora and Manohar Gidwani.

My special thanks to my friend Prakash Nath, his wife Shivrani, their son Sandeep Khanna (Pinkoo) and daughter-in-law Ritu, for their unstinting help.

Encouragement and assistance often came from my friend Kailash Nath, his wife Chaiji, their son Ravi Khanna, daughter-in-law Pratibha and grandson Sanjay (Baboo)—all of them helped to compile some source material.

In Montreal, Jehangir Guzdar, president of Daivam Transport Inc., placed at my disposal his organization to transport materials from many countries. Jehangir's questions also led me to a closer study of the pre- and post-Zoroastrian period of ancient Persia. Shirish Suchak, president of Chalais Holdings (Canada) and his wife Veena were also always ready with help.

My thanks also to B.N. Jha, Secretary to the Government of India in the ministry of heavy industries and public enterprises, for his encouragement and help.

In Chicago, Dial V. Gidwani, president of Intra World Travel & Tours and the founding president of the American Institute of Sindhulogy, helped in transporting massive documentation and archaeological records from all over the world. Dial also gave me many songs of the Vedic period collected by his father Dr Vatanmal.

In Delhi, Papu Chablani and her husband Gulu helped. In Bombay, Kala, Kiki and Pritam Punwani helped in many ways.

My salute to Marya Pushkarni, the gypsy girl I met in Prague, Czechoslovakia, thirty-four years ago. She was thirty-six then—small, slim and petite, with shining eyes and dark hair; and in the depths of her eyes was the same glint of a shy smile as in the waters of a deep well. No wonder, she was always called a 'girl'. From time to time, she sent me songs—over a hundred. She never put postage stamps on her letters, but somehow they always reached me. I received her last two songs a day after she died. Her songs did not help me in writing this novel as they are pertinent to a later period—when the gypsies migrated from India as wandering minstrels and singers. But her perseverance kept my spirits alive. Since then I have visited Prague twice to light a candle on her grave. Hopefully, I shall do so again.

Leah Allesandro of Mexico too! She gave me a thousand clues to the Hindu influence on art, architecture and sculpture of the Mayan civilization. I did not use the material in this novel as, so far, I have not discovered direct evidence of the ancient Hindu explorers having travelled beyond Europe to reach the American continent. Yet her patient and painstaking pursuit of the subject provides an inspiration to question the historians who have written to preserve not the fire but the ashes of the past. Leah is now no more; she died, trying to protect forests from urban encroachment; but then, she always believed that the dream survives even when the dreamer does not.

My thanks to Paloma Dutta of Penguin India, whose advice, expertise and valuable suggestions have made this a better book. Immense also is my gratitude to Shatarupa Ghosal, whose meticulous editing of the book is truly admirable.

I remember with affection my friend K.R. Malkani (author of *The Sindh Story*), who served as member of Parliament and finally as Governor of Pondicherry; and my friend Jashanmal Wadhwani, president of Vivekanand Education Society. Both Malkani and Wadhwani kept pressing that I should write an abridged version of my book *Return of the Aryans,* so that it could reach a larger audience. Malkani and Wadhwani are no more but their encouragement has served as a strong incentive for me to write *March of the Aryans*.

My thanks also goes to Gobind T. Shahani of New Delhi—Rotarian, banker, financier, scholar and my dear friend for the last six decades—whose encouragement and assistance was great and is continuing.

I am grateful to archaeologists, librarians and directors of archives and museums, here and in a hundred countries, who unhesitatingly helped to obtain material for the book. So many have also helped with translations of sources from foreign languages. Their list is endless, and if I do not individually mention them, I know they will understand, and forgive.

The responsibility for mistakes is entirely mine. Often, dates have left me confused, where I was not certain if poets, singers and others had the lunar or the solar calendar in view. Hopefully, the reader will permit an allowance of thirty to ninety years, in the case of many of the dates used in this book.